The Bard of Castaguard

Jane Welch was born at Foremarke, a hamlet in the very centre of rural England, exactly where more than a thousand years ago the Viking Great Army camped for the winter, their forces led by three of Ragnar Lothbrok's sons, including Ivar the Boneless.

Jane spent much of her childhood in a remote coastal wilderness in the Scottish Highlands. With no electricity, TV, and before internet, Jane immersed herself in reading the world's best fantasy novels and scribbling her first short stories on any paper she could find. School and work competed with her writing and it was not until taking a part time job teaching skiing in the Pyrenean mountains that she finally had the space and time to write. Surrounded by the magic of those ancient mountains, she embarked on the first of the nine books that make up the Runes of War Saga.

Jane has continued her travels and research and is now working on a new series, inspired by the beauty of the Mediterranean Sea and its remote islands. In particular, her imagination was caught by a climb to a lighthouse, ruined since antiquity, standing sentinel above twin harbours.

Jane lives and writes in beautiful Devon on the south-west coast of England with her family and noble dog, Odin.

Also by Jane Welch

The Runes of War Saga

PART ONE: *The Book of Torra Alta*
Vol 1. The Runes of War
Vol 2. The Lost Runes
Vol 3. The Runes of Sorcery

PART TWO: *The Book of Önd*
Vol 4. The Lament of Abalone
Vol 5. The Bard of Castaguard
Vol 6. The Lord of Necrönd

PART THREE: *The Book of Man*
Vol 7. Dawn of A Dark Age
Vol 8. The Broken Chalice
Vol 9. The Allegiance of Man

The Runes of War Saga

PART TWO:
The Book of Önd
Vol 5. The Bard of Castaguard

JANE WELCH

HARPER
Voyager

Harper*Voyager*
An imprint of
HarperCollins*Publishers* Ltd
1 London Bridge Street,
London SE1 9GF
www.harpercollins.co.uk

HarperCollins*Publishers*
Macken House, 39/40 Mayor Street Upper,
Dublin 1, D01 C9W8, Ireland

This paperback edition 2024
1

First published in Great Britain by Earthlight,
an imprint of Simon & Schuster Ltd 1999

A catalogue record for this book is available from the British Library

ISBN: 978-0-00-860904-7

Typeset in Goudy by Palimpsest Book Production Ltd, Falkirk, Stirlingshire

Printed and bound in the UK using 100% renewable
electricity by CPI Group (UK) Ltd

For Harriet and George with immeasurable love.

ENCROACHING ICE CAP
VAALAKA
THE STEPPES OF THE NOMADS
THE HORN OF VAAL-PEOR
SUMMER MELTS
THE DRAGON SCORCH
THE THREE BLACK DEVILS
COUNTRY BOUNDARIES
BARONIAL BOUNDARIES
ROADS, TRACKS & PASSES
BARONY OF TORRA ALTA
BOARCHASE FOREST
Torra Alta
BARONY OF JOTUNN
Jotunn Manor
BARONY OF NATTARDA
SILVER SALMON R.
BARONY OF OVISSIA
Loonsbury
Puddleswold
OLDHART FOREST
Wiglaf's Manor
Bleham
FARONA
Granham
R. DORS
BELBIDIA
BARONY OF FARONSHIRE
BARONY OF PISCERA
BARONY OF QUERTOS
GORTA
Dorsmouth
ISTHMUS
Northdown
BARONY OF CALDEA
SHIFTING SHORE
Ildros
Tartra
THE HOOK
HESPERA Is.
FARTHEST ISLE
THE CREST OF OPHIDIA
CABAL
THE SPIT
THE QUIET
DEAD GODS
OPHIDIA

ENCROACHING ICE CAP
CAIRN
Ceolothia
Three Sisters
The Tongue
Sea
Camallia
Lake of Tears
Frosted Peaks
The Serpent
The Smokies
Sea
Deserts of Glan

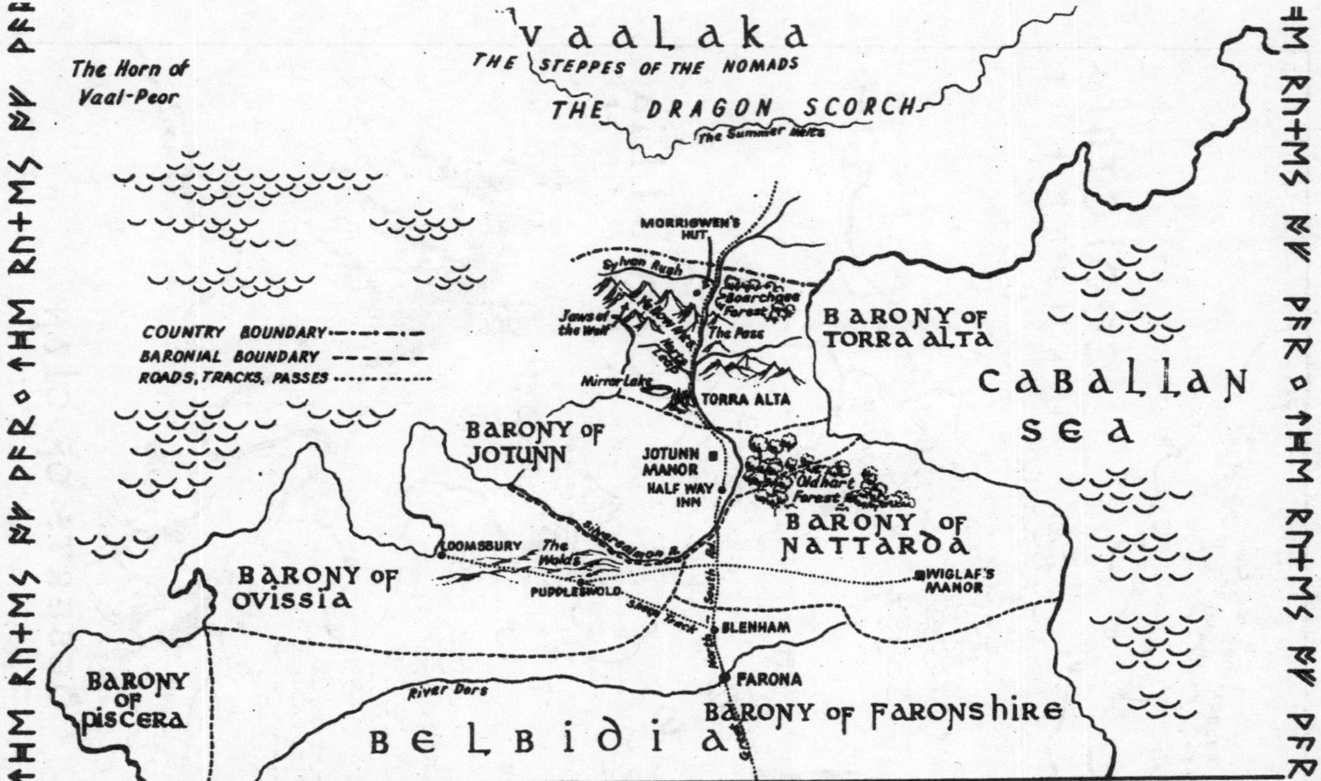
VAALAKA
THE STEPPES OF THE NOMADS
THE DRAGON SCORCH
The Summer Hills
The Horn of Vaal-Peor
COUNTRY BOUNDARY
BARONIAL BOUNDARY
ROADS, TRACKS, PASSES
MORRIGWEN'S HUT
Sylvan Rush
Boarchase Forest
Jaws of the Wolf
The Pass
Mirror Lake
TORRA ALTA
BARONY OF TORRA ALTA
CABALLAN SEA
BARONY OF JOTUNN
JOTUNN MANOR
HALF WAY INN
Oldhart Forest
BARONY OF NATTARDA
LOOMSBURY
The Wolds
PUDDLESHOLD
WIGLAF'S MANOR
BARONY OF OVISSIA
Sheep Track
South Rd.
North Rd.
BLENHAM
FARONA
River Dors
BARONY OF PISCERA
BARONY OF FARONSHIRE
BELBIDIA

PROLOGUE

Unblinking, his dazzling yellow eyes stared up into the glaring sun. Though empty of thought, his quiet face was strikingly handsome.

A web of silken ropes cradled his limp body and, pushed by a gentle breeze that penetrated the vaulted hall, they creaked against his worn leather leggings and verderer's green hunting jacket. The brilliant sunlight of Rye Errish, that world beyond life known to human souls as the Otherworld, blazed through the narrow void high above in the domed roof of the judgement chamber, glistening on the silvery ropes and playing upon the golden hair that framed his bronzed elfin features. The fierce debate that so concerned him swept on interminably while he remained oblivious to all.

"He should be sent to the sun, every part of him burned away forever!" Straif's voice was impassioned, the scratchy tone creaking and screeching. Furiously, the ealdorman stabbed his blackthorn staff at the verderer's suspended body above their heads. "It was decided! You are weak fools to overturn the decision." He swung his staff to point at a fellow member of the High Circle. "Saille, this is your doing. Your weak womanish emotions bring chaos."

Trembling, the ealdorwoman hovered higher, her glistening hair floating about her and her sunshot-eyes sparkling with emotion as the humming note of her wings rose to an inaudible pitch. An air of pity intensified her willowy looks and ethereal beauty. "We, who stand in judgement, must have compassion, understanding—"

A snort of displeasure cut short her words. Phagos, a tall ealdorman, with smooth greyish skin and beechnuts entangled in his beard, frowned at her in disapproval as he pointedly drummed his fingers on the cracked leather cover of a vast book. "Worldly foolery. To govern wisely, we need only turn to the knowledge of the law." He tapped the great tome. "The punishment for such treachery is oblivion. Talorcan's immortal being must be destroyed!"

The thirteen ealdormen fell silent. Resplendent and glorious, they hovered on vast dragonflylike wings high in the air about a circular marble plinth. A single central pillar set into the smooth floor of the chamber supported the plinth. For their shimmering gold hair, blazing yellow eyes, gossamer wings and captivating expressions, they might have been described as fairylike, only they were too regal, too substantial and, in particular, too aware of their own power. Some were childlike in stature. Others, though stout, were only a head shorter than the average human, and any unfortunate soul that might have suffered their judgement would have seen how each bore tribute to a particular tree.

Fingering a bunch of ash keys, Nuin rapidly beat her translucent wings to soar regally above her peers. Her shimmering feathery hair, swirling around her shoulders, shone more brightly than any of the others, and of all the thirteen members of the High Circle, that had sat in judgement since the beginning of time over the souls passing through the lands of spirit to reach the bliss of Annwyn, she was the most captivating.

"We must view his case in the light of all his deeds. We must look at the whole. Consider now how the dungeons are filling daily with those earthly souls that refuse to pass on from our world of Rye Errish to the forgetfulness of Annwyn. Have not too many been savaged by the ancient, hooded wolves that should be extinct from Earth's dimensions? The laws of equilibrium and symmetry between our worlds are distorting, crumbling and we, after all, are the lawmakers. We are the guardians of Rye Errish and yet can we honestly say that we are governing well?" Her bright eyes flashed accusingly at her fellows.

"Talorcan recognized our failure and so it is, in part, our fault that the sickening greed for power swelled in his belly. We removed him from office but even that has helped us little. The new chief verderer that has replaced him has not the same skill with his charges. The verderers ushering the souls to the gateways of Annwyn have lost entire columns to the commoners and the treacherous beasts of the forests. And though his methods of torture are more inventive and barbaric than Talorcan's, he has less subtlety and less success in persuading those stubborn souls who refuse to forsake their last lives to move on."

Saille winced. "And Talorcan was not all bad. He had great strengths."

"Too many strengths. He was too close to overthrowing us. He must be punished," Tinne snarled, thrashing his holly brand wildly.

"He must return to the stuff of the stars," Phagos, the tall ealdorman insisted, thumping the tome before him. "We cannot release him into the forests of Rye Errish. He knows them too well and has too much power there. His long service as chief verderer will have taught him too much. He must be obliterated."

"There is surely one other punishment so abhorrent that all might be satisfied." This feminine voice was calm and thoughtful. A plainer member of the High Circle, a crown of hazel leaves pinning back her golden hair, hovered a little higher on her gossamer wings.

"Force him to join the cycle of life as a human!" Uilleand, smelling sweetly of honeysuckle, guessed at Coll's plan and was appalled at the barbarism of such an idea.

"He would have to attain a soul," Coll continued to explain her inspiration. "We can send him to Earth and, if he should conceive a child, he will gain a soul and so suffer the inexorable misery of life, death and rebirth."

"But that must be with the loving consent of the woman," Saille interrupted in concern. Her expression was one of sympathy, her lean willowy body sad at having to pass so harsh a judgement. "Our sentence cannot cause the suffering of a human soul. That would be no justice at all."

"Quite so," Coll applauded. "We of the High Circle must, above all, be just."

Saille's long fingers soothed her willow staff. "In conceiving the child, he would pass on an essential part of himself into the human existence; a part of him would then live forever in the cycle of life, death and rebirth and he would attain a soul."

"But for an immortal being of Rye Errish to join the cycle of life . . . The very idea is terrible," Nuin exclaimed, jangling her keys, though she looked pleased rather than horrified. "Yes! It is a fit punishment for one who served so well and then deceived us with such evil purpose. He sought to conquer one of the three great talismans so that he might wrench apart the gateways between dimensions; and he consorted to tamper with the third power held in the precarious guardianship of man so that he might subjugate, not only the souls passing through Rye Errish, but those on Earth as well. He sought a power higher than ours! Now the forests are heaving with wolves awoken and crawling out of the distant corners of Rye Errish. They hover around the gateways, seeking a path back to their earthly lives. Talorcan has played a part in this stirring of souls and the punishment is just."

Phagos nodded sagely. "Since he began his scheming, the magic of Necrönd has sent disturbing ripples that distort the natural patterns of the universe. Let us hope that, with his demise, some stability might be restored. The punishment is just!" he echoed Nuin.

"It is decided. He is to be banished to Earth." Nuin's imperious tone boomed with conviction and the other twelve ealdormen nodded in acquiescence.

The shamed verderer was sombrely lowered to the marble floor. Saille touched his cheek and a spark of light flared up in his eyes as his body was freed from the ealdormen's spell of binding. He blinked at her.

"Thank you for your mercy," he said graciously, his honey-sweet voice musical and smooth, the tone at once mellow, soothing and intriguing.

She smiled in acknowledgement. "But remember you cannot use your powers as a verderer once you are on Earth. Your only salvation is to find love. The child must be conceived in love, freely given love; not love won through the falsehoods of spellbinding."

"Use the magic in your voice to win her love and you shall go to oblivion," Straif warned resentfully, "where, by rights, you should be now but the ealdorwomen are too weak-minded."

Talorcan merely bowed. "I accept my punishment."

Satisfied with the judgement, Nuin slotted a key into a low door carved with wondrous representations of the hidden paths that link the universe and the ways between worlds. Depicted in the simple wood of the ash door were the three artefacts of power that opened the barriers between Earth and the Otherworld: Nuin's Keys, Duir's Pipe, and, set apart, a seemingly harmless and fragile egg.

This egg, known as Necrönd, was shown surrounded by warring tribes of humans. And circling hungrily about them, though carved with less detail, were the slinking forms of beings of the dark. Whereas the Keys and the Pipe were illustrated amidst scenes of serenity, Necrönd centred a world of hatred and chaos, a man's world, destructive and unordered.

The door swung back and Nuin held out her hand to lead the verderer across the divide. They passed through circles of ice and fire and then into the dark, where Talorcan walked in awe of the infinite emptiness that stretched around him. The sense of nothingness pressed about him, threatening to tear him apart.

Then the silence was broken. Snuffles and pants sounded to both left and right and, far off, a lonesome wolf howled in the dark. A sudden growl and snap of large hungry jaws snatched at his face and was gone. The flash of a red maw gaped out of the blackness and the air was filled with the stench of rotting flesh.

"They walk the channels of magic. They are within the spirit ether, clawing their way towards Earth. Think of what evil you have done," Nuin said. "And listen to the souls flooding across the dimensions. So much death!"

Talorcan had heard nothing save the wolves' fearsome snarls until Nuin stretched her long lean arm into the darkness. Though he had witnessed much suffering and torment of the human soul before now and had always viewed it with a sense of superiority and detachment, he flinched away in shock.

"Listen to them!" Nuin insisted.

She thrust her hand deeper into the darkness and

Talorcan heard the ghoulish screams of dying men and the savage snarl of wolves as they tore at flesh and snapped bones in crushing jaws. Children screamed in terror. Men were shouting, desperate to save their loved ones. Then Talorcan heard their screams as they died in anguish, having failed to save their kin, the pain of that failure more terrible than the cut of death. The screams ripped his flesh as Talorcan felt the cold touch of a spirit passing across the divide on its lonesome journey to the forests of Rye Errish. The loss, the suffering cut through him like a cruel wind, sundering the steel armour of his heart.

Nuin's bright eyes flared at him savagely out of the dark. "Your punishment is not enough. Saille's request that the child must be conceived with the loving consent of a woman is insufficient. You must love her, too, and I curse that love! If you succeed in gaining a soul, you will suffer as these about you have suffered by your hand. Their greatest pain is that they cannot help their loved ones and your pain will be worse. To gain a soul, you must love this earthling, and your love will be her ruin, bringing with it the darkest evils to stalk her. You will come to understand the grief of these souls. Look for us, Talorcan: we shall be watching you – and your misery."

"I didn't mean for the wolves to be freed from their exile here in Rye Errish," he replied ruefully. "Their master has power; I wanted that power. I would have had it, too, if the Maiden had succumbed to my song of enchantment. Her power joined with mine . . ." He mused for a moment but then said firmly, "But I was wrong. Here in Rye Errish—"

Nuin interrupted as leaves rustled beneath their feet, "We are not in Rye Errish anymore. The Otherworld is beyond even your reach now."

The darkness ahead was split by a jagged bolt of searing white light.

CHAPTER ONE

Caspar's newly acquired mount stepped delicately along the forest track, her burnished golden coat rippling in the dappled sunlight. So quiet was their progress that the faint rustle behind sounded startlingly loud in the near silence.

He twisted round in the saddle but could see nothing untoward. Trows Forest was still. Even the fluffy balls of white flowers coating the leafless branches of the blackthorn trees were motionless in the quiet air. Narrowing his bright blue eyes, he sought to pierce the gloom to either side. A twig snapped some way back down the track but he could see nothing untoward.

While twisted round and not looking where he was going, a low branch scuffed the back of his head. Wincing, he turned back to concentrate on the route ahead. The way was little used and the trees were closing around the path.

"Speedwell," he muttered aloud, forgetting the sound of the snapping twig. "Why couldn't Brid have sent someone else to find it?"

He brushed his hand through his thick auburn hair and was surprised to feel it damp. Pulling his fingers away, he looked at the smeared blood in surprise.

"Blackthorn, wretched tree of ill-fate," he grumbled, resisting the temptation to slash at one with his knife, a particularly fine blade. He grinned at the knife in appreciation. Like Sunsprite, his mount, it was also newly acquired and without equal in this world, and though its value far outstretched that of the verderer's horse, he did not prize it as highly.

The workmanship of the knife only briefly distracted him from the scratch to his head, which troubled him far more than so slight a graze should have done. The scalp at the crown of his head had itched of late and now bled at the least provocation, though the small injury had been some time ago now and should have healed. The deranged man in the dungeons of the Otherworld had attacked him with violent intent but had only succeeded in tearing a few hairs from Caspar's head.

Hurriedly, he tried to put such thoughts from his mind. It was too disturbing, too frightening even, to think of how close he and Brid had come to being lost forever in the land of spirit. Talorcan had nearly caught them. The bright image of the verderer's face still haunted his nights, still lurked in his waking mind. The creature of the Otherworld had wielded such power that he had nearly stolen Brid's soul and Caspar could not shake his fear of him. What if the creature pursued them? He shuddered and turned his thoughts back to the task in hand.

Knowing that its blue flowers would not yet be out and so would be hard to recognise speedwell from the foliage alone, he concentrated hard on his search. Hanging low over Sunsprite's shoulder, he scoured the ground, seeing little other than last autumn's decaying bracken and tall, black-tipped toadstools, and was beginning to worry that he wouldn't find any speedwell. The little girl was gravely ill and he must find the flower soon. Too much depended on the child.

Yet another twig snapped. This time he drew Sunsprite

to a halt, listening intently. Far from home, beneath this oppressive canopy of dark pine, ancient oaks and vast beeches, he was growing despondent. The trees grew up tall through the fallen bodies of their ancestors that littered the forest floor, providing a home for foaming fungi and spreading ferns, and he found the enclosed world stifling and alien. He longed, more than anything, to escape the damp closeness beneath the thick dark foliage and return to the far-reaching vistas and rugged landscapes of his mountain home.

Remembering that Hal had warned of mysterious beasts abroad, he felt for his bow, strung it in readiness and searched on.

Again, something moved to his rear. The snowy blossom on the branches of a blackthorn quivered and a snouty sandy-coloured face poked through the spiked twigs.

"Oh, it's you," Caspar said in relief, looking at the short little man with spindly legs and curiously dun-coloured skin. He lowered his bow.

"Spar, we should be hurrying home, not dawdling with the wagons," the woodwose complained, with no deference to the youth's nobility. His horns were gone, reabsorbed into his curly-haired scalp and he looked less and less deerlike with each passing day since they had returned from the Otherworld to the Ceolothian forest. Though his limbs were spindly and his movements skittish, he had something of the appearance of an overexcited, emaciated dwarf. "Spar, I need to get back to Sorrel. We must hurry."

"Go on without us," Caspar suggested impatiently. He, too, wanted to get home but his sense of duty forbade him from leaving the others. He was eager to see May. He had something important to tell her. "You'll be much quicker. There's no need . . ."

Fern wasn't listening. His nostrils twitched and his eyes were wide and black. "Wolf," he muttered.

Caspar stiffened but then relaxed as he saw the squat white form of Brid's terrier, Trog, snuffling along the track after them. Flopping along behind at his heels was the white wolfling they had rescued from trappers. Though Brid had not wanted to name a wild beast, Caspar insisted on calling her Runa for the rune-shaped scar on her shoulder. The mark was shaped like the rune ᛒ; Beorc, which represented rebirth and was the rune adopted to signify the Maiden. Brid had taken one glance at the wound and declared it confirmation that this was the wolf they had set out to find – the wolf that would lead them to the orphaned child who was destined to be the new Maiden. And the search for Runa had led them to the little girl who so needed the speedwell.

Fern leapt up onto a fallen log, stretched his neck up long and thin and grimaced at the dog and his floppy-pawed companion. Trog glared briefly up at the woodwose before bounding after Sunsprite, the wolfling nipping at the dog's heels and skipping back and forth around him in delight. Fern ran ahead to stay level with Caspar.

"You can't be afraid of Runa," the youth told him. "She led us to the new Maiden – just as the runes prophesied."

Fern's nostrils twitched faster and he kept a disdainful distance from the dog and wolfling.

"Help me find some speedwell," Caspar said peaceably.

"You passed some a while back at the foot of a tall pine before we entered the blackthorn thicket," Fern told him. "Didn't you smell it?"

"No. Why didn't you say? You knew Brid asked me to find some," Caspar began but found he didn't have the energy to argue with this strange creature, half deer, half man who had returned with them from the Otherworld.

Whereas he and Brid had accidentally slipped through the channels of magic to reach the Otherworld, he still couldn't quite come to terms with the fact that, like Abelard the archer, Fern had actually died.

Fern was right. The short-stemmed plant was growing nestled beneath a silver pine whose limbs stretched up high above the surrounding trees. Caspar carefully knelt and picked a handful of the delicate herb. Although he knew it was desperately needed, a part of him was reluctant to hurry back with it to the column. Hal was there. It wasn't that he disliked his uncle. No, not at all, it was just that Hal had become so smug since he had rescued Brid from the chief verderer.

Nevertheless, he pocketed the speedwell without delay and hurried back to his horse. Fern trotted along close to his side as they wound their way back through the dense forest, dangling ivy twining around their necks and arms at every opportunity. Caspar shuddered, still unable to drive the fear from his mind that ghostly creatures lurked in the shadows, prowling the forest in search of him. He was certain they were after him in particular, since he was master of Necrönd, the means to their release from their eternal exile in the Otherworld. He needed the Egg on his person to protect himself and protect it from thievery. He felt naked without it. How could he have let the high priestesses persuade him to leave Necrönd in the dungeons of Torra Alta?

The sound of voices ahead led him back to the train of wagons and he broke out of the forest into the middle of the column. Hal was still at the fore of the escort, strutting his way alongside two princes, one of Ceolothia and the other of Belbidia. Caspar reined in, waiting for the bulk of the wagons to pass so that he could join Brid at the rear. Princess Cymbeline herself, daughter of the powerful King Dagonet of Ceolothia and the betrothed of King Rewik of Belbidia, was nowhere to be seen. He presumed she was in one of the central wagons, resting on the long journey.

He kept himself distant from Hal and the two princes, who brought out the worst of his uncle's nature. He couldn't bear their posturing and contrived conversation about who amongst them was the finest knight. In Caspar's opinion, Hal talked too loudly of his accomplishments.

The nodding draught horses plodded by, leaning into their thick collars to draw the vast sagging wagons, trails of grease dripping from their axles. They bore the princess's dowry. He had glimpsed some of it when Princess Tudwal had checked it over at night and was still amazed at the heaps of finely crafted jewellery, brightly coloured silks and satins and particularly the glistening sunburst rubies that were a deep red with a shining golden heart. He had never seen so much wealth.

"Speedwell," he said laconically, offering it to Brid.

She took it gravely, too worried to even raise a smile of thanks, and returned to stroking back the damp strands of thin blonde hair from the face of the bloodless child cradled in her lap. "She is the special child. The wolfling brought us all together at a point where we could bring her back from the Otherworld. There can be no child more special than this little girl restored from death. But she is still too weak to speak and, until she can give us her true name, I have called her Nimue, after the moon Goddess."

Brid's words were soft and warm but her eyes and the dark shadows beneath them belied her calm. Her soft brown hair, which turned to burnished auburn whenever a rare beam of Ceolothian sunlight penetrated the close forest, had worked free from her tousled braid and hung in knotted tresses. She had discarded the silken dress given to her by the chief verderer of the Otherworld and, in its stead, wore one of Hal's tunics over an over-large skirt borrowed from one of Princess Cymbeline's ladies-in-waiting.

Midst the fine Ceolothian courtiers that accompanied the Princess, Brid looked so small and peasantlike. They called her the little wren because of her small frame and brown clothes but she laughed at them for it. But like the wren, she too could blend into the background and become one with nature.

Caspar thought that once they had found the innocent girl that was destined to take Brid's place as the Maiden, she would be filled with relief. All omens pointed to Nimue being the one but, perversely, Brid seemed more burdened than ever, though she would not speak of it.

"Brid, shouldn't we ride on ahead? They will be eager for news of us at home. We should hurry," Caspar urged, gently squeezing her shoulder.

She shook her head. "Nimue is sick. Too much depends on her. She must ride in the wagon and I cannot leave her."

"If what Hal says is true, the wagon might not be the safest place." Caspar looked suspiciously round at the Ceolothian troops. "What of this plot he's uncovered to steal the princess and her dowry?"

Brid waved a hand dismissively, never once taking her eyes off the quiet face of Nimue as she tried to protect her from the jolting wagon. "Hal's just being melodramatic. Only a fool would attack Princess Cymbeline. It would be madness to risk the wrath of both King Dagonet of Ceolothia and King Rewik."

Caspar was surprised that Brid criticised her betrothed. The corners of his mouth lifted into a half smile, glad to see that her love of Hal had not clouded her judgement of him. But fearing that his smile would stir her displeasure, he turned and swung his legs over the tailgate.

Marching vigilantly behind, though with a pronounced limp, was a strangely dressed archer who nodded politely at Caspar. It was still hard to believe that this man, Abelard, had been born four hundred years ago and had fought and died during the Ceolothian wars. Like Fern and Nimue, Abelard had also returned with them from the Otherworld. It was easy, however, to see that he was different from the other troops, his distrust of Ceolothians obvious and intense – though that was hardly surprising since it was a Ceolothian arrow that ended his life.

Young Pip, who had never managed to march in any form of orderly manner, matched him step for step, his broad grin constantly flashing up towards the archer. Brock fell in line behind Abelard, in awe of the man, constantly reminding Pip that Abelard was a man of legend, sung about in ballads from a time of heroes, and that he shouldn't be so familiar.

Those Belbidians not from the Barony of Torra Alta found his manner strange and shunned him, and the Ceolothians, unable to ignore his black looks, stiffened when he was near and tried to avoid him. Hal, too, clearly did not like him and it took Caspar no time to realize that his uncle resented how Brock and Pip so respected the archer.

Earlier that morning Hal had sneered, "Hero! Abelard the hero! We should be grateful, of course, at a time like this. No doubt, his mere presence will thwart any attack on the princess." The raven-haired young man had sniffed scornfully but then his expression brightened and he leant from his horse to give Brid a tender kiss on the top of her head before riding purposefully to the fore of the column.

To ease his tension, Caspar jumped from the wagon and strode alongside Abelard. Few words passed between them, both pairs of eyes fixed on the Maiden and her charge, as if their gaze in some way prevented Nimue from slipping back to the Otherworld.

"Spar!" Brid demanded sharply from the back of the wagon and the light-boned youth started at the sound of his name. "I need bloodwort. Take Fern and find me bloodwort. Morrigwen swears by bloodwort. Nimue is ailing; her blood is weak. Be quick about it!"

Caspar wasn't troubled by her biting manner; she looked tired as if she had been up all night and he shared her concern.

He turned Sunsprite from the road into the umbra of the trees and stooped over her shoulder, scanning the ground. The trees quickly muffled the sound of the plodding draught horses, creaking wagons and the crash of the huge cartwheels as they jammed on roots and heaved and bumped over the uneven ground. As Caspar left the track and entered the thick of the forest, he was immediately aware of an unreality that permeated this gloomy world. It was so still and self-contained. Nothing much seemed to matter here. The rest of the world was hundreds of miles away, all the hustle and bustle of human life so meaningless in the ageless still of the forest.

"Bloodwort," he now murmured repeatedly to himself, trying to focus his mind on the new task. He so wanted to get home. He had been away too long, far too far. Anything might have happened. His thoughts centred on the Druid's Egg that the high priestesses called Necrönd, cocooned in its rune-bound oak chest, deep in the dark safety of the castle dungeons. Something was wrong and he felt its hold on him clawing him back home.

Both Hal and Ceowulf had lately been troubled by

mysterious beasts and had accused him of wielding Necrönd to summon them. It was typical of Hal to immediately blame him, though he was little troubled by harsh words from his young uncle – he was used to it. However, the criticism in Ceowulf's voice had unsettled him deeply. The big Belbidian knight from the barony of Caldea spoke only with consideration. Hal might accuse him of misdeeds, just to put him in his place, but not Ceowulf.

Caspar's quest for bloodwort was proving fruitless; not even Fern could sniff any out, and the youth was deliberating whether to go on or return empty-handed, when the sound of women shrieking from the wagons made up his mind for him. The ground was trembling with galloping hooves and the air was split by a blast from Hal's hunting horn.

The note called out again as Caspar raced back through the trees. He never once thought of the Princess Cymbeline. His concern was for Brid and Nimue.

The trees whipped by, scratching at his face and scraping over his spine as he hunched up low over Sunsprite's withers and raced for the wagons. His heart plunged to his belly, knowing that Hal had been at the fore of the column and there were fifteen wagons between him and Brid in the rear.

Horses squealed and the clash of metal screamed through the forest. Sunsprite's pace quickened, her hooves effortlessly gliding across the treacherous ground. Caspar struggled to unhitch his bow from his back, his ears already ringing with the clamour of battle. He burst out onto the road and raised his bow, seeking a target. Unliveried soldiers and men clad in skins, a force three score strong at least, had engaged the escorting troops on both sides of the wagons. Caspar loosed two arrows in quick succession but soon the men were fighting at such close quarters that it made the use of the bow nearly impossible.

Shrieking out the Torra Altan battle cry, he loosed three more arrows at the outflanking enemy as he hurtled to the back of the column, intent on reaching Brid. His hand moved to his belt, reaching for the verderer's knife he had brought with him from the Otherworld. A spike of a blue metal, the blade shimmered with stardust.

Sunsprite reared, her cream hooves lashing out at a black animal that streaked beneath them. Caspar faltered. He knew it at once: a hooded wolf! A huge granite-grey beast with a black face and mane.

In reflex to a shriek from above, he raised his knife just as a man fell on him from the branches overhead. The ruffian impaled himself on the terrible knife that tore through the soft tissue of his neck. Blood soaked down Caspar's arm as he threw the man aside to be trampled beneath Sunsprite's hooves.

He looked ahead to the wagons. Abelard stood atop the rearmost wagon, loosing arrows into the mêlée below. Two attackers had stout poles under it and were using them to topple the wagon. Caspar charged. "Brid, get out," he yelled. "Get out!" He could hear the feeble cries of the little girl within. Where was Hal?

Five men barred Caspar's way. He sheathed the knife and nocked an arrow to his bowstring, loosing one and then another into the bellies of the men before him. He reached back for his quiver but pressed his hand to his scalp as a sudden and acute pain sliced through his head. He was certain he had taken a glancing blow from a hurled knife. He expected blood to gush over his face but there was none. The pain deepened and he slumped for a moment, suddenly intensely aware of wolves running through the undergrowth, flanking the wagons. He gritted his teeth and forced himself to focus.

"Spar! Spar!" Brid was yelling and the urgency of her cry cleared his head.

The wagon toppled and a crash of splintering wood tore the air. Women shrieked and horses caught in their harnesses squealed and writhed on the forest floor. Crashing caskets burst open and jewels and fine trinkets rattled out into the earthy carpet of leaves. Attackers whooped and yelled with the frenzy of battle, their cries mingling with the cacophony of clashing steel.

Caspar's hands reacted faster than his mind and he had already nocked a new arrow to his string. Brid was out from under the torn canvas, crouched protectively over Nimue. A man ran at her from the cover of the trees. Caspar loosed his arrow, the sound clean and sharp midst the ranging cries of panic and disarray. The shaft buried itself in the man's chest, driving him to his knees, pink blood and saliva bursting from his mouth. Caspar spurred Sunsprite to Brid, who had Nimue clutched under one arm. He reached down for her upheld hand and half dragged and half swung her away from the wagons. The few Torra Altan men followed in his wake and helped Brid up onto the back of a loose horse. She gripped Nimue over the front of the saddle but could not flee with her into the forest for the wolves and bears still charging in from all angles. Caspar thrust his hunting knife into Brid's hands and turned Sunsprite to protect her.

The Torra Altans formed a protective knot to the rear of the escort as wolves and bears swarmed over the fallen, and more men leapt out of the forest and cut into the troops guarding the wagons. Belbidians and Ceolothians alike were cut from their horses; dragged off by billhooks or hacked through limbs and torsos with common scythes. Caspar looked down the length of the column and fired on any rogue or mercenary offering a target.

The fighting was concentrated around the central wagons but Caspar's thoughts were not for the princess. He could see Hal beating a path towards them, the sweeps of his great broadsword scything rhythmically to left and right.

Heavily armoured and distinctive in his red and white chequered surcoat, Ceowulf was still at the fore of the column, the fluid effortless motion of his sword-arm swinging back and forth distinguishing him from the cumbersome efforts of the other noblemen around. Caspar watched as the Caldean knight hacked at shoulders and heads and speared a wolf through the neck. Using the heel of his spurred boot, he raked down the back of a trapper's head, tearing away scalp and stripping the flesh from his backbone in a broad sheet before he turned his destrier towards the central wagon where the princess and her ladies-in-waiting cowered.

Caspar loosed arrow after arrow but it was not enough. The ladies-in-waiting were dragged from the wagons and trampled underfoot. Prince Tudwal, bellowing with fury, cut at a knot of wolves around him, thrashing savagely in hot panic. Prince Renaud, a sack thrust over his head, was screaming for help as he was dragged from his horse and stolen away into the trees.

Then seven trappers set on Caspar and his companions at the rear of the column. With his arrows spent, Abelard used his knife to stab manfully left and right. Brid's horse reared and she fought to control the beast while still pinning the ailing Nimue to the front of her saddle. Caspar could barely think for the screams of the dying and the howls of carnage. The fighting was too close for his bow so he drew the verderer's knife, stabbing it into the face of a trapper that grabbed at his ankle. The man fell, blood pouring from between his fingers that were clamped over his eye.

The attack was aimed around the central wagon concealing the princess but Caspar could no longer see it for the clash of swords. Hal fought his way to the back of the column to reach Brid, and three more fell to his great broadsword, not rogue trappers this time but soldiers in the unmarked black livery of mercenaries.

A billhook was thrust at Caspar's face and he instinctively lurched backwards before stabbing down ferociously at the bare head of a mercenary. His arm jarred as he smacked into solid bone that then gave as the blade split the plates of skull.

Through the screams and wails, he fought on in a daze of exhaustion and disorientation. Sweat stinging his eyes, he could barely see what was happening around him. Someone had his foot. He looked down at the determined bloodied face staring up at him as the man began to haul him off balance. Then a cudgel struck his shoulder, sending a jarring pain down his arm to his hand.

Someone gripped his tunic and held him upright. With relief, he knew his bones hadn't cracked though he slumped forward giddily and it was a moment before he could turn his head and grin gratefully into Hal's face. His uncle's sword was dripping with blood and the body of the man with the cudgel now lay in two pieces in the mud. Caspar nodded his gratitude and, with gritted teeth, concentrated on the work in hand.

There was panic. Wave after wave of attackers crashed out from the forest, hacking their way towards the central wagons and, as each wave struck, the small Torra Altan group became more isolated from the rest of the column.

Huge black bears lumbered in behind them, lashing at the horses. Caspar tried to count his men. He couldn't see Fern and hoped the little woodwose was still somewhere deep in the forest. Nearby, he could see Brock, Abelard, Hal, Brid and Nimue. But where was young Pip?

A bear lashed at the canvas hood of a wagon. Crates of pearls spilt open on the ground as the beast tore through the contents. An arm flapped from beneath one of the spilt pallets and clawed at the rutted forest trail. Keeping crouched and his head low below the level of slashing swords, Abelard charged bravely forward to grab the hand. He heaved at it, dragging Pip out from beneath the toppled wagon.

The boy gave the ancient archer a sheepish grin and yelled above the shrieks of battle. "I've never seen a Ceolothian bear before. They're big!" There was no sign of fear in the boy's face despite the carnage around him.

Horses bolted for the woods, scraping off their riders on low branches, the floundering men left to the wolves. A black bear lolloped towards them, the animal's slashing claws level with Caspar's face. He wheeled his golden horse and flung his precious knife, focusing on the blade that cartwheeled through the air, slicing into the beast's left eye. The youth was not so accurate with a knife as he was with a bow but the bear fell. Caspar's triumph was short-lived. Another was immediately behind it.

"Pull back!" Brid shouted.

It was the voice of reason. The great slashing sweeps of Hal's runesword cut through the outstretched arms of the bears as if they had been parchment and allowed the Torra Altans to pull back into the cover of the trees and reform their tight knot.

Shielded by Hal's sword, Abelard retrieved a quiver of arrows, drew his bow and fired thick and fast until neither man nor beast dared risk an attack. For a moment they stood in silence, gathering their senses, their blood still tingling with adrenaline.

"The princess!" Hal appealed to Brid. "We can't just hide here like cowards."

"We were doing nothing to protect her and could never have reached her side," Brid argued, raising her voice above the desperate cries of men and women ringing out from around the wagons. "Nimue is more important. The continuation of the Trinity is all that matters."

"I'm going back. You'll be safe here with Spar," Hal insisted.

Brid snatched at his hand and held fast. "No, you must stay. You have the runesword: you must protect Nimue. The child is vital to us. She is the future Maiden and Morrigwen has not long to live. The Trinity must not be broken."

Hal looked at her for one brief moment of uncharacteristic indecision before his bony jaw hardened into lines of determination. "Spar will protect you. There will be war if a Belbidian escort allows harm to come to the Princess of Ceolothia. If anything happens to her, King Dagonet will vent his grief on us and all Belbidia. Thousands will die and I will not stand back to let this happen. Besides Ceowulf is in the thick of it. He is my friend. I will not leave him." He withdrew his hand, turned his horse and cantered back.

"No!" Brid shouted after him in outrage. "Hal, no! For me, don't, please don't. I need you." Tears sprang to her cheeks and she bit her trembling lip.

The remaining Torra Altans withdrew into the denser cover of the woods, their weapons drawn and braced for attack, and waited. After long moments of tense silence, the bushes to their right rustled. A black snout poked out, sniffing the air. The hooded wolf froze as it scented them then burst forward. Abelard loosed one arrow that pierced its throat and cut short its wild cry of attack. But the cry had alerted others to their presence and, in seconds, a bear was charging towards them, flattening trees in its rush. Caspar drew his bowstring taught but, with cool-headed control, waited until the bear was clear of the obscuring trees and bushes before loosing his arrow. Neither his first nor his second arrow stopped the beast and it took three more, one from him and two from Abelard, to bring it down.

They stared into the forest gloom, listening to the wails and cries from the trail, until, at last, came the sounds of withdrawal, horses and wolves galloping away, the noise of their thundering retreat swiftly absorbed by the forest. After the clash of metal and cries of pain, the sudden silence was almost tangible, hanging thickly in the forest air.

Brid was the first to speak. "We must see what help we can give." She spoke no words of concern for Hal's safety though her eyes were wide and almost black with anxiety. Cradling the child in her hands, she nudged her horse to walk forward. Caspar retrieved his knife then hurried after her and the others. Abelard was hurt. He had masked his pain well but, as he started to walk, he stumbled, gasped and clutched at his arm.

"It's nothing," he grunted, turning his wounded side away from them.

"Let me see," Brid demanded, handing Caspar the girl and sliding from her horse.

"I've had worse," Abelard joked as Brid looked at the slash in his leather jacket.

Beneath the jacket, his shirt and skin were wet with blood and it was hard to tell what was split flesh and what was drenched and shredded cloth. Quickly, she cut away his sleeve and pressed the oozing flesh together with one hand while binding it tightly with the other. Pip had hurried to place himself at Abelard's other shoulder for support.

"Fine lad," Abelard praised him and Pip grinned. Caspar had never seen the boy so happy.

When they reached the road, they halted at the sight of the carnage. Crushed and severed limbs jutted from beneath upturned wagons, their contents spilt in swathes of bright colour over the earth that was now dark and puddled with blood. The bodies of men and animals, friends and foes lay side by side in the final equality of death, the heaped bodies of the fallen blocking the road.

But where was Hal?

Brid bit her lower lip, her eyes flitting anxiously back and forth over the scene. "There!" She pointed. "Hal!"

He stood up from behind a toppled wagon, acknowledged her with a brief wave and returned to the task of freeing a man pinned beneath one of the wheels.

Caspar took in the rest of the scene. The escort, two score strong, lay slaughtered with, perhaps, twice as many bandits and mercenaries strewn around them. Three wolves moved amongst the bodies, tearing at bellies and driving their pointed snouts into the warm offal within. Caspar aimed his bow at the nearest and it shrieked horribly as the arrow dropped down through its shoulder. The others fled.

He grimaced at the dead animal and the five other wolf carcasses strewn in amongst the men and wondered that only six hooded wolves had been killed when so many had attacked. Even dead, the hooded wolves filled him with horror.

Brid refrained from rushing to Hal's side as the raven-haired man looked up from the man at his foot. Turning her angry back on him, she started the cold business of laying out the shattered and torn bodies. Though her face was pale and solemn, she showed no revulsion at the cold touch of the dead.

Hal left the man he had pulled free and began shouting for Ceowulf. Some of the fallen shrieked and thrashed; others lay still, groaning softly with their pain. Horses, some with flanks rent by great gashes, others with white and jagged bones sticking through the skin of their legs, trembled on their feet. Two struggled in panic, entangled in their harnesses. Midst the strewn bodies and thrashing horses, it was impossible to see at a glance who lay amongst the dead.

"We were lucky," Brid spoke quietly, "so lucky to be at the rear of the wagons and furthest from the princess."

"Ceowulf!" Hal bellowed again.

He was yanking away bodies, digging and kicking his way through them. At last, he stopped in his track and, mid-cry, his voice cracked. The Torra Altans froze as the raven-haired young man dragged away a man by his boots and heaved aside the body of a wolf. There lay the body of a knight. Clad in his red and white chequered surcoat, he was instantly recognizable as Ceowulf, youngest son of Baron Cadros of Caldea. Blood oozed from his forearm where his gauntlet had been ripped from his hand. His helm had been knocked from his head and claw marks raked his face.

Brid fell down by his side and pressed her head to his chest, listening intently. At last, she sat back. "He's breathing," she whispered and soothed his brow. "Ceowulf, dear friend, it's Brid. Don't worry, I will help you."

Caspar's heart pumped in his throat.

"Why are you all standing there staring? There's work

to be done. Find the wounded and bring them to me," Brid demanded as she tended Ceowulf's wounds. She sent Pip for water and blankets from the wagons and the others to search through the bodies for those that still breathed.

Hal did not respond to Brid's orders. "She's gone," he said quietly. "I was too late. They dragged her away into the forest. And there's no sign of Prince Renaud or Prince Tudwal. Nor Tupwell and Hardwin for that matter though they might still be here amongst all this."

Brid toiled for many hours, preparing poultices and washing wounds. Despite his own wounds, Abelard worked constantly beside her, his ancient skill learnt on the battlefields of their forefathers making him adept at the task. With strong hands, he straightened twisted limbs and stretched broken bones so that the high priestess could set them in splints. Hal and Caspar solemnly took the bodies to a glade, which was split by the road ahead, and laid them reverently in a circle, placing Ceolothian by Ceolothian and Belbidian by Belbidian. It was some while before a true account could be made of their losses.

There was no trace of any one of the other noblemen and there were at least half-a-dozen troops missing. Hal was glad that Sergeant Ogden was not among the dead. He had admired the man's professionalism.

"Ransom?" Hal suggested.

Caspar nodded. "Why else would they take them alive? Though how such well-armed men could yield to mercenaries I can't imagine."

"They weren't that skilled," Hal told him. "We'd been attacked a few times in the forest and only myself, Ceowulf and Prince Tudwal knew how to wield a sword. The rest were easy prey."

"But why stop at the princess and the noblemen? Why not take the dowry as well?" Caspar asked.

Hal snorted as if the answer were obvious. "We're the only ones left, us and a handful of injured troops, whom we must get to safety. What are we going to do? Carry the wagons on our backs, I suppose, since there's no more than three horses fit enough to walk. We're deep in Trows Forest. It's a good three or four days' ride out and they will have returned to clear up the loot long before we can get help."

They glanced back towards Brid who was stooping over Ceowulf. The knight was grey and had not moved since blinking once or twice before dropping back into a cold sleep.

Hal knelt beside Brid, put his arm around her and squeezed her shoulder. For one brief moment she rested her head against him before stretching up to kiss his neck. Then she pushed him away and gravely returned to her charge.

"Best make a fire for the night," Hal said with forced brightness.

"If we hadn't have been right at the rear of the column . . ." old Brock muttered, staring at the circle of dead lain out in the shallow graves he had dug for them.

Fern finally appeared from the trees. He sniffed at their work. "I wouldn't have bothered; the wolves will dig them up before the week's out."

Ceowulf stirred as the woodwose spoke.

"Wolves," he spluttered.

His eyes rolled beneath drooping lids, scanning the ring of young faces before finally fixing on Caspar. "Wolf, Spar!" he said in accusation. "An unnatural wolf. It walked on its rear feet, Spar, and it had an empty skull for a face." He spoke in gasps and then slumped back in exhaustion.

Brid crushed stems of woad and used the ink to draw

runes across Ceowulf's brow. "He's delirious. Hush, Ceowulf, these are runes of healing. Great Mother, we beg your protection. This brave knight, devoted to your service, is in need of your mercy." As she spoke, her deep green eyes flashed angrily towards Caspar.

"It's not my fault! I didn't do anything!" he protested more fervently than he had intended.

Hal was suddenly on his feet and, without warning, swung a clenched fist at Caspar. The well-aimed and unexpected blow knocked him to his knees. A stunned silence followed. For once, Caspar didn't return the attack but slowly pushed himself to his feet.

"I didn't summon them. They are not of my doing," he protested nervously.

"You've been tampering with Necrönd!" Hal roared, rubbing at his fist where Caspar's teeth had split the skin.

The younger Torra Altan withdrew sulkily. He felt foolish and ashamed and knew that no one believed him. Taking himself off to the edge of the glade, he sat and pulled his thick bearskin defensively around him. His only comfort was that the little wolfling squirmed out of Pip's arms and stumbled after him to flop into his lap. Together, they watched as the light of the fire grew, casting out a bright circle within the dark of the forest. Runa's white fur was soft and it soothed him to stroke it. Carefully, he avoided touching the rune-shaped wound on her shoulder. He patted her, trying somehow to convey his thanks that she had found Nimue for them.

"I didn't summon the hooded wolves," he told her. "I haven't been near Necrönd in weeks. How could I?"

"What do you mean by summon the wolves?" Fern was suddenly beside him, holding a stick that he brandished at the little wolfling. Caspar shielded her head protectively.

"Stop it, Fern! She won't hurt you."

"Humph! That's only because she's too young yet. But what have you done wrong, Spar, and why did you let that man hit you?"

"I haven't done anything wrong," Caspar protested vehemently. "I've done nothing. Just because they can't explain it, they choose to blame me. Everybody always blames me."

"But I thought you were a powerful lord. I thought you were heir to Torra Alta. How can you let them treat you like that?"

"Because I'm no one, Fern," Caspar tried to explain but sighed, thinking there was no use. His uncle had always commanded a deeper respect than he had and Brid was a high priestess soon to become the Mother, the most powerful of the Trinity. It would not matter how many titles he held; they would never respect him.

Fern prodded the wolfling with the stick and the little white cub grabbed the end of it and worried it back and forth savagely.

"You're a child," Caspar snapped and pulled the stick out of Fern's hands.

"You haven't explained anything," the woodwose complained. "How do you summon these wolves?"

Caspar shrugged and subconsciously rubbed at his scalp. "To save Torra Alta from attack three years ago and to rescue my mother, the high priestess Lady Keridwen, I had to find a talisman. An egg."

"An egg!" Fern echoed contemptuously.

Caspar nodded. "But it is an egg of sorcery and within it is held the breath of life of all the ancient savage creatures that once roamed freely across this world. They were banished to the Otherworld, to the land of spirit by the First Druid. The Egg allows me to summon them back. It draws them as ghostly creatures that gradually form into solid creations. The Egg we call Necrönd."

"And you are its master?" Fern sounded incredulous.

"I don't believe any man can be its master. I am its guardian – though the priestesses do not trust me with its care," he added bitterly. "They believe it has too much power and that I have been wielding it."

"Have you?"

"Since the Vaalakan war, no. Since then, I have been tempted and just once or twice, I admit, I have summoned maybe one or two creatures but I have always sent them back. I am not that irresponsible."

"You sound uncertain." Abelard was suddenly standing over them, the firelight flickering on his frowning face.

Caspar's arms fell open in honest dismay. "No one else can reach the Egg. No one else tampered with it while I was in Torra Alta. I checked daily. But still the wolves appeared. Sometimes I fear I summon them in my dreams, though I don't see how; I can't conjure up any spirit without holding the Egg in my hands and I've been away from it!" His voice rose in passion.

"You fear your spirit might be able to leave you at night and wield the Egg?" Abelard asked.

Caspar nodded. He felt a weight being heaved off his shoulders as he acknowledged his guilt. "Perhaps all these deaths are by my own hand."

Brid was hurrying over to join them, acute as ever to anything of import. She offered Caspar her hand. "We must talk. Come, join us by the fire. What you suspect may well be true. I will cast runes of protection around you while you sleep. Then we must hurry you home to Morrigwen and Keridwen to perform a rite that will shield your mind from the power of the Egg. The ancient creatures, banished for thousands of years from this world, will all pine to rejoin the cycle of life. The combined will of so many beings, focused on one common intent will be overwhelmingly strong. It will create a magic that will travel through the dimensions. They yearn to be released and they will worm their desires into your thoughts when your mind is weak. And, Spar, stop rubbing at your scalp," Brid's tone suddenly became sharp. "That scab will never heal if you keep picking at it."

"I must have caught my head on a branch," Caspar muttered. "It's opened up again."

"I have too much to worry about here without worrying about a scratch such as that." Brid pursed her lips irritably and set about her runes.

Huddled by the fire, Caspar could not ignore the flickering shadowy presence of the trees. He didn't like them. They seemed to hang over them like giant vultures. He longed for the heights and the open skies of Torra Alta.

A rustle amongst the trees made them all start. Caspar's hand snapped up his bow in automatic reflex.

Fern's neck stretched up tall and his nose twitched impossibly fast for a human, then he relaxed. "It's not a wolf or a bear; just a man."

Hal was smartly on his feet at the sound of twigs snapping and branches being pushed aside. Without a word, he disappeared into the gloom only to reappear minutes later, supporting an old soldier under his shoulder. Two others stumbled close behind.

"Master Hal, thank the Mother you're safe," the old soldier was saying with relief before nodding in greeting at the gathering of Torra Altans. "I chased after them but four turned on us and killed our horses."

"Take your time, Ogden," Hal told him kindly. "No need to rush. Sit by the fire."

"They took the princess and all the other nobles," Ogden panted. "Bagged them and tied them to the horses. They've headed deeper into the woods, streams of wolves flanking them. There's devilry at work."

As he talked, Brid mixed him a calming potion of hypericum in a golden goblet taken from the dowry and then turned back to the more injured soldiers.

Once they had made all the wounded as comfortable as was possible, they returned to the fire. Behind them, the toppled wagons had spewed forth their rich cargo of jewels, the great spills of sunburst rubies glinting like fairy fires in the camp's torchlight.

"We could fill our pockets and be the richest men in Belbidia," Ogden joked.

The surviving companions laughed though none of them made the faintest gesture to do so. Surrounded by death in the great expanse of forest, the jewels seemed worthless, no more valuable than the leaf mould and rocks around them.

Hal looked from the treasure to the Torra Altans, Ceowulf and the eight other soldiers that had survived the attack. There was not one Ceolothian amongst them.

"It'll mean war!"

"War! How so?" Brid asked. "Surely King Dagonet and King Rewik will work together to raise the necessary sums to ensure the princess's safe return. Then their combined armies will scour the forests until the ransomers are found and punished. But not war."

Hal shook his head. "There will be war between Ceolothia and Belbidia." He patted his breast pockets and then brought forth some scraps of torn parchment. "Renaud is behind all this, I'm telling you. I knew even before we entered the forest that he had plans to set an ambush. They'll ransom all the noblemen; but Princess Cymbeline won't be found alive."

"How do you know?" Brid demanded.

Hal placed the pieces of scrunched parchment together in some form of order. "You remember this," he waved the parchment, "I discovered hidden by the carcass of a wolf. It speaks of the princess and her sixteen wagons and warns that she must not leave Trows Forest."

Caspar shrugged. "How does that prove that Prince Renaud is to blame?"

"It's obvious, Spar, isn't it?" Brid suddenly jumped to her feet. "King Rewik is elderly and never once showed any inclination to marry. Everyone expected his younger brother, Prince Renaud, to succeed but the announcement that he intended to marry Princess Cymbeline changed everything. Hal's right. It will take no time for King Dagonet to realize that only Prince Renaud benefits from Cymbeline's death and then he will have revenge on Belbidia."

"And you found that in a wolf's carcass," Caspar repeated. "There are wolves in everything."

Brid looked at him and then, as if suddenly remembering something, reached for her herb scrip. Impatiently she tugged open the leather thongs that secured it and pulled out a roll of skin. "We found this in the Boarchase," she told Hal. "It's a communication about a find of sunburst rubies in the Yellow Mountains." She nodded at a glistening sweep of jewels that had spread like molten magma from a cracked casket. "We found this message inside the body of a buried wolf as if it had been left for wolf trappers to find."

"There *are* wolves everywhere," Hal echoed, snatching the skin from Brid's hands. "Wolves everywhere!"

Caspar pulled his bearskin up around his ears. So, Renaud wants the throne for himself and someone else wants to steal Torra Alta's mineral wealth from his father. It was strange, deeply strange and Caspar wondered whether it was just a coincidence that both conspirators had used trappers to convey their message.

He felt in his pocket and found the chip of bone that

Morrigwen had given him, its surfaces worn smooth by generations of worrying fingers. "The rune of the wolf," he murmured.

Brid looked at him thoughtfully, the light of the fire playing in her wide pupils. "The rune Morrigwen gave you; the rune of the wolf that represents the savage side of nature. There has been too much of it about you of late. Come, you are near sleep. I must perform the rite that will protect your spirit from their will while you rest."

"War," Hal repeated. "And we are not strong enough. Not now."

CHAPTER TWO

Brid's breath was sweet in Caspar's face as her cool fingers smeared streaks of blue woad across his bare skin.

Hal glared at them, the muscles on his jaw flexing as he ground his teeth, but he could have spared himself the pain of his jealousy; Brid's caress did not have the same exhilarating effect on Caspar that it would have had a month ago. He no longer yearned for her in quite the same way.

Later she brought a cup of dark liquid to where he lay in isolation beside a small smoky fire some thirty paces from the blaze of the main campfire. The potion tasted acid and he grimaced as he sipped it.

"It'll help you sleep more peacefully," she told him, scattering rowan twigs in a circle around him.

Once more she traced out the nine bands of runes that she had drawn around his head, chest and belly. "Three bands to bind the three states of being of the mind, three for the soul and three for the body," she told him. "These will stop your spirit wandering beyond your dreams."

His sleep, when it came, was not restful. He dreamed vividly of Torra Alta's dungeons even to the point of being able to smell the dank of the slime-coated walls. He dreamt he was in the cold, airless cell that contained Necrönd and was stooping over the ancient oak casket that guarded the Egg. The cramped chamber reverberated with the hollow sound of panted breaths and padding paws. He turned to flee the ghostly noise and, with leaden legs, laboured up the steps to the clean air of the courtyard above but the sound followed him and he turned to see shadowy wolves sniffing in his footsteps. He tried to run but the faster he ran, the more wolves took form, squirming like lizards out of the cracked stone walls of the ancient castle.

He awoke early before his companions and, with still drooping eyelids, gathered what horses he could and set to, stripping out one of the wagons for the wounded. Soon he was joined by Ogden and Brock, who laughed as they swept out the sunburst rubies from the bed of the wagon. No one showed any inclination to keep one piece of the treasure that had brought such ill-fate. It was a long march home through Trows Forest and they were all eager to move on before the bandits returned to claim their spoils.

They passed few traders on the rutted earthen road. Caspar loathed the long slow hours of the days trudging through the forests but they were more welcome than the nights, haunted by screech owls and the screams of wild cats, when the dream would return to torment him. He would awake hot and sweated. He felt better when at last they left the forests behind and entered the barren, windswept landscape of southern Vaalaka where the horses' hooves chimed and sparked on the bare rocks. Still, they had many long days' ride ahead of them.

On a grey morning, when now all but two of the soldiers were able to take to the saddle, they reached a high plateau and looked south. The dawn sun caught the jagged peaks of distant mountains and Caspar's heart warmed at the sight. Rising up beyond the harsh steely landscape of wind-worn rock and ash that formed the plateau of Vaalaka soared the brilliant gold of Torra Alta's Yellow Mountains marking the northern boundaries of Belbidia.

"'Tis like a golden crown tipped with diamonds," Abelard sighed. "What a sight! Aye, it's been a long, long time." His face suddenly dropped. "Still, it's sad. They're all dead now. Everyone I knew is long since buried."

Brid shook her head. "But they're not, Abelard. They are still there in the spirit of their descendants. They are still the same brave men of Torra Alta."

"Though most of them aren't quite men," Hal grumbled. "Since the Vaalakan war all but a quarter of the garrison are underage; it will be many years yet before Torra Alta will be able to defend itself properly. Most are imbeciles with the bow."

Brock nodded ardently in agreement. "Kids! Squealing kids!"

Fern continually skipped on ahead out of sight and they barely saw him for hours on end. They turned the wagon towards the banks of the Silversalmon whose waters drained the southern slopes of the Vaalakan plateau and carved south towards the heart of Belbidia. At last, the green strip of the Boarchase forest that skirted the northern foot of the Yellow Mountains came into view. Caspar smiled; at last, they were nearly home.

Catching the youth's emotions, Sunsprite stretched her pace out beneath him, snorting and whinnying. May would be waiting for him; his mother and father too would greet him with joy. His hands trembled as he eagerly anticipated stroking the smooth glassy shell of Necrönd. The thoughts jarred in his mind as he realized with disgust that his burning desire to behold the Egg overwhelmed all his other emotions. From deep within the roots of the great castle, Necrönd was calling him.

"Where's that stupid creature gone, now?" Abelard complained in his burred accent.

Until Abelard mentioned it, Caspar hadn't even noticed that Fern was missing. He shook himself, trying to concentrate on his surroundings. The Silversalmon slipping through the leafy shade of the late spring forest, raced past, dappled light flecking the rippled surface. He peered into the gloom of the Boarchase Forest. Where at first, he had only seen ribbons of light and shade banding the tree trunks, he finally made out a herd of speckled deer and young fawns, and wondered if Fern had gone to join them.

The forest thinned and he grinned proudly at the sight of a herd of grazing horses with young strong foals. They snatched up their heads from the grass at the edge of the road and, following the lead of a well-muscled stallion, vanished behind a spur of rock. Caspar smiled appreciatively. They were fine healthy animals; a good crop of foals and, in a couple of years, they would be ready to train as war-horses. Two years more and they would be ready for export. It was common knowledge that Torra Altan war-horses were the most highly prized in all the Caballan.

His gaze stretched south along the great sheer-sided canyon and stopped on a massive needle of rock that lanced up from its floor, supporting the castle of Torra Alta. The blocky buttressed walls dominated the canyon, glowering down at all that dared to approach. Caspar, however, saw it as a welcoming guardian. The sun played on the pale whinstone walls and the wind tugged at the blue and gold Dragon Standard of the Barony. The narrow pass around the Tor was the northern gateway to Belbidia and the castle of Torra Alta was the key; he was deeply proud of it.

"Y' think," Abelard murmured, his eyes moist with tears at the sight, "what them Ceolothians must've felt four hundred years ago as they marched on such a stronghold. Their hearts must've sunk to their rotten feet, finding themselves throttled by the canyon and facing the Tor."

The castle battlements, like giant gappy teeth, stood stark against the endless sky. Caspar barely took his eyes from the castle as they rode onwards, past an ancient henge. In his childhood it had lain toppled and buried beneath a mound of earth and creeping ivy, an unnatural hump in the flat flood-plain of the canyon floor. Now the resurrected stones, a ring of sharply pointed obelisks, shaped like sharks' teeth and standing to twice his height, stood clean and proud. Whenever he passed them, his skin prickled with emotion.

Thin stakelike figures marched the castle walls and lined the crenellations above the barbican towers, which jutted tall into the deep blue sky. The note of long ibex horns boomed out the call to muster.

Caspar frowned. "What's wrong? They're calling the men to the castle."

"They're not," Brid said softly. "They're calling us. We set out a couple of months ago for a short trip into the forest and they'll have been searching for us ever since."

Caspar swallowed as he thought of his parents' grief. He was about to race ahead when Hal jerked his horse's head up and galloped for the Tor. Sunsprite lunged forward but Caspar reined her in. Someone would be needed to drive the wagon and its inexperienced team of horses up the steep road that spiralled the precipitous cliffs of the Tor and he couldn't leave Ceowulf to do it. The knight was still barely fit.

"Go on, Master Spar," Abelard urged as if reading his thoughts. "Happen it might be I'm out of practice but I still lived longer at Torra Alta than y'; I can get the wagon up. And Brock'll help."

Old Brock grinned. "We're really quite capable, Master Spar."

Sunsprite burst into a gallop and raced across the ground, overhauling Hal's mare in seconds. Effortlessly, Caspar tore through the fields at the base of the Tor, past where the cockhorses stood waiting to help supply wagons draw the loads up the difficult incline. Heads spun as he sped through, his cloak flying out behind him. One or two gasped, pointed and shouted in alarm, not knowing what had cut through their midst at such speed; but Caspar didn't hear their words. Sunsprite's quarters were tucked beneath her, her taut hocks angled to power her up the steep incline, though her hooves barely sounded on the solid rock. Like a hot wind, they swept over the ground. Caspar had never imagined a horse could possess so much lithe power.

"Father!" he yelled as he streaked beneath the open portcullis. "Father! Mother!"

Young voices clamoured in alarm. "Spirits!" someone was shrieking. "Fairy horses!"

A man of middle years, tall and lean with dark hooded eyebrows and a beaked nose, strode quietly forward from amongst the youths.

"Captain!" Caspar raised a hand in greeting.

"Master Spar!" the man saluted with a warm smile. "We were worried. Cracker came home riderless weeks ago," his voice trailed off and Caspar realized that he was not looking at him but at his horse. His eyes scanned Sunsprite's sleek golden coat, silvery mane and tail. "I suppose we shouldn't have expected you to return with any mount less remarkable," he said with understatement though Caspar was no long listening.

"Mother," he called in a choked whisper, leaping from his horse and shamelessly running towards her outstretched arms.

Keridwen, normally so dignified in her approach, was running across the courtyard, her simple blue gown flapping up around her slender firm legs. "My boy, my child, I thought I'd lost you." She sobbed into his shoulder.

Caspar gently pushed her away and hurriedly wiped the sleeve of his shirt across his face. His father was crossing the courtyard and Caspar was reluctant to be seen with tears on his face.

Branwolf held out both his strong, square hands and took Caspar's in his firm grip. "The others?" he inquired in a low voice. "Brid, Pip and Brock?"

The Baron's son sucked in a deep breath and drew back his shoulders, knowing that it was his duty to apprise the warlord of the events of his expedition. It was one of the first rules of command to be able to give and receive information with speed and clarity.

"They are well, all well. Hal too!"

"Hal?" The Baron interrupted. "But you went in search of a wolfling that would lead us to the new Maiden. You only went to the Boarchase." He showed no surprise at Caspar's statement but, rather, made the youth feel that he must somehow be mistaken. The Baron raised his hand to stem his son's explanation as Hal clattered into the courtyard, hotly followed by Brid.

"He can tell me himself. Brother!" he hailed across the courtyard. "You have brought my son home." He raised his hands in greeting, beaming a grateful smile, and Caspar felt ashamed that his father immediately presumed that he was only safe because of Hal. "Tell me of the events." Already he looked to Hal to provide all the details.

Hal saluted. He was barely three years older than Caspar

and a great many years younger than his half-brother, Baron Branwolf, whom he closely resembled in his dark looks and robust body. Branwolf, however, was now greying heavily around the temples and his skin was thickened and creased by the years in the high-altitude sun.

"We came across Spar and his party deep in Trows Forest in Ceolothia. It seemed they had been waylaid by trappers who had taken the wolfling they sought. After they joined our escort party, we were ambushed. Princess Cymbeline, her brother Prince Tudwal along with our own Prince Renaud, Tupwell of Ovissia and Hardwin of Piscera were taken and the rest, save all those you see before you, slaughtered. Worse, I bring news that the ambush was devised by our own Prince Renaud and that other parties are plotting to steal sunburst rubies from the roots of your mountains." Hal, as always, had succinctly summarised the situation.

"We shall talk more of this as soon as you are rested and fed," Branwolf said smoothly though his eyes were worried.

"But we weren't all taken by trappers," Caspar began to insist.

Brid nudged his elbow. "Now is not the time to explain. Sometimes people understand more if you tell them less." Still cradling Nimue in her arms, she turned to Hal and gave him a kiss. "I have work to do and must leave you," she said, her eyes lingering on his before she swept away with Keridwen towards the west tower.

Caspar felt no jealousy; instead, he smiled at their happiness and turned to look at the faces of the gathering crowd. Pip was already winding his horse between the excited youths. "And I took my dagger and slashed back and forth," he told them loudly, "cutting the very screams from their throats. I fought alongside the great and noble knight Lord Ceowulf and stabbed the wolf in the neck that was tearing at his arm."

"A wolf? A hooded wolf?" the young boys of the garrison asked excitedly.

"A huge black hooded wolf. Vast it was," Pip told them and they gasped in amazement.

Caspar smiled at the boy's tale while searching through the crowd to find one face in particular. And there she was! She had given a cursory glance towards her young brother, Pip, but was now eyeing him. Their eyes met and Caspar held out both his hands, welcoming her. She stepped forward eagerly then walked on more suspiciously as if still distrustful of his emotions.

"Master Spar, I am pleased that you have returned to us safely," May said graciously if not over politely.

"Sweet Merrymoon," he murmured, his voice trailing away. He wanted to explain that he was over his infatuation with Brid and that he truly loved her alone. He fought to express himself but somehow couldn't find the right words.

"I groomed Cracker for you daily," she said shyly. "He wouldn't let the grooms near him and kicked his way out of his stall three times but I sat with him, hour after hour, until he trusted me."

"You did!" Caspar was delighted but found himself effusing about his horse rather than saying what he wanted to say. His hand itched to reach out for hers. He wanted so much to take her in his arms and, at last, claim her for his own, to stoke his fingers through her luxuriant chestnut hair that fell in ringlets to her shoulders and framed the gentle lines of her caring face. He wanted to look lovingly into those deep hazel eyes that seemed so sad; but he could not. Somehow, he felt unworthy. He needed time and wanted to explain his feelings properly and fully.

They were both acutely aware of the curious and expectant eyes, Cook's in particular, studying them, eager for gossip.

"But perhaps you don't want Cracker anymore?" She looked at Sunsprite resentfully.

"Oh no, I shall always want Cracker." Caspar was awed by Sunsprite's speed but he felt no deep passion for the horse, preferring the savagery and wicked nature of the stallion he had tamed from a colt. "No, I shall make a gift of Sunsprite to Brid."

May's face fell at this and Caspar instantly realized he had said something wrong. "But, no, I meant . . ." he began but May was already making her excuses.

"I must welcome my brother, then I must see to the high priestesses. I am still their servant and I must not shirk my duties," she said humbly, her voice thickening to the more pronounced accent of the Boarchase as if she wished to stress the differences between them. Defeated, Caspar watched her fast retreat towards her brother. Pip still fondly held the white wolfling and May immediately began petting her. Shortly she was rushing to the kitchens to find Runa some food.

"A fine-looking lass." Abelard gripped Caspar's shoulder. "Very fine indeed," he emphasized approvingly.

Caspar gave him a pleased grin. He had shared much of his soul with this man. Only he and Abelard knew of the deep anguish of the dungeons of Abalone, the lone castle at the heart of the Otherworld. Only they two, of all men, knew what lay beyond death and the bitterness that came with the end of an unfulfilled life.

"Come, Abelard, I will present you to my father but first we'd better get you fed and cleaned up. Brock, take care of our friend here, and see that Ogden and the other men are given food and quarters so that they can rest before making their journeys home," he ordered.

Already there seemed much business to be done. The priestesses had hurried away to discuss the wolfling and the little girl they had found; Hal was busy with Branwolf, no doubt explaining about Princess Cymbeline in more detail; and he too had pressing business of his own. He left Sunsprite to the groom and worked his way to the quiet corner of the courtyard where a well of worn steps led down into the black pit of Torra Alta's dungeons. Tense with anticipation, he hurried down the steps, fumbling for the keys that he had never relinquished. The half-burnt firebrand was still where he had left it and his hand trembled as he struck a flint to light it.

It was barely two months since he had last feasted his eyes on Necrönd but it felt like a lifetime. The fears of his dreams had been so real that he needed to see for himself that all was well. He flung open the dungeon door and held his torch high so that the light filled the central chamber. His knees went weak at the sight.

For three years, he had daily passed through the dungeon filled with its rusted implements of torture. They had always seemed macabre and barbaric, his imagination filling them with tortured bodies, but now he knew his imagination had not been vivid enough. He had experienced the reality of torture in the Otherworld and vowed to have the stocks, chains, fetters and cages removed from the castle at the first possible opportunity. On weak legs, he stumbled through the chamber, which felt thick with the memory of ancient souls, towards the cell that lay behind the low oak door at the far end of the dungeon. His mouth was dry and his heart pounded against his chest.

The place stank and now he knew what that smell was – the deathly smell of hooded wolves. He sensed them everywhere about him, their hungry presence pacing this very same space but in the separate dimension of the Otherworld.

His breath came in panted gasps as he wrenched open the low cell door and crawled into the cramped hole dug into the solid foundations of the castle. He dropped to his knees, his slender shoulders brushing against both walls of the pit where the prisoners of ancient times had been crammed into dark and solitary confinement.

Barely daring to breathe, Caspar stared for a full minute at the casket, examining it in every detail. The runes of warning were still as stark as ever. He scanned the words without thought for their meaning, his eye searching for the strands of his own red hair that had spanned the body and lid of the casket. He had placed three across the crack just to be certain that no one had tampered with the casket in his absence and, with great relief, sighed as he saw they were all exactly where he had placed them. The lid of the blackened casket creaked as he opened it. He hunched forward, eager to see the simple blue marbling of the Egg nestled on its humble bed of moss. He stroked it, his fingers trembling as if he were caressing the smooth belly of a maiden that had come to his bed for the first time.

Such power, such terrible power lay beneath his fingertips. He need only cup the Egg in his hand and he could summon all manner of beasts into this world and marshal them to his command. He could send dragons to find Cymbeline and two-headed bears, like the one Hal had described, to rid Belbidia of the plague of hooded wolves. He could fill the skies with griffins and set them to guard the walls of his castle. No one, nothing could deter him in any purpose that he desired.

The Egg begged him to wield its powers, pleading with him to be as a god and summon the beasts from their captivity in the Otherworld. He could end the miserable suffering of their existence and give them life. All they desired was to breathe again and feel the warm earth of the Great Mother beneath their feet.

"Fool, Spar!" a voice split the dank air of the dungeons.

Caspar slammed shut the lid of the casket and fumbled to close the hasp.

"Fool, Spar, you have been home no more than minutes and you are down here meddling!"

The youth felt his freckled skin burn crimson. His mother's voice was terrible, sharpened by disappointment.

"But, Mother—" he started to protest, plucking out three more hairs to bridge the crack of the casket before climbing out stiffly into the wider chamber.

"I knew you would be here. When will you learn?"

"I have done nothing."

Keridwen wasn't listening. "I have been patient, more than patient. Have you no idea of the harm you are unleashing? The land is awash with wolves."

"It is not by my doing. But if you would let me wield Necrönd, I could drive them back."

"Others are blaming us for the slaughter, Spar. Have you no idea what that means?"

"But it's not me! I've done nothing!"

"How can you lie to me?" Keridwen's voice was cold with anger and Caspar shrivelled inside. He longed for her comfort and reassurance.

"But, Ma, I have done nothing." Why couldn't she hug him as she had done on his return? "Ma, I just had to check that it was safe, that no one had touched it."

"I do not believe it. The place reeks of necromancy."

Caspar had to agree: the air was stale and putrid with the decay of death. "But I have summoned nothing, no one," he insisted.

"There is hatred, hatred everywhere in these walls," Keridwen continued, her tone now more anxious than angry. She held out her hand for her son. Though he was bitterly resentful of her lack of faith in him, he longed for her comfort and took it gladly.

"Can't you see I'm afraid for you? These monsters loathe man. It is man that slaughtered them and man that banished them to the Otherworld." She was talking gently now, her free hand flicking out in warding gestures about them. "This much hatred is overpowering. In the end, their combined purpose will conquer you. Spar, you are my son; you must trust and obey me for I want only what is right for you."

"But I am strong enough to wield Necrönd! You only think I am not because you haven't noticed that I've grown into manhood. You still think of me as a helpless child."

"I notice more than you might like, Spar, very much more. I simply don't believe that any man has the strength of mind to be master of Necrönd, least of all one who wishes to do so much good." She smiled at him tenderly. "Come, your father has called an assembly in the upper hall; there has been a messenger."

The arched hall was warm and smoky. Three deer-hounds lay full length, roasting their bellies beside the blazing fire set deep into the west wall. Only the twitch of an ear belied their interest in the human activity around them.

Branwolf wouldn't sit until the oldest of the High Priestesses came to join the counsel. He paced back and forth before the fire with Brid's short-legged terrier, an Ophidian snake-catcher by breed, constantly at his heels.

He held in his hands the torn pieces of parchment and

roll of skin stained with writing that Hal and Caspar had given him, ruffling them as if feeling for an explanation. The Captain sat at a long table with all those Torra Altans who had returned from the Ceolothian forest, Pip beaming from ear to ear, his dark peppercorn hair brushed and shining for once. Brid sat slightly apart, stroking the soft white head of the Yellow Mountain wolfling they had rescued from the trappers. Abelard looked on with an unfathomable expression, while old Brock appeared anxious and fidgeted uncomfortably in the presence of the noblemen. Fern was not with them. In fact, Caspar had not seen him since he had skittered away into the Boarchase.

The youth stared into the fire, wondering what May was doing right at this moment and going over and over in his mind how best to proclaim his love. The moment had to be special. Should he kneel at her feet and ask for her hand? Should he grasp her in his arms, say nothing but kiss her passionately? Should he lead her by the hand to watch the sunset and whisper quietly in her ear of his devotion to her?

Morrigwen appeared at last. Caspar was so shocked by the change in her that his mind was jolted away from daydreaming about May. The Crone was carried by a burly young archer and Keridwen rushed forward to lead them to a couch while Brid hastily arrayed cushions.

"By the fire," the ancient woman ordered, her creased and craggy face like the dried hide of an old troll. The light of the fire shone through her wispy hair to her wrinkled scalp. "I must be by the fire. Branwolf, why do you let this place get so cold?" she grumbled, glaring at the Baron with frosted white unseeing eyes. She wheezed and spluttered and Caspar was horrified by how she had aged. "Why have you gathered us here? You should have come to my chambers."

Branwolf looked at her sympathetically but said in a low controlled voice, "Because I am Baron of Torra Alta and lord of this castle and will rule from my own hall." He turned to address the assembly. "I have received yet another message from the King and—" he stopped in his sentence as Morrigwen loudly scattered her bag of rune-carved bones over a low table beside her. "Morrigwen!" The Baron's voice was tinged with impatience and Caspar was instantly alert. His father was invariably steady and controlled in his commands. "May I begin now?"

The old Crone sniffed and waved a distracted hand at him while continuing to fumble and scrunch the rune-carved bones in her fingers. Caspar had thought she would be elated when they had brought Nimue home but it seemed not. A sudden draft swept wood-smoke back into the room and Morrigwen coughed, dropping her runes to the floor. Brid hastily gathered them up while Branwolf glowered thunderously.

"I have news of import." He unrolled a long parchment scroll and pinned it to the table with four tankards. Caspar leant forward eagerly. A rough circle of blue wax at the bottom of the page was stamped with the mark of the King. Alongside sprawled a spidery signature scratched in red ink.

"The King requires that I enlist the aid of all my men, be they noble or peasant, to slay every wolf that roams my lands. Every single one, be they a hooded or a Yellow Mountain wolf. And I am to send him the pelts as proof of our actions."

There was silence as the members of the counsel looked at one another.

"But that's madness; the King surely means us to kill only the hooded wolves," Hal interrupted.

Branwolf slammed down his fists in anger. "You have

been away, brother. This is the third message from the King in as many weeks, not mentioning the deputation from the Barons of Jotunn, Nattarda and Ovissia. They are suffering huge losses to their livestock. Our friend Baron Bullback alone has lost eleven prize bulls!"

Caspar found this puzzling. On their return, they had seen herds of deer and horses running free all along the fringes of the Boarchase. If the wolf numbers were so threatening why, then, hadn't their own livestock been attacked?

"Since the murdered carcass of the sacred she-wolf was brought within these walls, I have forbidden all trapping. And Baron Godafrid of Ovissia is livid," Branwolf told them. "I have scoured the woods but we have killed all of three hooded wolves. Three! And yet they complain of hundreds. More than half the boys of the barony are out in the mountains now, reporting daily that they see rare sightings of the hooded wolves but none are good enough shots with a bow to bring them down."

"We must go ourselves," Hal said forcefully.

"I have a hundred men out there! Do you think that you, Hal, will make any difference?" Branwolf's voice was strained and Caspar was aware of the heavy burden that lay on his father's shoulders. "A hundred men and they have killed three wolves in as many weeks. It's pathetic! Our neighbours are angry but I will not pacify them with the pelts of innocent and harmless Yellow Mountain wolves."

"You intend to defy the king?" Hal looked surprised though quietly pleased.

Branwolf sighed. "I do and I must. Just as I must do something about the hooded wolves that plague our neighbouring baronies."

"I can wield Necrönd!" Caspar stood up, speaking more

loudly than he intended. His chair toppled behind him, crashing to the reed-strewn floor.

The hall was suddenly quiet. Everyone stared at him, hope glistening in his father's eyes. The silence was broken by Morrigwen flinging her scrip of runes across the floor. "Never! This is where all this evil started."

"I did nothing!" Caspar protested. "I did not summon these wolves." Involuntarily, he scratched at his scalp where the crown was sore.

"The more you tamper with that Egg, the more hooded wolves appear. The correlation is clear. Perhaps the Ovissians are right to blame us for this plague," Morrigwen said harshly.

"Silence!" Branwolf boomed. "I believe my son when he says he has not summoned these wolves."

Caspar flushed a brilliant red, his hand springing to his crooked nose, which he nudged self-consciously. He feared the old Crone was reading his thoughts, probing for his sense of guilt.

Branwolf turned to study his wife's expression. Keridwen was calmly shaking her head and Caspar knew he would be forbidden from using the Druid's Egg to save them all. He looked at his mother resentfully, thinking that just once more would do no harm. The hall buzzed with whispered conjecture.

Branwolf raised a hand, demanding for silence. "Enough! There are other things to discuss for it seems that trouble comes in threes: prospectors after my minerals, the Princess Cymbeline ambushed, and the wolves. The minerals can wait. Hal, you will ride straight for the King's court in Farona with the heavy news of his bride. It might at least make him worry less about the wolves." He laughed ironically. "The rest of us had better join the wolf hunt."

*

The hunting party of thirty mounted men and youths rode out into the mountains at first light. Glad to be back in Firecracker's saddle, Caspar raced to the fore. The Oriaxian purebred was one of the fastest animals in the countries of the Caballan Sea. Though he lacked the pure energy of Sunsprite, Caspar welcomed the earthy solidity of his lean-legged stallion.

Their route took them south-west into the lower foothills of the Yellow Mountains that bordered Ovissia. The lower pastures were grazed by large herds of stocky mountain horses with broad backs and stoical natures that formed much of the barony's wealth. They were perhaps more wary than usual at their approach but not so much as to stop them grazing on the clover and grass that grew richly on the warm, well-watered slopes of the south-facing mountains.

"My, Lord Branwolf, you've lost no foals to the wolves?" Brid queried. She had insisted on riding out with the hunt and, since Hal had already left for Farona, there was no one to stop her.

"None," the Baron agreed. "I lost two foals this spring but not to wolves, just to natural sickness. It was the same when the plagues hit the rest of the country these past two years; we never suffered from them either."

"No, but that was quite explainable. In Torra Alta we let our animals roam free. Disease does not spread and fester as it does in the overcrowded sheds of the lowland stock farms."

"Still, they blame their plagues on us because we do not suffer them. But I can't explain why we are spared by the wolves. My foals are at least as vulnerable to wolves as Baron Bullback's young oxen yet he has lost eleven bulls. I cannot explain it."

"Look! Wolf! Wolf!" one of the young archers shouted, eager to alert the hunting party to their quarry.

The older men groaned but Caspar felt sorry for the overzealous lad who had spoiled the hunt. He had undoubtedly scared off every wolf for miles around but now he would have to suffer the taunts of the other lads and it could be years until he lived such an incident down.

"It was a black wolf," the red-faced lad was explaining. "I saw him up there on the skyline."

It was several hours more before they spotted any other wolves and this time it was a small pack of pale grey Yellow Mountain wolves. They were thin and rangy, scavenging right up in the higher peaks where there was little food.

"They'll die before the summer comes," Brid said with regret.

As her self-appointed bodyguard, Abelard tried hard to stay alongside her but clearly found the task difficult. Having spent most of his life with a bow in his hand and on his own two feet, he was not a strong rider. He couldn't begin to keep level with her as she galloped in circles around them, evidently thrilled by the speed of the horse from the Otherworld. Abelard eventually gave up the task and fell in alongside Caspar.

"Y' shouldn't have given her the horse," Abelard rebuked him, "Er, Master Spar," he added the respectful title as if in afterthought.

Caspar barely noticed. "Wolf, hooded wolf," he hissed. "Way up there." He pointed to a black speck.

With gestures of his hands, Branwolf silently spread the men out into one long thin line as they rounded towards a spur of rock that spat from the steep slopes into the valley bottom. With reins knotted and guiding their horses with legs alone, they drew short bows that could be easily handled in the saddle. Caspar groaned inwardly as he watched the younger lads struggling and fumbling, bows entangled with reins and quivers sloped over at precarious angles where they had been improperly buckled.

The Baron waved the line to a halt and patiently waited for them to right themselves. Caspar admired his father's consideration but knew that hours of gruelling practice awaited the poor lads on their return until they could all do this simple manoeuvre with ease. They paced forward again but when a few allowed their mounts to jitter or shy, he ordered them to a halt and waved only the experienced few forward.

The great black wolf was still a distant silhouette against the western skyline. After stealing forward for a slow minute Abelard raised his bow, a fine laminate of yew that Caspar had tested but had been unable to draw. It was an uphill shot and he seemed uncertain of the range because he lowered it again and shook his head. Caspar knew he needed to be another thirty paces closer to make certain of a kill so he and Abelard crept forward alone, keeping low amongst the boulders and scrub.

They were downwind of the beast and the wolf was clearly not yet aware of them. Squatted on its haunches, it had its back to them. Caspar drew back his bow, ready to take aim, his muscles tensing, filling him with that wonderful feeling of power in his chest and arms as he strained against the draw weight. He took aim and drew a deep breath, steadying the shot. It was, by anyone's standards, a very distant mark but he knew he could do it. He wanted to prove to Abelard that the men of Torra Alta were just as proficient as they had been in his day.

"No! Wait!" the Baron cried.

The wolf sprang for the safety of the scrub and fallen boulders that swallowed the light beneath. But as it leapt, it gave out a shriek and began to tumble, crashing onto the rocks. Caspar and Abelard sprinted back for their horses to catch up with everyone else who now sped towards the wolf, Brid on Sunsprite streaking ahead of the men like a bolt of golden lightning.

"Who shot that arrow?" the Baron shouted. "It wasn't a hooded wolf." With futile but determined attempts to catch up with Brid, Abelard was shouting at her to be careful. She made no sign of hearing him and, on reaching the fallen wolf first, while she slid from her horse and knelt beside it.

"It's dead." She looked up at them in sorrow as they drew to a halt. Close to, it was immediately apparent that this was a Yellow Mountain wolf. Though dark ones were rare and this male was exceptionally large and well-muscled for a Yellow Mountain wolf, it lacked the black mane that gave the hooded wolves their name and was still considerably smaller.

"Who loosed that arrow?" Branwolf demanded though he didn't bother to look at the line of inexperienced lads trotting up behind them. The idea that any one of them could have made the kill at that range was ridiculous.

Brid sprang back up onto Sunsprite and, like a winged unicorn, the animal dived up the scree to reach the rock on the skyline. There, Brid sat tall, scanning the next valley, then, with a single cry of pursuit, plunged away out of sight. Abelard hurried for his horse though he wasn't even mounted before Caspar was up on Firecracker and away.

Shrieking wildly like a banshee, Brid plunged recklessly down the far slope, closing rapidly on three riders galloping south for the border. Sunsprite swept through them and they howled and cursed as if they had been charged down by a demon. Caspar hurtled after her.

CHAPTER THREE

May crawled into the tight recess of the half-shuttered arrow slit. Pressing her face into the narrow opening, she watched the tiny figures of the hunting party race across the canyon far below and eagerly sought out Caspar's light athletic form.

Mounted on his flame stallion, she picked him out with ease and bit her lip in disappointment; he was galloping closely alongside Brid on her new golden mare. How could she compete? It didn't seem to matter that Brid was betrothed to Hal; she could see that Caspar still loved the young high priestess. Guiltily, she realized she was scowling at Brid's minute figure. She respected Brid – she was the Maiden and One of the Three – but she also resented her as a woman.

When Caspar had first returned from Ceolothia, she had thought for a while that something was different. She had sensed that he wanted to tell her something meaningful and perhaps, at last, would declare his love for her. But how could she have hoped for that when, there he was, riding jubilantly alongside Brid, just as before?

She hurt inside. Of course, as a woodcutter's daughter, she was never going to be his equal. How could she have let herself be so foolish as to fall in love with him? She sniffed and swallowed hard, trying to reason against her blasphemous resentment towards Brid. It wasn't Brid's fault, she knew that, though she thought that the priestess could have done more to discourage Master Spar. She looked down at her tightly clasped hands, furling in her emotions.

"Merrymoon, the fire! You've let it die back!" Morrigwen scolded, her head tilted to one side as she fixed May with her sightless eyes.

Turning her back on the scene below, May hurried to stir the embers and pile on yet more logs. She stumbled in the gloom before her eyes had time to adjust to the dimly lit interior of the turret room. Morrigwen preferred her chambers dark and allowed only the deep golden glow from the fire and a small chink of light to fall through from the shuttered arrow slit. The turret room was always hot yet the old Crone complained miserably of the cold.

Keridwen sat by her side and the two muttered constantly. May was too much in awe of Keridwen to feel a strong warmth for her but she loved the old Crone like a grandmother. Once, soon after her mother's death, May had hoped that Morrigwen would choose her as the future Maiden, but it was not to be. Though the old Crone had befriended her and taught her many of the priestesses' arts, she was still an outsider to their esoteric world.

The girl Brid had brought back from the Otherworld sat in the corner of the room, playing with the salamander. May understood her quiet sorrow since Nimue, too, was an orphan. Listless and pale, no one yet had heard her murmur a single word. Little Nimue had none of the priestesses' strengths but maybe it would come in time. May was worried for her and, picking her way through the fallen books, heaped herbs, scattered utensils and avoiding the heat from a spitting cauldron, moved gracefully and silently across the room to offer the child some comfort.

Kneeling, she patted Nimue's hand, trying to hide her revulsion at the feel of the girl's cold clammy skin. May didn't fully understand where Brid had found her, only that the white wolfing had picked her out as the new Maiden. She was to be publicly announced as Brid's successor at the fire festival of Beltane that marked the beginning of the light half of the year and the blooming of fertility in the land. Despite the efforts of the New Faith over the previous decades, Beltane's tradition as the day for courting had never been abandoned even amongst the most zealous men. Now, since the reinstatement of the Old Faith and with so much young blood occupying the castle, the religious festival was fervently observed.

Beltane was but days away, the preparations well underway, and the messengers sent out to discover whether Nimue had any living family had still not returned. If no parents could be found, it was certain that this frail child was the one that would fill Brid's shoes; only an orphan could become a high priestess.

May sniffed and listened.

Her attention sharpened; the two high priestesses had mentioned Caspar's name. Had they forgotten her presence here on the floor in the shadows? She didn't move so as not to distract them from their conversation.

"I fear for his soul." Keridwen's voice was tense. "How much of it is already devoured by the power of Necrönd? The will of the beasts on the other side is too strong for him."

"It is his doing. There is no other explanation. Spar must be summoning the wolves," Morrigwen reasoned icily.

"He swears to me he is not," Keridwen said defensively.

"Yet he will not give you back the keys."

Keridwen shook her head. "No, he tells me he is its

guardian. The Great Mother put that responsibility on him and he will not relinquish it."

"The Druid himself hid the Egg for a good reason; he could not even trust himself with its guardianship. Spar is young and innocent. How can he have the wisdom to guard the Egg? How many more of these devilish creatures need cross the divide before they have total control of him?"

"What can we do? At night, I have cast rowan about his bed and Brid has daubed him with binding runes but he has grown too strong for us. We can no longer contain him." Keridwen's voice trembled.

May felt her anguish; she too was deeply troubled for Caspar. She loved him more than all else and, if the priestesses could do nothing to save his soul from the evils of the Otherworld, she knew that she must. Though lacking the craft of the high priestesses there was one thing that even she could do.

It was late that day before the hunting party returned and, when it did, it was midst much shouting. Brid, her face aflush, sat astride Sunsprite's golden back, her indignant cries ringing through the courtyard. May hurried with Keridwen to see what the commotion was all about.

A great black wolf lay slumped over the front of Branwolf's saddle, its head flopping to the beat of the horse's footfall, blood dripping from its mouth. The little wolfling at May's feet sat back on its haunches and howled pathetically.

Branwolf met his wife's gaze. "It's the Black Wolf, my namesake," he said sadly. "They shot him. These three Ovissians killed him."

The accused were hustled forward into the courtyard, the last shoved roughly from behind by an overzealous guard. He tripped and fell heavily against the carcass of the wolf. Horses scattered in the commotion and May pressed herself back against the courtyard wall for fear of being knocked over. She moved to the steps of the kitchen and climbed them to see above the heads of the men and glimpse the prisoners. In surprise, she noted that one was no more than a young lad.

The Baron's voice boomed over the commotion. "I have decreed that no more Yellow Mountain wolves will be killed in my barony. Should I have you flung from the castle walls as an example that none can carelessly disobey me? I am Baron of this land. No one will defy me."

"Then you are a murderer! The wolves have slaughtered whole villages. Ovissian men, women and children still lie unburied with their throats ripped out by your wolves," the boy shrieked.

May was shocked that he dared to shout with such hatred at the Baron. The Captain slapped him hard across the mouth but the lad did no more than spit blood and sneer up at him defiantly.

"We wear the Ovissian colours. Strike us and you strike at Baron Godafrid," one of the older men grumbled at his feet, not daring to raise his eyes to meet the Baron's.

The youth's high-pitched voice cut through the crowd's murmuring. "You'd rather see Ovissians savaged than be rid of these mangy wolves? What are you, Baron Branwolf? Their devil leader?" He spat out the last syllable of the Baron's name.

Jeers echoed through the courtyard. "Throw him from the walls!" the cry went up.

Branwolf raised his hand for silence and, ignoring the distraught boy, stepped closer to the older of the two men, overshadowing him with his great bulk. "I am sorry for your distress," he said coldly. "But I will have no more of this madness. You are killing the wrong wolves."

Stuttering, the man found his nerve. "Look at the wolf's teeth. Just like the teeth that tore out my wife's throat. We in the Ovissian wolds are dying. Is it not strange that you and your witches are not? We saw horses and many young foals grazing peacefully and yet the wolves that pour out of *your* mountains into *our* pastures are killing men, women and children. You are a murderer, a treacherous murder."

"Throw them in the dungeons," the Baron bellowed.

"No!" Caspar shouted, his lone voice all but drowned out by the excited high-pitched yells from the garrison. "You can't. No one has been thrown in there for hundreds of years."

Only for the briefest moment did May think that the youth hesitated out of mercy. Caspar had paled and his eyes flitted towards the dungeon steps; he was thinking of Necrönd.

Branwolf glared down at his son, his eyes black with anger. "No one has dared defy a Baron of Torra Alta before. A cold dark night will set them straight." He held out his hand for the keys.

"But . . ." Caspar hesitated.

"The keys!" Branwolf thundered.

Caspar reluctantly fetched them from his inner breast pocket.

It was two days before the Baron let the men out again. Since, clearly, they were tough men – no lesser man would have defied a Belbidian baron in such a manner – and the punishment was by no means harsh, May had expected them to look, at the most, miserable or downcast. But it was terror that she saw in their white faces as they tripped and fled across the courtyard, booed and pelted by the Torra Altan garrison.

"Let that be a warning!" the Baron boomed. "Tell your comrades, if I catch them killing Yellow Mountain wolves, I shall lock them in the dungeons and forget about them."

Caspar anxiously retrieved the keys from his father and hastily disappeared, his eyes furtive.

May's stare followed him; she too needed those keys.

It was long after dark before she had the opportunity of acquiring them. The busy noises of the castle, the shouts of the boys, the constant scurry of feet and clatter of hooves in the courtyard, even the clank of pots from the kitchens had finally ceased.

Checking that the four kitchen maids, whose chamber she shared, were soundly asleep, she stealthily opened the door out into the corridor just a fraction and squeezed through. She crept along the dark echoing halls to Caspar's chamber, her heart fluttering in her throat as she put her hand to the hoop of the latch. The door was shut. She wondered if anyone had seen her. Tongues would wag and the kitchen maids would enjoy the gossip. Still, she didn't care so long as they didn't guess at her true purpose.

The latch moved with a creak and she was surprised to see light flood out from the room. At first, she thought Caspar must still be awake and began wondering what reasonable excuse she could give for her presence until she heard him moan in his sleep. Slipping inside the door, she blinked in the flood of candlelight that was reflected in a glassy pool of liquid surrounding the youth's bed. The candles were arranged in a ring around his bed, themselves surrounded by a ring of small stones, all within a ring of water-filled chalices. Sprays of rowan to ward away evil spirits encircled the entire pattern.

May took a step back. The youth on the bed lay half naked, his belly, chest and brow banded in runes written, no doubt, by Brid. She sniffed resentfully. For a second the sight of his tight chest muscles absorbed her. He squirmed and wriggled in his sleep as if fighting with an enemy. In his hand, he clutched the ring of three keys, his knuckles bloodless with tension.

She stood and watched, waiting for the dream to pass and for him to relax his fingers. Her breathing seemed to roar in the stillness of the chamber and the minutes dragged by; she dared not move a muscle. At last, he lay still though his hand was still rigid around the keys. She crept forward and hesitated, suddenly fearful of crossing the circles.

She swallowed hard, wondering what spells were woven into the circles and decided they had to be protective ones. She was uncertain of the meaning of the stones, water and fire but knew the rowan was there to ward away those of evil intent. But she meant him no harm, in fact the opposite, and she prayed that meant she could cross the guarding circles. The flickering candlelight played on the keys, the ancient rust worn away by the anxious rubbing of Caspar's fingers. A sheen of sweat covered his lithe body.

She tiptoed forward. Reaching into the circle for his hand, a tingling sensation thrilled through her. Elongated faces with vast shrieking mouths and empty eyes leapt out of the dark. Ondines of the elements, the girl thought fearfully, rooted to the spot.

"A curse on any that dares harm him while he sleeps in the consecrated circles," they sang, long-fingered hands stretching out to grapple with her hair.

"No, I— I— won't harm him," May stuttered through trembling lips. "I love him. I came to save him."

The strange, sweet smell of honeysuckle pervaded her nostrils and she felt the spirits enter her body, searching her soul for her secret. "She loves him," they murmured. "It's true."

May knew it was true though it hurt to admit it. The pain of her unrequited love soured each day of her life. "Yes, I love him and I must do this to save him. If I don't, they will hate him, all the world will hate him and Necrönd will destroy him. Help me. Let me take the keys."

The spirits swirled about the room, whispering and twisting, winding around the oak pillars of the great four-poster bed. Suddenly they centred on Caspar. With a feather-light touch, they caressed his skin, soothing his tight fist and lifting his palm gently from his chest. His hand eased open and May gingerly lifted the keys.

Once she had them, she turned and moved quickly from the room, taking a candle with her. She pulled the great oak doors to behind her, wincing as they clunked into place, and ran for the courtyard. Taking a deep breath, she plunged down the worn, winding steps towards the windowless chambers at the heart of the castle, the small candle fluttering in her hand.

The first door opened into a high vaulted cavern filled with macabre objects. She tried not to look upward at the stocks and chose to curl around the far wall, away from the iron maiden that hung motionless on its rusted chain. Her candle guttered in the damp air, giving the irons form and life. Her imagination filled the stocks with crying men, their eyes maddened by their miserable existence and, urgently, she searched for the door to the cell that Caspar had on occasions described to her.

The low oak door opened with surprising ease and she held the candle up high, expecting to see something monstrous but, within the cramped chamber, there was only a small wooden casket. Before attempting to open it, she hesitated to read the warning runes engraved on the lid.

"Use not the tools of the Gods lest they use you," she

muttered and, without absorbing the meaning, worked the smallest of Caspar's keys into the lock. Just before she opened it, she noted three hairs spanning the lock. She removed them and stuck them to the side of the casket with some spit. The lid creaked open and she shrieked.

A bodiless face stared up at her. Black eyeless sockets gaped out at her and a bestial mouth screamed. She leapt back, murmuring protective charms and swallowed hard. Once she had composed herself, she realized it was just the faint glow from her candle playing tricks in the light. It wasn't a face but an egg, only a little bigger than her fist, lying amidst a bed of moss. Berating herself for being so foolish, she sucked in her breath and tentatively stretched forward to touch it.

Her knees sagged and, overwhelmed with awe, she slumped against the wall for support. The solid bedrock that formed the cell walls wavered. What she knew to be black rock stirred and moulded into ghostly forms; creatures, great beasts of unnatural conformation with bodies of lions, heads of horses and wings and claws. "Free us!" they clamoured. "Let us roam the earth once more. We are all creatures of the Great Mother: set us free."

She had asked Caspar what he felt when he held the Egg but he would not speak of it except to say that he sensed hatred, creatures boiling with the desire for revenge. She sensed that too.

"Witch-woman, gaoler, child of murderers!" The words came out of nowhere. Then the ghostly form of a dragon's snout nudged at her from out of the shadows. Strangely, she felt no fear. Holding Necrönd tighter, she examined the ghostly beast that filled the same space as solid rock. A slit on its throat bubbled with blood and a crooked wing drooped at its shoulder. "Daughter of executioners," it spat at her. "I am your slave."

She slid the Egg into a small silver case and the image of the beasts faded back into the wall. Morrigwen had given her the silver casket in which to guard the tresses of hair that she had taken from her mother's head. Some considered it macabre but it was all she had left of her mother. The coil of red hair made a safe nest within the casket.

She set her mind to practicalities. She must leave everything as if nothing had been touched. Carefully she stuck the hairs that had spanned the lock back in place and, in doing so, dropped one on the dusty floor. It was impossible to find. She broke one from her own head, reasoning that in the low light no one could possibly see the difference. She locked the casket, retreated into the main chamber of the dungeon and shouldered the cell door shut.

Sweating with fear and effort, she retraced her hurried steps through the castle back to Caspar's chamber. With breath held, she eased the door open and approached the bed. Gazing at him through a blur of tears, she stretched her hand out towards him, yearning to touch him, but instead she stiffly held back and gazed at him through a blur of tears.

"Farewell, my love. May the Great Mother keep you safe," she whispered.

This time the Ondines welcomed her, recognizing at once that she had no malice in her heart. She let the keys slide into Caspar's hand and watched with sadness as his fingers closed protectively around them. She hurried for the door, never noticing the spray of May blossom that lay on his pillow. Clutching the casket to her bosom, she ran, knowing that she had no time to waste. A creeping sensation that something dogged her footsteps trembled through her spine.

She had everything ready and so hurried straight for the stables to fetch her pony, an old reliable mare that Caspar had chosen for her. The animal was almost pure white and so given the grand name of Rosalba but, as her plodding nature had emerged, it had naturally been shortened to Rosy. Quietly, she led the mare through the side door by the portcullis that was left open at times of peace. In the dark, she daren't ride on the steep road but led her right to the bottom and it wasn't until she reached the canyon floor that she realized that she had no idea where she might go. Dizzy with tearful emotion, she turned south towards lowland Belbidia, following the course of the Silversalmon. Morrigwen had always said that water chose the natural route and if in doubt to follow its lead.

It wasn't until the Tor was only a thin, distant needle, the towers of the castle ablaze as it caught the first rays of the morning sun, that she wheeled her pony to look back. "Farewell, my lord, I shall love you always." She choked on the words.

Wiping away her tears, she turned her back on her past life.

CHAPTER FOUR

Caspar gazed out into the soft mauve light, silence enveloping him. He couldn't sleep. Nothing stirred on the ribbon of road that snaked up from the canyon floor to the rocky heights of the Tor. Nothing had stirred in hours.

The pale outline of an ibex with long arching horns skittered across the road and disappeared back behind the blackness of the jagged rocks and mounded bonfires recently piled along the edges of the road. It was all he had seen move in hours. A sense of unreality, perhaps conjured from his lack of sleep, pervaded him. He felt lost, numb. Darkness meant he was unable to search for her. All he could do was sit in the watchtower over the barbican, scanning the road and longing for her return.

He had searched the surrounding land and villages for days, asked questions of even the youngest child and every merchant that had passed by, but none had seen her. He had looked everywhere for her and, despite his mother's anger, had even slipped down to the dungeons, to search for her. But she was not there and he had stopped only long enough to check that the three hairs were still in place on the casket.

But despite his distress over May's safety, he also felt a guilty and inexplicable ease, a sense of relief deep within his soul. He found himself imbued with almost unnatural energy. Even the infected scratch on his scalp was healing.

May was punishing him, he was certain but, surely, she would come home to him soon. Today of all days she would return. He resolved not to ride out to look for her that morning but to wait, his actions emphasising his faith that she would come back to him. She had to; he loved her.

The tuneful song of a blackbird thrilled the air and a pan clattered in the kitchens even before the cockerel crowed from the hen house, demanding to be let out. He dragged his eyes from the road and turned towards the courtyard. A slight figure stirred in the shadows. He recognized her at once and hurried down the spiral stone staircase to greet her.

Brid stood on Torra Alta's heartstone, arms uplifted to embrace the east as the rays from the pale sun fanned through the peaks of the Yellow Mountains.

"She's left me, hasn't she?" he said, his worry over May overshadowing all else, even on this morning.

"Mmm," Brid murmured distractedly as if she hadn't heard him. Caspar felt ignored but then had to admit that he had spoken of little else for days. He tried to forget his own worries and thought for the first time that Brid, too, was deeply troubled.

He was about to leave when she broke free from her own gloomy thoughts. "There's no point searching for her," she said quietly. "She has taken herself off and doesn't want to be found. Perhaps she will come home soon. She was dear to all of us – especially you."

"Today," he said wistfully. "I was waiting until today. I wanted it to be midst the great fires that will sweep up into the midnight sky. I wanted it to be special so that we might remember it until the end of our days. I wanted to tell her then that I love her and wish her to be my bride. But now she is gone."

"Perhaps she will come back soon," Brid replied, the uncharacteristic platitude letting Caspar know her mind wasn't fully on the matter.

"You know as well as I that May is not one to act rashly."

Brid nodded distractedly.

"I shouldn't have waited," he berated himself.

The beautiful young priestess patted his shoulder. "I'm sorry, Spar, but I must leave you; there is much preparation to be done before the ceremony."

Caspar felt abandoned by all. Everyone, it seemed, blamed him for the wolves and now they blamed him for May's disappearance as well. They shunned him. Only the little wolfling that skipped out of the guardhouse and stumbled across the cobbles, greeting him excitedly and nipping at his ankles, welcomed his presence without judgement.

Briefly, he considered going to help with the preparations for the day's wolf hunt but shrugged his responsibility away. He couldn't face all those accusing eyes. He returned broodily to the barbican and leant out over the stone crenellations. It was the morning of the Beltane festival; the first day of Merrymoon. In the crisp light of day, the dark mounds of the night were clearly discernible, the beacon fires set at intervals from the valley floor to the castle gates. More were heaped upon the three concentric circles of the castle walls. The flames would spiral up the Tor, embrace the castle and blaze from the battlements and tallest towers. Tonight, Torra Alta would be a tower of flame, giving thanks for the coming of the light half of the year.

He gazed into the distant canyon until the sun was warm on his back. He patted Runa affectionately and drew in a deep breath, thinking that he could not shirk his responsibilities any longer. Snatching up some dry bread from the kitchens as he passed, he gave half to the wolfling and nibbled disconsolately at the rest.

"Here, Master Spar, you'll have more than that," Cook scolded. "I've eggs and a fine bit of bacon sizzling in readiness for you. You're nought but skin and bone. You'll fade away."

He shrugged at her and ambled away, muttering his excuses. He could hear his father's voice ringing out from the stables, organizing the day's hunting. Caspar wondered what the point of it all was. They had killed no more than four hooded wolves in all. He saw little point to anything of late.

"I'd expected more," Morrigwen croaked as she asked Keridwen to describe the scene to her.

The Crone was huddled in a thick bearskin rug and groaned as she was carried by a solid-looking soldier towards a couch placed by Torra Alta's heartstone set in the middle of the inner courtyard. Caspar guessed that the bearskin weighed more than she did. Keridwen was fussily arranging cushions to ease the old woman's fragile bones. Caspar had never seen his mother show signs of anxiety before and he watched and chewed at his lip uncomfortably.

The day's hunt had, yet again, proved fruitless, and they had returned early to be ready for the festival. Thousands of pilgrims crowded the canyon road, keen to be present on the day the new Maiden was to be inaugurated. The hunting party had been forced to barge and weave their way through. Many pilgrims were already camped around the Tor, basking in the weather that was warm for the time of year.

"They have come from the breadth of Torra Alta, even from the very west coast where the choughs and kittiwakes scour the cliffs and they live in turf houses and caves," Keridwen chattered, covering up her distress. "But fewer than I had hoped have come from the south. A dozen or so from Jotunn and Farona, a few hundred from Quertos but none from Ovissia. I know they blame us for the wolves, but I had hoped . . ."

As the sun set and the mountains loomed blackly over the canyon, the last rays catching their peaks so that they glinted like rubies, Brid lit the first fire. The brazier set over Torra Alta's heartstone burst into crackling life and on her signal, those beacons on the battlement walls and crowning the barbican were set ablaze, bathing all in a flickering red light.

Brid turned to bring Nimue into the centre of the scene. The frail child tottered forward, her white shift snagging round her ankles, and stepped onto the circular slab of heartstone set into the cobbled courtyard. The wolfling sat back on her haunches and howled, the note strangely deep and adult from so young a pup. Trog looked startled and butted Runa with his blunt snout.

Frightened by the wolf's cry, Nimue tugged at Brid's skirt. The priestess knelt down and offered her more bloodwort before stepping regally forward to begin the ceremony. Her torch touched a ring of camphor oil blended with herbs; blue flames burst up in a circle around the privileged few gathered in the castle's inner courtyard. They gasped. Firecrackers snapped and squealed before bursting into showers of red sparks around them and Brid and Keridwen danced with their hair loose, spinning around and around the heartstone in a wild frenzy.

Nimue began to cry.

Morrigwen clutched Caspar's arm and, kneading it viciously, her brittle fingernails breaking on his skin, mumbled softly of ill omens. Then she seemed to forget where she was and the importance of the situation because she grumbled in her throat and said hurtfully, "It should be May here by my side not you. You drove her away. No girl will wait forever. You're a fool, Spar."

The rest of the gathering joined the dizzy dance. With no ceremony or pattern, they wheeled one about the other, shouting and whooping, their voices jubilant.

Caspar did not dance. He understood the Crone's heaviness of spirit and sat looking at his feet, wondering about May. Then sudden tension in the old Crone's grip made him look up. He followed her sightless gaze through the swirling dancers to a lone woman in black who was shouldering her way through the buffeting crowd.

Morrigwen's hand limply fell away from Caspar's shoulder.

For a moment, he feared she had died. She had told him over and over again that she only kept herself alive because they must find the new Maiden and that, now her task was nearly done, her life was gone. Then she gripped him fiercely and tugged him towards her with renewed vigour. "There is something wrong. Someone approaches."

Caspar wondered how she knew since she had professed to being able to see no more than the glowing light of the fires.

"There's a woman, a woman in black," he said slowly. "She's looking at Nimue."

The crowd drew aside and the other two priestesses halted abruptly in their dance, aware of the moment. Now that the woman was close, the light of the fires full in her face, Caspar saw the tears running down her cheeks as her hand reached out towards the child. Nimue tottered forward, then ran into her arms.

"Ma, ma!" she squealed. It was the first words anyone in

Torra Alta had ever heard her utter. The woman dropped onto her knees and scooped the girl up in her arms.

Caspar swallowed hard. The girl's mother lived! Nimue wasn't an orphan! Morrigwen dropped Caspar's arm. A light spring rain streaked the sky, hissing on the fires and a discontented hush fell over the crowd.

The woman spoke in emotional bursts. "I— You see— It were two months back now. I was bringing her here all the way from our home in Piscera, praying as you might heal her with your powers." She gasped, a sob shuddering her shoulders, then smiled with wonderment at her child. It was a moment before she could speak though no one hurried her. "The blood were never strong in her body and she died along the journey. Then, cruelty of cruelty, her body was stolen. They must've brought her to you and, now, I see it must've been the fairies. The Great Mother be praised, you have cured what were surely only a sleeping sickness and given her life, new life."

The woman swung her child comfortably round onto her hip, a peaceful smile spreading across Nimue's face as she kneaded her mother's shoulder.

The three priestesses stared speechlessly for a prolonged minute before the Crone spluttered and began to choke. Keridwen ran to her side while Brid brought her water. But the old woman was not strong enough to drink. Tears streamed down Brid's cheeks.

"There is no time left to me," Morrigwen gasped.

Keridwen cradled her frail body, rocking back and forth while Branwolf quietly ordered the crowd to leave. Morrigwen croaked and Keridwen bent to hear her.

"She says to let them stay. Perhaps here amongst them is the new Maiden who might yet come forward on this day."

But none came. Only the wolfling sat closer to Morrigwen, nuzzling her gently.

"You were meant to lead us to her," Morrigwen groaned after a few tense minutes when only her irregular breathing could be heard in the stillness of the crowd. "The runes told that you would lead us to the new Maiden but you only brought us a child back from the dead. First a mother wolf was killed, then the dead walk the earth and now I am dying. The Trinity will be broken." She looked to Keridwen. "My last task was to live until a new Maiden could be found but I am dying. I have failed you, my daughter."

"Perhaps all along it should have been May," Brid muttered. "Even if she could not point to the moon on a clouded night, she has the look of the old ways about her."

Morrigwen stared up at the sky. "When I die take me to the ancient henge. Let the ravens and eagles pick me clean. When my skeleton is white and dry, take the bones from my hands and feet and carve the runes on them in readiness for the new Maiden. Then take my skull and bring it here to Torra Alta's heartstone and, with a rock from the Yellow Mountains, splinter it to pieces. And on each piece carve the rune of hope, for there is nothing more I can offer you.

"I have lived too long. I leave my task undone and the burden is now on your shoulders, Keridwen. The power of two is not that of three. The Great Mother will not hear you and your powers will dwindle. You are but yourselves until the day the Trinity is restored. We have laboured long but have failed." She patted the wolf's head. "Oh, savage beast, may I return to my next life to see you still roaming the hills as you were born to do. These mountains belong not to the Baron and his descendants but to the wolves that have lived here for thousands of years, long before we ever marched out of the south, abandoning the caves of the ancient world for the fertile soil of the north.

"Spar," she murmured, "see to it that these beasts do not die. You chose the rune of the wolf, the rune of savage nature, and you are their guardian."

The youth felt for the smooth-edged chip of bone that he always kept in his pocket, while tears ran unashamedly down his cheeks. He wasn't just weeping for Morrigwen but for them all.

Those closest to her drew back, watching, waiting, barely moving. They waited all through that still, cloudless night and on through the next day, watching and praying. The sun arched overhead, warming the old woman's frail body, but as it crept towards the western horizon, the blood-red globe wept its twilight colours over the golden mountains and a chill wind blew in from the north.

The old Crone's eyes blinked open. "I follow the sun. The night air is too cold for me." She smiled peacefully. "I have done all that I can to teach you well. I have carried the banner through one hundred and fifteen years, far longer than is natural, and now the Mother calls me to her. I ache more than you can imagine and I long for peace. Keridwen, forgive me that I leave you with this burden." Her hands fell open, and the last flickerings of life in her sightless eyes were gone.

Night swallowed the canyon. The wolfling, ghostly white in the darkness, threw back her head, and wailed. The cry filled the castle, washed over the walls and swept out into the mountains, the clarion of grief taken up by answering howls from the distant valleys. High above the castle an eagle climbed high into the pale mauve skies, circling into the slanting rays that no longer touched the earth, and flew west into the last of the day.

Keridwen slumped over the old woman, peeling back

the bearskin to lie close to her body. Choking back sobs, Caspar tugged at his mother's shoulder, wanting somehow to draw her away from her grief but she paid no heed.

"She must cross the savage forests of the Otherworld," Abelard said gently. "May her journey into the bliss of Annwyn be swift. They should give her a horse so that she might gallop ahead of the trudging souls, revered by all, her body once more strong, just as her life was strong."

Caspar fingered the rune of the wolf in his pocket and felt the heaviness of responsibility as he wiped the tears from his cheeks. Too shocked to absorb the reality of Morrigwen's death, he stared at her corpse that was already blue, his hands shaking as he worried the rune.

"The Trinity is broken," Brid spoke shakily. "I am weak as I have never been weak before." She smoothed her hand over Morrigwen's wrinkled brow and, between quiet sobs, spluttered, "Morrigwen, we need you." She raised her head and looked south towards the Belbidian lowlands. "Hal, where are you when I need you?"

The fires burnt through the night while the women wept. Branwolf withdrew to his hall, Trog at his heels. Head down, Caspar followed soon after, the wolfling padding on floppy over-sized paws at his side. Reaching down, he ruffled her neck and she licked his hand.

The next morning the crowds still encircled the Tor, most lying in huddles around the fires. A few knelt in silent prayer. Only the Torra Altan women within the castle kept up their wailing.

The wind swirled around the castle, blowing smoke back into the towers so that the entire Tor puffed out plumes of black as if the ancient dragons still brooded within the hollow mountain. The pilgrims gradually stirred from their cold slumber and came now as mourners, to look on Morrigwen's dead body. She lay on a cradle of yew, her wispy hair entwined with may blossom.

The flowers reminded Caspar of May and he despaired at the sadness she would feel when she learnt of Morrigwen's death. Perhaps the news would bring her home; surely, she would want to pay her respects. Hope gladdened his heart. He stood on the battlements, watching the pilgrims file up the spiralling approach to the castle but there was no sign of May. He moved amongst them, asking if any had seen a chestnut-haired girl with big hazel eyes but most shook their heads. A few had pointed to girls who fitted the description but none was May.

He searched tirelessly all morning and then returned to the barbican for a better view. Soon a familiar figure caught his eye. Fern came skipping and leaping delightedly up the steep incline of the Tor.

"Spar!" he shouted up at him, his gleeful voice discordant amid the sombre dirges. "I've found her!"

Half running, half falling, the youth raced down the stairs within the barbican. He pushed his way through the crowd and lifted the little woodwose up off his feet. "Where?" he demanded frantically. "Where?"

Fern's horns had all but disappeared and were now no more than velvety nodules poking through his curly hair. But, with his big eyes, protruding nose and mouth, and sandy skin, he still had much of the look of a deer about him.

"In the old part of Brambletwine Wood to the east."

Caspar nodded, at the sense of it. Why hadn't he thought of it? Of course, May would go there. There was little habitation in the eastern ranges of the Yellow Mountains and the woods on its north-facing slopes were thick and tangled where there were few boar to root around and clear the undergrowth. Only wild men and hermits lived there.

"The wolves are leaving the forest and she will be safe now. I needn't have worried," Fern continued excitedly. "She's grown, of course, and so beautiful, just like her mother. She saw me. For a moment she stood still and stared right at me," he added happily.

Caspar slowly lowered Fern back to the ground, trying to hide his disappointment. The excited fellow was talking about his fawn, Sorrel. He wouldn't have even known about May's disappearance. "Fern, I'm glad for you. Truly, I'm glad."

Fern danced excitedly. "All that mattered was that she was safe. She looked at me long and hard." Fern stopped dancing up on his bare horny toes and looked sadly at the ground. "Then, Spar, she fled."

"You are grown like a man now. She will have seen you as a predator," Caspar pointed out, trying to be helpful.

Tears sprang to Fern's eyes. "I know." He looked down at his body in disgust. "That's why I have come here. I didn't want to but I can no longer live in the forest. I tried the beech and the birch shoots, which I used to love, but it all tasted . . . well, so woody. Can you imagine?"

Caspar thought he possibly could.

"And I'm hungry, Spar, and I've nowhere else to go." He looked dolefully up at the youth.

"Fern, you are welcome here. Of course, you're welcome," Caspar hurriedly assured him but the woodwose wasn't listening but examining the throng of people filing past the old Crone.

"A very big herd," he anxiously remarked, pressing close to the Baron's son.

Caspar shrugged at the woodwose and summoned a soldier to fetch some food for Fern. "Mind there's no meat.

A plate of herbs, fruit and bread would be good," Caspar instructed.

The soldier shortly returned with the required food plus a huge platter of one of Cook's specialities. Fern's eyes widened at the sight. He nibbled in turn at the bread, herbs and fruit but, once he had discovered Cook's honey cakes, he would touch nothing else.

"You'll get fat," Caspar warned.

The little man's greedy eyes bulged with relish as he took an enormous mouthful and chewed fast.

Fern's arrival only briefly distracted Caspar from his search and soon he was again weaving through the crowd, asking after May. Fern followed. Eager to please his new master, he ran amongst the mourners and, between mouthfuls, repeated Caspar's questions. Many looked at him in amusement but some with disdain as if his enthusiasm were inappropriate to the sombre mood of the throng. Caspar soon lost sight of the woodwose butting his way through the crowd and gave him no more thought as he pressed his questions on the next group of pilgrims, a small band of beef farmers from the east coast of Jotunn. They looked momentarily thoughtful but then shook their heads. No, they hadn't seen her.

His confidence was failing. "Great Mother," he prayed, "help me find her." The thought drifted into his head that he should wield Necrönd and send the creatures of the Otherworld out to find her but he resisted. After all, he had promised Keridwen that he would stay away from the dungeons.

Fern suddenly came hurrying back, pushing his way through the sombre file of people, unaware of the anger raised by his rude shoves. His nose twitched and his sandy skin was flushed.

"Wolf!" he panted in alarm.

Caspar looked at him in surprise, wondering what he meant. It was inconceivable that a wolf could be here midst the press of people.

"Calm down. There are no wolves here. Think hard and tell me what you really saw," Caspar demanded, trying to hide his irritation.

"I was asking after May as you directed but then I heard another asking. He stank of wolf," he expounded. "Tall, wearing wolf-skins, there was no scent of man about him, only wolf. A wolf that walked on two legs."

Alarm bells rang in Caspar's head. After the attack in Trows Forest, Ceowulf had claimed he too had seen an unnatural wolf that walked on its rear feet. Caspar couldn't fathom what either meant by this and could only wonder why anyone else should be asking after May? He barged his way through the mourners, in search of the supposed wolfman. Once, he briefly glimpsed the grey swinging shape of a wolf-pelt cloak on the back of a tall man but the crowd closed around Caspar and he was too small to see over the surrounding heads. By the time he had forced his way through to the edge of the road and climbed a boulder to get a better view, there was no trace of any wolf-skin cloak.

"Did you see a man in a wolf's pelt?" he asked those nearby. Most looked at him blankly though a small child crying in her mother's arms said she had seen a man with huge teeth that had growled at her.

"Pay her no heed, sir. She's tired, that's all," the woman explained. "You didn't see nothing, sweet one," she soothed.

"But I did," the child wailed, her eyes wide with fright.

Caspar was stopped from asking more by a trumpet blast and the sound of approaching horses. Someone shouted, "Look out!" Horses charged through the crowd, their riders kicking aside pilgrims and shouting angrily for them to make way.

"Hey! What do you think you're doing?" he yelled, recognising the red and blue colours of Ovissia. Ovissian nobles were the last people he would expect to come and pay their respects to Morrigwen.

He raced back along the road and caught them up in the inner courtyard where they were shouting angrily, their horses blowing and coughing from the effort of the hard climb.

"How dare you disturb the peace of our wake?" Branwolf's booming voice filled the void within the castle walls. "The word must be urgent."

"It is!" the nobleman thundered in return as he looked down at the great Baron in disgust. "While you mourn the loss of one woman, we suffer the loss of hundreds from your wolves. You even keep them here as pets." He glowered at Runa who slunk behind Keridwen.

Caspar studied his broach of high status and garish livery. He looked at the short jaw, round face and distinctive ears and instantly recognized the family resemblance. Branwolf hesitated for a moment, sizing the man up before smiling his greeting at Baron Godafrid of Ovissia's second son.

"Irwin, you've changed. You look more and more like your brother, Tupwell, every time we see you. Welcome on this sad day."

The man sniffed and rudely remained mounted. "I am not here to pass pleasantries with you. First you send wolves to destroy our livelihood then you return three of my father's men after having them tortured and terrorized by demons in your dungeons. It is the last outrage Torra Alta will commit against us. My father is gone to the King to see what is to be done with you."

Irwin's eyes narrowed and he leant forward threateningly. "In Farona the talk is all of your treacherous deeds. We've learned how Princess Cymbeline, Prince Renaud and my brother, along with other nobles are taken. The King believes that you, Branwolf, are at the root of this plot against his bride and holds your brother Hal, to ensure your speedy presence at court." He thrust a parchment into Branwolf's hand.

Caspar was gaping in disbelief and outrage but his father barely blinked. The parchment was stamped with the King's seal and he pressed close to read it.

"The King demands my presence," Branwolf announced calmly. "And of course, I shall obey, though the timing is inconvenient."

Caspar read the rest of the script to himself, gulping at the words. The King threatened to march his troops on Torra Alta if they failed to destroy every wolf in their Barony by the end of the month. He knelt down beside the wolfling and clutched her protectively against his sides.

"I came in person to deliver this message," Irwin declared, "to inform you that the shepherds are gathering to my father's army. And he will send them to swell the King's ranks to ensure that you comply with this order. If you do not comply, we shall know that these wolves are some devilry of yours, conjured to overthrow the throne and thereby force your vial paganism on the rest of Belbidia."

The garrison men pressed angrily close.

"Let him alone," the Baron ordered in cold harsh tones.

Reluctantly, the men drew back, jeering as Irwin and his entourage left, their horses' hooves slithering on the bare rock of the road down the Tor.

"We'll fight! We'll stand and fight!" one of the young soldiers shouted excitedly from the battlements.

Caspar looked up at the young faces around that brimmed with enthusiasm, eager for glory. He was young himself but not so innocent. He had seen the slaughtered of the siege and knew that Branwolf would not be keen to make such young and inexperienced lads stand and fight.

"There is no glory in fighting our King. Come!" the Baron demanded. "Spar, Captain, join me in the hall. Spar!" He strode off, leaving the women to their mourning. Caspar sprinted after him.

"I must leave at once," Branwolf told them once they were alone within his halls.

"But with Ovissia on the point of bearing arms against us?" Caspar's mouth was dry. Outrage against their neighbours coursed through his veins and he struggled to keep his voice steady.

"Don't question me, Spar! They think this is some form of devilry. They believe I am my namesake, the Black Wolf, and that I plot to overthrow Belbidia. I must go in person to reassure the King of my goodwill."

"Let me wield Necrönd," he suggested, his voice suddenly breathy and hushed. "I can stop all this."

The door creaked open and Keridwen glided into the room, her eyes puffy with tears and her normally glossy hair straggly about her shoulders. "Never! We are in this plight because of your meddling. The very worst thing you can do is release its powers. It must remain in place and as soon as our troubles are sorted," she said with conviction, "Brid and I will divine a way to have Necrönd hidden from mankind for all time."

"No," Caspar burst out. "I am its guardian! The Great Mother decreed long ago that I was to be its guardian."

"But you do not guard it, Spar. You seek to be its master," Keridwen pointed out.

Brid slid through the narrow crack in the door to stand by Keridwen, her cheeks wet with tears. "It's your fault," she bluntly accused Caspar.

The youth flushed red and looked away, grateful that his father's strong tones diverted attention from him.

"We have more immediate things to worry about. The King has summoned me to answer accusations of treason. I shall ride for Farona at first light. Spar, I leave my castle in your care though of course the Captain will see to the smooth running of the garrison. Keridwen will guide you. And you will listen to her!" the Baron ordered, his words heavy with threat.

"No," Keridwen gently interrupted. "Spar is old enough to live up to the responsibility of his birthright and my duty is to stand by you, Branwolf. I shall come with you to Farona to prove our honest intentions to the King."

Branwolf nodded. "It would be a brave statement but you put yourself at risk. Rewik has never knowingly tolerated a pagan priestess in his courtroom."

"We are all at risk," Keridwen said solemnly. "We must do all we can to keep the King's goodwill and persuade him that, like the rest of his subjects, we too yearn to be free of these hooded wolves."

Branwolf looked down into his son's eyes. "Ready yourself for command, Spar. We shall place Morrigwen's body within the henge at first light and leave directly after. Torra Alta will be in your hands."

Caspar gave him a lopsided smile. He was not bloated with pride at this trust: he knew it was an empty gesture and that the Baron was relying on the undoubted and tested competence of the Captain to keep his castle secure. Besides it was only because Hal was not here that his father had even thought to nominate him in charge.

More than half that night, Caspar fretted in the dark of his chamber, pacing up and down rather than making any attempt to sleep. They were wrong; he knew they were wrong. He had not tampered with the Egg as they accused. He had even proved his strength to resist it by refraining from visiting it for several days and he knew that, if he wielded it, he could solve their problems. He would wait until Keridwen had gone.

He was glad of the morning though it brought with it a sorry task. They bore the old Crone's body down the spiralling road from the Tor in the early hours and laid her body upon a stone slab within the ring of the ancient henge. Her clothes were stripped from her so that her blue grey skin would feel the wind upon it. Caspar found it gruesome but it was what Morrigwen had wanted; to remind them all of the truth of death and the mortality of the flesh. Keridwen took her sickle, cut away Morrigwen's crisp silvery hair and weaved it into a knot.

She smiled sadly at Caspar. "This way I can keep some part of her ever with me." She carefully placed the precious coil of hair into her scrip and then, raising her hands, summoned the spirits of the elements. In incantation, she called on the Ondines to protect Morrigwen's corpse from malicious harm. Caspar sensed a trembling in the atmosphere, a thickening of the air, and though he could neither see nor hear anything, he had the uncomfortable sense of being watched by critical eyes.

When all was done, Branwolf took his wife's hand. "We must leave."

Caspar rode with them as far as the end of the canyon and kissed his mother farewell.

"Promise me you will not wield Necrönd," Keridwen pleaded, her face still stiff with grief.

He felt her eyes probe deep into his soul and, for the first time, he saw her just as his mother and not as a priestess, her powers already diminished. She was suddenly vulnerable. He didn't want to promise but nodded all the same; he could cause her no more hurt.

"Spar, consult the Captain whenever need arises," Branwolf ordered. "And don't worry; no doubt, the minute I am in Farona, King Rewik will release Hal and in ten days, a fortnight at the most, he will be here to advise you."

"I'll be glad of Hal," Caspar said truthfully though he was resentful that his father should immediately presume that he would need Hal's help. "But I'll manage without him, don't worry. I come of age at the end of the summer."

"No man comes of age at eighteen." Branwolf sniffed. "At eighteen you have all your mistakes ahead of you and no humility. Now, your job is to find where these hooded wolves are breeding. They must be in the mountains somewhere. Let's have an end to them."

Grey clouds stewed on the western horizon, muffling the peaks, and Caspar suspected that even at this time of year it was snowing on the highest crags. The air was moist and spots of rain dampened his cheeks as if the great gods of the sky wept silent tears for Morrigwen's death and Keridwen's departure from the castle.

He rode out with the men for twelve days but they found no nest of wolves, though he wasn't surprised. He knew in his heart that, somehow, they came from Necrönd. By the thirteenth day he was longing for Hal's return. It was a week's ride to Farona but with a keen horse it could be done in less and he had expected Hal home by now at the latest.

With tired eyes and still dressed in her hunting leathers from the day before, Brid stood silently beside him, her eyes fixed on the road, anxiously winding her long plait through her fingers.

"I'm going to see Morrigwen," she said in a taught voice.

Caspar busied himself with other duties but continued to look out for her as, hour after hour, she sat amongst the ravens by Morrigwen's slowly rotting body. Abelard stood near her, his yew bow constantly in hand, warily scanning for danger. And so it was that Abelard was the first to warn of approaching horsemen entering the southern mouth of the canyon. Brid leapt to her feet and ran for her horse, spurring her way up to the castle to get a better view.

"Is it him?" she panted, as she clattered into the courtyard, leapt from Sunsprite's back and scrambled up onto the walls alongside Caspar.

"I'm not sure. He might be in the midst of them but all I can see is men wearing the red, yellow and black of the King's colours."

"He's not with them," Brid said in certainty. "He would be at the fore, galloping ahead of the rest."

They were indeed the King's soldiers but they didn't turn off the road to ride for the castle but continued north after stopping briefly at the stables at the base of the Tor. Caspar sent down a soldier to find out what their business was and waited impatiently for the lad to return.

"Master Spar, they stopped only to buy grain, saying they were heading north to search for Princess Cymbeline."

"And no word of Hal," Brid exclaimed, tossing her thick plait over her shoulder decisively. "I'm going to Farona," she announced.

"You can't," Caspar forbade her. "We've lost Morrigwen. Keridwen is gone. We need you here."

"You'll manage without me, Spar," she said dismissively. "But I shan't be long. No doubt Hal is on the road home and I'll meet him on the way." She smiled optimistically.

"But . . ." Caspar struggled for something to say. He

couldn't let her go. He felt certain that he couldn't cope without her. There was already a disrespectful and constant chatter amongst the young garrison that would have been instantly hushed by his father's presence.

"I'm going and that's an end to it," Brid said formally, underlining Caspar's lack of authority in the castle.

"I'll arrange an escort," he conceded.

She shrugged carelessly. "Abelard will come with me."

"That's not enough," Caspar protested.

Brid laughed. "Who can you send? I would spend more time looking after them than they me. Besides, you need every man you've got to find the wolves. Abelard will be better use than a hundred overexcited youths."

Caspar stared in despair as Brid trotted Sunsprite out under the portcullis with Abelard behind her on a stout old mountain pony. The archer looked uncomfortable in the saddle and Caspar thought he would be very saddle sore long before they reached Farona.

His heart sank as they vanished. He tried to straighten his shoulders and hoped he looked capable of command. The garrison of youths and fresh-faced men looked nervously at him, reflecting his own state of mind.

"Sir?" The Captain saluted, awaiting orders.

Caspar grinned sheepishly. No one within the castle had ever called him "Sir". He coughed. "Um, Captain . . ." he began indecisively then broke off. He was about to voice his orders about the day's hunt but was distracted by loud shouts and the clatter of hooves. The party he had sent out four days earlier to the outlying lands of Torra Alta was only just returning.

CHAPTER FIVE

"They won't say where they're from, Master Spar," one of the men from the hunting party shouted excitedly while the other soldiers struggled to hold three surly-looking men.

"Caught them in the Jaws of the Wolf, we did, digging in the scree slopes washed down by the avalanches. Trappers they are, their ponies loaded with traps, cudgels, knives and pelts. But they were digging! And that ain't what trappers do."

The soldiers were clamouring and arguing so loudly that Caspar didn't know what to think.

One turned on the three trappers held in the rigorous grip of the other soldiers. "We should set you in your own traps and stake you out in the courtyard. That'd teach you. Then you'd tell us what you were digging for!"

"Um . . . listen," Caspar began but too quietly. The soldiers continued to rage at the captives, jostling them roughly. The blood rose to his face and he raised his hand for silence but he was at a loss as to what to do. Pip was already dragging the baggage from the horses and rifling through it. "Pip!" he shouted. "Just wait until we've got some order."

"But, Master Spar, look at this." Pip continued to drag out pelts, garments, cooking pots and supplies while the other men gathered around him. A sense of imminent doom pervaded Caspar. A heavy hand pressed on his shoulders and he looked up into the Captain's face.

"Act decisively," he murmured. "You don't need to decide what to do about these trappers immediately; but at least set the men to a task, any task. They need the reassurance of orders."

"But—" Caspar stammered.

"Let me show you." The Captain was a kindly man who kept himself always to himself and Caspar had great respect for him. He carried out his job with steady devotion, never looking for acclaim, and Caspar knew how grateful his father was for the man's experience and easy manner. "Olwen, Rollo, see to the horse. Will, Bron, finish unloading the trappers' ponies and then take them to the stable."

He lowered his head and murmured to Caspar, "And this is most important." He then spoke out loudly again, "Pip, stand guard over those saddle packs and see no one touches them, you hear?"

Pip saluted smartly, grinning with satisfaction.

"Always give that lad a job he thinks is important," the Captain advised. "He does a fine job if he thinks he's valued but otherwise he does nothing but disrupt."

Before long there was order. The trappers were safely secured in the guardroom minded by old Brock. The contents of their saddlebags, which Pip had arranged – surprisingly neatly – were ready for examination. Caspar's eyes skimmed over knives and hatchets and fell on a small, tightly knotted leather bag. He slit the thong with his knife and poured the contents onto his palm. At first glance, he thought they were plain rough stones but, when he turned them over in his hand, he saw the small light grey pebbles glinted with specks of red. He scraped one against another to chip away the outer coating of dull rock and revealed the bright, glossy red of a gem beneath, a golden glow welling out from its heart. Instantly, he realized that they were raw sunburst rubies.

He marched to the guardroom and flung open the door. Old Brock's eyebrows rose in mild surprise at the force of his entrance. "Who are you working for?" Caspar demanded of the trappers that dwarfed him, anger lending his voice authority.

As one, the trappers scowled up at him from where they sat against the far wall. Old Brock yanked the nearest to his feet by his ears. Brock was a big man and, like all the old soldiers that had lived in the castle during Caspar's youth, he was tough, earnest and possessed simple objectives. "You, answer the Baron's son," he growled, twisting the ear in his grip.

The trapper was a tough man and didn't seem unduly perturbed by Brock's handling. "We work for the King, killing wolves," he replied with a sneer.

"So, what are you doing with these?" Caspar demanded, hefting the bag of raw rubies in his palm.

"Took them off a fellow that was messing about with our traps," he answered surlily.

"Why were you digging on the scree slope?"

"Found a den. Thought there might be cubs."

Caspar knew the trapper was lying but was also acutely aware of his ineptness to extract the truth. He was also sure that behind their surly sneers, they were splitting their sides with laughter at him. "Do you know what these are?" He held out a fist full of the uncut rubies.

"Of course we do. They're rubies. That's why we took them off the other chap. We wouldn't be so stupid as to leave a prize like that behind now, would we?"

"Who do you work for?" The Captain slammed the door closed behind him and, unsheathing his sword, began to closely examine the keenness of its raw edge. A horrible smile lifted one side of his face.

"Throw them in the dungeons!" Pip shouted excitedly.

Caspar groaned. How had that boy got in here? The last thing he wanted was to have these men thrown in the dungeons – so close to Necrönd.

"String them up from the portcullis," Brock offered, prodding one hard in the ribs with the butt of a staff. "They'll talk with the ravens hanging over them." He punched the standing trapper in the stomach, brought the staff up into the man's face and shoved him back against the wall. Spitting blood, the trapper slid down beside his ash-faced companions.

Caspar cringed. He knew they must get answers out of these men but he didn't want to see it beaten out of them and wished that someone else were here to take the responsibility away from him. Whatever, he could not allow torture. "Enough," he said softly, placing his hand on Brock's arm. The trappers looked at him with satisfaction.

"Take them to the henge and have them staked out overnight by Morrigwen's body," he gave the unlikely order to the Captain, who saluted smartly though he searched Caspar's eyes doubtfully. It was not a harsh punishment by any means since the nights were warm and no wolf ever came that near the castle.

Pip looked disappointedly at Caspar. "But, Master Spar, the Baron imprisoned the last lot in the dungeons."

"That was before Morrigwen died," Caspar tried to sound enigmatic to conceal his lack of confidence. All eyes were on him and he knew he must show no more signs of hesitancy.

"We should put them in the dung—" Pip began to insist but his words were stopped by old Brock picking him up by the collar and dragging him towards the door. "Master

Hal would see them properly punished. Abelard would know what to do," the boy called back over his shoulder.

Caspar knew old Brock would punish Pip for his insolence so he quickly turned his mind to more important matters. That night he kept vigil over the three trappers, who were tied to stakes pegged out around Morrigwen's shrivelled body. Her corpse lay untouched. Caspar had expected to see maggots heaving under the skin but she there was as yet little sign of decay. She lay peacefully in the summer sunset, blue runes of love and safe-keeping painstakingly drawn by Brid and Keridwen covering her flesh, only she looked so cold and lonely.

The trappers were not yet subdued. "This is all that's left of the great castle of Torra Alta? Just a mere boy," they taunted Caspar. "Do you really think that tying us out here with a corpse will make us tremble? You haven't got the stomach to command men. A frontier castle with a boy in charge! Ha! You feel sorry for us like you feel sorry for the wolves. It's no wonder the place is crawling with them."

Ignoring their taunts, Caspar began to chant prayers to the Great Mother, hoping that the nearness of Morrigwen's body, lying out naked in the canyon winds, would lend him strength. He felt strangely at ease with her corpse. She looked so peaceful with the breeze of twilight ruffling through her cropped hair.

He avoided the eyes of the men, who spat at him and called him a wolf-lover and murderer of children. Perhaps here in the henge some answers would come to him. He felt strangely peaceful as darkness drew its cloak over the land though he could hear one or two of his own men muttering that he was losing his senses. He ignored them and concentrated on Morrigwen's corpse. She was all that was left to advise him and his mind began to clear.

It was surprising that May had not returned. The news of the old Crone's death had surely reached her, wherever she was. Hal had not returned either. His thoughts were broken by the trappers talking in low whispers. Caspar didn't know how to deal with these men and felt deeply frustrated. He need only conjure some beast with Necrönd and he would have them petrified, prepared to tell him everything; but he had promised his mother he would not and a Torra Altan was a man of his word.

He sighed heavily, pulled his bearskin around him, and once more prayed to the Great Mother for guidance. Hours passed, fears rushing in and out of the recesses of his mind. He remembered how, only just before her death, Morrigwen had spoken of his mother's brother, Gwion, whom she had raised as her own son, and of how she feared their meeting beyond this life. "I feel his presence so close." Morrigwen's voice had trembled as she spoke of him. "It's as if he is still alive, still waiting for his opportunity to poison me."

Caspar had tried to reassure her. He had witnessed how the power of the runesword had flung the priest over a cliff to his death. But in the blizzard, he had never seen the body, only heard the cry as he fell. But it was impossible that he still lived.

A chill ran through him. Here, in the confines of the henge, there was a sense of death and brooding menace that he felt was aimed at him. He thought of all the people that might wish ill against him and the realisation struck him that he was responsible for countless deaths, all those tens of thousands of Vaalakans that had died as a result of his command when he had summoned beasts from the Otherworld to drive the Vaalakans back from Torra Alta. He pulled his bearskin tight about his shoulders.

It was beyond midnight before the full moon shone down directly into the canyon, touching the great towers of Torra Alta, which sent flashes of white light out into the depths of the valley. Then a strangeness came over him, a sudden sense of reassurance as if the burden of responsibility had been lifted from his shoulders.

Someone else was there. He sat up, instantly awake. One of the three captives moaned fearfully but Caspar felt no terror as the corpse began to stir. A thin hazy shape hovered over the body. He crept closer to the altar slab at the centre of the ring of stones and reached out into the filmy light. An eye opened in the ether and stared directly at him, glinting red in the moonlight. A face formed, the face of a beautiful young woman. Up out of Morrigwen's body she rose, her skin silvery in the moonlight, her breasts and belly ringed with symbols of stars and moons.

"Necrönd," she murmured weakly, her hand moving imploringly towards the youth. He grasped her fingers but, as her hand touched his, he felt the crippled bony fingers of an old woman. She gripped him and pulled him fiercely towards her.

The night air within the henge began to stir. Vapours oozed from the pointed obelisks and massed together into four nebulous forms that, at moments, resembled naked maidens and at others, were no more than swirling smoke. The fluid shapes were distinct from one another in that when they condensed into more recognisable forms, one had flames leaping from its fingers and trailing from its long hair, another dripped water, the third swirled in the air and howled like the wind and the last moved more slowly and was the most solid in form. The Ondines, Caspar thought, recognising that they represented the four elements.

They dragged him backwards by his arms and hair,

biting at his hands to force him to release Morrigwen's dead fingers. The young woman swept the Ondines away with a flick of her wrist and danced wildly around the circle, leaping as if rejoicing in the grace and freedom of her body. As she swirled and leapt, she sent the Ondines to swarm around the trappers, one Ondine vomiting a jet of water over them, another breathing fire into their faces. The Ovissians shrieked and gibbered.

A whirring and buzzing sound like swarming wasps filled Caspar's brain, making him giddy. The air turned stale and the young woman with the dark red hair slid back into Morrigwen's body as if she were being sucked in by some giant mouth. The body shook and the dead mouth gasped with pain.

Caspar smelt smoke and was aware of a distortion in the atmosphere before him. Somehow, the area around Morrigwen simply didn't match the surrounding henge. The air was suddenly hot and he could hear voices. At once, he knew that the veil between this world and the Otherworld had been ripped aside and he looked across into the of the dungeons of Abalone. Four of the yellow-eyed beings of the Otherworld gripped Morrigwen and drove long skewers into her knees and elbows, levering apart the joints. She shrieked horribly.

One of the three trappers retched with fear at the gruesome sight while the other two wailed of devils and demons. Caspar paid them no heed.

"That's enough," a female voice pleaded. The thirteen members of the High Circle were looking down at Morrigwen from a viewing gallery above the dungeons and it was Saille, the spirit of the willow, who had spoken. Caspar remembered her well.

"You cannot torture an old woman so, chief verderer. Stop!" the ealdorwoman commanded.

A small man with green leggings and bare from the waist upwards looked up at her expectantly. Caspar's stomach knotted into a fist of bitter hatred as he anticipated the sight of Talorcan, the chief verderer that had stolen Brid's love with spells of enchantment in a bid to steal her soul. But this was a different being, slightly taller and thinner with more narrowly set eyes though they gleamed as yellow as Talorcan's had. It seemed that Talorcan had been replaced.

"No, continue," Tinne, the aggressive spirit of the holly, ordered.

The verderer chose to respond to his plea rather than Saille's and took a steel iron from a pit of glowing embers.

"We should make no exceptions for this old woman. It is her own fault that she suffers the horrors of these chambers. All she need do is give up on her life and take the journey through the forest to the bliss of Annwyn," Phagos said calmly, crunching at a beechnut he had pulled from his beard.

Caspar was confused. He had thought that Morrigwen would be eager to move on and reach the bliss of Annwyn. He couldn't believe she was prepared to withstand such pain in her desperation to get back to them.

"She is One of the Three. The Trinity has never before been broken. She must be allowed to return," Saille argued.

"No!" Phagos was adamant. "The law is clear. She has lived far longer than most and it is her own fault if she has not achieved what she needed to do in her lifetime. If she could not find the successor to the Maiden in one hundred and fifteen years, there is no reason why she should succeed now. She had time enough. Verderer, continue."

"No!" Caspar screamed, through the smoke-filled doorway to the Otherworld while the three trappers shrieked and moaned as the verderer stood astride Morrigwen's stretched body.

The verderer nodded to his four assistants. For a moment, they eased their skewers out of the Crone's body and she gasped in agonized gulps.

"Old woman, move on; embrace your new life. Give up the responsibility. It is not your burden any longer to find this girl."

She glared straight back up at the verderer and Caspar felt the strength of her defiance and desperation sweeping in waves through the atmosphere.

The verderer spat on the tip of the red-hot poker, making it hiss, and he hesitated no more. Savagely, he thrust it against her stomach, bearing his weight down until it gouged deep into her abdomen. Her body curled up around it, her arms and legs writhing in agony. Her eyes bulged, and one hand reached out towards Caspar.

"Necrönd!" she shrieked before swooning.

The verderer stamped his foot on her ribcage, heaved out the poker and nodded to his men to have her limp body dragged back to her cell. "Bring her back if she still resists when she comes round."

The smoky hole in the atmosphere was gone. Caspar found himself staring down at Morrigwen's dead corpse. Gripping her skeletal shoulders, he vigorously shook her body, her head waggling violently. "Morrigwen, give up on your life. We will find the new Maiden. Rest. Rest in peace. It is our burden now, not yours."

The wolfling, who had all this time kept silent in the shadows, leapt up onto a boulder and, with the globe of the moon behind, threw back her head and howled.

Caspar stroked Morrigwen's papery cheek that shone silver in the moonlight. "Do not let them torture you."

Her head lolled, the tongue squeezing out from between

blue lips. Her eyelids slid back and Caspar wasn't sure if it were a trick of the light or whether he was really looking into the startling bright eyes of a young woman who was very much alive. He dropped back the body in horror and the thin skull cracked against the solid rock. The movement brought a bubble of blood up from within the throat. It trickled down the side of her dry mouth while a wet mumbling gurgled out with the blood. "Necrönd," it seemed to say.

A white maggot wormed half out of one tear duct. He choked back on the bile in his throat but was too fearful for Morrigwen's tortured soul to dwell on his revulsion. He had to help her! He couldn't possibly leave the old woman to be tortured in the dungeons of Abalone; he could save her with Necrönd. That was what she must have meant. He was to bring her back from the Otherworld. He knew he had promised his mother, but Morrigwen's plea exonerated him from his oath.

He ran up the Tor, the wolfling lolloping silently at his heels. The watch shouted out in alarm as he sprinted through the door alongside the portcullis. Someone had roused the Captain who was striding through the crisp air, his long dark figure quite vivid, almost blue, in the brilliant moonlight.

The Captain caught his hand. "Master Spar, what—"

"Leave me be. I must save Morrigwen," he cried, unaware that he sounded utterly mad, his eyes rolling as he wriggled free and ran for the inner courtyard, breathlessly tearing down the worn steps to the dungeons. They were torturing Morrigwen and he had the power to stop them. He heaved on the steel doors and ran across the dusty floor. Fumbling for his keys, he was faintly aware that the strange smell that had troubled him over the last few months was gone. The air smelt simply dank with the occasional whiff of sulphur wafting down from the wellroom.

He found the key to the studded oak door that crouched in the corner of the chamber and heaved it open. It was at least a month since he had looked at the Egg and he was trembling with the anticipation of once more feasting his eyes on its latent power. His mouth was dry as he fell down on his knees to release the hasp on the casket.

Noting that the hairs he had carefully stuck across the lock were all in place, he heaved up the casket lid and held the firebrand forward.

A cold sweat glistened on his forehead and his breathing became shallow and rapid. He steadied himself against the slime-coated wall. Save for a few tendrils of moss, which should have been cradling the white and blue-veined egg, the casket was empty.

He dragged the ancient chest forward, hoping beyond hope that somehow the Egg was lying behind. He searched through the moss again, certain that it must be there. But the chest remained empty.

This wasn't possible. Had Keridwen taken it? He knew in his heart that she had not; he would have sensed it on her when she left Torra Alta, as he would have done with Brid. Someone had stolen Necrönd. Suddenly he realized that Morrigwen had not been begging him to wield it for her but to warn him of its absence.

What evil would befall them now? If none of the high priestesses had it, who could have taken the Egg? The keys had been on him day and night. His mind raced.

So many people had come to the castle. He sat back against the walls of the cell, trying to think, trying to suppress his panic. He brushed away a sticky cobweb from his head, his hand skimming over his scalp. It was no longer sore! For the first time he realized that the irritating scab was healing and did not immediately bleed when he touched it. Now that he thought on it, the scab hadn't troubled him for a few days, only he had been too preoccupied to notice and now couldn't say exactly when this change had taken place.

He was startled by a cough at the door.

"Spar!"

He knew the voice.

"Spar, what's happened? The castle's astir and the Captain's had some trappers locked in the guardroom, gibbering fools all three. Everyone says you've gone mad."

"It's gone!" Caspar looked forlornly at the little woodwose. Was Fern really the only one left to help him?

The creature's nose twitched and he sniffed around the casket in disgust and curled his lip up. "Wolves," he complained in revulsion.

"Just damp and mildew," Caspar corrected him.

"No, it stinks of wolf."

Fern jolted something in Caspar's memory. The woodwose had seen a man amongst the mourners and claimed he smelt of wolf. He looked at Fern. He still went barefoot, his toenails grotesquely black and horny. He lifted the little man up by his collar and shook him fitfully. "You remember that man?" he asked fiercely,

Fern's nostrils flared and his eyes flitted around the room. "Wolves!" he repeated as if oblivious to Caspar.

The youth dropped the little woodwose to the stone floor and thought. It had to be the man smelling of wolves that had taken it. He couldn't wait for Hal to return; they couldn't let the trail get any colder. They had wasted too much time as it was. He touched the crown of his head and remembered that it must have been around the time of Morrigwen's death that the wound on his head had last irritated him. It was obvious now. His complacency had come as the Egg had left.

"We'll leave now! At once! Before the garrison is up," he told Fern. "Collect your things."

"I don't have any," Fern shrugged.

Caspar thought of what he might need and hurried to find his bow, some food and blankets, and to saddle Firecracker. Fern, he knew, wouldn't take a pony and would prefer to run. He strode into the kitchens and collected some bread, a particularly good round of Jotunn cheese, a ham, some salted beef and some salted venison, then decided to put the latter back for fear of upsetting Fern. Fortunately Cook had baked a whole batch of honeyed oatcakes. Guiltily, he scooped them up, thinking that Cook would have wanted them for breakfast and would have to bake soda bread instead. Wooden spoons, rolling pins and sharp words would be flying. He paused to leave her a note but could think of nothing good enough to say.

There were just a few more things he had to collect. Hurriedly, he made the long climb to Morrigwen's turret room in the west tower. He opened the heavy door into the circular room. Without the Old Crone's blazing fire, it felt cold and forbidding. The room was tidy, which it had never been when Morrigwen was alive when a constant brew of infusing potions had bubbled away on her cauldron and a scatter of herbs, books and utensils had lain higgledy-piggledy on an unswept floor.

Now everything was cold and neat and Caspar didn't have to be vigilant to avoid treading on anything or wary of the cauldron that would unexpectedly spit out dark staining liquids. He peeped over the cold rim down into the pit of the great pot to see a thick treacly liquid congealing in the bottom. A chalice and sacrificial knife and sickle lay neatly arranged on a three-legged table. At least he hadn't had to look far, he thought, as he picked up the sickle that was little bigger than his palm and slipped it into his belt.

The dragon's claw was gathering dust and large spiders busied themselves in the alcoves. Dried herbs hanging from a beam gave a sweet scent to the air and the disarray of newts' tails, shrivelled tadpoles and wrens' feet that were usually scattered over the floor, were heaped into separate piles. The natural chaos was gone and the room felt sterile; he preferred it as it had been.

Morrigwen's books, normally precariously piled by chairs and tumbling from the mantelpiece, were neatly arranged on shelves, evidently by someone who could not read since they were neither in alphabetic nor subject order but in size.

Where was it – that little black book that Morrigwen never allowed any to touch? Even when her eyes had failed her, she would fumble blindly through the pages as if feeling for the words. Brid and Keridwen were gone but, though Morrigwen was dead, he had seen that she was still in the Otherworld; while she remained there, perhaps he could reach her. But only if he could find that book.

He was grateful that the room was tidy as he ran his eye over the bookshelves and saw it, right at the top. He dragged a stool across and, standing on tiptoe, eased the book out then, without looking at it, he put it straight in his pocket.

Now for her runes that were always out of the bag, either in the Crone's fingers or scattered over her divining circle. It took years to learn the art of divination but Brid had managed to teach him something of runelore and, though he had no true understanding, he prayed that, if he found them, instinct would guide him in their use. After all, he was the son of a high priestess. He searched the room three times but to no avail. He left the room and re-entered, trying to look with new eyes. Where would someone who knew nothing of the arts and had little sympathy for pattern put Morrigwen's runes or their scrip?

He would have put them in the bag and left it centrally within the divination circle but that was on the floor and the floor had been swept clean. He lifted every cushion and sought through every drawer. Her rune stave, which Caspar had no purpose for, was lined up by the fire next to the poker. He gripped it and it felt positive in his grasp. Although he had no use for it, he knew it made him look wiser and appearances, as Hal had so often told him, counted for much. He had never before thought that was true and had always laughed at Hal for his pretences and particularly for his constant desire for a suit of armour. After all, wouldn't heavy armour only be a hindrance in their mountainous terrain? But now he was the one who felt inadequate and in need of something to prop his confidence. He took the rune stave.

He finally found the rune scrip amongst a miscellany of other oddments tidied up into a sewing basket belonging to May and took one last look around the room. He paused; a bone comb, arranged like an ornament between an eagle's wing and a horse's jawbone, rested against a little frosted vial of what he knew to be oil of camphor. He loved the sharp, cleansing smell of the white liquid and had seen once how Morrigwen had taken the tiny pure crystals and made them burst into flame by flicking them into steam over her cauldron. The comb was May's, left behind in her haste to flee him. Running his fingernails over the prongs, it rasped in a series of dull notes. He sighed deeply, thinking of her rich chestnut hair, and slipped it into his pocket. How could she have left him, when he needed her so?

He had all he came for and fled down the stairs, two at a time, his light feet drumming on the worn stones, and dizzily sped across the courtyard to the stables. Caught up in his sense of urgency, Firecracker banged him against a corner post and hauled him out into the courtyard, squealing and snorting as they hurried to join Fern, who was already waiting by the portcullis.

Head down in thought, the Captain was striding towards the guardroom but halted at Firecracker's bellowed challenge to the early morning sun. "Master Spar!" the Captain hailed. "The guards say the prisoners are demented. You had best—"

"I'm sorry, I've no time," the youth blurted. "The Egg is gone and I must find it." What more could he say? There was no time to waste. Firecracker tugged at the reins and swung him round sideways. "Hal will soon be home. Tell him—" he faltered, uncertain. "Tell him I'm sorry."

He clattered under the portcullis only to be pursued by excited yips and barks. Firecracker bucked and Caspar looked down to see Trog nipping at the stallion's heels, the white wolfling weaving back and forth beside him. The two were now inseparable.

"Go home!" Caspar ordered.

The dog wagged his tail furiously and appeared to grin but showed no sign of turning back. Caspar scolded him and ordered him to the watchtower but Trog laid his ears flat to his head, as if refusing to hear, and the youth gave up on the battle. Hal was right; Brid had spoiled the dog.

By the time he returned to Morrigwen's body it was fully dawn, streaks of gold radiating through the banks of cloud lazing on the eastern horizon. The pale blue of the sky overhead was streaked with thin ribbons of pink cloud though the canyon was still in cool shadow. A thick dew tipped the lush spring grass with silver, and spiders' webs, like garlands of jewelled silk, sparkled in the filtered light. Damp seeped through the cracked leather of his boots. Somewhere an owl hooted, reluctant to end its night hunting.

Morrigwen's body was damp though soon the sun rose above the clouds and fell between two peaks to the east and a slit of light slashed across the canyon to warm the corpse. He tiptoed into the ring, clutching the black book like a shield before him to ward back the Ondines.

He held high Morrigwen's rune stave. "I do not come in malice," he protested but still they swooped aggressively towards him, screaming in his face and clawing with airy fingers at his eyes and hands. "Morrigwen would want this of me!" He wafted the stave at them. Fire spat into his face and, instinctively, he ducked beneath the upheld staff. They squirmed around his legs and tugged at his hair. Gritting his teeth and girding his mind to ignore their chilling shrieks, he waded on, the black book in one hand and the sacramental sickle in the other.

He had often wondered at the purpose of the tiny golden sickles that the three high priestesses carried and the answer came to him instinctively as he thought on his own purpose. The curved blade was ideally suited to his needs. Both hands trembled as he leafed through the pages, searching for the runes of augury that would guide his hand.

Fern shrieked fearfully from beyond the edge of the circle, "Only carrion do such evil."

Caspar ignored him and read the ancient text. *With golden blade slit open from throat to belly and peel apart the skin.*

Forcing from his mind the thought of what he was actually doing, Caspar made the first cut. There was no spurt of blood but just a slow moistening of the tissue but he was sickened by the amount of force it took to tear the loose skin. His cut was jagged and the Crone's ancient body flapped about as he heaved and worked.

At last, the slit was made and, flicking his head to the side at the stench, he wormed his fingers into the soft tissues and wrenched open the belly cavity. Maggots wormed and laced through the perforated tubes of her gut. His fingers squelched in the purply tissue as they sought through flaps of lung and spleen and a great slab of an enlarged liver, no creamy yellow fat beneath the skin. He pulled out the guts that slithered like live snakes in his fingers and, for the first time, his control left him and bile spumed into his throat. He retched in his mouth and nudged his clammy forehead against his shoulder, willing himself to be strong.

The guts came out easily but he had to use both hands to tear the gristle of her chest. It gave suddenly, the chest and throat ripping open all as one in a rush that sent him forward as the pressure gave, his nose stopping barely an inch from the white bones of her ribs. He sat back in horror. Though his fingers were clear of her body, the heart had heaved and the entrails squirmed. At first, he thought some large parasite was being birthed within her body but then he realized he was looking at her insides as they were in the Otherworld, where her heart still beat and where the guts of her drawn body were being stirred by the verderers' tools of torture.

He turned his eyes to the book for guidance, smears of blood and tiny congealed lumps of tissue clinging to the crisp pages. The book instructed him to look at the size and position of the liver and the heart, and to draw out the intestines. Directions could be divined from the size of the liver, purpose from swellings in the gut; but it was meaningless to Caspar since he had never seen the entrails of a human displayed before.

Fern was being sick.

Looking into the old woman's face, he beseeched, "Morrigwen, you must tell me how I can find Necrönd." He drew out the entrails as the book told him and stretched them out to encircle the corpse. Then the book instructed that he found a spray of ash and he looked hurriedly around for the nearest ash tree. With a word of apology, he snapped the end from a low branch and took the small spray laden with feathery leaves and placed it in Morrigwen's mouth. The ash would show the truth of the larger pattern of the world reflected in the smaller pattern of her body. He laid out her arms and legs, her body just an empty sack now that he had disembowelled her.

"Your heart was here in Torra Alta," he told her. "Perhaps your body, therefore, corresponds to the rest of Belbidia."

A wren flitted out through the undergrowth and popped up onto one of the standing stones, its short tail bobbing. Caspar snatched up three runes and, twirling himself round withershins, cast them into the air while breathing aloud the ancient name of the Great Mother, a word never to be spoken lightly. His voice sounded strange as he spoke, aged and croaky. A shudder ran through him and a sense of great life and energy crammed his being, bringing with it a momentary but overwhelming flash of enlightenment regarding the linking of all things and the purpose of being. As he turned, the tiny wren swooped and, hawklike, snatched up one of the stones.

Caspar was about to curse when he remembered that the bird was believed to communicate with the dead.

Morrigwen must know and, surely, she would tell him somehow where he must look.

Two of the runes fell upside down at Caspar's feet so that their symbols could not be read but the wren still hopped about with the third one in its claw. The bird pecked at it and then hopped on a little further, evidently intimidated by the presence of the Ondines that hissed at it, the air blowing through its feathers, making it fluffy like a fledgling. Caspar thumped the rune stave down on the alter slab with a resounding crack to distract the Ondines. They buzzed angrily around his head, spinning him round and around, his throat suddenly a blaze of pain as the fire Ondine breathed into his mouth.

He shrieked and leapt back, beating them off with the stick and the wren hopped bravely up to Morrigwen's body and dropped the chip of bone on her shoulder. The bird twisted its head sideways and looked quizzically at her face. Then its tiny beak stabbed forward and pecked at her eyelids. Caspar brushed the bird away and studied the rune.

It had been placed east of the heart, which he had designated to be Torra Alta, but still it made little sense to him. He picked up the rune, certain that it would enlighten him, but swallowed back his disappointment. Morrigwen's scrip was somewhat weightier than Brid's and contained runes that the Maiden had not shown him. He studied the rune's outline and then flipped through the black book for reference to it. There was none.

He studied the rune again and laughed to himself. It was always like Morrigwen to make life hard. It was not one rune but three tree runes linked together: Nuin, the ash; Duir, the oak; Huathe, the hawthorn.

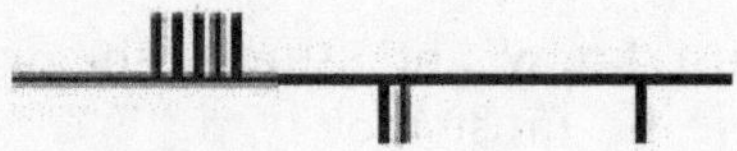

He knew nothing of their combined meaning, only that it must be very powerful.

Wondering how a priestess might interpret such a casting, he sat down to think. Nuin was the key to understanding how the universe was linked, all things being a part of one whole. Duir offered strength, protection and a doorway to the inner mysteries. Huathe was the tree rune of chastity, cleansing and restraint. His mind hurt as he tried to form one meaning out of the combination of all three but he came to no conclusion. Then he remembered Brid's advice, never to search too deeply for meanings but let them come to you. She had said that often the most simple answers were the right ones and were easily overlooked if we try too hard to find them.

What then was the simple meaning? Go east to the ash, the oak and the hawthorn? But that was too easy! It couldn't be right. But why not? Beyond the first jagged escarpment of the Yellow Mountains to the east were many woods lying low in the dark shaded valleys: Stag Run, Rook Wood, Brambletwine and Fey Grove to name but four. Fey Grove, but of course! Could it really be so simple? There, the ash, the oak and the hawthorn grew so densely together that often their boughs joined and knotted as one. Such trees were known as fairy trees and Caspar knew from May that no woodsfolk would ever go near them.

He smiled. Yes, it would be a good place to hide out with Necrönd. Hardly anyone ever roamed into the eastern mountains and Fey Grove was only reachable over the steepest terrain or through Brambletwine Wood, which was dense with interwoven thorns. Moreover, Fey Grove was in the middle of bear-country. No one in their right minds would travel that way. It would be an excellent place to hide out with the Egg.

"Morrigwen, I'm sorry for this." He looked remorsefully at the savagery he had committed to her body and stiffly retreated, signalling to Fern that they should leave.

"Why this way?" Fern demanded. "The wolfman was heading south. We should go south."

Caspar growled in his throat. "Because I have divined that we should go east to the forest."

"Toadstools!" the little woodwose muttered. "Death cap toadstools and poisoned ivy." Evidently to deer, this was one of the ruder comments that could be made. "What will the Lady Keridwen say when she hears of the horrible things you have done to the old woman?"

Caspar tried to avoid the thought. He had spoken aloud the sacred name of the Great Mother and She had guided him through the wren. He had to have conviction. Brid would. Hal would . . . He couldn't let himself be swayed by Fern.

The woodwose looked at him and sniffed. Somewhere he had picked up an irritating habit of constantly needing to chew and seemed to have an endless supply of something green in his mouth.

"Fern, if the Great Mother has told me to look east to Fey Grove, do you think I'm going to look there or follow you?"

Scowling, Fern followed after Caspar. "What have you got in that pack? Your kind are all barbarians; I can smell meat." He stabbed an accusing finger at Caspar.

Though his sharpened awareness of danger might prove very useful, Caspar already wished he had left the little being behind.

"I told you they went straight south down the road,"

Fern persisted as he trotted alongside Firecracker, whose lean muscular legs swept Caspar north to the stone bridge above Foals Ford, the nearest crossing of the Silversalmon.

"Perhaps Morrigwen knows more than you. Who are you to nag so?" Caspar snapped.

"Who are you?" the woodwose retorted. "I've seen nothing yet that tells me you're more important than me."

Caspar pursed his lips. He didn't feel important. Perhaps Fern was right but he was still going to cross the Silversalmon and follow the path from there east right into Fey Grove. "You don't have to come. You can stay here."

Fern looked back at the high Tor and shuddered before racing after Caspar.

CHAPTER SIX

"Y' should never have come, Pip." Abelard checked his rising irritation with the boy. "Y' should never have abandoned your post without first seeking permission of Master Spar. He's in charge."

"In charge!" Pip sniffed disrespectfully.

Abelard couldn't understand such impudence. Imagine Pip just walking out and racing after them like that! He left Brid to scold the youth, which she did with insincerity, while he wondered whether it wasn't a terrible mistake to have left Master Spar alone in Torra Alta. It wasn't his decision, of course, but he could have said something. The boy had great inner reserves of character and a driving sense of purpose, which he would defend with a passion, but he was still too reserved and unsure of himself when it came to command. Still, the Captain was there and he was a good man.

"Can't I ride Sunburst now?" Pip demanded of Brid.

"No, Pip, I don't want her ruined," she said without taking her eyes from the road ahead. "He should be riding home towards us by now. What's keeping him?"

Pip scowled and plucked his bowstring broodingly. He reached for an arrow, raised the bow and took aim at a bulbous knot on the bowl of a tree. He hit the wart but was a good eight inches off centre.

"Y' just go and fetch that arrow," Abelard told him.

"The fletcher don't spend his days labouring away for y' to leave them marking the miles to Farona."

"If it matters to you so much, you get it," the boy replied with a challenging glint in his eyes. "And while we're on the subject, everyone says you're such a great master with a bow, yet you've never proved it. I don't believe you are at all." Pip's respectful tone towards Abelard had evaporated since the archer had been so disapproving towards him for abandoning his post at Torra Alta.

Abelard raised his hand to take a swipe at the back of Pip's head. Someone should have thrashed some respect into this lad long ago and he was surprised at the Baron's laxity in this. Still, he had heard how Pip's father had given his life to save Caspar and he suspected this was why Baron Branwolf tolerated such leniency towards the loud-mouthed youth. The thought slowed his hand and, though he had fully intended to knock the lad from his horse, Pip managed to duck and avoid the full force the blow.

No longer trusting his temper with Pip, he kicked his horse on to draw alongside Brid. He had made the journey to Farona twice before in his youth, and well-remembered toiling along the muddied tracks; but much had changed in four hundred years. The Halfway Inn was still standing, which made him smile as he recalled his last stay there; but the country they rode through was not how he remembered at all. Gone were the dark wild woods thick with boar and in their place sprawled vast open fields. He even had to refrain from gasping at the sight of the Jotunn oxen with their huge white bodies and black faces. The brutes were enormous with huge rolls of flesh around their shoulders and necks. He had never seen so many beasts in one field, their vast black horns rattling against each other. The treeless field was tightly roped so that they would graze one area before being moved the next day to scythe through another.

"In my day there were an oak for every acre," he said. "After all, ain't that what an acre means? Them beasts have no shelter against sun nor rain. What happens come winter? It'd be right unhealthy to barn so many beasts."

This prompted an outburst from Brid who spent the rest of the journey berating the tyranny of Belbidian farming practices, which became especially vehement as the road cut through the great windswept plain of Faronshire in the heart of the country. Here dust devils stormed over the huge fields. The air was stuffed with dried chaff and fine soil; and the horses wheezed while the riders buried their faces in the crooks of their elbows.

"But 'tis not yet summer, my Lady Brid. How can they be harvesting grain now?" Abelard wondered at the madness.

"They plant two crops a year and have done for decades now," she sighed.

Abelard pouted. "'Tis plunder."

Brid nodded distractedly.

The archer pointed off to the side of the road. "Here, I remember, stood acres of tall beeches and coppiced oaks, their trunks swollen, twisted and gnarled with age, that produced regular timber and many good days' work for the carters, wheelwrights and carpenters, not to mention the bodgers."

"Bodgers?" Brid asked.

"Men that worked and turned beech-wood for chair legs," he explained. "There were still the wheat fields, of course, and millers naturally, always millers, but there were herbalists and mushroom pickers and those what search for truffles. And the wheat was always brought in at the *end* of summer – at its rightful time."

"I know," Brid murmured in that wondrous soft voice of hers. Abelard wished he were younger. She was so beautiful, so . . . He checked his thoughts, quietly aware of their impropriety.

In all his years he had rarely met a man and a woman that he thought well-suited and, when he did, he often later judged their love to be shallow as if the lack of conflict between them somehow meant there was little chance for passion to develop either. But never had he been more surprised by a match than that of Brid and Hal. She was sensitive, so in tune with everyone around her and cared passionately about the world, while Hal . . .

Abelard found himself growling in his throat. Hal was an angry young man. Of course, he was dashing and capable, and he could see how most young girls might be attracted by his smooth confidence and easy manner – but not Brid. She had too much depth of understanding.

"What's the matter?" Brid asked him and he smiled in embarrassment, realising he had been staring straight at her.

"I was just thinking how the world has changed. People stay the same but the world has changed."

They passed through sweeping plains dotted with windmills and by early afternoon reached the cross-roads at Bleham where the four ways were lined with granaries whose tall shadows overlaid the busy town. They halted outside an ostlery.

"Right, lad, off your horse. It's a farmer's mare for you."

Pip frowned. "Oh no, it's not! I'm going to Farona looking as fine as a feather."

"No y' ain't and nor are the rest of us," Abelard told him, dismounting stiffly.

"But we should approach the King's palace with the

Torra Altan flag aloft and fanfares blasting to announce the Maiden's presence."

Abelard laughed in amusement, whipped the cloak off his back and stuffed it into his saddlebag.

"No Torra Altan goes anywhere without his cloak," Pip chastised him.

"I know that better than y' lad. In the old days, it were no different. The snows were thicker then and the roads not so good; a fellow could get cut off and he'd die as quick as a naked fledgling from the cold without his bearskin. His bearskin and his bow have always been his most precious belongings and that's why we're leaving them behind."

"That's nonsense."

"No, it ain't, lad. The Faronans will spot us directly as Torra Altans and we won't to be able to move freely in the city. You forget that this plague of wolves has put our lord and all others of Torra Alta under suspicion. We need to make our plans."

They rested at the inn while Abelard explained to the ostler that they wanted their horses to rest here where they could run out in the fields during the day rather than having them stalled in Farona. "Can't have them losing condition. We'll need a horse and cart though."

He negotiated a fair deal for a cart and an old nag and soon they were on their way. He couldn't get used to the constant groan and whirr from the windmills that they passed every half-mile along the road.

After many uncomfortable miles sitting on the boards of the cart, he saw in the distance a tall thin spire spiking heavenwards out of the treeless plain. He wasn't prepared for Farona and stared in disbelief.

"I know! It's horrible, isn't it?" Brid said quietly. "And that's where they're keeping him."

Soon the cart was banging and thumping on the narrow, cobbled streets of the city. Overhead, much of the sky was shielded out by the tiered houses that leant towards each other like bowed old men straining forward to catch each other's words. Barrows and carts clattered along the cobbles and urchins worked hard in the light rain to scrape the streets of the slurry of horse droppings. Abelard remembered how, in his day, Farona had been a circular city of mud huts thatched with reeds from the River Dor but now it consisted of tall stone houses broken only by the occasional brown and cream timbered pub and it was totally without a splash of green vegetation or brown earth anywhere. The streets echoed with the sound of sellers' cries and the stench of the open gutters trapped down in the cold breathless alleys, where the sun fell only in the swelter of midsummer, was overpowering.

Brid looked silently ahead.

High in the west wing of the King's palace, Branwolf marched up and down the length of the luxurious gallery. Much to his annoyance, the thick wool rugs dyed in vivid colours that carpeted the broad oak floorboards muffled the sound of his heavy tread, the echo swallowed by the pelts of Yellow Mountain wolves that lined the walls. He scowled at the bright flowers in their blue painted vases that sat on the polished side-tables. He missed the sweetly scented straw that littered the stone floor of Torra Alta's keep.

There were no draughts howling under the doors and the big staring windows let in floods of light. No smoke escaped from the fire and no pestering dogs whimpered at his back. No sound of whistling arrows nor thud of barbs embedding in straw targets wafted in from outside.

Instead came shouts from the distant markets and the sound of soft-soled shoes shuffling along the servants' corridors. The palace itself suffered from an uncomfortable silence as if noise or chatter might give offence.

Goblets of fine Caldean wine and pitchers of Quertos cider were laid out on a carved dresser by the flickering fire. A low table with an inlayed chequered pattern of ivory and ebony was dotted with carved figures, a game of warlords in progress. Branwolf slumped down in the plainest chair he could find and kicked his feet up onto the table, scattering the carved figures onto the floor. He glared resentfully at the nearest window with its grid of bars imprisoning them into their luxurious gaol.

Keridwen sniffed.

"Don't sniff at me woman! I'm a baron and a warlord. He kicked the table and sent it skittering across the room to thump into a cushioned footstool.

"Losing your temper will do no one any good."

"I'll lose my temper if I want to, you hear!" He sprang to his feet, his head a savage rage. His eyes focused on tiny objects around the room, vases, statuettes, even a clock, a very rare sight in Belbidia. Beside one door was a gleaming suit of armour, painstakingly polished, a ceremonial piece with a swan's crest crowning the helmet, fluted gauntlets and wide skirts to protect a mounted knight. Above it on the wall hung the stuffed head and antlers of a rather moth-eaten stag. He yanked the head from the wall and used it to swipe at the armour, the crash and clang of metal echoing painfully within the chamber.

Keridwen glanced briefly at him and, even through his rage, he was aware of her cool gaze. Annoyingly unflustered, she sat calmly studying the contents of her rune scrip. He marched over and ripped it out of her hands.

"How dare you chastise me?" he roared, totally aware of his appalling behaviour.

"You're a fool. Charging around like a bull is going to do you no good at all," she said calmly and held out her hand for her scrip. "I can't just sit here doing nothing; give me back my runes."

Branwolf dropped the runes at her feet and marched to the window, leaving his wife to pick them up. He didn't know what he would do without Keridwen. Everyone thought he was such a great man, a powerful man with cool-headed decisiveness but, in truth, he was no more sensible than Hal. He clenched his fists and tried to rein in his rage.

"I am a baron and here I am imprisoned by the King. A weak king at that! And no news of Hal in days. What are they doing to him?"

"The others won't desert us," Keridwen said mildly. "They will come. Bullback will come. Ceowulf's brother, Cenward will come for us. They will not leave us here."

"Rewik promised he would release my brother when I arrived." In a burst of frustration, he tore down the wolf pelts from the wall and then looked around for something else to attack. The toppled armour! He punched his fist into the breastplate and grinned at the dent he created. Satisfied, he stood back and sucked at his knuckles.

"You're behaving like a child."

He smiled sourly at her. "I know but there's no one to see me but you." Suddenly quite calm, he took his wife's hand and clutched it. "I'm worried; there appears to be no natural explanation for these hooded wolves yet we are being blamed and shall be made scapegoats for this plague."

Keridwen gently brushed him off and moved about the room, setting things straight. He grunted and reluctantly began to help her, fixing the armour back in place while Keridwen re-hung the wolf skins.

"Rearrange the games-board," she said as if nothing untoward had happened. "We'll sit and play."

Branwolf grunted. "I don't want to play games."

"They'll be here in a moment," she told him while scrunching the runes in her scrip, which Branwolf found annoying. Her eyes were flitting about the room in that way that meant she was sensing things he could not. Sorrowfully, he noted how much she had aged since Morrigwen's death.

Once the games-board was straight, he took a curved horn from a dresser that was half full of wine, which he tipped into one of the many vases, and refilled the horn goblet with water. He wanted a cool head. He placed himself by the chequered board and arranged the pieces as if they were mid-game, carefully ensuring that his hand was in a considerably stronger position than Keridwen's. She was apt to beat him too easily and he couldn't risk Rewik suspecting such a thing.

Keridwen sat opposite him, took one look at the board and threw her eyes heavenward, instantly aware of his plot. He winked at her and she grinned back. That was the wonder of Keridwen. Though she was often serious, with higher things on her mind, she never failed to see the amusement in any situation.

Just as she had warned, the triple looks on the door soon ground and clanked as the bolts were shot back. The door swung open. Branwolf very deliberately did not look up.

"A good move, my lady," he spoke to his wife, "but I shall better you."

Keridwen kept her head down, intent on the game and laughed delightedly. "Oh, but you didn't see this move. My raven takes your bear here."

Branwolf groaned heavily, still refraining from flicking his eyes up to see who had entered.

Someone coughed loudly and impatiently tapped their feet. Branwolf studied the games-board ever more intently. Damn, he thought. He had deliberately placed the pieces to guarantee himself an easy victory but still Keridwen had seen a slot where her raven could swoop in for the kill. He growled in his throat and chewed hard at his lip until a cunning move came to him. With a confident grin, he advanced his horse.

The move produced a delighted giggle from Keridwen. And to think he had taught her this game in the first place! Now he had lost a fox, a bear and a swan. It was too much. He sat back and looked up over his goblet, taking a long draught of water, then lowered it and smiled congenially.

"Cousin Rewik! What a pleasurable surprise. I'm sorry to keep you waiting but my wife is getting better at this game." He kept his voice low and well-modulated. "Perhaps you would like to challenge her. You might find it very entertaining to see how the female mind tackles such problems."

Keridwen looked at him coldly before turning slowly and rising to face their sovereign. She didn't bother to curtsey or even bow her head but stared at Rewik levelly. "Welcome. Come join us. A glass of wine perhaps?" She spoke as if she were in her own domain and, when the King shook his head, she moved and sat by the fire. "Please," she nodded at the chair opposite, "make yourself comfortable."

The King's eyes narrowed as he watched her, his thin lips whitening. He clicked his fingers and several priests entered the room, ostentatiously wafting incense and muttering verses from the Holy Scriptures.

"Do not play games with me, lady of the Devil," Rewik spoke in harsh, staccato tones, his eyes flicking around the room as if judging how they had fared over the last few days.

Anger boiled within Branwolf but, apart from a twitch in his jaw, he kept himself perfectly still. Keridwen didn't need him to fight her battles and the King would be more disconcerted if he didn't.

"I am gratified to see you are afraid of me." The priestess flicked her fingers at the priests who began to chant louder, averting their eyes from her piercing glare.

"You talk to your king, woman." Rewik's voice was filled with threat though he barely spoke above a whisper. "Fear me! I need no more reason to have you burnt or beheaded."

Branwolf sprang to his feet and stood threateningly over the King.

The priests and four soldiers advanced menacingly. Keridwen shrieked out a fearful sound deep in her throat and the air shimmered about her, a circle of blue fire springing into life before the soldiers' feet. The priests leapt back in fright. Branwolf could never quite see how she managed to break open her vial of camphor and flick it about her without him seeing. He still suspected that it might truly be magic.

"Do not play games, devil woman." Rewik had not flinched. "I come to speak with you and see if you will bargain for your husband and his brother."

"Bargain!" Branwolf did not like to be excluded from this conversation. He felt for his sword and then remembered that it had been taken from him.

"Send these wolves back, devil woman, and return Princess Cymbeline and I will release your husband and his brother."

"You promised you would set Hal free the minute we

arrived," Branwolf thundered. A big square man made bigger by his bearskin cloak, he looked like an oak tree standing over a reed as he advanced on King Rewik. "You have reneged on your promise. A king of Belbidia and you have come to such shame!"

Rewik shrugged. "I want my realm free of wolves and my bride returned."

"I know nothing of Princess Cymbeline and the wolves are not our doing," Branwolf insisted in quiet but assured tones though within he felt like a savage wolf himself, lusting to shred these men to pieces. "I gain nothing by endangering Belbidia. This is my country."

"So why is it that your own lands do not suffer? And why have you and your kin removed my bride and brother? It is plain you wish to ensure I have no successor! You know better than any that after Prince Renaud, Baron Godafrid of Ovissia and yourself share an equal right to the throne."

Branwolf's eyebrows raised. "I do not want the throne of Belbidia. I want only my lands."

Rewik waved a dismissive hand. "There's no man alive that doesn't want more. You want the throne so that you can spread the Devil's word. You cannot fool me however complacent you seem, arriving at my palace."

"And how fares my brother?" Branwolf demanded.

"Oh, he is still here," Rewik replied in a well-mannered tone. "I think it is time you joined him." He signalled them towards the door.

Keridwen, her runes in her hand, marched beside Branwolf down the endless white corridors to the heart of Rewik's palace. Everywhere was a scrubbed white furnished with carpets, tapestries and finely carved ivory chairs each no doubt worth as much as a war-horse. They were escorted past the kitchens where the walls were bare and pitted and clearly of greater age than the rest of the palace. The corridor curled downward and they entered a pillared chamber where the air stank. Branwolf knew it at once as the entrance to some dungeon.

"You're going to incarcerate me without giving me a chance to explain myself, not a murmur?" he shouted as they separated him from Keridwen, threw him into a small side chamber and locked the door. Raging silently, he listened to his wife's footsteps receding into the distance.

He was forced to wait only minutes but it felt like hours. The door was yanked open and he burst out onto the point of a spear.

"This way," the guard told him curtly. Another dozen men, all bristling with spears and swords shouldered him, and Branwolf had no alternative but to obey. Giddy with fear for his wife, he was led to a small circular chamber lit only by a hazy shaft of light that fell from a grille in the ceiling.

"What have you done with her?" Branwolf screamed in attack at the sight of Rewik before him.

Then his focus was drawn by a second man who was also regally dressed with straight blond hair cut cleanly at his shoulders. Long pointed spurs stabbed out from the back of his pointed boots and a sickly-sweet smell of incense clung about him. His hauberk was studded with brilliant jewels and the motif of a rampant raging bear marked his breast. Clearly this proud man was a Ceolothian.

CHAPTER SEVEN

Like ranks of giant wizards beneath tall, coned hats, the black outline of the Yellow Mountains dominated the evening skyline. The Tor stood like a lance-bearing knight between them.

From the border between Torra Alta and Jotunn, May gazed back at the blocky silhouette of the castle and watched an orange flame leap up from the keep into the night sky. Silent tears streamed down her face as the great beacons upon the castle ramparts crackled and roared, plumes of magenta smoke rising into the night, the entire castle a torch blazing to the heavens. A great sense of loss gnawed at her soul; instinctively, she knew the old woman was dead.

Soon the mourners would come and pay their respects but she would not; there was no place for her there. She had nursed Morrigwen through three long years from the time when the priest Gwion, Keridwen's brother, had poisoned her with Vaalakan fang-nettle. She had spent many long days reading from her endless heaps of books, stories upon stories, detailed descriptions of lore, herbs and physics. Many thought Morrigwen austere but she knew different; it was the stories the old woman had delighted in most.

She grieved for Morrigwen and was sad that she could not be there amongst the mourners. She had so much wanted the old woman's blessing before she died. Morrigwen would have given her something, some token of her love, but now she had nothing to remember her by; it was like losing her mother all over again.

May turned away, distracted by the awesome power of Necrönd that tingled through her veins. It nagged constantly, demanding, pleading, threatening, all at once. It oozed consciousness, a vast presence of souls; she felt like a helpless queen facing a starving nation demanding that she fed her subjects when she could not.

Breaking away from the main road to Farona she wound along a grassy track until a glow through the trees to the south beckoned and, thumping her heels to encourage something more than a plod from her pony, she set off in that direction. Roaring fires blazed around the perimeter of a small Jotunn village and once within its bounds she felt safer. Hastily erected hurdle fences surrounded the village and were reinforced in places where great teeth had rent the wood.

She frowned. They had put up only physical defences and no one had thought to protect the village with runes or tree magic. She sighed, aware that she had some of the knowledge of a priestess and wondered whether she should spend a few minutes casting runes of protection and sweeping clear a barrier with oak branches. She looked at the hazel hurdles and shook her head in despair. Oak would be better.

The villagers were about to close the gates when she slipped through, vastly relieved to reach the safety of the area well-lit by braziers burning outside each dwelling. Calves moaned and whimpered in the confines of a central barn outside which eight men with pitchforks and bull-whips stood guard.

There was little talk and an air of expectant fear hung

over the village. A busy inn squatting by the roadside beneath low eaves tempted her. Songs swam out through the shuttered windows and chinks of bright light told of roaring fires within.

But the inn was a luxury beyond her means. She had only a few copper coins and cursed her lack of foresight. She should have borrowed some from Pip but, there again, it was extremely unlikely that Pip would have any money saved. Wanting to attract the least attention, she headed for a small dwelling at the far end of the village.

She raised one hand to knock at the door while the other moved to clutch at the silver casket beneath her robe to give herself courage. But as her hand drew close to the Egg, her heart felt sick with the fear, images flashing into her thoughts of monstrous beasts and horned men, fangs snatching out of the dark of her mind. She felt their fear and their terrible sense of loss and loneliness but also their hatred and savagery. Like the hooded wolves, they were intent on destruction.

But beneath these feelings, a part of her mind swelled with a vast sense of power. She was mistress of these beasts, an empress; all she need do was wield Necrönd and they would fall to her every whim. Now she fully understood the priestesses' fears for Caspar. She snatched her hand away and again knocked at the door, timidly this time. It was a long while before anyone answered and, when they did, the light from the brazier shone deep into the villager's face while May's was cast into black relief.

It was a young man who opened the door. He leapt back in horror and slammed the door on her. There were shrieks of 'Wolf!' from within and May felt a cold terror shudder through her, fearful that a great wolf was at her shoulder. She spun around but there was nothing there.

She knocked again. This time a pitchfork was pushed out into the crack of the open door and then a white face followed it. "Who's there?" It was an older man and he held out a lantern into May's face. She blinked.

"You fool, son, it's only a young lass. What are you doing out there after dark?" he asked May, opening the door wider and glancing out into the blackness behind her.

"I'm travelling south," May mumbled, suddenly aware of her foolishness. "I have no money and would beg of you just to spend a safe night sleeping by your fire."

"Don't let her in." The young man held a pitchfork. "I saw a wolf right on her shoulder, father. I saw it as plainly as I see you."

The hairs on the back of May's neck stood on end.

"She's from the north, one of the devil Torra Altans. Look at her cloak. Don't let here in," a woman's voice rang out. A gust of wind blew at the man's lantern and the flame was flattened for a moment, leaving a black well of darkness before May's face. The old man leapt back in fright and slammed the door in her face.

"Wolf-woman!" the cries went up from within.

She ran for her pony, flinging herself onto Rosy's back just as the doors of the hut were thrown open and men and boys came yelling out, thrashing pitchforks and blazing torches that left streams of sparks in the air behind them.

May whipped Rosy to a lumbering canter, doing her best to charge for the southern end of the village. The gates were still open as the last of the villagers brought in the prize oxen and pregnant cows that were slowest to come in from the fields. One limping bull bore vast gashes along its flank where it had suffered a wolf attack.

Men were now pouring out of their huts, shrieking

abuse. One hurled his pitchfork like a javelin and it landed inches from her horse. Rosy lurched in her slow, flat lumbering stride and, grunting, doubled her efforts. She was a farm horse, an old mare with a sagging stomach from bearing too many foals, but she had a sweet temperament and had always greeted May with a whicker. But, with these men on her heels, she needed no encouragement from May to gallop flat out, the heavy beat of her feathered hooves pounding the hard oxen-rutted track.

A man thrust a torch into May's face and she lay flat to Rosy's neck and hooked her fists into the coarse mane, praying that she had the strength to hold on. The old mare stumbled as they barged through the oxen, a horn grazing May's thigh, but she was too relieved to sense any pain as they fled out into the enveloping night.

Once she was beyond the village, the men gave up their chase and Rosy quickly slowed and began to wheeze. They had gone less than half a mile before the lumbering canter became a jog that jolted May's spine and she pulled to a walk, wondering where she should rest for the night. Rosy plodded on wearily, swinging her head low by her knees and May became intensely aware of her own breathing coming in urgent shocked pants.

After a short while she thought she could hear someone else breathing heavily just behind her. She turned but could see nothing but shadows from the trees lining the road and, beyond them, where the moon cast its light down on the undulating fields, several vast humped shapes that she recognized. She relaxed. She must be hearing the oxen grunting in the field, steam rising from their backs and nostrils as the night cooled.

She urged Rosy on, hoping to find a barn where she could sleep, when again she heard a faint echo of breathing directly behind her. She glanced over her shoulder and, seeing nothing, berated herself disgustedly for letting her imagination get the better of her.

An ox snorted and let out a long low moan, the chorus quickly picked up by the rest of the herd. They lumbered anxiously away from her, their horns clashing. May wondered what had disturbed them. Nervous of the night noises, she hurried on, a cold sweat breaking out on her brow. The field of oxen was some distance behind but she could still hear panting. She touched the casket at her breast and the sound grew louder.

She had thought the villagers foolish for trying to protect themselves only with hazel hurdles and yet she had done nothing for herself. She snatched her hand away from the Egg as a shriek filled the air. It came from somewhere to her left; neither human nor bestial, a devilish sound of anger and pain.

"Great Mother, save me," she murmured as the night was broken by a low howl that wailed higher and higher. When it finally dwindled away, the rest of the world was silent, holding its breath, fearful and expectant. Wolves, she was certain, no doubt attracted by the oxen. She stared around and decided to cross into what looked like a small wood on the far bank of the Silversalmon.

The river was high with the spring melts, the water a white foaming ribbon in the moonlight, but she soon found a place to ford. Putting her trust in Rosy, she wondered how she had the nerve to cross the river in semi-darkness. Caspar would never have let her. No! She sniffed. But he never hesitated to ride off into the wildest of places with Brid. May sat tall, thrusting away all thought of the Baron's son. She was a woodcutter's daughter and the woods would be kind to her. She understood them, loved their cradling embrace that would shield her from the world. She would be safe there.

Thankful of the moon piercing the lightly leafed dark of the small wood – pasture was precious in Jotunn and the number of trees limited – she wound her way towards its heart. There she found a small clearing with an oak at its centre and smiled; the oak was the tree of protection. A grand tree, its boughs were spread wide and on one side clasped hands with the feathery leaves of an ash. Somehow, it seemed significant to her. She patted its rough bark and immediately felt better.

On the far side of the tree the huge trunk had been split by lightning and May was aware of her lack of learning. Brid would have known the significance of a lightning-struck oak but she was uncertain whether it boded good or evil.

She unsaddled Rosy then, uttering words of apology, snapped off a branch from the ash and, with the fresh leaves of its feathery tip, marked a circle around the base of the oak. She had witnessed many times the three high priestesses performing rites within the sanctum of Morrigwen's high turret room and now, with a great sense of satisfaction, she realized that she knew which runes to write; runes to protect her from physical enemies and runes to protect her from evil enchantment and night spirits. Her skin tingled and she was certain that, the moment her last circle was complete, the air shimmered with the power of her spell.

Then she gasped with shock as hot, crackling energy scorched up from the earth, over her feet, up her legs and body as if she had been caught in a blast of flame from the great furnace in Torra Alta's wellroom.

A spark of white light sizzled up from the roots of the tree and flashed out into the night. Panting and gasping, she expected to find herself singed but, as the shock subsided, found she was completely unharmed. She took steady even breaths and looked at her hand that still clutched the ash stick with which she had drawn the runes. She grinned and laughed giddily, deciding that she must have unwittingly directed the great magic with the branch. Perhaps it was in her after all to be the new Maiden. Bitterly she shrugged away the thought, knowing the path she had chosen ended all such possibilities.

Too tired to eat, she took a sip from her gourd before pulling her bearskin around her and curling up in the deep valley between two roots of the old oak. She pulled the bearskin tight over her head so that she would be completely camouflaged against the brown earth and closed her eyes. She was certain she had been asleep only a few minutes when she was roused by a peculiar sound. She blinked into the still darkness. She could hear singing!

Pulling back the bearskin, she peaked out into the night. In surprise, she saw that she must actually have slept for some hours because the moon had set and a thick blackness shrouded the silent wood. The singing must have been a part of her dream; not even an owl stirred.

Still blurry with sleep, she blinked, thinking her eyes were playing tricks with her. Ghostly flecks of light sprang out of the darkness, swooped towards her and danced about the oak. Necrönd shuddered and throbbed with energy at her breast and May instinctively placed a protective hand over the casket.

The lights faded and she told herself firmly that they were no doubt only glow-worms. Slowly the night noises returned, a gentle wind rustling the leaves and for a while she was comforted by the snuffles of a badger rooting through the undergrowth until the sound of rasped breathing disturbed the peace. She could not place where it came from. Trembling, she curled up into a tight ball and prayed, her flesh creeping as she became acutely aware of every sound, the snuffle of hedgehogs, the distant low of oxen, the far shriek of a vixen. Her stomach tightened, making her feel sick with fear as she waited for fangs or the cold dagger of a highwayman to stab out of the night; but none came and, at last, she heard the first shrill notes of the dawn chorus.

With daylight came a new sensation. Someone was watching her; she could feel it. The sweet notes of a blackbird calling from the branches of the oak above imbued her with enough courage to peel back the bear-skin from over her head. Rosy was happily munching on the few wispy shoots of grass that grew in the shade of the great tree. A sigh escaped her lips. If Rosy were safe and relaxed, then all must be well; though the uncomfortable feeling of being scrutinized persisted. Hastily, she stood up.

"Who's there?" she demanded and quite distinctly heard a sigh, unmistakably human. Rosy's ears pricked up; she hadn't been wrong. "Who's there?" she called again.

She looked round, her eyes instinctively drawn to the graceful ash tree, its feathery leaves fluttering in the light dawn breeze. She felt naked and vulnerable and wished she had never left the solid protection of Torra Alta's walls. How could she have taken Necrönd? How could she have been so stupid? What vainglorious madness to think that she could protect herself from the savage power of the Egg when all three high priestesses had refused to touch it. Like a childless maid snatching a baby from its crib, she had stolen away Necrönd without knowing what it might grow into.

Rosy was once more contentedly cropping at the grass; surely, there was no one there. She wondered whether her fear of beings prowling about her stemmed from the

Egg and her awareness of the animals imprisoned within it, watching her, willing her to summon them across the divide. Tentatively, she opened the casket and was horrified to see a black streak that zigzagged down one side of the shell. The mark was new, no doubt caused by the blast of heat she had released by drawing the runic circles. She flushed guiltily. Awed by the burden of responsibility, she snapped the casket shut and stuffed it into to her shirt.

She had only just put the casket away in time when she heard something rushing through the undergrowth towards her. The blood drained from her face and limbs and it was all she could do to pick up a broken branch at her feet and brandish it before her. A bestial shriek filled the wood and whatever it was retreated into the undergrowth. Something prowled the woods and she began to fear she had summoned beasts of power in her sleep just as the priestesses had feared Caspar had done. A wind rushed past her face and she breathed in stale air. A howl of rage screamed through the wood followed by a yell of attack. She cowered beneath her bearskin; the wolves were coming for her, she was certain.

But nothing attacked. When at last the wood was silent and grey morning light filtered through the leaves, she crawled out. The perimeter of the circle was surrounded by footprints, the long-clawed prints of a wolf pacing around and around her; yet, she had seen nothing. She stood shivering in her bearskin. Where was Rosy? What would Baron Branwolf think of her?

She was a Torra Altan; she couldn't stand there trembling. Squaring her shoulders, she called out for her horse, her voice thin and wavering.

Her shoulders drooped. She wasn't a Torra Altan warrior. She was just a woodcutter's daughter running away, alone and frightened and she didn't even have her brother with her anymore. She hadn't thought she'd miss Pip but she did.

An equine squeal of fear answered her from the road and, fearing that Rosy was in distress, she forgot herself. With dagger in hand, she dodged through the trees until she saw a flash of hooves and sprinted faster to see Rosy bucking and kicking, a black shadow snapping at her cream side.

"Leave her be!" May screamed.

A long claw lashed out from the shadow and a deep gash of red sprang up on Rosy's flank. May even thought to hurl her knife as she ran forward, incensed, but she stopped dead in disbelief as a little man rushed out of the trees. Brandishing a holly branch, he smote at the shadow.

Small and lean, he moved with speed and grace and her impression was of an elf. She glimpsed leathers and green jacket and a flash of golden hair. The sight brought her up short.

Though many tales spoke of elves, Morrigwen had told her many times that no such thing existed and had once even brought out the *Book of Names* to prove it.

The shadow and the elf were gone. Bewildered, May held out a quivering hand towards the pony.

"I'm sorry," she murmured, thinking that somehow in her sleep she had summoned the black shadow. The gash on the animal's flank smelt as if it had been touched with the cold hand of death.

She led the limping beast to a stream and rinsed the wound with water. "The elements will clean a wound as well as any herb," Morrigwen had told her. "Clay will draw out infection, water will help rinse it away, fire will burn it out and even fresh air will dry a wound faster than gauze." But May still chastised herself. She should have loosestrife and melilot in her scrip just as Brid always did.

Despite her ministrations, the horse trembled violently, its eyes wide with pain. May didn't know what to do. She sat down by the water's edge and began to cry.

She was a fool. She should go back. She could not cope even in the neighbouring barony. How then could she hope to travel far enough so that Caspar would never find her? Her sobs caught in her throat. She had tried not to think of him. She hadn't cried over Caspar for many months, not since the day he had promised to take her riding with Firecracker but then forgot, going off to help Brid instead. May tugged at her long chestnut hair. How could she compete with Brid? The girl was so dazzlingly beautiful with such penetrating green eyes. She had only plain hazel eyes.

May tossed back her hair. What was she doing brooding over such things? That part of her life was over. It was all behind her now and she must make a new life for herself. She had to protect all those she loved from Necrönd. A cold shudder ran through her as she thought of the Egg.

After packing the wound with fine alluvium soil from the edge of the stream, she led the limping animal out into the light and back onto the road. The sun was up above a cloudy horizon and pilgrims were already marching north in quiet possession. Most ignored her but those who looked into her face hurriedly made the sign of the Mother or crossed to the far side of the road, whispering fearfully.

She couldn't understand what it was about her that they feared.

The peaked roofs of the next village pushed up above

a line of hedges and she quickened her step, hopeful that someone could help Rosy or that they could safely rest there. She couldn't ask the mare to walk any further.

After her last experience, she thought it more prudent to stop at the inn. The door to the *Cow and Calf* at Longmeadow was slightly open and a man with an apron over his large belly and a cloth in his hand was peeing out into the twilight, taking a breath of fresh air. May took him to be the innkeeper. His whiskered face with its grey eyes looked down at her.

"I have no money but I beg that I might rest in your stables a while. My horse is injured," May said in her most appealing voice.

"The stables are full, lass," the innkeeper told her. "Pilgrims everywhere. They say the old witch is dead."

May tried not to let her grief show. She had known it in her heart but hearing the words spoken was almost more than she could bear. "But—"

"I have no room."

"My horse is hurt," May repeated more insistently. Pip wouldn't have taken no for an answer; why should she?

"What's a young lass like you doing out on the road alone?" The man gave her a friendly smile but May felt intensely vulnerable under his leisurely stare.

"I had to leave home," she said.

"You're from Torra Alta though, aren't you?" He nodded at her heavy bearskin that was pushed back from her shoulders.

"Aye, I'm from the forest to the north beyond the castle. My ma and pa were killed and the woods became unsafe," she spoke truthfully though the events were more than three years ago now.

"Wolves everywhere! And you look too well-dressed for a forest girl. What are you running from? Did you not go to your lord at the castle for protection?" the man asked suspiciously.

"Oh, yes, I went there but it wasn't possible to stay. Unwelcome advances . . ."

"Aye," the innkeeper replied in understanding.

An earnest-looking woman with a mop in one hand and a dripping cloth in the other nudged him aside. "Here, husband, we're busy today. Give the lass somewhere to stay and be done." She smiled at May sympathetically. "Them lords putting themselves on you and you in no position to turn them aside."

The innkeeper grunted, May presumed in agreement. "We'll make room in the stables for your horse and you can sit by our fire. One customer with no pay will hardly break us. Must have been a hundred pagan pilgrims through here last night. It ain't our way, the old ways, and maybe as it'll bring bad luck harbouring the witch's mourners, but you can't turn away good custom when there's taxes to pay. The death of that woman's been the best thing that's come out of that barony in years."

"Oh aye," the wife agreed, pointing May towards the stables. "'Tis gone to the bad has Torra Alta. Now you make your horse comfortable, lass, and then come in by the fire."

May settled Rosy in the crowded stables with some hay and a bucket of water and when a young groom grinned broadly at her, promising to take special care of her pony, she felt happy to leave her pack and bearskin there and return to the inn. She was comforted by the number of people within and the sense of so many worshippers of the Old Faith about her. She smiled tentatively at them and got warm smiles back. Relaxing, she sat close to the fire, trying not to think of her loneliness.

"A story!" a young man demanded in general. He was

well dressed in a tailored jacket and sat comfortably on his chair, eating an expensive plate of quail. He chinked his purse. "Someone entertain us with a story," he said loudly. "I shall pay for it."

May kept her head low. She knew many stories but she didn't want to attract attention.

"I'll tell you a story," a traveller offered in the burred accent of southern Belbidia as he rose from his chair to sit on a central table. His skin was well tanned and his hair dark like Ceowulf's. May guessed he was probably Caldean. "My master's a wine merchant and I sailed the seas and once, in years gone by, we took our fair vessel up the Narwhal Ria into Ceolothia."

"Oh, 'tis a fair journey!" The crowd sat back, raising their goblets, eager for the tale.

"Oh, aye, a long journey and the seas were high and the wine did not travel well that year. Many barrels burst open and others ruined by salt. But my master's a wise man and he says to us we'll make the journey pay by buying Ceolothian silks to sell back here in Belbidia. He's a smart man, my master. Well, we went deep into the river with our ship and, as luck would have it, ran aground. They say Ceolothia once had big ports in its interior but their rivers are now mostly silted up by the tons of slurry running out from their mines.

"We had to put our wares onto wagons and drag them inland where we were attacked by giant bears that stood on their hind legs and charged at us but we escaped. And just as I thought my very flesh would rot away for the rain, there, sparkling like a diamond in the middle of that muddy plain, were the white city of Castabrice. There we met a man that had lost his hand training bears, terrible sight it was. He came from the ends of the earth, from the hollow mountains of Kalanazir where the deepest mines are found, and he had been to the very roots of the mountains where the earth belched fire.

"He told of the thousands of men and women that are swallowed by the mines never to return and he described the magnificent, yellow-hearted rubies that they dug for. His woman had been stolen away by slavedrivers to work the mines and he had never seen her again. Slaves never come out, they say. Only those employed by the mines for some special talent get to see daylight again. Anyway, this man, he became a bear trainer, hoping that one day the great beasts would destroy him but they had not killed him yet, though perhaps he would be eaten little by little, one limb at a time."

The storyteller went on with his tale of adventure into Ceolothia but May was no longer listening. She had grasped one pertinent fact: the mines of Kalanazir would take her to the depths of the earth, towards the womb of the Mother. That surely was her answer. And the bear-trainer's woman had never returned. If she could just get herself there, she would never be able, even if tempted, to come home. She would need no will power.

The young man paid the storyteller handsomely and, one by one, the people in the crowded inn settled to sleep, mostly where they were by the fire since the rooms were full. The tavern reverberated with snuffles, grunts and the deep steady breathing of sleeping folk. May could not sleep for the drunken snores and, since the night was warm, she thought she would return to Rosy. The mare greeted her with a whicker and, to May's relief, was standing four square.

She settled down close by and, kept warm by the thick straw and her bearskin, soon began to drift off. Shortly, however, she was disturbed by loud breathing rasping close at her ear. She shook herself awake and crawled into the corner of the stall. The breathing stopped.

Content that there was no one close to disturb her, she settled down to sleep again only for the sound to return. She could smell hot stale breath.

"Great Mother, help me," she whispered, horribly afraid that the rasping breaths came from herself.

She stayed awake for another hour before exhaustion overtook her and she fell asleep to dream she was pacing round and round in a tight cell, driven mad by the loneliness of her existence. She sniffed about her at the crack in the door, knowing that out there lay freedom. Squatting down, she scratched at her ear and was suddenly aware of her long grey fur. A long and mournful howl, startlingly close, woke her from her dream.

Four men were standing over her, one holding a pitchfork and another a riding whip. "Get out of here!" they screamed.

She sprang to her feet, clutching her bearskin, a growl coming up from her throat. Terrified, she yelled but her voice came out as a howl and she lowered her head and ran, dodging between the men. One hurled a pitchfork but it clattered uselessly over the cobbles. In her panic, she tripped and sprawled to the ground. A whip lashed her ankle.

"Wolf!" men shouted.

Terrified, she screamed and, again, the sound of a bestial howl filled the air. The whip caught her arm, swung her round and dragged her backwards. Rosy began to kick her way out of the stalls and, finally, the rope at her head collar snapped. She bolted, scattering the men in her wake. Steel stabbed from all sides. Blood gushed down May's face where the whip caught her cheek and her side was numb where a pitchfork had caught her but, somehow, she still managed to run after her pony.

Then her exit was blocked by a further man who raised

his knife ready to hurl it. May froze, unsure which way to run.

Hooves clattered on the cobbles and a mounted figure galloped out of the dark at the man's back. With one kick to the back of the head, the rider knocked the man to the ground and the knife clattered across the cobbles. Though the horseman was small and slight, his grip was fiercely strong as he lifted May from her feet, wheeled his horse and galloped back towards the road with her dangling from his fist. She had glimpsed his eyes in the dark and they had flashed yellow. Her body banged against the horse's flank. Once he had sped a little distance down the road, he lowered her to the ground and turned to see off the six men who charged after, yelling and shouting.

Too frightened to stop, May kept running though her side throbbed and her forehead was moist with blood. Rosy was just ahead and fortunately stood still long enough for her to grab her bridle and drag her off the road. Instinctively, she was drawn back to the sanctuary of the woods.

Too terrified to rest, she kept on moving throughout the night. Dodging branches, she ran, glad that it would soon be morning.

CHAPTER EIGHT

A booming crash peeled out across the rugged mountains. Fern's ears pricked up.

"Ibex," Caspar told him as the rams' horns clashed again and the tinkle of scree tumbling from beneath their warring feet echoed through the mountains. He slapped the muscled crest of Firecracker's neck and moved on but Fern halted uncertainly.

"I still think we should go south," the woodwose grumbled. "Why won't you listen to me?"

Caspar ignored him. He wasn't surprised that Fern was uncomfortable. The high mountains weren't a natural place for deer; they, like the boar and bear, preferred to forage amongst the lower forested slopes and valleys, not amongst the bare shoulders of the crags where tumbling waterfalls threaded through the land like silver sashes. The cascading waters fell joyously towards the valleys, polishing the rocks that glinted in the sharp sunlight. A distant rumble warned of avalanches to the north. The bellow of a lone bear roared back its challenge.

"Bear country!" Fern trembled.

"When my ancestors first came to Torra Alta, it was a land of three beasts: the dragon, the bear and the wolf. The dragons are long since gone; the wolves are now threatened; only the bear remains," Caspar said sadly.

Firecracker's hooves slipped on the loose scree, which

littered the slopes of the juniper-clad mountain. The young man slid from the saddle, drew the rune stave from his pack to use as a walking stick and, grinning foolishly to himself, led his horse further into the wilderness. Somehow, the staff really did make him feel wiser.

Of course, he had been into the eastern range of the Yellow Mountains before but only rarely and not for many months now. There were no dwellings as such though a few old men were rumoured to live here – outlaws and hermits or those just running away from their madness into the wilderness. When they did, they went cautiously. This was the domain of the Torra Altan brown bear, the only place in the known world where the species existed.

He fingered the long fur of his bearskins. The harsh winters in northern Belbidia saw to it that most Torra Altans, men and women alike, wore such cloaks. The bearskins were long-lasting, handed down from parent to child so that very few bears were hunted or killed. Only when they strayed west and threatened the peace of the villages in the Boarchase or the lowland farming communities on the southern slopes were hunting parties sent out. The brown bears were respected, almost revered, and their numbers were protected for future Torra Altan generations.

A fall of jagged boulders blocked their path, forcing them upwards and, as they breathlessly scrambled around the shoulder of the mountain, a new valley opened before them. Peaks and ridges climbed endlessly away to the east, their rich golden colour catching the sun.

"You should have listened to me," Fern insisted.

"Why should I listen to you when Morrigwen told me to go this way?"

"Morrigwen is dead," Fern retorted bluntly. "Do you have any more oatcakes?"

Caspar groaned. "You eat all the time." His hand on the rein jerked as Firecracker kicked at the wolfling who had run too close while chasing and nipping at Trog's flank. The once nimble snake-catcher had grown more sedate in his later years, carrying a full round belly and an eager desire to lie full length in front of the fire, but he was considerably more lively since the wolfling's arrival.

"Why don't you ever listen to me?" Fern continued. "You listen to everybody else, particularly Hal though you swear to me that you outrank him." Fern sniffed in disgust. "You listen to Brid, naturally, but you listen to that horrid archer just as much." Fern exuded an intense dislike of Abelard. "You even listen to Morrigwen's dead body but you never listen to me!" He stamped his foot and twitched his nose.

"Fern, I don't listen to you because—" Caspar faltered, trying to conquer his exasperation with the creature. He didn't really want to hurt the poor thing. "Because, because!" he finished as if that were meaningful.

"You'll regret it. You'll say you were sorry."

Caspar wasn't listening. Below lay Brambletwine Wood and soon they would reach Fey Grove where he hoped to find Necrönd, and his mind was absorbed with the thought. When he next looked up, he found he was following Fern and, since the woodwose appeared to have a natural gift for picking a route through the untrodden terrain, Caspar let him lead. They were dropping down towards a river that disappeared into a dense wood of rowan, birch and tall, red-stemmed pines cradled in the rocky valley. Indeed, the wood was congested with brambles and Caspar thought it would take them a long while to cut their way through.

The woodwose stiffened and pointed. Ahead, beneath

the trees, shadows shifted. Something large moved amongst them. Caspar caught a glimpse of long branching antlers. Then there was a squeak and a yip and Trog crashed forward.

Fern squealed in alarm and threatened him with his stick.

Caspar laughed. "Trog won't hurt the deer; he's much too slow."

The dog suddenly changed track, snuffling close to the ground, his tail wagging excitedly. Fern dropped his stick and looked white and sickened.

"What's the matter?" Caspar asked.

"Blood," he replied and pointed to the river's edge.

With Fern in the lead, they moved on, cutting their way along the course of the river as they made their slow progress through the wood. By the time the branches thinned, Caspar's hands were ribboned with scratches and tears. They broke out of the wood but the woodwose halted and would go no further; before them lay the source of the blood. The skin, feet, head and guts of a hind lay straggled over some rocks. The carcass was gone.

"Fern, man has to eat," Caspar tried to placate him as the woodwose sidled up to the remains and sniffed around it in distress. He snorted and, grunting away to himself, marched off, looking back disgustedly at Caspar as he went.

"Stop it!" The youth was suddenly angry. He didn't see why this creature should constantly make him feel apologetic. "Man has always eaten deer; there's nothing wrong with it."

"Nothing wrong with it! You didn't even notice, did you? It's no good me telling you anything because you never listen. No, you only listen to the men you're supposedly in charge of. Mother knows what's happening here," the woodwose continued. "Wolves moving south; men moving north."

"What do you mean, men moving north?"

"It's no good me telling you anything, high lord and master of Torra Alta. I've been telling you all day that we're going the wrong way; the wolfman went south. I told you but you won't listen. You listen to the entrails of an old woman but you won't listen to the entrails of a deer, will you? Oh no, because to you a deer is nothing, just food growing on the hoof. Well, I'll tell you something, young man," he sniffed and twitched his nose. "In the eyes of the Mother we're all one. You and I, there's no difference between us."

"But there is," Caspar replied indignantly. "I have responsibilities. I will have a castle and a barony to run one day."

Fern sniffed in disbelief. "You'll always have other people running it for you."

Caspar's spirits dropped. "So, what about the carcass of the hind?" he asked to appease the woodwose.

"It wasn't killed by a Torra Altan." Fern sulkily refused to tell him more. They passed more than a dozen deer carcasses, each lying much like the first; gutted, the meat removed the and skin discarded. Caspar could understand one or two deer being killed but this was enough to feed a village. There had to be a hundred men living out here in the mountains. He stooped to pick up a broken arrow lying on the ground.

"I told you they weren't Torra Altans. They always use grey goose quills and their arrows are very much longer. Pip told me that. Everyone knows that," Fern told him knowledgeably.

Caspar ran his fingers over the feathers, which were white with brown speckles, goose probably but certainly not Torra Altan. Fern had been right.

"These men must be the ones that have Necrönd," Caspar said thoughtfully.

"What on earth makes you think that?" Fern asked disdainfully.

"It's obvious, isn't it?" Caspar snapped, tossing the arrow aside. "Morrigwen sent me this way and I find evidence of a large band of men living up here in the mountains. They must be the ones. Why else would they be living here?"

"I've told you that Morrigwen said nothing," Fern retorted.

Nose snuffling the ground, Trog ran ahead, the tip of his tail wagging furiously above the juniper bushes that thickly covered the terrain, and Caspar hurried after him, searching for tracks. "We must find these men."

"See them punished!" Fern added with enthusiasm. "Deer killers! Let the dogs have them. Only good reason for keeping dogs."

Caspar nodded towards a conical peak to the north. A plume of cloud twisted and coiled out from its summit, showing where winds eddied and whistled around the exposed ground though where they stood there was only a light breeze. "We'll go up there," he announced. "We'll be able to see for miles."

The youth tethered Firecracker and climbed slowly, using the coarse stems of the juniper bushes to pull himself upwards. The juniper had a wonderful fragrance that lulled his mind. The five Mares' Tails stood erect and distinct on the eastern horizon. Five peaks sharpened into horns by the cruel elements, snagged at the clouds that were caught by the rising winds and whisked up into tails like galloping horses.

Another plume climbed from the ground halfway between them and the five peaks though this one was a smoky dun and rose lazily from the warm valley. "Look! A campfire!" Caspar pointed. "And it's right by a wood, by Fey Grove. These have to be the men that have Necrönd."

"We should go back," Fern advised. "We should go back and get men. Get the Captain; he'll know what to do."

Caspar pouted resentfully. "I don't need any help."

"Well, I'm not going any further," Fern repeated several times as they returned for Firecracker and began the trek east towards the fire. "I just won't."

When they approached the camp some while later, Fern was still complaining but showed no inclination to turn back. They worked their way into Fey Grove and hid midst the curious trees where the oak, ash and hawthorn, heady with the scent of spring blossom, were woven tightly together. From the fringes of the wood, they looked down into the valley. Over a score of men and about half a dozen women were busy around the fire, preparing meals and gathering wood. Caspar congratulated himself for his skill in interpreting the signs given to him by Morrigwen's body. His fingers trembled as he thought that Necrönd must now be near.

He waited until dusk, when the shadows blended with the darkness, before making a move. He pulled his bear-skin over his head and, keeping to the shadows, crawled stealthily forward. A song drifted out from the camp, a shepherd's song no less, he thought in amazement.

In the wolds, by the babbling brook,
With fire stoked and hand on crook
We count our sheep and count again
For we are shepherds; all good men!

The ram is strong, the ewe is fat – and her coat is woolly.
We're not afraid of Big Bad Wolf, nor any other bully.

The night is long, the air is cold
When Big Bad Wolf he stalks in bold.
But my fire is high, my crook is long
And my ram is very strong.

We're not afraid of Big Bad Wolf nor any other bully
Though the lambs are young, the ewe is fat and her
coat is woolly.

The end of the song was greeted with appreciative laughter that lulled Caspar into sense of security. Surely, men that sang such harmless songs would be no trouble. He crept closer.

"Do we have to sing songs about wolves?" One sounded particularly irritable. "We haven't seen a wolf in days, not since we got here, in fact, and I don't want to be reminded."

Caspar frowned. The accent sounded Ovissian.

"I came here to kill wolves. They said: 'Join up, Naith, and get to kill wolves.' But I've not seen one," a younger voice cut through the grunts of the older men.

Caspar frowned. Surely, these men were nothing to do with Necrönd.

A sudden shriek from Fern made the hairs on Caspar's neck prickle. Howling like a demon, the woodwose rushed into the middle of the camp, thrashing wildly at them with a branch. Caspar held his breath, uncertain as to what to do. What madness had possessed the woodwose? One of the men caught Fern by the arm and swung him round; another wrenched the stick from his hand while another cuffed him across the face with a closed fist.

Fern spat blood but kept struggling. Caspar restrained himself from rushing in, prudently realizing there were far too many men for him to tackle and decided to march into their midst and apologize. He was pushing himself to his feet when a jarring pain slammed through his shoulder. Instinctively, he rolled over, an arrow latched to his bow to ward off his attacker. He aimed straight in the face of a young man. The man had evidently meant to hit him across the back of the head and knock him flat but instead had clubbed his shoulder and the worst of the impact had been absorbed by his bearskin.

Caspar thought the arrow would dissuade him from further action but a bullwhip cracked out from his left and snatched his hand away from his bow, leaving a red cuff around his wrist. Four other men pounced on Caspar and dragged him into the circle.

"Bloody Torra Altan." One of them spat. A large side of deer was roasting over the fire and Fern was gibbering, tears streaming down his face. "My Sorrel," he cried. Though only small, the men were still having difficulty holding him as he thrashed in anger and despair. "To come back to this. My Sorrel! You devils, you fiends!"

Caspar felt his limbs go weak.

A tall man with spiky hair wiped the blood from the back of his hand. "What kind of creature is this? More evil beasts coming out of Torra Alta." Long scars furrowed his arms where, Caspar guessed, he had been clawed by a wolf. He looked around at these men; they weren't trappers; there were no wolf pelts in sight.

"Hold your tongue, stupid creature, or I'll shut you up for ever." The man piled his fist into Fern's stomach and the creature folded.

"Hey!" Caspar shouted but found himself unable to move with four men pinning him down by each of his limbs. They stripped him of his bow, verderer's knife and hunting knives.

"What kind of creature is he?" the spiky-haired man

demanded, looking with curiosity at the blue steel of the spiked blade.

Caspar's brain raced and he shrugged to give himself a moment to think. "Just a regular man, only he was bitten by a wolf and it touched his mind. Now he thinks he's a deer."

The man's shaggy grey eyebrows rose and he laughed sarcastically. "Bitten by a wolf, eh? I don't believe it. No Torra Altan's been bitten by a wolf."

Caspar sensed their hostility and racked his brains for what to do. Hastily, he looked around the group and was amazed to see more men and women joining them, holding picks and shovels. These were Ovissians, surely, judging by their smocks and woollens. What were they doing digging in Torra Alta's mountains? Had he found the men that were seeking to steal his father's mineral wealth? Ruefully he decided that, right at this moment, the knowledge wasn't going to do him any good.

They clearly hated him as a Torra Altan and it took him no time to realize why; most bore claw marks or deep wounds where hunks of flesh had been bitten out. A little girl had an eye and ear missing on the right side of her face. Evidently, they blamed Torra Alta for the wolves and their suffering.

"I'll prove it to you if you let me go," Caspar bargained.

The man rubbed his spiky-haired scalp thoughtfully and then nodded to the others who released their grip. Caspar staggered over to Fern, pulled aside the red kerchief that he wore at his throat and then pulled open his vest to expose his chest. The men gasped.

"How did he survive that? Such wounds to the jugular!" one exclaimed.

Caspar clutched Fern's violently shaking hands and looked into his wild eyes, that shone hugely black. Gently, he covered the blackened raised scars to his throat and chest.

"Listen friends," Caspar said, "we too are enemies of the wolf and have suffered as you have."

The tall spiky-haired man stood back and looked at them sceptically. "But you are Torra Altans, clearly."

Caspar nodded. "What of it?"

The men looked away and began muttering amongst themselves. "We can't trust him. We should wait until Mamluc returns to see what's to be done with them."

Caspar's fingers closed rigidly around Fern's shoulder, digging into his flesh as he wondered whether this Mamluc had Necrönd. As the men continued to argue, he sensed no leader amongst them. "We'll have to wait for Mamluc," one repeated and it was the only thing they agreed on.

Caspar's hopes of talking his way out of their predicament were shattered by a yowl from above. All heads jerked upwards to see Trog set to launch an attack from the top of a boulder not far from the camp. The wolfling beside him sat back on her haunches and howled. Several of the men snatched for bows and catapults. Caspar's heart pounded but he needn't have worried. These were not bowmen by any means and their arrows fell well short though they did send the two animals back into the wilderness. Those with slings had better aim but they still lacked the range.

"Tie them up," the eldest man said. "It'll do them no harm and we can wait for Mamluc."

Caspar and Fern were tied by the hands and feet and forced to sit by the sweltering fire. The men warily kept their distance.

"He's a wizard, a warlock," one muttered. "Look at his staff. He might curse us."

Caspar wished he could.

Listening to grunts deep in the valley, he fretted at his bonds. He didn't want to be tied and defenceless if anything attacked. He had seen a brown bear stand on its hind legs and tower to nearly ten feet. He would feel safer with a bow in his hands. He snuggled against the soft bear-fur around his body, thankful for its warmth in the cool of the mountain night. He had not killed this bear. The cloak had belonged to his grandfather, Baron Brungard who had died before his birth.

The men stirred from their sleep and were quickly on their feet, muttering and whispering, chains clinking softly in the dark. The camp emptied, leaving Fern and Caspar tied up alone like lambs staked out to catch a tiger. The grunts grew louder accompanied by heavy footfalls.

Fern whimpered.

"Shut up; you'll draw it to us."

"It's a bear!" the woodwose whimpered. "A bear!"

"I know that." Caspar tried to sound calm. "But he won't come near the fire."

"He can smell the meat," Fern moaned. "Bear will come for meat. Bad as wolves, they are. Worse! Monstrous!" He trembled.

Somehow, Fern's dread made it easier for Caspar to keep his nerve. "They won't leave us staked out like bait; no human would do that to another."

He was wrong. The crunch of feet accompanied by snuffling grunts became a rumbling run as the bear lumbered into the camp. He caught its outline, the vast hump of its head low to the ground, foraging through the camp, one great swipe of its paw sending bedding rolls flying. It made towards the fire and circled it warily, jaws chomping as it eyed the remains of the spitted carcass. Fern let out a low moan and buried his head into Caspar's shoulder. The youth gritted his teeth.

Lights flickered around the circle and, with relief, he sensed the men creeping back. The bear was moving slowly away, grunting and swaying backwards and forwards, before breaking into a lumbering run. Suddenly Caspar heard splintering wood, a deep scream and a heavy crash that shuddered the ground. A moment's silence was followed by snarls and wild thrashings that echoed strangely. Caspar had little time to think what had happened as the men rushed forward, wafting their torches. His eyes were dazzled but he heard the sound of rattling chains being dragged over the ground. Low and terrified screams came from the bear mixed with the peel of hammers on steel. The noises went on for some time while the shouts from the men slowly became less panicky and more gleeful.

"Everyone all right?" one asked.

He was answered by exhausted grunts. The bear raged on, the sound still hollow and muffled. In all that time Caspar was able to think and realised the bear must be in a pit. As dawn approached, he found that, if he strained his neck high enough, he could just manage to see that they were hammering down a chain net over a gaping hole in the earth. He was too tired to worry about what madness had driven these men to capture a bear. The animal snarled and growled but gradually quietened until finally, it hit the ground with a heavy thud and became still. The excited chatter from the men ceased and, after a short pause, they gave out a triumphant cheer.

Caspar and Fern were given water and a little bread but were left in discomfort, tied to a stump of a tree. They could do nothing but sit and watch while the men congratulated themselves, drank a little too much ale and continually peered over the edge of the pit to check on their prize.

The revelry continued for most of the morning and was only broken by the arrival of a strangely dressed man. Caspar twisted round in interest. He had never seen the like. The man's skin had a reddish hue and his eyes squinted and were deeply sunken. He wore a heavy black bearskin on his shoulders much like a Vaalakan. Torcs gripped his bare arms and leggings laced with leather thongs clad his legs. A long, barbed club was strapped to his back.

Caspar was so intent on the man's dramatic eyes that he hardly noted anything else about his face. One was black and the other pale green and they moved independently of each other. The instant Caspar saw him close up, he was doubtful that he had Necrönd. This was not the man they had seen in the crowd at Torra Alta.

The squint-eyed man exuded an air of self-worth. "You have a bear for me." His voice was confident. "I can see it in your frightened eyes. You Belbidians are always so afraid."

Caspar bristled but as he scanned the camp, he did indeed see the fear that this man induced. As he studied the Ovissian shepherds, he noted again their shovels and picks that he had thought were for mining but now he saw they were probably just for digging bear pits.

"Oh yes, Mamluc, sir! A great beast. You will be pleased," one of the men said excitedly.

They moved towards the pit. "You have done well," Mamluc conceded. Caspar could not place his accent though he was certainly not Belbidian and, by the reddish-brown colouring of his skin, not even from the countries of the Caballan Sea. Caspar strained up higher to see until the muscles in his neck threatened to cramp and was amazed as this stranger dropped into the pit. Silence hung over the camp until he eventually reappeared. He strode away from the pit to stare down at Caspar. The youth was acutely aware of the size of his great black boot that was planted right by his ear.

"Who are these two? I came for bears not boys." He stepped over Fern and wrenched up his face, staring deep into his huge eyes. Mamluc's face whitened in horror and he leapt back, muttering curses and lurching to sweep his fingers across the ground and fling dust into Fern's eyes. "I am Mamluc, the Bear-tamer and now I shall be Mamluc, the Accursed. I have looked into the living eyes of dead man." He stepped back and loudly ordered the men to keep Caspar and Fern tied up while he saw to the bear.

The men muttered anxiously while a cold shudder trembled through Caspar's body. This Mamluc was uncomfortably perceptive. The shepherds handed over Caspar's weapons and Mamluc avidly seized on the verderer's blade. "He will be pleased with me for such a gift," he said softly to himself, touching the point of the blade with respect.

By the next morning, the bear was awake and bellowing like a demon.

"What do you want with a bear?" Caspar demanded of the large youth that yesterday had called himself Naith and today came to give him food and water. The bread was stale and the water tasted as if it had been stored too long in a gourd. The thin sliver of meat was dry and very tough and, naturally, Fern would not touch any.

Naith had hazel eyes, a trait he shared with most of the population of lowland Belbidia, and ruddy cheeks that spoke of a life outdoors. His hair flopped over his eyes and a dusky down sprouted from his young chin. A young girl half his age, her eyes bloodshot with tears and her fingernails black with earth, kept close at his side. Despite the mud and worn-look of harsh living, it was impossible to hide the prettiness of her delicately neat features. Nervously, she sat and watched all around her, constantly fingering her long brown hair that hung in tangled ropes about her face. She looked tired.

"I don't know why we trap the bears," Naith finally told him. "I joined to kill wolves."

"That was my plan," Caspar added, thinking that would endear him to the youth who was very much his own age.

"After they killed my mother and father that's all I've thought about – killing wolves – but I've still got Lana to think about and it's not right for her here. What's bears got to do with wolves?"

Caspar shook his head and shrugged. "What do they do with them?" he asked.

"Take them over the mountains." Naith pointed east.

Caspar's attention was drawn by Mamluc, who, at that moment, began to set about the bear with chants and potions, throwing coloured dusts into the pit.

Fern hissed, "He's not the wolfman. I told you he went south."

The Belbidian outlaws heaved on ropes, dragging the great bear out and lashed further chains around its paws and neck. They heaved and strained even though the animal was drugged and one was flung to the ground, clutching his arm, after it weakly swung at him.

The young man, Naith, who had briefly spoken to Caspar, disgustedly took his place on the left hind leg while his sister stayed close to Caspar. He smiled at her and she smiled nervously back. "I'm frightened of the bears," she murmured.

Caspar could think of no comforting reply as he watched the men struggle to hold the bear. Mamluc took out a pipe and began to play. The bear was mellowed by the music and followed the squint-eyed man as he led the animal east out of the camp. The women and remaining men hastily loaded their belongings onto a few scraggy ponies laden with clanking picks, shovels and one or two rusty cooking pots and followed. Fern and Caspar were tethered by a length of rope to the back of one pony and forced to walk behind.

They cut north towards the whispering forest where swathes of silvery aspens fluttered their leaves and then climbed steeply over the crest of the mountain, sweat pouring off the men's backs as they laboured against the bear. One or two of the women sobbed with their efforts but when Mamluc yelled at them, hefting his barbed club, they doubled their labours to drag the bear through the ravines, using whips and lengths of chain to cajole it. Circles of blood oozed around its paws where the chains dug into its flesh.

Caspar was unaccountably exhausted by the climb and was relieved as they looked over the crest of the first ridge to see a wide path that tracked alongside a stream stained deep golden with minerals and flowing like honey over the ground. For a moment, Caspar questioned whether it might be the height that made his head swim. He laughed at the idea; he was a Torra Altan! His legs still worked for him, plodding one step after the other but his mind was dazed, unable to focus on anything else except Mamluc and the sweet music that sang from his pipe.

The sound was magical and silky smooth. Caspar's eyes swam back and forth, following the swing of Mamluc's bearskin cloak that moved to his confident stride.

The little girl, Lana kept close to Caspar as if recognizing in him an aversion to this brutality. She was crying. Her brother continually looked back at her anxiously and caught Caspar's eye, giving him a nervous half-smile.

Mamluc called a halt and cast back down the valley, flinging dust in the air that sparkled like a thousand miniature rainbows. Caspar slumped to the ground in exhaustion, holding his head, and tried to focus though the world swam about him.

Fern was grunting in disgust. "I've told you this man is not the wolfman. What are we doing here, Master Spar? We must escape."

Caspar groaned. "How?" Fern had an irritating habit of rubbing his head at his bonds and Caspar thought to tell him that it was no use but he just didn't have the energy. Vaguely, he wondered how Fern managed to look quite so sprightly. "It must have been in the meat," he murmured. "If only Brid were here, she might be able to cure us. Even May might have an idea about which herbs would help."

Fern's spinning head flicked toward him, jaws twitching constantly. He sniffed as if Caspar were a fool. "In the meat! I thought humans were meant to be intelligent."

The woodwose still managed to crane up his neck and look into the far distance though Caspar could focus no further than the tips of his swirling fingers and his thoughts revolved only about his stomach and that at any moment he would retch.

"It was in the water," Fern continued. "Couldn't you smell it?"

"Why didn't you say?"

"Because we had to drink," Fern replied.

Caspar was confused. "But you don't feel sick?"

"No, of course not." Fern stood up, sniffing the air.

Caspar didn't understand. He was beginning to see why Abelard had found the creature so annoying. "They're following," the woodwose informed him.

"Who's following?" Caspar insisted.

"The others."

"Fern, can't you speak plain Belbidian?"

The woodwose looked at him. "It wasn't like this in the herd. I spoke one or two words and everyone understood but with men I have to go into great tedious explanations."

"But you don't explain anything!"

"I do. I told you it was in the water."

"But that doesn't explain anything. That doesn't explain why you don't feel ill and I do."

"You feel ill?" Fern was amazed. "Haven't you been eating doe's fescue?"

"I don't eat grass," Caspar objected.

"But everyone knows that if you eat marsh ramswort when the tips have turned black you must eat lots of doe's fescue." Fern looked at him as if he were a fool.

"You knew what had poisoned us; knew the cure and didn't bother to tell me!"

Fern frowned and pouted. "Well, no," he admitted. "It didn't occur to me that anyone would need telling. It's so obvious."

Caspar's toe itched to kick him, but he restrained himself. "Well, do you have any?"

Fern nodded and brought out a clump of bright green broad-stemmed grass veined with black from his pocket. "It has to be the mountain variety, of course," he added.

Caspar chewed hard at the dusty tasting leaves and his jaw quickly began to ache. "Who's following us?"

"I told you; the others," the woodwose repeated.

"There was no one else with us, Fern," Caspar reasoned.

Again, the woodwose flicked his head round at him and frowned in confusion. "They have names, they talk to you but you don't even remember them." He nodded disgustedly as if suddenly enlightened. "Of course, I forgot.

They're not human, so you don't consider them. You don't consider the noble Firecracker, nor that scoundrel Trog nor the murderess Runa as part of your company. Humph! You only ever consider yourselves."

"But, Fern, they wouldn't follow. Trog might, and Runa might follow him but never Firecracker. A horse would always go home."

"See for yourself."

Caspar's vision hadn't yet cleared though he was feeling less giddy. He had to take Fern's word for it. Fern, he had discovered over the last few months, had no understanding of storytelling, lies or invention.

Mamluc leapt down from the rock and snatched Caspar up by the collar. "Warlock!" he shrieked, the noise caught in the narrow valley, echoing back and forth. "You succumbed to the poison but already you have overcome its effects. What devilry are you conjuring?" Again, dust that flared into specks of fire flew into Caspar's eyes but he caught the distinct stench of singed hair and sulphurous firecrackers. Knowing that the magic didn't come from the man's fingers, he laughed nonchalantly, though the rest of the party cowered.

The young girl squealed and the older men growled at her to be quiet.

Mamluc snorted and regained his composure by ordering that they set up camp. Fern was excited, giving out little barks every now and then. Again, Mamluc approached, his squinted unlatched eyes seeming to swell. He snatched at the air as if catching butterflies, excitedly drawing the atmosphere to him.

"Sorcery!" Mamluc accused, though with respect. "Your eyes are clear." He laughed almost in delight as if he had at last found a worthy opponent.

"Let us go or I'll unleash my true powers on you,"

Caspar threatened, reaching into his pocket for the camphor. Hoping that the bluff would work, he broke the lid off the vial he had taken from Morrigwen's chambers and flicked a pinch of the volatile liquid into the moist air. It ignited into a spray of flame.

Mamluc laughed. "A good trick, sorcerer." He snapped his fingers in Caspar's face, walked stiffly away and began ordering the men to dig a large pit so that they could secure the bear for the night.

Exhausted, Caspar slept heavily. When he awoke, it was still dark. From amidst the whispering aspens came cries of greeting. He sat up to see a line of lanterns weaving through the trees to join the camp. Another gang of men leading a chained bear emerged from the darkness. This bear made no attempt to escape.

Caspar blinked in the firelight. A girl, young, strong and scantily clad, led the animal who shuffled submissively after her. She bowed to Mamluc. The two groups merged around the fire, all asking about sightings of wolves though none had seen any.

"That's not true, of course," one from the first party exclaimed. "The Torra Altan lad we found, he had a wolf with him though it's gone now."

The second party were suspiciously curious and three rose to examine Caspar and Fern.

One was older and generally better dressed. He thrust a firebrand into Caspar's face. "You fools, you peasant shepherds. This ain't no common Torra Altan woodsman. Look at his clothes. I've traded with them long enough, taking my wool up to the castle. I've seen them close at hand. He's a high born Torra Altan if ever I saw one. He's a wolf-lover; he's one of the devils responsible for the carnage."

"Slit his throat!" another shrieked.

Hands snatched at Caspar. Someone cut him loose from the tree where he was tethered, though his hands were left strung up behind him. Fern shrieked, wriggled and kicked more like a rabbit than a man and his slender limbs slipped through the men's grip. Screaming like a cornered animal, he charged with his head down, ramming his skull into the belly of the first man that stood in his way. The man rolled to the ground while, with one quick bound, Fern was up and away, running like a true stag though his hands were still tied.

"Let him go," an Ovissian cried. "He's just a commoner and he'd been savaged by wolves. But this one," he pointed at Caspar, "he's a bloody high born Torra Altan."

"Throw him in the pit. That's what he deserves," the spiky-haired shepherd snarled vengefully.

CHAPTER NINE

He lay perfectly still. Pressing his head into the earth, he smothered his breathing and stifled the scream that crammed his throat. A huge paw nudged at his thigh, hot breath rasping close to his head. Again, the bear snarled.

A claw pressed inquisitively between his shoulder blades, then scooped underneath him and rolled him over onto his back. The crowd of faces rimming the pit gasped in morbid anticipation. With enormous self-control, he lay limp and lifeless, staring at a long snout that sniffed at his face, the cold, wet nose prodding his cheek. The bear's breath was sour with fermenting meat and its teeth yellow. One was loose, the gum red and swollen around it. Though he tumbled and flopped, trying to appear dead as the bear prodded him, his eyes remained fixed on that great mouth.

The bear lashed again, raking him across his arm. Razor-hot pain screamed through him and every muscle tightened but still his will prevailed and he kept perfectly still. In frustration, the bear swung its weight from one foot to the other, a puzzled growl rumbling in its throat.

Great Mother, he silently prayed, *let this old bear know me for its friend*. He guessed it would only be moments before it attacked in earnest, those savage claws tearing him limb from limb.

A great paw pressed down on his chest and Caspar tensed his muscles against it as it applied more weight. He couldn't draw breath and thought that any second it would crush his ribcage. Staring fixedly at the beast, the corners of his vision blackened as he fought for breath. His limbs grew weak and his tongue felt thick in his mouth. The bear rocked backwards and he gasped in breath that rasped loudly in his throat. He knew at once his mistake as it raised a huge brown curving paw above his head.

Caspar closed his eyes, anticipating at any second the cruel and final blow. Just as he prayed it would be quick, a long high bark echoed into the pit. He blinked open his eyes to see the bear freeze and rock back onto its haunches.

Someone stood in the dark of the pit between him and the bear, neat short boots reaching halfway up slender golden calves, the legs indisputably feminine. The bear slumped onto its side and raised a paw like a puppy in supplicated greeting. Caspar again heard the bark but it wasn't the bark of a dog. In amazement, he realized it came from the girl. Rolling back against the side of the pit, he looked up at her slender body.

The girl, for she was not yet a woman, tossed his bow and hunting knives at his feet but evidently had not been able to retrieve the verderer's blade. He thrust one knife into a sheath in his boot, one in his belt and gripped the third in his hand. "Master, we should leave now," she informed him.

He looked up at the ring of faces jeering and booing at him from above and felt doubtful. Trembling, he pushed himself to his feet and pressed his back against the cool earth of the pit wall. The bear was nuzzling at the girl as she hammered out the pins that locked its collar. It didn't register at first that she had addressed him as

"Master". Somewhere he heard a horse squeal and he knew that Firecracker was nearby.

"Get her out!" someone was shouting from above the pit.

The bear growled viciously and stood protectively over her.

"We can't without hurting the bear!" another shouted back.

"I want the bear and my slave alive!" Mamluc ordered.

The angry shouts continued to rage above their heads, Mamluc vainly yelling for action.

Once free, the bear launched itself from the pit in a frenzy of savage growls. The shepherds scattered. Caspar scrambled out as it thrashed its way through the men, tearing out throats and trampling others. One swipe at Mamluc sent him rolling into the fire. His coat was quickly aflame and he rolled in the dirt, struggling to rid himself of the garment. Men and women screamed and ran hither and thither, some rushing for the trees and others scrambling and half-falling to reach the river at the bottom of the valley. Caspar wondered whether they knew that brown bears could climb as well as swim.

Only Naith and his little sister Lana remained, having hidden beneath Caspar's bearskin. The long-legged girl, who had so extraordinarily controlled the bear, tugged at Caspar's arm, urging him towards the edge of the trees where Fern stood like a shadow. The bear charged back and forth, clearing the way and bellowing out his challenge. And there, standing by Fern, was Firecracker. The stallion tore at the ground with its hoof and snorted furiously at the bear. With pains shooting through his side, Caspar ran forward, gripping his injured arm.

As he put his hand to Firecracker's bridle, Trog, hotly followed by Runa, burst through the trees. While the dog snarled and growled ferociously at the bear, Runa nipped at his side in her excitement.

"Not a sorcerer? How then did you summon them?" the girl in the lionskin shouted above the noise. "You have power; a man with a woodwose in his thrall, who can summon wolves. Great omens, Master."

"I have no one in my thrall," Caspar protested.

"We must move," the girl said quickly, curiously eyeing the wolfling who was nuzzling Caspar's thigh. "They'll be back soon, Master." She looked at Caspar. "Which way will you take us?"

He heaved himself into the saddle and lowered his hand to pull the girl up behind him.

She shook her head. "A slave cannot ride with her master. Hurry. We must go before Mamluc reorganises the shepherds."

Taking a handful of Firecracker's mane to steady himself, he nodded weakly. His whole side ached and he was too tired to argue.

The girl halted and pointed at the bear. "Go home!" she said firmly with the manner of someone commanding a hound and reluctantly the bear lumbered slowly away between the trees.

Though she had asked Caspar for directions, she seemed to forget and nodded after the bear. "He will know best where to hide from these trappers. If we follow him, we'll be safe."

Caspar nodded and urged Firecracker forward, the slave-girl trotting alongside with easy strides that he would have been proud of himself.

They crested the valley side and dropped into the next that was thick with feathery-leafed rowan bearing floating clouds of white blossom. A cool stream swept through the valley bottom and they decided to rest. Caspar slid from his horse to bathe his wounds, wincing as the ice water coursed over his broken skin.

Hiding his pain, he looked at the slave-girl curiously and said, "Tell me what they are doing with the bears."

She shrugged. "Taking them to the sea. I know little of it. I just do as my master bids."

For the first time Caspar noted the scars on her bare arms, some white and long since healed, others red and bruised. Her thick straight black hair was cropped level with her shoulders and about her head she wore a leather band with beads knotted through the ends, which kept her hair back off her olive skin. A black cross was tattooed onto her forearm, which Caspar imagined to be the mark of her slavery. Her upper arm was marked with three more tattoos, though these were ornately drawn in rich reds, purples and golds and he guessed these symbols were the brand mark of her owner.

"He discovered my talents long ago," she murmured, "and we travelled south to Salise where he would hire me out to train bears." She heaved a sigh. "These animals are wild and the pain of their slavery wretched. Some men like to watch them dance and others to see them fight. A bear fight is a terrible thing." She lowered her eyes to the spongy moss that lined the banks either side of the mountain stream. "Then late last year my master brought me here where he said he would quickly grow rich because none had yet tamed a brown bear. The dun bears of the continent are a third bigger but none, not even the Ceolothian black bears, are as savage as the long muzzled brown bears of these mountains."

"What is your name?" Caspar asked.

The girl shook her head. "I don't know my real name. They call me Ursula after the bears. It matters little for I am a slave."

"And you have no idea what Mamluc wants with these bears?"

"He did not tell me and I did not wish to ask him. I spoke to him as little as I could. But you have saved me from him. You have the power, Master Sorcerer, to protect me." Her dark eyes filled with hope and fixed on his. He snatched his gaze away.

"They'll never track us, not now. We've crossed two scree slopes and no one can track over solid rock, not without a dog." He mounted Firecracker and without a word turned east up the valley.

"Spar, why do you insist on this?" Fern complained. "The Egg was not to be found in Fey Grove."

"Because Morrigwen told me to go east. I might have been wrong about Fey Grove or perhaps the thief has moved on but I must go east as Morrigwen said."

"You'll pay for what you did to her. We should go south but you are a fool and won't listen to me. And remember I smelt him the day May disappeared? What if he's got her? Don't you care about May?" Fern paused and looked hard at Caspar. "Your face has gone oddly crimson," he commented, his voice echoing high up on the bare crags that lined the valley and Caspar shook with the effort of restraining himself from kicking the woodwose.

"Hush!" the girl warned.

A kite, gliding on it huge wings, shrieked in anger at their intrusion. Angry and anxious, Caspar pushed a hard pace and they climbed steadily. Ursula, kept up remarkably well, stoically marching a pace behind, but the terrain steepened and she shortly began to labour.

"You'd better get up behind me," Caspar ordered more harshly than he would normally have spoken.

"It's not my place," she insisted.

"It is if I order it," Caspar snapped, reaching down for her hand.

She looked at it for a second and then, with a brief smile that flashed across her lips, took it and placed a foot in his stirrup. She swung up, clutching at his injured arm to steady herself. Caspar bit his tongue against the pain but was slightly placated that at least someone obeyed him. Too many people – he glowered at Fern – spent their energies arguing against him.

She wrapped her arms around his waist to secure herself and Caspar felt himself flush with the touch of her bare flesh. Guiltily, he thought of May and concentrated on the broken path ahead.

Already the wind was growing fresher as they climbed and, as Caspar's hand accidentally brushed against Ursula's, he was shocked at the coldness of her skin.

"You're shivering! Take my bearskin," he urged, freeing the clasp but she would not.

"You cannot give that to me, Master!" She sounded alarmed by the thought and pressed away his hand. Caspar did not insist since he had more troublesome things to think about. Surely, there were people in the mountains that you would help him, a hermit or an outlaw perhaps that had seen the wolfman, as Fern had named him. Caspar was convinced that the thief must be somewhere east of Torra Alta as Morrigwen's body had told him and he had been wrong only about Fey Grove.

"If you're not here for wolves or bears, what are you doing in this wilderness, Master?" Ursula asked.

Caspar tried to explain that he a lost something of great value and that it had been stolen, possibly along with the girl he hoped would be his bride, by a man with the smell of a wolf about him. His words sounded mad but Ursula made no comment. He looked up at the rising eastern peaks ahead that had grown taller and more vicious looking as they had approached, great cracks now visible in the mountain sides as if a giant had hacked down their rocky spines with a clever and torn open the earth's crust. No vegetation softened the outline of the wind-abraded mountains.

From one crack, a waterfall tumbled, spray bounding back into the atmosphere that glistened with a myriad of fragmented rainbows. The fall spread wide into a vertical white sheet, dropping a hundred feet into a churning maelstrom of foam and rock on the edge of a black pool. Hardly able to think for the roar of the water, Caspar looked up at the peaks. The shadow of a bird played over the face of the mountain. In the sky above, an eagle glided on spread wings, the still kicking body of a young ibex in its claws. It climbed high above them and dropped its prey, the kid cartwheeling down to splinter on the jagged scree below. The bird fell from the heights, its wings furled, only spreading them wide to break its dive and pick up the shattered carcass.

The mountains were wild, remote and inaccessible. Surveying the split and craggy terrain, Caspar guessed they must be near Old Man's Mountain which was said to be the very oldest mountain in the range. Surely the thief had chosen to hide out here in the harsh wilderness with Necrönd, though the thought continually nagged at the back of his mind as to why this wolfman had not yet wielded the dreadful power of the Egg.

Ursula caught his hand and pointed downwards. "Master, look!" she shouted above the roar of the waterfall.

Caspar looked down at a bare footprint in the soft ground by the pool, the toes pointing towards the waterfall. At once, he thought of the many stories with men hiding in caves screened by a wall of falling water. He slipped from Firecracker's back and led him forward, his face quickly becoming damp from the spray.

He found more prints and stooped to examine them. They were all the same, just a little bigger than his own prints, but he was uncomfortable at the breadth and shape of the unshod feet. He picked his way forward towards the sheet of dark water, determined to prove himself right, but with little thought of what he would do if he were suddenly faced with the man that had stolen Necrönd.

Close up, the sound of the water was quite terrifying and Fern simply would not go near it. He took Firecracker's reins and declared that he would be most useful waiting further back. Caspar edged around the pool and soon found himself soaked by the spray and his senses dizzied by the roar. A narrow ledge disappeared behind the sheet of falling water and he sidled along it, gingerly placing his feet on the slippery surface. As he drew close, the rainbow of colours danced and swirled before his eyes and he was overwhelmed by the beauty of its natural but majestic power.

Behind the molten silver of the falling sheet, Caspar could barely breath for the rush of air. The dancing patterns in the water drew his imagination and the patterns darkened in a central circle before his eyes as if he were looking through a round window.

He blinked. The image of a gleaming white castle with golden gates appeared in the midst of the fall, tiny golden-haired creatures dancing like fireflies in the spray to each side. He wondered at the central vision and realized he had seen the castle before, the castle of Abalone in the heart of the Otherworld. Miniature people mounted on golden horses rode in and out in a bustle of colourful pageantry. Trumpet fanfares blasted through the roar of the water that was suddenly strangely distant.

Like a hawk swooping to the ground, his vision rushed on the castle, plummeting down into the castle's depths until he was gazing at the bent form of an old woman. Around her cackled the yellow-eyed verderers of the Otherworld.

"Morrigwen!" he cried in anguish.

The verderers dragged her from her cell. She kicked and struggled, turning her withered face to Caspar, her eyes reaching for his. Her lips moved and he thought she would beg him for help but, instead, her tortured cry filled his mind with agony. "The wolf!" He heard her voice ringing through the waterfall. The verderers dragged her by her arms, her frail body bumping along the ground towards a chamber filled with fires and the cruel instruments of torture.

"No!" Caspar yelled, his whole body shaking with rage.

Still dragging Morrigwen into the chamber, the yellow-eyed verderers looked up as if they had heard him. Caspar's stomach churned at the sight of men strapped to racks, twisting and screaming as their arms and legs were pulled from their sockets. Others shrieked, dangling above oily smoking flames that licked at the black withered stumps that had once been their feet.

The incongruous sound of laughter snapped up Caspar's attention. Across the fug of the hall, a man in a head brace shrieked in manic delight at the Crone's torture. He jerked and wrenched at his bonds, shouting at the old Crone, his foul obscenities squeezing past the iron spike that pegged his tongue and gagged his mouth. It took six verderers to shackle him but even the tightened screws gouging into his eyes and the blood pouring out in twinned ruby streams down his cheeks could not stop him hooting with glee. "I will have her! Soon, I will have her. And then you will all suffer a thousand times the pain I suffer now."

With miraculous strength, Morrigwen turned her face toward Caspar, though the verderers hung onto the thin strands of her hair. "Spar!" she called, before a garrotte closed around her neck.

As if the twisted rope were about his own neck, the vision blurred. Some force turned him towards the viewing gallery above the torture chamber. There, the assembled ealdormen looked down on Morrigwen's torture, most in stern judgement though Saille, clutching at her staff of willow, wept and begged for them to stop. Caspar felt weak with the thought of Morrigwen's suffering and, forgetting entirely where he was, involuntarily reached forward to catch the Crone's outstretched hands.

"Remember the wolfling!" she cried as he began to tumble, his hands grasping vainly for a hold on the slippery rocks. As he fell, a snatch of Trog's bark reached his ears before he was dashed into the pounding roar of the waterfall. His breath wrenched from him by the pummelling water, he was hurtled downwards, falling at horrible speeds into the tumult.

Down he plunged into a churning cauldron of bubbles, each fighting for the surface beneath the pounding power of the fall. He grazed against the bottom, cushioned by the roiling waters that rebounded from its worn surface. He fought to kick upwards but the downward drive of the water was too much for him. Helplessly, he struggled, his lungs bursting for air. Skeletons of deer, ibex and bear littered the quiet pool, a silent lake cupped beneath the white foam of water above. Exhaustion chilled his body and his world dimmed.

He was drowned; he knew it. There before him were the brilliant yellow eyes of a being from the Otherworld. She was fantastically beautiful with swirling golden hair, gleaming eyes and an aura of magical radiance. Dimly, he recognized her as Saille, the otherworldly spirit of the willow. Tenderly, she wrapped her long, graceful fingers around his wrist.

"It is forbidden for me to help Morrigwen but, because you are at the threshold between worlds, on the brink of life and death, I can help you." He thought she would kiss him as she drew him towards her and closed her mouth on his but instead, she breathed air into his lungs. Clutching him tight, she unfurled her wings and flew through the water, her delicate gossamer gown clinging to her slender figure. She took him to the very edge of the still pool trapped beneath the waterfall. "This is the edge of the gateway," she said and pushed him up through the battering waters.

Hands grasped him and naked silvery-skinned beings with strong limbs snatched him rapidly through the water. The light above glinted on them as they flitted through the water, silvery blue hair streaking out behind.

Saille's breath within him was exhausted and the cold dark of unconsciousness crept into Caspar's mind but he was still dimly aware of the figures swimming swiftly and powerfully on. He sensed their thoughts flowing through the water around them, the web of their swirling hair joining their minds wherever it touched. They were the water spirits, the Ondines of the water, and they clutched hold of his mind, begging him to hold on, to fight for life just one moment longer until they reached the edges of the water where their sisters of the earth would help him. "Oh, the frailty of humans," they complained. "Why does the Great Mother allow them so much power when they are too weak to wield it?"

Caspar remembered nothing about the last few moments except for the silvery white of the surface above that seemed so impossibly beyond reach. He feared he would never reach it.

The next he remembered was hearing deep gravely voices. Sounds returned to him long before vision. Strong firm hands were stroking his naked body. He was numb for a second and then a dreadful pain heaved through his chest as he coughed and wretched up water. Big dark eyes stared into his, breathing warm earthy air into his face. They seemed strong, too, like the Ondines of the water and he realized these must be their sisters of the earth. They plucked him to his feet and, tossing him into the air, carried him above their heads like a dead man being borne to his funeral.

For a moment, he felt the mountain winds about him and then the world became still, no more than a distinct echo chiming around him. The naked beings laid him down on a mossy bed within a cave, and began stroking his head and his feet, an experience so pleasurable that it stole away his worries and he sank back into sleep.

Sometime later, he was aware of them watching over him, muttering continually amongst themselves in a language that Caspar neither recognized nor understood. No more than black, brown and grey shapes, he could barely see them in the faint light that fell through from a shaft to glance off stalactites hanging like daggers from a red ceiling, domed and smoothed by an ancient river that had long since abandoned its course.

He tried to move but found himself leaden with exhaustion. "The wolfling," he muttered, repeating the words of the old Crone.

Barely visible before the cave walls, the Ondines stirred around him. They pressed against his body, wrapping around his limbs and, as Caspar looked towards his arm, he stared, fearful that it had been devoured by the rock. The Ondines laughed at him and one unwound her caressing body from his limb and he breathed a sigh of relief to see the glow of his white flesh in the gloom. A sense that his memories were slipping from him troubled him only vaguely as the pleasure of being caressed by these strong females overwhelmed him.

"Lie still," they breathed at him in deep reassuring voices. "Lie in our cave. We shall keep you happy."

Dimly, he thought that it must have been their footprints that had led him to the waterfall. His sense of urgency slowly evaporating, he felt no need to move as they began to smother him with warm kisses, the strength of the earth pulsing through their bodies into his.

"Lie still," they whispered. "They are searching for you and Saille begged us to protect you."

Caspar had no understanding of what they meant until he heard men's voices and the sound of rocks being heaved aside and the tinkle of scree as feet scrambled on loose stones. A horse shrieked and the chime of hooves peeled against rock. Men swore and cried out in alarm. Caspar's spirits sank. Only Firecracker could squeal in quite that belligerent manner.

A young voice, anxious and insistent, rang out. "I saw him, the sorcerer. He floated in here. Look! There's his clothes."

"This is devilry," a gruff voice said in lowered tones.

Another snorted in disgust. "We'll have this Torra Altan. Turning bears loose on our men and keeping a wolfling as a pet! I'll stretch his guts to bait the bear traps."

"Search the cave," Mamluc's voice echoed angrily. "Come out and show yourself, sorcerer, or I'll slit the slave-girl's throat."

The cave rang with the sound of a frightened squeal that Caspar recognized at once as coming from Fern and not Ursula. The deep blood-curdling notes of Trog's growl reverberated through the hollowed rock followed by the crack of a bullwhip. Ursula yelled out in anger.

The wolfling, Caspar thought in despair. He had heard no evidence of her. He squirmed round in the Ondine's tight grip to see the whip slice into Trog's flank, splitting open the white fur into a scarlet seam. Caspar struggled and tried to yell out but the Ondines wrapped round his face and closed rigid around his body, preventing any movement. Fear of incarceration gripped his mind.

Hands pressed over his face, leaving only his nostrils and eyes uncovered. Men searched the cave, thrusting torches into crevices. Mamluc gripped Ursula by her hair and wrenched her head backwards.

"You ungrateful slave, I should slit your throat. Where is the Torra Altan?" He held up a scimitar like the ones carried by the nomads of Glain and his threatening voice was deep and stilted. Firecracker squealed and lashed out against the steel chains around each of his legs. Mamluc threw a cloak over the animal's head and twisted his ear to calm him. Caspar swore he would rip this man's throat out.

Mamluc left another two men to handle Firecracker and moved on Ursula. He snagged his fingers through her hair and sharply jerked back her head. "Where is he? Tell me, girl, and your death will be less painful."

He kicked her feet from under her and she fell heavily, her head cracking against the stone floor. It was too much for Caspar. He could not let the girl take such abuse on his part. He struggled and gave out the loudest yell he could muster only to find it absorbed by the rocks.

"What was that?" one of the men asked nervously and moved towards where Caspar lay.

"I heard something too." Another shepherd joined him and they began heaving aside boulders and snapping one or two of the stalagmites that had taken thousands of years to form. One raised his pick to smite at the rocklike being encasing Caspar's knee. Held steadfast by the Ondines, he could not move and his muscles spasmed as he watched the pick hammer downwards. The Ondines merely tensed and the pick clanged against them as if they had been solid rock. Locked into this coffin of stone-like flesh, Caspar sensed the Ondines' anger and pain.

"It's growing darker in here," one of the men murmured anxiously.

"Ignorant slaves, just find him," Mamluc raged.

"We're Belbidians and no Belbidian has ever been a slave," one shepherd muttered stiffly but they continued to search.

Caspar, too, sensed it was darkening. The men looked around them anxiously and, in that brief unguarded moment, Trog launched at the slave master's leg. Mamluc yelled as the curving jaws sliced into the flesh of his shin but he managed to raise his barbed club and swung it against Trog's skull. The animal fell weakly to the ground.

A girl's voice gasped in sympathy. "But he's a dog, not a wolf. A dog!" she declared, kneeling by Trog. It was Lana.

The slave-driver flung her slight body across the cave. Her brother stiffened, flashing a look of dark anger towards the man in charge, and defiantly moved towards his crying sister.

"Leave her," Mamluc thundered, cracking the bullwhip across the youth's back.

Whimpering, Lana crawled deeper into the cave towards Caspar. She scrambled over the Ondines' bodies, unaware that they were any more than rocks. He sensed the Ondines shift sympathetically to cup her body as, crying for her mother, she snuggled into a cleft between the stones. Then her breathing stopped in a sudden gasp of fright and her eyes opened wide. She pulled herself slowly back and then gave out a terrified scream, pointing at where

Caspar's eyes and nose poked out from the surrounding rock.

Caspar's world went black. He couldn't breathe. Ondines covered his nostrils and eyes, entombing him within the mound of their bodies. Though struggling and kicking in breathless panic, he sensed they were trying to help though they could not understand his plight. The one covering his mouth gripped hold of his tongue. He jerked and strained and, for a moment, his nose and mouth were freed. He gasped in air only to have his eyes and mouth smothered again and he fought to draw enough panting breath through his nostrils while the Ondines cramped his chest.

When his eyes were finally uncovered, he saw the cave was indeed darkening rapidly and the rock walls appeared to be closing in on them. Mamluc and several shepherds ran for the light as the cave mouth narrowed. Those who remained within began to scream in terror. Caspar could see the Ondines slowly worming their way to form a solid wall and trap the shepherds within. The men panicked and reached for their tools. Their picks swung silently against the closing surfaces and, where they struck, the Ondines gave and absorbed, gripping an ankle or an arm and holding it fast as if setting it in stone.

Then the mouth of the cave sealed over and it was dark. One of the shepherds struck a torch and in the dark Caspar saw that along with Fern, Ursula and the animals, only a few of the shepherds remained within the cave and they were held firmly by the Ondines.

A way opened up deeper into the mountainside. What Caspar had taken to be rock at the rear of the cave must have been an interlocked wall of Ondines. The light fell on crystal beds with glorious coruscating patterns that toyed with the torchlight, sending dancing beams onto the ceiling of a deeper cavern beyond. He was slowly released and, still trembling, found himself pushed upwards to be exuded out of the rocklike creatures. Ursula staggered backwards and pointed speechlessly.

The Ondines ignored her, Firecracker and Fern, both of whom squealed and kicked out, allowing Caspar to run for his clothes. Hastily he pulled them on while the shepherds cleaved with picks and shovels to avoid the insidious creep of the Ondines. Those who were still free when the cave closed were slowly absorbed into the Ondines, which smothered them like rising quicksand. Caspar looked in horror at the terror on their faces. Many Ondines pulled Fern, Ursula, Firecracker and Trog, who stumbled giddily, forward as if sensing their loyalty towards Caspar, while others contemplated the little girl, who still lay trembling on the bedrock. Then one Ondine reached out hands and pulled her deeper into the cave.

"Naith!" she screamed in terror, her arms reaching out for her brother.

Caspar looked back to see him locked to his waist, his long arms thrashing to fight his way out of the rock. "Lana!" the youth yelled back. "Get yourself out of here! Lana!"

Caspar could not bear the girl's anguish nor watch the youth's terror. He reached out a hand to pull him towards him and, as he grasped the youth's fingers, the Ondines released Naith and he staggered forward.

The men's piercing screams of terror became muffled cries and distant moans and finally silence. All that could be heard was the heavy breathing of Caspar's companions, Firecracker's snorts and Trog's painful breathing. He slumped back, unable to think straight for several moments but then realized that the others were staring at him in dismay.

"The wolfling!" he suddenly demanded as Morrigwen's urgent words rang through his head.

Fern sniffed. "We've been through hell and all you care about is the wretched wolfling."

"I've got her." Ursula lifted up the shaggy lion's mane that was draped around her shoulders to reveal Runa coiled around her neck. The white beast flopped out and padded softly around the cave without showing a hint of fear. She nuzzled Trog and snuffled her way deeper into the cave.

The Ondines watched her with interest, scooped up Trog and then pulled the others deeper into the cave while the wolfling inquisitively padded ahead. Water dripped all around them, giving out a pitter-patter of notes as it plinked on crystals or thudded onto solid rock. Green slime and moist and deformed ferns clung to the ceilings and walls, proving that at least some light normally found its way into this cave.

"We must hurry," Ursula pleaded. "Mamluc will not give up."

The gentle deep voices of the Ondines rumbled, "Go down to the feet of Old Man's Mountain. Follow the water. Always follow the water." They stopped and waved Caspar on.

"Come with us," he begged. "Please, you must."

They slowly withdrew. "We are not like the water Ondines that flow across the world or the fire Ondines that play and skitter, sparking into life in the most unexpected places, nor the moaning Ondines that ride the winds. This is our cave and we are happy to remain here. We do not like to stray from our roots."

A firm hand pushed Caspar onwards. He wondered

how often he had touched on an Ondine of the earth while thinking it was solid rock.

"Hurry," Ursula hissed. "You do not know Mamluc. He will not rest. He never loses slaves."

CHAPTER TEN

"I'm here to escort you to the King's counsel," Keridwen spoke warmly as if nothing were amiss.

Ignoring the five sour-faced guards that crowded at her back and were, no doubt, hand-picked by the King himself, she smiled calmly though her eyes flitted over the purple sores around his wrists, where he had been strung up, and the great gashes across his neck and chest, where he had been lashed with a cat-'o-nine tails.

He had almost welcomed the heat of the beatings. Somehow, it was almost funny that the real torture, the solitary confinement of the windowless cell and the constant dousing with cold water, which left him shivering through the night, left no mark on his body.

To his infinite relief, the high priestess didn't exclaim at his condition nor offer him pity. Given strength by her presence, he hauled himself painfully to his feet and croaked his welcome.

"Take my arm," she told him as he stumbled towards her. "The floor is slippery and you must guide me in case I fall."

Hal grinned at her, determined that none of his pain would show on his face, and reached for her arm. Leaning on her, he drew on her strength. She was small but strong, just like Brid, and her arm stiffened to support him as he held up his head and staggered past the guards.

Rewik may have hoped that, as a woman, Keridwen would be deeply shocked at the sight of his injured body. Pitiful exclamations would have been so humiliating. But Keridwen was the Mother and wasn't easily shocked.

The guards, two preceding and three behind, marched them up a tight spiral of stone steps and Hal asked loudly and cheerfully for news of home. Keridwen replied lightly that all was well and Brid was looking forward to seeing him soon.

Slowly they climbed upwards, the curve of the steps distancing them from their escort. "Thank you," Hal murmured. "Thank you for not pitying me."

She smiled in understanding.

The guards directed them along several corridors into a chamber dimly lit by a smoking brazier and a patch of daylight that entered through a small grille in the ceiling. Hal's heart caught in his throat at the sight of his brother's broad back cloaked in his heavy Torra Altan bearskin. The presence of Branwolf, who had been more like a father to him than an elder brother, was too much. For the first time, he admitted to himself that he had been afraid down there in the dungeons, not of the pain that would next be inflicted on him but simply of the not knowing when his incarceration would end and what might be happening at home.

Branwolf span round, his eyes flitting over Hal before grasping at Keridwen. He opened his mouth to speak but then closed it and smiled with quiet composure. Hal had great respect for his brother and was reassured that, now that Branwolf was here, everything would be all right.

Branwolf's gaze returned to his young half-brother. Hal sensed the scrutiny, aware that Branwolf marked his thinness and the sores around his hands and the look of general pain and degradation but, like his wife, he did not humiliate Hal further by commenting.

The Baron kept his composure, though Hal noted the subtle signs of strain. He looked older somehow and occasionally his hand moved to nurse the back of his head. The change in Rewik was more notable. He was not quite so upright in Branwolf's presence and he fidgeted uncomfortably.

Without asking for the King's permission, Branwolf strode towards a solid table set with simple stools that dominated the cold circular chamber. He sat and drew back another stool beside him. "Sit beside me, brother, and explain to our King why you are here so that we can unravel this misunderstanding."

"Quite so, cousin, we should sit in comfort to discuss this matter." Rewik's voice was thin and reedlike.

Hal sat and, for the first time since entering the chamber, noticed the presence of a big man who stood apart from the guards and kept himself hidden in the shadows.

"I'll tell you again, cousin," Hal said, sitting heavily beside his half-brother, his voice slightly slurred from a cut lip. "As I see it, we were ambushed at your brother's instigation. Clearly, Prince Renaud did not want Princess Cymbeline to enter Belbidia because, if she produced an heir for you, he would lose his direct claim to the throne and all that he had expected to inherit. He must have arranged for himself and as many other nobles as possible to be taken for ransom to make the whole affair look more authentic."

"If this is so, it will mean war!" The big man, his blond hair red in the light of the braziers, stepped forward out of the shadows and thumped the table with his enraged Ceolothian fist. "My father has lost two children in this outrage, this Belbidian plot and, though our nations have been at peace for four hundred years, there will be bloodshed!"

His teeth gritted against a scowl, Hal looked darkly at Turquin, King Dagonet's eldest son.

"We have men scouring all the northern lands for them," Rewik said hurriedly. "Assure your father that my heart goes out to him. I too have lost a brother in this and we shall find them all."

"How? You don't know where to look," Turquin sneered. "This youth has admitted nothing in the weeks you have kept him, while my kin are still lost. If you cannot get him to talk then I suggest you find another method."

"I have told you all I know and freely," Hal insisted. "It is not I that has done this."

"You lie!" Rewik shrieked, the nostrils of his sharp nose flaring. He turned from Hal and, half-rising, stabbed an accusing finger at Branwolf's face. "This is a simple Torra Altan plot to undermine Belbidia. In one move you have stolen my bride and ruined Belbidia by turning Ceolothia against me. And for what? So that you can wait out the war in your heathen home and emerge to claim the pieces after Dagonet has harried my army and lands."

Branwolf sat back and spoke calmly. "History speaks well for my barony. We have served our countrymen valiantly through the ages against many foes. Our loyalty to Belbidia cannot be doubted. Besides, I would not be such a fool. You forget that if King Dagonet marches on Belbidia, it is Torra Alta that stands in his way. I would lose more than you, cousin."

"Perhaps you have a further scheme that I have not yet guessed at. You could flee to the mountains and let him sweep through."

Branwolf snorted at the absurdity of the idea.

"My father already gathers an army," Turquin continued

in a low menacing voice. "You will deliver to me my brother and sister within a month or face his wrath! And that will mean the annihilation of Belbidia!"

Rewik sat motionless, only his eyes flitting between Turquin and the Torra Altans. Finally, he blinked fast several times and turned on Branwolf. "I will not allow war. Our country is already plagued. You will all go to the dungeons, you, your brother, your wife, until you tell me what you have done with my bride."

Turquin rose. "You are wise Rewik; your action will help my father to hold back his vengeance for a little while longer. Be warned, however, you must return my kinsmen by midsummer."

With his eyes burrowing into Rewik's, Branwolf stood to counter Turquin. "This is madness. I am a peer of the realm; you cannot condemn me without the signature of three barons at the very least. You know you cannot do this."

"Who's to stop me?" Rewik retorted.

"Cadros, Bullback to name but two."

"I could name another four that would instantly support me." The corners of Rewik's tight mouth curled upward into a sneer. "In my dungeons, you and your witch will cause no more trouble and I shall keep friends with my Ceolothian allies."

"You will achieve no long-term peace like this," Branwolf said calmly and without temper, his deep voice ringing through the chamber. "However long you keep me and my wife imprisoned, it will not bring back Dagonet's lost children and, I warrant, he will not be appeased for long."

But there was nothing Branwolf could say to stop Rewik from ordering his guards to remove the Torra Altans. Keridwen pulled away from them and turned threateningly towards Prince Turquin who blinked, his mouth slightly agape at the ferocity of her stare.

"Ceolothian," she said, her words reverberating, giving substance and power to her words as if many spoke and not just one. "Remember, you will not find the truth about your sister's disappearance if you listen to just one counsel. In making scapegoats of us, you make fools of yourselves."

Rewik followed them down into the dungeons and each Torra Altan stared at him steadily as they were forced to crouch on the cold damp stone and were tethered by a short length of chain to a low hoop on the wall. Branwolf pressed his back against the stone wall and looked up at Rewik. "Cousin, you are king of a great nation and yet you reduce yourself to this. You degrade yourself. Your fear-fired actions prove you a mindless pawn."

"You think you are so important?" Rewik thundered. "Remember you are nothing but my prisoner now, and you and yours are mine to do with as I please."

"Yes, I am important," Branwolf said, looking hard into the King's eyes. "I have a wife, a son, a brother and many friends that love me and you can never take that from me."

Barking instructions to the guards, Rewik turned and left.

To Hal's relief he was not separated from his brother but placed in the main dungeon where many curious, surly and bloodshot eyes studied them. No guard came forward to douse them with buckets of water or lash them with whips and they were even brought sour water and bread. It seemed that Rewik still held Branwolf in some respect.

Wrinkling his nose against the stench, Hal looked at the prisoners around them. They cast dull eyes in their direction but none stirred; or moved from where they propped their slumped backs up against the damp, fungus-coated walls. The extent of their straggly hair and unkempt beards, and the filth clinging to their grey skin and tattered clothes clearly showed that they had languished here a long while.

While Branwolf and Keridwen murmured hushed words to each other, he sat in silence, aware of the eyes of the other prisoners fixed on them.

He glared back. "So, we break some of the boredom for you," he snarled, "but we're not a freak show."

"Here, lad, we've done you no harm," one spoke up. "There's no need to look daggers at us. It ain't us that's locked you in here."

Hal was jolted back to himself and raised his hands in a gesture of apology, the chain heavy about his sore wrist. "No, good man, indeed."

"I guess you think you're too fine a folk to be thrown in with the riffraff," another growled less charitably.

Hal grinned at him. He admired such bold front, such honest aggression and understood a man that spoke his mind. He had been maltreated by his cousin, the King; why then should he feel animosity to these simple folk who had done nothing – that he knew of, at any rate – to harm him?

Hal snagged angrily at his chain only to jar his wrist.

"I wouldn't do that if I were you," the first man spoke again. Crusted sores festered around his mouth and Hal found it very hard to look at him without focusing on the infection. "It only hurts. So, what brings you three to this sorry state?" he directed his questions at Hal since the other two kept their heads down.

Hal wondered whether he should answer but, judging by their expressions and their predicament, decided it was quite safe to speak relatively openly.

Briefly, he introduced himself and his companions. "We're accused of treachery." He had expected a dramatic response or at least a widening of eyes but he was disappointed.

"Aren't we all?" another complained. "Treachery for not paying taxes is what we're all here for. He demands an impossible levy that goes up every year. This year the excuse is he needs more money to build a grand palace for his new bride. I couldn't pay without selling my seed crop and, for my son's sake, I wouldn't do that. Chose prison instead. So here I am beneath the king's splendid feet and there's nothing to be done about it. Last man that tried to escape was hanged. We were all marched out to witness it."

The others were muttering and it appeared they had suffered similar fates. "I've been here six months," one of them croaked, "and I doubt I'll ever see my children again, though I still wouldn't have done no different." He spoke defiantly as if fearing to be accused of regretting his actions though Hal had not quiet gathered what those were yet. "No, sir, I would've done the same again and again. I could have done nought else. The only payment I could give was ergot-poisoned rye. They threatened to hang me at first save I told them it had the mould. They said I was out to poison the King. Ha! Wish I had."

There was much muttering and agreement amongst the folk. "Them noblemen have no idea what it is to be on hard times. Seems they get upset if they have but three rows of ermine on their cloaks stead of four. Each year they squeeze us a little tighter and we squeeze the land tighter but the soil is already sick. My land is sick and each year it gets sicker."

The other prisoners didn't press for the details of the Torra Altans' crimes but fell back to commiserating with each other at the state of farming in the heartland of Belbidia.

Hal would not have guessed that night had fallen. There was no change in the light, but the other prisoners became quiet and closed their eyes. He could only sleep fitfully and was soon longing for morning and breakfast to break the monotony. He had been fed sparingly during his days in isolation and the horror of the loneliness and hunger swept through his restless dreams like a wild horse with tearing hooves. He shifted from one side to the other, trying to get comfortable on the hard stone and his fettered arm hung awkwardly. He alternated between crouching, kneeling and sitting to try and relieve the discomfort but, with each passing hour, the sharp stabs of pain that ran from his wrist through his elbow to his shoulder grew worse.

At last dawn came. No daylight penetrated the foul-smelling dungeons but he knew it was morning from the cries of the household guards echoing above and the way the scratching mice disappeared into silence. At the far end of the chamber, a trace of orange light appeared around a stout oak door accompanied by a faint smell of wood-smoke; the torture chamber was already being warmed for use. Some time later food arrived and was passed along the line. He hungrily slurped up his bowl of grey gruel, which was cold and gritty, and drank long draughts from a pitcher of water before grunting his morning's greeting to Keridwen and Branwolf.

"I thought noble folk were above eating porridge," remarked the surly prisoner that had been so forthright yesterday.

With his mouth still full Hal retorted, "I've eaten porridge most days of my life."

"I was told the likes of you ate only peacock and swan," the peasant continued though he finished with an amiable laugh.

Hal turned to his brother and nodded at his bowl of

porridge. "Our dear cousin could mistreat us a greater deal more if he really suspected treason."

Branwolf nodded. "I suspect much of this is to prove to King Dagonet that Rewik is doing all that he can to find his beloved daughter. He must fear war with Ceolothia more than anything. After the Vaalakan war, Belbidia is no longer in a position of strength. Our resources are stretched as it is."

"Yeah, that's all very well," Hal conceded. "But unless someone finds Cymbeline and brings home her captors, we might well be here forever."

A shrieking howl of pain echoed up from the oak door whose frame was outlined by cracks of orange light. The fires in the dungeons were evidently roaring and Hal imagined that the branding irons must be white hot. He tried to blot the screams from his mind.

Keridwen smiled. "What about another story to pass the time?" She sounded flippant but Hal knew her attitude was right when the other inmates answered her with a cheer.

Keridwen's stories kept everyone's minds off the sounds from the closed door; telling stories was something she did better than anyone else Hal had ever met. But after several vivid tales, Keridwen was interrupted by an old woman with warty hands who vigorously rattled her chains at the Baron's wife.

"Witch, no one wants to hear your blasphemous tales. 'Tis sinful to listen to the words of a heathen," she warned the other prisoners.

"Hush, woman. I've been here a miserable sight longer than you and I welcome the joy in her voice. 'Tis a beautiful voice and when she speaks 'tis like roses grow up out of the stone," a rough looking man croaked through his beard.

"Hear, hear," several others shouted in agreement.

Ignoring the woman, Keridwen began a story about a hare that chased after the moon. Each night, he ran faster and faster until his legs grew longer and longer and he climbed higher into the mountains to get nearer the pale light. For his devotion, he was blessed with a silvery coat during the winter months but to prove that he was still a creature of the earth, the white hare must still wear his earthy brown coat every summer and keep close to the ground that would always protect him.

"Have you no stories for the men?" another prisoner asked. "Though sweet enough, these tales are not the stuff to keep a man's attention for long."

Keridwen laughed and Hal let a grin spread over his starved face. She would surprise them, he knew; she could tell tales of knights with sharp blades and long shields that even Ceowulf had never been able to match. But Hal's grin did not last; without exception, all Keridwen's heroic knights wore shining armour. Forgetting their situation for a moment, he scowled at Branwolf. It was a chafing-point between them that Branwolf refused to allow him the money for a suit of armour, always complaining of the enormous cost of rebuilding the castle that he had to bear. Hal was certain that no one would pay him any proper respects until he had that suit of armour.

The prisoners were enthralled by Keridwen's tales and, if it hadn't been for the discomfort in their stretched arms, their hunger and thirst, Hal would have listened to their sighs and cheers and believed they were all back in Torra Alta's great hall during the winter festival. Then tales were told from dusk until all but the teller were asleep, their stomachs replete and their heads woozy with good ale.

Even the prison guards were enraptured by Keridwen's

tales. She was charismatic, her voice well-modulated but, most charming of all, she had a tale to suit every request. Soon even the woman who had warned against her was gradually beginning to smile. It dawned on Hal that Keridwen was drawing the guards into her tales, making them laugh and encouraging them to tell their own tales. And with every story she told, she seemed to turn the person who had requested it into the hero, whether the hero were a hare or a mighty knight charging onto a muddy battlefield. In time, all those present knew what it was like to see the air thick with arrows, feel the ground shake with the thunder of war-horses bearing their vast steel-clad knights. They could hear swords clanking on armour, see steel spurs gauging sweating flanks and smell the stench of blood in the air.

The stories reminded Hal of Ceowulf and he wondered where he could be. He was certain that his friend could not simply have abandoned them and hoped that he had gone to rouse the support of the barons loyal to the Old Faith. But after the recent plague of wolves, Hal was no longer confident that even Bullback would speak for them.

Days passed and he became increasingly worried for Branwolf who developed a raw bubbling cough. Keridwen barely took her eyes off him though she didn't neglect the other inmates around her. Not content with just telling stories, she began to preach the word of the Great Mother and of the balance of Nature. To Hal's amazement, these millers and ploughman still hung on her words and an increasing number joined her in prayer each morning. Won over by her fabulous tales, they were enthralled, hungry for her words, and eager to believe them.

She was in the middle of prayer one morning, when the peace was rudely interrupted by guards dragging in new prisoners who were shouting abusively and kicking like mules. One, a merchant by his attire, was exclaiming loudly that if any of his silks were stained or torn, he would see to it that the guards' children and grandchildren would suffer ingrown toenails and that their wives would have nits in their hair and scratch like beggars until the end of their days. A tall bulky man, he looked quite absurd in his golden gown and light scarlet slippers that were trimmed to a point and curled up at the ends. His voice was also rather too high for someone of such stature.

"By all accounts they are not your silks, thief," a guard responded.

The silk merchant was accompanied by a young girl and, but for her veil and his scarf about his mouth, they were similarly dressed and smelt of expensive oils. Even in the dull light of the dungeons, their clothes glinted with sequins. In high excited voices, they cursed the guards in the name of the Saint Merchantus, patron saint of all merchants. Hal had never heard of such a saint and wondered from what part of the Caballan this brightly garbed pair hailed. Their voices, so sweet and high, were vaguely reminiscent of the highborn Ophidian tongue though they didn't sound quite authentic. Hal was quite entertained by this new company that broke their tedium until the small girl peeled back her veil. Two vivid green eyes peeked out.

He looked clean into those eyes and nearly yelped in dismay. It was Brid. Instantly, he knew that the other figure was Ceowulf. He couldn't believe he had been so blind. Keridwen showed none of his surprise and he guessed she must have sensed Brid's approach. He stifled his dismay and said nothing until the guards were gone. Then he took a deep breath to speak but was silenced by a sharp kick from Branwolf, who coughed and spat phlegm into his hands before raising his dark-rimmed eyes towards Ceowulf. "Tell us your story, stranger. Down here, we're eager for any news."

Ceowulf scowled. "Ain't none of your business, Belbidian. May your socks forever be plagued by holes and your boots leak! I'm not talking to no foul-mouthed person of this wretched country."

Hal's gaze touched Brid's. Briefly they held the stare, showing no outward form of devotion, though Hal sensed the strength of their bond like a steel cord between them.

Ceowulf and Brid were shackled to the wall just the other side of Keridwen and did nothing but complain of the dreadful fashions in Farona until all the other prisoners were asleep. Only then, and in hushed whispers, did Ceowulf reveal their tale.

"I spent a ridiculous amount of money on these even more ridiculous clothes and we stole quite openly from the markets to ensure we would be caught."

"How could you have been such an idiot?" Hal exclaimed in anger. "How could you have dragged Brid into this? How dare you put her in such danger?"

Ceowulf raised quizzical eyebrows at Hal and continued, "Originally, I set about this plan myself but somehow Brid found me in the markets and insisted on joining me. She'd come all the way from Torra Alta, worried that there had been no news of you, Hal, in weeks."

"It was my idea," Brid said firmly, "so leave him alone. We had to get you out. There is word that King Dagonet himself will shortly arrive and is demanding blood. We have to get you out and find Cymbeline and her captors before it's too late."

"Get us out!" Hal snorted. He was warmed beyond hope

to see his Brid again but he was livid almost to the point of madness that she had put herself in such danger.

Ceowulf ignored him and turned to Branwolf. "Sir, we have a plan already in action. Early tomorrow, hired mercenaries dressed in identical clothes to our own and a few with bearskins – a very costly undertaking, I might say – will ride through the south gate and, with some degree of conspicuousness, head south where my father will give them sanctuary. This should draw the King from our scent while we get out of the dungeons and ride north. We've left our own horses at Bleham where we can no doubt get more for yourselves. From there, we ride for the safety of Torra Alta, get provisions and then on to rescue Princess Cymbeline and so vindicate ourselves."

Hal thought he was making light of the last part. The King had been searching for Cymbeline for weeks and he didn't know that they would fare any better.

Branwolf shook his head. "It is an excellently conceived plan and I hope your plan to actually get us out of here is equally well thought out. It's a big step from here to the horses at Bleham. And I'm afraid neither myself nor my fair wife will accompany you."

Brid started to object but Keridwen cut straight through her. "Branwolf is right. We show fear and guilt if we all run: we show faith in our innocence if Branwolf and I remain."

"But why you and Branwolf? Hal and I could stay," Brid insisted, her eyes full of concern as she scanned their thinning bodies. "Branwolf is not well."

"It's nothing," the Baron insisted. "I am Baron of Torra Alta and it shows better faith if I and my wife remain."

Hal knew this was true but also suspected that Branwolf and Keridwen wished to spare the young any more suffering.

"I will not leave Keridwen," Brid insisted and they argued long and harshly though, in the end, the Mother's calm insistence won.

Sulkily, Brid revealed the plan. It seemed that in Ceowulf's many travels he had met a mercenary that had spent a long while detained in these very dungeons and had finally escaped through the chimneys above the torture chambers where fires blazed to heat branding irons.

"He said that the deepest chambers are lined with skulls and that it was the most gruesome dungeons he had ever visited," Ceowulf recounted. "He was an unlucky man and apt to be injured or captured more than most of us. He carried the most horrible wounds from King Rewik's torture chambers. The fingers on his left hand had been cleaved lengthways and his shinbones had been split with an axe then pierced with spikes, the flesh left to heal around it."

"And what about your injury? I doubt you're fit enough for such madness. And did he say how he magically undid his chains before he climbed the chimney?" Hal asked scathingly, thinking the plan a little thin and the mercenary's tale a little tall. He rattled his chain and grimaced as it chafed on the sores around his wrist.

CHAPTER ELEVEN

The night was dark, the moon no more than a slit of silver hanging in the black sky. May's flesh crept with fear. Every night-sound was amplified. Creaking crickets, a distant hoot of an owl, hedgehogs snuffling in the undergrowth, all were loud and jarring in her ears.

Rosy was frightened. The old mare jerked and jolted May's arms in their sockets. She spurred her into a canter, and bouncing painfully in the saddle, headed for the road.

The woodcutter's daughter had never been comfortable on horseback. She had known it was a continual disappointment to Caspar and possibly was one of the reasons why he had never quite been able to give Brid up for her.

Rosy's pace became wilder. Desperate, lonely tears pricked at May's eyes and streaked back across her cheeks. Fearing the speed, she sat back as Caspar had taught her and hauled on the reins. In response, Rosy dipped her head between her knees and kicked up her heels in an effort to throw her.

Ahead in the darkness lay the open fields of Jotunn but May could not see them. Rosy's speed increased and May dropped the reins, flung her arms around the pony's neck and clung on, her eyes screwed shut.

Caspar's instructions as to how to deal with a bolting horse flashed bewilderingly through her mind. "Always guide the bolting animal into space then draw it into ever tighter circles to force it to slow."

Her face bumped hard against Rosy's neck, coppery saliva flooding around her bitten tongue. How could she turn without reins? Even with her eyes tight shut she knew the pony was not slowing.

She remembered how Hal had sniffed at Caspar's advice. "In my experience, May, if a horse bolts there's never any space to turn them. Jump! That's what I'd do."

"Hal's never jumped from a bolting horse," Caspar had said. "It takes more than nerve to jump when the ground is flashing by five feet below you. What you mustn't do is panic."

She must try. May forced herself to bite back her panic and open her eyes. The ground raced by in a blur; the pale trunks of the trees lining the road flickering in the edge of her vision. The pounding hooves beat out in her mind the rhythm of Caspar's words, "Brid is the only woman alive who can calm a bolting horse." Reaching forward, she snatched up the reins. She would show him. She wasn't a high priestess; she was just an orphaned woodcutter's daughter but she would show them all.

Rosy lurched left and right, pitching May forward onto her ears. Slipping, she grabbed handfuls of mane, every muscle straining to keep herself upright. Though she clung on with all her strength, she could not stop herself from sliding precariously to one side. Rosy's hooves drummed faster and she knew her grip would not last. Then drumming thundered all around her, bringing with it the sound of heavy excited breaths and yips like hounds on the scent, and she knew she was no longer alone. Sick with fear, she buried her face in the mare's coarse mane.

Bracken ferns whipped at her legs as Rosy charged into the vegetation at the side of the road. Jaws snapped at her face, giving her the strength to push herself back up into the saddle. They were the jaws of wolves.

Rosy galloped on, her heavy pounding footfall accelerating to a lighter and more graceful stride, the sound of her hard hooves suddenly muffled. May slitted her eyes against the rushing speed of air against her face that pulled her hair into a banner behind her and whisked the tears off her cheeks. Her eyes smarted in the wind.

She dug her fingers into Rosy's wet hide. The coat felt suddenly soft and long, a great shaggy black mane around her neck. Blood was whipping back into her face. She couldn't believe that Rosy had the sudden strength to accelerate.

The mare gave out a terrifying noise, halfway between a shriek and a howl, a most unnatural sound from a horse. May closed her eyes and began to pray. "Great Mother, I am ever your faithful daughter," she cried out loud and Rosy shrieked even more.

A shrill blast, a clear perfect note, sounded across the land and galloping hooves pounded the ground at her heels. The long mane slipped through her fingers and she lurched below Rosy's shoulder – but did not fall. Strong arms hauled her up and away from her mount. A man swung her up onto the back of his saddle where she bumped uncomfortably behind him and clung tightly to the sacking cloth covering his back, instinctively finding the material out of place on him.

She had ridden behind her brother and always felt precarious. Few of the common classes in Belbidia were accomplished horsemen, using the animals more for draught work than for riding. She had also ridden behind Caspar on occasions and immediately felt his confidence and the huge sense of control that he instilled over the horse. This man had the same manner. This man could ride like Caspar yet he wore the sacking cloth of a peasant.

Three wolves, black shadows in the night, circled away from Rosy who bellowed out an unnatural noise, long and low, rising to a shriek that split the night. The man before her reached for a bow hooked to his saddle, nocked an arrow to the string and skewered the first beast straight through the chest. The rest swerved away.

May was stunned. Until then she would have believed that only a Torra Altan could fire so quickly and with such accuracy but clearly her overlords had misplaced confidence in the uniqueness of their skill. Then, for a brief and heart-stopping moment, she thought that the man might be Caspar in disguise, come to her rescue; but she knew, however much she willed it that, the horse was not Firecracker and its rider was not her lost love.

The horseman raised his bow again but the wolves were gone. Dawn was rising, the clouds to the east fringed with pink. He drew to a halt, dismounted and pulled May after him, holding her tightly to him, soothing her hair and murmuring soft words of comfort. For a long minute she could do nothing but bury herself in his chest and let her fearful sobs flood out before she remembered herself and her situation.

She pushed him away, muttering words of thanks. She could trust no one.

"You cannot travel alone," the man rebuked her in the softest and most musical of voices. He spoke Belbidian perfectly but his accent was strange and she wondered where he had come from. "The wolves are abroad and you must not risk yourself, fine lady."

"I'm not a lady and there is no reward for rescuing me. I'm sorry to disappoint you but I have no gold either."

"You do not disappoint me, fair lady. You are far more beautiful than I ever imagined."

May instantly distrusted him. "You cannot know of me."

"Oh, but I do, fair lady. You're betrothed to the Baron's son."

"I'm betrothed to no one. No one has asked me to be their bride and I most certainly have not given my word to anyone." She wondered why she was telling the stranger these things about herself except that it was dawn and she was suddenly feeling very much safer. Still, she didn't like the way he pretended to know her. "Now unhand me!" She struggled free from his embrace, though he still would not release her hand.

"Let me at least help you find your horse," he said, smiling radiantly and releasing her hand.

May shrugged dismissively. "It is almost light now and I shall be perfectly safe, thank you, sir. It won't be far to the next village." She looked at him sideways. The dawn sun caught his smooth bronzed skin and glinted in his eyes that shone with a curious yellow tint. She knew him at once as the man from the *Cow and Calf* and pushed him away. "You followed me!" she accused, suddenly frightened.

Why would anyone want to follow her if it wasn't to get to Necrönd? This stranger was clearly not the brave rescuer he was pretending to be. The sacking cloak sagged over his shoulder, half covering his cream smock beneath, and struggled to give the impression that he was a miller of sorts. But no miller would ride or speak like that.

"My lady, of course I followed you. I could see you were in distress and what man, if he had half a heart, would let so fair a maid go alone in such difficult times as these."

Despite herself, May couldn't help but enjoy his words.

She had been in perilous danger and he had come galloping to her rescue. It seemed almost churlish to spurn him now. She had hoped in her heart that her rescuer had been Caspar but she knew he would not come for her. Caspar's words of love had always been empty. In fact, she thought bitterly, they had brought her nothing but heartache. The other girls had begun to shun her, resentful that she was so favoured and complained that she no longer did her share of the cleaning in the kitchens. She had explained that Morrigwen had set her other tasks of collecting herbs and making candles. Though the melting tallow stank quite horribly, she had come to enjoy the task, learning to mix the tallow with herbs to produce special prayers to the Great Mother. It had been her retreat.

The yellow-haired man stepped back from her. She brushed down her sleeves and pulled her bearskin around her tightly and tried to stand firmly though her knees sagged. She could not allow this stranger to think she needed help.

"Thank you, sir," she said politely, edging away from him. He had such fine features and curiously almond-shaped eyes. She tilted her head, studying him. He looked like an elf! She suddenly felt vastly uncomfortable. Morrigwen had insisted that there were no such things as elves; she had said so a hundred times when the girl had begged her for a story about them. But May had seen pictures of elves in books and this man was too like them, slight with those same slanted wide eyes. Morrigwen had to have been mistaken. This man with his radiant hair and astonishing eyes had to be an elf.

She felt herself tremble and turned slowly and determinedly to walk away. During her earlier childhood, the old folk of the woods had told tales of elves; how they dwelt in the heart of the forest and came out only to steal the souls of virgins.

She didn't dare look over her shoulder to see if he were following though she could feel his eyes on her back. As if walking on knife blades, she painfully stepped towards the road, hoping to find Rosy that way. The verges were lined with lush grass that the mare would find more enticing than forest ferns. She told herself the wolves had merely been the product of her frightened imagination. After all, she'd never ridden out alone before and the fearful dark of the night might have been too much for her.

Plodding hoof-beats sounded behind her. She stared ahead, determined not to encourage the elflike man by looking round. Feeling the need for courage, she put her hand to her chest and felt for the silver casket that held Necrönd. A dark giant hand seemed to embrace her, cloaking her in fear. The trees to either side appeared to lean closer and she sensed eyes, red glowing eyes staring resentfully and yet fearfully at her from the umbra. Silvery shapes of ghostly unicorns glided through the trees on silent hooves and the wispy shades of laughing goblins danced around them. All eyed her warily and for the first time she was aware of the power she held.

The horseman rapidly increased his pace and she swept around and commanded in a cold voice suddenly full of power, "Leave me!"

His eyes flicked towards her silver casket and she knew instantly that, whoever he was, he understood Necrönd's dark magic. She turned, almost tempted to summon the ghostly beasts around her to be rid of him, but then remembered Morrigwen's warning against meddling with such forces. She had stolen the Egg to save Caspar from the seductive power of Necrönd and already she was being tempted to use it. She jerked her hand away.

The man dismounted. "Merrymoon," he said in the softest of whispers, "do not be afraid of me. I have no wish to harm you. But do not touch the Egg; you are safer if you leave it be."

May's hand hovered over the latch on the casket. She was so absorbed in wondering how he knew about the Egg that she barely noticed that he had called her by her real name. No one but Morrigwen and occasionally Keridwen had called her by her real name since she was a very small child.

May pouted and again decided that the best thing she could do was simply ignore him. She marched stiffly away, increasing her pace as her shoes slapped on the beaten earth of the road, and hurriedly rounded a bend. She stopped dead.

Rosy's head hung down amongst stems of the long grass though she was not feeding. May gave out a little moan of despair and ran towards the pony that threw up her head in alarm at her approach but, exhausted and shaking with pain, did not move away.

"Oh, Rosy!" May moaned and very gently raised her hand to take the pony's bridle, moving slowly to avoid alarming the poor creature further. But the moment her hand touched Rosy's bridle, the mare squealed and jerked back its head in fright as if May had suddenly pressed a branding iron to its cheek.

"Easy, now," she soothed but the pony still snorted in terror.

A hand reached over her shoulder and firmly grasped Rosy's bridle. The elflike man murmured in soft lullaby notes to the animal, instantly soothing it. The flattened ears pricked forward.

"Leave us," May commanded angrily though she was grateful that the man had calmed her pony. She looked back at Rosy and soothed her long straggly forelock, and with trembling fingers brushed it back, searching for the source of the blood. She stifled a shriek, unable to understand how the animal's eyes could have been so damaged. Both bled from the very centre, runnels of blood oozing from the black pupils.

She stepped back in alarm, her hands shaking, and turned to fall into the arms of the elflike man. Still holding Rosy's bridle, he wrapped his other arm around her and voiced a soft and comforting song. It was indeed strange that he might sing but May did not dwell on it; she was too shaken and found the song comforting.

"Poor Rosy." She began to sob. "What can I do for you? I've been an idiot. I should go home." Weeping, she crumpled to the ground.

The man, though small, was strong and swept her up and carried her towards his horse. "I shall find somewhere safe for you," he murmured.

"No!" May regathered her courage and wriggled free from his grip. "I can't leave Rosy like this. Thank you for your kindness," she said firmly and politely though with that timbre of aloofness she had heard Ceowulf's wife use on occasions when she wished her own way. "Kind though you are, sir, I must do this myself. I am on a pilgrimage."

He nodded, the dry smile on his lips clearly announcing his disbelief. "Indeed?"

"Yes, indeed! I have a hair from the old Crone's head which I must take to the to the east beyond these shores where I intend to spread the word of the Great Mother. It has long been lost in those lands."

"How extraordinary! I am going that way myself."

"Indeed!" May replied with equal scepticism. "And why would that be?"

"Oh, I go to seek my fortune," he replied.

She sniffed, losing some of her cultivated composure. "Well, you can seek your fortune without me." She turned back to examine Rosy, soothing her neck and wondering what best to do for the animal. Taking a gourd from her pack, she rinsed the animal's eyes before examining her all over. There was no other mark on the animal. Though sweated and nervous, Rosy could still walk and May tugged her on, hoping that she would soon find a village where she could get help.

She wished she were going east to spread the word of the Great Mother – her heart was always filled with such joy when she repeated Morrigwen's tales about the power of the earth and the forces of the rivers, winds and fire. But her task was an inglorious one. She sniffed again and thought of Hal building spirit amongst the men and encouraging them to unite as the toughest garrison in the known world.

He had muttered to May once, "It's a thankless task for, though I do it well" – Hal was never one to underestimate his abilities – "it's Spar who'll get the reward and the praise. They'll write ballads about him but no one will write a ballad about me."

"No doubt you'll write one yourself," Keridwen had teased him.

He had glowered at the high priestess disrespectfully and swept from the room, but not before giving May one of those playful winks. He was quite wicked and she had no idea how Brid put up with him.

May had scowled then and she was scowling now. The stranger had his hand on hers. "You need me," he said gently, persuasively.

"I need no one," she replied grandly though her voice quavered just a little. "Good day to you, sir. I pray only for the Great Mother to protect me."

"May the mother find me," he said so softly that she barely heard him.

She wondered what he meant. He took in a deep breath as if to say something more or perhaps . . . no, the idea was ludicrous. For a second, she thought he was going to sing again, which seemed too curious, but then he stopped, his mouth agape, and dropped her hand.

She turned east, following the road that ran through the north of Jotunn and parallel with the southern foothills of the Yellow Mountains, Rosy stumbling behind her, the pony's breath hanging heavily in the still air. She would indeed continue with her plan to go east beyond Torra Alta's coast and on to the depths of the great Ceolothian mines. To the hollow mountains of Kalanazir. It would be like returning to the womb of the Mother and, surely, she would be safer there than anywhere else. Surely, she had some skill the Ceolothian miners might need. She knew much of herbs and healing, after all and there must be many injuries at the head of a mine. She brightened a little at her plan but then looked down at the verge side again in low spirits, wondering how she would pay for her passage.

Scouring the verges, she eventually found some purple-stemmed eyebright, its white flowers marked with purple veins and a yellow heart, to go with the moles-leaf she had already harvested. She bandaged Rosy's eyes with cloth soaked in the plant juice and after another hour the slow ooze of blood was stanched. Experimentally, she waved her hand in front of the mare's face but she seemed quite blind.

May doubted there was anything that anyone else could do for the pony so, when she passed through a number of villages, she kept her head down and kept going. Her feet began to ache and a blister burned on her heel. Rosy stumbled behind, her nose pressed against her hand. She seemed calmer now though she tripped on ruts and stones in the road. May hoped the blindness would soon pass.

By the time the shadows lengthened towards evening, she was weary and very footsore, her soft soled boots already beginning to crack across the top of the toes. Again, she had found nowhere to stay the night.

The road cut deep into the ground, hollowed out by great oxen carts. Once she climbed up the green banks to look north where, far on the horizon, she could just make out the great peaks of the Yellow Mountains, which from here were a deep rich gold glinting beneath the azure sky.

Homesick, she sighed and pulled her gaze back towards the steep banks of the road where the swathes of bluebells were already beginning to stoop and wither. Even this far north in Belbidia, farmers grew wheat and those fields not given to pasture were a deep blue green where the fresh shoots of corn were pushing up through the earth. Celandine and pimpernel grew in clashing colours along the side of the road and in places the black spandrels of crow's foot were out. There were nettles everywhere; she had never seen so many, their great fleshy leaves smothering even the tough-stemmed comfrey.

Rosy's eyes had healed miraculously quickly and May was pleased with herself, thinking sadly that even Morrigwen would have been impressed with her herblore. Many might have known about eyebright because the name made it easy to remember but fewer would have heard of moles-leaf nor perhaps even recognized the velvety black plant. Very satisfied, she decided it would be quite safe to ride Rosy now.

She never really felt alone in Jotunn. She could never

walk more than a quarter of a mile without hearing or seeing one of the barony's great oxen, huge white beasts with black faces. The next field, which dipped towards a stream lined with flag irises, was crammed with a vast herd, all except two lying down to chew the cud. They seemed curious at her slow passage and one clambered to its feet to investigate. Once one had moved, the rest seemed compelled to follow and soon they were all lined up along the fence, inspecting her. She was quite frightened by these huge beasts, that made such a noise with their clanking horns, groaning, lowing and grunting. She had no idea that their breathing could be quite so loud. They were so much more noisy than horses. They followed her to the end of their field, their dark faces watching until she was out of sight.

With every step, she became increasingly desperate for somewhere to stop but, after her last experience, she was wary. She didn't want to stay in an inn but thought it would be better than retreating to the woods. She passed through two hamlets but decided not to stop, reasoning that isolated communities tended to be very suspicious of strangers. At last, through the twilight, she saw a large village ahead nestled in a natural hollow where two rivers converged. It was surrounded by many small enclosures, each containing one solitary bull with a vast head and huge horns. She thought the cows had enormous horns but they were rather thin and spindly compared to the great bull oxen.

Rosy had become calm and her usual placid self but, now that evening was drawing in, she began to stumble in the ruts. May dismounted and rebuked herself for her arrogance. How could she have imagined she was skilled in herblore? She had been studying it for just three years and was not blessed with the sight or the wisdom of the three high priestesses who were able to perceive things that others, however learned, could not see.

The village in the distance had seemed much closer when she had first glimpsed it. Darkness hugged the hollow of the road. Rosy was jittering and snorting nervously, and she feared that the horse might bolt again. To her dismay, she saw blood ooze from the pony's tear ducts.

The oxen in the surrounding fields no longer lumbered towards her in their curiosity but began to low with the persistence of calves separated from their mothers. She even began to wish for the company of the small, yellow-eyed man with the lean chestnut horse. Almost hopefully, she craned around to look but he was not there.

She shook herself. What was she thinking! He must want Necrönd; why else would he have followed earlier? No one would mistake her for a noblewoman and kidnap her for ransom.

The road plunged into the umbra beneath the heavy canopy of leafy chestnut trees, their boughs laden with red and white lantern flowers. The mare reared and shrieked, lashing out with her hooves while May struggled to hold her. The oxen bellowed. Something lurked in the shadows. Two pairs of bright red eyes stared out of the dark, one from either side of the road. Trembling, she tried hard to calm Rosy by soothing her muzzle only to be bitten for her troubles, the horse's teeth grazing her knuckles. Snatching away her hand, she looked in bewilderment into Rosy's ghostly white face.

The twilight shadows were long and the trees blocked out much of the crimson light of the last of the day. Rosy bucked and, with jets of blood spurting from her eyes, she dragged May with her into the pool of darkness. She reared over May, knocking her to the ground and into the ditch.

The girl crouched in the damp hollow, nettles stinging her exposed skin, as she cowered from what had been her placid pony. The animal was raking at the ground, its teeth, now curved and fanglike, tearing at the grass. May covered her head with her hands, her face pressed down into the cold mud. One great long screech, sounding more like a great bird then any four-legged beast, filled the air. The cry was answered by a series of thin distant howls.

Her hand quivered over her silver casket as she battled with herself. Should she or should she not wield Necrönd to protect herself?

Unwilling to plunge down the steep sides of the ditch, the animal swung away from her but soon she heard it sloshing through the waters, its breathing snuffled and thick as if blood partly blocked its nostrils. May's legs would not respond. She knew she must get up and run from the demon that had possessed Rosy but she could find no strength.

All she could do was look up and scream at the silhouette of the old mare standing over her, its head stiff with pain and blood dripping from its eyes and mouth onto her face. For a second it paused and then with a shriek of rage reared up ready to pound her to a pulp with its hooves. The shriek twisted to a squeal of pain and suddenly the whole body of the animal was crashing towards her. May flung her hands over her head just before she was crushed into the soggy ground, the great weight of the animal pinning her down.

She could barely breathe beneath its weight. Water was slowly creeping up around her face. She tried to scream for help but, as she opened her mouth, she drew in water. Spluttering, she strained to raise her head higher and, struggling frantically, her hands clawed out around the sides of the horse. Then suddenly something gripped her fingers. With determined frenzy, she closed her hand around it and found herself being dragged out from under Rosy, water slurping and sucking around her. The light from a firebrand blinded her. Coughing and trembling, she stood weakly, trying to gather her senses.

"Here, let me take your wet cloak. You'd better have mine," a gentle musical voice implored her. She knew at once it was the strange slight man who had followed her previously and looked up angrily into his eyes that, in the dusk, glowed with golden light.

"You demon. It's your doing, all of this. You did this to my horse so that you could rescue me and win my favour."

"What madness, Merrymoon! " He sounded almost frustrated with her.

May could not fathom him, nor understand what he was doing, only that she instinctively distrusted him. These fearful things had started to happen the moment he had first crossed her path.

"Come, we must get you to safety," he said, tugging her towards him.

May pushed him away and turned back towards the white heap of her pony lying twisted in the ditch. Rosy was quite dead, shot through the back of the head with an arrow, a very clean neat shot. He was a marksman, that was certain. Even Caspar would have been pleased with the shot.

May hurt. Her hands were throbbing and her entire body was beginning to stiffen with bruises. Nevertheless, she gritted her teeth and slithered down into the trench. She had seen her brother fight in the practice arena covered with bruises from staves and blunted swords but he had still fought on harder and longer than any of the other lads, not because he was bigger, stronger or more able but simply because he was more determined. Well, she wasn't going to be any less determined than her brother.

Mud sucked around her calves, soaking the hem of her dress. With fumbling fingers, she began to unbuckle her saddle pack and heave it out of the ditch. The stranger did not immediately protest at her labour as she would have expected but sat back watching her – with admiration, it seemed.

"Leave me alone!" she snapped at him.

He laughed. "You are ungrateful. I could have left you to drown to death in the ditch. Think of it."

"Why are you following me?" she demanded. Grunting under the weight, she heaved the pack over her shoulder and began to stumble towards where she had last seen the flickering lights of the village.

"Because you need me – amongst other reasons," he added enigmatically, which did nothing to ease May's troubled thoughts.

It was dark and she needed to hurry. The man rode right behind her, his lean horse plodding with steady hoof beats. He held his firebrand so the circle of its light encompassed May and she could not help but be comforted by his presence. He had a competent and confident air, which was what she craved in this dark lonely world, but she was not so easily won over. He was there by design and not accident; there was no doubt. Still, if he were after Necrönd, perhaps it was better that she kept him within sight so that she could see what he was up to.

"Stop!" he hissed suddenly and, despite herself, May found she was compelled to obey. There was something in the urgency of his voice.

Ahead on the road, she could just make out a shape snuffling along the ground. She looked back at the bright-haired man in alarm. He drew his bow in readiness but May suddenly relaxed and laughed. It was only a great pig; she could hear it grunting.

"I don't need rescuing from a pig." She sniffed and marched hurriedly on though, the moment she stepped beyond his circle of light, she was swamped with fear. She would stay only a little ahead of him until she found shelter for the night.

The village gates of Oxmead were barred and two farmers brandishing long pitchforks swung lanterns in their direction.

"Who's on the road so late?" one demanded.

"I'm on my way to the eastern ports," May replied. "And I need a place to stay for the night." Not wanting to attract attention, she didn't complain when the strange elflike man said he, too, was heading for the eastern ports, hoping to find a passage home to his country of Gorta.

Forgetting that he had changed his story, May was comforted by this since everyone knew that the inhabitants of Gorta were most particularly strange and that might account for his peculiar manner. She headed straight for the inn, determined that this time she would find a safe place to rest and devise a way to give her clinging companion the slip.

CHAPTER TWELVE

It went against his instincts to delve down into the earth. He wanted to be up in the air where the hawks soared on the rising thermals, not burrowing like a mole into the unknown. The sound of water was everywhere around them, dripping and seeping through the rocks, the entire underground world leaking like a colander.

Their own dark shadows swelled against the walls of the caverns, hunched shoulders bowing on the ceilings. Noses grew long; grotesque fingers like those of hobgoblins, skeletal and dangling, stretched out from elongated arms. Caspar strained to hear over the noisy progress of his companions. He had heard what he dreaded most – footsteps, he was certain they were being followed.

Caspar stopped and listened more intently. Yes, certainly that was the sound of boots on rock. He held up his torch in one hand and stave in the other.

"Who follows?"

He was answered by the sound of panting. Straining his eyes, he stared into the gloom and finally made out the shape of a man hurrying after him.

"Devil, sorcery," the man was muttering in alarm. "They swallowed them whole! Whole! I saw it."

"It's Melkin, one of the shepherds." Naith said. "We can't leave him to perish in the dark. Over here! We're over here!"

"You think I'm blind? Your torch is the only thing visible." Melkin stumbled to a halt and glared hard at Caspar. "Accursed sorcerer!" he accused. "Not only are you a wolf-lover but a devil-worshipper too! Well, sorcerer, get us out of these caverns."

Caspar snarled at the shepherd, who had somehow escaped the Ondines, but decided not to confront him. The man had no doubt been led astray by Mamluc and couldn't possibly cause any trouble on his own. Since he could never abandon a fellow Belbidian down here in the roots of Old Man Mountain, he decided he would allow the man to join their party.

"You can't! No! Naith is bad enough but not another vile murderer! Get away from us!" Fern violently objected to Melkin. "Spar, do something."

"Like Naith, all I've done is try to drive the pestilence of wolves from Belbidia," the shepherd defended himself.

Fern seemed somewhat appeased by this and grunted at the Ovissians to express his tolerance. "Anyone that kills wolves cannot be all bad. But you didn't have to kill deer to do it," he said bitterly.

"We've no time for arguments," Caspar said, trying to sound calm and reasonable. Their torch was nothing more than a fagot of twigs lashed together and burnt quickly and he was fearful that they would not find a way out before the light was gone. Fern continued to snort and grunt with fear at his surroundings, though Trog showed no sign of concern, sniffing every stalagmite and arrogantly lifting his leg on those he found appropriate.

Hurrying after the wolfling, Ursula uttered words in a strange tongue over and over again. Caspar studied her for a moment, thinking how beautiful she was beneath the scars and short-cropped hair that emphasised her muscular face belying a rugged life. He could only guess at her age; she looked young like himself but her eyes were aged by sorrow. Bringing up the rear with Melkin, Naith bitterly cursed Caspar and quoted great sections of the scriptures that warned against devils.

"I could have left you in the cave to die," he rounded on him.

The flames guttered, plunging them into momentary blackness, and his voice fell flat. They dropped down a series of broken levels in the rock's strata and the channel briefly narrowed before entering a broad chamber split into two levels by a fault in the rock. Light leapt back at them. Dazzled, Caspar flinched and blinked, waiting for his eyes to adjust.

"It's amazing!" Melkin seemed to have momentarily forgotten his anger. "I've never seen anything like it. The heart of the mountain, it's . . . well . . ."

"Rubies, fiery rubies!" Caspar couldn't believe it. He crept forward, his hands feathering over the seams of rock all around him where the solid brown stone held tongues of brilliant red gemstones that glowed yellow from within. It struck him that his father would be richer than King Dagonet himself once he knew about the rubies. In the middle of the chamber, a single stone throbbed with energy as if the sunlight trapped within it struggled to burst out.

"Hurry!" Fern urged.

The wolfling snuffled close to Ursula's heels. The little girl, Lana, looked weary and clutched onto the rock walls for support.

"I never dreamed . . . !" Naith starred around him. "A man would never have to work again." His eyes swam in their sockets.

"What's the use of them?" Fern grumbled. "They're only rocks; you can't eat them."

Caspar reached out and stroked the nearest cluster, disbelieving of the gems' beauty; but it was the central stone that drew all his attention. Kneeling, he examined it closely, dazzled by its radiance. His blood ran cold. Chisel marks scored the base of the great nugget. The firebrand sputtered and a trill of smoke gave out into the still atmosphere as it smouldered towards the handle.

"Hurry! Please!" Fern piped anxiously.

Caspar stood up slowly, looking around him and wondering why someone had abandoned such a prize when they were so close to holding it in their grasp. The fist-sized nugget must be worth a kingdom. He had seen sunset rubies once or twice before but they had been the size of a freckle and he had heard rumours that King Dagonet's crown was encrusted with gems the size of a thumbnail but this! And it lay within the barony of Torra Alta, his father's by rights.

Firecracker jerked the lead rein in his hand and snorted, his breath extinguishing the last of the light. They were plunged into darkness, the sound of the dripping water suddenly loud.

"Master, what now?" Ursula's deep voice whispered in Caspar's ear. "Great Sorcerer, I've seen you rise from the dead and walk through stone. Lead us now through the dark."

"I'm not a sorcerer," Caspar snapped angrily but instantly regretted his tone when he sensed her withdrawal. He hated to hurt her; she seemed to bear so much sorrow already.

He sensed the others were waiting for his lead but he was at a loss. The rocks around groaned in darkness. Unnerved, he wondered again what had interrupted the men in the process of chiselling out such a prize. Sunburst rubies were so rare, durable and beautiful that they were more valuable even than blue diamonds.

"Follow the water," Fern muttered. "Those creatures said follow the water."

"We can't leave that ruby behind," Melkin insisted.

"We! I didn't think you were a part of our company," Caspar snubbed him.

"I'm not but . . ."

Tinkling scree slid from the roof above and they drew closer together. Again, the rocks grumbled. Lana began to cry and Trog barked loudly.

"Follow the water," Fern repeated. "That's what they said. Why don't you ever do as folk suggest?" he demanded of Caspar, butting him in the ribs with his head.

It flitted through Caspar's mind that, if Hal had been here, he would not have tolerated Fern for a moment longer. In the darkness, he orientated himself by turning towards the sound of a waterfall tumbling through the rock.

"We can't see!" Lana moaned.

"Don't fear," Ursula said confidently. "We're in the hands of a master sorcerer; he will lead us out into the light."

Caspar felt foolish and stammered, "Well, first we must stay together."

"That's obvious," Fern grumbled at him. "Come on! We must hurry." He was tugging at Caspar's arm.

"But we can't see," Caspar protested.

"Are these the words of a great sorcerer?" Melkin sneered.

"Don't touch the gemstone," Caspar snarled. He couldn't see the man's hand move towards it, but instinctively he sensed his avarice thick in the air.

"I don't know who you are beyond a murdering Torra Altan and I see no reason to listen to the likes of you."

Caspar hesitated, wondering how to assert his authority.

Fern tugged at his arm. "Spar, this way."

The woodwose and the animals seemed better able to

make their way in the dark than the humans so Caspar let Fern guide them. He stumbled forward, gripping hold of Ursula's arm who in turn clutched at Lana. His thoughts lingered long on the little girl; perhaps it was because of her that Morrigwen had sent him this way. She was young and an orphan after all. Could *she* be the one destined to replace Brid?

The rocks groaned and Caspar felt a tremor and feared that the great fault in the cavern was shifting. A chill shuddered up his spine.

"Here, Naith, we can still get this gemstone out of here," Melkin's rough voice echoed from behind them.

"No, stay with us," Caspar ordered. They would leave Melkin; his instincts were to get out of that cavern, whatever prize was to be had. The chisel marks around the gem had been warning enough.

Gradually, he saw that it was not as dark as he had at first thought. After the initial blackness when the torch went out, the rubies had begun to emit their own soft glow. He had a sense that they radiated sunlight trapped within their hearts. Slowly his hands and then Fern's outline in front of him became darker shapes in the surrounding gloom and at last, he could make out a great pillar of rock formed by the joining of stalactites and stalagmites. The structure gave the illusion of holding up the roof.

With Firecracker's hooves beating out a steady chime beside him, he stumbled after Fern, away from the sound of hammer against rock that rang from the cavern behind them. The roar of an underground river boomed ahead.

Naith hesitated and then ran back to help Melkin. Lana started after him but Caspar caught her hand.

Ursula said softly, "Master, you can't keep her from her brother."

Caspar's conscience was pricked and in that moment

of hesitation, Lana slithered from his grasp. He let her go. "But he's irresponsible. He won't look after her properly," he exclaimed, wondering why he felt compelled to seek Ursula's approval.

Firecracker was becoming increasingly difficult to handle, refusing to pass close by any pillar of rock, and Trog growled and tucked between Caspar's legs, tripping him up. Runa whimpered and refused to go forward. When Caspar stooped to pick her up, she bared her teeth and nipped him quite sharply, drawing blood.

Fern sniffed as if this action confirmed everything he had ever said about wolves. Ursula placed her hand on Caspar's.

"Let me," she murmured.

The wolfling coiled herself around Ursula's hand and then snuggled around her neck, burying her head in the shaggy mane of her lionskin. Caspar felt almost jealous. A groan and creak sounded from the fault line in the rocks. Ursula stopped in her tracks, jarring Caspar's arm. "Master, we need your sorcery." Her voice trembled.

"I've nearly got it," Melkin's voice echoed towards them only to be smothered by a shattering cry. Lana's scream froze Caspar's heart. She was a Belbidian child, helpless and frightened; he had to go back for her. Besides, what if she were the one . . .

It took little time to retrace their steps. Naith and his sister stared in horror at the gemstone still embedded in the pillar. A thick reddish liquid seeped from the wounds made by Melkin's hammer, which now lay shattered into fragments at his feet. The shepherd tugged and heaved at the rock with his bare hands.

Caspar's heart plummeted. "Great Mother, forgive us," he murmured. "You're bleeding." He ran forward, gripping at the man's hands and yanking him round.

"You get away from me, boy," Melkin menaced, pushing Caspar's lean body away with no effort. "I'm having this ruby."

Caspar stood back. "Leave it," he ordered in cold urgent tones. He raised his bow. "Can't you see you're making the Great Mother bleed?"

"I lost my flock, a thousand head of the purest white sheep that ever grazed the green meadows of the Ovissian wolds. I lost them all and, with them, my fine house. My father built up his flock and I doubled it and then doubled it again. A big flock it were and I bought a mighty fine house with the money from the wool. Naith will tell you what a fine house it was. Torra Alta took it all away and Torra Alta can pay for it. This ruby will do me – and Naith of course," he added hurriedly though the youth had evidently sensed that he was not to be included in the winnings. He was edging his sister away from Melkin who gave out a squeal of triumph as the nugget broke away in his hand.

"Leave it!" Caspar ordered loudly.

His voice was suddenly lifted to a great roar, rumbling and groaning like rolling thunder overhead. Caspar froze. The sound had not been his alone but had come from behind him and he dared not turn. Fern moaned pitifully and sank to his knees. Trembling, Melkin's hand dropped limply to his side, letting the ruby roll to the ground.

A warm breeze played on the back of Caspar's neck, wafting in gusts like slow deep breathing. A dark shape stretched over his shoulders and spanned out into the form of a vast hand the colour of rusted bronze. Tenderly, the hand cupped the gemstone and set it back where it had been. The oozing liquid that seeped from the cracks slowed and congealed to set the gem back in place. The hardened liquid beneath the gemstone crusted before his eyes into a thousand miniature red rubies.

Slowly Caspar craned his neck round to see a huge hunk of rock leaning over him. Then it moved and he made out its ogre-like shape and oversized head. Caspar expected the living rock to move with a great lumbering effort but, in fact, each pace was almost silent as if the creature feared to bruise the skin of the Mother. More huge shapes loomed closer out of the dark.

They were surrounded. Giant hands clasped around Caspar's neck. Others scooped up the dog and wolf and wrestled for holds on the rest.

Deep voices trembled the rocks around them. "Thieves!" they roared.

"I tried to stop him," Caspar protested.

One of the huge beings reached out a hand for Firecracker's bridle but stiffened as the clang of metal on rock echoed through the chamber. The horse reared up and lashed out again. Several of the rocklike ogres pressed in closer to surround the horse, hands grabbing out of the dark to steady him.

"Easy, Cracker," Caspar breathed and lifted his voice to address these underground creatures. "We are not enemies of the Mother. We mean no harm."

Dissatisfied grunts rumbled around the chamber but, once the horse was firmly held and Trog had finally stopped trying to crunch his way through the finger of one of these stony beings, they looked around only to see that Melkin had gone.

"Thief!" the beings roared. "He has more in his pockets."

Melkin raced off, his pockets chinking. Pushing past Lana and flinging her to the ground, he pounded towards the roar of the underground river. Several black mounds swept after him, while Caspar and the rest were dragged after by their captors. The more Caspar kicked and struggled, the more he hurt himself. It was like pounding against solid rock. Trog's teeth ground and scraped painfully as he persisted in gnawing at the huge thumb around his neck.

The sound of the river drowned out sensible thought. The air became moist with spray as they were dragged up a ramp of stone rising above gushing silver waters that roared past far below. There was no trace of Melkin.

A solid grip pinched Caspar's shoulder and plucked him off his feet. Rumbling and grunting, the giant stone-men retreated from the brink and stole them away into a tunnel of blackness. There was little air and Caspar dared not think where they were going or what these creatures might be.

The swaying strides numbed his nerves and disorientated him but he was sure they were going down, deeper into the earth. "Thieves must be punished," the rumbling voices threatened.

Firecracker's hooves kicked and sparked on their stone-like flesh though even the fiery stallion did not have the strength to break free from their grip. Caspar stared into the dark.

Stunned by events, he was uncertain of his senses when he at first heard singing, a deep unmelodious sound that rather reminded him of Hal's humming. A green light crept along the smooth rock towards their feet, like the waves of a slowly encroaching tide that swelled and ebbed to the rhythm of the song. The darkness receded and Caspar found himself in a vast cavern where three waterfalls tumbled down to fill a rippling pool. In the centre of the pool was a flat island of rock where huddled figures sat around a glowing fire.

The figures were half the height of the stony ogres that had captured them, being only a little taller than himself, but they were twice as wide as any man. Their clothing was greenish brown, reminding him of moss rather than any fabric he knew and their grey skin coarse and grainy like granite. At the approach of the huge stonelike men, the smaller creatures jumped up and began to remonstrate, "You've disturbed the story-time. You always ruin everything. Always!"

The giants tilted their heads contritely. "I'm sorry," one said ponderously. "We thought to please you."

The smaller beings sniffed in condescension, muttering and grumbling in their deep gravelly voices. "Bringing us presents won't make any difference, none at all."

"Nevertheless—" One of the giant stone-men approached the pool. Behind him Caspar noted three more standing guard. They closed ranks to form a solid wall trapping them within the chamber. The singing stopped. Though inharmonious, it was homely and comforting and Caspar found the place strangely hollow and quiet without it.

Even the waterfalls made too little noise, falling with the delightful sound of fairy bells, a tumbling chime that echoed faintly throughout the chamber. The three cascades created ripples that mingled and stirred through the pool in conflicting waves, sending an extraordinary pattern lapping around the small central island. The smaller creatures lowered their square hands into the rippling waters, flexing and stretching their short fingers as if meditating on the texture.

The giant stony beings waded into the water and, appalled at the idea of being presented as a gift, Caspar squirmed to break free. The pool swirled around the creatures' thighs, then waists and rose towards their chests. He feared that they would submerge altogether until slowly they began to rise up again, water cascading from their shoulders.

The curious green firelight filtered down through the water, reflecting on soft white coral-like structures resting on the bottom. Caspar shuddered as the creatures' feet crunched, turning over a skeleton that rose to the surface – a deer. Fern had already seen it and was shrieking horribly.

The remains of a larger beast stirred in the depths and the half rotted bloated head of a bear broke the surface, its empty eye-sockets staring blankly up at them. Ursula caught her breath but said nothing. Lana squealed and buried her face into Ursula's side.

"Presents will make you happy," one of the massive beings said in placatory tones to the huddle of creatures on the island.

"They never last," one retorted. He, too, had craggy features and grey stony skin like a rhinoceros whose hide had hardened and cracked. Morrigwen had shown Caspar a picture of a rhinoceros in her *Book of Names*.

"They pine away or starve or—" the smaller stonelike creature stared at Caspar and his companions and faltered in his complaint. "But these are different."

"Humans!" another exclaimed. "Surely humans!" He looked around excitedly. "Aren't they?" He seemed to need confirmation from his fellows.

"Yes, brother," the first smaller creature replied. "Though I haven't seen one since before the dragons left."

"Since before the dragons," another whispered in amazement. "The dragons were the storytellers, the great song masters and second only to them is man. They must tell us a story. Bring them to our fire."

The squat creatures, perhaps forty of them in all, sat down cross-legged around the perimeter of the fire. "You must tell us a story," they chorused.

The larger creatures grunted happily. "You are pleased with your presents?"

The huddle of grey-skinned creatures did not answer but watched expectantly as Caspar, Ursula and the others were placed amongst them.

The biggest of the creatures on the island stepped forward, prodded Naith and eyed the animals knowingly. "We can eat the horse, the dog and the wolf of course; they have never proved good storytellers. We have wasted many good years waiting for such animals to tell us of the bright world above."

"We'll tell no stories if you hurt the animals," Ursula was quick to answer. "Is that not right, Master?"

Caspar nodded at her, still wishing that she wouldn't address him so.

"A story then!" the creature persisted. He pointed at Fern. "You, begin."

"But I—" Fern stammered and turned to Caspar. "Spar, I know no stories."

The creatures' faces fell. "We stonewights must have a story," the youngest looking of the creatures complained in disappointment. "It's not a nice present at all. I've waited years. Tell me this story," he demanded, dipping its hand into the pool and cupping up water. "It tells of bears up above. It is a close story. The water hasn't travelled far."

Caspar wondered at the meaning of these words.

"Perhaps that is my story," Naith offered, casting anxious glances at the floating carcasses in the pool. "I can tell of the bears."

Caspar relaxed his gritted teeth as the smaller stonewights settled contentedly and began to hum and grunt. "Tell us then. Begin at the beginning. Nowhere else will do."

Naith pushed his sister deeper into Ursula's embrace. "It is a story that starts with wolves." His voice deepened and mellowed and Caspar, who had heard a great many excellent storytellers, was impressed. "And since you ask me to begin at the beginning, I must tell that story first."

The stonewights grunted and nodded in satisfaction.

"For generations, we in Ovissia peacefully minded our sheep. Then the wolves came from the north, spilling out from the mountains of Torra Alta and roving into the quiet wolds in search of the flocks."

"This has nothing to do with bears," Fern interrupted.

Caspar tugged at his hands. "Sit down and behave. We must please them if we are . . ." His words faltered.

"When they had finished killing the sheep, they then turned on the poor women and children of the villages," Naith continued. "When they came to our wold, I hid in the trees like a coward and I watched them tear my village apart. Soon a thatch caught alight in the panic and the village burnt like a great funeral pyre. By morning the wolves were gone and I ran home to find only my sister alive. Her eyes were white and staring and she told me of how she looked on a wolf and saw the face of a man."

Excitedly, Lana interrupted. "Ma hid me in the bread oven. It was still warm and I could barely breathe till I moved the latch from inside. Through the crack in the door, I heard it all." She choked and trembled, and a flood of tears burst into her eyes and streamed down her face. "I heard Ma's terrible screams and then silence except for the slowly padding footsteps around the room. I peeked through the crack. A vast grey wolf with a black mane—I saw into his face, an eyeless face but the face of a man. I-I-I saw it. And Ma—" Her words were choked by racking sobs and shuddering gasps for air.

Naith took her from Ursula's arms and hugged her tight while the stonewights dipped their hands into the water and nodded. "Oh yes, the waters have whispered of him."

Caspar's head jerked up but he dared not interrupt.

Naith wiped his own eyes. "So, we fled the village and on the road we met soldiers, Baron Godafrid's men it seemed. After I spoke of the wolves, they told me I could find work killing them. If the Torra Altans couldn't do it, we would go into their mountains and do their job for them. Readily, I agreed. I had no means of living and was eager for revenge, just like the other men we joined. There were many of us. The wolves had caused such havoc."

He looked down despondently at his hands. "But we found few wolves and they moved me from one band to another until we came here to the eastern ranges. The men in charge no longer spoke of wolves as if they had been forgotten and we saw no more of Baron Godafrid's men but only strangers from abroad. I was afraid we had fallen in with a bad lot except that they paid us well." He chinked his purse. "Rather than hunting for the elusive wolves they sent us after bears; we could catch a bear a week. We trapped them and dragged them across the mountains to the bear handlers." He nodded at Ursula. "It was rough work and took our minds off the wolves but I was glad of the money. And . . . well," he faltered. "Here my story ends; I can tell no more."

The stonewights' eager faces were like those of children allowed to stay up late and sit by the fire on feast days. They had looked delighted throughout the tale but Naith's closing caused general dissension.

"That is not a story. That is just a happening." One stood up and, like a spoilt child in fury, hurled down a rock onto the slab of stone. The greater stonewights, who had waded back to the edge of the pool watching with indulgent expressions, muttered in disapproval at this behaviour. "We bring them presents and this is the thanks we get."

Ursula stood up and began to stutter nervously, continually looking to Caspar for approval. "I can speak . . . I know more of this tale for the bears are like kin to me. Once the likes of Naith had procured the bears I, you see, I would lead them overland." She worried her fingers. "Overland to the ships on the eastern coast. I saw them crated and sent away by sea." Unlike Naith she stuttered and fidgeted. She had no gift for storytelling.

"The sea, the great wide sea," the stonewights chanted. "Oh, to touch the greatness, the wholeness of the water." Again, many of them dipped their chunky hands into the rippling pool and then sucked at their fingers. "The great wide waters." They sighed collectively before looking back to Ursula.

One pointed. "But you are a little being; how can you command a bear? We want stories not lies!"

"It's not lies. But I do not know how I do it. I am of no rank and I have no name that is my own, they merely call me Ursula after the bears though I know in my heart this is not my name."

The stonewights sat up tall in eagerness for her words. Caspar agreed this had the makings of a most intriguing story.

"They found me on the eastern coast of Oriaxia."

There was a general stirring at this announcement.

Ursula ignored them and her speech became more fluid as she was absorbed in the telling. "And that's as far east as anyone from the Caballan knows of the world. Against its shore crash vast waves that lash the beaches, waves sometimes forty feet high, and sometimes higher, whipped up by tumultuous weather far away in the great unknown. My first memory is of the face of a woman, very old, I think. She was waving farewell and there were tears in her eyes. I remember the tears and the taste of them as they rolled onto my face and trickled down to the corner of my mouth. Then I remember a great burning sky, a terrible whiteness of heat. And days, endless days. In that time, I lost all other thought and knew only the symbols on my arm."

Caspar looked at this girl in wonder. "They say I was found on one of the great white beaches of Oriaxia where the desert runs into the sea. The man who found me took me into his family, which was loving and generous, and they treated me as their own. And I loved them, for they became my parents and my brothers and sisters. We played on the beaches and I would draw bears in the sand, huge vast pictures like a great message to the eye in the sky, though I had no memory of such beasts."

Absentmindedly, she was scratching out patterns in the slime of the rock with her fingers. "My new family were traders in pearls that were to be found along that part of the coast. They harvested them throughout the spring and summer, and then in the autumn we would make the long journey hundreds of miles inland to the eastern desert oasis where the great fairs are held. We considered ourselves well-off though it would have taken more than a thousand of our pearls to buy one Oriaxian purebred." She nodded disdainfully at Firecracker. "We did well each year at these fairs and I was glad and danced in the sun.

"On one such journey we met with a travelling act that kept a dancing bear. To my knowledge, I had never seen one but I ran to it and it played with me, I laughing and cuddling and it following me around like a dog. And at the fair was a man who traded in horses and slaves alike and he said to my father he would give him a herd of purebred stallions if he would sell me. And my father spat and held me close and said I was his girl." Ursula's voice quavered at this.

"We went home and came back to the great fair for three more years but in those years the ocean currents had turned cold and many more men had moved south to work our oyster beds. Each year my father made less and less money and my mother would weep, saying she had six mouths to feed. Then came autumn again and, though we knew how little money we would make, we began our long journey and I played with my brothers and sisters and they laughed and danced with me. Father carried me on his shoulders, trotting like a horse or swirling me around like a desert dust devil. He made little money at the fair but he bought me a trinket, a little doll."

She fetched in a pocket and brought it out. Faded and grubby, one arm was dangling by a thread. Tears rolled down Ursula's cheeks. "Then he took me by the hand and told Mother that, for a treat, he would take me to see the bears. I was so excited. But he didn't," she said flatly. "He took me to the slave trader. Father said not a word to me. He put me at the man's feet and shook hands with him before leading away fifteen purebred stallions." She glared angrily at Firecracker, stood up, and pointed with trembling fingers. "You see, I'm worth exactly fifteen times that horse.

"The slave trader took me many miles on the back of a camel and I remember so little of the journey for I could barely see for the tears." She slumped down again. "But you see, I wasn't Father's true born daughter so perhaps it was right to sell me to help the others. It's understandable, isn't it?" She sniffed quietly. "Anyone would have done that. Anyone would have looked after their own first."

Caspar was amazed by her forgiveness, her lack of bitterness. He would have raged in madness against such a terrible twist of fate.

There was little need for her to tell any more of the story for the lash marks on her arms told the rest, speaking of the harshness and misery of her slavery.

"I served my master as a stealer of bears but it was more the work of a murderess until this great sorcerer found me." She shuffled closer to Caspar and looked up at him dutifully. "He saved me and is my master now."

His heart ached for her, as evidently did the stonewights' for they wept and sighed and muttered that never had they heard such a good tale. Never! One by one they began to fall contentedly asleep.

The prisoners sat nervously, looking around them at the smaller stonewights who lay sleeping in heaps like monstrous puppies. Humming, the giant stonewights waded forward into the pool, and looked over their little charges, crooning softly of how sweet they were when asleep, and wasn't it peaceful, and aren't they just the most precious little things that had ever been born. They gave out deep sighing moans and gave each other great embracing hugs of congratulations.

Cold and ravenously hungry, Caspar sat in bewilderment, huddled up between Trog and Fern. He alternately eyed the stonewights and Naith suspiciously.

"Why don't you tell us your story?" Caspar asked the huge doting stonewights.

A grey and crumbly looking stonewight looked quite taken aback at the idea. "Our story? Well, what is there to tell? We have been here in these caverns since the beginning of time. We know only what the water tells us."

"Oh!" Caspar found this remarkable and put his hand into the pool. It felt like plain cool water but he most certainly wasn't prepared to taste it because of the number of bodies lying in the depths.

The smaller stonewights frowned. "You mean you understand nothing from it?" one asked.

A giant stonewight grunted. "They live such short lives. They have no time to learn of the patterns of the world, so little time to gain true understanding."

Those young stonewights still awake looked at Caspar curiously and he felt like some sort of freak. One reached over, dipped his hand into the water alongside Caspar's and fiercely gripped the youth's fingers. A peculiar look, contemplative and faraway, filled his grey eyes.

"There's a dungeon in Farona. The King speaks to your father with distrust."

Caspar's stomach knotted. Suddenly, instead of staring at his own reflection, he was staring at the rippling image of his father and mother, Keridwen's face drawn with anxiety and pain. Branwolf looked weak and sick. They were in some sort of dark cold cavern, the walls seeping with slime. Chains circled their wrists. Caspar swallowed hard. The image swirled and changed and he saw a hooded man riding a tall horse. The man turned slowly to glare at him but most of his face was heavily in shadow and Caspar could make out nothing but his mouth, the lips peeling back to reveal a black hole that gaped open wider and wider into nothing. And in the blackness ran hooded wolves and Caspar sensed them seeking him.

The wolfling beside him put its paw on his shoulder and suddenly gave out a long moaning howl. The image of the hooded man stiffened and jerked his head up as if he had somehow heard her. The picture shimmered, retreated, and was absorbed into the depths of the black pool.

"They seek you out," the stonewights said. "Beware the nights! Beware sleep! Then they come!"

Caspar shrank away from the pool and sat back next

to Naith, who was cradling his sister protectively and staring at the stonewights as if they were demons. "They could keep us here days. Have we nothing to eat?"

Not forgetting that this man was an Ovissian who had been employed to steal Torra Altan bears, Caspar rose to search his saddlebags that he had long since stripped off Firecracker's back. "We should have plenty of Cook's best oatcakes," he murmured, opening the straps. "A soft cheese and several loaves. We've already eaten the last of the salt beef." Caspar knew how travelling made for a keen appetite and he had packed as much as he could. Undoing the buckles, he thought it felt suspiciously light. He peered inside to see only a handful of crumbs at the bottom and a squashed piece of cheese. He turned swiftly on Fern.

"You couldn't have." Caspar knew now why he had been silent for so long; Fern sat amid a scattering of crumbs.

"I was hungry. A fellow must eat."

"But you've eaten all the bread and oat cakes." Caspar looked at the cheese while all eyes were turned eagerly on him. A thought suddenly flicked through his mind and he hurriedly checked the other saddlebag. That too was empty. "You've eaten Cracker's grain! How could you?"

"Cracker was eating the grass. He didn't need the grain. You always get cross with me if I eat grass."

Caspar closed his eyes, clenched his teeth, and began to count slowly to ten. "If I ride Cracker all day, he doesn't have enough time to graze. He needs the grain." He smoothed Firecracker's red coat. "How could you do that to him?"

Fern's mouth was twitching rapidly and Caspar realized he'd got another mouthful from somewhere. He advanced on the woodwose who hurriedly stuffed his hand into his pockets to pluck out a last oatcake and cram it into his mouth before Caspar could take it from him.

Caspar stumbled for words. "You're lucky Hal isn't here to deal with you."

The woodwose swallowed hard and licked his lips, his eyes like two black saucers.

"That would have fed us for two more days; what shall we do now? How long do you think we'll be here for?" the youth scolded, nodding at the stonewights who still showed no sign of stirring, their breathing ruffled and contented. He warily eyed the macabre skeletons that rose and fell in the rippling water. "We could be here forever! And there's nothing for us to eat."

"But there is!" Fern replied defensively. "I wouldn't have eaten it all if I thought you would starve. Look, there's moss and trailing bracken everywhere."

"Fern, we can't eat that!"

"You can't?" The little woodwose seemed genuinely surprised. "I thought you only preferred the oatcakes. There's honey in them, you know," he said almost conspiratorially. "Besides, I don't see why you are fussing. You have the dried, burnt flesh to eat. I thought that was your favourite."

Caspar sighed in resignation and turned back to the misshapen piece of cheese and withered meat. Hoping that fortune would shortly provide them with another meal, he took his knife, cut slices from the grey flesh and lumps from the cheese, and handed pieces first to Ursula and then Naith for him and his sister. "As a fellow human I offer you this though I still haven't forgotten that you came deliberately into Torra Alta to murder wolves and steal bears, my bears!"

"Your bears!" Naith sneered. "Just because this poor girl flings herself at your feet and this deranged man follows you like a dog, it doesn't mean you can play heavy-handed with me. I had my own flock of sheep once!"

"We're in the Barony of Torra Alta. These are my father's lands. They are his bears."

Caspar had not anticipated Naith's reaction nor that of Lana's. The youth looked at him with utter hatred while the girl launched herself at him, her fingers hooking into the flesh of his cheeks and tearing at his eyes. He tried to prise her off gently but was unsuccessful and it was Ursula that pulled her away. Naith spat at the piece of beef he had been offered and then flung it at Trog who bolted it down with the same gusto that Fern had eaten the stolen oatcakes.

The two youths circled each other, sleeves pushed up ready to fight. Naith, though only a couple of years older at most was, like Hal, very much bigger than Caspar. The shepherd snarled through bared teeth, "You murderer. You killed my mother with your wolves."

Trog growled and made a lunge at Naith's feet but Caspar caught his collar before Trog could sink his teeth into the Ovissian.

"I swear by my father and mother and by all that I hold dear, Torra Alta itself, that I have not brought these wolves on Ovissia."

Naith launched himself at Caspar, his hand aiming to grasp his throat, but the noble youth was quick, agile and had spent many years training to fight. He ducked and brought his arm up, sweeping Naith's hands aside to land a quick but effective rabbit punch to the chin. "I don't want to hurt you," he growled as the shepherd lumbered backwards.

"Hurt me! You don't want to hurt me, you wolf lover?" Naith kicked out at Trog who latched firmly onto his boot. "You've ripped out my heart."

"Trog, drop!" Caspar ordered but to no avail. Trog's eyes were closed and he showed not the slightest sign of having heard. Caspar lunged forward and grabbed Trog's collar, unperturbed by the violence of the growls as the big terrier worried the boot. Finally, Trog let go only for Naith to attack again while Caspar still held the dog. The Ovissian grabbed him from behind, yanking his head sideways and punching the small of his back with his knee.

Caspar hit back in rage, his fists flying fast and accurately. Standing by, Trog yipped and wagged his tail in approval at this display.

"I didn't summon them, I didn't!" Caspar shouted, his own fears and frustrations amplifying the attack. He felt a rib give beneath his clenched fist and Naith gasped, clutching his side and doubling up with the pain.

Panting, Caspar looked on resentfully. "I didn't summon the wolves. I am not a sorcerer. I am guardian of Necrönd and I have kept it hidden and safe and I have not used it to draw these wolves out of oblivion." He could feel hot tears of anger pricking at his eyes and it was as if he faced the jury of the entire world, but most especially his mother, father, Brid and Hal, all of them blaming him for this wrong.

Suddenly he was aware of the staring silence around him. The squat stonewights were awake and alert and the larger ones had drawn close, breathing in slow, troubled murmurs.

"Tell us your story," they great beings rumbled.

Caspar hesitated. He had been warned against speaking of the Druid's Egg but, in his rage and indignation, he had blurted it out like a fool. "Put his hand in the water again. Let us learn more. Let us observe what the rhythms that flow around the world reveal of him," the giants urged each other excitedly. Caspar was reluctant but could do nothing as a stonewight gripped him and, though Trog's teeth rasped and scraped on the stony skin, the creature held his hand in the cool rippling water. All the other stonewights eagerly dipped their own fingers into the pool.

"These are ripples that circle the world," they said in some awe. "Tell us your story."

Caspar sighed. He had said it all anyway so what did it matter? "There is little to tell. I am guardian of the Druid's Egg but it has been stolen away from me. At about the time of Morrigwen's death we saw a man, a strange man." Caspar paused wondering how to explain it.

Fern butted in. "He wasn't a man at all. He looked like a man but he stank of wolf. Men are not what they appear; it's better to smell them out."

Caspar nodded lamely, accepting this description. "He was snooping around at the time of Morrigwen's death, hiding himself amongst the huge numbers of mourners. He must have stolen it away. I must find it. Necrönd is a terrible power in the wrong hands . . ." He felt the weight of their eyes on him. "The Great Mother entrusted me with it and I have failed Her."

"He will summon huge monsters from the Otherworld and conquer wherever he goes," an ancient-looking stonewight, its small eyes cradled in grey bags of sagging skin, mumbled ominously.

Again, Caspar nodded lamely and slumped his head into his hands.

Naith's expression softened. "If you retrieve this thing, this egg, you will be able to crush the wolves?"

Caspar nodded.

The larger stonewights began muttering anxiously

amongst themselves, striding back and forth through the waters, creating great waves that splashed over the island and washed at the smaller stonewights who shrieked angrily.

"Necrönd! A word we have not heard since the dragons were young. This thief who holds it, he could enslave us. We are the old creatures of the Earth but, since we were of no threat to man living so deep down here beneath the rocks, we were not banished to purgatory outside of the Great Mother like most of the other old creatures. But Necrönd will command us, so strong is its sorcery."

"Master has great sorcery," Ursula said with conviction.

Caspar could not help but smile at her. She had such faith in him and no one had ever held him in such esteem before. He appreciated her adulation even more because he had won it by rescuing her rather than gaining it through his noble position. He smiled and she beamed back.

"This story of bears and wolves is now our story," the stonewights rumbled amongst themselves. They glanced sidelong with their grey stony eyes at the smaller stonewights. "For the sake of the children we must help."

They dipped their hands back into the pool, chanting softly as they stroked the water. One or two dropped off to sleep and then, at last, the oldest ogre creaked to his feet. "It's in the water. I feel it now. East, east of here. Nearing the sea."

CHAPTER THIRTEEN

In self-absorbed silence, Ursula sat cross-legged, drawing patterns in the slime covering the rock.

"What do the patterns mean?" Caspar asked, trying to distract himself from his worries and hunger.

The slave-girl jumped as if she had been lost in meditation. "Master, I don't know. They simply give me comfort." She returned to her drawings.

"East of here. East!" Fern grumbled. "But that didn't make me wrong." He was clambering over the rocks to find brackens, which he offered contritely to the vast stonewights, who were becoming increasingly agitated by his interruptions.

"How long can they take to decide?" Naith scraped the heel of his boot back and forth over the ground in frustration. "We'll starve if someone doesn't do something soon."

Light-headed from lack of food, Caspar staggered to his feet, braced his shoulders and coughed loudly. "Please listen; we are going to die if you keep us like this. We cannot go for days without food and the more time you waste, the further Necrönd is from us."

"We don't meter our time in days; that is the time of the sun. We feel only the pulse of the Earth. We've only just begun to discuss the problem. Have patience, little fellow. You're like a hectic firefly buzzing, buzzing,

buzzing. Keep on like that and you'll burn yourself out in a flash. Be still like the pool. Think of the waters and how long it takes them to make the cycle, to flow from here down deeper, seeping away under the subterranean lake and into the great hot rivers before welling up again, forced up by the pressures below, and rising into the riverbeds. Then they rush overland to the sea, which swells and sweeps across the curved belly of the earth, thence to be drawn as droplets into the air by the heat of the sun. The droplets mass into clouds before raining down on our mountains and trickling down to our pool again."

Caspar barely listened in his frustration but clenched his teeth and fists against his anger. "Necrönd," he hissed through his teeth, hoping to draw them back to the subject. "I must find it."

"Ah, we have been discussing that, indeed we have. For though you say you kept this thing of power safely hidden, you still managed to lose it. We feel it might be better that you remain here. Perhaps you are not the one that should wield such power."

Caspar slumped down; there seemed to be nothing he could do.

The stonewights returned to their bickering. "The man seems ill-suited to the task; if only we could go . . . But we cannot leave the grand caverns. Our old bones would dry and crumble in the sun."

"Perhaps the children could go," one argued.

"They are not responsible enough. It's unthinkable!" another exclaimed.

Several young stonewights sprang excitedly to their feet. "Oh, but to see the world, the sea, the great expanse of the sky! Surely, we are old enough."

"But we bring you offerings and sometimes they tell

stories of the sea. The stories are enough," an ancient stonewight said knowingly.

"But if you are all too old, then surely, we younger ones must go. We are quite old enough."

There were grunts of disapproval from the great rocklike beings. "I don't know about old enough. Oh, no now! I don't think so."

"But we haven't had a proper story since the dragons."

"Since the dragons!" Caspar exclaimed.

They pointed into the murky depths of the pool and Caspar squinted, following their gaze until he made out a vast skeleton lying on the still bed.

"One or two came here injured a little while back and told of battles with man. They died. They lasted longer than most creatures but, in the end, they died. They all die," the smallest stonewight wailed. "In just a blink of an eye. They moan and weep and, like you, complain. And then they die."

Caspar felt extremely uncomfortable.

A particularly squat and round-faced stonewight spoke for the first time. "We need not all go. One stonewight can accomplish the deeds of many men. If one of us accompanies these frail creatures, we can ensure the task is done. I shall go with them."

One particularly creased-looking ogre wrung his hands. He too had a round face and the family resemblance was clear. "But Perren, it is dangerous out there. You cannot go. As your father, I will not allow it. Indeed, I forbid it."

"I've lived two hundred and thirty dragon lives and that is time enough. I shall make my own decisions."

Oddly the other giants hurriedly nodded their agreement, telling Perren's father that he worried too much. Caspar saw they were eager for Perren to take up the quest since that meant their own offspring need not go.

"When he goes, the others will soon follow and we shall be alone again," the father warned. "Don't you remember how it was before them?"

A smirk spread wide on one ogre's face. "We all remember the night the Ondines came."

"Ah, we all remember that. They came, and we talked about nothing for a dragon's lifetime until they returned with our little ones in their arms and left them here for us."

"Oh, but if we had known what a trial, what a worry they would be. Only two hundred and thirty dragon lifespans and it's felt like an age! There's never been any contenting them."

"No, never!" There was general agreement.

Caspar was working out that, since a dragon was reputed to live three hundred years, the younger stonewights were . . . He couldn't work that out right away and hummed quietly for a moment before figuring that they must be sixty-nine thousand years old.

"I've had enough." The young round-faced stonewight stood up purposefully. "I'm going to take them out of here to find Necrönd." He turned to Caspar and his companions. "Come, we shall go."

When no other stonewight moved to stop them, Caspar smiled with relief and began gathering up their belongings. Perren's father grunted uncomfortably and said they must talk longer about things. He turned to his son. "Perren, such a hasty decision is not right, it's not natural. Perren, listen to me!"

Perren grunted and hunched his shoulders against his father's voice while the other great stonewights supported his decision. "Now young lad, we'd best wrap you up a bit, protect your skin from the sun." He tossed the young stonewight a grey-green mat that appeared to be woven from ferns and moss and, hastily, the other stonewights wrapped it around Perren's wrinkled body and tied it fast at the waist.

Once Perren was prepared, the older stonewights swept up their captives, waded out of the pool and marched into the dark of a tunnel. It took three of them to carry Firecracker but Caspar was still amazed by their strength. The horse was ferociously strong and kicked like a demon.

They curled upwards through the dark, then through the soft glow from the chamber of precious stones and onwards into a steep and narrow passage. As they climbed, the stonewights became increasingly wary, moving more and more reluctantly with each step until, at last, they stood in the circle of grey light that wound down from a deep shaft.

"What's that smell!" Perren exclaimed.

"It's the upper air!" his father muttered anxiously. "Now, be very careful."

Perren shrugged him away and waited while Caspar and his company were heaved up the shaft and pushed onto the surface. Firecracker gave a last kick at the stonewights who had been restraining him, sparks flying as he skittered away. Caspar lunged after him, catching his reins only just in time. Following Trog and Fern, who ran ahead, they squeezed through a narrow crevice and out into a ravine. Caspar didn't stop to say farewell to the stonewights but hurriedly coaxed Firecracker up the side of the ravine.

The ravine was thick with gnarled and half-formed hawthorns, and he did not stop until he had reached the top. He needed to be out in the fresh air; he needed to see and he needed to hunt; they were all ravenous.

Already his hand was twitching for his bow. It was a windy day, a faint moistness from low lying clouds, clinging in the air. It smelt good. Tall mountains, green with spring vegetation on their lower flanks, stretched their sheer-sided, golden heads high above him.

They were still in the Yellow Mountains but far from Old Man Mountain. He turned to look back west and saw the hazy outlines of five peaks topped with trailing clouds. The Mare's Tails, that had been ahead of him before he had been carried into the caves, were now a good distance behind. They had travelled miles and must have passed right under their roots.

"East to the sea!" Perren declared and marched off but no one followed. The stonewight faltered in his tracks and turned questioningly.

"We've got to eat first," Caspar explained, gesturing with his bow towards the close thickets that hugged the lower slopes. Greener trees and a sinuous grey line marked where water weaved its way down the mountainside. "That way first," he announced, quietly moving forward, and was gratified when all followed without questioning him.

They clambered over rotted logs coated with moss and lichens while, above them, leaves rustled in the breeze. The path cut by the creatures of the mountain was squeezed narrow with bracken, forcing the party into single file. A stag's bellowing groan echoed through the valley.

"They're rutting," Caspar whispered.

Leading Firecracker, he crept forward, his boots and thighs green with lichen after brushing past the older birch trees. He pointed through the feathery veil of leaves to a muddied clearing and turned to the others, gesticulating for silence. The grass in the clearing was scored and churned to mud by hooves. A broad shallow scrape showed where stags had battled, the earth deeply gouged by their lowered antlers.

Caspar smelt success. The marks looked fresh and a stag that had been rutting was an exhausted stag. The wolfling snuffled forward, nosing at the ground, and licked enthusiastically at one particular patch of earth. Blood, Caspar surmised. Nose down, Runa followed the trail and Caspar motioned Naith to sweep round to the right while he followed the wolf. A high scree slope on their left meant that the stag was unlikely to run that way.

Caspar eased forward, concentrating on Runa, and froze when she did. Her snout stretched forward. She had seen something. At first, he saw nothing through the interlocking boughs laden with shimmering leaves then, at last, what he thought had been the broad trunk of a tree stirred. The stag stood with its head down by its knees and its antlers resting on the ground. Carefully, he pushed the leaves aside to get a better view.

Its great chest heaved, blood dribbling from one nostril. The poor animal was nearly spent with exhaustion. Judging by the antlers, it was an old stag, great white wounds across its flanks bearing testament to a cruel spring of rutting. He raised his bow, taking slow controlled breaths, and concentrated. There was only a small gap between the interlocking branches; his only target a narrow patch of throat. He drew the string and held his breath to steady the shot. That moment, a distinctive yelp of excitement shocked the still of the valley and the stag's head jerked upwards out of his line of sight.

Caspar pushed forward as the stag tottered on exhausted legs and lumbered into a wobbly canter straight towards Naith's post. He caught a glimpse of white and heard a grunt and a squeal, and swore; Trog had ruined yet another hunt. He clambered over one branch, slid under another and got his bow entangled with dangling ivy. Finally, he stumbled out onto a narrow track to see Trog yelping excitedly in pursuit of the stag. Antlers lowered, the animal charged straight at Naith.

For a second, Trog had his curving fangs into the beast's hock but the stag lashed out, catching the dog's cheek. It bucked its way free and charged on towards Naith, who foolishly waved his arms and blocked the stag's path. The shepherd stood his ground though Caspar yelled at him to move.

Stumbling to a halt, Caspar spread his legs to steady himself and sucked in his breath to aim. The animal's head was lowered and it offered only its rump as a target but he had no option and loosed his arrow.

Wide-eyed, Naith leapt back from the beast that fell in the dirt at his feet, its great antlers tearing at the ground as it swung its head and tried to heave itself to its feet. Caspar sprinted forward and at close range made a clean kill through the back of the head.

Naith looked sheepishly at Caspar. "I didn't want to show myself a coward by letting it get by but I had no idea they were so big and powerful."

Caspar grinned, appreciating his bravery.

Naith smiled back. "I'm used to the odd ram becoming wayward but that stag was a little bigger."

They laughed, sharing their relief and triumph; they would feast well tonight.

Trog and Runa ate then and there, wrenching at the offal, while Caspar gutted the deer and, with Naith's help, heaved the carcass back through the wood to where he had left Firecracker. Not caring that the saddle would be drenched in blood, they slumped it over the horse's back and returned to the others.

By the time they got back, the light was fading and the chill evening air was already rolling down the mountain sides to loll in the narrow valley. They were greeted eagerly by Ursula who had lit a crackling fire and, in no time, they had hunks of meat skewered and roasting against the heat of the glowing embers. Lana helped and proved an able cook and was evidently pleased to be of value.

"Murderers! Butchers! Barbarians!" Fern squealed in Caspar's ear but the youth had no time for him. In disgust, the woodwose turned away, kicked out at Trog and the wolfling, who were sat by the fire contentedly cracking bones, before withdrawing to sulk and nibble at the grass and fresh shoots some feet away.

The venison sizzled and singed and the end of Caspar's stick became aglow where he had held it too close to the fire. Perren was shifting round behind him, surveying their darkening surroundings.

"I had no idea anything could be so incredible. They never adequately described the height, the majesty of the mountains, nor the emptiness of the sky, nor the stirring air nor the stars and the moon and how time goes from light to dark. It is ever constant in the caverns. Even the dragons didn't have the words to describe this!"

Caspar noted how he had taken a small nibble of the meat with his rounded gappy teeth but had discarded it and now sucked at the roots of a heather that he had unearthed, licking his lips in delight as if it had been festival goose itself. Torra Altans indulged in a great deal of goose over the period of the winter festival. It was a very popular dish and certainly one of Caspar's favourites, he thought hungrily.

With his face tight with the heat of the fire, his mouth scorched from the charred venison and his stomach full, he became concerned that Fern's normal accusations of brutality had been missing in the conversation for some while. He turned round to see Fern still at the edge of the camp but no longer nibbling, his body still and his neck stretched up high. He crept over to join him. "What have you seen?"

"I'm not talking to you," Fern growled but nevertheless pointed to a flickering light lower down the valley. "It's been working its way towards us for quite some time. Since Ursula lit the fire, I think."

With the heat of the fire prickling his back, Caspar stood and watched the swinging light. Slowly, it dawned on him that his body was cast into black silhouette by the flames behind him. At that moment, Ursula placed a fresh branch on the fire and he turned to see the coiling tongues of brilliant red flare up from the fresh wood, sizzling pine needles leaping into the air, caught by the vortex of rising heat and dancing like coiling fireworms into the twilight sky.

"What an idiot! How could I have been such a fool to light a fire here?" Caspar groaned.

"Forgive me, Master." Ursula seemed almost afraid. "It was my fault." Her hands were trembling though she stood stiffly, freely offering her guilt.

Caspar looked at her, acutely aware of the white scars striping her dark skin. "It's not your fault." He knew she had lit the fire but it wasn't right to blame her. He was supposed to be in charge. "It's too late now. But we need to think how to lose these men."

"They're not men," Fern said indignantly.

"What do you mean, not men? I can see lanterns."

"Well, of course there's a few men; wolves don't carry lanterns."

Caspar shuddered, instantly recollecting the image he had seen in the pool. "How do you know they are wolves?"

"Of course, they're wolves." Fern twitched his nose and stretched up taller while Runa pressed close to Caspar, her raised hackles like a comb down her spine. She sniffed the air and, with her tail between her legs, ran fearfully to Trog, who was now only a little taller than the lanky pup. The heavy snake-catcher put his blunt muzzle protectively over her shoulder.

"Quick! Naith, douse the flames," Caspar belatedly roused everyone to action. "Ursula, help gather everything up. We must leave at once."

"You're frightened of wolves!" Perren exclaimed in some astonishment. "And that's no way to put out a fire."

Naith was sending showers of sparks into the air as he wafted a branch at the flames. Perren rocked forward on his great flat feet and stomped into the fire, treading out the flames without showing the least sign of pain.

Caspar stared in disbelief for a second before remembering the urgency of the situation. Hastily, he loaded their bags onto Firecracker's back. Fern ran round in excited circles, urging them to hurry.

"Well, do something to help!" Naith snapped at him but to no avail.

The woodwose scooped up a roll of bedding and flung it messily over Firecracker's back, accidentally thumping the horse's sides. Firecracker snorted and tugged at the reins, sending Naith, who was wisely wary of the stallion's vigorous hooves, flying for cover. Even Caspar had his foot trodden on.

"Fern, just sit down and wait!" he snapped.

But the woodwose couldn't and fled along the path, squealing at them to hurry. Caspar lifted Lana up onto Firecracker's back and then, with the others jogging behind him, headed after Fern. Even if they had more horses, he doubted they would make better speed because of the terrain. Fern, at last, waited for them and Caspar's irritation with the woodwose eased when he saw how quickly he found paths that lead them deep into the folded landscape, swallowed from view by ridges and craggy outcrops.

Thankful of their recent meal though uncomfortable to be moving so soon after such a feast, they jogged on through the chill night as best they could. Perren, by contrast, seemed exhilarated.

"Such excitement! So, this is fear," he panted. "I can smell it on you, hear it in your breath." He seemed fascinated. Caspar felt quite ill.

Low moaning howls grew loud behind them. He knew at once that they were not Yellow Mountain wolves by the screech of painful loss in their song. Every minute they sounded closer. Then suddenly one was up above them on the ridge to their left. The wolf, his thick mane easily discernible above the scarp, was silhouetted by a great half moon scything behind it. The animal stretched out its neck and howled. Sweat trickled down Caspar's back.

The padding footfalls of another wolf were audible to their right, edging towards them. Caspar had the sense that they were being herded towards the head of the valley where, no doubt, more wolves lay in wait.

What was he doing dumbly following Fern? His instincts might have taught him an acute awareness of wolves but not how to escape them; that was all too obvious.

"Stop!" he yelled and wasted no more time. He loosed his arrow at the black silhouette on the high scarp. If they were going to be attacked, he would rather it was now before they were surrounded by the entire pack.

The wolf stumbled to its knees and then fell into blackness, the valley echoing with the crash of its body onto rocks. Caspar swirled round, anticipating an immediate attack from the second wolf.

The air was thick with howls though he could see

nothing in the blackness and swung round. A disembodied red glow of eyes floated towards him, one pair to the left, another closer ahead. He concentrated on the one running straight at him and loosed his arrow. The red glow of the eyes went out.

Ursula's screams rent the air. He span on his heel but couldn't get a clear shot at the two wolves stealing towards her. Though weaponless, she yelled out her defiance at the beasts.

"Perren, grab her!" Caspar yelled, fearing there was nothing he could do. The great square shape of the stonewight stood motionless and didn't react. "Perren!" Caspar yelled again.

Just as one wolf sprang into the air, Perren strode forward and shoved Ursula to the floor. With a deep grunt, he smashed his fists down on the wolf's skull, the crunch of stone against skull horribly loud. Caspar fired at the other wolf and heard the squeal and shriek of the injured animal as it turned and fled.

"Lana!" Naith squealed.

In the confusion, Firecracker had bolted into the dark and Caspar stared helplessly into the blackness, praying that they wouldn't stumble across the girl's slender body lying on the ground.

Naith sprinted ahead but to Caspar's surprise, Fern had reacted faster and soon was swallowed into the dark. It wasn't long before his voice came drifting back to them, "I've got them. She's fine. She clung on!"

She must share some of Brid's bloodline, Caspar thought in relief. Again, the notion that she was the new Maiden nagged in the back of his mind. Breathless and with cramp stinging his sides, he caught Fern up, took Firecracker's reins and turned on Perren. "Why didn't you act sooner?"

The stonewight shrugged. "You humans do everything in such haste." He dismissed the criticism and pointed ahead to a brightening glow in the sky. "What's that?"

"Dawn," Naith told him petulantly. "Don't you know anything?"

With the sounds of baying wolves still behind them, they turned left to climb out of the valley and avoid the pass ahead where they suspected more wolves lay in wait. Below, the valley still trapped the night but dawn was already warming the higher peaks. Nearing exhaustion, they dragged themselves upwards, weaving back and forth on the steep slope until, at last, the sun washed over the valley's walls, soaking the mountains around in rich burnished gold that was divided by deep chasms of shadow.

Fern halted abruptly. "They've gone!"

"What do you mean they've gone?" Caspar asked patiently.

Naith sneered. "There's no use listening to the fellow; he's quite mad."

"No, the wolves have gone," Fern insisted, his whole body now relaxed.

Caspar noted that the wolfling's hackles had also smoothed. He frowned. It didn't make sense for the wolves to vanish simply because it was dawn.

Ursula tugged at his arm. "The wolves may have gone, Master, but what's that?"

"Where? I saw nothing."

"I saw a flash of light," she insisted. "Something, glass or metal maybe, caught the sun."

Caspar squinted into the west but could see nothing but mountains, their lower slopes swathed in scrubby trees and brackens that poked through thinning mists. He might not have seen anything but that didn't mean there was nothing there. "Come on, let's get off this ridge."

They scrambled down the far side, heading for the cover of the lower slopes, but without tracks to follow and, since the ground was steep and broken with boulders, the going was hard and slow. Caspar feared that Firecracker's hooves would be bruised and spilt by constantly marching on the stony ground though the burden of the little girl was a slight one. Fern moved with as much sprightly verve as ever and Naith was as strong as he looked. Perren marched gaily – for a stonewight – exclaiming loudly at plain clumps of heather or common sweet-scented woodbine with extreme delight. Ursula, however, was not so strong as the others. She stumbled to her knees once or twice with exhaustion and Caspar took her hand, pulling her to her feet.

She wrenched away from him. "You must not help me, Master. I am your slave."

Though the idea was absurd he didn't bother to argue with her; the girl had too much resolve. "Well, get up behind Lana and ride," he coaxed her gently.

She looked horrified. "Ride an Oriaxian purebred, a stallion at that!"

Caspar thought that, for one that always professed to be a slave, she was extremely argumentative. She did, however, readily accept a helping hand from Naith.

Caspar continually cast behind them but it wasn't until noon that he saw what Ursula had seen; a bright flash of reflected sunlight. They had crossed valleys by climbing the steep ridges dividing them, something that no one would do in their right minds unless it was to throw someone off their trail, and now he was certain they were being tracked.

Pushing their way through the scratchy birch trees,

their legs drenched from the dew off the thigh-high bracken, they naturally fell to following Fern. Caspar hoped his weaved path and unexpected turns would confuse their pursuers, though his main hope lay with outrunning them. However, Fern's pace proved impossibly fast and Ursula began to lag behind even with Naith's help. Caspar called Fern to halt and waited for them.

"Keep going." Naith waved him on. "I'll stay with her."

Caspar shook his head. "We must stay together."

Naith nodded and firmly took Ursula's hand to help her. Caspar didn't blame him; Ursula was a beautiful girl.

Fern dropped down into the next valley, its bottom clad in graceful rowan trees and the air sweet with spring blossom, and splashed through a bright stream. Perren paused and dipped his hand into the waters, a glazed expression smoothing his round stony face.

"What is it?" Caspar asked.

"There's no sense of wolves. Last night the mountains were overrun with them but today there's nothing."

Rather than feeling relief, Caspar was more troubled. He'd rather be aware of the enemy than have them spring out of nowhere.

For a while, Fern led them along the line of the valley bottom, where the going was easiest, then, when the climb steepened towards the pass at the head, he turned north, hauling himself up the side wall of the valley towards the ridge. They zigzagged back and forth, Lana being lifted from Firecracker's back several times while the horse was encouraged to leap up the worst sections. Caspar's hands were scratched and raw from pulling himself up by the coarse stems of juniper. Even Fern was beginning to sweat and Trog lay down and panted at every opportunity.

It was tough crossing the grain of the land like this

but they needed to avoid the passes at the head of each valley, which were exposed and devoid of scrub, the rocks worn smooth by the rush of wind. The passes provided the best opportunity for attack.

Once over the ridge and slithering on bald rocks down into the next valley, joints jarring on the descent, their spirits rose, knowing that their harsh climb was over until they reached the head of this valley. They picked their way across a stream, using the natural stepping stones formed by boulders and fallen branches, and continued east. Perren strode happily alongside Firecracker, whistling and taking snatches at the air then running his fingers down the smooth bark of the birch and rowan trees and stooping to closely examine the fingerlike petals of honeysuckle that grew vigorously over the undergrowth. Aware of their quickened pace, Caspar turned to check on Naith and Ursula. The girl came stumbling towards him but here was no sign of Naith.

"Where's Naith?" he asked when she caught up.

"He's coming," she panted. "His knife fell from his pocket when he was helping me across the stream and he was finding a stick to fish it out with. I'm sorry," she apologized. "It's my fault. He was helping me."

Caspar smiled at her. "There's no need to be sorry."

She would not return the smile but continually cast back for Naith, evidently more comfortable in the company of a shepherd than a baron's son and looked pleased when he caught them up again.

Throughout that day, they broached ridges and slithered down into new valleys while always keeping a general heading of east towards a tall dark spike of rock. It was not the usual yellow stone of the mountains but the ancient core of a huge volcano that had stabbed up from the heart of the Great Mother and was called the Dog's

Tooth for the way it curved like the eye-tooth of a hound. Caspar estimated they would be in the foot of its shadow by sundown.

A broad stream fed by a mountain tarn blocked their path, the ground boggy and marshy to either side. Perren was always the first into the water and the last out and, by now, all of them were soaked to the top of their thighs. Firecracker waded across, the water boiling beneath his belly. He snorted in rage at the invasive power dragging at his hooves.

Naith chivalrously carried Ursula across while the stone-wight stood in the ice-cold water, watching the wobbly shape of his great grey bare feet flexing and stretching over the rocks on the riverbed.

The valley wall above them was steeper, broken by sections of sheer rock between the green bands of rough vegetation. It was going to be difficult to break out of this valley and over the ridge that was spined with thin-edged boulders, vaguely reminiscent of a dragon's back. Caspar pouted at his horse and pondered over his decision before turning to the others.

"Perren, if you carry Lana and climb straight upwards, I'll take Cracker. He won't make this climb. I'll go down and work him round this ridge. It'll take longer but I'll meet you on the far side underneath the black crag." He pointed to the Dog's Tooth and the others nodded in understanding.

An outcrop of rock and another scree slope blocked Caspar's path and eventually he found a way round though, by now, the others were high above him, heading directly for the sharp peak. As he watched, they passed as little dots into its shadow.

Caspar gripped Firecracker's bridle and led him between treacherous scree slopes. At last, he had found a grassy section that cut diagonally upwards and the horse grunted and heaved, bucking its way up from one ledge to the next. Exhausted, Caspar paused a moment to draw breath, scanning the miniature valley below, which had shrunk away from him.

Blowing and heaving, they scrambled up another section only to find their path blocked by sheer rock that Firecracker's hooves couldn't tackle. He scanned upwards, searching out a route but could see none and was thinking he would have to work his way further over to the left. That was when he saw them, a line of hunched silhouettes creeping along the spiny ridge and climbing to intercept his companions. Caspar swung his gaze to the right and counted more closing from that quarter. Steel flashed in the red rays of the sinking sun.

Amongst the soft outline of smocked shepherds, he saw rounded helmets with distinctive nose-guards and the unmistakable outline of men dressed in the garb of Ceolothian soldiers. Caspar had no trouble recognizing them. He could not imagine what a Ceolothian soldier was doing here in the Yellow Mountains until he thought that King Dagonet must be sending his own men to search the wilderness for his daughter. But why would they be trailing him?

Unconsciously he raised his bow but the shot was too long. He lowered it, watching with gritted teeth as the soldiers climbed steadily towards his friends. Fern, at any rate, was already deep in the shadows cast by the fissured rocks at the base of the black crag but they were dangerously close to the rearmost figure, whom he presumed to be Naith.

He tethered Firecracker to a coiling stump of juniper and crouching low to keep himself hidden, scrambled higher to get within range. He could hear them now, their laboured grunts and angry shouts of Ceolothian loud in the mountain air. Glimpsing plumes and lances, he guessed they numbered a score at least. Two groups worked along the ridges towards each other, centring on the black peak. Soon they were tightly closed around the spot where he had last seen his friends though there was no sign of them now. Puzzled, he crawled closer, scratching his face on the twiggy heathers and juniper bushes.

His companions were nowhere to be seen and appeared to have simply vanished. His heartbeat in his throat and he crouched down into a scrub-filled hollow, for once thankful of his slight stature.

Naith! At last, he had seen him, crouching low in the shadows, a soldier advancing on him. It was a long shot but Caspar thought he could make it. He raised his bow only to find his breath taken from him by a cold solid hand that clamped over his mouth. He tried to struggle but the arm was strong and held him firmly.

"Spar!" a rumbling voice murmured softly into his hair. "Keep still."

It was Perren and Caspar realized after that he must have been standing on the stonewight's toe for some while. The chunky grey-skinned being was so still and craggy-looking that he had simply melted into the gloomy landscape and Caspar had never noticed him. Perren edged aside to reveal a hollow in the rocks behind him and pushed Caspar in before nestling back over the top to conceal the entrance.

Beneath Perren, it was cramped and hot, only a thin thread of light working its way through a crack in the rocks above that was shielded by juniper branches. Fern and Ursula were squashed against the earth underneath the stonewight. Lana was shaking with sobs and kicking at Perren to let her out. He ignored her as best he could, mumbling that it was for her own good.

"Where's Trog and the wolfing?" Caspar breathed.

"Trog ran off but the wolfling's here." Ursula shifted her pointed elbow, jabbing into Caspar's shoulder, and he caught a glimpse of the tip of Runa's white tail, the rest of her body lying snuggled down beneath Ursula's lionskin cloak.

"And what about Naith?" Caspar protested. "He's out there."

Lana whimpered fearfully.

"I was standing in the stream when he waded past me," Perren told him solemnly as if the words were meant to mean something important to Caspar.

"I don't understand."

"I felt his treachery. So, I hid the rest in here while he was scouting back along the trail. He believes you are the master of the wolves and has probably been marking our trail at every opportunity."

"I thought he cared about me." Ursula sounded downcast. "I should have known that no one would care about a slave."

They sat there for what felt like an eternity, the sounds of stamping feet above thudding through the earth as the soldiers tramped around, searching. Fortunately, Lana suppressed her sobs and kept quiet though Fern wriggled and squirmed, chewing at heather roots that pushed down through the rocks. Caspar nudged at him to stop. Fern's constant munching was getting on his nerves.

"You don't complain when Perren munches on roots," the woodwose whispered resentfully.

"Yes, but Perren doesn't do it the entire time nor quite so rapidly. It makes my jaw ache just watching you."

Fern nibbled all the faster but then froze with his

mouth stuck open as a stick jabbed through the thick juniper cover overhead and voices grumbled above them.

"You fool, Ovissian. You've betrayed us."

"They were here, I'm telling you. I was right behind them. Would I have gone to all that effort to mark a trail for Melkin so that he could lead you to us if I did not want them caught?"

"They must have second guessed you," the Ceolothian taunted.

"They couldn't have; they're all too simple. And even if they had, they couldn't just disappear." There was a long pause before Naith spoke again. "Unless . . . It's sorcery! Just like he raised the wolves, this is more of his necromancy. They were everywhere last night. Though he pretended to fear them, we escaped with no trouble at all."

"*He* is not master of the wolves." A sneer edged the Ceolothian's voice. "Poor little shepherd thinks he's been leading us to the Wolf Master all this time. Ha!"

Naith suddenly gave out a scream of horror. "Then he wasn't lying! You . . . You—"

After that Caspar could only hear the sounds of a struggle that ended with a heavy thud and more grumbles and yelled expletives. "Well, little Belbidian, we're just going to tie you up and leave you. The wolves will come for you the moment it's night," the Ceolothian voice promised.

"You bastards! You cold-hearted miserable creatures, you're not fit to squirm beneath the ground."

"There's nothing wrong with creatures that live underground," Perren muttered while Ursula wrapped little Lana in her arms and smothered her cries in her lionskin. Fortunately, Naith was making too much noise for his sister's muted wails to be heard.

"Shh!" Caspar told them all to lie still until he was certain the soldiers were gone. Naith's desperate cries for help rang out above them. When he felt the chill air close in around them and knew that the sun had set, he prodded Perren's back. "Let us out. With all Naith's shouting, every wolf for a hundred leagues will be headed this way. We've got to find a safer place fast and I've got to get Cracker and Trog."

Perren stood up and Naith gave out a squeal of surprise. "Where the hell did you come from?"

"Traitor!" Perren growled, raising a rock above his head.

"No," Caspar softly commanded.

"But he's a traitor." Perren's grey shape advanced in threat on the prone form of the pegged-out shepherd. Lana wrapped herself about his legs, begging him to stop.

"No," Caspar repeated. "He doesn't understand what's happening. The Ceolothians were using him and he's confused and hurt. Leave him be."

"A traitor should die." Fern supported Perren.

Ursula nodded at this. "I have been in no country in the Caballan where a traitor would be allowed to live."

Caspar had the sinking feeling that he was no longer in charge of the party.

CHAPTER FOURTEEN

May had little money even for the Oxmead's simple inn, and she pensively fingered the coins until the copper was warm from her touch. Unused to handling money, it felt alien in her palm. She didn't want to spend one coin of it but knew it was the only way to keep herself safe from the stalking evils of the night.

"Please, won't you join me?" she invited, nodding towards the stool opposite, her voice smooth and full of aplomb despite her trembling hands. If she couldn't be rid of this man, she would at least know exactly where he was. She felt it to be a wise decision and was impressed with herself.

The man's curious sun-shot eyes strayed from her face to her hands. She snatched them under the table.

"The nettles," she excused herself. Her fingers were tinged green where she had rubbed them with dock leaves but they still throbbed.

He looked at her sympathetically and again she reminded herself to be wary.

"I cannot sit yet, sweet Merrymoon; I have no money for a meal and I must earn it first." He smiled at her. "Come, you and I will eat well tonight." In a loud and confident tone, he spoke out, "Friends! I am a traveller from distant shores and have seen many wondrous sights. Your faces are sombre; would you care for a song to lift your hearts?"

"Aye, 'twould be fair," a traveller agreed.

A merchant, by his richly dyed woollen cloak, thumped the table. "And if you can make me laugh or cry, I'll pay you in silver."

A few of his companions nodded but one challenged, "A song would be fine but I've never heard one yet that would make me cry."

The rest of the inn remained absorbed in their own affairs. May thought them ungenerous. If this had been the halls of Torra Alta, the entire throng would have been clamouring for a song.

Though her strange companion winked confidently at her, she still thought they would be eating plain bread tonight – that was until he began to sing. His voice, which she might have guessed from his speaking voice, was powerfully beautiful and he sang of a lost love with such captivating sadness that before long she found herself thinking of Caspar, tears pricking at her eyes.

Through a blur of tears, she looked towards the door, longing, hoping, praying that he might suddenly step through it. But it was hopeless; life seemed hopeless, pointless without him. The tears brimmed over and ran freely down her cheeks as her strange companion sang on. Strangely, it was not the words that moved her, for they were commonplace, but the emotion behind them that stabbed straight to her heart. When at last the final notes slipped quietly from his lips, he gave out a heavy sigh and hung his head. The company of the inn kept silent for a long moment before clamouring for more, their faces bright and eyes spangled with tears.

May, too, found herself begging for him to sing. What was she doing? The man had an unnatural power in his voice and she remembered the woodsfolk's stories of how elves would steal away souls with the spell of their songs.

Well, she had a spell of her own. She reached beneath her plain shirt for a small scrip and brought out a withered spray of rowan that had been there since last autumn. If he were the spirit of an elf, the wood of the mountain ash would ward him away from her. She placed it on the table opposite her where he would sit after finishing his next song, which was bright and merry, a simple tale of a foolish man with a foolish dog. For some reason, the way he sang it sounded quite ridiculous and the inn was soon merry with laughter and showering him with coins. He was right; they would eat well that night and though the crowd protested and begged for yet another song, he tugged himself away from their imploring hands and returned to her table.

On seeing the rowan branch, he gave her a tight-lipped smile. "You play odd games with me, my lady. You have some understanding of the properties of the world around you and the hidden strengths in all living things but you are not a priestess." Tentatively pinching the sprig firmly between thumb and forefinger in a way that one might grasp a nettle, he pushed it back towards her. A surprised smile spread over his face and, reaching over, he stroked the rowan's leaves. "The mountain ash, with her feathery leaves, is indeed a very beautiful tree."

"What do you mean, I am not a priestess?" May asked, snatching back the spray of rowan. "You thought that would harm you, didn't you?" she demanded.

"I was merely suspicious of your intent. The berries are dark and I wondered if you had some design to poison me. Come!" he clapped his hands. "Landlord, I will have strong ale and fine bread." He looked about him at the tables to see what others were eating. Steaming pies, potted meats and roasted duck gave out tempting aromas, the portions generous. May had to admit that she was famished and couldn't refuse when he offered her a choice of such wholesome and delicious foods.

He studied her as she ate and, somehow, she warmed to him. She couldn't help it for the smile on his face. She could not fathom him, could not read the emotions in his curious eyes as she could with other men. He seemed to delight in pleasing her and surely, if he were after the Druid's Egg, he would have taken it when she lay helpless in the ditch.

"Why are you following me?" she asked directly, watching him closely and waiting for his reply.

He held her stare and chewed slowly until he had finished his mouthful before saying, "You summoned me. I thought at first that I had been summoned by a high priestess, the magic was so powerful." He gave her a teasing smile. "Still, I didn't do too badly."

May was offended. "You were hoping I was Brid," she snapped. Was she forever to be plagued by Brid and constantly in her shadow? "You thought I must be Brid because only a high priestess should have the power to carry Necrönd."

"Don't say it!" Suddenly his hand was on hers and a tingle ran through her. Though she could not read the emotion in his eyes, she was certain of that touch. It was protective. "No, I didn't mean that, Merrymoon. Besides, a high priestess would have been well enough advised never to have taken such a thing of power into the open and into such vulnerable surroundings."

May flushed. "You want it!"

"And just what good would it do me now?" He sniffed resentfully. "Once, yes, but not now."

May turned her attention back to her food, wondering how she would best be rid of this man, or if she should be rid of him at all. There now! Already she was thinking favourably towards him. Standing up stiffly from the table, she thanked him curtly for the meal.

He caught her hand. "Lock the shutters tonight and, if you are at all frightened, call out for me."

"What do you care for me?" she demanded.

He smiled almost apologetically. "My dear lady, I need you."

"Need me!" She sniffed.

"More than you could possibly imagine." He smiled, letting her fingers slip through his.

Thinking him slightly deranged, she hurried up the stairs to her room, glad that she did not need to share it with anyone. Panting hard, she broke the rowan sprig into pieces, scattered them around the bed to protect her from evil spirits and dived beneath the blankets, pulling her bearskin over her head. Fidgeting nervously with the broach that fastened the cloak, she listened to a twig beating against the window pane.

The bearskin and its clasp were given to her by Caspar and she was particularly fond of them. The clasp was solid silver wrought into the design of a great dragon with outspread wings and was of some value so she kept it pinned to the inside so that none could see it.

This was not a new habit for her journey but one she had long since adopted since she did not want Caspar to see how much she treasured his gift by constantly wearing it. She loved to have it against her skin and often stroked it for comfort, regretting that he had never again shown her such romantic tenderness.

The familiar hoot of an owl preceded the cold scream of a vixen. In the long silence that followed, the wind died back and May could hear nothing above her panicked heartbeat, but she was certain there was someone in the room, standing in the deep shadows. She had a preternatural sense that she knew that person. Trembling, her hand moved towards Necrönd though she girded herself against touching it. The priestesses had warned against it and she must trust in their judgement. Praying for comfort, she wished Caspar would burst through her door and rescue her.

She could not halt her imagination and became convinced that there was something in the corner, sitting and waiting for her to go to sleep. "Spar," she sobbed. "I need you."

She gritted her teeth, ashamed that she, a Torra Altan who had survived the siege, could tremble at shadows. She stared hard at the shape. Surely, it was just a chair with clothes thrown over it, fleshed out by shadows. She pulled her bearskin tightly around her and clenched her eyes shut but soon was convinced that something was creeping towards her bed. She peeked through her fingers and shuddered in horror; the thing in the corner had moved closer.

Just when she was about to scream out in terror, the musical notes of her self-appointed guardian's voice wafted up from the hall below. A sudden ease relaxed through the entire inn. The shadows lightened and the chair returned to the simple silhouette with her clothes thrown over the back. She slumped back onto her pillow, which crackled and rustled as the straw inside the sacking moulded to the shape of her head, and listened to the man's song. It was so gentle and reassuring.

Again, it made her think of Caspar and tears slid across her pale cheeks. For three years she had kept him aloof, waiting for him to throw his unbridled affections at her, waiting for him to come charging up the road to the castle from a hunting trip on his dashing horse and sweep her off her feet and kiss her. The castle would have cheered with delight.

But it was not to be. She sniffed. As the elfin man's song was filled with the words of a love lost, the tears flooded down her cheeks and she turned over and buried her head in the pillow.

She must have sobbed herself asleep because the next thing she knew it was very cold. The bearskin had slid from her bed and lay bridging the circle of rowan. The moon had set and no light sliced through the shutters. The sound of breathing filled the darkness. Paws padded the floorboards about her bed. The slobbering chomp of a mouth sent her trembling. She was not a priestess but she hoped the rowan would keep at bay whatever evil prowled her room.

Her hand moved towards the Egg. Perhaps she could use it to repel the spirits that had crossed the divide from the Otherworld to this in the dead of night. Her hand hovered and she knew how strong Caspar's compulsion to wield the Egg must have been. Thinking of Morrigwen's warnings, she clenched her fist and drew it reluctantly away. She must trust in the Great Mother. The creatures were but shadows and could surely do no harm.

She had almost convinced herself that the shadows and ghostly noises were born from her imagination when the dark shape in the corner disturbed her again. She fancied it was creeping forward and that other hunched shadows gathered around it. Then, suddenly, it rushed at her. May screamed.

The door flung open and a lantern swayed on the threshold. The shadowy shape swerved from its attack turned and glared straight at the silhouetted figure who stood in the doorway, singing out a slow wailing song, terrible and fearful, that sent a chill through May. Every sinew set hard as if she had been turned to stone. The shape gave out a moan of pain and then began to shrivel away. The figure walked forward, the tone of his voice changing, slowly filling with soft warm tones that allowed May to relax. It was the elflike stranger who had befriended her. He lit her bedside candle.

"What was it?" she begged tremulously. She felt invaded as if the thing had crept into her dreams and manipulated her thoughts. How long had it been sitting in the corner?

He shrugged. "The Egg does strange things."

At that moment, May did not care where he got his knowledge from and, when he held out his arms, she fell into his embrace. Exhausted after so many sleepless nights, it was easy to be rocked to sleep in his lullaby. When she awoke it was morning and he was still singing softly. Her fears gone, she pushed him away in sudden embarrassment.

Unfazed, he smiled. "Come, I shall buy you breakfast."

May hesitated only briefly. He led her downstairs and it was only then that she noticed that he had changed his odd smock and sacking clothes for a leather jerkin with silver studs worn over a green silk shirt. He looked very fine indeed, the attire far more appropriate for him, she decided.

Soon they were on the road again, sharing his horse and heading east towards the coast. She spoke little for several miles for her mind was busy, wondering who this man was and where he came from but eventually, she had to satisfy her curiosity.

"If I am to travel with you, won't you at least tell me your name?" she asked.

He smiled warmly, as if this invitation meant that she might finally accept him, but did not immediately reply. Self-consciously, she stroked her thick chestnut hair. She had a certain intuition that this man was truly only after herself. But why? She had never considered herself beautiful – standing in Brid's shadow saw to that – but this man clearly found something of attraction in her.

She nearly smiled back but checked herself in time. Already his flattery was beginning to work on her and she saw that she was losing her protective scepticism. He couldn't possibly want her simply for herself; he was too clever and even with his voice alone he could have princesses bowing at his feet.

"Amaryllis," he told her after a long hesitation as if he had not wanted to reveal something so secret as his name.

She nodded, feeling more trusting of him now that she had a name to call him by. How he had persuaded her to ride behind him on his lean chestnut mare she could not fathom but she was not uncomfortable. They were making good progress towards the eastern ports and the ships that traded across the Caballan. Once there, she would seek passage alone to Ceolothia.

The road steered gently north-east, skirting the Yellow Mountains and following the border between Jotunn and Torra Alta. The road split, one fork heading for the crowded ports of eastern Jotunn that exported the famous Jotunn cheeses, and the other north to the small fishing villages of eastern Torra Alta. Being born and bred in the quiet woodlands, May was naturally wary of large towns and opted to head north. The small track twisted and turned through chalk hills and, as evening approached, brought them out above the brightly coloured houses of Kittiwake Cove.

They looked out from the cliff tops at the crystal green of the deep sea. Closer to land, the creamy colour of the seabed, patched by dark seaweed and rocks, became visible where it sloped up to reach the shore. A good mile out, the shallow waters of the cove were protected from the swell of the deep water by a ring of jagged rocks. Beyond them, three huge ships were anchored in the darker white-capped waters.

May gasped at the sight of the vastness of water. She had heard tales of the sea, of its mysterious ways and colours, but nothing had prepared her for the enormity of it or how its movements were like a monstrous animal munching hungrily at the land. The huge body of water stretched away, the colours gradually fading until they were no more than a grey line in the distance. Such a sweeping view was alien to May and it frightened her. The sea was alive and even smelt somewhat like a sweaty animal, its swell like steady, slow breathing. Choughs, gliding and rolling in the air beneath her, brought her gaze back to the road at her feet.

A path broke off it, descending towards the village. Cut into the side of the cliff, it weaved back and forth, in and out of sight, taking advantage of every ledge or outcrop on which to turn and twist. Large engines strung with chains and pulleys lined the cliff tops, clearly used to lower goods to the village when the goods were too bulky to be loaded into donkey panniers.

She had expected Amaryllis to show some trepidation at riding down the steep track, which was at least as steep as the Tor, far too steep for wagons, and very much narrower in places, but he proved her wrong. Unflinching, he rode firmly down, though his horse was sweated and grunting by the time they reached the upper levels of the village that clung to the cliff-face. Here the track was widened by wooden platforms that jutted out from the rock face and were thankfully lined with railings.

They zigzagged down, squeezing past troops of donkeys labouring under great baskets strapped to their backs. The houses were small with tiny windows that squinted against the glare of the sun reflected off the silver sea.

The houses were not houses as May knew them but rather ancient caves from a time when a swollen ocean must have bitten into the cliffs at a higher level. A series of ladderlike steps were cut into the cliff, leading up from the narrow quayside to the dwellings above. Pulleys, like those that swung from the gables of tall mill house, heaved up barrels and pallets. The inhabitants were lean from the constant climb, their faces red from the abrasion of the salty spray and they had a way of shouting even when quite close to one another to make themselves heard above the strident cries of the kittiwakes that mocked the port and glided gracefully along the line of the cliffs. May was glad to reach the foot of the cliffs and the quay front where they dismounted.

"We must find a passage for you, my sweet lady Merrymoon," Amaryllis said gallantly though May could not tell if he were teasing or not. "It will be good to cross the sea. Very much safer."

She frowned at him.

"The sea is a barrier to spirits. The Dark Shadow will find it harder to cross it."

They surveyed the seafront. Two inns plied for trade at either end of the village. May noted at once that the nearer one, *The Hungry Fishermen,* had a constant stream of young fishermen staggering in and out. She couldn't quite read the sign swinging above the door of the second pub but she could see that the doors were closed. It stood nearer the ranks of rowing boots that were carrying cargo to and from the three large ships out beyond the bay. Evidently, the pub was frequented by the traders anchored in deep water who didn't have time for the inn just yet.

She turned her attention back to the fishermen. Two knots of men were gathered alongside a jetty clad in seaweed and barnacles that appeared to be the focal point of the village. The men in the first huddle were smartly dressed in clean leggings and jackets, one or two carrying staves. The other group wore heavier woollens and thick jackets, clearly fishermen dressed against the harsher weather of the sea.

May studied the smarter group and one man, who was doing most of the talking, caught her eye. By his smart black cloak and peaked hat, she guessed that he was the village prefect.

"Strange man, he was, and a noble if ever I saw one. The Baron's son, he claimed. Baron Branwolf's son himself. Showed me his ring, he did." He paused in his tale, waiting for an appreciative gasp from the gathered villagers. "Arrogant and stiff on a great black horse, I've never seen a fellow that thought himself so grand. Gave me a warning of trouble-makers roving the mountains to our west. Wanted men apparently. We're to stand a watch above the cliffs and look out for them. He said they'd be coming from the mountains. Oh, and he said there's a reward."

May's heart pumped. The Baron's son! Her heart rejoiced then she checked herself. But not on a black horse! All the same, she had to leave here at once just in case it was Caspar. She couldn't risk letting him recover Necrönd. Troubled by her torn emotions, she never questioned why he was asking after a band of ruffians and not herself.

The group dispersed, gossiping excitedly about what they would spend the reward money on. May's curiosity was drawn towards the huddle of fishermen and their women who were gathered about a brazier below the low eaves of the *Hungry Fishermen.* Their conversation was of an altogether different vein. It seemed that there had been no moon last night and the superstitious fishermen had not put out to sea.

May looked round her and saw no church or priory and hoped that this was a place that had turned back to the ways of the Great Mother. The charred remains of a large bonfire, no doubt lit for the recent Beltane festival, confirmed her thoughts, and her spirits lifted.

"Will you be safe if I leave you at the inn?" Amaryllis asked. "I'll need to make enquiries with the traders."

She nodded uncertainly. She had planned to travel on alone but hadn't yet worked out how she would rid herself of her eager companion.

He looked unsure. "Perhaps, my little one, you should give *it* to me. I will be better able to protect it than you."

A cold smile grew on her lips. "I see it now! You cannot take it from me by force, can you?" Her fingers worked nervously over the silver casket. "You cannot steal it from me so you plan to win it with grace and favour. You will not win me over," she said coldly and dispassionately. "You will not seduce me. I love another deeply and truly."

Her hand felt for the broach at her throat and she thought of that wonderful summer in the first year she had spent at Torra Alta after the siege, when she had still been too innocent to see how Caspar's infatuation with Brid was a permanent barrier to her happiness. She had been so flattered by Caspar's attentions, thrilled by his delicate touch, by his breath on her face when he came that fraction closer, and the trembling in his hands when he brushed against her. She had been so happy until she saw how he yearned for Brid and how he would sigh with pain when he beheld her.

How could she compete with Brid? May hated her and was consumed by guilt. It was unthinkable that she, a devout follower of the Great Mother, could hate one of Her high priestesses.

Amaryllis held out his hand. "It has no power to help

me now. I need only you," he told her lavishly, "and I want only to protect you."

May flushed at his flattery but clutched her bearskin ever more tightly over the silver casket. He withdrew from her. She sat by the *Hungry Fishermen's* crackling fire and listened to an old sailor talking excitedly about a creature he had seen on the cliff tops. "It was up near Granny Grebe's place, up above the grey cliffs."

"Like the rest, you didn't have your boat out last night and you were in here until nigh on dawn," the innkeeper laughed. "It were no wonder your saw strange beasts on your way home. The wonder is they weren't pink."

The crowd tittered and the old sailor puffed out his chest. "We all know folks farther south along the coast near Jotunn what's seen wolves. Maybe they're headed our way."

This was waved down as ridiculous.

"And, here's old Granny Grebe herself to tell us what wolves were a prowling at her cottage last night," the innkeeper announced.

A chill swept into May's heart as a very tall woman with steel grey hair stooped under the lintel of the low door and stepped into the room. The fire seemed to darken for a moment.

Granny Grebe turned her eyes, hooded by whiskery eyebrows, coldly on the company and ordered of the innkeeper, "A whiskey."

He frowned. "A whiskey, Granny Grebe? You know you don't want to drink that. It gave you terrible ulcers last year after the festival."

"I've had a nasty turn," she growled, "and I need a whiskey."

"You see, I told you there were wolves. She saw them too," the old sailor said in triumph.

"Wolves! I saw nothing of the sort. I just tripped on a cobble." She sniffed and pointed at May who was mortified to find herself the centre of attention. "Only thing I saw was two strangers come out of the plagued inland and they came bold as bears down the road. It's not so often that strangers come here by way of the land." She looked directly at May. "Is it now, young lady?"

Granny Grebe sat opposite May and looked at her curiously. The girl shrank back, horrified by her yellow teeth and the stench that came from them. The woman's eyes were sore and bloodshot and she rubbed at them in irritation.

"Don't be afraid," the old woman said in discomforting tones, her words crackling and spitting in her throat. She touched her thumbs and forefingers together, making a quick and brief sign of the Mother as if to tell May she were in safe company. "I would have made the pilgrimage to pay my respects to the old Crone but my legs are too weary. I see you are returning from there. I see in your face that you are a child of the Great Mother."

May was stiff with fear. Though this woman spoke lovingly of the Mother, her instincts screamed out against her.

The other villagers nodded kindly to the old woman and one or two brought forward children with ailments that she tended and, in May's opinion, offered sound advice, telling of herbs and roots that would mend their sore teeth or their fishhook wounds, the latter being remarkably common.

But May could not trust her and explained she must leave and find her friend. Her heart missed a beat as she realized she had genuinely described her feelings towards Amaryllis.

Granny Grebe reached out and snagged at her arm, the

touch cold. "Do not trust him, child," she warned, her eyes rolling to show the whites. "He seeks only your power, seeks to win your trust so that you can freely give him the power. Even from you it would be hard to take such a thing."

"How? What?" May stammered, wanting to ask more but fearing that she might fully reveal herself if she did.

"You must not trust him."

"Trust whom?" May asked coolly.

"Him of course," Granny Grebe nodded out towards the pier. "The one in a smock and sacking." She snorted as if finding the idea ridiculous then turned her accusing stare on May. "You don't like me." A laugh bubbled up in her throat. "I can see it in your eyes, child."

May did not like the way she spoke so much like Morrigwen, piercing her with an intense glare and holding her head at an angle just in the same way that Morrigwen used to.

Granny Grebe cackled louder. "It's ironic, isn't it, that here you are distrusting me because I'm old and ugly." She looked down and flicked at her grubby red dress in disgust. "But because that man is daring and handsome, you are prepared to believe every word of his velvet tongue?" The old woman pouted at her. "Don't you think that's just a little foolish?" She rolled back her eyes and chanted meaningless words before suddenly sitting bolt upright and glaring deep into May's eyes. "I've seen signs – you are in danger from him. You must leave at once but do not cross the sea. Head back into the mountains towards your own lands where you will be safer."

Granny Grebe took three swigs of her glass and moved away. May knew she had to act quickly before Amaryllis returned. She wound up her hair into a twist at the back of her head, securing it with a large pin that instantly worked free. She tied it again, wondering how to react to Granny Grebe's advice. Certainly, she must lose this curious, yellow-eyed stranger.

She wished Morrigwen were there to guide her. Once, when she had first come into the old Crone's care as an orphan, she had thought that perhaps she was the one destined to be the new Maiden. She had sensed Morrigwen had wanted that, so often calling her "my child" and doting over her, something she never did to anyone else except Brid. But near the end of her life, Morrigwen had admitted that, though the runes had spoken favourably of her and, clearly, she had a large part to play, she could not point to the position of the moon on a cloudy night as could all the high priestesses.

Instinctively drawn towards the sea, she ran quickly down to the quay. She did not trust Amaryllis but nor did she fully want to take Granny Grebe's advice. She must find her own passage without Amaryllis knowing. She looked out at the little fishing boats nuzzled up against the quay and then out at the dark majestic traders beyond the barrier of toothlike rocks. Somehow, she must reach the mines of Kalanazir.

She found herself standing before a group of fishermen, their cheeks flushed with drink. One, who was a little older than the others, perhaps in his late twenties, and with bright fun-loving eyes, sat back and grinned, revealing his large teeth. "Now there's a sight for sore eyes. They've been talking on about wolves creeping out of the mountains but they said nothing about earth sprites. Now that's a far better tale."

May blushed. "I'm seeking a passage and—"

Another sailor nudged the elbow of the one with the toothy grin and engaging eyes. "Here, Danny! What do you want to go about chasing after your sulky wench when there's a doe-eyed sweetheart like this stammering before you?"

They all laughed roundly and May bit her lip nervously. "I-I need to get to Ceolothia."

"Ceolothia!" The men laughed and May wondered what she had said that was so ridiculous.

"I have relatives there." She struggled for a good reason. "My folks fell fowl of the wolves and I have nowhere else to go. I must seek my future abroad and find my cousins."

"You don't need to trouble yourself by crossing the seas, sweet lady, when there's Danny here on his knees begging to look after you." The sailor thumped his toothy friend on the back who stumbled forward grinning in embarrassment. "Besides, do you think we sail that far when the best fish are in our own waters? Nought but smooth-hound off the shores of Ceolothia."

"Please, I need help." She looked up at them honestly, hoping to appeal to their better natures but they were interrupted by an older sailor with a thick beard and short striped shirt who came striding down the quay and stood legs astride before them. "Here lads, what do you think you are doing tormenting a poor lass like that?"

May turned towards him hopefully. "I need to get to Ceolothia."

"Ceolothia!" The man tilted his head to one side. "You want to be asking the merchants, now, not us fishermen."

"Oh, I know but I thought someone could take me straight out to the ships. I don't want to go near where they're loading their cargo onto the boats. There's someone down that end of the quay that I wish to avoid," she said honestly. "If I ask there, he'll see me." She fetched in her pockets for a brass coin – one that Amaryllis had left her for fare in the inn – and held it up.

Danny put his tankard down still half full and smiled

congenially at her. "Well, my nets are done long since and the tide's on the turn now so it ain't long before we can get through the Mermaid's Door. I reckon I'm nigh on ready to push off just as soon that Derry shows himself. A coin is a coin after all." He nodded at a ketch with a bright red sail moored at the end of the quay. "She's mine," he said proudly. "One of the biggest in Kittiwake and I have two lads as well as Derry what sail with me."

"His old uncle left him the boat," one of his fellow fishermen explained. "Though he didn't deserve it. Ain't his own hard work that's earned it." He grinned and punched Danny on the arm.

"Well, I thank you, sir," May said to Danny, hurrying after him down the quay with her head low, hoping Amaryllis wouldn't spot her. She never saw him but did catch a glimpse of Granny Grebe, her red frock fluttering in the breeze at the head of the quay. The old woman lifted her head, throwing the briefest glances towards May.

The red-sailed ketch had no room in the small pilot-house for her and May took shelter from the wind amongst a heap of canvases stowed in the stern. Two young lads were already busy arranging nets and coiling ropes neatly on the deck, ready to pay out when they reached the fishing banks.

"Like I said, I've just got to wait for my mate, Derry," Danny told her, "and then we'll set sail." He busied himself about the vessel for some time, helping the others to sort through the nets, ropes and baskets. He swore colourfully when at last his mate came rolling down the quay, and groaned, "Drunk already!"

Derry merely scowled and jumped aboard, staggering to his knees and clutching at halyards for support. He hauled himself upright and staggered through the neatly coiled nets towards the pilot house. He sat shivering in its lee. May kept her hood pulled over her eyes and tried to hide from Danny's generous smiles and the drunkard's scowls.

The sea along the coast was calm but further out dancing white caps rode a green swell, warning of a squall over the deeper waters. The cruel bite of the sea was softened by the line of jagged rocks about a mile offshore that rose like sharks' fins out of the water. Around them the sea boiled and clashed, sending puffs of spray high into the air and, in horror, May saw that they were heading directly towards the tallest of these jagged rocks.

"The Mermaid's Door," Danny shouted, nodding towards the crack between two rocks. He pulled in his sails and shouted for Derry to help but the drunkard merely turned green and flung himself to the side of the boat, retching violently.

Danny's face blackened with anger and he worked frantically, hauling in the sails while pulling on the tiller to steer a true course for the gap in the jagged rocks. May looked back at the twinkling village lights and caught a glimpse of a white sail atop a sharply heeled-over boat. Someone was waving frantically from the deck.

Moonlight flashed on the sails, a pool of light falling through the clouds, brightening the water around the pursuing craft. May knew Amaryllis was aboard.

May was startled as the deck of the ketch lurched beneath her. Danny shouted at his crew to grab a grappling hook. The two lads were hanging over the side, pointing and shouting. Danny heaved to in the lee of the rocks that plunged down into the green depths. Long ribbons of seaweed, like the arms of drowned men reaching imploringly upwards, were washed to and fro by the pull of the sea.

"What is it?" one of the lads asked nervously.

May's curiosity drove her to the gunwale and she peered into the frothing waters. A body, washed out by the tide, was floating face down in the water, straggling grey hair stretching out like the tentacles of a jellyfish around the head, and grey, bloodless arms bumping against the rock. Small fish, the bright silver slivers of their bodies glinting in the grey light, nibbled daintily at her toes. The woman was dressed in white as if for a wedding or festival but then May realized they were merely undergarments. The grappling hook snagged into the woman's hair and Danny pulled her upright.

May shrieked in terror. She had seen that face before, alive and well, no more than a few minutes before they had put to sea.

CHAPTER FIFTEEN

Something large and white bobbed in the angry waves. Ignoring Danny's shouts to keep seated for fear of the swell, May hung over the stern and stared in horror. The body of an old woman floated face up, the corpse grey and bloated as if it had been dead some days. But that wasn't possible. May felt weakly sick. It was Granny Grebe, the same woman she had seen on the quay just before they left.

The ketch lurched in the buffeting swell that was stirred by the crescent of toothlike rocks and May gripped a slippery rail to steady herself. "Danny, out there in the water! Look!" she at last managed to shout.

Again, the deck beneath her feet rolled violently. She lost her footing and her grip failed on the rail. She tumbled across the narrow deck and thumped into the gunwale on the other side. Terrified that she would be thrown overboard, she cried out for help.

"Hang onto something!" Danny yelled, struggling with the wheel.

The black, foaming waters either side of the Mermaid's Door churned and rolled, lifting and twisting the small vessel as if it were parchment rather than the timber of eighty-year-old oak. The short-handed crew battled to steady her, every effort centred on negotiating the narrow passage. Derry was no use to them. He reeled drunkenly and hung on a loose rope dangling from the rear mast while the others heaved purposefully at halyards and sheets. May yelled out louder.

The drunken mate looked at her stupidly and groggily gathered himself together. Working against the lurch of the swell, he staggered towards her, tripping on the aft-hatch cover as he went. "Don't worry, lass, I'll save you," he slurred.

Though he was clearly still intoxicated, he was better able to keep his feet than May and, gratefully, she held out her hand for him. He stiffened, a horrible smile splitting his ale-reddened face, the crinkling of his cheeks forcing tiny drops of blood from the corners of his eyes. May shrank back against the gunwale and stared in horror at the glinting blade that appeared out of nowhere into Derry's palm.

"Jump," someone shouted from the following boat that carved towards them through the dark waters. "Merrymoon, jump while you've got the chance! The waves will protect you." It was Amaryllis's voice.

Danny yelled for one of the lads to take the wheel so that he could help her but she knew there was no time. The knife slashed back and forth through the air before her eyes and Derry gave out a fiendish laugh.

"Possessed!" The word hissed unbidden from May's lips.

Leaning back out over the stern, she strained away from him, clutching at her silver casket.

"Merrymoon, woodcutter's daughter," he sneered. "It is not for you. Never for you! You do not have the strength." He reached out a hand and she felt the air shudder with the presence of a thousand hungry minds willing her to touch the Egg.

"Derry, get away from her!" Danny shrieked, his strong hands yanking back the madman's arm.

With a flick of his wrist, Derry threw the skipper across

the deck and, with menace blackening his bloodied eyes, turned back for May.

"Jump!" Amaryllis pleaded again, his voice rising in song. "Trust in the sea, the tears of the Great Mother."

Derry faltered, his eyes searching out across the sea for whoever sang those deep commanding notes. Seizing her chance, May hesitated no longer, took a deep breath and plunged into the churning green-black waters. The cold snatched her breath. For a moment, foaming bubbles caressed her skin, then the huge power of the sea caught her slight body in its all-enveloping embrace and tossed her back and forth like a child punishing an unloved doll. She fought upwards and broke above the surface not more than ten feet from the ketch.

"I'll have you!" Derry yelled from the boat's stern and threw a grappling iron. The hook snagged her shoulder and, grinning broadly, he pulled her in.

"Leave her!" Amaryllis shouted, his command stronger now that his boat drew close.

Derry gave out a twisted bestial wail, his attention slipping from May. She snatched the moment to tear the hook through her dress, twist and plunge away, fighting though the cold water that dragged at her clothing. Her skirts heavy, almost solid, clasped around her thrashing legs. The possessed drunkard squealed in anger and lurched over the side of the boat to grab her but cringed as the salt water splashed up. He snatched away his arm as if scorched and the skipper grabbed his opportunity to tackle him. They wrestled savagely and, through the spray May saw how Derry was thrown overboard and swallowed by the sea.

She valiantly kicked towards the rocks, her vision blurred as the waves rolled around her, one in every seven towering over her and punching her down. The cold weakened her. Spluttering and choking, she kicked up again, scrabbling with her hands for the silvery light that played on the surface, but the power of the sea pummelled the strength from her. The weight of her bearskin dragged her down and she scrabbled to undo the clasp but it was pinched too tightly together and awkward to reach on the underside of her cloak. Frantically, she wrenched at the hide but it would not yield.

Lapping waves closed their silvery skin above her upturned face. She watched the bubbles rising from her mouth and soon ceased struggling to free the broach. In the back of her dimming mind, a curious thought awakened. It was her love for Caspar that was drowning her. Mother, help me, she prayed as her strength left her and the numbing sea sucked her body down.

Someone was in the water beside her. Strong hands lifted her head, pulling her upwards. She gasped air, daylight bright in her face, and glimpsed golden hair and knew her saviour was Amaryllis. He swam strongly, his hand cupped beneath her chin, pulling her with him towards the wallowing hull of the other boat that lay hove to, bow into the waves.

Burly arms heaved her up, her legs hanging like leaden weights as she was banged against the hull and scraped over the wooden bulwark. With a thump, she was landed onto the decking. Horribly cold, she welcomed the closeness of the body beside her. Amaryllis held her tight and, in exhausted surrender, she let her head slump against his shoulder.

"Do not run from me any longer," he murmured. "You are too precious to lose, far too precious."

She did not protest when he dragged off the sodden bearskin and started to loosen her bodice. She no longer had the strength to do anything but trust him.

The boat danced in the water, holding its position while the men threw out ropes and raked the water with grappling hooks to dredge up Derry's body.

"We've got him," one of the sailors from the other vessel cried out, reaching over the gunwale to claw him aboard. One grabbed a hand but the flesh tore away as if long since rotted. The rest of the corpse slid back into the water and plummeted unnaturally fast like stone.

"Has he gone?" May spluttered as Amaryllis drew her close, feeding his warmth to her. The blood slowly heated in her veins, though not painfully as it would sting after coming into a hot room from the freezing cold but just as if the sun had gently melted away the frost.

Amaryllis's lips brushed against her ear. "Don't trouble yourself. You must rest."

May was too exhausted to question him further. All she knew was that for some while the sailors of both vessels had been toiling to retrieve Granny Grebe's body and now had turned back for the shore and were struggling against the out-going tide to bring the corpse back to Kittiwake Cove. A nervous hush hung over the boat.

"Will he come back? That man, that creature?" May asked, when at last she had the strength to remember Derry's maddened expression and the look of absolute terror imprinted on Granny Grebe's dead face.

"Perhaps, though not for a while. After the tears of the Great Mother have taken him, he must find a route back from the Otherworld. But such strength of purpose! I doubt he will rest until he finds a way." Amaryllis looked distracted but May couldn't summon the energy to puzzle out what he meant.

"The men say he drowned without trace," she said through chattering teeth as he rubbed at her hands. She didn't know that flesh could turn so blue. "Why did he sink so?"

"The tears of the Mother are a great purifier and spirits cannot be borne up in them."

"Spirits?" she asked, searching deep into his yellow-tinged eyes.

Amaryllis nodded.

She felt comforted. "I feared you were an elf sprite but you dived into the water for me."

He laughed but with a strangely sad note. "My sweet, I am *nothing* but flesh, mortal flesh." He looked at his hands as if this idea was somehow strange to him.

The sailor working the helm said, "There's an old saying that a spirit can only cross the sea in an eggshell so we sailors, who don't care much for spirits or anything of ill-luck, always take great care to crush them after we've eaten an egg."

Amaryllis smiled indulgently. "A wise precaution but it's not the egg but the bird they seek. If they cannot find a boat, the spirit must enter the body of a bird and fly across the waters. It is strange how traditions are born."

May accepted his words without question, only wondering that this man knew so much. She was only used to women being learned in the ways of herblore, folklore and mysticism.

"Where do you come from?" she asked as he wrapped her in warm clothes and then cradled her, rocking her back and forth and humming so sweetly. She could not protest but welcomed his attention. Again, she let her head nestle against his shoulder and closed her eyes, listening to his mellow song. Tears rolled down her cheeks; still, she wished it were Caspar holding her.

But it was not Caspar. He had not been there to save her. If she were ever to live again and take each breath in happiness rather sucking in black sorrow, she would have to forget Caspar. She snuggled closer against Amaryllis's firm chest. And perhaps this was the best way. She had seen many lovers hurt and bruised at the castle. The folk that had replaced those massacred by the Vaalakans were mainly young; courting was high in their minds. She had seen how all wounds of love had healed fast as soon as they were salved with another's attentions.

She had to start a new life – for her own sake and for Caspar's. Slowly she reached out and squeezed Amaryllis's hand. She felt his instant reaction, his sudden jolt of trembling joy. It shocked her and she snatched her hand away, though within her something warmed. She had just a twinge of satisfaction that she could bring someone such pleasure.

She closed her eyes and didn't open them again until they were wallowing in still water alongside the quay. Countless black and white terns skimmed the waters and kittiwakes cried out with that unmistakable shriek from the cliffs above.

"We'll go to the other inn where we'll draw less attention. It's not so popular with the locals, it seems, and only frequented by passing traders," Amaryllis said. Sweeping her small frame into his arms, he carried her towards the inn. The sign of a blindfolded puffin swung above the door, the paint faint and cracked from exposure to the onshore winds. "You can rest upstairs while I ask around and find us a passage on the morning tide."

"Why are you helping me?" she asked weakly.

He smiled disarmingly and replied with an open face, "Because you mean life and soul to me."

May laughed. How could she possibly trust someone who made such outlandish and ridiculous claims – yet she wanted to. He was her protector and she needed him. She concluded that, so long as she was vigilant to keep Necrönd from him, she was safer with him than without.

"A room for the lady and a maid to help her," Amaryllis demanded of the old woman that came to serve them. May welcomed the bath and the sweet syrup they offered to help her sleep but could not rest until Amaryllis returned and sat by her door. She awoke with the tingling numbness gone from her feet and fingers though she was still exhausted. The yellow-eyed man was standing over her. "I'll get you some food," he offered.

She shook her head. "No, just some company. I– I– don't want . . . Her face . . . Granny Grebe's face."

"There's a roaring fire downstairs," he told her. "You'll feel better there."

She nodded unenthusiastically and sent him out so that she could dress. It took her a long time, fumbling with buttons and laces, since she was still so weak and shaken, but she refused to ask for help. When she was ready, she called him back and allowed him to lead her down the stairs.

"Well, little chap, what food can we prepare for you and your lady?" the innkeeper of the *Blind Puffin* asked, welcoming them into the dining hall.

"Little chap," Amaryllis echoed with some indignation and May realized that she had forgotten how small he was; he had such presence and it was easy to overlook the fact. "What else but your best fare."

May tugged at his hand and shook her head. "No, no, I'm not hungry."

Amaryllis nodded in understanding. "Your best fare for me and some hot soup for the lady. We'll sit by the window in the sun," he said considerately.

The innkeeper led them to a fine table set against one of the small porthole-style windows that overlooked the sea. It was tucked away in a recess. "The inn's quiet now but it'll soon fill with men when the tide brings in the sailors of the traders. They don't like the *Hungry Fishermen* half so much as here." He nodded as if this were very satisfactory. "Now sit you down where you won't get crushed in the crowd."

She gazed out of the window past the ring of rocks to where the great ships bobbed and tugged restlessly at their forward anchors, their finely cut prows pointing up-tide all in the one direction, like deer-hounds scenting prey. The innkeeper brought a great rack of ribs for Amaryllis and soup for May but she couldn't face even that. She could only think of Granny Grebe's half-rotted face bobbing in the water.

Amaryllis was talking to her warmly and patting her hand. "You must eat to keep warm," he urged with obvious concern for her well-being.

Numb with the cold that had crept deep into her bones, she paid him little attention and, instead, was absorbed in idly watching while the pub gradually filled with foreign faces. Then his voice stopped. May started. A young girl draped in a blue cloak of the softest material was standing by their table as if she had appeared out of thin air. At least, before May had studied her properly, she had thought she was a girl for she was shorter even than Brid and very fine-featured, but now, on closer inspection, she could see she was a woman of middle years.

Amaryllis sat motionless and May was beginning to think him quite rude for not acknowledging the woman's presence when, suddenly, he pushed back his chair, rose to his feet and gave her the most disarming smile. Her amber eyes gazed piteously back at him and then May.

"You carry such a burden for one so frail," the woman purred at May and heaved a deep sorrowful sigh.

May frowned, suspicious of her meaning and intent.

Could she mean Necrönd and how did she know of it? And she might be small but she certainly wasn't frail and what was this woman doing accusing others of being frail when she was so tiny herself? Then the wind must have swept aside the clouds for a shaft of light fell through the window, slanting across the woman's face that was suddenly so fair, so pure and yet so sorrowful. Awed by the sight, May immediately felt inadequate and, thinking she had no right to any opinions any more, swallowed her indignation. She had thought Morrigwen wise, Keridwen sensitive and Brid uncomfortably perceptive but this woman appeared to be all three. Those eyes . . .

"Well, little Merrymoon, you've come a long way and proved yourself wise, too, finding such an experienced fellow as this to be your guide and protector." She looked at Amaryllis meaningfully. "I am sorry for you, truly I am but there is little I can do for you except give you this." She reached inside her scrip made from some very soft leather and produced a tiny scroll of greyish brown bark.

"Willow bark," May said weakly, recognizing it instantly.

The woman nodded in pleasure. "Oh yes, but more potent by far than anything you can find in the— in the Caballan."

May nodded, took the bark in her trembling fingers and chewed at it tentatively. It tasted just the same as the willow bark Morrigwen administered but she was amazed to find how quickly the vigour returned to her body. Her skin flushed with sudden warmth.

The fair woman turned her strange doleful eyes on Amaryllis. "Fair fellow, if ever you are to walk the long forest road to Annwyn, you must heed what I say. Even far off, we heard your song and you sang not in melody, which is your right, but in power. You have transgressed. Perhaps it is already too late but, if I am to plead your case, you must keep your gifts to yourself else the terms of the bargain are broken."

Somewhat subdued, Amaryllis nodded at her and she smiled back with deep compassion. May watched the woman's back as she weaved her way through the crowd though most people barely seemed to notice her, giving her a brief nod perhaps but that was all. Near the door, she stopped amid a brilliant shaft of sunlight that slanted through a nearby window and turned to look at May through the spirals of slowly falling dust that sparkled in the light. She smiled and then was gone. May blinked. It was as if the woman had simply been absorbed by the light. May decided she must have been dazzled for a second while the beautiful woman slipped away into the crowd.

"Who was she?" May demanded and then looked more sternly at Amaryllis. "And more to the point, who are you?"

"Your fairy godfather," he replied with a half laugh. "Now we don't have time. We must cross the seas and slip away silently, leaving no trace. And try not to even think about the Egg. It draws attention. They sense it, you know. The spirits and ancient creatures are pulled to it. Its presence is as obvious to them as you find the coming of dawn after the terrors of the night."

May knew what he meant. She felt the presence of a vast army of creatures, sensed their resentment and the pain of their yearning for life, sometimes coming in great battering waves and, at others, the steady pressure of their one purpose leant against her will like a bull against a rickety gate. Not for the first time, she wondered how Amaryllis knew so much of the Egg and what he had to gain by helping her. But despite herself, she was beginning to trust him. The willow bark had worked miraculously and, shrugging away her problems, she stretched and began to eat her soup hungrily.

Amaryllis looked around the now close-packed inn and nodded at a black-bearded sailor wearing short sleeves and wide trousers with broad blue stripes. He was bellowing at several men and would have no one sharing his table though the room was crowded. Clearly, he considered himself a man of status among the sailors. He caught Amaryllis's eye, scowled and then turned to May, giving her a lecherous wink.

"We must find a passage and that looks like as good a place to start as any. He's a ship's master if ever I saw one. And sure of himself too," Amaryllis remarked with approval. "I'm happier at sea with a man that's confident." He squared his shoulders and approached the seaman with less of a swagger than was normal to him. "We seek passage across the Caballan, master," he said smoothly.

Somehow, whenever Amaryllis spoke, the people around would fall silent as if unable to resist listening to the musical quality of his voice.

The ship's master looked him up and down. "You're no Belbidian. Never seen a blond Belbidian in my life. What are you running from in your fine clothes? You smell like trouble. Can't risk trouble aboard ship."

May saw that Amaryllis was having little joy in finding a passage and decided that, now she was feeling so much better, she would make enquiries of her own. Soon she was in conversation with a rather more respectable-looking ship's master whose hands were clean and his clothes fresh and white. She felt they could trust such a man far better.

"Escaping the wolves, lass?" he surmised, his accent foreign. "Well, I've already got a few of your fellow countrymen joining us on this trip. And I'd be glad to take—"

"It won't be necessary," Amaryllis interrupted, his voice cold as stone, and tugged May away.

"But he wasn't even going to charge us." She yanked her hand away in indignation.

Amaryllis's eyebrows rose as if to tell her she was a fool. "Didn't you see his earrings?"

"What was wrong with them?"

"He had a silver bear's claw dangling from them," the elflike man replied as if that were highly meaningful. "Come on, we can board the *Dolphin*. There's a few men preparing to row out to her now with more cargo. She's not sailing until late morning but we can take our cabin now. Her draft being too deep to navigate the small rivers, she's headed for the mouth of Skuas Ria, one of Ceolothia's northern ports. She's carrying spinning wheels, looms and woollen fabrics, all exported from Ovissia, I'm told. It's a fine ship but I don't suppose you're going to thank me for finding us so perfect a vessel?"

He was right of course but that did not mean she had to like it and she sulked all the way out to the ship. While the oarsman heaved at the oars, pulsing the boat out into deep water, she gripped the slippery bench beneath her and whitened as they fought through the churning waters of the Mermaid's Door. A sudden swell of black water buffeted the boat. She was still angry with Amaryllis for laughing at her choice of ship and refused to draw closer to him for comfort. Then they rowed past a dark, red-hulled ship with the motif of a bear's claw painted on her prow. Canvases covered her cargo and a sickening stench, the smell of terrified animals, wafted from her hold. May shuddered and shuffled closer to Amaryllis.

"You're grateful now and so you should be," he scolded her lightly. "You could be aboard one of those slave ships, laden with Torra Altan bears, but instead we're headed for northern Ceolothia and the semi-frozen steppes where the white seals breed. I have found you a good route, have I not?" he preened.

"Yes, it is a good route."

"Then you should be grateful."

"I am grateful," May conceded.

"Then you should be pleased."

"Don't you see? I don't want to feel grateful," May told him and then laughed at herself, though without joy. Somehow, it had been easier to bear the pain of leaving Caspar when she had been pursued and frightened. Now she felt too safe and secure. Everything seemed to be working too well just when she was finding herself leaving the security of Belbidia and could no longer just turn around and run home.

She was uncomfortable that they had to share a cabin but there was no alternative and very soon they were underway.

"Will you never tell me about yourself? If we must spend this voyage alone together you must tell me. How else am I to trust you?" she questioned her companion.

He shrugged. "I told you my name and that I am from Gorta; there is nothing more to know."

"But that strange woman knew you. She spoke as if you were somehow on trial," May continued, pushing the question.

The ship was heeled over, cutting into the winds, and she found the only way to feel comfortable was to sit firmly on the floor with her back against the underlocker of the lower bunk. Amaryllis, however, seemed quite at ease. "People from Gorta are always on trial; it is part of our training."

"Tell me about Gorta?" she insisted, eyeing him sceptically.

"It is the ancient isle of the Druids and covered with cairns," he said in wistful reminiscence. "They eat mayfly, oyster-catcher's eggs and cakes of seaweed that they rake off the long beaches because the interior is barren of any thickness of soil. They say it was originally unpopulated but the druids took it as their sacred isle so they could study without distraction during their long apprenticeships. Only once they had studied for twenty years were they allowed to leave and spread the word and the ways of the Great Mother. But the population has been greatly in decline for the last three hundred years since the Old Faith began to dwindle."

May did not believe for one moment that he was a druid. She didn't know why but she was certain that any druid must be very old and have long bushy eyebrows.

"But I am not a druid," he announced as if reading her thoughts. "No, their order is all but gone and their buildings and texts taken over by a new school where I trained. You might say we have some of the ways of wizards, learning to tap into the laws of alchemy and the properties of the elements. But I was blessed with a talent that I was born with and did not have to learn and the master wizards resented me for it, saying they I must not use this natural magic but must learn like everyone else. They were jealous of me you see."

"Your voice of course."

Amaryllis nodded. "Of course. But I couldn't help being myself. Finally, they exiled me from the school and told me never to return unless I did so with a great prize, the freely given love of a maiden."

May scowled. This sounded to be the most implausible of punishments. Then the full meaning of Amaryllis's words hit her. "I am the prize?" She was outraged. "I am the prize!"

He shrugged and nodded. "I thought I must be honest with you."

"But you said I summoned you," she pointed out a hole in his story.

Amaryllis paused for a moment and hid his face in his mug, taking a long slow draught. "Well, yes, I did, didn't I? You see, the wisest amongst the ancient truth-givers, the one you saw today, took pity on me and said her divinations had told her of a maiden in need that was trying to summon help and protection and that I must do all I could to help her."

It was quite the most ridiculous tale and the fact that Amaryllis told it with such a wicked glint to his eye made May want to burst out laughing. The only part that did ring true was that he did have a certain mysterious power and indeed his voice was magical.

Bad weather kept them below deck for the first part of the week. Throughout, May continued to question her self-appointed champion though she could not extract anything approaching a plausible explanation from Amaryllis. Every day, he promised he would follow her to the ends of the earth and, if it weren't for the bright glow of delight in his eyes whenever he beheld her, she would have believed that his tales had not one single ring of truth.

On the evening of the fifth day, when the sun turned the Caballan Sea to rippling molten copper, he leant beside her at the ship's side and sang softly and it was only then that May felt life was bearable. She was certain of one thing, however, and that was that he did not come from Gorta. Ceowulf had been there once and told of how the air was thick with the cries of choughs and guillemots since the entire island was surrounded by high cliffs, which were the birds' habitat. There were no beaches and so nor could there be any oyster-catchers that thrived on them. It was a simple mistake and she wondered at his nerve for telling her such a lie.

But she also wondered at her own motives for tolerating his attentions. And what of the small mysterious woman with the amber eyes who had appeared from nowhere beside their table? Strangely, she had liked her and had felt a certain curious recognition as if, in her distant past, she had met that woman in a dream.

The sea was still and, as the sun set, it was as if the ship sailed at the centre of a huge shield of molten gold. With the night came a soft wind bringing a smooth gentle swell, the ship rocking in the cradle of the sea. Soon, the light of the moon struck the water with its silvery wand, allowing the quieter, more potent powers of night-magic to ooze out of the elements and stalk the earth.

"Moonlight's not really silver at all," May observed. "Cream perhaps and often it has a soft red glow to it if the sun has only just set. Look how it brings life to the water." She thought it was as if a host of white-veiled mermaids were leaping and dancing on the surface but wouldn't have dreamt of saying such a thing.

She reached her hand out towards the light as if to catch it but it did not fall on her. She wasn't surprised but was still disappointed. Often, she had noted how the moonlight fell on Brid, anointing her with its magic, a breath-taking sight. It seemed to seek her out but not so May. She sighed and let her hand drop. She was just the orphaned daughter of a woodcutter, why should the moon touch her?

Amaryllis was watching her. "You are crying for the moon," he half-laughed and May nodded, aware that her cheeks were wet with tears.

"The moon does not sparkle in my eyes nor ripple

through my hair like it does with Brid. He would have loved me if I had been like her. But he does not love me and I must go away."

Amaryllis sat close, his arms brushing against her. Distrusting him, she shrank from his touch, and yet some small part of her wanted his comfort and his help to shoulder her burden. Necrönd was too much for her; she knew that now. He came no closer but simply said, "You will feel better when the sun rises."

She did not. Overnight the clouds rolled in and the sea darkened. An albatross perched on the rigging and Amaryllis started and looked at it distrustfully for a long, concentrated moment before relaxing. Clutching onto the rail at the edge of the companionway, May studied him quizzically.

"They travel far over the sea without settling on the water," he warned.

The next few days were again rough and May felt sicker than she had ever felt in her life. Spreading herself on her bunk, she clung on tight and was more tempted than ever to raise the powers controlled by Necrönd just to take her away from storm and the nauseous roll of the sea.

She was already exhausted by the burden of the Egg and the relentless sea wearied her further. Sweat prickled on her fingertips. She itched to wield Necrönd. It looked harmless, quite harmless yet the patterns, the silvery blue threads that marbled the creamy gloss of the shell absorbed her thoughts and she spent hours simply tracing out the line of one thread and wondering whether the scorch mark had in any way harmed it. She wondered if the patterns would stir to form some magical sigil at the moment of command. She yearned to find out the truth and felt a thousand wills pushing her hand towards the shell.

Her fingers were hovering over it when she heard a sigh right behind her. Hurriedly, she covered the Egg and glared up at Amaryllis, his eyes strangely aglow in the semi-darkness.

"Get out!" she shrieked at him.

He shrugged and sat down on her bunk, ignoring her protests. "It's growing on your mind." He made no move to snatch the Egg away, which at least allowed May to relax a little. "It is not yours, Merrymoon," he warned her. "The Great Mother gives you no protection from it. You endanger yourself. They will overcome you. Believe me, they have great strength."

"How would you know?"

He paused before saying thoughtfully, "I think we all know in the depths of our hearts. They are the nameless beings that come out of dark memories to haunt your nightmares and make your afeared for you soul. I have seen it on the faces of many men. I had not realized until now how deep a fear that must be." He sighed regretfully, remorsefully even.

May had no idea what he was talking about but resolved that she must lose him as soon as they stepped onto dry land. In trusting him, she had grown weak and allowed him too close to her precious Egg. By crossing the water, they had shaken off the shadow that had been stalking them and, no longer needing Amaryllis's protection, she would be safer without him now. Even if it meant using the Egg, she must be rid of the stranger who spoke so little truth about himself. She was resolved. This man would use her; she was certain. Why else was he following her?

Dawn found her towards the prow of the ship, watching a grey line that was gradually taking form out of the surrounding mist to become a spur of land. Dark clouds, swirling and churning in a heavy sky, glowered over it. She shuddered. She had never before set foot beyond Belbidia and she was scared of the cold grey world before her.

CHAPTER SIXTEEN

"The dragon, though it had claws and teeth like scythes, did not breathe fire but the scent of delphiniums that gave all that smelt it the most astonishing dreams – dreams that would come true if they were ever brave enough to capture the dragon's breath in a bottle."

Keridwen wove her story well, feeding it with every ounce of her energy and, it seemed indeed that a blue vapour slipped from her mouth with each word. As planned, Hal drew his head down into his cloak and breathed in the acrid and vile scent of the weed, spinster's hope, to counter the blue vapour that permeated through the chamber. Certainly, Keridwen would sleep for several days after inhaling so much of the hallucinogenic concoction but he, Brid and Ceowulf would keep their heads clear.

It was late and the sounds from the torture chambers had long since ceased for the night. They hoped that the fires were damped down. The coals would still be hot but if they moved quickly . . .

It seemed to take an age for the vapours to work but when the last of the guards slumped dreamily and happily to the floor, Brid reached for the knot at the end of her thick hair and uncoiled her braid. All of them, of course, had been searched on entry to the dungeons but the guards had found nothing on Brid. Her thick hair was a soft coppery brown, the streaks of red catching the light, and it was so long, right down to her waist, that she had been able to conceal several useful items within the knot. No one had thought to search her hair. After all, it was not as if she were a mercenary, an assassin, or a political criminal. She had merely been stealing silks from the market.

Some hours beforehand, she had already extracted from her tresses a twist of cloth containing her essential herbs and then busily concocted the two potions needed. Now, as the surrounding prisoners began to doze and the guards' eyes grew blurry and heavy, she produced a thin length of hooked wire. "Let's see how much trouble these locks give us," she said cheerfully.

Hal grinned at her, "Brid, you're a marvel."

"It was Abelard's idea," she confessed.

Hal groaned. "You don't mean you've brought him along?"

Ceowulf answered for her, "Of course. He's waiting for us just beyond the palace grounds with a cart full of wine barrels all bound for the fine barony of Jotunn. Cybillia won't approve of course. She'd rather I drank ale but I can't get used to your northern customs. She spices the wine and warms it. Such a terrible thing to do to good Caldean wine," the knight complained. "Mind you, it's a good thing he came; no one else can take care of Pip."

"Not Pip too! It's a disaster!" Hal exclaimed. "That boy should be banished to Salise, sent as far away from Torra Alta as possible."

Choking on the spicy vapours that Brid had given them, they set about unfastening their fetters and, without the guards watching them, the task was far easier than they had hoped. Once free, Hal immediately moved to close Brid tight in his arms. She hugged him back but they quickly broke apart in their haste to escape and, still possessively clutching each other's hand, they made their brief farewells to Keridwen. Though more heavily exposed to the sleeping vapour, she had experienced its effect many times before and had managed to stay awake. She gripped Hal's arm.

"How will you find the princess when both Rewik and Dagonet have failed?" Her eyes were full of suspicion. "You're thinking of Necrönd. Don't let Spar use it," she warned him stonily but Hal would not reply. Keridwen glowered at him. "Of all people, you are the one he will listen to most. You must not encourage him. It must remain locked away."

He turned his back on her fury.

"Hal, listen to me! It will do terrible evil."

He stiffened, trying to shake off the uncomfortable sense that Keridwen's eyes scorched deep wounds into his back, and refused to turn around. It was unnerving that she read his mind so well but she was not always right. In his opinion, her decisions were made with her religious duties uppermost in her mind and sometimes he considered that might be at the expense of the welfare of the people. He respected what the priestess said about Necrönd and what should be done about it but he could not allow her to put her fears of the Egg above the safety of Torra Alta. He would not let those he loved suffer again.

Keridwen spoke coldly to his back, "Spar will not do it, Hal. I made him promise and he would never go back on his promise to me."

Hal could not stop himself from looking round at her. "That doesn't matter. I shall tell him that you have changed your mind and beg him to draw forth the ancient monsters of this land to find Cymbeline. He will believe me –

especially when I explain that the King has chained his mother in his dungeons."

"I shall remember that you have vowed to go against my wishes," Keridwen threatened.

He could hold her gaze for only the briefest moment before he was forced to break away from those cerulean eyes. Though she had certainly lost some of her mystical presence since Morrigwen's death, there had been an urgency born within Keridwen that had given her a determined strength and he was strangely afraid of her. He turned and ran after Ceowulf.

It was not far to the iron door that separated the torture chambers from the slime-covered walls of the dungeon. Ceowulf expertly worked the lock free and nodded back at Hal's appreciative grin. "A mercenary learns many tricks," he said, lightly.

Brid crossed the room without pausing. Hal, however, faltered at the sight of the rack and flogging posts and the stains of blood on the stone floor. A half-rotted corpse hung supported within the confines of an iron cage, eyes dripping from its sockets. Even Ceowulf broke his stride at the sight before hurrying towards the raised bed of fires set against one wall. A range of pokers and branding irons stood propped up beside raked embers.

Brid found water in a butt and drenched strips of cloth that she wrapped round her hands and face. Trepidation quickened Hal's breath; he was suddenly afraid – not for himself but for Brid.

He grabbed her more roughly than he had intended. "You can't do this. There has to be another way."

She looked at him indignantly. "You're not afraid to climb the chimney, are you?" She didn't seem to need a reply. "Well, nor am I. But I am afraid of being caught here in the morning and facing the gallows."

The sound of tortured timber broke their exchange. Ceowulf grinned guiltily and brought over two thick planks, which he had torn from the stocks, and placed them across the fire cage to provide a platform from which to begin their climb. Hal noted a stiffness in the knight's movements and suspected his injury still pained him but Ceowulf was a man and would cope, he was sure. Brid, on the other hand, was a delicately boned maiden. He glared at the smouldering embers, raging within at his impotency to spare her pain as he helped her up behind him to balance on the planks that were already beginning to char. The wet cloths did not protect them fully and the air was breathless, singeing their nostrils and lungs as they blinked up into the enclosed blackness. He was vastly relieved to find a rope dangling down not more than a foot above his head.

"I'll go first," Brid said, immediately taking charge. "I can climb a rope easily but it'll be much harder for Ceowulf so, Hal, you bring up the rear." Nimbly, she scrambled up Hal's back and snatched at the heavy knot at the end of the rope, hauling herself up into the sooty void.

Grunting and gasping, Ceowulf made heavy weather of the climb.

"It's much easier if you put everything into one concerted effort and pull yourself up fast," Hal advised, "otherwise the grip in your fingers begins to fail." It was the third time Ceowulf's great boot had slammed down onto his fingers and Hal was seriously worried that they would not make it. At least the bricks around them were beginning to cool and he no longer scorched himself as he was bumped into the brickwork.

Side flues offered them occasional resting points but Ceowulf's laboured breaths betrayed his exhaustion. Hal guessed they must only be halfway through the climb when they found a wide ledge on which to rest, all three huddled and crouched into the dark side opening.

"You go on without me," Ceowulf grunted, massaging his right shoulder. "I'm slowing you up."

Neither Brid nor Hal bothered to make any retort as they urged him to take up the rope and follow Brid again. Gritting his teeth against the strain, Hal hauled himself up behind his friend, pushing his shoulders up towards Ceowulf's feet to help give the knight a platform from which to work against.

Hal thought his grip would finally fail when at last Brid's voice whispered down from somewhere high above. "I'm nearly there."

He was still in the pitch black of the gradually narrowing chimney. Wriggling his shoulders to squeeze through the soot-covered bricks, he was beginning to worry that Ceowulf might get jammed but, from the sudden cry of jubilation, he knew the knight had reached the top. Starlight flooded in through the chimney.

Swearing with the effort, Hal pulled himself up the last few feet to be met by Pip's beaming face. He didn't feel in the least like smiling back. "Next time you have to drop a rope that long, make sure there are knots all the way along its length."

"Yes, Master Hal," Pip replied smartly, evidently too taken up in the excitement of the escape to worry about being surly for the moment.

Exhausted, Hal and Brid sat panting on the tiles to regather their strength while Ceowulf lay back, cradling his right arm and moaning softly. From the palace roof high above Farona, the view was spectacular. The moon had swept behind the great spire of the cathedral, casting its tiered and turreted architecture into fine relief. Far below them, house lights illuminated the capital's narrow streets, the intricate pattern like a golden web around them. Hal felt exposed. Hastily they clambered over the roofs towards the mews where lower buildings butted up against the palace.

"The rope!" Ceowulf called softly from the edge of the roof.

Quietly, they lowered the rope down into the dark of the yard. Hal went first, followed by Brid who, light and athletic, had no trouble coiling down. Ceowulf brought up the rear and, with a heavy thud, dropped the last eight feet. They paused, listening intently, but no one had yet raised the alarm. Seconds later, they were climbing down into the moat. The ice-cold water rippled as big carp wafted their golden fins to swim away from the intruders. Shivering and with tendrils of weed still caught around their legs and arms, they crawled up the far bank. Presently, a covered cart drawn by a large horse nuzzling into a nosebag rolled out of the darkness.

Spluttering with the cold, they piled in, one on top of the other, and wriggled between the barrels and under a canvas sheet as the cart rolled off. Brid immediately began digging furiously for new clothes while they stripped off their wet and conspicuous attire. The carter whistled a tune, an air that Hal didn't recognize though he knew at once that the sound came from Abelard. None of them spoke as they nestled themselves between the jostling barrels and ripe-smelling cheeses. Hal scratched at his back where he was being tickled by some straw stuck in his smock, an authentic touch no doubt. No one said a word until they were beyond the city gates, which opened at dawn, and, at last, they were rolling north into the open countryside.

"Phew!" Pip exclaimed, his eyes wide and sparkling.

Hal had a strange urge to laugh but it was instantly

repressed by Brid when she said, "Poor Keridwen, poor Branwolf. Let us pray they do not suffer for this."

"Branwolf," Hal repeated solemnly. Another thought struck him. "I can't leave! I can't go without my sword! I knew there had to be something wrong with your plan, Brid. It's hopeless. I have to go back for my sword. The Great Mother entrusted it to me."

Ceowulf laughed. "Good to see you have your priorities straight as usual. Nothing like putting your sword before . . ." He shrugged, not needing to continue with the insult. "But, friend, you underestimate how well your betrothed knows you. We retrieved the sword first."

"Oh Brid!" Hal gave her a big hug and made to kiss her but she pushed him way.

"I get no thanks for saving you but am smothered in praise for saving the runesword," she said airily though Hal paid her no more attention.

Ceowulf was rustling under the pallets of cheeses and drawing out a long sack-wrapped bundle. Slowly he peeled back the cloth to reveal a plain scabbard collared with fleece. His eyes fixed on the finely crafted hilt wrought into the design of two warring dragons.

Hal grasped it. "Mine!" he said zealously, unsheathing the great runesword to check that it was unscathed. The edge was as keen as ever and the runes of war and sorcery that decorated the central groove of the fuller were just as stark and daunting as he remembered.

Hal grinned at Ceowulf, his white teeth pearly in the thin morning light. "You got it from the weapon room?"

Ceowulf nodded. "There's nothing that the promise of a good case of Caldea's finest red won't achieve. Unlocks the rustiest of chastity belts," he laughed. "And I saved the sword from the furnaces. The King had ordered it destroyed and the gold refashioned."

Hal gasped in horror.

"I had to offer the armourer my own sword to replace it."

"Your sword!" Hal exclaimed, knowing full well how much it had meant to Ceowulf. Forged in Salise, he had won it in a tournament. It was said to have once belonged to the tall race of men that, many thousand years ago, had crossed the countries of the Caballan. They had left behind a legacy of great monuments and canals but, as suddenly as they came, they were gone, marching out of their lives into the unknown. Hal was never sure whether he believed Ceowulf's tale of the sword's heritage.

The knight shrugged. "You owe me, friend, and you will find me a greater sword than the one I have lost."

Hal kissed his blade and pulled Brid towards him but she was unyielding and he released her in defeat.

Recognizing the signs of a brewing argument, Ceowulf coughed and politely moved as far away as was possible in the tight confines of the wagon. Hal didn't understand what it was all about. Of late, it had proved impossible to please his betrothed. When he had crossed the barrier between this life and the Otherworld to rescue her from the verderer, Talorcan, he had shown beyond all doubt that he loved her. The muscles of his jaw tautened as he thought what might have been if he had failed.

Though he had proved that he loved Brid truly and that their souls were joined, she had seemed distracted and angry with him ever since. He wondered whether such passionate love might have burned so intensely that it had burnt out.

Sulkily fearing the worst, he pushed her away and concentrated on his sword. Neither spoke. The dark shadow of their tempers unsettled the others and even Abelard's attempts at light conversation fizzled out. The five sat in silence.

It was Brid who finally broke it. "How could you have been such a fool as to let Rewik take you prisoner? Look what it's done. What will happen to Keridwen? You saw those implements of torture!"

Anger jetted through Hal's body. "What? You can't blame me for Rewik's deeds!" He saw the look of accusation in Brid's eyes and wondered how she could misjudge him so. He had done everything he could. He bit his tongue and for the next four leagues sat with his feet dangling over the edge of the cart, watching the road rush by underneath.

"I'm sorry," a soft voice eventually whispered behind him. "You have suffered and I was worried for you." Brid didn't need to say more. She crept into his arms and snuggled down against his chest. "I was so worried for you but now I am terrified for Keridwen."

They took it in turns to drive the cart through the night and, when Hal had finished his stint, he handed over to Ceowulf. Carefully, he stepped over the sleeping bodies of Pip and Abelard and took his place at the rear of the cart next to Brid. She held up a slice of buttered bread topped with soft cheese and slid it into his mouth.

"You need feeding up," she said tenderly.

Grinning, he put the bread aside and pushed her down onto his bearskin that he had laid out in the bed of the cart. He lay alongside her and put his arms around her waist, pulling her tight against his body. She felt warm. "I hunger only for you."

She kissed his neck and he shuddered with pleasure. Then she wove her hands in between the layers of his clothing, seeking flesh. "Oh, Hal, you're so thin," she said in distress.

He kissed the top of her head, feeling so comfortable with her that he found no need to search for words.

Brid's hands feathered across his torso. "I was so afraid for you." She peeled back his tunic and kissed his chest.

He glanced over his shoulder and saw that Ceowulf was tactfully staring dead ahead at the road and whistling quietly to himself and the others showed no signs of stirring. He rolled Brid over, pressed down on her, kissing her mouth, and eased his hands under the belt of her leather hunting breeches.

She caught his hand. "Hal, no," she said softly. "You know I love you but I can't: I have a duty. I am One of the Three; I am the Maiden. Not until the new Maiden is found. Don't test me so; it's not fair."

She had firmly explained this to him many times before but for the first time he sensed a weakening in her resolve. "You know you want to," he murmured.

"Of course I want to," she agreed, squeezing the firm muscle of his upper arm.

"Well then?" he cajoled.

She kissed him and for a moment he thought she had finally succumbed. Then she suddenly stiffened beneath him and turned her head away. "Hal, I'm sorry but no."

"We shall be married so soon," he continued persuasively.

Someone tapped him on the shoulder and furiously he snapped his head round.

"Master Hal, when a lady says no, y' must respect her," Abelard said calmly but firmly.

"How dare you!" the nobleman snarled, rising to his feet, fists raised.

"She is a high priestess to the Great Mother; I would give my life a thousand times to protect her!" the archer proclaimed quietly. "I know you mean no real harm, Master Hal but—"

"She is to be my bride!" Hal bellowed, thinking he

would kill this sanctimonious busy-body. "How dare you interfere!"

Ceowulf stopped the cart. "Now steady there, Hal. I'm sure this is just a misunderstanding."

Brid tugged at his arm. "It's all right, Hal. Leave him be. He was doing what he thought was right."

Ceowulf sagely pushed in front of Abelard and put a hand on Hal's shoulder. "It's just a misunderstanding; let it drop."

Hal swatted Ceowulf's hand away. Fearing that he would do someone serious damage, he jumped from the cart and punched his fists into the wooden boarding to relieve some of his anger, never noticing the pain as the skin split over his knuckles.

After a couple of hours brisk walking, he was calm again and understood that Abelard might have misinterpreted the situation. Of course, he would never force Brid against her wishes. He'd waited three years already; wasn't that proof enough of his love and his chivalry?

Ceowulf joined him. "Listen, Hal. Abelard has taken it as his duty to protect the Maiden and that's why he has overreacted."

"It's my duty," Hal snapped. "She's my woman."

"Of course, but it's important that we don't fight amongst ourselves. Things are tough enough as it is."

Hal reluctantly agreed. He wasn't about to forget what Abelard had done but he was big enough to rise above the situation and pretend that nothing had happened. He gave Ceowulf a jaunty smile, his teeth bright in the moonlight. "I'm tired," he announced. "I'm going to get some sleep."

The next morning, they reached Bleham and pulled into the back of the ostler's. Hal noted with envy that Ceowulf's armour was wrapped, ready to be packed onto the back of his horse. The young man fingered his plain hauberk in disgust, jealously eyeing his friend's armour as they prepared to leave. Still, it pleased him that Abelard looked uncomfortable on a horse. Nevertheless, he took pains to behave with what he considered to be impeccable grace towards the archer after what had happened and congratulated himself on his self-control.

It was only four days before they reached the canyon of Torra Alta, Brid's golden mare having pulled all the way to get ahead of the others. With the Tor in sight, it seemed she could no longer contain her own urgency to get home and gave Sunsprite her head.

"Don't you dare gallop away!" Hal yelled after her, beating his horse into a foaming sweat in a vain attempt to catch her, while Abelard charged behind. Defeated, Hal reined in and cursed Caspar for giving her such an animal while Abelard persisted in the hopeless attempt.

Ceowulf grinned at Hal. "She's a free spirit. You'll only make yourself bitter trying to bridle her."

Hal scowled and continued to scowl when he caught up Abelard, whose horse would gallop no more and now wheezed along at a plod.

"I'm sorry, Master Hal," the archer apologized for his failure.

Hal's frown deepened in concern when, within the hour, Brid came galloping back. She pulled to a halt, the golden mare dipping down onto her haunches, sparks flying from her iron-shod hooves.

"Ovissians!" she warned. "The place is swarming with armed Ovissians stationed all around the root of the Tor. And the flag is down! They've stripped the Dragon Standard from the keep! It seems Rewik has already confiscated Branwolf's lands. And Spar! He must be held prisoner!"

"I knew Master Spar wouldn't cope," Pip muttered.

"We'll get him back, don't you worry, Master Hal." Abelard made an attempt at optimism then turned to grab Pip's collar and yank it sharply. "Now lad, I've had it with your lip!"

"But Spar! And what of Necrönd?" Hal could not think for a moment and certainly had no time to consider Pip who was complaining bitterly about Abelard's brutality. It was no use trying to rescue Caspar, not from Torra Alta; the castle was impregnable. All the underground tunnels had been fully sealed after the Vaalakan war. What could they do?

"What are we going to do about Spar?" Brid asked, sniffing back tears.

"Nothing," Hal said stonily. "Without Necrönd we can do nothing except see to it that Rewik reinstates Branwolf. And the only way we can do that is to find Cymbeline, though just how we are going to do that without Necrönd I don't know."

"We'll think later," Ceowulf told him "But, first, let's get off the road and into the mountains."

All nodded at this. Zigzagging up the sheer walls of the canyon into the cool of the Yellow Mountains, Hal fretted over how they would find Cymbeline. With all the resources at their disposal, neither Rewik nor Dagonet had even managed to locate the lost wagons. But on further consideration, he wasn't that surprised. Ceolothia's forests were vast and their route had taken them off the main highways. Perhaps Ogden had been unable to lead Rewik's men back to the exact spot. He was certain, however, that he could find it. Well, perhaps he couldn't himself but Brid surely would; she had an uncannily good sense of direction for a woman.

As they climbed through the trees, he assessed their

situation. At least they were properly dressed against the mountain weather but their supplies were low since they had anticipated going only as far as the castle. Now they would have to wait until they were in the Boarchase beyond the mountains before they could hunt and make provisions for the journey ahead. And then there was Abelard and Pip – and, of course, Brid. He had planned to leave them all in Torra Alta; the last thing he wanted was to thrust his betrothed into danger.

"Abelard and Pip will only cause trouble," Hal grumbled to Ceowulf.

"I completely fail to see what you can possible hold against Abelard," Ceowulf defended the archer. "He is a most honourable fellow in all ways."

Hal grimaced by way of reply.

"Now, Pip then. We all know Pip is trouble."

For some reason Hal found himself perversely wanting to defend the boy. "Pip's done nothing wrong of late," he argued, contradicting himself. "Everybody gets at Pip. They *expect* him to do wrong, so he does. And just because they wrote a ballad about Abelard, everyone thinks he's a champion."

"Yes, but you can't hold that against him." Ceowulf fell pensively silent and then laughed. "I thought you had forgiven him for earlier but now I see why not. He's a hero, an enduring hero from the days of old when men were men, and battles were fierce, and honour was everything. He's everything you want to be! But that's no reason to resent him."

Hal scowled and kicked his horse forward in search of somewhere to camp since it was already twilight. All that night, whilst huddled in a cave for shelter, he brooded over Ceowulf's words and it wasn't until they reached the green swathe of the Boarchase Forest, lying like a strip of deep sea lapping at the feet of the Yellow Mountains, that he knew why he resented Abelard.

He commented to Brid, "It's because he's unnatural, shouldn't be here at all. A man back from the dead after four hundred years! And he's so smug about it. He thinks that, just because of that, he has the answer to everything."

"Well, you have to admit, Hal, that he would probably know more than the average person," Brid said laughingly. Though his betrothed, she would never indulge him by taking his side in any argument.

"You would take his part," Hal said bitterly. "Just because he dotes on you like some lap dog. I suppose I'm not good enough for you now. I suppose I'm a shallow fool with a blind temper and you prefer the all-knowing, deeply spiritual Abelard." His eyes blackening with anger, he put little thought into his words; he just wanted to hurt her just as he was hurting. He blamed himself that he had not been able to persuade King Rewik of Torra Alta's innocence and so didn't feel charitable towards anyone. And to make matters worse Abelard was nice to him, *sympathetic*!

They slew a deer or rather, much to Hal's aggravation, Abelard slew a deer, for which everyone was *so* grateful. It had been a long mark and he had brought it down in one beautiful shot that had passed behind the animal's shoulder and embedded in its heart. They roasted it then and there over a crackling fire before deciding on their next course of action. A full belly comforted Hal and soothed his temper.

"Where could Renaud possibly have taken Cymbeline and why hasn't he asked for ransom yet?" he pondered out loud, pulling Brid close who rested her head against the muscle of his chest, one hand gently kneading his thigh. "It makes no sense."

Abelard, who, despite his limp, was pacing up and down like a sentry, stopped and offered, "If he asked for ransom, it'd happen everyone would see as it was him who had done this evil. If, as y' say, what he really wants is the throne of Belbidia, he'd best get that by disposing of Cymbeline and then claim that he too was held prisoner and could do nought to save her."

"But if that was his plan, he should have seen to it that *someone* demanded ransom, otherwise it is too easy to point the finger at him," Hal argued.

"What other possible reason could there be for stealing away the princess other than ransom, or for the throne of Belbidia?" Ceowulf asked.

"Reasons are often only obvious in hindsight. When we have the answers, we'll think how stupid we were not to see them earlier," Abelard remarked philosophically.

"Well, that's obvious, isn't it?" Hal sneered, gently pushing Brid away so that he could reach for some food. He sank his white teeth into a hunk of meat, the red juices dripping over his hands and onto his leather leggings. Though he had eaten like a ravenous hound since their escape, he had barely put on half the weight he had lost.

Brid hugged her knees and commented with gentle criticism, "Hal, you're not being helpful."

He could not stand it any longer and got up to march away into the trees.

Muttering, Brid came after him to see what the matter was. "Hal, wait!"

"It's all right for you. You get all the praise but I get all the blame. Have you no idea what it's like for a man to be rescued by his betrothed? If they write a ballad about me, I'll be a laughing stock."

"You'd rather I'd left you there?" She sounded hurt.

"Why couldn't you have just sent Ceowulf down the chimney in the dead of night? You didn't have to bring Abelard and Pip along as well, did you?"

"Abelard insisted. He wouldn't let me go on my own."

"No, he seems to think it's his job to protect you since, clearly in his oh-so-wise eyes I'm not man enough to do it myself," Hal added vehemently. "I shall be your husband soon, Brid, and I hope that then he won't be traipsing after you like some lovelorn lapdog."

"He's a fine man," Brid said lightly, "and it does you no credit at all to be sour towards such an honourable fellow."

Hal felt dismal. He had lost face – and in front of Brid of all people, whom he adored to distraction. Just for once, she could have taken his side. His brooding thoughts ceased, however, as the leafy boughs of the Boarchase thinned and the escarpment of Vaalaka loomed up before them.

"All we can do is pick up the trail where we were ambushed," Ceowulf said, gazing into the grey wilderness.

Hal grunted his agreement. "It's a long ride."

As Hal had anticipated, Brid had no trouble picking her way through the maze of forest tracks north of the main trade routes to the very spot where they had been ambushed though it lay a hundred leagues deep within the Ceolothian forest. She took a peculiarly deep interest in the lay of the land and looked on each tree as an individual, recognizing many particular ones on the way. Hal had not expected to see the heaped spills of gems still lying there undisturbed, the shaded ground glistening with sunburst rubies. It seemed incredible that no one had returned for such easy loot.

Pip was immediately on the floor, gathering up gems

and stuffing his pockets. Hal gripped his collar and snarled, "Touch one of the stones and you'll find yourself buried six feet under with piles of rubies for a tombstone."

Pip reluctantly obeyed, the stones dribbling from his pockets as he turned them out. "But, Master Hal, no one would know and it seems nobody wants them."

"Just search," Hal ordered. "Just scour the ground for any signs of who made this ambush. There must be something. A shred of clothing, a weapon, anything that might have some mark on it."

Brid had already started to organize the search. "Hal, you look around Cymbeline's wagon. Since you were closest, you might make the most sense of the scene."

Hal objected to being ordered around by Brid but it would have sounded churlish to protest, especially since what she asked was only sensible. He left Secret to gaze with the other horses and began to kick around midst the pine needles. A heard of boar had been this way, trampling through the debris from the upturned wagons and all he found was a snatch of Cymbeline's torn gown hanging from the corner of the wagon.

Ceowulf looked at the scarlet strip of cloth and then blankly at him. "What now?"

Before he could answer, Brid was at his shoulder. "So, we know they were last seen heading north but we don't know if they continued in that direction. If there were just one clue to the nature of the attackers, it would be easier to trace them."

"We'll never find them," Pip said gloomily. "The ground's overrun with boar prints and it's been raining. I've not seen a single hoof mark other than our own leading out from here."

"So helpful, Pip." Ceowulf grimaced. "We have to find them. All we can do is track north until we pick up some trace of them. Even after so many weeks there must be some mark since they'll be no other riders to confuse them with."

Hal's eyebrows rose sceptically. "The forest is huge. They need only have veered fractionally one way or the other and we'll never find them."

"If I were hiding out, I wouldn't leave the forest," Abelard said. "But certainly, they've gone a goodly distance, otherwise some of them would have come back for the wagons, wouldn't they? Whatever their orders, mercenaries are mercenaries and there's more to be earned filling their pockets here than stealing princesses."

"Well, they haven't come back yet, have they?" Hal pointed out rather scathingly.

"They haven't," Abelard conceded. "But human nature is human nature and they will. Someone will come back. I say we wait."

"We could wait forever," Hal objected.

Ceowulf shook his head. "It's better than wandering aimlessly through the forest. They can't be long now. They won't risk leaving all this treasure around."

They waited in fact for four days. Hal was almost disappointed to be proved wrong, since that proved Abelard right. They heard whistling and hurriedly retreated into the woods, Hal hissing fiercely at Brid to keep herself out of trouble.

"I'll look after her," Pip said brightly, wafting his short sword.

"Just watch that you don't take your horse's ears off with that," Hal said quietly, his attention already drawn by three riders garbed in black surcoats that floated over clanking armour. They had just come into sight through the trees.

He reached for his bow and nodded at Abelard. "You

take the one on our right and I'll take the one on our left. Then we've only got one to deal with."

Abelard nodded.

"Ready? Now!" Hal ordered.

The two flanking mercenaries never knew what struck them as both toppled without a cry to the ground. Their horses bolted. Hal hadn't worried that his man wore a capped helmet; he knew the Torra Altan arrows would pierce metal plate and hammer straight through the skull. Abelard's arrow pierced his man neatly between the eyes and the lifeless body toppled and, with one foot trapped by a stirrup, was dragged through the heaps of rubies. The central mercenary wasted no time but yanked around his horse's head and fled. Ceowulf and Hal spurred after him in hot pursuit, swords drawn.

The mercenary was weighed down by armour so, even though Secret was not the fleetest of Torra Altan horses, she slowly closed the distance while Hal concentrated on guiding her between the trees. It would have been easy to kill the mercenary but they needed him alive. In desperation, the mercenary flogged his animal viciously. The distance lengthened again and Ceowulf was even further behind. Hal could ask nothing more of Secret who was beginning to labour so, on entering an open glade, he pulled to a halt and remorsefully drew his bow.

He aimed for the horse's quarters since that was the only way he could be certain of missing the man. It fell with a squeal and a sickening thud, the mercenary catapulting over its head and lying twisted in the ground. Ceowulf was quickly on top of him, knife at his throat.

"I swear I don't know, sir," the man said hurriedly in a husky Camaalian accent. "We never ask who's paying. Our sergeant just gave orders but once we'd done our bit of fighting, we couldn't stick to them and had to break away from the back of the column to get back to princess's wagons. Couldn't leave that lot just lying around, now, could we?"

"Where were you headed?" Ceowulf growled, his knee grinding into the man's chest.

Hal knew there was no need to interfere and left the Caldean to his interrogation while he set about the unpleasant task of putting the horse out of its misery.

Ceowulf was soon finished, apparently satisfied that he had extracted every ounce of knowledge from the mercenary. He stripped him of his weapons, leaving him to wander the vast forests alone, and returned to the others.

"They've gone north of Dagon's Gutter, the great river that drains Trows Forest," Ceowulf explained to Brid, who was waiting anxiously in the thick of the thorn woods. "They've got both princes, Cymbeline, Hardwin and Tupwell. That was as much as the fellow knew. He thought they would cross the river at some old stone bridge above Rainbow Falls."

There were no paths cutting that way and the going was slow. Their hands and faces were scratched by trailing branches and tempers were wearing thin when, quite unexpectedly, they came across a lone hunter tending a small fire and stirring a bubbling pot. The man was pleasantly talkative and, obviously glad of company, shared his hot lunch with them. The meal over, he pointed them in the direction of a track that he claimed would take them clear to the river though he cautioned that it was a hundred leagues or more.

Hal looked doubtfully at the narrow strip of dark mud. Recent rain had muddied the ground but it slowly dried out as they moved north. Eventually, they picked up the first tracks.

Brid slid from her golden mare to examine them. "Hooded wolves," she declared laconically.

"Well, that's something," Hal said dryly. "The forest was swarming with them when we were attacked. It seems Princess Cymbeline has a four-legged escort now."

Contemplating the wolves, they rode on in subdued silence, the wolf prints becoming more obvious when they reached higher ground where the soil was better drained. Here the spoor pitted the width of the track though they found no other clues.

Travelling light as they were, they made good time and after three days reined in at the sight of a great sheet of tumbling water where a broad river fell from a plateau.

"Rainbow Falls!" Hal pointed.

There was no mistaking it. The spray rebounded a hundred feet into the air, the tiny droplets of water catching the light and forming a myriad of miniature rainbows. Dagon's Gutter fell a hundred and fifty foot where a black scar of rock divided the forest into two levels. The arch of a vast bridge was visible high above them on the skyline. There was no place to cross the river below Rainbow Falls so, soaked in the sparkling spray, they worked their way back and forth to climb the escarpment and reach the stone bridge that spanned the head of the waterfall in one easy arching sweep.

The ancient stones of the bridge were pitted, the massive slabs notched and carved with figures and lettering all but worn smooth by the passing years. They wondered at the huge architecture and the fate of the civilisation that had built it. A wide track fed by many other forest paths led to the bridge and they trotted across. The roar of the river drowned all sound until they were some distance beyond it on the one road that led north.

"There must be some tracks left by the kidnappers even

now," Hal insisted. "The trail might be weeks old but they were made during the end of the rainy season and it's been dry since."

"We'll never find them," Pip continued with his monotonous theme. "Not amongst all these wolves."

Hal kicked the ground. "Wolves everywhere!"

"Hooded wolves," Brid corrected him. "The air still has that reek to it. And look at the size of the footprints."

"They're nearer the size of a lion," Pip exclaimed.

"You've never seen a lion's footprint," Hal corrected him, "let alone a lion."

"I have!" Pip protested.

"Stop it!" Brid snapped. "I am trying to think! There are too many wolves in all this."

"And too many rubies," Hal added. "What do wolves and sunburst rubies have in common?"

Brid shrugged. "Nothing except trappers, who seem interested in both." She played with the end of her plait, tickling her cheek with it.

She was so beautiful, Hal thought, too beautiful to be allowed out into the wolf-infested forest.

She seemed to read his thoughts. "I admit I'm unsettled. They seem to move with driven purpose. And clearly, they were used to help capture Cymbeline."

"But Spar is the only person who could control them!" Hal accused. "It has to be Spar meddling with the Egg. Perhaps, in his captivity he can't get to it but is bending his mind towards it and somehow . . ." Hal couldn't quite form a logical argument and prayed the Ovissians had not found Necrönd. "But I will not believe that he would summon wolves and, even if he has, someone else is somehow controlling them now."

"Then who? Without Necrönd no one has the power. Certainly not Renaud," Brid said firmly.

"But why not Renaud?"

"Because I've met the man and he does not have the power within his soul."

"How would you know? It might be a part of his cunning to keep the strength of his character hidden from you," Hal argued, always looking for a logical explanation.

Brid sniffed. "You have no empathy. None at all."

Hal grunted. It was no use arguing with her. He leant forward to kiss her but she pushed him away irritably.

"There is too much on my mind," she told him sharply. "All I can think of is Keridwen in those dungeons and what will happen to her if we are unsuccessful. Will they torture her, Hal?"

"No," Ceowulf said firmly. "I fear they will torture Branwolf but they will not bother with Keridwen when they have him. By hurting Branwolf, King Rewik will prove to Dagonet that he is taking the loss of the princess seriously. He'll do it simply to appease the Ceolothians and avoid war."

Brid looked deep into his dark brown eyes covered by straight brows and smiled sorrowfully at him. "It is little comfort to me to think of Branwolf's suffering but I know you're trying to help. You are a sweet man, Ceowulf, but you know they will hurt Keridwen too."

"They will not. There is nothing to be gained," he insisted.

Brid turned back to Hal. "And what do you believe?"

A thin strand of a hazel branch whipped his face before he had time to duck. "Rewik will torture her because she is a pagan priestess and because it will hurt Branwolf more than anything else," he said with flat honesty. "He'll think to break him that way."

Brid nodded at him. "I know. I saw it in their eyes before we left. Both Keridwen and Branwolf knew what awaited them."

They rode on in silence, having little difficulty tracking the wolves that had left a great river of prints behind them in the soft soil north of Dagon's Gutter. The horses snorted and squealed but struck a good pace through the permanent half-shade of the woods. Daylight was precious to them; the sun's rays were quickly swallowed by the thick trees, though when they reached the top of a rise just as the sun rested on the horizon, it cut horizontally through the tree trunks, making the entire forest seem alive with firelight.

They stopped for the night, keeping warm by a small fire, and were quickly asleep. Hal awoke first while the mists still swirled along the path and, without rousing the others, went off to study the tracks for a while. With great personal gratification, he eventually found five or six crescent-shaped hoofprints overlain with the paw prints of wolves, finally confirming that they were on the trail of several riders. He hurried to wake the others.

"Heavily laden, too," Brid remarked, after examining the prints. "I would guess they lost too many horses and have doubled up."

Ceowulf nodded as he hastily divided out rations for breakfast. "Looks like it."

"Can I lead now?" Pip asked. "I'm always at the back."

"Y're not!" Abelard laughed.

"It can't do any harm to indulge him." Hal smiled charitably towards Pip. "We can hardly miss this great trail. Not even Pip can get us lost."

Brid had an almost permanent frown on her elfin face as the day wore on. At first Hal regularly checked Pip's tracking but there was no missing the trail and he soon became distracted by studying Brid. The dappled light played in her hair, the ends of her plaits swishing around her waist that was so slender he could close his hands around her. The firm curves of her hips swayed to the steady roll of her horse's gait. She was beautiful, tantalizingly beautiful. His thoughts strayed into daydreaming. He could ravish her then and there, pull her from her horse and into the bushes. She would refuse him as she always did but, at last, she would yield, unable to resist his passion. He ground his teeth, trying to restrain his thoughts, and shifted in the saddle, tossing back his head and cracking his knuckles to relieve some of the physical frustration. It wasn't fair!

They had crossed three fords and carefully picked their way over one half-rotted and creaking bridge and still there had been very little change in the surrounding woodlands.

"What's the matter?" Hal asked after a while.

"Nothing," she assured him though she sounded lost in thought.

"You're frowning," he told her.

She smiled sweetly at him and nudged Sunburst alongside so that she brushed against Secret's flanks. The two horses flared their nostrils, both interested in the other's peculiar smell. Hal was intensely aware of Brid's close physical presence and increasingly frustrated by it. Of course, he was worried sick about Branwolf and Keridwen and furious with Caspar for his misuse of Necrönd, but what nagged at Hal most at these times when he brushed up against Brid was finding the new Maiden. It was that problem that affected him personally. Until the new Maiden was found she would not come to his bed.

He decided that as soon as he had vindicated the name of Torra Alta, he would force Caspar to use the Egg and find the girl that would fill Brid's office. He had wrongly thought that when the old Crone died, Keridwen might take her office, allowing Brid to become the Mother, which meant that at last they could be married. He had once thought that she would come to his bed anyway but he had been continually proved wrong; Brid held her religious duties above all else. He was glad that no other temptations had come his way of late. He doubted that he would resist.

"Am I?" Brid asked.

Hal had forgotten what he had said to her though it came back to him in a flash. "Yes, you're frowning. What's wrong?"

"Well, apart from everything else," she said with her usual humour, "these tracks just don't seem right anymore."

Hal looked down at the ground. After letting Pip take the fore, he had paid little heed to them in a long while. Hurriedly, he slid from his horse and went to the very edge of the path where it was easier to pick out individual prints that weren't merged all into one mass. He paced alongside them, counting and judging distances.

Brid watched him intently. "See, there is a difference, isn't there?"

He nodded gravely. "A very clear difference. Pip, you idiot, get back here."

Abelard and Ceowulf cantered forward from where they had been lagging a polite distance behind.

"What's the matter?" Ceowulf asked.

"This idiot has just blundered on without looking," Hal accused Pip.

"I was looking!" Pip protested, his face red and his fingers twining uncomfortably through the reins. "I was following the tracks just as you said. You didn't tell me to look for differences."

"Don't be impertinent," Hal snarled. "You were posted to the fore. You should have reported anything unusual."

"I thought you were checking him," Ceowulf murmured to Hal.

Hal chose to ignore him. He wasn't going to admit that he'd been too distracted by his physical frustration. It was too demeaning.

Pip stared blankly at the forest track and shook his head, though both Abelard and Ceowulf groaned.

"Why didn't I look?" Abelard berated himself.

"We should have noticed," Ceowulf commiserated him, sharing the blame.

"If it's anyone's fault it's mine," Hal was now equally determined not to be outdone in taking the responsibility. "I let Pip go on ahead. I was wrong; he just doesn't have the experience."

Pip was looking more and more downcast and studied the tracks in earnest. "But I just don't understand."

Abelard sighed. "It's like this, lad. When we set out, we picked up just the slightest tracing of hoofprints, quite heavy hoofprints in places where one horse bore two riders. The wolf tracks overlaid them."

Pip nodded. "Yes, I understood that."

"Well, look at the prints now," Hal said in frustration. "Can't you see the speed at which the wolves are running? Far faster than they were before and the horses, especially such heavily laden animals, couldn't possibly have kept up. And, if the wolves are ahead of the horses, then we should see the horse prints clearly over the top."

"But there aren't any," Pip protested, still defending himself.

"Which means, Pip, that at some point they turned off the track and not one of us ever spotted it," Brid said with a sigh.

They retraced their tracks, winding through the great sweep of the forest, their spirits becoming increasingly depressed as the day wore on.

"They must have broken away at one of the fords,"

Abelard raised his voice above the heavy breathing of the horses and the thump of hooves on the soft turf.

It was in fact the second ford and, by the time they reached it, their horses were exhausted and they had wasted half a day.

"It wasn't my fault," Pip continued to protest. "No one would have noticed from one side of the river to the other that the wolves had suddenly speeded up."

"They would have done if they had taken the lead and boasted how good they were at following tracks." Hal ground his teeth, restraining his anger. How could he have been such an idiot as to let Pip take the fore and then be so lax as to be distracted by Brid and so fail to check Pip's tracking at least every mile? He glanced sideways at Brid: women were nothing but trouble. "When we get home, I'll see you demoted to the kitchens," he threatened the boy.

Pip did not cringe or scowl but, in his infuriating way, shrugged as if he didn't care.

"Here!" Abelard shouted from downstream. "They've merely waded down river and turned into the thick of the forest. At least a dozen horses moving quite slowly."

Though they were overlain by the prints of many boar, the tracks were easy to follow until the ground became sodden underfoot. The path dipped towards a swamp in the middle of the woods where fallen trees lay like lazy monsters lolling in the grey waters.

"They must have waded through it," Hal said, his voice echoing strangely over the black waters that laced around the roots of tall trees.

"Careful," Abelard shouted. "Y' let me go first. We don't know how deep it gets."

"Always the hero," Hal muttered, urging Secret straight into the boggy marsh before Abelard had a chance to show off his fearless spirit and selfless chivalry by testing the ground first.

They kept in single file behind Hal with Ceowulf bringing up the rear, water swirling around the horses' flanks. Hal's boots dragged through the murky water and he could feel the wet seeping through the soles. There was a strange hush over the marsh, not even the sound of a moorhen clucking or reed warblers piping out their own distinctive song, disturbed the quiet. The great fallen trees, lying half in and half out of the water, disconcerted Hal. As soon as his back was turned, he had the sense that they were rolling and swimming along behind them.

They had gone no more than a short distance into the swamp when it became quite clear that they had lost all sight of their trail. What Hal had thought to be the far side of the marsh was just a mud bank whose far side plunged back into a forest of trees waist high in dark water with a silver glint to the surface where it was touched by the sun.

"I thought it was just a small marsh and, if we crossed, we could look for their trail on the other side but it seems unending," he complained.

"We'll get lost," Pip said woefully.

"It's getting deeper," Brid observed quietly.

Hal took every one of these statements to be an insult against his judgement. Goaded into proving his abilities, he urged Secret forward, the swishing, slurping sound of the other horses plodding through the water following after him. It seemed loud in the still of the marsh.

"What's that?" Pip exclaimed.

He was craning around to the right and Abelard already had his bow drawn.

"I didn't see anything," Ceowulf said calmly. "Don't let the marsh spook you."

"I'm not spooked. I saw something," Pip insisted petulantly. "Something swinging up in the trees."

The men laughed. "Swinging through the trees! We're not in the Endless Continent, Pip. This is only Ceolothia."

"I saw something," Pip repeated his eyes narrowing to slits. "And you're all fools if you don't believe me."

"Now steady there, lad," Abelard warned. "Y' can't—" His sentence was cut short by Brid kicking Sunburst on to rush through the water in great surging leaps, heading for a large water-locked willow. Its curving whiplike leaves fell from its flat crown, weeping into the water to form a dome.

Hal charged after her, yelling at her to be wary of deep pools while Pip shouted again that he had seen something in the trees. No one listened.

"Look!" Brid exclaimed to Hal. "What do you make of that?"

"But it's Renaud's mark, surely! A wheat sheaf surrounded by a coronet." Hal frowned in puzzlement. "Why would Renaud possibly leave his mark hastily scratched in the willow?"

He turned to look deeper into the marsh and glimpsed another mark on the next willow. Without thought, he kicked Secret towards it. Her forequarters dropped from under him as she wallowed into a hidden pool and he was flung onto her neck, a great wave of muddy water washing over him. Spluttering, he heaved himself upright while Secret swam and struggled for a firm footing.

"Look out! Master Hal! My Lady Brid! Watch out behind you!" Abelard's voice rang across the water.

CHAPTER SEVENTEEN

Mustering all his authority, Caspar contradicted the others, "I won't leave Naith there."

The shepherd's tendons stood out like drawn rope as he struggled to wrench himself free from his shackles. "Then untie me before the wolves come!" he shouted, his voice hoarse with terror.

Lana clawed at the ropes. Hardening his heart against his emotions, Caspar jerked up her arm and held her fast in his grip.

"Murderer," she screamed.

Fern showed none of Caspar's compassion towards Naith. "You killed deer to trap wolves. You killed my Sorrel! I hope they rip out your guts and eat them in front of you before you die." He stamped on Naith's pinned hand.

Ursula was even more terrifying in the viciousness of her emotions. She stood over him. "You befriended me. I thought you cared for me. But you were just using me; all the time you were laying a trail for your comrades." She kicked him sharply in the ribs. Though troubled by this, Caspar was impressed to see Naith swallow his wince.

Caught up in the human emotions, Trog was growling over the shepherd's head, his lips peeled back. He lunged, snapping his jaws viciously, his curving white teeth closing a hair's breadth from Naith's nose. Lana shrieked and struggled.

Caspar saw little point in revenge. Naith might know things about the bear trappers that he hadn't yet disclosed and, surely, after the outlaws had staked him out like this, he would no longer side with them.

Trog stalked the length of Naith's body and sank his great teeth into his boot, heaving it off and shaking it madly as if it were a rat. The wolfling was soon wrestling Trog for it, the two of them tugging and snarling playfully. Runa, though still floppy-pawed and gangly, was becoming quite a challenge for the stocky terrier who looked alarmed by the wolf's force. But when the dog refused to give in and finally ran off with the trophy held high in his mouth, Runa returned to sniff at Naith's bare foot and nip his toes. For the first time, the shepherd screamed.

"Please, please, Sir, take that wolf away from me, I beg of you. I thought I was doing right for the sake of Belbidia."

They had stood arguing for too long; Caspar had finally had enough. "Fern, fetch Cracker. Perren, help Naith up but see you keep a good hold on him. And Ursula, get that damn boot off Trog so that Naith can walk. We must find somewhere to hide for the night. Already, we are out too late without a fire."

To his mortification, not one of them stirred. Only the wolfling sat obediently at his feet, nudging at his hand with a cold muzzle and giving him an affectionate lick.

"You are not ordering me about." Fern was indignant. "Not when you're wrong. Hal would not have shown pity on this traitor. Hal—"

"Don't you Hal me!" Caspar yelled, losing his composure. "I could have left you in Torra Alta for the men to treat you like a freak but I took pity on you."

"Took pity on me! You needed my help!"

"Help, Fern? You've been nothing but a hindrance. You think like a scared rabbit and you never do what I say."

"Why should I listen to you when no one else does? You may one day be lord of Torra Alta but you're not my lord, nor Ursula's and not Perren's either."

Perren guffawed at the absurdity of the idea. "A man, lord of a stonewight!" He spluttered through his words and finally got control of himself. "But Spar is right. The shepherd may tell us much about our enemies and we have little time to waste. Ursula, get that boot and Fern, fetch the horse. The wolves will be here soon."

While the others obeyed Perren and rushed off, Caspar released Lana, who ran to fling herself over her brother and hug him tight. Sighing, the Baron's son used his knife to cut Naith's bonds and the shepherd struggled upright.

A howl close by set the hairs on Caspar's neck pricking. "Hurry!" he shouted. They had knives and only a few arrows, scant defence against a pack of hooded wolves.

The sun was now no more than a cap of deep red on the western horizon and, ahead to the east, the sky blackened. They ran into the growing gloom, Caspar's mind racing to make a plan. If they could find some rock face, crevice or perhaps the head of a ravine, they could at least shield their backs while he held the wolves off with his arrows.

"They're getting closer," Fern warned tremulously. "You must run faster."

"We must hide," Spar corrected but he didn't know where. Soon, like the others, he was looking to Perren for help.

"You'll be safe underground where I can protect you like I did from the trappers. The wolves won't attack me," the stonewight said.

"How do you know?" Ursula asked.

"No animal has ever attacked a stonewight. The old ones told us that."

Caspar guessed he was referring to the great stonewights.

"And are old ones never wrong?" Ursula sounded sceptical. "I thought I had a father once that I could trust."

"They say that even a hooded wolf would break its teeth on me. Now don't waste your breath; we must hurry like Spar says."

It wasn't until they crossed into the next valley that Perren pointed to a blocky mountain half a league away, which was a goodly distance over the harsh terrain. The setting sun at their backs lit the huge block of rock ahead, its bulk split by several tumbling waterfalls, silvery-red in the twilight. The crack of a gorge showed as a dark slit.

Holding Lana under one arm and tugging Naith along by a rope, Perren's large silent feet swept him over the ground. He pointed to the mountain. "We'll head up there towards the gorge; that's the safest."

Ursula finally gave in to Caspar's demand and mounted Firecracker. With lungs bursting, the youth jogged alongside. Firecracker jittered and crabbed sideways, yanking his arm. Soon it was fully dark, the moon a mere slit and the stars barely visible for the humps of hungry clouds that, like great whales, scooped them up into the abyss of their black mouths.

"Wolf, wolf!" Fern piped, running close to Perren. "Hurry, hurry!"

An owl screeched out from the valley behind them and Firecracker, bursting with energy, his great hocks springy beneath him, snorted and half-reared, pulling Caspar off his feet. Ursula squealed but somehow managed to remain seated on the stallion. Like a ghostly shadow, the wolfling was lopping beside them but Trog was beginning to lag.

Caspar feared what a wolf might do to poor old Trog who had grown fatter in middle age and had never been good at covering large distances. Fern pressed close to Perren and continually looked down into the black bowl of the valley.

"Wolves!" he shrieked, unable to contain himself any longer. His neck was stretched long. "Run! Run!" He squealed with panic that infected Firecracker. The stallion reared and plunged, lifting Caspar off his feet. He feared for Ursula and, knowing that he could not control the stallion from the ground, scrambled up behind her.

They scattered. Fern vanished into the darkness above while Firecracker lowered his head and burst forward along the ridge, his hooves sparking on the treacherous boulder-strewn terrain. It took all Caspar's strength to hold Ursula upright before him, her body quite rigid with fear, and he never saw what happened to the others. Black shapes leapt out from behind jagged rocks and Firecracker shied and weaved.

But the wolves didn't attack. As before, he sensed they were being driven to where other wolves lay in wait. He had to do something. With his heart in his mouth, he yanked Firecracker's head round and spurred him down the plummeting slope, hoping to split the pack.

The stallion skidded, leapt and stumbled, grunting hard with the effort of bearing both riders who slid forward onto his shoulders. Like this, the horse could not run but kept his legs out before him, slithering on flexed hocks and wrenching up his neck to maintain balance. Gripping Ursula to his chest and leaning back in the saddle, Caspar guided Firecracker down into the dark of the trees, blinking as pine needles whipped into his face. He glimpsed the blurred white ghosts of Runa and Trog tumbling beside him.

Ursula stifled a scream. A wolf was on their tail; he could hear it give out a low moaning whoop as it caught the scent of their fear. He pressed Firecracker on, hoping that the purebred Oriaxian could outdistance the hooded wolf. Quickly, they left Trog and Runa far behind and he hoped the hooded wolves would ignore the two smaller animals for the horse, which was a more natural pray for a wolf.

They slithered and bounced from one tree root to the next until suddenly they reached the valley bottom where the trees were thinner and the ground relatively even. Once clear of the wood, at least he could see more in the twilight. They splashed through a stream and Caspar turned Firecracker to run along the valley floor and gave the stallion his head. The horse needed little encouragement as the black shapes of two wolves closed, one streaking across at an angle from the other side of the valley.

In the gloom and at this pace and with Ursula stiff before him, Caspar didn't have a hope of using his bow. He didn't try, knowing that all he could do was to get far enough ahead so that he could halt and take proper aim.

Firecracker was fast and willing, perhaps even faster now than he had been as a colt since the rough terrain of the Torra Altan mountains had hardened his muscles. But he carried an extra burden and Ursula, though clearly brave, bounced awkwardly, thumping down onto Firecracker's back mid stride.

"Cracker won't make it," she cried to him, her words snatched away by the roaring wind as they galloped. "Not with both of us."

Caspar felt her grip loosen and hugged her tighter about the waist, fearful that she would let go.

"You must make it," she insisted, struggling to get free. "You have to find Necrönd."

Caspar strained to hold her fast. "We've got time to make the gorge," he grunted. He could not sacrifice another human being, not one that depended on him. His fingers clawed deeper into her flesh. "Don't you dare let go," he hissed at her through gritted teeth.

They galloped on, stumbling and splashing through marshy hollows, plumes of steam puffing from Firecracker's mouth and rising off his flanks. The wolves were not as fast as the hot-blooded stallion, not over this distance anyhow, but Caspar feared that the horse's stamina would not last. The terrain was steepening and, heavily laden, Firecracker's long lean legs would lack the power to drive them upwards.

The horse heaved and panted and Caspar feared he was driving the animal to exhaustion. He steadied him slightly, believing that if he controlled his pace now, he would still be on his feet when they reached the top.

But he misjudged his timing and didn't have enough left in hand when a fresh wolf, unhindered by the chase, sprang out from the right where it had been perched on a grey ledge projecting from the valley shoulder. Firecracker could not increase his pace though he heaved and snorted. Caspar struggled for his knife and flung it into the dark and the wolf shrieked. But in that time another wolf, which he had not seen, sprang from the dark. Firecracker's quarters gave beneath him. The stallion bellowed in rage rather than fear, bucking and kicking. He fought his way free but lurched forwards awkwardly.

Wolves snapped at the horse's heels until one got a firm hold, biting into the ridge of tendon above the hock. Firecracker was down. Caspar hit the ground hard and rolled, Ursula's boot catching him in the mouth. He rolled again and came upright with his bow in his hand and an arrow nocked to the string. He fired at the wolf whose jaws raked through the horse's flank while Firecracker dragged himself forwards on his forelegs.

As he prepared to fire again, pain exploded through Caspar's leg. Dagger-long teeth sliced through the flesh of his thigh. He yelled at the wolf, his mouth wide in a ferocious scream, and hacked with an arrowhead but he could do nothing. With alarming strength, the wolf dragged him back, claws tearing through his leather leggings to the tender flesh beneath.

Jaws gripped his shinbone and his only thought was that the spare knife in his boot might prevent the beast from crushing his leg entirely. He could not move and knew that the wolf was pinning him down, waiting for another one of the pack to latch onto him, probably by the throat by which time he would know very little about it. He kicked out with his free foot, smashing into the animal's teeth and, for a moment, its grip loosened only to snap on a little higher up, this time around his knee cap. The teeth dug deep and grated against bone.

"Great Mother, mercy!" he cried, aware now of a white shape bounding towards him and the high-pitched squeals of a dog in pursuit. Only Trog could attack with such ferocity. The snake-catcher lunged straight for the wolf's neck, his eyes slitted to protect himself. He had a good hold and the wolf's grip on Caspar's knee weakened. He tore himself free and pushed himself to one knee but the hooded wolf and Trog were such a twisting tangle of black and white fur that he could not use his bow without risking the dog.

Runa, snarling like a banshee, came streaking to Trog's aid and sank her teeth into the wolf's foreleg. The noise of squeals and howls was horrendous, the sound so alien that Caspar couldn't tell who was making it. Though far smaller and despite being tossed and shaken as the wolf writhed, Trog held his grip on the hooded wolf's windpipe and the beast slowly sank to its knees. All were splattered in blood.

Ursula dragged at Caspar's arm. "Get up!"

Trog beat his tail feebly as the wolf collapsed under him, a thin trickle of blood oozing from its nose. The dog looked up at Caspar as if waiting for great appreciation but Caspar had no thought to praise him for the pain in his leg.

Firecracker scrambled up off the ground onto three legs, blood streaming down his quarters and puddling beneath his raised hoof. When Caspar tried to push himself upright, the pain shot up from his knee to his thigh. He slumped back, gritting his teeth.

Trembling with fear, Ursula stood over him with her knife raised, watching the hooded wolves approach with horror. "Come on! Get to your feet," she urged.

Caspar hastily tore a strip from his shirt and wound it around his knee, hoping that in some way it would make him able to cope but it did nothing to relieve the pain. "Ursula, go! Leave me!"

She sniffed at him as if he were mad. "I can't leave you, Master."

Caspar sensed the close presence of wolves. He glared into the darkness but could see nothing but the rounded black humps of rock and scrub. Then some patches of scrub began to move and he made out the shape of five wolves, low on their bellies, creeping forward out of the darkness. Trog stood with him, his back a bush, the thin moonlight slicing down to anoint his white coat and that of the wolfling beside him who continued to nudge at Caspar's elbow, urging him to his feet.

He reached for his bow, the quiver still heavy with arrows. He had perhaps twenty left but doubted that was enough. Shaking with pain, he pushed himself to his feet, the wet blood soaking down his leg. With his strength fading, he glared into the gloom, daring the wolves to move. He fired. A thrum and whistle sounded the arrow's flight that was followed by a muffled thud, then an unnatural scream, which rang out louder and louder, rising to a shriek. Wolves growled and one wailed out its lonesome song. Runa pressed close to Caspar's leg while Trog answered with a snarl so savage that it daunted even Caspar's spirit.

He fired blindly into the dark and fired again, hoping to deter them. But they rushed them in a whirlwind of fur, teeth and snarls. Trog leapt at the throat of the first while others streaked out of the dark in its wake. Caspar knew he could not kill them all. He fired, missed and fired again.

Ursula, who had flung herself to the ground at the first attack, now had gathered her courage and was seemingly incensed with the frenzy of battle. The screams, howls and smell of blood drove her fear into madness and she launched at a wolf to Caspar's left.

Weakening with pain, he swung giddily round to help the girl and loosed another arrow. The wolf screamed a hollow scream as it clawed its way forward on its belly, thick foul-smelling blood oozing from its mouth. Its anguished wail grew deeper and longer until it seemed that a thousand wolves screamed from the one throat and he knew that he could hear them in the land of spirit, clamouring for their freedom in this world, screaming in wretchedness to return to the Great Mother.

Its cry was answered by a bellowing roar. Startled, Caspar realized the noise was coming out of Ursula. The wolves fell silent. The night fell silent though the air still shimmered with the aftershock of that unearthly bellow.

Finally, the silence was broken by a deep grunt. A dark shape towered above him and Caspar slumped onto his hands with no strength left to him to draw his bow. After that, he heard nothing and fell to his side, watching his world fade away into a darkness tinged with red.

When his senses slowly returned, he heard only Firecracker's screams, his thrashing hooves tearing at the ground, and the grunts and heaves of some huge animal. Gone were the snarls and savage howls of the wolves. Trog's snarls became a cough and then a yip followed by silence. Caspar didn't have the strength left to open his eyes. He lay face down in the stony ground, wondering if this was what it was like to die in the midst of battle, confused by clashing sounds, his senses distorted by pain and fear. Slowly, even those sounds receded until, he was aware of nothing but the firm solid earth pressing against his cheek, the pain in his leg somehow distant and outside him.

The next he remembered was being aware of a swaying motion and great thick warm hair around him. It was comforting – just like being wrapped in his own bearskin. It dawned on him gradually that he was being carried. He could hear Firecracker's uneven footfall alongside him and someone, whom he thought to be Ursula, making strange ululating sounds. After a time, he was laid down and wrapped up warmly. For a moment, he heard the trickle of running water and smelt damp moss and ferns before the darkness of his mind welled up and he sank back into oblivion.

He awoke at dawn, his head clear. Blinking in the gloom, he saw he was in the back of a narrow cave or fissure, water trickling down the rocks. Ursula's long bronze legs, clad only in short fur boots and the tattered lionskin skirt that stopped halfway up her lean thighs, stood over him. Beyond her, blocking the mouth of the cave, was a large dark shape that gave out a series of low grunts.

A soft cold nose snuffled at Caspar's neck and he blurrily focused on two white snouts, one thin and long, the other blunt and somewhat smellier, lapping at his face. He could also hear the steady rhythmical munch of an animal grazing. He stirred and the big rock-shape silhouetted against the morning sun also stirred and he saw it was not a large boulder but a big creature, which stood to its two feet. The vast body of a brown bear filled the doorway.

It was strangely unperturbed by Ursula, Firecracker, the wolfling or the dog but, as soon as it was aware of his conscious state, it gave out a savage howl, swung one pendulous claw at a rock and sent a clash of scree toppling down from the mouth of the cave. Growling in threat, it approached with swinging steps. Caspar froze.

Ursula gave out a sharp cry and sprang in front of him, singing out a rhythmical, poetic chant. The bear sank down onto the ground like an obedient hound and almost purred as she rubbed its huge shaggy head. She patted it dismissively and the lumbering animal waddled back into the dawn light. Ursula waved her arm almost in farewell.

She was crying. "I didn't know that he would come, not after what I had done." The sobs overwhelmed her. "Will they ever forgive me? They would not have taken so many without me. It's my fault," she gasped. "I led them into captivity." She tore at her short black hair and looked at Caspar with red-raw eyes. "But he came." Dried blood streaked her arms, one or two wounds still gaping and moist. She looked for all the world like a savage cave-dweller. Taking a deep breath, she gathered her control. "You are better?"

"I'm awake," Caspar corrected, eyeing her nervously and wondering whether this strange creature would not herself turn into a bear at any moment. She glanced back towards the mouth of the cave and he elbowed himself up to see that they were in a narrow ravine lined with moss and ferns that climbed the sheer walls.

"Where are we?" he asked. "And Cracker? How's Cracker?"

"We made the gorge which Perren pointed out," she told him. "He will come soon. I remembered it was the last thing he said that we should head for the gorge. The wolves, surely, will not touch him."

Caspar thought, just as Ursula must have done, that neither Naith nor Fern could have outrun the wolves. He felt no sorrow at the loss of Naith but he felt an unexpectedly deep grief over Fern. He closed his eyes and prayed that Perren had looked after Lana. "And Cracker?" he croaked.

Ursula shrugged. "He's grazing but he can barely put any weight on his hind leg. He has angry wounds but I can't get anywhere near him to wash them."

Determined to help his horse, Caspar heaved himself to a sitting position but his head swam. He gritted his teeth. However ill he felt, he must get to Firecracker and wash the wounds. He slumped back and, trying to gather his strength, began to count. With great effort, he pushed away the bearskin that covered his legs and looked through the tears in his shredded breeches in horror at the blood-soaked mess of his knee. Ursula sucked in a sharp breath at the sight.

Strangely, Caspar felt less sickened by the wound than he might if it had been on someone else. First, he would have done something to heal himself before he could set about Firecracker. "Some water," he told Ursula who stood hovering over him uncertainly.

After such close liaisons with the three high priestesses, he was unaccustomed to women not knowing what to do and a broad though painful grin spread across his face, cracking the dried mud and blood that had caked his cheeks. In his early childhood, he had been taught to believe that women were in some way more delicate of nature and less able than men, however, he had suffered a rude awakening when he had met Brid. She had made a deep impression on all the other women in the castle who had learnt by her example that a woman could possess great knowledge. Even May, though she was always humble and reticent, had a quiet way of getting things done.

Caspar sighed, thinking how much he missed May with her beautiful thick hair and the smell of spices and herbs that surrounded her. Why had she run off like that at a time when he could not go after her? He slumped back and sighed with the pain of his tortured emotions.

"It's just not fair," he suddenly blurted at Ursula. "Though I love May with all my heart, I have to put my duties before her. She will understand, won't she? I must find Necrönd first before I can search the world for her. She would understand, wouldn't she?"

"Master, I don't know," Ursula replied. "I have never been in love nor am I bound by any duty. I merely am that I am and must do as I am bid."

"Oh," Caspar said weakly, his head reeling. He looked down at his knee and, with trembling fingers, peeled apart the torn strips of his leggings to look at the mushy flesh. "I need water. Bring me water. And in the saddle packs I have a selection of herbs."

"I can't get to the saddle packs," Ursula told him. "Your horse still has a vicious kick on him."

Caspar groaned. "All I need is willow bark to deaden

the pain and lower the fever so I can think . . ." he muttered. Already his skin was beginning to burn and his mind was clouded. His memory of how he got here was hazy. He knew there had been a great brown bear though that seemed quite ridiculous now in the daylight. The fever must be twisting his mind.

Ursula returned with the water and sat beside him, drawing strange shapes in the dust of the cave floor with a long, elegant finger. After he had drunk long and slaked his thirst, Caspar's head cleared enough for him to know that he must eat. He managed to pull himself to a sitting position; now he just had to get to his feet. "Poor Cracker," he murmured.

Ursula flicked a smile at him. "Master, you care."

"Care?"

"Yes, about the horse."

"Oh yes!" he replied ardently. "Of course."

She smiled. "I have lived long in Oriaxia. They admire their horses. They take great pride and cherish them for each is worth a fortune. But they do not care for them. They do not touch their hearts."

Though Ursula supported him under his arms, the effort of trying to stand exhausted Caspar. Sweat drenched his back. He pushed her away and slumped back onto the cold earth, while Ursula began to pace back and forth. "I don't know what to do," she admitted.

"Wash it," he gasped. "Wash the leg often."

He was kept warm by the wolfling and Trog, who both snuggled comfortably close to him, and felt himself drifting down into a sickened almost drunken sleep, his head slowly spinning. Ursula continued to pace distractedly. She had washed the wound and the touch of her hands had surprised him. He had expected her touch to be sensitive and tender but instead her hands were uncertain and fearful, as though unaccustomed to touching others. She sang as she tended him and this seemed to soothe her. Soft and melodious, her voice was not at all what he would have anticipated from her Oriaxian accent, the sound so haunting as if drifting across from the far side of a misty valley.

As she sang in her deep rich voice, the wolfling began to lick Caspar's wounds, the rhythmical sensation strangely comforting. He had not expected the wound to cause him so much trouble. He had been cut before – and often – with knives, swords and even suffered a wound from a crossbow bolt. In Torra Alta in fact, the size and nature of one's wounds was a matter of some bravado. Hal, of course, proudly displayed his scars at every opportunity, particularly his sliced earlobe and hand with its missing finger but none bore quite so many wounds as Ceowulf, though he was reluctant to show the marks of battle except when he seemed to feel that Hal needed putting in his place. Caspar wondered whether he would ever get the chance to display his new wound that now burnt as if the wolves were still tearing at his skin. He could not close his eyes without seeing them race towards him.

It had grown suddenly darker and he realized that Ursula's singing must have sent him to sleep though he still felt no stronger. In fact, he felt worse. The wound still bled and he knew he would die here if he did not move.

"He will come," Ursula said with certainty as she paced up and down. "He said he would come."

She fell silent for a while, watching the mouth of the cave, then looked thoughtfully towards Caspar's bow and finally moved to pick it up. He wondered for a moment whether at some time during her enslavement she had been in the gladiator ring. He had heard of sickened men who enjoyed the viciousness with which women were made to fight. Perhaps she would know what to do with a bow. She looked at the plain arc of wood, held it up one way then another and quizzically studied an arrow. Caspar was reminded instantly of the new recruits at Torra Alta.

Carefully, she placed the bow back at his side. "Perren will come."

Caspar was too weak to even wince. At last, the thin strip of sky that he peeked through the mouth of the cave turned to the violet of evening. The wan light of an evening star twinkled in the twilight.

"The wolves," he muttered. He knew it would not be long until they came. His jaw chattered uncontrollably.

Ursula wrapped his bearskin tightly around him and, though he could feel the sweat sliming his skin, he was still horribly cold.

"You are hot," Ursula complained, her face contorted with worry. "They should be here. I cannot call on the great Gods every time. They are angry with me for what I have done."

Caspar looked up helplessly at her. "I'm cold." His own voice sounded distant within his head.

She rubbed his hand and, when he continued to shiver, she slipped under the bearskin with him, fingering the soft fur pensively before finally wrapping her legs and arms around his body. She cuddled up to him but not as he had expected. Her embrace was neither like a mother's, nor sensual as a lover's, but was rather the clinging hug of a small frightened child. She tucked her head down onto his chest. After a while he realized she was crying softly but he did not have the strength to either question her or hold her tight for comfort.

She seemed so lost and utterly frightened but still her

close presence lent him strength. Nevertheless, he wished throughout the long hours of waiting that it was May's head resting against his head, saying she was sorry for running off like that and begging him to hold her through the night. With thoughts of May uppermost in his confused mind, he found the strength to close his arms around Ursula. She felt warm and strong against his sweating body.

Then at last he heard a voice.

"Hurry! Oh, for pity sake's hurry!"

Caspar sighed with relief. He never thought he would have been relieved to hear that high, excited voice again.

"We are hurrying," the slower deeper tones of Perren rumbled into the ravine.

"Look, the horse!" Fern squealed. "They are here. They are! I told you they would be."

"You did no such thing," Perren grumbled.

"Just because the horse is here, it doesn't mean that the others made it," Naith's more reasonable voice argued.

Trog growled low at their approach but soon stopped and gave a pleasured yip before returning to snuffle up against Caspar. The cave mouth blackened with the silhouette of four figures and he saw with relief that Lana was cradled against Perren's square bulk.

"What are you doing curled up with Ursula?" Fern piped indignantly. "The noble Cracker needs tending and look at you!"

"I knew you would come," Ursula said with satisfaction as if their arrival renewed her faith in life. "I knew you would come. Master Spar would not believe me but I knew."

Naith took his sister from Perren's arms and looked at Caspar in disgust. "She's a slave. She has no way to refuse you."

"I was cold," Caspar replied weakly, annoyed at having to explain himself.

"You've done nothing for the horse!" Fern snapped, standing in the mouth of the cave. "Nothing! I don't believe it. Lying there cradling the girl and the dogs. Dogs and girls are all you think about."

"I couldn't, really I couldn't," Caspar found himself trying to explain his actions to the woodwose and stopped himself. "Fern, just fetch Cracker in and wash his wounds. Thank the Mother you found us."

"You need me. You see, there are things that others cannot do. I am needed," Fern said grandly and looked sharply at Naith. "I am needed. And you are still a traitorous murderer. You should have been left for the wolves. But I'll fetch his horse; no one else can do it, you see."

Fern's glee was soon subdued by a sharp kick from the Oriaxian purebred but at least he managed to unsaddle him and bring over the packs. There was no food but there were medicines. None of the others knew how to use them except Fern who immediately pulled out some bloodwort. "Chew this," he suggested to Caspar. "It always makes me feel stronger."

The cave was plunged into darkness as Perren settled into the entrance and they all spent a long cold night, listening to the howls of wolves outside. Lana clung close to Ursula and Caspar continually gave silent prayers of thanks that the little girl was alive and well. He hoped it wouldn't be long before he could take her back to Keridwen and Brid.

He had little strength to listen to Fern's convoluted tale of how they escaped but it seemed that the wolves had turned to pursue Caspar and Ursula, forsaking the others. Perren had carried Lana and surprisingly Naith also, insisting that the shepherd still had a story to tell them. It appeared that other than Perren's desire for stories, Naith would have been abandoned or in some way finished off by the stonewight.

"I led them away," Fern insisted.

"You did nothing of the sort. They merely chased after Master Spar." Naith sounded irritated and Caspar noted a subtle change in the way the Ovissian referred to him. *Master* Spar, indeed!

"Nobody is listening to you," Fern insisted. "You're a traitor and now Spar will pronounce judgement over you."

Caspar felt disinclined to do any such thing. He barely had the strength to even understand what was going on.

Perren insisted on hearing Naith's tale and was disappointed when the hefty youth protested that he had told all he knew.

"I've told you," he began. "We thought we were helping Baron Godafrid by going to kill the wolves in their Torra Altan breeding grounds. He said, too, that we should capture the bears lest you, the wizards and warlocks of Torra Alta, sent them next to plague us. Soon we were caught up with Mamluc, the slave-driver and his bear trade. Ursula would take the bears from us and after that I have no idea what happened to them."

"You have no idea who was organizing it all?" Caspar found the strength to ask. Throughout that night, the cold had crept back into his bones though his skin was afire as if the elements warred over him.

Naith shrugged. "Mamluc, I thought."

Caspar found that unlikely. Any man planning such a grand scheme would be unlikely to get his hands dirty with it. Caspar tried to fix Naith with his eyes to see if he could read the truth but could not hold his gaze for his sick headache.

"His blood needs letting," Naith said with conviction.

Fern shuddered at the very thought. "Blood!"

"I'm cold," Caspar moaned.

Perren put his hard hand on his forehead. "In my opinion, earth's surface creatures die all too easily," he said with some lack of emotion and sighed regretfully at this inevitable fact. "Once there was a man that came from the northernmost reaches where the world was blue-white with ice and he survived long enough to tell us five hundred tales or more but even he died in the end. He lasted the longest."

"Perren, that's not helpful," Ursula rebuked, again sliding alongside Caspar and wrapping him up in her arms for the shared warmth.

The next morning, they knew they must move on but it was clear that Caspar could not walk and that Firecracker could not carry him. The horse limped severely and could bear no weight on his off hind.

"Gentle exercise will be good for him; help clear out the poisons," Caspar said, trying to cover up his distress at the sight of Firecracker's injuries. He had to content himself by being carried, along with Lana, on Perren's broad shoulders. Naith was pushed to the front of the file where all could see him.

They set out eastwards towards the sea where Perren said he sensed Necrönd. At last, they broached the head of a valley to see the ground sloping away and the deep golden reflection of the sun rippling on the wide expanse of water.

Perren gasped, a strangely deep and hollow sound. "The sea!" he cried. "The great waters of the Mother, the great womb, the great oneness that links all parts of her body, flowing, linking,, seeping together, bringing us all together," he exclaimed with passionate exuberance. The rest admired the sparkling expanse simply for its beauty.

A sense of hope grew in Caspar that here at last his journey must end; Morrigwen had sent him east and here he was on the very eastern shores of Torra Alta. The lights of a coastal village blinked ahead and he was hopeful that they would soon find help and Necrönd.

The lights were not those of the village but a watch tower on the cliff-top. When they drew level with it, they peered down to see the great scatter of twinkling lights lining the cliff-face and lanterns bobbing from masts and rigging on the ships at anchor beyond a bay sheltered by a line of rocks. Craning forward from Perren's shoulders to look down at the village that clung to the cliff, Caspar knew instantly that something was wrong. Great plumes of smoke rose from beacon fires all along the beach.

"You'd best bandage your face and hands," Caspar told the horny-skinned stonewight. "We'll say you've been scarred by the pox but you must cover yourself otherwise folk will panic."

They waited while Ursula and Perren shredded a blanket taken from Caspar's pack and patiently wound strips around the stony-grey of Perren's coarse-grained skin. Once they had finished, Perren slung Caspar's bearskin over his mossy clothes to disguise the strangeness of his great body. Fern, in the meanwhile, was snuffling at the coarse grasses sprouting along the top of the cliff.

"Wolf, wolf. He's here! I can smell him," Fern was shrieking like a madman.

Men disgorged from the watchtower, brandishing boat hooks and gutting knives at Caspar and his friends.

"That's rum company." A man glared as the dishevelled party approached. "Like as not it's one of them as drowned old Granny Grebe."

CHAPTER EIGHTEEN

Grappling hooks and gutting knives rattled in Caspar's face.

The prefect of Kittiwake Cove scowled suspiciously. "The Baron's son indeed! And what would the Baron's son be doing travelling with the likes of these fellows?" He warily eyed Perren bandaged in cloth and muttered about pox and skin diseases, before fixing more aggressively on Fern. "And some kind of dwarf."

"I'm not," Fern blurted in offence but Perren nudged him to be quiet.

"There's been too many strange folk about of late," the prefect continued, tapping his staff on Caspar's shoulder. "And the last one – a grandly dressed man looking for all the world like a proper nobleman, I might say – left us good money to look out for the likes of a quirky-looking band like you. Outlaws, rogues, villains, he said, wanted by the Baron for treachery. He said to stop you going by." He snorted disdainfully at Caspar and then turned to his fellow men. "Do we believe this ruffian, who comes limping out of the mountains with a band of misfits, that he's the good Baron's son or do we believe the finely dressed gentleman with the purple robe and the purse of gold?"

He prodded Caspar's chest with his staff. "You look like rogues, the lot of you. And look at your horse! No respectable Torra Alta would allow his horse to walk on such an injury."

Caspar wanted to explain that the injury was superficial and that the gentle exercise would help loosen Firecracker up but he was too confused for clear thought. He wished that Hal was with him. His head was giddy and his leg throbbed with pain. He had tried, in stammered exhausted sentences, to explain himself but no one was going to believe him. If only Hal were there. Just like Caspar's father, Hal exuded confidence – whatever his attire. A wound would only add to his plausibility. In fact, Caspar couldn't understand why Hal continually moaned that he needed a suit of armour to be taken seriously. The idea was absurd.

He looked uncertainly at the prefect and nudged at his crooked nose while Trog marched stiffly forward and officiously sniffed at the man's calves. The prefect tapped his staff decisively on the ground and then swung it to point along the road to the village. "It seems you had best come with us till this is sorted."

With knives at their backs, there was little they could do but comply and allow themselves to be marched down into the village. Caspar leant heavily against Perren for support. They were brought to a halt outside an inn called the *Hungry Fishermen* that overlooked the seafront. The doors were wide open, revealing a fire roaring within. A buzzing crowd was gathered without.

It appeared that the villagers had not mustered for their benefit but had been formed for some while, gossiping excitedly over a recent event. One man, with a broad toothy grin brightly engaged their attention and, even as they arrived, he was made to repeat his story.

"Went overboard, he did. Some devil or perhaps the ale or maybe both got into poor old Derry and he went berserk and tried to murder our passenger. I tried to stop him but he fought me so hard and fell overboard in the struggle. Then he was drowned and gone in seconds and we had no chance to pull him out. And old Granny Grebe! We found her washed out to sea, body all bloated and floating near Mermaid's Door yet she'd been seen on the shore when we left!"

"It was the moon! You should never have gone out so soon after a new moon," an old woman scolded. "'Twould never have happened under a good moon."

The men of the inn turned to stare at Caspar and his company who were thrust into their midst. One of the older fishermen said with an air of doom, "Weren't we warned to look for trouble and a band of ill-looking ruffians just like this. And we got it. Within the last three days we've had Derry mad and dead, and Granny Grebe drowned! Someone should take them through the Mermaid's Door and fling them overboard before they bring more disasters on us."

"I'm Baron Branwolf's son. Touch me and my father will wreak his vengeance on you!" Caspar threatened.

The prefect shook his head, looked at his feet, seemingly studying the shiny brass buckles on his shoes, and shifted his weight to and fro. "Perhaps we shouldn't be too hasty." He cast a sideways glance at Caspar. "If you are what you say then you should have no problem proving it."

"I heard the Baron and his men were all a head higher than six foot," someone muttered from the crowd.

Caspar hastily pointed out the clasp of his cloak and the insignia on his ring but the villagers shrugged. Any noble of the Caballan would have understood their importance but clearly it meant nothing to these isolated villagers.

"Fine work, mighty fine, but it could be made of tin for all I know."

"How else can I prove myself?" Caspar asked in exasperation, wondering how he had allowed this humiliation to happen. His leg hurt and his head swam and he found it impossible to find an argument that these idiots would believe.

The village prefect looked long and hard at Caspar and his five strange companions. "Never, in all my life, have I seen so odd a bunch of travellers. By rights, I should have you locked up just for the way you look, yet there's something about you I like and I won't sleep easy till I know the truth of the situation. I'd ask a fisherman to prove his worth by catching fish or see him knot his nets. Now a nobleman from Torra Alta would be mighty handy with a bow, would he not? And where's yours? Everyone knows that the warlords of Torra Alta are the finest archers in all the world."

Caspar couldn't help but grin, warmed at the respect these people held for his household even if they didn't credit him with such talents.

"My bow's in my pack," he said with confidence. "Show me your mark and I shall prove myself."

The crowd evidently did not agree with their prefect and began shouting irately. They had recently lost two villagers and were sorely in need of venting their anger. "String his girl by her hands and hang her from the mast of the far ketch there. "One pointed to the end of the pier. "And let's see if he can cut her down with his bow. It's a good distance and there's a swell. If he misses, they're all guilty and we'll hang the lot of them by the neck. If he can cut the rope, then none of us will doubt him."

"What if he hits her, though?" the prefect objected.

"Then he ain't a Torra Altan lord," one of the villagers happily pointed out.

Perren moaned threateningly and Caspar felt his stone-hard muscles twitch. "No," he hissed, tugging back the stonewight's arm, fearing that he would crush one of the villagers in his huge fists. "These are my people and I'll have no bloodshed. Let me prove myself."

Ursula's dark eyes glanced pleadingly at Caspar. "It's too far; you'll, you'll—" She left her fears unspoken and raised her chin bravely as she was marched to the end of the pier. Her hands trussed up above her head, she was hauled up the mast that swayed to the soft rhythm of the harbour waves. Caspar was to cleave the knot between her wrists though they had put Ursula at an almost impossible distance.

Naith protested that he would never do it. "Never! You'd be a murderer to try. I've seen men go after deer and they've missed them at fifty yards. That's nearer a hundred. You'll never do it. And look at you. You're shaking and sweating."

"Just hurry up, Spar," Fern twittered, apparently oblivious to the severity of the situation. "I can smell him. He was here."

Caspar blotted all the clamour from his mind, breathing evenly until he was aware only of Ursula and the tension in his trusted bow. He needed just one moment of strength and lucidity. From here he could not see her expression but was glad because he knew the fear in her eyes would daunt him. Abelard had told him that archery was nine-tenths practice and one-tenth faith. Caspar had practised every day of his life and forced the thought of Ursula's doubts from his mind. Of course, he could do it! He could hit a moving target from the saddle, he could do this; the sea had rhythm. Synchronising his breathing with the swell, he tensioned the string and let the arrow fly.

The crowd gasped. Ursula sagged to her knees and Caspar stumbled forward as Perren slapped him roundly on the back, his ears ringing with cheers from the crowd.

Now that the ordeal was over, he fixed on a mooring post and lurched towards it, sitting with his head slumped between his knees before he would faint.

"Split the rope clean in two!" men hollered from the end of the quay. Brushing off helping hands, Ursula plucked out the arrow from the wood and lithely leapt ashore, walking with grave dignity back towards him. She tossed her head and raised her eyes to his. He had expected to see resentment and anger for putting her in such danger but instead she smiled with admiration.

"Master, your arrow," she said with respect.

Naith was still choking in disbelief. "There's not another man in the realm could have hit such a target."

"Well, there's a few," Caspar said truthfully.

The prefect brushed down his clothes, red-faced with consternation. "The other man was so believable, sir. Accept our apologies."

Caspar tried to wave his blusterings aside but the effort and fatigue got the better of him and he slumped to the ground. Faint with his injuries, he gripped his knee and tried to make sense of the spinning world before him.

"If Granny Grebe were here, she'd like as not have a cure for you," one of the villagers said regretfully. The fishermen all nodded and many of them held up healed scarred and cut fingers from knives and fishhooks, an impressive array of wounds that would have won acclaim at the castle.

"Best put some spirit over it, I guess," someone else suggested.

An old woman sloshed neat brandy over his leg and he stiffened, swallowing a scream; he had not expected the sudden pain. They held him down and doused him again, raw hot pain burning his leg. He slumped in resignation and let himself be carried to a bed where he lay and slept solidly for two days without knowing anything of it.

When he awoke, he felt a good deal better though he was still limping as he stumbled down creaking stairs for some breakfast. His companions were already eating and Ursula jumped to her feet to welcome him, expressing her joy at his regained health. Caspar did not like fuss and hurriedly told her to sit down while he drew back a chair and grabbed some bread and creamy butter that no doubt had come fresh that day from neighbouring Jotunn. Alerted to Caspar's restored health, the village prefect soon entered the inn and smiled apologetically, bowing awkwardly and ushering forward the old woman who had doused Caspar with brandy. She shuffled forward, offering him a murky-looking potion in a green vial.

"Tincture of melilot, sir. Granny Grebe used to make it. I believe it's good for the blood. And here's some fresh herbs I picked in case you have need of more."

Caspar studied the suspicious-looking liquid doubtfully and forced a grateful smile onto his face. "I won't forget such kindness." He reached out his hand to take the gift, put the fresh melilot into his pocket and placed the vial by his drink. "I'll take some with water in just a moment," he told her.

She grinned, evidently pleased to have been of service. Caspar was relieved when she left since he had no wish to touch the potion. He had little faith in her herblore and didn't want to poison himself. As soon as she had bobbed a curtsey and left, he pocketed the vial so that she wouldn't know he hadn't drunk the contents. She had been kind and he had no wish to offend her.

He turned back to the prefect who was waiting ceremonially behind the woman. "Where did this stranger go who was so determined to blacken my name?"

The prefect shrugged. "Back into the mountains as far as we know."

"But the wolf?" Fern insisted. "What about the wolf?"

"There's been no wolf." The prefect looked puzzled.

"He doesn't look like a wolf," Caspar said dismissively, his temper made short by the dull ache that remained in his leg, and unaware that his explanation sounded ridiculous. "We're looking for a tall man who was dressed in wolf-skins but it seems he's got himself some finery now."

Fern sniffed at the description. "He's no man. He smells of wolf. Unmistakable."

"I saw a wolf," an old sailor spoke out in triumph. "I told everyone I'd seen a wolf though no one listened. Up by old Granny Grebe's dwelling."

After breakfast, they climbed to the spot, Caspar breathing heavily, his limp worsening. Fern dropped onto his knees, sniffing the ground and then leapt up as if he had been stung by a bee.

"He was here." He sniffed around for some while, tracking north along the cliff top. "He's been here once – maybe twice." Fern was joined by the wolfling who sat back on her haunches and howled.

A few outlying dwellings, hunched behind the lee of outcrops and shaded by trees permanently bowed by the onshore breeze, were visible some distance ahead. They hammered on several doors to no effect but then a young man, who apparently gathered gulls' eggs for a living, approached from the cliff top. While studying the eggs in his basket, he shyly said that he rarely saw any folk but certainly, a tall man in a purple robe had headed past. "Went that way." He waved his hand north along the cliff top.

*

The villagers made up large packs of dried, salted and pickled fish, the latter stuffed into gourds and, with some relief, waved Caspar and his companions on their way. Firecracker was fresher and eager to pace out but Caspar still led him to spare his injured hind-leg. They had gone no distance before Fern was tempted to nibble at the fish, claiming it wasn't at all the same as eating real animals.

Though Ursula, as usual, kept her head bowed and her thoughts to herself, Perren and Naith accused him of being quite mad and the argument only abated when Fern excitedly announced that they had picked up the trail again. Scampering in circles, he rushed backwards and forwards, every few minutes crying, "Wolf!" which Caspar soon found very tiresome.

On their second day out from Kittiwake Cove, the ground dipped more gently towards the sea, the thin soil of the cliff-tops turning to softer turf. Here, they saw the first actual footprints. They were made by long thin boots, slightly pointed at the end, and surely, they belonged to a tall lanky man, Caspar guessed.

"It might just be an innocent shepherd or the like that made them," Naith said sceptically as they waded through a shallow stream where Firecracker stopped to drink.

Fern looked at him in disbelief. "Have you no nose? Oh, I see! You're still trying to lead us off the trail to stop us finding your master. I have not forgotten that you are a traitor."

Naith lifted one side of his upper lip and snarled at Fern who leapt back in alarm. Perren's slow eyes roved past Naith and settled on Caspar. "He doesn't want to be a traitor. He believes you are the Baron's son and thinks that there is good in your heart but still distrusts you. He doesn't understand why your father hasn't ordered these wolves exterminated, these hooded wolves that are till savaging their way through Ovissia and he is angry."

Naith jumped in surprise. "How did you know that?"

Perren kicked his foot through the shallows, sending up a spray of water. "Your thoughts are in the water."

Caspar pouted but had little thought for Naith, wondering instead whether this wolf-smelling man had not already tampered with Necrönd. "I knew I could trust Morrigwen when she said to go east."

Fern snorted. "This is the very same scent I picked up at Torra Alta. He could well have skirted the southern edge of the Yellow Mountains and we would undoubtedly have caught him up by now if we hadn't struggled through the mountains."

Not for the second time, Caspar wondered whether Morrigwen hadn't sent him this way so that he might find Lana. He remembered that the wren had chosen a rune marked with the combination of symbols for the oak, the ash and the hawthorn. At first, he had thought that had signified Fey Grove but clearly he had been wrong and the meaning more profound. Perhaps the third part of the rune representing Huathe, the hawthorn, which carried the meaning of chastity and restraint, was actually meant to signify the Maiden though he thought that was the role of Beorc. He pondered on this thought for some time but could come to no logical conclusion; he simply didn't have the knowledge.

He could not walk fast and leant heavily on his staff for support as they followed the rolling coastline, startling gulls and puffins that suddenly swept up unexpectedly from the cliffs below. Perren was some way ahead when he raised a hand in warning and strode purposefully back. "There's a line of men in the valley ahead."

Ursula cursed as they crept forward on hands and knees

and peered over the brow down into the next stony valley that cut its way towards the sea. "My bears!"

Clanking chains were pulled taught around the necks of four snarling bears. Teams of men struggled to restrain them. Whips cracked viciously.

"He's close!" Fern squealed, excitedly jumping up and pointing. His high voice rang through the valley and a few of the men far below looked up curiously. Caspar pulled Fern's legs from under him and dragged him back out of sight.

"More Ovissian shepherds and more Ceolothians," Caspar observed. "They're a harsh people, the Ceolothians. I might have guessed it would be Ceolothians taking the bears. They consider the meat to be a great delicacy and—" He stopped short at the sight of Ursula's expression.

"Don't you talk to me about bear-murdering Ceolothians!"

"So, the wolfman has joined Mamluc's bear trappers." Caspar considered the thought. "He's surrounded himself with a hundred men. How now do we get to him?"

"My bears! They've got my bears! I can't let this happen anymore," Ursula wailed emotionally. "We must attack!" Her voice was a snarl of passion.

Naith sneered at her. "We're a ragged band and they're a strong force."

"They have my bears."

"We can't attack," Caspar said reasonably. "We must follow them and wait for the wolfman to make a move away from the column."

"What about my bears?!" Ursula's voice was impassioned and she thumped the ground with clenched knuckles.

"I'm sorry," Caspar apologized. "If there was anything I could do . . ." He screwed up his eyes, trying to make out which one of the distant figures might be the wolfman, but he could not.

Unobserved, they followed the bear traders all that day without once seeing anyone break away from the line. The following few days were the same and, though Caspar gradually grew stronger, he was becoming increasingly frustrated that no opportunity arose for them to get at the wolfman. Every night Ursula wept for her bears despite Fern and Lana's best efforts to comfort her. Caspar avoided her company, wary of her accusatory looks as if it were his fault that the bears were chained and dragged across the landscape. She seemed most unslavelike in her behaviour.

Twice in the days that followed, the bears managed to hook their claws over their chains and jerk men towards them. Three men in all were struck, the last one so heavily that, even from that distance, they saw his neck was broken, his body left to rot on the cliff top. Gulls swooped from the sky to mob it.

The coastline gradually became less rugged and the cliffs gave way to rolling hills. Still, Caspar could think of no plan. He knew he must do something soon, though, because out to sea he could see ships, long-nosed crafts without sails, oars blinking in the sunlight. They were headed straight for the coast, no doubt to pick up the bears.

He looked down on the flat sea that encroached into a deep inlet, the surrounding land covered in reeds and patterned by black water lying in grey hollows and veiled with ribbons of mist. The mist sapped the colour from the land that lay in lazy milky shades, sometimes swallowing the feet of islands, their wooded heads emerging like monsters from the flat sea. The air was damp and cold.

Across the marsh three chained bears, followed by a cub that screamed like a human baby, were dragged toward the approaching boats. Long and thin with their oars pointing straight upwards to clear the banks, they slid silently up to a rickety platform that rose above the reeds and overlooked the flat salt marshes. The bears were not immediately loaded on board but were thrown into a huge, covered cage alongside the jetty. Men disgorged from the boat and joined the others to erect tents around the cage. A large octagonal tent stood centrally midst the lesser canvases.

"We shall wait until twilight. The boats will need time to take on water and they won't disembark tonight. I'll investigate the camp and creep up on this man that's stolen Necrönd," Caspar announced his hasty plan, wishing that he had taken action much earlier. Now he had the men in the boats to contend with as well. "Let's get off the brow, cut inland before working our way down into the estuary. We could hide out upstream of them amongst the reeds."

On reaching the mudflats, they crouched low and watched the tide go out, leaving the boats lying helplessly on their sides. Then they waited for the sun to go down behind the Yellow Mountains that turned from a brilliant gold, fired with points of red, to black angry teeth gnashing at a violet sky. The ripples and folds in the shallow mudflats caught the sun's rays, pools of water trapped in the shadows lying like ribbons of molten gold in the black sand. They could still hear the rhythmical pulse of the waves far out across the mudflats though the sea was now cloaked in darkness.

Caspar got to his feet. "It's time to make a move," he said, looking around for approval from his strange companions.

"You shouldn't go alone," Perren told him.

Caspar examined the blade of his hunting knife that he drew from his belt. "Necrönd is my responsibility. Alone, I have a better chance of creeping into the camp undiscovered." He looked around at them all and his heart fell to the pit of his stomach. Ursula was missing.

He snatched up his bow. "Oh, that fool girl! She's gone after the bears. Naith, give me your smock."

Slipping the garment over his head, he concealed his bow beneath and ran down towards the camps, his short knife ready for action. The salt marsh was more difficult to cross than he had imagined. The tide left sheets of wallowing water trapped in the hollows and, though in daylight he had seen how the network of marram grass banks had criss-crossed above the dark water, he was now lost in the maze of paths and was forced into the water to keep his course. Wading up to his thighs, he was careful to hold his bow up clear of the water to keep the string dry. By the time he reached the camp, he was feeling fearful and confused. He experienced none of the weightiness that he always felt when Necrönd was close; he wondered whether that was because he had failed as its guardian and it no longer called to him.

Shivering, he wrung out the hem of his over-sized smock that had dragged through the water and assessed his position. He did not like this place. The moon was not yet up and, apart from the orange glow of the fires, and grey-white will-o'-the-wisps that hovered over the flats, blackness enveloped the land.

He knew what he must do and, straightening the smock, he ambled nonchalantly into the camp as if he belonged there. Surely no one would question a man in a shepherd's smock. With so many men in the camp he trusted that no one would wonder that they didn't immediately recognize him. Naith had said how the groups of Ovissians were always being moved about. He headed purposefully for the largest tent, assuming that the wolfman would naturally take the grandest sleeping quarters. If he had Necrönd, he commanded power.

He stopped short as he reached the back of the octagonal canvas.

"A fine blade, Mamluc. Extraordinary metal. A present for me, no doubt."

There was a shuffle and grunt and Mamluc's deep husky voice said with embarrassment, "Well, no sir; I meant it for—"

"Of course, you mean to ingratiate yourself with your master," the other man said with sneering condescension. "Now, have I made myself clear? The bears must go. Every one," the sharp Belbidian voice ordered. It had a chilling edge that made his flesh creep. Caspar knew his countrymen well but could not place the accent. It was bland, neither rustic nor educated. It continued, "I have discussed the matter at great length with your esteemed master and those are our instructions."

"But I must point out that this exercise is costly in men. Isn't it possible that we have taken enough bears now to make each and every one of us a fortune?" Mamluc argued. Caspar would never have imagined that Mamluc could sound so unsure of himself.

"Do you dare defy or question me?" the Belbidian said with menace, a grumbling growl sounding in his throat. The hairs on the back of Caspar's neck stood on end.

"As you so rightly reminded me, I am my master's servant and I follow only his instructions," Mamluc replied hastily.

The other man laughed derisively. "My dear man, you have no need to worry; I have his seal. Look for yourself." The unmistakable scrunch and rustle of parchment reached Caspar's ears. "His wishes are for all the bears, every one. The rest of Belbidia is too slow to rise up against Torra Alta, complacently hoping that these problems will vanish. If we ship them down into Quertos then every baron will soon be demanding that Torra Alta be taken under the crown. There will be no more tolerance towards the pagans of Torra Alta when they find the brown bears of Branwolf's Mountains in their vineyards and orchards."

Caspar was certain he was right. The lowlanders would cry that Torra Alta's devilry was spreading across the country. The poor bears would cause havoc through the populated farmlands before they were all speared and burnt. Then the people of southern Belbidia would rise up in anger against Torra Alta.

He was about to slither out of the camp and bide his time until the occupant of the octagonal tent slept, when a terrible shriek pierced the air. It came from the bear pens. All about him men leapt to their feet, brandishing firebrands that left behind them streaming trails like the tails of miniature comets.

The bears were loose, crashing through the camp. Men screamed. A strange ululating sound followed them. Ursula! What mad havoc was she causing? Like the men around, Caspar too fled back from the three bears that pressed close around Ursula, rampaging through the camp towards the central tent.

"Slave!" Mamluc's terrible voice rose above the uproar as he burst out of the tent. "Your crimes exceed even your worth, slave-woman." He raised a spear and flung it but Ursula leapt aside before it could harm her.

Like a bear herself, she turned and let out a roar, a scream so deep as if the very soul of a bear lived within her. The bears paced protectively around her, the woman exuding a certain power. Even so, Caspar was distracted by a prickling sensation that ran up his spine and he found himself compelled to turn back to look at the tent.

The tent flaps were pulled back and several men

emerged into the firelight to surround Mamluc, whose ghastly squint-eyed face was twisted with anger and made darkly mysterious by the flickering shadows cast by the fire. He roared at Ursula. But it was not the sight of Mamluc that filled Caspar with fear. A tall man in a purple robe, a great wolf mask over his head, had slipped out behind them and was gone, striding away from the commotion into the shadows. Despite his height, he was almost invisible in the veil of mist that coiled around him.

Caspar was convinced he was the one they sought. Instinctively, he ducked into the shadows. There was something terrible about the man and it was not simply the wolf pelt and skull that gave a chilling aura about him. No, it was what was behind that mask that was so terrible, something that he could sense but could not see.

Ursula was crying in terrible tones, "Men of Ovissia, stand aside and the bears will not harm you. Don't you see, you are being used by your Ceolothian masters?"

The men faltered, uncertainly.

Mamluc brandished a thick bladed spear and in a deep, husky voice encouraged them to attack. Though some threatened with firebrands and short spears, none came too close for fear of the bears and most seemed uncertain.

Suddenly another voice rose amongst them. "Fellow shepherds, she speaks true!" Naith was pushing through the men to stand between them and Ursula's bears. "We are being betrayed by these men; they have no intention of destroying the wolves, rather they welcome them; they welcome anything that stirs up resentment against Torra Al—" His last word burst from his lips unfinished, the point of a spear stabbing out through his ribs. His hands raked awkwardly at the point of entry midway up his back while he looked in bewilderment at the sliver of metal protruding from his chest as if unable to accept his mortality. Blood oozed from his chest and trickled over his fingers.

"Naith! But it's Naith!" a trapper shouted.

He stumbled to his knees, the gurgle of his blood-filled lungs loud in the shocked silence. Then in splutters he croaked, "Ursula, beware the wolf-master." His trembling hand rose to point at Mamluc.

Ursula shook her head and reached out her hand to him. Naith sank back onto his haunches, leant his head against the girl's thigh and stared unblinking at Mamluc. The light was gone from his eyes.

Caspar looked on in horror. Poor Naith! Whoever Mamluc was, he was no wolf-master, that was certain. He had limited powers. Sweating, Caspar gripped his bow but had no idea what he could do to help either of them. He was on the point of bursting forward in rage when Perren, without his bearskin and standing in such a way that he appeared in the gloom to be no more than a rock, appeared at his elbow. The stonewight held him back.

"The man is finished and the girl mad. You will achieve nothing but your own death; you have a greater purpose still to achieve."

"But they – they need me," Caspar stuttered uncertainly. Perren's grip was far stronger than a man's and he had no way to free himself.

"The tent, Spar," Perren said slowly. "You can do nothing for him now but you can take this opportunity to search for the Druid's Egg. Only that matters. The old ones were right when they said we could not trust this quest to a man."

Caspar nodded and worked his way forward to slide behind the tent flaps. Once inside, he looked around, his heart racing. The place stank of animal, though that was hardly surprising for the number of pelts lying uncurled and bloodstained in heaps on the floor for bedding. There was little by way of furnishing and it took him no time to rifle through the skins and belongings. He was in such a hurry that he almost overlooked the circle. It was scratched into the earth around the bedding and clearly had some magical purpose. Small scratchy sigils marked the perimeter of the ring. He looked at them carefully but they meant nothing to him.

Runelore was an involved and complicated art to learn and, though he had mastered the basics, he did not recognize the rare sigils before him. Still, his flesh crept at the sight and he was certain they served some evil purpose. He rummaged through the tent again but was already convinced that the Egg was not there. Hurrying back to Perren, he shook his head in disappointment and turned to look for Ursula.

His spear poised, Mamluc stood facing her and the three bears that she held at bay. As Caspar watched, he plunged it into Naith's belly, twisting it savagely. A great sadness swelled in Caspar's heart. The young shepherd had been a traitor but had repented and Caspar was deeply grieved that there had been nothing he could do to help him.

It was too much for Ursula. The bears towered up over the crowd at her command and the Ovissians shrank back. Caspar thought that she and the bears would charge free until an icy shriek sounded from the perimeter of the camp. At first, he saw nothing, then he made out what he thought to be the hump of wolf. Then he saw something slithering towards the camp as if it had no strength nor form, a darkness blacker than the night. Giving out a spine-chilling shriek, the blackness gathered speed and, like a poisoned arrow, flew at the bears.

The bear nearest Ursula began to shiver and quake, black foam bubbling around its mouth and dribbling in shafts of thick saliva to wet the earth. It reared up and lashed at its face, half tearing out an eye. Its convulsions ceased abruptly and it dropped to all fours and charged at Ursula. The colour washed from her face.

CHAPTER NINETEEN

May snatched away her hand as if she had been scorched by fire. Biting her lip and cradling the fingers of her right hand, she eyed the silver casket for a long moment before gingerly stretching out towards the shell a second time.

As before, the atmosphere became charged with the energy of life. Soft warm breath caressed the skin at the back of her neck. Hazy outlines of spiny creatures with horns, long snouts and protruding teeth stooped over her, their minds bent on hers.

"Get away from me," she snapped peevishly and swung her arms about as if warding off a swarm of wasps.

They obeyed her command with malicious sloth and none of the respect she had anticipated. She had thought she would feel like an empress or least command the respect of a high priestess but she did not. She felt like a hated slave-driver.

"I'm-I'm sorry," she stammered feebly, her hands falling open in a gesture of helplessness.

She sensed no softening towards her, only loathing which, like the hatred that fires a feud through generations, ran so deep that they no longer even knew the reason for it but accepted it as a part of their very existence. With predatory stealth, the hazy images were soon pressing forward again, their combined presence of mind so strong that it all but cracked the air.

It was the terrorising closeness of the beasts that finally goaded her daunted spirit into action. Though no more than ghosts, she could feel them sucking on the power of the Egg, desperate to claw their way back to life. She snatched it up, fearful that they would take it from her.

The energy within the Egg jolted against her touch, a deep nerve pain jabbing through her body. Determinedly, she closed her fist, telling herself that the small oval shape was designed to fit her hand. The pain receded slowly, leaving her with an unexpected sense of vulnerability. She had anticipated a surge of power to charge her body as if she had grasped at a bolt of lightning. Instead, she felt only fear. The creatures' loathing grew in a burst of blackness that stabbed at her hands, peeling her fingers back from the shell. When her grip held fast, she sensed their hesitancy, an expectant hold of breath, and then their grudging acceptance of defeat.

Adrenaline gushed through her veins, her stomach fluttered, and her mouth went dry, every muscle of her body taut with anticipation. She held the Egg at arms' length, eyes agog, staring at the marbling of blue veins and the jagged scorch mark marring its creamy surface, waiting for something to happen. Acutely aware of the bloated tension, she realized that everything was waiting on her but still she did not know what to do. She had so little time.

Amaryllis said it would take him an hour at the most to buy horses for them. He had left her alone in the Ceolothian port of Skuas Ria, sitting in a quayside tavern with her back to a wall where the vast skin of a white bear covered the cold stonework. The skins of white seals carpeted the floor and a huge fire roared against the bitter wind that threatened snow.

Shying from the Ceolothians around her, she had kept

her head down until she was certain Amaryllis was long gone from the inn before creeping out the back and into the open, pulling her bearskin close about her against the cold. Pockets of tired snow still lay in the hollows on the north faces of the surrounding hills and the air was ringing with the bark of seal pups.

The port stretched in a narrow ribbon of low dwellings inland, busy streets crowding down to the water's edge, the houses built of an unfamiliar dark reddish stone. Above the inn, the ground rose rapidly to tilled fields and she only needed to weave through a couple of back alleyways to find herself in the countryside.

The chink of coins within her scrip made her think of Amaryllis. She wondered how long it would take him to notice that his purse was not as heavy as it had been. It was one thing she had learnt from Pip. Amaryllis had left the purse on the table after paying for their meal and, with a seemingly accidental gesture, she had swept it to the floor. Hastily, she had gathered the spilt coins, offering them back, but not before pocketing a few for herself. She had forgiven herself this crime, reasoning that she was driven by higher needs.

The red soil beneath her feet had smelt unfamiliar and was thin and stony. The few trees that she could see were stunted and slanting, telling of the fierce winds that blew from the west over the spit of land, adding to the impression of bleakness. The nearest tree had been an oak, the upper branches bare of leaves and the bark peeling away to show the bare pale wood beneath. Ignoring the ill-omen that the tree was sick, she had made her way across the field and settled down beneath its twisted limbs to contemplate drawing on the power of Necrönd.

Sick to her stomach, she had felt such action was a betrayal of Morrigwen's trust. She knew no one should use it; that was why, after all, she had taken it from Caspar. Still, she had seen no other solution. Stiffening her shoulders, she told herself that just once would not matter. It had taken her no time to decide that she would summon the smallest of the beasts of power, the smallest and least terrible that she knew of, a unicorn. Her choice was made when she remembered the legend that, though the great unicorns were dangerous to men, they could be seduced into submission by the power of a maiden. A unicorn would be fleet of foot and would bear her across Ceolothia's interior to Castaguard, outrunning the very fastest of any horse that Amaryllis might procure.

With her head tilted to the side, she gazed at the Egg, still wondering how she might command such a beast to appear. She had seen unicorns in the tapestries before the great siege. Some were small and goatish in appearance, but what she wanted was one of those large lean beasts with long legs like Firecracker's. She concentrated on such an image drawn in her mind.

Claws slashed out of the air and the deep moans and cries of large, ferocious beasts, clamouring to be freed, forced their way forward into her thoughts. Tears pricked at her eyes as her courage crumbled and she clutched the Egg tighter to steel her will. Hungry thoughts stalked her mind. She felt a cold hand touch her neck but, when she spun round, she saw nothing. A stab of blackness flickered across her vision and an excruciating pain stabbed behind her eyes.

She gritted her teeth, swallowing the bestial scream that came from somewhere deep inside her. Digging deep for her sense of control, she sought to reach the protection of the Great Mother by visualizing the Trinity of high priestesses that represented Her. A distant white light spread pinkly through the red pain.

Shuddering, she prayed she could keep the image of the hooded wolves from her mind but, even as the thought formed in her head, so could she hear a lonely chilling howl; though she was uncertain whether she heard it in her mind or that it came from across the flat grey plains sprawling beneath flat grey clouds. She gave out a little moan and thought more forcefully on the unicorn she desired, though the thought was hard to fix. Breathing in shallow gasps, she screwed her eyes up tight and blotted out the images of the other animals by thinking on those Ceolothian clouds, using them to fill the over-active parts of her mind before attempting to picture the unicorn.

She saw now how easy it must have been for Caspar to conjure up the wolves. Just by trying not to do so, she had created their images in her mind. She bit her tongue, pressed Necrönd against her forehead and, with a grunt of effort, at last, saw the unicorn in her mind's eye.

Something snorted, the sound distinctly real and outside her head. Jumping to her feet, she clutched the Egg to her bosom. Within the canopy of the sickened oak tree, the air grew hazy and began to shimmer. At its centre, a brilliant whiteness flickered and shone, growing in intensity until, before her, stood a most splendid equine beast. Jutting from its forehead was a pearlescent, lancelike horn, ten foot long, that snagged in the branches. The creature gave a savage shriek, snorted and raked the ground. May stepped back in horror though the animal did not advance but backed out from beneath the tree and made the very faintest bow of its head towards her as if acknowledging her power.

It was very much taller than Firecracker, its muscles and sinews more pronounced. Its dazzling white coat was flecked with silver that caught the sun and made her blink. She looked hard into its dark, liquid silver eyes and swallowed hard, worrying about what to do next when the sound of shouting drifted up from the port. Amaryllis was calling her.

The sound of his voice made her catch her breath and she acknowledged that a part of her wished to run back to him. Stiffly, she told herself that it was simply her fear of facing the future alone that made her cling to him. Ashamedly, she admitted that no one would expect her to cope alone. She didn't even expect it of herself. Perhaps now was the time to start believing in herself.

She seized her welling courage and, holding out her hand, stepped towards the unicorn that stood stiffly before her, and gently brushed her fingers across his cheek. Rather than pulling away, the animal snorted nervously and sniffed suspiciously at her hand before allowing her to guide him to a low branch so that she could mount.

Once up on the creature's back, she was afraid of the height and the sudden speed with which it leapt away. Clutching a fistful of mane, she murmured, "Castaguard," and the unicorn swerved to head east in response to her wishes.

She dared not look down; the unicorn, wrapped up in its own thrill of speed, careered across the open countryside at a terrifying pace, too fast for her to take in her surroundings. She sensed his sheer delight at his sudden freedom. Snorting and bellowing, he seemed thrilled simply to draw breath, rejoicing at the feel of the turf beneath his cloven hooves. May kept herself crouched over his neck, the stride so smooth and easy that she found no difficulty in keeping her balance.

They passed a shepherd and sent his bleating sheep scattering. Hearing the angry shouts at her back, a small smile crossed May's face; for the first time in her rather unremarkable life, she was creating a stir.

Gradually becoming accustomed to the speed, she grew less nervous and was able to think. The sea and the port of Skuas Ria on the spit were soon far behind and, with a guilt-ridden sense of loss, she knew that Amaryllis would never catch her now. She stiffened her lip, urging the unicorn faster, at last enjoying the rushing speed, using the sensation to outrun her emotions. Not even Cracker could catch me now, she thought, then realized that made her far beyond Caspar's reach; her heart sagged. The unicorn slowed to a walk in response to her wavering thoughts.

It was beginning to rain. A dun valley opened before her, the low ground dark with slippery mud. Even the unicorn left deep slurpy hoofprints. Defiantly battling against her uncertain thoughts, she gritted her teeth and slammed her heels into the unicorn's sides. With a shriek of anger, the beast burst forward at an even faster rate.

She sped on through the day and into the night, stopping only for water and rest when she could no longer hold herself up. The unicorn did not wander at all and when she slept, he stood guard over her. All the next day she rode on, the speed numbing her mind, but neither that nor her exhaustion could ease her sense of loss for the life she had left behind. She forced herself to think of Amaryllis in the vain hope that he could drive away her longing for Spar.

It continued to rain. The soft but persistent drizzle soaked through her clothes to her skin, but she hardly noticed it for her grief and her fear of the speed.

The third day passed much as before as she galloped on through dusk and into the night, the moonlight sparkling like silver frost on the unicorn's back. Then the soft light touched the spires of a distant city, whose walls and rising citadel glowed white like a lantern. So, this was the Ceolothian capital, the bright city of Castabrice that the storyteller in the inn had described.

Knowing that Castaguard lay but a few leagues further north, she decided she should stop and rest. The light trunks of an aspen wood beckoned and obediently, the unicorn took her into its depths. The widely spaced trees and the sound of their constantly rustling leaves were reassuringly familiar and soon she found a leafy spot in which to rest. In her exhaustion she fell into a deep sleep the moment she closed her eyes but it was not restful; disturbing dreams plagued her night. A shadow was hunched in the farthest corner of her mind. She was aware of it but could not quite picture it, since it slid to a deeper part of her unconscious brain the moment her inner eye sought it; yet she knew it was there, stealthily creeping closer. She sensed its sneering delight at her solitude. It stalked her. She tried to run but her legs were bound and her hands too weak to untie the knots. Then she dropped Necrönd and the shadow pounced on it with a howl of victory. Hooded wolves, with torn pelts and rotting flesh squirmed from the black perimeter of her mind, their eyes glowing redly as they guiltily glanced at her before slashing out wildly with their jaws and escaping into the void beyond the edge of her dream.

She awoke with a start at the sound of the unicorn snorting and pawing the ground. Shuddering, she held the silver casket close to her chest. She felt violated. Something had crept into her dreams. She knew she must keep awake. It wasn't safe to sleep.

She stood up and braced herself, pinching her fingers to stop them trembling and telling herself she was not afraid; she was a Torra Altan, after all. "Find yourself water and something to eat," she ordered the unicorn.

His head shot up in eagerness, the great horn again

becoming entangled in the trees and the girl thought that it must once have been an animal of the open plains and not of the woods as she had once imagined. He sniffed the air and trotted a short distance to a nearby dew-pond where he drank thirstily. She took pity on him, thinking how heartless she must have been to ride so furiously without considering the animal's welfare. They must have leapt ditches, earthworks, and streams without her noticing. The unicorn's once-glimmering coat was smeared with sweat-streaked mud and his ever-watchful eyes were duller than she remembered.

While it was still dark, she risked skirting the capital and then struck north following a road alongside a canal that cut directly towards Castaguard. The road surface was drained by deep ditches and so was free of the worst of the Ceolothian mud and it was so much easier for the unicorn that, even before dawn, they were well along the north road.

Ahead, a black tower poking up from the surrounding plain marked the position of Castaguard. A pale sun that crawled reluctantly into the cloud-muffled sky failed to bring any colour to the grim tower but in the thin light she could just make out the hazy outline of a range of saw-toothed mountains some twenty miles to the north that rose out of the Ceolothian plain. She needed no one to tell her that these were the hollow mountains of Kalanazir.

May was loath to do it but she knew that she must soon send this great unicorn back to the Otherworld. At once, she sensed his hostile disappointment. How could she repay his willing service by sending him back to the fleshless existence of the Otherworld where his meaningless life never touched on the Great Mother?

How could she misuse the trust of any animal so,

allowing it the taste of freedom that it had been denied for thousands of years and then taking it away again? She drew off the road and down towards a fast-flowing river that rushed off a series of low hills to her right. The water was unpleasantly green in colour. She let the animal stand in the stream, cooling its legs, and watched how it nuzzled the water and sucked and blew, as if delighting in the substance, before taking long and steady draughts. She patted its neck that was bone-solid. It paid no heed though she sensed its awareness, its intelligence.

Feeling quite foolish, she stammered at the unicorn, "I can only do right as I see it. I was taught that a kindness deserves a kindness, and that no bad man ever laboured hard for a just cause, and . . . and . . ." she looked at him helplessly. "What I'm trying to say is that you've laboured hard for me and I don't have it in my heart to send you back."

The unicorn arrogantly tossed his head and snorted almost in disbelief.

"Go," May said firmly and waved her arms at him.

The unicorn looked at her long and hard and then slowly began to back away and, only when he was on clear of the stream, did he turn and tear away, a streak of silver heading east for the unpopulated plains.

May was pleased for it until she remembered herself. How could she have been so foolish? The Egg was not for someone with compassion. She thumped her palm against her temple. Was this the mistake that Caspar had made? She had sensed its thoughts, how it wished to spear sheep with its horns and gore the shepherds who had hounded it into extinction.

Ashamed of her weakness, May returned to the road and made the last few miles on foot towards Castaguard. The multi-walled city lay below her on an island in the middle of a broad flooded hollow. The road left the canal, which was punctuated by locks and cut straight to the south, instead skirting down the steep sides and leading onto a raised causeway. The causeway formed a dark line through the silvery wetlands surrounding the city, the ground flooded by the great rivers pouring off the overshadowing mountains to the north. The black line of the stinking canal cut around the eastern edge of the city and from Castaguard's dark centre protruded a black tower whose lower walls and foundations sank from sight into the dipped heart of the city.

The mountains beyond were unwelcoming peaks of grim black with bare shoulders and heads capped in snow and blue ice. The clouds for once had lifted during the morning and were high and wispy but the blue sky made the mountains no more inviting. May fancied that their bulky shapes looked like the huddled forms of grim ogres shut out in the cold.

There was none of the fine stone that graced the buildings of Castabrice. Its twin city of Castaguard was built out of the local grim rock, the black walls streaked with red stains that she presumed had been washed out of the mortar salts onto the surface. May studiously tilted her head and reconsidered. No, surely once they had been painted a brilliant red so that the city must have glowed like a setting sun against a bank of smoky clouds. The constant Ceolothian rain must have washed most of it away and no one of late had cared to return the city to its former splendour.

The walls were tall and smooth and completely lacking in ornamentation, the vastness of their planed surfaces only broken where peaked arches rose above the few bridges spanning the stagnant moats. From the top of the rise, she had noted how the central part of the city around the black tower had five curtain walls and that unlike any other castle she had heard of – and Torra Altans had a large appetite for detailed descriptions of castles – each section was dug down deeper into the earth than the previous one, so that the root of the central fortress was sunk out of sight into a well. May thought it was as if the earth were affronted by the black scar of the city and was trying to swallow it from below. Pushing back her shoulders, she marched boldly towards the south gate, uncomfortably aware that the causeway had been far longer than she had at first thought and that she had drastically underestimated the scale of the city.

She had a simple plan. She would tell the mine owners of how she had lost her parents and needed to find work. Naively certain that her skills were of some worth, she was sure they would take her on. Hurrying over one of the bridges, she raised her head to gaze at the towering black pillars beside the gate that reared above her. She gave an involuntary shudder; the red streaks in the stonework gave the impression that the city wept tears of blood. Looking closer, she saw that the monstrous structures of Castaguard's walls were dotted with barred windows and must be hollow, housing many thousands of men.

No one questioned her entry. Far from it. The guards questioned only those leaving the city, especially those travelling alone. The areas between the five curtain walls were devoid of stone buildings but cluttered with stalls and slum dwellings built from upturned carts, old gates and skins. Even old oxen bones draped in sacking were used to give shelter from the relentless rain. Everywhere she looked, children with glum faces loitered along the edge of the road. The urchins pestered every passer-by, offering their services as guides to the auction square and best stalls. Most people hurried by to avoid them, though the mud-drenched merchants often shoved them aside though they sobbed and implored for help.

"We cannot pay our rent and my father will be forced into the slave mines. Please help," the ragged children cried in broken Belbidian, quick to learn the language of commerce.

The merchants seemed mostly oblivious to the protestations, but some turned their faces painfully away as if there were nothing they could do.

May picked her way through the crowd, following a snarling travel-worn merchant right through into the core of the city where the sun was barred out by the overshadowing walls.

The sound of a cracking whip stopped May in her tracks. All those on the streets were roughly swept aside by a troop of soldiers in creaking, thigh length boots and peaked helmets with nose-guards that hid their faces. They lashed whips, clearing the way for a huge, covered wagon. May imagined the cargo was of great value and when it stopped outside a low building with barred windows, the jeweller's sign of cut ruby painted in dark reds hanging over the guarded door, her suspicions were confirmed.

At last, she entered the central quarter dominated by the black tower that was curiously sunk into the ground rather than raised on a motte, as might have been expected. Though the arch over the portcullis was carved with figures studded with jewels, the upper parts of the tower were austere and functional and virtually windowless apart from a half dozen arrow-slits cut into the black rock. The flared walls of the tower narrowed as they rose to a mean spike rimmed with crenellations.

To the left of the tower, lying in its harsh shadow, was a cobbled square. At its centre rose up the statue of a dancing bear that looked, by the way its muzzle thrust upwards, that it might once have spouted a fountain of water. From somewhere beyond came muffled cries of pain and sorrow. May hurriedly turned away.

She had expected the centre of Castaguard to be even grimmer than its outskirts but, apart from the tower and its immediate surroundings, she was wrong. Through a pointed archway to her right hummed a busy market set about the four sides of an immaculate lawn. The market was full of marquees and tents, all of wonderful striped colours vying for the most attention, and the air was thick with the cries of bartering.

The stall vendors would shout twice, once in the Ceolothian tongue, and once in the fair tongue of Belbidia, which was the practice in the Caballan. She drew comfort from the sound of her mother tongue and steered her way through the stalls of silks and fine dresses studded with lesser jewels.

Everywhere about her were examples of exquisite craftsmanship from silversmiths, whitesmiths and goldsmiths. The wares were bartered for with much tussling, the incoming merchants seeking to favourably exchange silks, woollens, furs, satins and rich foods for the minerals. May could not help smiling as she saw how well the Belbidian merchants fared.

Though tired and hungry, she lingered long in the market. She had much to buy and did not relish the thought of returning to the cobbled square at the foot of the tower. She found a spice stall, which she browsed through carefully but, to her chagrin, she knew nothing of the properties of nutmeg, mace and cassia and hurried off in search of a herbalist. She was far more conversant with herbs and, though she knew she was paying an exorbitant price, she bought sage, hyssop, loosestrife, speedwell and a bag of poppy seeds, which the vendor informed her came all the way from Ophidia. Now all she needed to find was some honey.

The honey, which Morrigwen had always sworn by for the healing of infected wounds, took the last of Amaryllis's money and May knew that the time had come for her to seal her fate. She took a deep breath, girding herself for what lay ahead, and reluctantly left the hubbub of silk and spice markets for the deep gloomy shadow at the foot of the sunken keep.

Though she thought she was prepared for what she knew she would face, she was not. On passing the statue of the bear surrounded by a stagnant pool of greenish water, she knew she would see the crowded numbers of people penned in cramped silence into stalls but she had not imagined the depth of their misery. She had expected suffering and had seen men waiting to die during the Vaalakan siege but there had been a closeness between them, a bond born out of the misery. Here, men, women, children, the sick, the old and the hale, were huddled together but each looked in on themselves, sitting with heads bowed, sinking under the weight of their own personal grief. They looked lost, abandoned and alone.

Her heart went out to them and it flashed through her mind that she had the power to release them from their slavery. An inner voice of cold reason that she did not know she possessed told her she must not. If she did, she would reveal the whereabouts of the Egg and risk having more than just Amaryllis pursuing her. Moreover, she could not allow more creatures to escape from the Otherworld; she could create worse than a plague of wolves.

She laughed at her foolish arrogance for thinking she could save them. I'm like Hal, she thought. Everyone at heart wants to be the hero, for their deeds to be sung.

But no one must ever know of her sacrifice, otherwise she would have failed. At home in Torra Alta, if they remembered her at all, it must be as a foolish lovesick girl who ran away. No, her deed was not one of heroism but of sacrifice and she would add her own despair to the ranks before her.

Even as she wrung the last ounce of resolve from her tortured soul, her heart was chilled; drawing into the square was a wagon bearing crying women, their arms stretched through the bars, clutching in desperation at the air. Like cattle, they were dragged from their cages, branded with a black cross on their upper arms and thrust into the waiting pens. Some kicked and bit at each other, screaming terribly, while others stood silently, their mouths gaping.

She closed her eyes, hardening her resolve, then blinked them open, and searched beyond the guarded pens to the quieter ranks of people beyond. They sat on benches and did not shriek or cry but accepted what was to come with barely a shrug for they had nowhere else left to go. A soldier seated on a platform, listed details of those brought in front of him so that they could then be moved on to the appropriate pen. Judging by his braided uniform, it was an officer who stood by his side, assessing each individual. They barely spoke Belbidian, the flat tones of Ceolothian dominating the exchanges, which seemed short and to the point.

Her mind a daze, she joined the queue to enlist, ignoring the depravation around her and concentrating only on her feet and moving them one before the other. After mounting the steps to the platform and reaching the soldier, she said meekly, "I come willingly to find work."

The soldier was writing with a scratchy quill, the ink

blotchy and smeared. After examination, many of the people before her had been turned away or dragged, screaming, to the slave pens and she prayed she offered something that would be valued.

She looked into the soldier's face and smiled. In return, he stared stonily at her. She was utterly disconcerted. Never in her life had someone failed to smile back; this man didn't even smirk or leer but just gave her a flat and unemotional glare.

"I come to offer my services," she explained sweetly.

"Belbidian," he groaned. "Too many Belbidians of late. Too many by far. There is no call for shepherdesses in the mines. Turn aside and be gone! If you can find nowhere else and are still begging in these streets in a week you will be taken to the slave pits," he raised his hand that gripped a stamp marked with a black cross. "You can be properly branded later."

She snatched her hand away before he could mark her and she sucked in a deep breath, thinking of Brid. No one would have spoken to Brid like that. Brid had presence. Brid had faith. Brid believed that, come what may, the Great Mother walked beside her. If only she could find such faith, May believed that she, too, could achieve what she must.

"No!" she shouted, meaning to be authoritative, but in fact sounding startled and alarmed.

The soldier grabbed her hand and threatened. "I need not wait the week. I have the authority to throw you straight to the slave pits, girl," he threatened in practised Belbidian.

"I am not a shepherdess nor a farmer but," she tried to raise her head to meet the man's eyes but instead looked down at her feet, "a healer." She lied, hoping that the carefully chosen herbs would be convincing. She had studied long under Morrigwen's care and, though she knew little of runelore and barely grasped the rudiments of reading, she had the knowledge of the commonest ingredients used to heal infected wounds.

"A healer. What need have we of healers? Those that are sick do not last long and are easily replaced."

May tried not to react to this callousness. "But there aren't just slaves in your mines. You have skilled workers and soldiers too. Do they never have need of succour?"

"We have physics already and need no more."

The officer was watching them intently. A gold chain draped across his black uniform, he bore himself with an air of command and position. A smile spread across his lips as he studied May and she did her best to return the smile, her eyes bright and twinkling. She knew that such a response, though it might get her entry to the mines, would undoubtedly bring trouble.

"I am not just a healer," she said hastily and racked her mind for any other skill she might possess. At last, it came to her. She thought how Amaryllis had earned his way and remembered her hours at Morrigwen's bedside listening and telling stories. "I am a storyteller," she said firmly.

There was a great guffaw from the soldier though the absurdity of the idea seemed to please the officer. "Let her pass. Why not a storyteller? If you do not have Ceolothian, you must learn it fast. There are few storytellers who speak our tongue and the soldiers will be glad of the entertainment." The soldier daubed her with a red circle and pointed her toward the black tower.

Proud above her, the keep facade was clad with black stone, the arches and pillars around the portcullis studded with glinting rubies. Like eyes, they seemed to follow her as she passed through. She shuddered and then cringed from the carved stone heads of hobgoblins, bulging-eyed griffins and fanged wolves. Retreating into the hood of her bearskin, her instincts urged her to feel for the Egg.

She wondered briefly whether she could call Morrigwen back form the dead. She wasn't sure; as far as she was aware the Egg summoned only those in the Otherworld and she felt sure that so old a woman, who had done so much in her lifetime and had long since been weary of it, would have hurried on to the bliss of Annwyn and be beyond her reach. Besides, the whole point of running away with the Egg was to save Caspar from the seduction of its powers. It would be equally terrible if she was lured into mishandling it. Already, she was succumbing to it, looking to it for quick easy solutions.

The entrance passage to the tower dipped deeper and deeper into the earth. The sounds from the city became dull and distant, the cries wafting away above her head until she could hear only the monotone call of the soldiers ordering them to hurry and divide into lines, and the constant trudge and shuffle of defeated feet.

She pulled her cloak tightly around her and fingered the broach that Caspar had given her. "Give me the strength of a dragon to go on alone," she murmured while in her heart she prayed that Caspar would come for her. Perhaps, after all, he did love her; perhaps, even enough to cross the great expanse of Ceolothia to find her. Perhaps he would drop everything that was dear to him, even his wonderful castle and his onerous responsibilities and seek her out. She clutched the broach so tight that it left a deep imprint in her hand, producing a sweet, distracting pain, the pain of her love.

No daylight penetrated the lower corridors that were paved with slabs of cut stone that became steadily more worn as they descended, finally turning to beaten earth beneath her cracked boots. The stonework around her crumbled away to leave bare the compacted earthen walls of a tunnel shored up by vast planking, some old and split with age, others straight and pale where they had recently been renewed. The walls were broken at intervals by little doors with pointed architraves.

Puzzled, she was aware of eyes watching her as they trudged deeper and deeper underground. The shoring was no longer necessary as the tunnel walls were now of solid rock bearing the countless score marks of chisel, hammer and pick. She looked around. No slave or soldier paid her any particular heed and she had the peculiar sense that it was the rocks themselves that noted her passing.

On nearing two large double doors in the side of the tunnel, May was singled out and dragged through them by her collar into a smaller brazier-lit corridor. The air was thick with smoke and she covered her hand with her sleeve. Eyes smarting, she was hurried along. After a steady descent, she heard laughter and singing of sorts, the tones unfamiliar and quite painful to her ears. Many Torra Altans could not sing well but at least they put passion behind their voices and never had she heard a sound so discordant.

Here the corridor levelled somewhat and the number of braziers lighting the way increased, banishing the blind pools of blackness between them. The singing was coming from the end of the corridor where an archway was filled with double doors. May was thrust through the doors into a smoky hall filled with Ceolothian soldiers, their faces flushed red in the firelight. Evidently, this was a soldiers' resting station between the mines of Kalanazir and the slave markets of Castaguard. A stench of sweat and strong ale and the tang of vomit assaulted her and she felt intensely vulnerable.

She was used to rough men. She came from a frontier castle where the greatest prizes and accolades were given to those that could fight with bravery and stamina, and often with savagery. Before that she had lived amongst the woodcutters and they, too, were rough men used to a hard physical life. But in both cases their women lived amongst the men and never before had she felt so alone and vulnerable.

The chamber was tall, a smoking fire winding up into a central chimney, but the room was dim and devoid of furnishings save for long trestle tables and benches where the men sat drinking beer.

The moment she entered and was introduced, the soldiers demanded a story.

"But I've had no chance to learn any Ceolothian," she protested.

Though most jeered at her, one or two were helpful enough to speak in Belbidian to see that their wishes were understood. Hands tugged at her bearskin to pull it from her shoulders and they demanded to see her better in the hope that this would improve her tale.

May quaked. She had been very foolish. Her story would have to be good and she longed at once for the magical voice of Amaryllis.

They threw her up onto a table, one man ripping the sleeve from her dress in the process and clinging avariciously to her bare arm, his tongue sliding over her fingers. She closed her eyes, seeking courage while his companions pulled him off and lifted him bodily, passing him over their heads to the back of the hall. She was not a storyteller though she had listened avidly to the way Keridwen would tell great tales of heroism, her voice softening and whispering, then becoming loud like a terrible storm. She thought of how the woman could spin around and seem small one moment and then large at others, fearsome like the men she spoke of or seemingly vile like the evil villains who crawled through her tales.

Her heart pumped in her throat and she opened her mouth, trying to find words. The men were jeering already. In a mouselike voice, she began her story though she knew she was not audible above the raucous jeers. She began again.

"Before the days of the dragon lords—"

Boos burst out in the back of the chamber. "Ceolothian!" they ordered, grumbling and muttering and one or to threw the remains of their sloppy food at her. May's legs grew weak. She could not speak Ceolothian barely well enough to string four words together and they were not particularly useful words. "The cat is black" and "Your face is ugly." Pip had taught them to her.

Slimy brown sauce splattered her shoulder and slithered down her arm. One had his hand on the hem of her dress and, egged on by his fellows, was pulling at it. May knew she would not last long under their treatment. They would abuse her until she died but, worse, they would take the Egg. And to think she was such a fool as to bring it here to be plucked from her by some nameless Ceolothian soldier. It was the worst place on earth she could have possibly chosen.

But she had to do something and reached inside her silk shirt, flicked open the casket with her nail and grasped the Egg.

"Before the days of the dragon lords," she roared in a fierce and determined voice, "there lived a red dragon that roamed these very halls." As she spoke, she summoned such a beast, keeping the image half-ghost, half-real and allowing it to spurt flame that consumed an empty table beside her.

She commanded instant and aghast silence. Carried away by her power, she continued her tale. It seemed to matter little what she said so long as she summoned images of beasts. She spoke of dragon hunts and the brave men that slew the great worms and then of the winged unicorns and flying horses whose ghosts she made dance above their heads, and of mermaids with enthralling voices whose music thrilled the air. The soldiers begged for more.

May was exhausted and, when she tried to draw three beasts at once, they eagerly broke through the divide between life and death, hungrily snatching at the air, like newborn babies gasping and wailing at their first intake of breath. She felt others behind them, eager to be summoned, and was flustered by their demanding presence. Her concentration slipping, she sought to choose only the smallest and least harmful, but somehow a fire-breathing lion with dragonlike wings appeared and coiled around her before she had time to prevent it. The soldiers looked on with wide eyes.

While she was trying to send back the fiery lion, a goat with a fish's tail and claws instead of hooves sprung out of the atmosphere fully formed and solid onto the table. With it came the black shadow of a wolf. A sudden shriek of terror screamed out from the nearest soldier as the goatlike beast charged. May was quick, her panic turning to action, calling the beast to heel as if commanding a dog. Immediately, it obeyed.

Her eyes flitted around the room, searching for the shadow that had crept out with the goat. She commanded it to her side but it resisted her, stalking the outer perimeter. The soldiers gasped in amazed appreciation, clearly believing this was all a part of her story.

She was uncomfortably aware of one soldier that had

worked his way forward from the middle of the room and had taken a seat at the table on which she stood. He was leering at her, his tongue protruding from his mouth.

Panic gripped her. She had lost control of one of these beasts and did not know how to draw it back into the Egg. Her heart pounded. All she could imagine was being mauled to death by that fearful shadow and then having to face Morrigwen's acerbic looks of disappointment. "This, child," she would say, "is why you are not the one to be the new Maiden. You have no sense, no sense at all. How could you have been such a fool as to think someone like you could protect Necrönd better then Spar who was chosen by the Great Mother Herself to be its guardian."

May could not see the shadow but could sense it rippling through the crowd, stalking towards her. She tried to gather the other beasts to her but, with her mind so confused by guilt and terror, she could not focus sufficiently.

The soldier before her abruptly stiffened, a twisted smile sweeping across his face, his mouth opening to reveal black and rotted teeth that grew to sharpened points before her eyes. His eyes bulged, a trickle of blood winding out from one corner. Stiffly, he rose to his feet, a dogtooth blade the length of a short sword gripped in his white-knuckled hand.

CHAPTER TWENTY

Ursula stood proud and fearless before the raging bear, her tattooed arms outstretched and her lionskin cloak swept back off her shoulders. Strange words of command sang from her pale lips.

Fern squealed, "Wolf!" over and over though Caspar could see only the threat of the maddened bear.

He had to save Ursula. It didn't matter how many men there were or that he had not yet found Necrönd, she would die if he did nothing. He struggled for his bow beneath his smock.

"There's more at stake here," Perren reasoned, snatching at Caspar's arm. "She's lost to madness already."

"You heartless monster." Caspar kicked at Perren's legs and struggled to break the restraining grip but had no effect on the stonewight's solid skin. He could only suppress a moan as the towering brown bear dropped to all fours and charged Ursula, the force of its blow lifting her from her feet and flinging her across the camp. The slave-girl folded lifelessly around the ropes of a tent.

In maddened effort, Caspar twisted within Perren's grasp and loosed an arrow. The twang of the bow went unheard amidst the cries of the men and the horrendous bellowing of the bear. It skimmed the bear's shoulder, managing only to enrage it further and sending it spinning round in search of its attacker. Caspar's second shaft buried into the back of its neck. It arched backwards, vainly thrashing its claws to fight off the sting, but the arrow had done its work and, before Perren dragged him away, Caspar saw the animal crash to the ground.

The air behind rang with the shouts and hollers of alarm. Fern was almost out of sight, running inland, his peculiar gait made more distinctive as he leapt the many boggy rivulets. Perren dragged Caspar after him.

"You foul-hearted beast! We can't leave her; she might still live," Caspar yelled, only to be unceremoniously swung over Perren's shoulder.

With Lana under the other arm, the stonewight padded over the wetland at a most extraordinary rate. "You're a fool. Your span of life is so short and you have only one worthy purpose to fulfil and yet you would throw it all away. I cannot allow you to give your life in a futile attempt to save that girl when so many depend on you. Think of Necrönd and what might happen. We could all be enslaved by its misuse."

Caspar kicked and struggled until the stonewight abruptly stopped and flung him and Lana down into a reedy hollow shouldered by rocks before throwing his dark bulk over them and crushing them to the ground. "Be quiet," he growled softly.

Whips cracked and bears roared. Caspar reasoned that the bears must have fled in the same direction. The running rattle of a chain being pulled through a hoop and snapping taut and an exhausted half-hearted cheer from the Ovissian men announced the bears' recapture. Caspar fell still; Mamluc was yelling above him.

"She's alive!" Mamluc's voice was gleeful, lusting for power. "I have an escaped slave alive. Woman, you will be taken to the slave markets of Castaguard and have your hands, feet and ears cut off. Then you will be chained to the fountain at the centre of Castaguard's slave square until the end of your days, as a warning to any slave that might attempt to escape. In fact, I shall have the pleasure of taking you there myself. I have business in Castaguard." A whip cracked followed by a soft moan.

By the sharp intake of breath from the men, Caspar had no doubt that the whip had slashed across Ursula's bare skin. It was impossible to shift Perren and so he could do nothing as the sounds around him slowly dwindled. He had to strain his head round in the black mud to draw air and one leg was completely numb where it was squashed beneath him. Cramp pained his shoulder. When Perren finally moved it was no longer dark.

Spuming words of anger and staggering up out of the hole, the only thing Caspar could do to vent his frustrations was to lash out and slam his fist into Perren's broad face. He regretted it instantly and reeled away, his knuckles split and throbbing.

When he and Perren returned to the jetty, there was no soul to be seen; the tents were gone and so was Ursula. Only the empty pens and the bodies of the bears marked the spot. The bear cub lay dead on its back, arms and legs splayed, flies mobbing the great lines of split hide that striped its face where it had been lashed by a chain – but Caspar doubted that the chain would have killed it. The eyes stared open in fright. The other bear, which he himself had killed with the arrow, lay like a great folded rug beside the fire. Grunting with the weight of it, he pulled round its head and looked in revulsion at the bleeding eye sockets. A ball of flies was clustered at the corners of the eyes and mouth.

"Wolf!" a familiar voice whispered from above.

Caspar straightened up and squinted irritability at Fern. "What do you mean, wolf?"

"It stinks of wolf."

"Anyone can plainly see it's a bear."

"Anyone can plainly smell it's a wolf, and a bad wolf at that," Fern huffed.

"How can you not believe your own eyes?"

"How can you not believe your own nose? Many men wear many disguises to deceive the eye but they all smell as they smell." Fern sniffed at him in disapproval. "Well, he's gone now." He sniffed the ground and looked east towards the blazing sea and the shape of three narrow boats all heading south for Belbidia's barony of Quertos.

"He's crossed the sea?" Caspar asked with forced patience, trying to understand the woodwose.

Fern shook his head and nodded towards the opposite bank of the estuary where Trog was barking effusively.

"How did he get there?" Caspar asked.

The answer was obvious. Since the wolfling was already swimming the narrow channel of water trickling through the mud-flats exposed by the retreating tide, Caspar resolved that they must follow. Black mud clinging to his thighs and his clothes sodden, he led the others up onto the opposite bank after wading across. The wolfling was hidden behind a sculpted mud-bank beyond, snuffling at the ground and, when she saw their approach, she set off, loping purposefully along the shore, looking back only once to check that they were following.

Caspar limped after them followed by Fern and Perren, who struggled with a distraught Lana. The young auburn-haired nobleman stopped in his tracks and examined the area that had been of so much interest to the wolfling. Hoofprints! And he would recognize those neat round prints anywhere. "Cracker's!" he said looking up at Fern and Perren in horror.

"They've taken the noble Cracker and Ursula along the shore," Fern wailed.

Caspar stared gloomily down at the prints. Along with the crescent marks made by his horse were the smaller prints of a woman. The marks were interspersed with long grooves as if she had been dragged. Larger booted prints ran alongside. One set had to be made by Mamluc and the other, which was long and thin, no doubt were those of the wolfman, Caspar presumed.

"The boats must have taken them across the estuary when the tide was in," Perren remarked practically. With his bandaged arms, face and blanketed body now dripping with mud, he looked like some shapeless monster emerged from the sea. Judging that he now looked more of a sight like that and without fresh white linen would never pass as a man marked by pox, he decided to discard the bandages.

They trudged beyond the borders of Belbidia through endless sand-dunes on the southern margins of Vaalaka, coarse grey-blue marram grasses rustling against their thighs for many weary days. To his frustration, Caspar discovered that since Perren carried Naith's sister, who had fallen into shocked silence since her brother's death, he was the one that slowed them up. They were forced to stop early the first night because his knee ached horribly and he feared he would be unable to walk at all by the next day. Once rested, however, the sight of Firecracker's hoofprint, the off hind dragging through the sand, urged him on. The prints were still firm in the soft ground and he knew they were gaining on them.

Though he was worried for Lana and tried to soothe her with gentle stories and assurances that she would be welcome at Torra Alta, her quiet sobs unsettled the peace of the deserted Vaalakan landscape. But nothing distracted him from his worries over Necrönd. He was more convinced than ever that, in collaboration with Mamluc, the tall man in the wolf pelt had stolen it. How else could he have drawn out an ancient spirit into that bear? He satisfied himself that this man was unskilled at controlling the power and was soon convincing himself that only he had the required skills and sensitivity to the channels of magic to wield it properly. Still, it wouldn't be long until the wolfman gained in ability; he was certain of that.

By the third day, he had to content himself with being carried alongside Lana. This perturbed Trog who yelped at Perren's heels and nibbled at his boots, anxious that the stonewight might be harming his master. Time passed without mishap until, on the sixth day, they changed direction. A wide delta of marshy reed-bordered rivers had forced Mamluc inland, and they followed Firecracker's stumbling tracks to a fording point. Fern stopped suddenly while Trog and the wolfling bounded eagerly forward.

The dog sniffed at the edge of the river and then leapt like a cat, all four feet together, into the reeds. The wolfling watched him for some while, her head cocked to one side in amused puzzlement and then tried to copy his dance only to trip over her own feet. Being an Ophidian snake-catcher by breed, Trog was an adept murderer and had snapped up three toads and dispatched them neatly while the little wolfling was still taking great, ungainly leaps and splashing into the shallow water. For the first time in days, Caspar laughed and even Lana chortled when a red toad shot a great jet of black ink into the wolfling's face, splattering her coat. Runa shook herself indignantly.

"You won't laugh later," Perren told them. "You won't get rid of the smell and the ink has a way of smearing itself onto everything."

"How would you know?" Fern asked critically.

"A half-naked man carrying no other tool than a stone axe wandered into our caves sometime back now, his face blotched black, and he reeked from head to toe. He complained that his wife had developed a sudden appetite for ink-squirting toads but he couldn't live with the smell any longer and was running down into our caves to be free of the woman. Though a strong-looking man, he died far more quickly than most, vomiting black bile. Very ugly! The whole cavern stank for years."

Trog was in his element. Quick and speedy, he appeared to be taunting the bulging long-legged toads, waiting for them to shoot their black ink and leaping aside at the last possible moment, his tail wagging furiously and giving out curious little yips of uncontainable excitement. Runa watched him and tried hard to mimic him, following his every movement with great devotion, bowing her front legs and swaying from side to side before a great red toad. But the wolfling was too slow to avoid the squirt of black that sprayed over the brilliant white of her left flank. She squealed in dismay and began to lick at it but then howled in horror, spitting violently at the taste and running to the water's edge to lap at the marshy waters.

"Stupid animals," Fern said in disgust. "How can you find any amusement in watching them torment defenceless creatures?"

"A wolf is a wolf and a dog is a dog and their instincts are their own. It's no use me trying to stop them from hunting any more than it is to make you a hunter. And I wouldn't sit there," Perren told him.

"Here's as good a place as any."

Perren's heavy eyebrows rose. "Well, the man that told us of the red toads and his wife's passion for them explained that once the ink sacs are removed, they are apparently as sweet as parsnips. Marsh lizards also have a passion for them. Great big thick snakes with six small legs is how he described them."

Caspar looked down at his feet and hurriedly whistled Trog to him. "Snakes! Trog, heel. Heel!" He was immediately intent on getting away from the water; he had a particular aversion to snakes. Trog, however, was too intent on a small movement that stirred the reeds.

The wolfling shrieked, her quarters dipping as her tail was dragged down into the marsh. Trog dived into the shallows at her side, plunging his nose into the black water while Caspar lunged for the wolfling and grabbed her around the neck, pulling her to him. He caught a glimpse of a gnarled black snout clamped about her tail, the rest of the creature's body submerged in the muddy waters. The wolfling suddenly came free and Caspar fell back into the mud with her soft white body on top of him.

Trog's mud-blackened snout came up from the water, his teeth dripping with blood. He strutted proudly towards Caspar and the others, waiting until he was no more than three foot from them before shaking himself wildly and throwing the stinking slime of the bog and toad juice over all of them bar Perren who had stepped back and prepared himself for just this eventuality. Though he was pleased that Trog had seen off the marsh lizard, Caspar looked in horror at the thick blobs of toad ink. Perren had been right; it stank – and far worse than the hen house after Pip had neglected to clean it out – as was his wont.

They crossed the river set out at a steady pace, feeling unutterably miserable and only cheered by the fact that Firecracker's footprints were now more marked. The ink proved impossible to remove; Caspar had tried everything, rinsing in the river and scrubbing himself with reeds but still the vile-smelling liquid stuck fast to his clothes and skin. He growled at Trog, blaming him for this atrocity. The dog, however, seemed quite delighted with his new smell and strutted ahead proudly, sniffing left and right in the hope of finding new toads to conquer. Perren appeared smugly pleased that he alone had avoided contamination.

"We'll never get within an inch of anybody smelling like this," Fern complained, wrinkling his nose.

They marched on and by mid-afternoon were clear of the marshes and passed through low lying water meadows where slow streams wound through tall grasses peppered by flag iris and campion in brilliant display. Caspar was amazed to see such lushness even this far south in Vaalaka. A small herd of scruffy-looking cows grazed lazily, some lying down to chew the cud, and it wasn't long before they saw the tiled roofs of a village. It was an idyllic scene: perhaps half-a-dozen circular stone houses huddled around a low arched bridge spanning the bright water of a shallow river. Caspar sighed. He could see children playing merrily, chasing chickens and clambering on and off an overgrown ruin of stone arches and roofless cloisters. Huge, cleanly cut slabs of stone footed the buildings and indicated the grandeur of their former glory.

A man in a wide-brimmed hat and a long silvery-black cloak was chasing after the children with a stick, spurts of flame apparently bursting forth from his fingertips! The children shrieked but with delight, not fear. And when they spied the approaching strangers, they turned as one, pointing and shrieking with laughter and abandoning their sport with the chickens. The chickens squawked indignantly and began to peck each other, two cockerels leaping up into the air and kicking out with their spurred feet as if to vent their anger at being chased by the children.

There was a gleeful hoot from one of the older boys, who was pointing at the bedraggled company.

"Toady, toady, you're a stinking toady!" the children cried in unison and then shrank back from the sight of Perren's bulk and his rocky face. "What's that?" one screamed though the rest were driven forward by curiosity and soon began their taunting chant again when Perren made no threatening move.

Caspar, who didn't register that these Vaalaka village children were speaking to him in clear Belbidian, scowled at them and then, too late, remembered Trog. "Heel!" He snapped his fingers but Trog was not of an obedient nature. The snake-catcher merely cast back guiltily over his shoulder before setting off, dirt kicking up in spurts from his heels as he sprang after the chickens.

Yipping with delight, he plucked out tail feathers, the hens giving out satisfactory squawks of panic. Runa slunk forward, preparing to make her own pounce but, though she sprang and leapt enthusiastically, she was no match for the long-legged fowl.

The man who had been playing with the children did not look pleased. "Knaves! Villains! The world is full of you. Already this week my chickens have been savaged. They won't lay for a fortnight now and someone has to pay."

Impressed by this booming outburst, Trog forsook the chickens to cock his head at the stranger. The wolfling imitated her mentor.

Though he had shining yellow hair, Caspar found it hard to believe that this man was of Vaalakan birth. All the Vaalakans he had ever seen had been heavily built with thick sturdy muscles, their hair worn long and straggly to the shoulders. Even though despite his bright hair he was clearly of considerable age, the man was too slight and well-groomed and had none of the hard-bitten look of the northern nomads. He spoke Belbidian with educated ease, and now that he thought of it, Caspar realized that the children also possessed this skill. Though Belbidian was second nature to the peoples of the Caballan, used exclusively for commerce, surely it was rare for a Vaalakan to speak clear Belbidian since they practised little trade. Evidently, life was very much easier along this thin strip of land south of the Dragon Scorch and bordering the Caballan where the soft climate of the coast dulled the edge of the harsh winters that sliced through the rest of Vaalaka.

"How dare you attack my chickens?" the man cried angrily, flashes of purple light bursting from his fingers. Like the children, he too eyed Perren suspiciously and Caspar gave the man great credit for his composure since he did not exclaim in fear or even amazement.

Trog was so impressed by this flash of light that he hurtled back to Caspar and stood quaking behind his legs. Conversely, Runa padded forward in total disregard of the fireworks and sniffed around the ground where the flames had left little purple scorch marks, wagging her tail and cautiously sniffing towards the old man.

He was more impressed by Runa than he was by Perren. "A wolf!" he exclaimed in amazement. Caspar was surprised at the note of appreciation rather than revulsion in his voice. "A little wolf cub!"

Runa lifted her head and snuffled at his hand when he bent down to examine her. Caspar had never before seen a man so unafraid of a wolf. He also thought him unwise. Runa had a way of nipping strangers. She still had those puppy-sharp needle teeth that, though they would not crush like an adult wolf, would draw blood at the slightest contact.

He looked up and smiled. "Well, I've not seen strangers in these parts in years and then, all of a sudden in the same week, I meet two groups, as rum a looking lot as you would ever see, and both covered in toad juice."

The children laughed, pointed and gurgled out their cries and taunts. Caspar retaliated by sticking out his tongue. The children were greatly amused by this though the elderly man seemed unimpressed. "What are you doing trespassing here?"

"We are merely heading east. That's hardly trespassing?" Caspar replied indignantly.

"You've been stealing valuable ink juice!" the man said officiously. "You're lucky that the hunters are out; they won't take lightly to you stealing our ink."

"I will gladly pay for it," Caspar said apologetically though he thought the man mad for making such an absurd accusation. "I only wish we could give it back. We can't get it off us."

The man laughed. "Pay you shall. You have good manners, young man. The others refused to pay and they will stink and suffer for it. They were not what you might call friendly. Never offered to pay for their damage and threatened me instead with a plague of boils and tooth rot. But the curse will die with them and I'm not concerned."

"What did they look like, these others?" Caspar asked feigning mild interest.

"An odd pair, though perhaps no odder than yourselves." He glanced at Fern and Perren. "They had a limping horse and a girl with them. But come, you had best have the cure otherwise your stench will draw the toadeaters to us and the hunters are in the marshes and, I tell you now, we don't want to be caught unprotected."

Caspar thought not. He had no idea how gruesome a toadeater, as the man called the marsh lizard, might be and he didn't want to find out. His chief concern at that moment was to rid himself of the stench; he could barely think for the nausea it gave him. They were led to the central house that was peculiarly large and grand for such a remote village, following the man in the broad-brimmed hat who waved his great stick about and dramatically chanted strange words while emitting more flashes of blue light from his fingers.

Caspar grinned in amusement.

"You are not impressed by the fearsome magic of the arch-mage in exile?" the old man demanded. "That is only one of my names; I have many more, all of them terrible."

"Indeed," Caspar laughed. "An arch-mage? Where then is your magic?" Many times, he had heard the three high priestesses murmur spells and, when they did, the air trembled with magic. He had also sensed such power in Ursula but curiously, he had not realized it until now. This man, however, plainly spoke words of his own invention that did not draw on elemental powers.

"You speak no tongue belonging to the world of men," Perren accused him, his voice deep and gravelly.

"Indeed not," the man replied grandly. "I speak the hidden magic of the language of the hobgorms."

Caspar's grin broadened as he stared the man full in the eye and watched him blink. "The hobgorms?"

"Oh yes, it is a fearful magic dragged down from the thunderclouds," he said in a tremendous voice that had the children squealing with awed delight. "Have you not heard of the fiery beings that live up in the firmament? They are born of thunder and lightning and, be warned, they spit their revenge on those that do not revere them." Again, flashes of bright light sprang from the man's fingers and Caspar could not but help himself any longer and began to laugh vigorously.

"Please, sir, do not waste your camphor oil. Save it for others that might be better impressed."

The man looked at him, aghast. "You are a mage then?"

Caspar saw no reason to disillusion him as the man opened the door to his house. They were still close to the coast and Caspar had expected to see stores of potted fish or seashells or perhaps ducks and geese off the marshes. He had expected a simple peasant's room with a small fire and a bubbling pot with a woman, toothless and warty, stirring an unappetising porridge. He had expected stale-smelling, lazy dogs with flea-bitten coats scratching by the hearth. What he did not expect was this fine interior nor its cool sloping floor of flagstones glistening with oil that led down beneath an arch into another room that beckoned them with flickering firelight.

The flagstones were smooth with use and in Caspar's opinion the fine hairlike lines between them indicated that they had been laid by worthy craftsman. The room beyond the arch was an open hall with huge, curved timbers that supported the roofing rafters. Upon the fire, a pot was simmering with the steady rhythmical gluck and burp of a treacly liquid. A long sword, beautifully crafted and adorned with lettering etched into the fuller, hung above the fire's bressummer beam. Caspar struggled to read the lettering. He was never very attentive to such lessons in his childhood but, deciding the words were Ceolothian, wondered how the weapon came to this remote Vaalakan village.

The vapour from the cauldron wafted in their direction and, over his own stench, Caspar caught the scent of something overpoweringly sweet. A black-haired woman stood before the pot, stirring slowly. She wore the same shimmering black material as the man in the hat, hints of silver twinkling magically within the thread. Quite priceless. His eyes roved and, everywhere he looked, the hall was hung with rich clothes of vibrant colours. The walls were clad with shelves bearing any number of vials filled with bright liquids of all colours as well as bowls of berries, insects, crushed rocks and bark. Young women and girls busily loaded fabrics into vats and poured carefully measured mixes of dye from the shelves, singing as they worked. All of them had a similar look, being golden-haired, long-limbed and blessed with graceful movements. The only thing that detracted from their beauty was that mostly their jaws were a little too square.

Huge barrels, neatly stacked in one corner, half-obscured the entrance to a darker chamber cluttered with even more barrels. To his left was another windowless chamber lit by torches, the flagstones whitened by constant scrubbing. There was a hollow in the ground and runnels that led away from it to another dip in which lay a vast bronze dish that glinted in the torchlight. Caspar wondered at this extraordinary place.

"So, at last Elergian, the sovereign's servant, the great mage in exile, has impressed you," the golden-haired man declared.

"Indeed!" Caspar replied honestly.

Fern was trembling beside him. "Spar, we should not stay here. It would be better to smell, would it not?"

The tall woman in the shimmering black dress turned very slowly and Caspar found his eyes drawn towards her. She was compelling, not like the three high priestesses but rather in a humbler and more gentle way – more like Ursula who gave the impression of harbouring many long-silent secrets. Unlike all the other women, she had dark hair, very rare indeed in Vaalaka and, though probably well into her forties, she appeared to be with child. Her hand rested on her small bulge as she assessed Caspar and his companions at length, and she smiled sympathetically.

"Oh dear, poor things. You'd best strip your clothes off right now and put them in the pot there." She nodded to one at the back of her fire that slurped and bubbled at a faster rate. "I'll get you cleaned up and, poor man," she looked at Perren, "the process will help heal your—" She faltered and smiled.

With less sensitivity the man continued, "I have seen such grey and warty scars before. I have been beyond the Diamond Seas and seen men burnt and pocked by searing volcanic dust that hardened their skin. You have travelled far, stranger."

Perren looked at him as if he were mad but merely grunted and Caspar was at last enlightened as to why the golden-haired man had shown no alarm at the sight of the stonewight. The young women drew Lana aside behind a screen to give her some privacy while the rest of the company were expected to bathe in the centre of the open hall. The pregnant woman gave them each a black cake of soap, which Caspar had thought would make them dirtier but instead it seemed to absorb the foul slime into its spongy texture.

Perren would not take any. When everyone insisted, he grumbled that he had been smart enough to avoid being splattered by the toad juice.

"But it'll heal you," the woman insisted.

Perren looked affronted. "I like myself just the way I am," he said and stubbornly withdrew to sit down with his back against the wall to watch.

Caspar examined the soap. "Charcoal," he said in surprise, recognising the substance from the wellroom in Torra Alta.

She nodded. "Yes, but with the pellets from a toadeater's gizzard. It's the only thing that really gets the smell out."

"Poor Cracker! Poor Ursula!" Fern said unexpectedly. "They will still be covered in this." He showed more concern that the slave-girl was covered in the foul-smelling ink than he had at her capture and the torture she was likely to face. Caspar decided the woodwose only understood people's suffering if it directly related to his own.

The woman shrugged. On closer inspection, her long hair was an unnatural black that matched her gown and Caspar suspected they were both dyed with the same substance.

Unashamedly, he pulled off his clothes and, standing quite naked, threw them into the pot. In other circumstances he might have blushed at exposing his slight frame but, right now, he didn't care what he did so long as he was rid of that intolerable smell. Fern, on the other hand, was less than keen at the idea of stripping, and squealed anxiously when the woman tugged at his coat. Only on Caspar's insistence did he finally disrobe. The woman gasped and even Caspar was surprised to see that he was covered in a soft down similar in colour to that of a red squirrel.

She did not comment but urged them towards a huge cauldron splashed with many multicoloured spills that had dried over the rim. The pot was now filled with warm water and rested close by the heat of the fires. They sat submerged up to their necks in the water and were told that they would have to remain there for at least an hour.

It was soon clear that they were not immersed in water alone. For a start, it was thicker and more silvery than water but more so, not only did it clean Caspar's skin to a depth that it had never been since he was born, but it also refreshed his aching joints. The mage in exile, as Elergian called himself, appeared from time to time to stir in various sweet-scented herbs as well as arnica and hyssop for wounds, aches and sprains. On balance, Caspar decided that it was well worth falling prey to the dreaded toad ink just to receive this treatment.

Elergian insisted on pacing around and muttering charms just before scooping up the warm syrupy liquid into a ladle and anointing their heads with it. Perren's snores rumbled through the proceedings, evidently much to the mage's annoyance since he clearly enjoyed an awed audience and more than once tripped over him as if he had never seen the stonewight.

Predictably, Trog would have nothing to do with the bath and howled with fury as several girls dragged him towards a smaller basin. It was only when the lady with the silken black hair took the less protesting wolfling and began to gently wash her that Trog looked like he might be missing out on something and succumbed.

Towards the end of their long soak, when the black patches had at last begun to fade and Elergian had finally resigned himself to the less ostentatious duties of crushing herbs, berries and beetles to add to the toad dye, there was a sudden burst of excited shouts from outside.

"Elergian! Elergian!" young voices were shouting and continued excitedly in a foreign language.

Caspar frowned, trying to concentrate on the words. But surely, they spoke Ceolothian not Vaalakan, something about "a big one". Boots thumped the flagstones accompanied by the sound of something heavy being dragged. The mage hastily looked up as half a dozen youths and young men came panting into the hall, dragging a large reptilian carcass by its thick tail. Caspar strained his neck up to look over the brim of his cauldron and grimaced at the sight of a white-bellied lizard with six legs and a stumpy horn on its duck-billed head. It looked to be the weight of a large stag.

"We have visitors," Elergian warned the young men who strode hastily into the hall but politely spoke in Belbidian to avoid excluding Caspar and his friends. "You've grown brave or foolish, my hunters. You risked much attempting to catch one of such size." The mage was evidently concerned for the returning hunters. Caspar guessed by his air of protectiveness that these youths had once been playing around his feet and chasing chickens much as the children they had seen earlier.

"We were neither. The beast was already dead."

"Dead?" The mage looked at him aghast.

"He was. Look! You can see for yourself that there's not a spear mark on him."

"Stand back! He might only be sleeping," Elergian shouted in alarm, wrestling a long knife off one of the hunters.

The toadeater showed no signs of moving when it was prodded with the knife and the mage relaxed a little. They heaved it over, its six legs splayed out wide like a dead mole's and Caspar glimpsed at its slit eyes that were weeping blood. He shuddered involuntarily.

"Take it through to the far chamber for opening. We shall have celebrations tonight." Elergian was beaming as the young men dragged away the carcass, the scales rasping on the smooth floor.

Still soaking in his barrel, Trog was whimpering for mercy against the cleansing suds though Runa was lapping at the liquid and taking a childlike delight in splashing vigorously.

Caspar was beginning to worry that his skin would rot away and that the prunelike wrinkles in his palms and soles of his feet might be irreversible when he was distracted by the disembowelling of the giant duck-billed toadeater. Eight men pinned it upside down by its head, tail and each of the six spindly legs. The mage in exile, after chanting more of his rhymes and waving a curved and ornate blade in a ritualistic fashion, slit open the smooth pale belly revealing the dark glistening viscera within. The men stared anxiously as if they had prised open an oyster and were looking for a pearl. Then there was a great gasp of satisfaction and, in a sanctimonious voice, Elergian called for the golden plate.

"Careful now, be very careful," he warned as they eased the great dish under the toadeater. Delicately, he sliced and separated the bloody innards, his fingers squelching amongst the organs and membranes. "I have it!" he cried with satisfaction. "Reyna, help me," he called urgently and the pregnant woman hurried to him, a great beaming smile brightening her otherwise careworn face. She held out her hands to help him support the bladderlike sac and together they eased it onto the dish.

"It's bloated and ready to burst," he warned.

Reverently, they made their way to an altar slab where the mage rang a series of light-noted bells. Caspar watched in fascination as Elergian returned to the carcass armed with several hooked implements and a grim expression. With gritted teeth, he began sawing and tearing, emerging occasionally from his labour with his arms bloodied up past his elbows, to have his brow wiped.

"It's lodged against the spine," he said sternly and there was a general intake and holding of breath while he worked on. Finally, he emerged with a smaller sac, vivid green in colour, which he slid onto another plate. "We were lucky to get this one. He must have eaten himself to death. I've never seen a foul sac so swollen."

He carried the foul sac gingerly to a scrubbed cauldron in which a brew of silvery liquid gently simmered. He caught Caspar's eye. "If it bursts at this point, the smell would knock everyone in this chamber unconscious for a week. Worth a thousand times the toad ink when we've finished with it. Worth more than all these fabrics."

Caspar was impressed. The fabrics were of fine silk and spectacularly coloured. "You mean all these wonderful colours come from the toad juice too."

The man nodded. "With some additions of course. It's quite brilliant, isn't it? The amount of dye in the toad is minute and it would take years to gather up this quantity from them. Moreover, the foul-smelling substance is mixed in their ink. But our great friend, the toadeater, he munches the toad and his body separates the toad juice into pure dye in one sac and the poison in the other. In this state, I could probably sell the foul sac for a small kingdom since it is quite deadly but we have discovered that by boiling and distilling and with use of herbs, we can render down the poisons and drop by drop make trinoxia." He spoke the word with great reverence.

Caspar felt a snort rising in his throat. "But that's just a story. Trinoxia indeed!"

Perren grumbled and shook himself awake. "Er, a story? Someone mention a story?"

"No, it's not a story." Elergian nodded at a row of silvery vials on the wall. "It's so potent that it will cure all but the deepest of wounds and has been known to have a great effect on plague but I get a tenth of the money for the trinoxia than I would for selling the raw poison. I get requests daily for that but—"

"Naturally," Caspar interrupted, "conscience forbids."

He nodded in acquiescence. "Well, particularly Reyna's," he added, a smile growing as he studied Caspar's intent face. "You believe me!" There was childlike delight in his voice. "No one yet in the Caballan has believed me and either I or Reyna's good husband, Calyx, have had to take the journey ourselves once every few years to the Diamond Seas to sell our wares. But the dyes, of course, we can sell everywhere even to Oriaxia and beyond." He gestured vaguely towards the unknown worlds that lay to the east. "Calyx has been gone a good month now with the last batch."

Reyna looked down at her swelled belly and sighed. The mage looked at her with the same concern he had shown towards the hunters. She was old to bear children, Caspar thought, and judging by the faces of young women and girls around, he suspected that most of them were her offspring.

"I have washed in trinoxia every day to give me strength to bear this child so that the curse might be lifted." There was gleam of hope in her eyes and she stared deep into the silvery pool of the bath water as if staring far beyond. "Has every part of you been fully immersed?" she questioned. "Come, you must now drink of trinoxia, which will bring on the three deep sleeps. Nothing else will stop the poison, which though slow acting will weaken you gradually and eventually, though it takes a few months, will work through your skin into your blood. And none will nurse you through the agony of your last days for the stench of the boils erupting around your neck. A most ugly death."

The skin at Caspar's neck suddenly felt hot and he scrubbed more vehemently. When he finally emerged, he was delighted to find his muscles springy and his knee free of pain for the first time in days. He grinned but then remembered that Ursula and Firecracker had also been sullied by the insipid and foul-smelling poison. "We must go after them now. We've no time to lose," he told his companions.

"Only after the three sleeps," Reyna insisted. "Your clothes will be dry then as well." Turning to Elergian, she said quietly, "Perhaps our exile will shortly be over."

"I have searched the skies nightly and there have been no such omens," he replied.

"Pah! You wouldn't know the omens written in the stars any more than you can cut slivers from the moon to enhance our dyes." She laughed.

He nodded his head. "There is a smidgen of truth in that, my sovereign."

As Reyna had prophesised, Caspar was beginning to feel quite woozy and was carried by the hunters to a lavish hall decked with couches and strange artefacts that would not have looked out of place in a castle. Tapestries of the most extraordinary colours, depicting armoured men bearing swords, pikes and huge lances, all pointed for battle not tournament, caught Caspar's eye; but he was quickly distracted from the wall hangings by a glass-fronted cabinet. Within, was a crown set on a red velvet cushion. The crown was fashioned in white gold and set with sunburst rubies on each of its twelve points. He was pondering on how such an object could come to be there when sleep overtook him.

On waking, he found himself ravenously hungry and thirsty. He hurriedly dressed and helped Perren to bandage his face and hands in fresh cloth and chose a large black cloth that could be fashioned into a cloak, while a table was set with laden plates. The stonewight had become fed up with constantly denying that he had been burnt with volcanic ash and decided that he would resume his disguise.

Evidently, the dye-makers were not used to such appetites, even for those partaking of the cure, because they stared on wide-eyed and were most particularly amazed by Fern's habit of picking bits from other people's plates to either side of him. The woodwose eyed Caspar's bowl of fruit, stealing it the minute the youth was distracted by Reyna.

During the meal Caspar had several times heard Elergian addressing Reyna as "My Sovereign", and he found the title especially odd since she appeared so straightforward and busy and no one as yet had bowed and scraped at her feet.

"Where are you heading, Caspar?" she asked, seeing that he was gazing at her.

He took a deep breath while deciding what to say. "We are hunting a wolf, a very evil wolf." It was as easy to believe as the story of their trinoxia and their own extraordinary circumstances and not very far from the truth. "But when the third sleep is past, I must buy from you, at whatever cost, enough trinoxia to cure my friend and my horse and hasten after them. They are headed towards Castaguard in—"

"In Ceolothia," Reyna interrupted, groaning with the effort of pushing herself to her feet. She looked down mysteriously at her rounded belly and smoothed the growing bulge. "My price is that you take me there."

The old mage exclaimed in dismay that such an idea was quite ridiculous; Reyna was not travelling anywhere in her condition and besides trinoxia was worth fifteen sunburst rubies a vial, and she couldn't just give it away. "What would Calyx say? He would stop you."

She sniffed at him, unperturbed by this outburst. "Calyx isn't here!" she said with a degree of triumph that made Caspar suspect that she had engineered his absence. "I have to get to Castaguard before my time! That is my payment and this youth will take me."

Caspar didn't want any strangers with him. "I have burdens enough of my own—" he began to bluster excuses.

Reyna would not listen. "Few travel this way as it is but to think you are going to Castaguard . . . It is an omen!"

"You know no more of omens than I do," Elergian protested.

"Ah, but I am pregnant and a woman with child taps into latent powers, especially," she said in a grand and imposing voice, "one that carries within her the rightful heir to all Ceolothia."

Caspar spluttered on his drink, wondering at what stage King Dagonet had befriended this woman. This news, however, had a more stunning effect on his hosts than he could have imagined. They stood on their chairs and danced and screamed and leapt with delight, some of the younger ones evidently so overcome that they rushed to the antechamber, no doubt to be sick, while others emptied wine over their heads. Another juggled bunches of grapes while the eldest of the girls moved towards the crown and lifted it to offer to her mother who, laughing and as childlike as her offspring for the moment, placed it on her belly. There were shrieks of delight and riotous clapping. The mage rammed his staff onto the stone floor, commanding silence.

"My dear Reyna," he said reprovingly and took the crown from her hand and placed it ceremoniously back on its cushion. He blew off any dust and dabbed at it with a cloth to remove the smudges, tutting in disapproval. The rest sat down contritely. "You have borne twelve children like your mother, your grandmother, your great-grandmother and your great-great-grandmother before you and so on and so forth, back for twenty-seven generations. I begged you not to have a thirteenth. The twelve have weakened you and you are old and weary."

"I will succeed!" she said in fierce determination. "I shall. I must. I will not let my eldest girl go through this as I have done. I care not that the boy be a prince or a pauper but I will break this wretched curse that is a upon us."

Elergian patted her hand and Caspar at once saw the unutterable, unspeakable pain cloistered in his heart. He turned and looked at him. "But she will die. It was prophesised that only the thirteenth child will be a boy and only a boy will succeed to the throne but all the mothers have died with their thirteenth child before birth. The generations stretch back and all have died, in torment, in agony, the child too strong, too big for its own mother, destroying her from within before it could be born. And so, the curse and its burden have passed to the eldest daughter."

"And it is a curse I will break." Reyna stamped her foot determinedly, her jaw set. "I will live. I have taken trinoxia every day, bathed in it and fed on it and I am strong," she said determinedly though Caspar could see she was not. "And he must be born on Ceolothian soil. A prince cannot be born in exile." She turned on Caspar. "And you will take me." Her words were a steady and certain command.

All Caspar could think was the last thing he needed was to be encumbered by a maddened and pregnant woman. "I will take you nowhere," he said, trying to keep calm, "until I understand what all this is about."

"Sit back and drink your wine because I can tell this story." It was Perren who spoke, his voice muffled by his bandages. "It was but seven hundred years ago when the King of Ceolothia shunned his apparently childless wife. And all the world knew of it, and also where he begat the child that he presented as his chosen heir to his court, for it looked not at all like his wife but every bit like his sister who had been in supposed religious retreat for the best part of a year. Since then, the Ceolothian royal house has lived with a curse; each generation, the eldest son has been unfit to rule due to a weakness of the mind brought about by this incest. So, ever since, it has been the second son who has inherited the crown."

Perren paused for breath and cracked his knuckles, the sound alarmingly loud. "Now all of us know that in human terms the king's deed was a sin and a wrong."

There was a general nodding around the chamber.

"But what few know is that the wife of this king did in fact bear a child – a little girl – and this is possibly why the prince turned to his sister, for he was displeased that he didn't receive a boy and it was rumoured that the birth damaged the mother so that she could bear no more children. Although a girl, this baby was the rightful heir to all Ceolothia. But the custom dictates that she could not rule in her own right but could only allow her husband to command in her stead until she bore a son.

"The king's sister learnt of this baby and naturally wanted her own son to inherit and had the baby girl sent away with its uncle, the mage. It was an easy thing to do since the populace of Ceolothia would accept a boy without question and be unsettled with the offering of a female heir.

"Fortunately, the king's sister could not bring herself to kill this child but put a curse on her, saying that she would bare twelve daughters before she bore a son that could claim the throne; and that not until wolves are welcomed back into the hearts of men shall that son live – which naturally was tantamount to saying never."

Reyna turned to Caspar. "And, in the glad company of a wolf, you pass through our village on your way to Castaguard

– of all places – during my thirteenth pregnancy – of all times. You will take me there."

"Are you telling me that you are the descendants of an ancient king of Ceolothia?" Caspar spoke indistinctly, his mouth full of food.

She nodded.

"You should claim the throne in your own right rather than wait for a son," Caspar told her, picking suspiciously at a giant grilled frog's leg on a bed of marsh marigolds. "There have been many queens, many successful queens in the Caballan."

"But not in Ceolothia. The people would revolt," Reyna explained. "Besides it is not the throne I seek but to break this curse by bearing a son so that my daughter can live as other women do. I would not have my daughter and her line suffer this curse for another seven hundred years." Her teeth were fiercely gritted and Caspar shrank back from the vehemence of her emotions.

"I cannot take you," he said, surprised at his decisions. "Any other time . . ." Aware of all the pleading eyes looking at him he tried to excuse himself. "There are enough of you. You can surely get to Castaguard without me."

The woman shook her head. "But you carry the wolf."

"You mean Runa?" He nodded at the white wolfling curled up and snoring softly against Trog's chest.

She nodded. "Yes, but more than that. You are the protector of the wolf."

Caspar wondered how she could possibly know this.

"The first mother," she said referring to the queen that had been shunned for the king's sister, "practised the ancient arts before the New Faith overwhelmed Ceolothia and we have been waiting long for the old religion to rise again. We have kept true to the Faith in our hearts and our learning." She fetched in her pockets and clutched something small in her hand. "I'm afraid you won't forgive me. I took the liberty of searching your pockets before washing your clothes. I found this." She opened her palm to reveal a smooth piece of carved bone. "It's marked with a rune, the rune of the wolf. The wolf is welcome in your heart; my time has come!"

Caspar abruptly rose and lunged across the table, knocking over his goblet of wine in his haste to snatch back the rune Morrigwen had given him. "But I cannot take you. My errand is vital! Urgent!" Though his voice was sharp, his heart forgave him. Here was a woman likely to die in childbirth, if family tradition were anything to go by, and leave twelve girls of the Old Faith – all orphans.

Reyna sat back and smiled at him slyly. "But you *will* take me with you to Castaguard. You are the one that holds the love of the wolf in your heart and that will protect me from the curse. Besides, if you do not take me with you, I will not give you the trinoxia needed to cure your friends." She smiled with triumphant sweetness.

CHAPTER TWENTY-ONE

May sank to her knees, overwhelmed by exhaustion and terror. Fearsome notes filled with magical command rang through the refectory hall, the song directed at the beasts around her, subjugating them into cowering shadows. The crazed soldier before her dropped his dogtoothed blade and fled.

When a firm hand clutched her wrist, she crumpled entirely, relief sapping her last strength. "Amaryllis! Oh, Amaryllis, sweet mercy!"

The fleeing soldier banged into tables and tripped on the uneven floor and was soon lost into the smoky haze that obscured the far end of the chamber. Amaryllis turned his song on the nearest soldier, who stiffened and then ran after his colleague, only to return moments later, saying he had vanished into one of the deep shafts.

Extraordinarily, the rest of the Ceolothian soldiers sat peacefully and listened to Amaryllis as he turned his song to gentler notes. To May's amazement, he sang one of the soldiers' own Ceolothian songs that she had heard them sing earlier but it was almost unrecognisable, such was the passion and beauty that Amaryllis gave it.

He hugged her, enveloping her in his strength, and in a pause between songs, murmured softly in her ear, "My sweet Merrymoon, fear not, I shall protect you. But before you left the port of Skuas Ria, you could have conjured a great winged horse for me so that I could have kept pace with your unicorn. You have made me run hard and fast," he scolded jovially.

May could not begin to understand how Amaryllis had caught up with her so quickly. Nothing could have moved as fast as the unicorn. And how had he known about it? Right now, she barely cared. She let him wrap her up in his arms and rock her back and forth as he sang a gentle ballad.

The soldiers watched and listened attentively and applauded loudly at the end of each piece. Finally, he sighed, "Though it is good to sing, I'm tired of these Ceolothian ballads. They have no nobility in them." Laughing playfully, he began a lullaby that was so sweet and soft, it lulled her into drowsiness. She could see that it had the same effect on the soldiers. One by one, their heads drooped towards the tables and a few were fully slumped and snoring blissfully.

May could barely keep her eyes open and she sank back into Amaryllis's embrace. He brushed her hair back from her face and kissed her cheek. She didn't care. She didn't have the strength to resist him anymore. Amaryllis made her feel safe and she was glad he had found her.

"Poor, sweet, Merrymoon," he soothed, "but I cannot use my voice on you." He stroked her cheek and the sleepiness left her. When she looked up, however, she saw that every one of the soldiers was asleep.

"How did you get here?" she asked.

"I ran!" He laughed.

"Your legs are too short," she remarked in teasing then wished she hadn't.

"In your terms, I am short," he conceded, "but I am strong and fast – though not so fleet of foot as a unicorn. Any other creature that runs on the earth I might have overtaken but not a unicorn." He picked up a piece of bread that had been left at one of the tables and nibbled at it. He pulled away and looked at it, his nose wrinkling in disgust but then took another bite and searched around for more appetising scraps. "Reduced to this! But a fellow has to eat."

Chewing at a stringy joint of meat, too undercooked for her taste, May noticed with surprise that Amaryllis was also daubed with a painted blue circle on the back of his hand.

"What special trade did you offer them? Your singing?" she asked innocently.

"Singing!" he scoffed. "They'd have been as much interested in a singer as they were in your storytelling."

"But I was taken on as a storyteller!"

"Were you now? Seems to me you were taken on as a maiden with a pretty face and a fine body. Storytelling and singing indeed! No, I told them of my thaumaturgy and alchemy. After all, I am a wizard of Gorta and, sweet Merrymoon, I told them that my beautiful though rather muddled assistant had preceded me and they recognized my description of you easily enough. So, until your deed is done and we have buried this thing in the deepest shaft in the furthest corner of King Dagonet's ruby mines, my assistant is what you shall be. But do not look so glum, there is more," he added, his tone suddenly frivolous. "We shall not leave here empty-handed; the rewards for a true alchemist are very high. Mountains of gold coins, I am told." He laughed at the thought as though such wealth were of no interest to him before his face fell sombre and he looked around at the sleeping soldiers.

"Couldn't you put them all to sleep? The whole mine?" May asked.

He smiled softly. "I wish I could put all the world to

sleep so that just you and I remained. But the song is only a trick and I need to be close to someone to have an effect on them. And some hearts are hardened against it. No, my Merrymoon, we will do this your way, with stealth and cunning, not with singing." He looked at her, a beaming smile spread across his handsome face. "You are glad I came for you?" It was only half a question.

May looked at the dark stained stone floor. She had prayed that Caspar would come but, for now, she was glad of Amaryllis. Looking up, she returned his smile. She did not understand his purpose nor his extraordinary powers but he had saved her several times now. And when he had wrapped her in his arms, he saved her from the deepest agony of her loneliness, dulling the acute pain of losing all hope of Caspar.

In the days that followed, Amaryllis never let May from his sight as they made their slow journey through crumbling worked-out tunnels that cut under the mountains. May learnt that the profitable seams nearer Castaguard had long since been mined out and, over the centuries, the shafts and tunnels had delved further and further north and down beneath the cold of the Kalanazir mountains.

With the help of Amaryllis, who remarkably already knew the language, she passed much of her time struggling with the rudiments of Ceolothian. The soldiers insisted on using their own tongue and, out of necessity, she found she quickly grasped a few phrases and after several days began to understand a little of what was said even if she could not find the right words to express herself.

In places, the mineshafts were in such disrepair that they were forced to return to the surface and continue overland where the going was tough. Biting winds stung her face and she screwed her eyes up against the pain.

Stumbling wearily, she clutched at Amaryllis for support as they laboured around the steep stony shoulders of the mountains.

After half a day's forced march overland, May was thankful to be herded down again into the sheltered tunnels that now followed an underground river, the path no more than a narrow slippery ledge overhanging the churning waters. They were driven in bands and May cringed as stock whips split the air, often slicing into the back of some poor slave. Several even threw themselves into the river to be dragged under by the rolling waters rather than endure any more misery. Judging by the way the guards made no effort to retrieve them, she doubted that any survived the river.

Amaryllis gripped May's hand tightly as they wound through the cool passageways. Though they themselves could walk upright, as they were both smaller than average, most of the slaves and workers with them had to hunch their shoulders to avoid cracking their heads on the ceiling.

They stopped each night at staging posts where they were fed dried bread. May's spirits dwindled in the constant gloom and, already, she had completely forgotten the harshness of the weather above and was glad when at last they were driven up a succession of steeply rising passages and staired shafts.

When the final stair disgorged them into the brightness, the sudden cold air stole her breath. She was grateful of her bearskin and even more grateful for Amaryllis's strong hand pulling her on. She knew she would not have made the journey without him. The weak that fell at the side of the rocky track were left to survive in the mountains alone – something they were unlikely to do. She had no strength to help them.

As that afternoon continued, the wind swung round into their faces bringing snow and soon shallow drifts collected between the rocks, making the broken terrain even more difficult to cross. Weak with exhaustion, she stumbled on the loose stones and was shoved angrily from behind by a soldier. Amaryllis tugged her forward and when she stumbled again, he scooped her up and carried her on his shoulders in the same way that her father had done when she was a little girl. All had marvelled, not only at his strength and stamina, but also at his sacrifice. Most pushed others aside in their own attempts to survive.

Amaryllis never left her side and growled softly in his throat if any came too close. May wondered that she hadn't truly found her guardian angel. At night, though she was grateful of his presence, she would not let him lie too close. And if she awoke from a nightmare, as she so often did, or roused from a wonderful dream where Master Spar came riding to her rescue, she would force herself to think of Amaryllis, striving to drive away her fears or her aching want of the Baron's son.

Her clothes were stiff and her skin purple and puffed with cold. Head down, and tugged along by Amaryllis, she trudged between deep banks of snow that had drifted down from the higher peaks to clog the valley. And so, it wasn't until the head of the new working mine was upon her that she saw it.

The entrance was cut into a vast single block of rock that had been carved into the shape of an ogre's head with troll-like teeth protruding from a gaping mouth. A great wide tongue, split into nine smaller tongues at its end, formed the footing as they walked into the gloom of the maw. Before entering, Amaryllis stared up unblinking into the sun and appeared to nod in reverence.

And that was another thing that was strange about him; May hadn't thought of it before. Without so much as squinting, he could look directly at the sun, the rays washing over his face and bathing him in a fabulous wash of gold. His eyes glinted. The warmth seemed to stay with him as they passed into the working mines though, clearly, he did not like being underground.

"Losing the sun is worse than the lack food," he complained.

It wasn't the gloom that made May feel uneasy but rather the thought that the maddened soldier, who had vanished into a shaft, might still be seeking her. She shrugged the feeling away, realizing that she was probably simply aware of the slaves that looked at her resentfully since she was spared the beatings and floggings they suffered. Those hired for special talents were also given an extra ration of food each morning.

They were kept to the edge of the mine shafts at the sight of small shaggy ponies shuffling nose to tail towards them, bearing panniers laden with grit. To either side, long seams had been chipped away and great tunnels built to extract the thin layer of rocks containing the precious rubies, thousands of tons excavated for the very few ounces of jewels. The echoes of picks pounding rock swam back to them along the shafts whose mouths dotted the length of the passage.

"Looks like they're opening up old shafts again to glean out the last of the rubies. They can't be finding many new seams," Amaryllis remarked.

Too staggered by the condition of the dust-coated miners, May was hardly listening. Most coughed and sputtered, many stooping over and gripping their sides with the pain. She wondered if it were dust or disease that afflicted them so.

The male slaves were permanently stooped, their joints bowing from the weight of the great baskets they carried. Worse, she deduced that they could not have been down here long since they still had some colour in their faces. One or two particularly stout men were almost sick-white with the lack of sun and Amaryllis winced at the sight, saying that he hoped her onerous task would not take long.

Curiously, May preferred this grumbling Amaryllis. He was less perfect, more human. He patted her hand as if he sensed her emotion and she turned spontaneously to smile at him. She was wondering what she would have done without him, but instead said, "What are we going to do when they find out you can't discover any veins of sunburst rubies?"

"My sweet Merrymoon, you doubt me? I am hurt."

She laughed, unsure whether he was teasing her or not. "Amaryllis, no one can find minerals like that. Diviners indeed!"

"Have faith, Merrymoon. I am not your guardian fairy for nothing."

"You're an elf," she teased with a grin, "whatever Morrigwen thought about them. But I still don't believe even an elf can detect buried gemstones."

"Ordinary gems, no, I can't. But I can find sunburst rubies," he replied with an assurance that May felt was almost genuine.

As they worked deeper, the caves kept their steady ambient temperature, the sound of dripping water constant about them. May found the sound peaceful.

"It's like we're in the womb of the Great Mother, the dripping water like her pulse. Surely this will be one of the safest places for – for it."

Amaryllis looked at her sadly, pushing away her curling hair from her eyes to look at them. Unexpectedly, he asked, "Merrymoon, will you ever love me? I need you to love me."

"What? I— But—" Though she did feel something for this strange man, her heart belonged to Caspar. Amaryllis had chased after her and saved her time and again, whereas Caspar had not. But that had been the whole point after all. If Caspar had come after her, she would never have been able to save him from the terrible seducing power of the Druid's Egg. Again, there was a nagging doubt at the back of her mind about Amaryllis's intentions. She looked deep into his curious eyes but could not read them for their strange gleaming light; she could not see the truth in his soul.

"You must love me!" he said, suddenly gripping her arms.

May pushed him away, not knowing what to say. She was grateful but gratitude was not love.

He seemed to realize that he had transgressed because he slowly withdrew his hand. Still, May was pleased. If she could not have Caspar, at least she had Amaryllis's company. She had thought at first that the pain of not being with Caspar was the worst pain she would have to bear but she had been wrong. The pain of loneliness was crueller.

They were taken to the newest face of the mine where the air was thick with dust and the ceilings even lower so that even Amaryllis had to stoop. They could barely hear for the hammer of picks and the rumble and grind of tumbling rocks. Men worked with levers to prise open seams and hammered in tapered oak pegs to spilt the rocks before pounding them with great mallets. The men here were strong though they worked with resentment and their bare backs, glistening with sweat, were striped with whip marks.

Small men with narrow chisels worked away delicately at the threads of exposed seams that May presumed held the prized rubies. From the way the soldiers paced up and down gloomily at their backs, it was clear that the seam was running out.

When Amaryllis was announced as the new thaumaturge they were met with both shouts of joy and sneers of disbelief.

"Fail and you'll be pounded with the hammers," the guard in charge of the digging threatened in Ceolothian. "We've had three of you so-called wizards of late, halting the line and wasting time, sending us on wild goose chases into black pits of crumbling rock. We lost many men but found no rubies. You will be well rewarded if you succeed but fail and you die. Now, get to work."

May looked at Amaryllis urgently and hissed, "But you don't know where they are?"

He sniffed. "Have faith. I know exactly where they are. We are no more than twelve feet from a rich seam and probably forty foot from another but that's the direction I want. It's a narrow seam but I sense that it swells out and is hollow at the centre. From that I deduce that there must be a cavern lined with the gems. If we can tap into a natural system of caverns and tunnels, we can engineer a way to seal ourselves off as well as find a way out to the surface once we are done. But first, I must persuade them that this is where to dig; and, with respect to our predecessors, we shall need to put on a good show." He turned to the guard and spoke in Ceolothian. "Your thought patterns cloud the air. You must retreat so that I can probe the elements."

"Yet another madman," a slave groaned, looking sorrowfully at his callused hands and bleeding knuckles.

"Now concentrate, Merrymoon," Amaryllis said aloud

in Ceolothian and, pressing his forehead to hers, added in a whisper in her tongue, "I need you to feign a trance. Moan and roll your eyes or whatever you can do. Behave as you imagine a sorceress might."

"I know three very well," she replied stiffly, "and they are quite matter of fact about their craft and rarely moan and groan. If they knew where the gems were, they would simply point at them and then probably roll up their sleeves and start digging."

"Well, most people don't know that. They will expect some dramatic display of divination. Dance, sing, use your imagination, but whatever you do, don't even begin to think about telling a story. That was disastrous last time."

Well, if she had to do this bizarre act, she would make a good job of it. May sat crossed legged on the floor, uncoiled her hair from her twisted braid and pushed it forward over her face. She didn't know any magic charms so she began by chanting the names of the horses that she loved most at the castle.

"Firecracker, Secret, Blueblood and Troy." She moved onto the dogs. "Fleetfoot and Warfang, Rag-Ears and Boy." She moaned softly then ran through the names of the very best of the laying hens, "Higgledy and Blackeye. Two Toes and Scratch. Piggledy and Longtail, and old Black Patch." It was the best rhyme of conjuring that she could imagine.

Rolling her head from side to side, her hair swishing in the loose scree, she clawed at the dusty ground and chanted louder. Then suddenly she sprang up and flung out her hands, dust flicking out in a cloud around her, her voice rising to an ear-splitting screech. Snatching in her arms, she began to spin and leap and crouch and, again, shouted the names of the hens. She caught Amaryllis's eye as he produced his own ululating sound from his throat, stroking the walls around the cavern, breathing in shallow bursts and echoing May's scream. He flashed her a grin, evidently pleased with her attempts at spell casting.

May did not know how long she should keep up this energetic act. Amaryllis nodded at her to continue though she was already quite exhausted and running out of ideas so she decided then that she must repeat the long poem of the spiritual properties of the trees. Amaryllis looked at her in disbelief as if surprised by her knowledge. She went on to recite the medicinal properties of the twelve most essential herbs but this had less effect on him.

At last, he took from his pocket a short hazel staff and rapped at the rock beneath his feet. "We dig down at a steeply shelving angle," he declared in Ceolothian, his voice rumbling and deepening to a booming note that shuddered the loose rocks.

May watched with a degree of satisfaction how their display had impressed the miners. She wanted to laugh except that she still did not see how Amaryllis could possibly know where the veins of rubies were to be found. Warily, she eyed the soldiers with their great clubs and wondered what would happen when they failed to uncover a single ruby.

"This is soft rock," the engineer complained, prodding the brown seam that Amaryllis had indicated to be their point of attack. "Rubies are never found in soft rock."

"That may be so. They are beyond the soft rock."

"It's too dangerous. The walls will crumble and it will take weeks of shoring just to go a matter of yards."

Amaryllis looked untroubled. "By the powers invested in me by the great lord of Agarth that gave me the sight of the underbelly of the world, the richest seams in this mine are below my feet. We dig here!" His tone was imperious, unafraid and May wondered at his charms.

"Ha!" a voice shouted out from amongst the ranks of slaves. "We know nothing of this diviner's skills. The Master Engineer said the rock was soft. It'll crumble on us for certain."

"A slave speaks. Silence him," the soldier in charge snarled.

"Wait, listen! T's too much of a risk for nothing. Test him first. Conceal a ruby and see if he can find it. It would be simple enough."

"The slave speaks well," the officer conceded.

"You treat us with a great deal more humanity when there are rubies in our baskets."

A slow smile spread across the slave-driver's face. "Indeed, that is so. Blindfold the diviner and his apprentice. Blindfold them both."

May was roughly gripped by strong hands that bruised her skin. A smelly rag was wrapped tightly about her eyes, partially restricting her breathing. Immediately afraid, she stood stiffly still, listening intently. She could hear the men scrabbling about and then, after a pause of silence, the slave-driver spoke. "Find the ruby."

"My apprentice must sing." Amaryllis's tone was confident and assured though May's voice quavered as she again began her chant of the trees. She hoped none would listen too clearly to the words while she sang of the properties of oak, ash and holly and, with particularly feeling, of hawthorn, Huathe, the may tree, with which she identified.

"Unbind their eyes," the slave-driver growled. "Diviner, find me my ruby."

"Sing louder," Amaryllis commanded and he spun around the room in a mad dance. Passing close by May, he gave her a warm smile and a wink.

He moved towards the smallest soldier in the group. A general hiss and booing from the gathered men told May at once that the slave-driver had not hidden the ruby there. Her heart thumped fast in her throat.

She was stunned when the soldier Amaryllis had pointed to drew his club. A flicker of fear blackened his face as he snarled at Amaryllis to get back.

Amaryllis turned to the slave-driver. "His top right inside pocket," he said with a smug smile.

The soldier went white and turned to run but was grabbed by two others behind him, who twisted his arms to the point of dislocation until he squealed for mercy. The slave-driver snatched up a fistful of his hair and jerked back his head before plunging his fist into the man's pocket. With a triumphant snarl, he plucked out an uncut gem. It was a pale rough-edged nugget about the size of a hazelnut.

The soldier sagged to his knees and mumbled about finding it dropped somewhere and how he had meant to hand it in directly. He was dragged away, a solemn look left on the remaining soldiers, one or two twitching uncertainly. For a moment, May had thought that Amaryllis really could see the stolen ruby but then realized he must have spotted the soldier picking up the nugget earlier. The slave-driver, however, was impressed and didn't bother to see if he would retrieve the gemstone that he had officially hidden. She was surprised at such gullibility but perhaps he wanted so much to believe in Amaryllis' skill that he was easily deceived. Those that found new rich seems were handsomely rewarded; it was a constant topic of conversation amongst the soldiers.

They began digging right away, picks whizzing dangerously close to May's feet before she had time step back. Seeing this, the slave-driver hurriedly had his prized diviner and assistant removed to a safe place of keeping and kept under lock and key with a guard outside the door. "Can't have our valuable diviner falling foul of ruffians. We have some rum fellows down here," the guard mumbled. "You'll be a rich man if you've found good seams – as will we all. But, of course, you'll both join the slaves if you prove false."

It was while May sat huddled up in her bearskin, aware of Amaryllis's gaze on her face, that she first heard the creaks, groans and knocks that seemed to shudder right through the very rock and tremble the walls of the cell.

"What was that?" she asked in alarm.

"Oh, just the earth shifting; like an old man stirring in his sleep to get more comfortable."

She nodded at his explanation and settled down for the long wait while the men mined, their picks sounding like muffled chimes as they struck rock. Over the following days she kept herself very much to herself and occupied her mind by chipping at stones to make her own set of runes, which at least gave her something to do. She knew many characters but by no means all of them. They felt warm in her hand as if they had a life of their own.

"Will they find rubies?" she asked on the third day of their incarceration.

"Of course, they will. Would I put you into such danger by sending them into blank rock?"

"You are too good," she said critically. "Far to good to be true."

"My dearest Merrymoon, the moment I saw you, I knew that I breathed only for you, that my only purpose was to make you happy."

"There! You see what I mean! Men just do not say things like that. I've been surrounded by men for many years and of course they pay me attention but not one of them has ever fallen at my feet, so to speak."

"Then they must all be blind."

"There must have been hundreds of other women that you could have chosen. Why me?" she demanded, though she was still flattered. He was a very handsome man with a voice that could melt rock. She had been silent for days but needed to talk to him to take away her fear of the groaning knocks in the walls around them.

"Because you are special, May."

She smiled dismissively. "Everybody's special."

"I've told you before. You summoned me in your hour of want. You needed me. There is much in being needed. It gives security between us and in the end, it brings love."

There was a horrible screech and a blast of air that swept back May's hair followed by a choking cloud of dust. She knew at once that something had gone wrong. The tunnel must have collapsed as the slave had feared. Soldiers came quickly and roughly dragged them out of the cell to witness the scene. "There's several soldiers and the engineer trapped somewhere in that rubble. Get him out!" they were yelling in Ceolothian.

There was no mention of slaves though there must have been many under the rubble.

"I cannot," Amaryllis replied firmly and slowly.

"You are a diviner!"

"I can see only the sunburst rubies. I cannot see men."

A pick was thrust into his hand and May was given a broad sack for dragging away rubble. Though small, she worked hard, determined to do what she could to rescue the men. When the first was free, she knew she could do more by healing wounds than continuing to struggle with the rubble. She reached for her scrip, shouting for water to cleanse the wounds and thanked the Great Mother that she had collected plenty of Caballan hyssop and willow bark to ease their pain. She was most glad of the honey paste to draw out the poisons from their wounds that were thick with rock dust.

She was pushed deeper into the rubble of the collapsed and sharply shelving shaft. Soldiers ahead called out in pain but she stooped to help a slave whose foot was crushed. She was shoved harshly down into a crack between the tumbled rocks.

"Don't you touch them. We've no time for you to help the slaves. There's plenty more where they came from." The soldier smashed his barbed club down on the slave's face, the barbs gouging deep, splitting open the skull as if he had cracked open an egg with a spoon.

May steadied herself against the crumbling walls, her world spinning, and fought to stop herself from fainting.

Whips lashed, driving the uninjured slaves into the tight tunnel to free the engineer and twelve soldiers that had been buried deep at the end of the shaft. "Get the engineer out. We must have him," a slave-driver cried.

May looked in horror at the three hands and two feet that stuck out of the wall of rubble before her and knew there was nothing she could do for those men.

One of the soldiers grabbed Amaryllis and punched him full in the stomach. "It's you that's done this, led us to this rock-fall."

Amaryllis stooped and momentarily stiffened under the pain, curving his neck, the muscles in his jaw twitching though he should have been on the floor spitting blood and groaning. The Ceolothian was twice his weight and had put all his force into the punch but Amaryllis remained on his feet and stared at him, a sneer twisting his elfin face.

May closed her ears against the misery and tried to concentrate on helping those she could. She worked quickly, wrapping wounds, applying salves, but knowing that the most she could do for many was to take away the pain with poppy seeds that grew in the far north of Oriaxia.

"In here. Further down!" another was calling from within though there was only the tiniest of gaps for May to squeeze through. She wriggled in to see the white rims of flesh surrounding a man's eyes, the rest of his face barely visible for the smothering of rock dust. She blinked at him and reached back for a lantern so that she could see better.

His leg was pulverised by the fall of rock though he had managed to use his pick to lever it free. He was not groaning or screaming though she saw from the way he trembled that he was in deep pain and suffering from shock. His hands were cold to the touch. Dark blood seeped from his leg into the rock dust to from a dark slurry. May had long since lost her squeamishness – Morrigwen had always been furious with her if she paled at the sight of an injury – and, without hesitation, she pressed hard against the mushy knee to stem the flow of blood.

Still, this crushed leg was quite abhorrent and she knew there was nothing she could do beyond stanching the wound and giving him a vial of Oriaxian poppy juice to ease his pain. The leg would have to come off, she was certain, though that was beyond her powers. He clutched at her and murmured words of thanks and she held his hand, not knowing what else she could do as they waited for the next section of the tunnel to be cleared.

Behind her, the repeated lashes of a whip and Amaryllis's stifled cries rang through the dust-choked air as the soldiers beat into him. She gritted her teeth, fighting back the tears, knowing there was nothing she could do for him. "Great Mother, spare him," she murmured and suddenly in her heart knew she would miss him very deeply if he were gone.

One by one the trapped soldiers were brought free and only when, at last, the engineer was dug out did the whipping cease.

Grasping for breath, Amaryllis called out to her in Belbidian, "Merrymoon, come back to where it's safe."

She was about to turn and wriggle back when she heard a groaning coming from the solid rock beyond the blocked tunnel. The sound was quickly blotted out by a shriek of excitement and babbling shouts of delight around the last soldier to be carried out. Though injured, his elbow twisted out of his socket, a stupid grin stretched his face. In his good hand he clutched a rock.

"I found it! I'm telling you this one's got to be bigger than the ruby in King Dagonet's crown itself," he cried in Ceolothian.

His words were greeted with sudden silence and then more shrieks of excitement. Amaryllis was being loudly praised and, from their gabbled shouts, May learnt that this find could be the soldiers' passport out of this hell-hole. They were speculating on how they would be rewarded, evidently hoping for farming lands in southern Ceolothia where the weather was clement and the sun shone for at least four months of the year. By the way they spoke, none appeared to believe that such sunshine was possible.

"There's still men in there," May called out to them in her best Ceolothian though the soldiers didn't seem to care. She crawled as far as she could into the rubble until she could see a tiny crack ahead and began pulling at it with her fingers. She could distinctly hear sorrowful moans and knew she must help. Tearing her nails in her efforts, she freed a large rock. Beyond was a blackness that echoed with the tinkle of falling pebbles. The moaning grew louder.

"Help! There's more men here!" May cried out while struggling to move another rock. "In here. Bring your picks." She could hear muffled voices now, begging for mercy. Distressed at their plight, she struggled harder and managed to enlarge the hole fractionally but could see nothing of what lay in the pitch black of the void beyond. She reached back for the lantern that the last man had left at his feet and thrust her arm into the hollow. Still, she could see nothing and wriggled her shoulder in a little deeper. She caught the glimpse of a limb beneath rubble and a brilliant golden flash as the torchlight bounced off a seam of gem-studded rock.

She gasped at such brightness after the dark. It was like looking into the sun. For a second, she thought she saw eyes all around her, red eyes staring out of the rock. Then something caught her arms and was dragging her, screaming, through the small opening, scraping her over the rocks. She knew at once that the hands were not human. The fingers were too long and cold. Struggling, she glimpsed long thin limbs and bare reptilian-shaped feet in the lantern's wavering light.

A foul-smelling hand covered her mouth, stifling her scream. The rattle and crunch of bones sounded beneath her feet.

She was being dragged down into the tunnel, her captor shrieking with maddened laughter, stumbling and reeling his way through the dark, leaving the tiny glow of the lantern far behind.

CHAPTER TWENTY-TWO

Hal groaned. He knew now why the wolves and the horsemen had separated; it was quite obvious in hindsight. Swinging in a wicker cage suspended from the boughs of a willow, he had had ample time to reflect on the situation. Pip kicked at his cage in frustration while Ceowulf slumped back against the bars of his, chewing thoughtfully on a short length of reed.

Hal was irritated by the knight's composure but even more so by Pip's persistent taunts of, "You should have listened to me." Now he was saying, "You think you're so superior and see where it's landed you."

"Hasn't anyone knocked any manners into you yet, lad?" Ceowulf asked amiably. "All you said was you saw something swinging in the trees, which isn't quite the same as 'run, there's a score of men so uncivilised that they don't have one word of Belbidian between them, about to truss us up in wicker cages', now is it?"

Hal growled through his teeth at the boy then turned to glare at the little men of the marsh on their long poles who vaulted between rafts of floating vegetation and raised mud-banks without once getting their feet wet. Their movements were quick and unfamiliar but they were not wood goblins as he had at first feared. Thin and short of body, they all wore long straggling beards and wide-brimmed hats that were pulled down so tight onto their heads that their eyes were barely visible. Most annoying of all, they apparently understood no Belbidian and Hal was forced to delve for what Ceolothian he could. Ceowulf, however, had shown a strong grasp of the tongue but had still failed to negotiate their release.

"Let us out!" Hal roared in his best Ceolothian.

"Belbidian intruder," one responded in his native tongue and pointed his bony finger at Hal, "what do you mean by this invasion?" His pole was planted firmly in the marsh and he hung from the top of it with seemingly no effort. Hal finally spotted that there was a little ledge on each pole that gave them a foothold but he marvelled at their balance.

"We mean no harm nor trespass," Ceowulf assured him loudly over Hal's demands that they should be released at once.

"I will not be silenced," Hal shouted. "This is an outrage. Let us out right now and tell us what you have done with the woman!"

With much shaking of heads, the men of the marsh conferred amongst themselves, and Hal saw with relief that they had captured neither Brid nor Abelard. Nevertheless, they were obviously incensed that two of their number had been injured by arrows.

"Meant no trespass!" they hissed. "Yet you storm us with arrows."

"In self-defence!" Hal argued. "You attacked first, netted us in the water and dragged us to these cages."

A cuckoo flew overhead, no doubt searching out a reed warbler's nest in which to plant its offspring. The man of the marsh followed its looped flight in silence before accusing, "You invade the king's marshes."

"What does King Dagonet care of marshes so far from Castabrice?" Hal demanded. A marsh was surely of little worth but he was even more certain that Dagonet wouldn't maintain a fanatic bunch of men with large hats unless it was worth his while.

"What does King Dagonet care? Haven't you heard of the marsh fish with their prized roe? There's nothing like it in all the countries of the Caballan Sea. And then there's the cuckoos' eggs." The men all nodded at each other, proud of their riches. "Though he trusts us to deliver the roe, he sends someone every spring to collect the cuckoos' eggs."

Hal frowned, deciding these men were quite mad. Cuckoos' eggs! King Dagonet would never pay good money for cuckoos' eggs. And if Renaud had so carefully planned the ambush, he surely would never have taken the princess through an area populated by Dagonet's men. And he certainly knew what lay ahead because he had sent the wolves on a different route to avoid the marsh, which they would not have managed to cross as easily as the horses and, clearly, had taken a longer route round. He couldn't puzzle through the problem. In fact, he could barely think for his worry over Brid.

The men left them hanging helplessly in their wicker cages while they poled their way out of sight into the misty marshes.

"Cuckoos' eggs!" Hal exclaimed in disgust. His knives and his sword and his horse were gone but far worse, he had lost Brid. "Cuckoos' eggs," he repeated and, in his frustration, began to swing his cage back and forth and, in the absence of the marsh men, set about worrying at the coarse rope that secured the door of his cage. Pip, too, began to rock his own cage.

Ceowulf shook his head at them both. "All that will do is make you sick."

Someone tittered overhead, a girl's voice certainly. Hal

looked up and groaned. He thought they had been left alone by the men of the marshes but it seemed they were to be watched over by women. The insult of it! Like their men, they wore big-brimmed hats woven from reed that shaded their pale eyes.

The one immediately above Hal grinned. She wore a fabulous necklace, the oval beads of varying shades of white and blue. All the women jingled with them and further strings of the glossy beads were hung up from the willow branches. Another dressed in the same manner as the men, wearing breeches, stockings and lightweight clogs, slid down the rope supporting Ceowulf's cage and prodded at him provocatively with a stick. A few of the other girls tittered in excitement.

Well, if this was to be their fate Hal could think of worse tortures. Pip looked bright-eyed and expectant while Ceowulf coughed in slight embarrassment and winked at Hal. "I could think of worse predicaments. Cybillia's been pregnant a long time; it seems like forever."

Hal didn't feel like joking; he was worried for Brid, and yet at the same time had the unnerving and slightly annoying feeling that she was watching him – and undoubtedly with criticism. He looked up at the branches to where large platforms like vast rooks' nests swayed in the treetops. They were capped by wicker domes, evidently providing the living quarters for the marsh folk. The women were working industriously with fronds of willow, weaving all manner of wicker objects, such as baskets, hats, rafts and the structures for their platforms.

He wondered that they had not noticed the platforms when they first waded into the marshes but agreed with Ceowulf that they must have been so busy seeking a safe route through the shallow water that none of them could have once looked up.

Pip was standing up, clutching the top of his cage and looking towards the girls. "You can't deny us some water," he said in bold Ceolothian.

Hal glanced at the boy in pleasant surprise. So, he had been paying a great deal more attention during his tutorials than anyone had given him credit for. Branwolf had insisted on the best education for the wayward lad after promising Pip's mother that he would look after her children.

"We can't give you anything till the men get back," the eldest woman told him sharply. "They'll be away all morning collecting eggs and you'll get nothing until they return."

The day wore on and Hal was becoming increasingly frustrated. "Stop singing," he growled at Ceowulf when the man launched into yet another song. He had a fair voice, well modulated, but that did nothing to pacify Hal.

He suddenly stiffened at the sound of a deep hollow bark, a strange sound here in the depths of a marsh, though there was no mistaking it.

"A stag," Ceowulf confirmed, his deep voice rising above the anxious squeals of the women. When Hal looked up again, two figures were sitting cross-legged and comfortable in the crook of one of the higher branches above the women. Hal could have guessed that no one other than Brid could have climbed so quickly but he wondered who the old woman might be and what had happened to Abelard.

"I shall show you baskets that you have never dreamed of," the old woman sputtered, addressing the women of the marsh.

Though she spoke in Ceolothian, Hal immediately recognised her as the mysterious woman who had helped the kobolds just before the princess was ambushed. He couldn't believe that such a strange ragged-looking woman would have the mastery of more than one language. Before, he had judged her to be Belbidian but now she spoke Ceolothian as well as the women of the marsh. She took a basket from a girl's hands and wove with such speed and skill that in minutes she had formed the shape of a bird in flight.

"You must suggest to the old willow what you want from her and she will gladly oblige. She is a soft-hearted tree, particularly well-disposed to women and if you weave by the light of the moon your baskets will be magical," she said in a creaking voice.

Brid swung down from the upper branches. "With such skill you need not depend on your money from the king once a year. It's a long lean wait between payments, I imagine."

Hal's eyebrows rose. Brid had a better mastery of Ceolothian than he did.

"We will get money for these three men," one of the marsh women replied. "The king especially sent word to be wary of trespassers. We are to hold any. It is an important job."

"The king cannot weave baskets as well as I can," the old woman, who looked much like a willow tree herself, promised.

Hal wondered what that had to do with anything though he conceded that the women of the marsh seemed impressed by the statement.

"Indeed, you weave fine baskets but you cannot find cuckoos' eggs like our men can," one told the old woman.

She laughed, her voice crackling like branches groaning in the breeze. "You wish to test me? I tell you the biggest cuckoo's egg you will ever see is right at the roots of this willow." She slapped the grooved greenish bark of the tree.

The women of the marsh laughed. "We have searched the roots a hundred times but the water is too murky here so, even if there are any, we would never find them."

"The young man in the cage will," the old woman told them confidently and gestured with a crooked finger at Hal.

One of the women lay aside her weaving and accused, "This is merely a ploy to make us free him."

"And would that be such a problem," Brid said in a pleasant voice, "after all in the marsh you can always catch him again; he has no pole or stilts. However, if you do as I say, he *will* find the cuckoo's egg. The finest one you will ever see is down there; I shall prove it."

She snapped her fingers and at precisely that moment an arrow whistled out from behind one of the tree trunks footed in the marsh and thumped into the knot of rope that bound Hal's cage. He nudged the wicker door and it swung outward. A second later another whistling arrow streaked through the air and, before Hal knew what was happening, the rope suspending his cage was severed and he was plunged into the thick dark water beneath him.

It was dark under the water and he struggled frantically to find the open door. With breath held, it seemed an age before he could find it and kick free. His one immediate aim was to swim straight for the surface but something caught him around the foot. It felt distinctly like a hand. He twisted to free himself but strands of weed stirring in the water wrapped around him, pulling him back harder than he could swim for the surface.

Struggling stirred up more mud. Then through the murk he saw it, resting within a gnarled curve of root that looked for all the world like a hand reaching out towards him. He couldn't help but reach back towards the shining object. He grasped it, brushing against the root as he did, which felt strangely warm.

His legs were instantly released and he kicked furiously upwards, gulping in air as he broke the surface. He swam for the bole of the tree and clung on. A rope was quickly lowered to him and, as he reached for it, he heard the marsh men hurrying back to their camp to see what all the shouting had been about.

Still gasping and spluttering, Hal held in his hand a silvery-coloured egg though, judging by its weight, it wasn't an egg at all but some kind of precious stone.

"Look, look!" the men shouted in such excitement that they clearly forgot to feel any alarm at Hal's escape. "Never seen the like! Look at the size and the colour! What a prize!"

Pip and Ceowulf's cages were hastily pulled up onto the platforms above and they were freed without any of the discomfort that Hal had suffered.

"You could have suggested that Abelard dropped one of the others into the muck," he scolded Brid though he didn't really mean it.

"Ceowulf would have sunk and Pip would never have found his way out of the cage. It had to be you," Brid said without apology. "You wouldn't really have wanted it any other way."

Twittering with excitement, the marsh folk all sat cross-legged on the largest platform that was evidently their meeting place. "They told us to guard the marshes. They warned us that dreadful men would come but they said nothing of these fine people or that the old master of the forest himself would be with them," one said excitedly, stabbing his finger towards the sound of someone sloshing towards them through the marsh.

All looked where he pointed. A man wading chest

deep moved into the pool beneath them. With agile ease, he climbed the broad willow supporting the platform, water streaming from his long-legged body. Something about his manner gave him an air of nobility and power though his dress announced him to be no more than a common woodsman. An unstrung bow hooked into a leather strap sloped across his back, the string no doubt in his pouch to stop it being spoilt by the water.

He smiled at the old woman. "Mother, you have done well." He bowed his head deferentially at Brid.

Hal nodded at the man without commitment. So, this must have been the fine archer who had shot him down. At least he wouldn't have to thank Abelard for rescuing him – if Abelard ever returned from wherever he had fled to. Hero indeed!

At the behest of the peculiar old woman and the tall archer, food was hastily provided by the folk of the marsh. The dish of pan-fried duck did not take Hal's mind off this tall fellow whom he found so strange. Dressed as a woodsman, he was unkempt, his beard and hair straggling and tangled with burrs, and he had a peculiarly deep voice and moved with too much grace. And then there was the matter of smell; the man smelt strongly of animal; not an unpleasant smell in itself, quite like horse, but very peculiar coming from a man.

Brid showed not the least surprise at any of this. "Harle!" she greeted him warmly.

The tall archer bowed graciously. "I owed you and it was good to repay the service so quickly. There are troubles in the forest all over the Caballan and I have been busy." He chose to speak Belbidian to her.

"I don't understand any of this," Pip burst out in Ceolothian at the men who had caged him, having given only a second glance at the tall archer. "What is all this fuss about cuckoos' eggs? That's definitely not an egg." He pointed at the oval stone that was now in the hands of one of the men from the marsh. He was beyond his prime, his hair greying and his whiskered face lined by age, though his arms were muscular like those of a much younger man.

"It is," he replied and, laughing, gave out a cuckoo's call. "Well, no, of course it isn't a *real* cuckoo's egg. We only call them cuckoos' eggs because no one knows how they get there into the nest of roots at the foot of the willows. We are as unknowing of their origin as the reed warblers are of the cuckoos' eggs in their nests."

The old woman laughed as if they were little children believing in elves that would do their chores overnight. "You don't know where they come from?"

Hal looked at Brid who shrugged, seemingly also ignorant for once.

"Well, where do they come from?" she asked.

The old woman chuckled. "Well, now it's not my task to give away the secrets of old Willow Woman, now, is it? But I'm surprised at you, Brid, not knowing, and to think that the willow stands under the moon night after night, drinking up the moon-lit waters."

Brid took the cuckoos' eggs, smothering her fingertips over their wonderful silvery blue iridescence. "A strange name for so beautiful a jewel."

"So valuable too. Perhaps valuable enough to one day enable us to buy back our lands from the king," the old man from the marsh told them, closing his palm tight around the stone and looking down at the sound of someone else approaching.

"That I doubt." The tall stranger, whom Brid had addressed as Harle, broke off to greet Abelard who was now struggling up the tree and onto the platform. Harle thumped him appreciatively on the back. "What a shot, good man. I doubt that I could have done it at half the distance."

Hal groaned inwardly. He was going to have to thank Abelard after all.

"We'll be writing new ballads about you soon," Ceowulf laughed good-naturedly, adding to the chorus of praise for Abelard. "Hal, wouldn't you say it was a great shot?"

Hal forced a smile onto his tight lips and nodded at Abelard who nodded back. Hal resented him, resented the steely look of reservation in his eyes, resented his devotion to Brid. Instinctively he clutched at his betrothed's hand and pulled her tight to his side.

The musty-smelling Harle apologized that he must briefly leave them. Soon they could hear him whistling as if calling a dog. The sound of sloshing hooves shortly followed and Hal was amazed to see their horses placidly ambling chest deep through the mire, following this curious man. Hal was pleased to see that Secret still had his sword on her back, and it was only moments before Harle tossed it up to him.

Hal caught it neatly in his left hand and eased the blade from its damp scabbard. Lovingly smoothing the glistening metal, he looked at the old man holding the cuckoo's egg. "Who exactly ordered you to hold us?"

"We were given word that by order of the king we were to let no one through the marshes," the man stammered and plucked at the ends of his beard that were knotted into five plaits.

"Who gave you word?"

The man watched Hal's sword as if it were a snake. "Why, the men who rode through here at the beginning of the last moon. Of course, we were to tell no one and here we are telling you."

"They will forgive you," Hal said lightly. "You have no choice."

The marsh folk looked frightened.

"We are but serfs," the man with the cuckoo's egg said almost by way of apology.

Brid took his hand and soothed it. "Listen to me, fine fellow."

"Robin," he told her, "Robin Longpole."

"Robin, they were bad men that passed through here before us. They stole King Dagonet's daughter. If you help us rescue her, the king will look kindly on you. Do you know where they took her?"

"Of course, we know. We know everything that goes on in the marsh," Robin told her indignantly. "But they said the king would have us hunted down and gutted if we told anyone." He shrugged helplessly.

"How do y' know they bore the king's words?" Abelard asked.

"Because the young lady and the grand man showed us the king's seal."

"Curious," Abelard said. "Y'd have thought that such feisty young nobles would have been less co-operative. If Princess Cymbeline and Prince Tudwal had thrown away their seals 'twould have been harder for Renaud to bluff his way through."

"And even more curious that Renaud would mark the tree with his own emblem," Hal remarked.

The Torra Altans fell into pensive silence that was broken by a spluttering cough from the wizened old woman. Ceowulf eyed her curiously. "Who are you?" he asked.

"I'm Harle's mother," she told him.

"But you're so much like . . . well, like this old willow. I've been all over the Caballan and met all sorts of queer folk but I've never met anyone who had the very essence of a tree about them."

"No?" The woman raised her long drooping eyebrows in surprise. "No, I suppose you haven't, have you? But there again you haven't lived very long or travelled very widely either. There are few of us. We are a long-lived people and, like our counterparts in the Otherworld, though their job is to rule and ours to serve, we have certain powers." She turned to the marsh folk. "We struck a bargain that if these fine people were to produce for you the very largest and most precious cuckoo's egg then you would release them. Come, you must fulfil your promise."

"Yes, but we said nothing about helping them," one of the women of the marsh objected while fingering her necklace. "We could all be hanged."

"Then you must come back with us to Belbidia and be free of the marshes," Hal told them. "Free of your serfdom."

"But we can't leave the marshes and our great willows!" she objected. "There are none so old or beautiful in all the countries of the Caballan, is that not so?"

Harle's mother nodded her head.

They debated long into the evening about how much they could help the Belbidians while Hal and Pip saw to it that the horses were comfortably corralled between hurdles on one of the mud banks and given grain and fresh hay. They gave up grooming them since their coats were too stiff with mud, reasoning that they would get just as grimy the next day. When they returned to the others, the people of the marsh would come to no conclusion even when Ceowulf, who was best at these things, provided the details of the ambush and how they had been a part of the escort party. He mentioned, too, the wolves.

The marsh folk shrugged as if they cared little. "We have never had trouble from wolves. They can't get to us here; it's too deep for wolves."

Unable to come to a final conclusion, all agreed on one thing; that it was time for bed. Ceowulf and the Torra Altans were led via a series of rope bridges spanning the boughs to a number of vacant platforms each supporting a domed wicker structure. Ceowulf went white as he gingerly shuffled along the swaying bridge though the rest, born to giddy heights, barely looked where they put their feet as they skipped across. When they reached the first platform, one of the women pulled aside a hanging mat of woven reed that protected the entrance to a wicker dome. "Would a couple of you good folk like to rest here?" she invited. "It's big enough for two."

Hal crawled in, hoping Brid would follow but naturally she did not.

"We have prepared a more comfortable shelter for you, fair lady, just three trees distant," the woman of the marsh said to Brid.

"That is most kind," Brid said graciously.

Hal fancifully thought he detected a note of disappointment in her voice but then groaned from within the conical beeskep-shaped structure. It was Ceowulf that crawled in after him to share the nest of reeds and blankets, while Abelard and Pip climbed into a neighbouring dwelling. Though claustrophobic at first, the wicker shelters were wonderfully cosy. Nevertheless, the men spent the night in peculiar purgatory.

It seemed the marsh maidens lived according to a different code to the rest of Caballan society and were overly eager to make close acquaintance with the strangers.

It was not long after Hal retired that a girl, with a very sweet face and light mousy hair scooped back and decorated with a number of fine plaits, wriggled into their sleeping quarters. Her friend, who was younger and with a fuller figure, followed. Hal's stomach tightened.

"Great Mother, give me strength," he moaned, wondering how he was going to cope with this awkward situation.

Ceowulf coughed in deep embarrassment. "My dear ladies, of course we can make room for you to sleep here, but wouldn't you be more comfortable in your own beds?"

Neither girl spoke but clearly, by the way the elder girl snuggled up to the knight, she was going to make herself perfectly comfortable right there next to him. This was going to be more than awkward, Hal corrected his original summary of their situation.

Despite the men's protestations, the two girls were soon tightly nestled within the shelter and the older, slimmer one explained in a soft husky voice, "We are a small, closely related community. We often marry cousins but it is healthier, you see, to seek fresh blood whenever it is available."

"It seems we would be doing them a service." Hal moaned weakly. Brid could not be that far away but his frustrations were building and he didn't know how long his defences would hold out. It was too unfair. How could fate test him so? He just prayed that Ceowulf would not weaken, knowing that would certainly be too much for him.

There were a few protestations from the neighbouring platform. "Here, that lad's too young. You are not taking advantage of him," a woman's voice objected. "He'll do himself a damage."

Then Pip's indignant voice came back. "Who says I'm too young? You can judge after but not before."

The giggles and sighs that followed were difficult to ignore. Hal groaned in miserable frustration. But what was he going to do? He knew the obvious thing was to tell these young girls to leave but that seemed too rude in the face of their hospitality. And they were so persistent. He needed Ceowulf's support, which was clearly fading as kisses were lavished on his neck and he was rather feebly trying to keep the sweet-faced woman at bay. It was just too much.

"Think of Cybillia!" Hal told him sharply.

"I am! Believe me I am," Ceowulf replied lamely. "But she's pregnant and," he muttered conspiratorially, "she needn't know, need she?"

"She will if I tell her."

"You wouldn't do that to a friend."

"I will if you do this to me," Hal threatened. "I need your solidarity."

Ceowulf looked perturbed then smiled conspiratorially. "But Brid doesn't need to know either," he said practically, persuasively.

"She'll know!" Hal told him vehemently. "She knows everything."

"I'll say it was all me," Ceowulf offered. "I'm not sure I'm up to both of them," he joked, "but Brid will believe me."

"Mmm, but then she might tell Cybillia. They're very good friends."

Ceowulf frowned. "I'm obviously not thinking straight." Hastily he pushed the girls away. They looked rather hurt. "This is agony!"

Hal laughed. "Well, as long as I've got to suffer, I'm glad you're suffering too."

The next morning after a cold night above the marshes, Hal awoke and clambered out onto the platform to be greeted by a very pleased and sprightly looking Pip and a relaxed looking Abelard. It did nothing to relieve his frustrations or soften his temper. Nor did it help when Brid marched straight up to him and hit him hard across the face.

"What was that for?" he demanded.

"You know exactly what for. You cannot treat me like this, Hal," she told him firmly. "I will not be humiliated, do you hear?"

"I did nothing," he protested. "Ceowulf, tell her."

"Do you think I'm going to believe Ceowulf when he has as much to lose as you do! And don't think I won't tell Cybillia!" she threatened. "What a thing to do, Ceowulf, when your wife is pregnant too." She sniffed haughtily.

"But Brid— Hal, back me up here. You must tell her. Have you no control over your woman?"

"I am not Hal's woman!" Brid tossed back her plait indignantly. "I am a high priestess. No man owns me!"

They rode out into the marshes, Harle and his mother insisting on following on foot though the water came up to their chests. Hal was finding it very difficult to concentrate on the matter in hand. The horses were perturbed, at first, by the men on their long stilts swinging above their heads like vast cranes and both Pip and Abelard were having difficulty controlling their mounts that shied every time one of the stilted men came too close. Hal tried to keep level with Brid to plead his case but she simply would not entertain any notion that he was innocent. Glumly, he pulled back to the rear and slouched alongside Ceowulf.

"She won't tell Cybillia, will she?" Ceowulf asked. Hal had never seen him look so worried.

He shook his head. "No, I'm sure she won't; she would never do anything to hurt Cybillia."

The knight lifted his head with an immediate upturn

in spirits. "Sins of the flesh, you see, are never so truly bad as sins of the mind."

Hal frowned at him, thinking that he had gone completely mad and grumbled away, wondering how on earth he could ever redeem himself. And to make matters worse Abelard was now riding beside Brid, chatting happily away. Who did he think he was, a common archer like that ingratiating himself with his betrothed? The heat of his blood rose to a simmer.

It took more than a day to reach the borders of the marshes. They knew dry land lay ahead even though they could not see far through the cloudy veil of mist that sighed out from the willows and caressed the still water; the howl of a wolf penetrated the mist and the wolves did not enter the marsh.

"I hate this mist," Pip said to Robin Longpole, who had become their guide and was evidently the most eminent man amongst the marsh folk.

He shook his head. "Do not fear the mist but what lies beyond it."

"Wolves," Abelard warned.

"That's obvious," Hal retorted. "We hardly need your valorous self to tell us such things."

"I meant hooded wolves," he explained without rebuke, giving Hal that unreadable look.

Hal hated him as he had never hated anyone before. He hated the way he ingratiated himself with Brid and, no doubt, was poisoning her against him.

The willows thinned and, not wanting to emerge all at once, they halted where the ground began to rise towards drier soil. Here the mist turned to wispy veils and finally dissipated.

"Ceowulf and I shall make a reconnaissance," Hal declared. "The rest of you wait here."

"You'll do no such thing," Brid retorted imperiously. "Abelard, you will come with me. Your eyesight is good."

Hal was furious but could do nothing about it. He would only look more foolish if he tried to argue with her; she never gave in.

They returned shortly. "We could see only a short tract of flat land before the mist thickens again." Brid turned to Robin. "What do you know of the lands beyond?"

"There are many legends. But with my own eyes I have seen a great lake too big to see across, and brackish it is too. They say it's an inland sea."

"Brackish!" Hal interrupted. "This far inland!"

"It's believed that water from the great northern sea flows under the earth to fill it. The lake water is near cold and sometimes chunks of ice float on the surface and strange fish are caught. They say there's an ancient sluice to let the water in and out."

Hal looked at him sceptically, wondering whether he had understood the Ceolothian aright.

Robin Longpole coughed and, with a nod of insistence from Brid, continued, "Near to this shore is an island, but you can only ever see its great black cliffs for the mist. There's a submerged causeway, they say, that rises out of the lake when the tide's at its lowest. No doubt that's where they've taken the princess."

They moved tentatively forward, climbing to a heathered plain where they were at last greeted by a warm sun. The muscles in Hal's neck and back ached; he hadn't realized how stiff the damp had made him. The leather of his leggings was stiff and creaked, and he rued how he had neglected to oil them. The plain was but a mere strip of land that soon dropped away down a steeply shelving scarp, densely wooded with hazel trees, back into more mist.

The flat lands below the scarp were bathed in the milky light, the sun no more than a white ghostly globe shining wanly down through the veil of cloud. The mist deepened. It was cold and clung to them, drenching them over time in a permeating way that was worse than heavy rain. The sound of the horses' footfalls gradually began to change, crunching as they eased off the short, nibbled grass and onto a shingle beach at the edge of a silvery lake. Only the fringe of the water could be seen, its expanse quickly swallowed by the mist. Wolves howled, unseen, the haunting wail travelling easily across the still waters.

Hal flared his nostrils at the kelplike smell. The waters couldn't really be brackish, could they? He sent Pip to investigate who promptly reported back that the lake was indeed salty.

There was little they could do that night other than make camp and wait for the mist to lift so that they could see which way to go. Brid watched the trill of smoke from their fire coil upwards and gradually drift east where it was caught by a rising breeze.

"The mist will clear soon," she predicted.

But the mist hung heavily, foreboding like a damp warning for them to hold back, and not even Hal's thick brown bearskin could keep out the cold. His joints began to ache and his shinbones felt tender and brittle. He wondered if that was what it felt like to be old. He shook himself, deciding he was thinking stupidly, his mind distracted by Brid's coldness to him. The moment she stood up, Abelard would rise to his feet, follow her, and give him that inscrutable look of disapproval.

When the mist still persisted, they decided to continue searching despite it. They skirted the lake, the mist making it impossible to judge its size though the lapping waves gave the impression of vastness. The eerie sound of their horses' hooves crunching on the pebbles echoed over the water. At a similar sound in the distance, they stopped at once, all holding their breath. As the crunching sound drew closer, they hurried for the cover where the black gorse grew thickly at the lake's edge. Brid was the first to relax.

"Only wild ponies." She sighed with relief when the group trotted out of the mist, their heads high and alert as if something had startled them. They were a pale misty grey, short-legged and heavy-headed, keeping firmly to the edges of the mist, knowing that they were barely visible within it. The leading mare shrieked at the sight of the Belbidians and waded deeper into the shallows to skirt around them.

"The mist should have cleared with this light breeze," Brid said emphatically after they had crunched several more miles around the lake shore. Being brackish, the horses showed no desire to move towards the water and drink but Hal thought them wary of it.

He dropped from Secret's back and picked his way over the pebbles to the water's edge. There certainly was something peculiar about the lake. He dipped his fingers in.

"It's freezing!" He sucked the salt from his reddened fingertips.

Robin Longpole grinned. "I told you it's linked to the sea. Look how the tide is going out. The ground is wet above the water-line and there's a rim of debris."

"Well, no wonder the mist doesn't clear. Such cold water is bound to make the moist air turn to mist." Brid looked enlightened.

They were reassured by this logic for some while but Hal could not shake the feeling that there was still something more peculiar than finding a brackish lake in the heart of Ceolothia's vast forest. The air was becoming increasingly warm and sultry. And the further they travelled northward along the gentle curve of the lake, the more aware he was of the mist's strange greenish hue.

Even Brid was beginning to look nervous and, moving a little apart from the men of the marsh, returned to Belbidian speech. "It's unnatural." She stuck out her red tongue, tasting the air. "I need to stop and think."

"We can't wait!" Hal also dropped his efforts at Ceolothian. "Think of Keridwen; think of Branwolf. Every second we delay . . ." Hal didn't need to make the notion more vivid by spelling it out.

"No, Hal. Something is controlling the mist. I must sit and prepare myself and learn more of this mist. I can't allow your rashness to hurl us all into danger."

Hal could do nothing to dissuade her. Any delay for whatever cause was wrong in his opinion. They should simply be looking for signs of Renaud and the princes rather than worrying about the mist; after all, it might have nothing to do with them.

Sulkily, he withdrew from the body of the party. He loved Brid, of course, he loved Brid, but that wasn't enough. She had made him look a fool. Around her, he could not be a man, not in any sense of the word. His whole being hurt as he considered this. He would love Brid to the end of his days, but it was bringing neither of them happiness. Slowly and painfully, he was coming to the conclusion that, if in the immediate future she did not change her attitude towards him, he would leave to make his own life, that is once he had dragged that fiendish traitor Renaud home to face King Rewik.

As Ceowulf had done in his youth, he would go away to fight as a mercenary for any good or noble cause. He knew he was deluding himself since mercenaries were rarely sought for noble causes but rather for the dirty work that no one else cared to sully their hands with. But certainly, he would go away and, naturally, he would enjoy as many women as possible. That would make him forget Brid.

Brid turned, caught his eye, and frowning, waited for him to come to her. "Hal, you must see that at the moment there are so very much more important things than you and me."

Hal did not see at all. He couldn't understand why she should be distant from him, so distracted, why they couldn't work together. She showed no faith, no respect in him, when she refused to believe he had behaved impeccably overnight above the marshes. He could not let himself be abused like this. Where would it end? Abelard was looking increasingly youthful and buoyant and she turned to him more and more for advice. It was always Abelard, what do you think about this? And Abelard, what do you feel about that? It was deeply irritating – deeply. But what could he do? As far as he could see, his only choices were to lap at her heels or break away entirely. It seemed that, ever since he had proved his love, she had taken him for granted.

Him, Hal son of Brungard, taken for granted! He stiffly turned away from her and glared into the murky green of the mist to brood. No one had ever taken him for granted, not Spar, not Branwolf and he wasn't going to start with his future wife. The very idea of it galled him to the core. After many minutes, he sulkily followed the others who had retreated inland and lit a fire. They sat in a circle, all eyes on Brid as she sat humming gently to herself. She was always the centre of attention! Could a man really play servant to his wife and be happy? Someone would write a ballad about him and it would begin, *Hal, the meek; Hal, the humble; Hal, the lily-livered.*

He winced at the thought, too self-absorbed to care what everyone was saying but curiosity finally drove him to listen in case someone was talking about him. Surely, he must figure largely in the plans.

"I cannot make the connection between Renaud and this mist," Brid said frankly. "It is a curious magical mist full of hidden powers. Where has he learnt to draw on such knowledge?"

"Perhaps there is more to the New Faith than you thought, Brid," Hal told her calmly. "After all, it has been powerful enough to all but overthrow the Old Faith. Perhaps this mist is a miracle of his god."

"There is no god in this," Brid said with conviction. "There is no taste of the ethereal or the sublime, nor even of elemental or metaphysical magic." Her eyes slowly widened as she contemplated her words. "Abelard, what do you think?"

"Abelard, what do you think?" Hal mimicked with a sharp cut of sarcasm. "What does he know of magic, Brid? What does he know of anything?" He got to his feet. "There is an uncanny fog hanging over this place but is it anything more than unseasoned firewood sprinkled with potions? What the good folk of the marshes have told us is that the lake is shallow and easily crossed at a causeway when the tide is low. They say there are sometimes great cliffs of a black island to be seen from this shore. I don't need to know more; I'm going to find it. I've come here for one purpose and one purpose alone: to rescue Princess Cymbeline and so prove the innocence of Torra Alta. And I'm not waiting while you all just sit around gossiping and singing Abelard's praises."

"But, Master Hal, I truly meant no offence," Abelard apologized.

Hal didn't detect one note of sincerity in his voice.

Harle's mother spoke at last. "Someone on the island shuns us. This mist is unnatural and I smell wizardry."

"Wizardry!" Hal snorted. "Do you think Prince Renaud would have consorted with warlocks and witches?"

"I didn't say that," the old woman pointed out calmly. "I said wizardry. There's a very big difference."

"But there weren't any wizards even in my day," Abelard argued. Hal wasn't sure that he liked this man taking his side.

"No, not in your day. It's a long time since their kind walked the earth. They sold their souls, you see," Harle's mother said, picking the dirt from under her broken fingernails.

"I don't understand," Hal said irritably. He turned to look into the mist and decided that he would go alone to find the causeway as soon as the tide had retreated a little more.

"They sold their souls. They made a bargain with the ealdormen of the Otherworld. The wizards were a race of men that were here long before the Druids. They were learned and wise in all matters of physical properties but they were frustrated that their lives were so short, preventing them from gaining full understanding and knowledge. They swore allegiance to the ealdormen, promising to help them control the souls of men when they passed on into the Otherworld in exchange for a thousand times their natural lifespan. When they died, they did not cross the forests of the Otherworld to pass into the bliss and forgetfulness of the oneness that is Annwyn but returned immediately via Nuin's Door."

"That would make them as good as immortal," Abelard said. "But y' said it's been an age since they walked the earth."

"Indeed. You would only meet them in the Otherworld but you might not know even if you did," Harle's mother replied. "Not unless he was casting his magic at that time. It is not like Brid's magic that is based on the laws of nature and devout prayers to the Great Mother who then might bend Her will to Brid's purpose. No, this is man's magic generated from within his own mind. You see, gradually as the years passed, there was a darkness that overcame these wizards."

"A darkness?" Brid repeated in question.

"Since it had been so long since they had completed the full circle of life, death and rebirth through Annwyn, so long since they had returned to the Great Mother, they forgot their love of Her and the love of the Earth itself and they drank up Her energy and cared not what evil they might do so long as they gained in power."

"Wisdom is a terrible tool in the hands of an evil man," Abelard said solemnly and Ceowulf nodded in agreement.

Hal threw his eyes heavenward. "Trifling, empty proverbs! Wisdom might prevent a man from evil: innocence causes as much harm." He turned to Harle's mother. "So, what happened to these great and terrible men? Did they meekly take themselves off to an island in the middle of a misty lake in northern Ceolothia never to be seen again?"

"No, of course not! They were banished by the Druid's Egg," Brid interrupted.

"Necrönd!" Hal exclaimed.

"Spar," Brid murmured ominously, her mind evidently one step ahead of his.

"No," he said firmly. "Spar might be easily led but he can have nothing to do with this. He would do nothing so harmful."

"But Master Spar must be involved," Abelard reasoned. "He is Necrönd's guardian. No one else can use it while it's in his keeping."

"How dare any of you judge him? I love Spar like a brother and I know him better than anyone." Hal was suddenly furious. Doubting Caspar was like doubting himself and, as Keridwen had said, Caspar had promised her not to wield Necrönd. Hal was convinced that only the boy's mother or himself could persuade him otherwise. Spar could be very stubborn. He knew he had himself doubted his nephew's innocence in this but that was different. He could allow himself to be critical of his kinsman, but not others and certainly not Abelard.

"You're fools the lot of you," he snarled. "You can sit here until eternity for all I care but I am not going to let Branwolf and Keridwen rot away in Rewik's dungeons, nor leave Spar in the hands of the Ovissians, do you hear? Not for a moment longer!"

He marched off towards the horses that he could no longer see for the darkening mist, though he could hear them. Their steady munching at the short tough grass bordering the lake seemed louder than before. Secret, with her bright liver chestnut coat, was at last visible as a dark shade in the mist and he wasted little time catching her. Once mounted, he turned for the shores of the lake and continued along its edge in search of the causeway.

CHAPTER TWENTY-THREE

Caspar sulked. Why on earth had he agreed to this woman coming along? Her belly swelled with the child within it and she could barely walk for the sickness that overwhelmed her each morning. Obviously, she would get slower as the journey passed; and how long could he stand her arguing?

She was again demanding that they give up following the wolfman and Ursula, and instead head direct for Castaguard by boat. That way, she was arguing, they would at least have a chance of intercepting the wolfman since they had, in her opinion, no hope of catching him as they were. Caspar felt the last threads of authority slipping through his fingers.

Reyna waved her hand in the direction of a stretch of woodland between them and the sea. "We've just passed the small fishing village of Slakwater over there. I'm sure we could borrow or hire a boat," she said firmly and to Caspar's discomfort persuasively. "Elergian can handle a boat in his sleep."

He girded his resolve to refuse her. "We'll lose them if we stop following the trail," he insisted.

Reyna shrugged her shoulders. "We'll never catch them," she prophesied with disconcerting certainty.

To add to Caspar's growing frustrations, the old mage, who had already proved himself to be both pompous and irritating, had begun to argue with Perren. Fern, on the other hand, seemed to like both Elergian and Reyna, and agreed with anything they said, which was even more irritating.

Perren had discarded his bandages for the moment, since he complained that they irritated him, and tried hard to persuade Elergian that he had never been near a volcanic island let alone suffered any burns, and was in fact a stonewight. The mage, however, was reluctant to believe him though Reyna was more generous and intrigued by the idea. Perren persistently plied them for their story, wanting to know every detail; the names of every one of Reyna's daughters and on to as many great-grandmothers and their daughters as she could remember, and how much ink they extracted each year. He seemed particularly interested in the smaller details such as whether blackberries or crushed beetles produced the more interesting dye.

At length Caspar could bear it no more. "Perren, do you really want to know?"

"Of course, I do. The longer and more detailed the story the better. You humans rush too much. Now, I remember how it was during the time of cold when the ground was white and the permafrost so deep that we felt the chill even down in our caverns. The old ones could do little hunting for roots and soft rocks, and so they told us the story of the yak. And by the end, we knew even the number of hairs in its coat and how many tics were behind its ears. That's how to tell a story. That's how to live life."

Caspar took a deep breath and ignored him. Arguing with Perren took a very long time and a great deal of stamina that he simply didn't have.

While Fern trotted on ahead, Reyna was lagging further

and further behind and Caspar was distressed by his inability to keep them together. He was just going to call out to Fern to wait yet again when the little man stopped of his own accord and began running wildly in circles about one particular spot on the ridge of the softly folding coastline. The wolfling, her back a comb of hackles and her nose snuffling the round, galloped to the same point. Caspar broke into a run to investigate their find and saw how Runa's hackles smoothed when she reached the spot that Fern found so interesting. Her forelegs folded under her and she rubbed her head in the soil before rolling in delight. Even Fern was grinning.

"What is it?" Caspar asked.

"He's gone. Vanished. The air is clean."

Caspar looked at him in bewilderment. "What do you mean?"

Runa sat back on her haunches, threw back her head and howled, evidently enjoying the hollow wail that sounded in her throat. She stopped rather short with a squeak and looked at Caspar as if checking she had his attention before skipping up onto her floppy paws and bouncing up at his chest, knocking the wind from his lungs.

He had forgotten how much she had grown – in leggy height and strength! She looked at him with steady eyes, as if trying to meet his soul and then rushed away to sniff at the ground, finding some strong smelling Vaalakan mud to roll in, apparently by way of celebration. Once her fluffy white coat was streaked with mud, she slid up beside Caspar and wiped her long muddy flank against his thigh. She looked very pleased with herself.

"You've spent too much time with Trog," he scolded her playfully while trying to puzzle out what Fern was talking to Elergian about.

"I'm telling you he was here. I can smell his foul footprints. Dark they are, foul-smelling, reeking of wolf. They are here and here and here but from here on," he stamped his feet alongside the spot, "they are gone, vanished!" Fern exclaimed, waving a hand forward along the line of continuing footprints to illustrate his point.

"That's just senseless. There's no sign of a struggle and the footprints go on," Caspar objected. "Look, there's that same long, thin, pointed print. There's one print and there's the next. There's no difference."

"Isn't there? Smell for yourself." Fern was indignant.

The wolfling raced back and forth along the line of prints and, each time she retraced them to the point where Fern stood, her hackles rose and she growled in her throat, a deep blood-curdling growl, her lips rolling back to reveal the needle-sharp teeth that crammed her mouth.

"I shall do a divining test," the mage declared, ostentatiously dribbling water from a gourd into several of the prints.

Caspar sniffed. He knew magic when it was being performed; it made the hairs on the back of his neck tingle. This was nothing though Elergian rolled his eyes and swooped back and forth, murmuring complicated words in a most impressive manner.

"Tell us, oh great mage," Reyna urged.

Perren sat down laughing, a curious deep rumbling sound, and quietly said to Caspar, "Does she really believe him? There's not an ounce of sensitivity in his fingers. Few men have it of course. It is mainly women that understand the energy of magic. It isn't just learning, remembering lists and properties. It's the—"

"Tingling in the blood," Caspar finished for him. "But why should it just be a female characteristic? I can sense it."

"I didn't say it is. I said it was commonest in women. And I'm surprised she's deceived by him."

"I don't think she is," Caspar retorted. "I think she's being kind."

"It's kind to let someone live with delusions about themselves? That's ridiculous. Think how much worse the blow when they finally discover the truth."

Caspar shrugged. "Few ever find out the truth. And if they do, they rarely believe it." He spoke without thought. He was worried. He didn't understand what this discovery about the footprints meant but the best they could do was hurry after them. The footprints, whether they smelt of wolf or not, were all they had to go on.

As expected, Elergian found nothing and they trudged on following Ursula and Firecracker's distinctive track and the footprints of the two men but only for a short distance. Caspar suddenly paused and studied the prints again, retracing them to the point where Fern had exclaimed about a change. He followed them forward again.

"You know, there is something different. The wolfman's stride has changed. He's wandering from side to side." He strode on vigorously.

"I can't go at this pace," Reyna gasped. "You must wait for me."

Caspar suppressed a groan. "I'm sorry, we have to hurry otherwise we'll never catch up with them."

Reyna sat down. "I shall go no further today." She wasn't imperious but simply exhausted and spoke a statement of fact. "I cannot risk overtaxing my body. I have to survive this last pregnancy. I will bear this son."

The old mage wrung his hands and looked at Caspar. "She should not have gone on to have this last child. She and Calyx could have lived happily as they were long into old age. But what is done is done and she must rest."

Caspar didn't have the heart to press her and, seeing a singular rock in the flat landscape, scrambled up it and sat down to survey the area. The trail was now leading them across dried up salt flats that bordered the sea. To the west about a league inland, the ground rose sharply to an escarpment running parallel to the coast. He was thankful that, though the ground was soft and marshy in places, the going was generally easy – maybe not easy enough for a cart but it was good terrain for a horse. And without horses, it was going to take them forever to reach Castaguard. "We need horses," he said decisively.

"I'm not riding in my condition." Reyna was adamant.

Caspar was impressed by her sense of focus. It appeared that nothing mattered except her baby. He should have been as focused on the Egg. Now it was gone, little else mattered to him, except that he had been forced to forgo his search for May. That guilt played heavily on his mind and now his search for Necrönd was becoming embroiled by his need to rescue Ursula, a woman he barely knew. He wondered how he would ever explain that to May when he finally found her.

"I could carry you, Reyna," Perren offered. "You would barely slow me at all."

Reyna looked at him uncertainly. "I'm not sure. Prolonged contact with your rindy skin might have an effect on my unborn child. I can take no risks."

Caspar groaned. Ursula would die if they did not find a way of moving faster but he had to content himself with the slow march that Reyna dictated. As they moved on, he concentrated on the footprints but took little comfort that they were clearly slowing; Firecracker's hindleg left a dragged trail where the stallion's limp was worsening. He bit his lip in concern.

"What's that sound?" Fern asked anxiously.

Trog and the wolfling stood stiffly, their noses pointing to a nearby hillock. Caspar could hear nothing at first but could just see a thin trill of smoke being wafted by the wind. When they rounded the edge of the heathered mound, he heard the crackling of a fire and smelt meat cooking, which no doubt had attracted Trog and the wolfling. A grubby, long-haired man, wearing nothing more than a loose bearskin draped around his shoulders, the skin of his face and chest flushed with heat, sat too close to the fire. He spun round at their approach.

"Who passes by? More strangers? I've come here to be free of the madness of men. Now twice in one week. Be gone with you. Get away!"

"Please," Caspar cajoled, "tell us of those ahead of us. I'll pay you handsomely."

"He's not to be trusted," Fern warned Caspar. "He's a meat-eater."

"I don't want your money," the hermit protested.

"Some shoes," Reyna offered, frowning at Elergian who looked at her blankly before nodding in sudden understanding. He made to strip off his solid boots but changed his mind and reached in his pack for lighter, more decorative footwear.

The man grinned. "Well now, some shoes!"

Caspar smiled at Reyna, glad of her astuteness.

"A man leading a horse with a girl tied to its tail. Strange he was, tall, dark-skinned and not properly dressed." He looked down at his own naked body and laughed apologetically. "Squinty eyes. Unmistakable. But I saw more of the other man. Deranged, I'd say. He shouted fearfully of demons and a terrible blackness. A tall man, all thin legs and arms, shrieking maniacally. As I watched, he stripped off his wolfskin then rolled onto his back to pull off his trousers, which he then whirled about his head. Not even I could take his clothes for fear I might catch his madness." The hermit nodded to a distant hillock where folds of clothing softened the outline of rock.

"He ran about naked, wailing on about this devouring blackness and then about a bird landing on his shoulder what sucked the blackness from him. Quite mad. He ran off as if running from his own soul."

The hermit took the shoes and Caspar fretted over the information. Had this wolf creature somehow slipped away from the man to possess the bird? Though the notion was absurd, it was all Caspar could think and, in the absence of any other ideas, even began to make sense.

They had only travelled another mile before Reyna forced them to rest again. Using his softest tones, Caspar endeavoured to persuade her to see sense. "Can't we find some horses? It would be so much easier."

Reyna shook her head. "I've told you, no. And as I've said before, there's no point us trying to catch them before we reach Castaguard. We should turn back for Slakwater – it's still the nearest village and there's not another for leagues. We could sail ahead to catch them as they enter the city. There's still time."

"But what if the toad's poison overcomes them before they make it?" Caspar argued.

"Then we'll be too late anyway. But at the moment they are just getting further and further ahead," Reyna argued.

Perren nodded at him. "She's right, Spar. You must make the decision."

Much to Caspar's annoyance, Reyna seemed capable of moving much faster when she had her own way. They retraced their steps and headed for the darkly wooded and swampy shoreline, the sea bright and glistening beyond it. As they neared the coast, Elergian warned them to be careful.

"Why?" Caspar asked.

"Toads."

"Oh." Caspar didn't need to know more. He kept in line behind the mage who was shaking a jar that he said was full of toadeaters' teeth to keep the toads at bay. This time the little wolfling was very wary and pressed close to Caspar. They threaded their way through the swamps to Slakwater where Elergian took charge of the negotiations to procure a vessel.

"You spoke of fishing boats at the least," Caspar reminded Reyna. "We can't put to sea in one of those!"

The mage again spoke to the fishermen in the harsh, guttural language of Vaalaka and again they were pointed to what Caspar took to be a row of under-tarred, over-sized coracles fixed with flimsy sails.

"I wouldn't feel safe in anything more than two inches of water."

"They have nothing else," Reyna said, firmly handing over four silver pieces for the vessel whose only promise was that it had seating enough for ten men and a spread of canvas for shelter.

The sail hanging from a flimsy mast was tattered and threadbare but still managed to pull the round-bottomed boat heavily to one side. Caspar gingerly climbed aboard and dubiously kneaded the tarred reed with his fists before settling himself into the rounded bow. The mage in exile took his station at the rear of the vessel and, looking like he knew what he was doing, lowered a long thin board into the water behind the stern. He assured everyone that it would give the craft stability but Caspar had little confidence. He considered the craft unseaworthy and that was that.

The rest clambered aboard, the boat rocking violently and sinking alarmingly as Perren boarded. Elergian hurriedly ordered him to sit centrally and keep still. Caspar was given an oar and stood near the blunt bow as they pushed out into the current. The boat swirled in the eddies and Elergian struggled to direct it with the large paddle at the stern. No amount of his chant and spell-castings eased their way.

Perren's eyes glazed with tears. Ignoring the mage's orders, he hung over the side to dip his hand into the water. The boat leaned precariously.

"The sea," he exclaimed. "I am within its cradle. Spar, can you imagine? The sea!" He grinned, his excitement spread from ear to ear like a young child.

"Well, if you won't keep to the middle, you can at least have a paddle." Elergian handed him one but he pushed it aside.

"Oh, I won't be able to use that. I shall be too busy. I can feel thousands of people," he exclaimed. "Thousands of wants and fears and needs all at once. It's so confusing, so . . ." He was lost for words, his eyes sparkling with excitement like a child with a new toy. "Reyna, put your hand in the water," he begged.

"Perren!" Caspar snapped sharply, straining against the current with his paddle, and trying to follow the mage's bidding by paddling like fury to keep clear of the rocks that loomed beneath the water as they rounded the headland. Perren's weight, as he lurched towards the very edge of the reed and tar boat, did nothing at all to make it manageable. Once they were past the rocks, the mage waved Caspar to sit down and rest.

"I think you're hindering, lad, rather than helping," he complained though quite amiably.

Caspar placed himself firmly in the very centre of the

boat and held onto the bench as if he were gripping to the edge of a precipice. Both Runa and Fern sat trembling before him and, in a gesture of trust, the little wolfling placed her long snout on Caspar's knee and looked up pleadingly into his eyes.

"It'll get us there more quickly," he told her, speaking his thoughts out loud and then cursed when Perren launched himself across the boat and draped himself over the opposite side. The waves lapped up and over the edge of the boat.

"Reyna, Reyna," he cried, "put your hand in the water."

"You'd better do as he asks otherwise he'll capsize the boat," Caspar urged.

She dropped her hand gracefully into the water while Perren stirred it excitedly. He grinned at her. "I can read more in the sea. It *is* a boy and he is well." His smile seemed to fade on his lips and a look of regret filled his grey eyes but then it returned a little more forced and he repeated too enthusiastically, "He is very well; I rejoice for you . . ."

"But I am not," Reyna supplied his unsaid words. She spoke matter-of-factly and gave a self-deprecative smile. "I already knew that."

"You told me you were well!" The mage was furious and angrily jerked at the tiller. The boat swung across the current and was buffeted by waves that hit them broadside on. Caspar's grip tightened and he concentrated on trying to soothe the wolfling.

"We should have walked," he complained and begged Elergian to concentrate on his sailing.

"I will live," Reyna bravely insisted and patted his hand. "But only if you do as the young man says and look after the boat."

The old man grasped the tiller and stirred them as close to shore as possible, following the contours of the land.

The cramped, spray-chilled days wore on uneventfully though Caspar never lost his distrust in the vessel. The sunsets on the water were dazzling and the sea glittered a brilliant red. Then, when the sun was nearly drowned in the ocean, only the caps of the waves caught its rays, becoming like gold and red jewels lying in a bed of black velvet. At night the stars over the sea shone brilliantly and the moon seemed to be at one with the water, melding with it, drenching her silvery fingers deep under the surface, caressing and stroking.

Not for the first time, Caspar noted how the moonlight fell on the wolfling, her white coat becoming aglow, casting off a silver aura around her. It reminded him of how moonlight seemed to seek out Brid, blessing her with a magical quality. He looked towards Lana and his hopes that she was the new Maiden crashed. He should have noticed before. Perhaps he had been too involved in all the other problems but he could not recall her ever showing any interest in the moon.

How could he have been so arrogant? He admitted to himself that, after the disappointment of Nimue, he had so much wanted to be the one to find the new Maiden that he had never really questioned that Lana might not be. Now he had to be sure.

"Lana, put your hand in the water." Caspar nodded at Perren who eagerly stirred the swell with his rough hand.

"I sense the fear of the wolf, particularly horrible nightmares of a wolf with a man's face. A deep sorrow, so much loss and a yearning to return home." Perren said sadly.

No wonder the girl was so quiet, Caspar thought. He had not considered the depth of her grief. "She has no special power?" he asked quietly.

"No more than you."

Caspar gloomily stared up into the face of the moon. "I'm sorry, Morrigwen. I've failed you." Quietly he remembered how he had imagined Keridwen and Brid's praise when he returned triumphant with the new Maiden.

They sailed on and, after several days in such close quarters, tempers were becoming frayed. To Caspar it seemed that all his attempts to keep a cordial fellowship were met only by abuse from all sides. The only one he didn't argue with was little Lana who spent her time in the bottom of the boat, petting the ever-appreciative dog and the more wary wolfling. Having held such high hopes for her, he now felt responsible for the poor orphaned child. He would see to it that she had a safe home.

By day he watched the shore relentlessly but never once glimpsed Ursula or his horse and he fretted for them both. The time passed slowly and he became fearful that they would never reach Castaguard. The woven reeds were becoming waterlogged and with each new day the vessel became more sluggish. But there was nothing he could do other than sleep and worry and when he was too exhausted to worry, he dreamed deliciously of May rocking him back and forth in her arms while they lay in a field of bluebells. This particular time he woke up with a warm feeling of cosiness that quickly evaporated as he remembered that May had run away.

He wondered whether the men of Torra Alta did not think that he, also, had abandoned them. He had always been taught that the people of the barony were his primary duty and he believed that. They were his people and he would do anything to protect them and yet they must think he had deserted them. Why, Great Mother, he silently asked, why did you lay this burden on me? Any one of the high priestesses would have fared better. Even my father, even Hal. "But why me?" he blurted out loud.

Perren was watching him. "Put you hand in the water," he urged.

Caspar had already done that at least twenty times already but the stonewight's over-excitability and great weight made him too much of a liability in the boat and he was forced to oblige or spend another hour bailing.

"You have an honest heart, Spar, and little ambition. You were born with more than you wanted and would be unlikely to seek your desires through the Egg. From all the stories you've told me, I'd say Hal would have wanted power or recognition, Branwolf a greater and more secure garrison, any one of the high priestesses to spread the word of the Great Mother. So, as unlikely as it might seem, you were chosen."

"But I've always wanted things. I've wanted to be bigger and stronger and more decisive."

Perren laughed. "Well, Necrönd won't give you any of those things so you can't misuse its power."

Caspar smiled faintly. It seemed a poor reason to him.

For two nail-biting days, the mage steered out into deep water, insisting that it would cut weeks from their journey. Caspar prayed every moment that the shore was out of sight.

At last, Caspar knew the discomforts of the open boat were at an end. The first glimpse of land lay ahead; slate grey clouds smothering an equally grey line upon the horizon. As they neared, the clouds lifted and the land gained its earthy colours until Caspar could make out the two promontories that marked the entry to an estuary. Closer still, he saw how the occasional sliver of sunlight slipped down between breaks in the clouds to gladden a valley with golden light, quite beautiful in the dun landscape. It was like the promise of hope, a glimpse of better things, of how the world should be.

"Narwhal Ria," Elergian announced with satisfaction. "And you presumed to doubt my seamanship."

The Narwhal Ria was lined with reeds so tall that, once they had made some headway inland, it was virtually impossible to see what was water, riverbank or rush-covered meadows. Men, up to their waists in water, worked with scythes, gathering reeds and laying them in bunches onto long rafts. So intent were they on their task that, even when Perren stood up and stared at them inquisitively, they barely looked up from their labour. They navigated inland, the river gradually becoming busier with other craft though most, like the reed-cutters, were too intent on their business to pay any attention to the small round-nosed vessel, however odd it might look.

At the first opportunity, Elergian moored up alongside a village jetty so that they might bathe in the fresh water and rid themselves of the abrasive salts that encrusted their clothes, skin and hair. They rested only briefly before taking on fresh supplies and continuing upriver.

By mid-day the river was congested and the mage had to work hard to avoid the other vessels, especially the boats that dragged long nets out between them to scoop up the fish. Caspar, now much happier that land lay within swimming distance, leaned over the side and watched the silvery shapes flashing by.

Dotted along the muddy banks, villages, with their huts of brown daub walls and drooping thatch that was steeply shelving to shake off the heavy rains of the winter, added interest to their journey. The Narwhal was not an easy river to navigate for the spits of land and sand bars and, even if it were fuller during the rainy season, it would be treacherous for the unseen hazards beneath the water. There was little wonder that Ceolothians favoured the roads over the river to move their cargoes.

Away from the silted coast, the river narrowed and deepened. Struggling upstream against the current, Perren's strength came into its own as he tirelessly tugged at the oars. Soon they had left the coastal region behind and entered a region virtually devoid of civilization.

A week since they had seen any village, the river became blacker and more turgid as they sailed, rowed and punted upstream into the vast pine forests where rafts of needles caught between logs and floating vegetation slewed against their craft. Caspar shuddered, seeing water snakes wriggling and rippling on the surface. He hated snakes and concentrated his vision on the forest. Many times, he saw forest bears coming down to the water's edge to drink and, once, he thought he saw kobolds but by the time he had alerted the others the little creatures were nowhere to be seen.

The scenery barely changed for days on end until at last, the forest thinned and, in the distance, they could see a tiered and gleaming city. The river narrowed, the banks becoming sheer and rocky as they were diverted into a canal where they joined a line of other vessels waiting to pass through a series of locks.

The water only half filled the stone-walled channel whose sheer sides stank of rotting vegetation and were coated in green algae. All that was visible beyond the narrow world of the stinking canal wall was a strip of sky overhead. It was horribly oppressive.

Thus they entered Castabrice, like rats on a raft in an open sewer, the canal cutting right to the edge of the bright city. Reyna looked longingly at the tall, airy white spires that rose above the canal, while Caspar rewrapped Perren in his bandages that gave the impression he had suffered a hideously disfiguring pox and curiously examined the sluice gates that fed into the canal from the city.

"Flood precautions," Elergian explained laconically.

"It is not the original capital, of course. It was always the most beautiful city, built with the wealth of the largest sunburst ruby mines, but it is not a city of learning or law. Its twin city, Castaguard is the ancient heart of Ceolothia. It's extraordinary; I have never been here but still I've read so much about the place and imagined myself here so often that it feels like home."

It took many more days to negotiate the numerous locks that barred their way to the multi-walled city of Castaguard. Black mountains, with voluminous clouds gathering on their flanks, glowered at them from the horizon, adding to the sense of gloom as they slid into the shadows of the city walls. Furthermore, it was raining.

Reyna's reaction to Castaguard was very different to that of the capital. She had been very sick that day, which Elergian said spoke well for the child but ill for the mother. She had little strength. When she saw the black rocks of Castaguard, which had just the hint of a burnt red smearing their sides, she gasped in dismay.

"It should be a brilliant red that would flush gold and crimson in the sunset. The entire city walls should be clad in red Ceolothian bauxite but look what they have done to it."

Centuries of soot and grime from the pits and the fires had created a dour and sinister place. Caspar had no desire to enter. The canal stank and so did the moats. Already the wolfling's hackles were up and Fern was twitching.

Entering the city from the south, the broad canal curved round to the east though smaller channels split from it, leading to low arches in the outer curtain walls and into the city. The canals were sluiced against flood. Taking one of these channels, they steered past the heavier vessels and made for a rickety little-used jetty where they moored. Before they left, Perren put his hand into the water.

"Sadness, horrible sadness and despair. Men come to this city to die," he said heavily.

"But this is my city!" Reyna was near tears. "The beautiful city of Castaguard with its shining red walls."

"Reyna, please don't distress yourself, please," the mage begged. "There's only one thing that matters now and that's your health."

"But what has become of my people?" Reyna wrung her hands in distress.

Caspar studied the huge city walls and raised his eyebrows in surprise. Beyond the banked walls of the canal, the ground dipped towards the heart of the fortified city where only the upper sections of a grim black tower poked above the surrounding buildings. He would have expected to see a towering keep set upon a motte but, from here, nothing was visible beyond the cliff of black wall before him. A huge garrison, he concluded, seeing that the upper regions of the walls bore windows and no doubt were hollow, and provided sleeping quarters for a vast number of men. Coming from a castle himself, he was impressed by the scale of Castaguard's defences.

He cut a length of rope to make a leash for the wolfling so that there would be less outcry at her presence. She spat and fought and squealed, twisting upside down onto her back and frantically gnawing at the rope as if suspecting some terrible treachery. Only when Fern offered her a piece of gnarled black root, which the woodwose said was known amongst deer as Fawn's Bribe, was she placated.

Perren laughed at the name. "It tastes deliciously sweet. The old ones would bring it for us since it kept us quiet for weeks if they gathered enough. Always does the trick," he said cheerfully and Fern nodded and smiled in solidarity.

In the end, Runa allowed herself to be tied so long as the rope went from her collar to her mouth while Caspar held the other end. He had the sense that she was far more in control of him than he of her. She wasn't like Trog. Caspar understood Trog. He was cheeky, mischievous, devious and loved attention but the wolfling was none of those but always mysterious, always watching, always aloof.

The moment they moved away from the canals and took the straight wide road lined with sandbags into the city, Fern was up on his toes, stretching up his neck and peering around for danger. "He's been here. I know he's been here."

"Fern, don't be ridiculous. He can't have got here before us. Not unless he flew." As the words passed Caspar's lips, he had a horrible sense that he had hit on some truth though he could not understand what. His skin prickled.

Fern was so indignant and upset about the smell of wolf that Caspar, despite his sense of logic, could not help but believe him and decided that, once he had secured rooms for the night, they would investigate the scent.

He was just deliberating on exactly how they would approach the search when they entered the first of the markets that dominated the centre of the city. Caspar was suddenly horrified to see he was holding a limp rope and that Runa was gone. He'd been so busy thinking and watching Fern that he hadn't noticed the wolfling slip her collar. Trog was whining and sniffing the ground and suddenly sprinted down a dark alley and away from the populated heart of the town.

"I don't imagine the wolfling's ever been near a city," Reyna said. "I'm not surprised she's run away."

Caspar looked after Trog anxiously. "Runa! I must—"

"Trog will look after her," Perren assured him. "He's devoted to her. No doubt, she'll find her way to the outskirts of the city and wait for you. They'll find us again."

Caspar wished he could enjoy everyone else's lack of worry. But even he forgot the wolfling when he strode through the brightly coloured market square to the sunken keep. The sights that lurked in its shadows horrified him; men and women squatting on the bare earth in rows, many shackled by the neck, sores and wounds marking their bodies and showing obvious signs of fever and ill health. Slave masters, big strong men with large whips, walked up and down the ranks.

Caspar could not sleep for the crying. He sat in the window overlooking the square that was lit from a dun moon half obscured by the clouds. Below, he could see slaves who had no room to lie down, sitting with heads down between their knees, backs hunched against the rain. Perren sat beside him and wept at the story of human suffering. They had sat in their rooms for four days now, waiting for any signs of Ursula.

Caspar had fretted over whether they should search the incoming roads or sit and watch the central slave markets. In the end, he was persuaded by Reyna that, however frustrating, they must sit and wait. "You'll never find her and it's unwise to roam in Ceolothia without clear purpose. The authorities are fussy about such things."

"Fussy!" Caspar snorted. "I've seen them fill three wagon loads of men and women since we've been here. Just rounded them up off the streets like stray dogs!"

After four days of Fern's continual pacing and Perren's insatiable appetite for stories, they were near throttling each other. Caspar wouldn't have minded Perren's love of stories so much if he didn't have that infuriating way of interrupting and asking inane questions so that the whole thread of any story was lost.

Exasperated by his companions' lack of storytelling, Perren began to tell his own tales. He started with the story of the march of the stones, of how they formed their great circle dance across the earth; then the wars of the dragons of a thousand years ago and then of the year when the verderers of Rye Errish flooded the world to learn about the men that they would later usher across their lands to the afterlife. The stories never ceased and Caspar eventually fell into the rhythm of his style, which was slow and convoluted and gave no more importance to the heroes of these great events than the simple folk who witnessed them. It was a curious view of the world, lacking in perspective, but Caspar wondered whether Perren's view was not more truthful than his own.

He sat by the window all that time, keeping a constant vigil over the slave-market guarded by the statue of a bear that stood in a muddy stagnant pool. Its dank aroma wafted up to them.

A week later, Perren had been reduced to naming, in full and in as many languages as he could, every animal and insect that had ever walked the earth. Caspar was dozing lightly, prevented from proper sleep by his fear that Ursula and Mamluc would never arrive in Castaguard. He was almost resolved to head back along the coast by foot.

All this while, Reyna sat with her puffy legs up, panting gently while Elergian paced around her, muttering charms. "This is not a healthy place to deliver a child. The air is full of spoor and infections. And the damp!"

Caspar was suddenly on his feet, pointing and stammering. "Ursula!" he exclaimed, his voice strangled in disbelieving horror.

Firecracker, his head low, lash marks on his rump, limped ahead of her. Though subdued, he was still able to take vicious kicks at anyone who came close. Ursula was being dragged by her ankles behind the horse, her bare shoulders thumping and scraping on the cobbles. She didn't seem to be moving.

His knuckles whitened as he clenched them around the bars of the window, his muscles shaking with anger. The others pressed close around his shoulders, gasping. The mage pulled Reyna away. "You must not upset yourself, my queen. You are exhausted already."

She nodded weakly but would not be pulled away from the window. Horns sounded around the city and soon a mob had gathered in the square below, some faces alight with excitement, others taut with outrage. The slave-drivers seated on huge coal-black horses, barged to the front, swinging and cracking their long whips above the heads of the crowd. Caspar recognised the horses at once as Torra Altan bred war-horses and vowed that no more would be exported to Ceolothia.

Ursula was dragged to her feet, blood weeping down her back. The great bullwhip lashed her again. She did not cry out, though Caspar knew that the bravest of men should have cried aloud from the pain.

"Maybe the toad juice has numbed her, subdued her," Reyna said, her voice catching. "Perhaps there is some good in that poison."

Ursula's apparent bravery had a subduing effect on the staring crowd, who watched in morbid silence as ropes were attached to her arms and legs and then tied to two of the slave-drivers' horses. Clattering on the cobbles, the powerful steeds were ridden away from each other, lifting Ursula from the ground.

"They're going to stretch her between them." Caspar's voice was dry and disbelieving. "We've got to do something."

Ursula made no noise. She was quite silent and stared defiantly into the face of the slave-driver. He snarled and cuffed her across the mouth. Her head swung and lolled down for a moment before she looked back up and continued to glare.

The crowd moved forward and soldiers gathered around her, their crossbows raised to keep them at bay. Caspar knew there were bears in the city and wondered that she didn't call them to her aid but, seeing the crossbows, decided that she feared they would be injured. Evidently, she preferred to take her punishment silently and alone. She had lived a life alone and would expect no more in death.

But he would not let that happen. He had no idea what he could do or how he would do it but yelled out from the window at the top of his voice. His cry was chilling in its urgency and all looked round.

He fled the room, threw himself down the steep slatted steps to the lower floor and sprinted from the house to the square. By the time he was passing the stagnant pool with its rampant bear, his hand was on his bow. Thirty crossbows were turned on him as came to a halt before Mamluc.

He disregarded the crossbows. "That is my woman!" he shouted levelling the shaft of his arrow at the man's throat. "You will untie her."

"She is an escaped slave," Mamluc shouted back in Belbidian, holding up her hand to show the tattoo mark on her arm, a simple black cross. "We caught her running and now she must face the consequences of all recaptured runaways."

For a moment Caspar faltered for words. Mamluc was showing no sign of poisoning. Had he escaped contamination or did he really have powers of sorcery that would protect him from the toad juice? Caspar racked his brain for something convincing to say. "She was not running. I sent her to gather herbs for me. She is mine!" he yelled. "This is an outrage. You cannot damage my property!"

"You are a Belbidian. Everyone knows that Belbidians don't have slaves."

"I have been in Ceolothia for a while, gathering rare herbs. See!" he held up his fist and produced the wilted stem of yellow melilot that the old woman at Kittiwake Cove had given him. "It's easier to find slaves than servants in Ceolothia. What else was I to do?"

"You must prove ownership."

"Er—I—" Caspar stammered. He did not know how it was customary to prove ownership of a slave. "She is my woman because she has my horse." Firecracker had jerked his head up and was snorting at the sound of his master's voice.

"She is a bear tamer," Mamluc roared. "And my slave! I came here to show these slaves what happens to those who run away."

"You can't prove it!" Caspar yelled, replying in attack.

"Possession! She is in my possession; therefore, she is my slave."

"She is in the possession of my horse," Caspar retaliated. "She is tied to my horse."

One of the Ceolothian slave masters interjected, "Then you must then prove ownership of the horse."

Caspar smiled confidently. "There is a mark on the underside of his saddlecloth stained in blue woad." He drew the sign in the mud. It was ᛖ, Ehwaz, the horse rune and he had asked Brid to place it there to give him strength and luck while riding.

"Unsaddle the horse," Mamluc yelled at one of the guards. The man approached only for Firecracker's head to snake around and menace with bared teeth.

Caspar slung his bow over his shoulder and, with a murmur of welcome, slid the saddle from his horse's back. Firecracker snorted and whickered but did not attempt to kick him. There was a cry of approval from the crowd as he lifted the saddlecloth for all to see. The rune he had drawn was clearly visible and a cheer roared out from the ranked slaves.

"So, he proves ownership!" Mamluc scowled. "I must have mistaken this wench or forgotten that I had sold her on. But that makes none of this better. I caught her wandering alone and we all know the laws on slavery in this country. A slave cannot be left to roam without supervision. Think of the threat to the good honest folk of Ceolothia. They could have their throats cut in their sleep by a slave. The punishment for such laxity is clear; to the slave mines with them!"

"To the mines with them!" the mounted slave-drivers roared.

Caspar had no time to think before he was being dragged backwards by his arms, cursing his own stupidity. Hal would have rushed in just as he had but he would have rushed in with a plan.

A sudden shriek of fear stopped the men in their stride though they did not let go. Someone was shouting in Ceolothian and Caspar had to think to translate it. "Flood! Flood!" He then saw it was Reyna who screamed the words of alarm.

There was a moment of sudden silence and stiffening

in the crowd followed by a shrieking squeal of metal and a growing roar. Reyna was close at Caspar's side and had screamed before she could have imagined what was about to happen. A wall of black water, crested with white, was channelling down one of the side streets, snapping up lines of washing that blocked its way, tearing out doors and windows and swallowing discarded barrows, in its destructive path towards them.

Caspar tried to grab hold of Reyna, Ursula, Lana and his horse all at once but could not get to them for those fleeing the square in mad shrieking panic. Instead, he stood his ground and waited. The moment the water hit the square, it would spread rapidly, its energy dissipated, and he was probably only at risk of getting his feet wet. Perren had Lana so he shoved his way first to Reyna and, holding her hand tight, dragged her against the tide of townsfolk, merchants, slaves and soldiers to his horse, telling her to hold fast to a stirrup while he freed Ursula.

He cut Ursula's ropes and, with her arms weakly looped around his neck, strode through the rising water. The rushing mire buffeted his booted calves, sloshing up over his knees. She looked up at him with a misty faraway expression, brimming with gratitude.

"Master," she said dreamily, almost happily. "I hadn't dared hope you would come for me. You cared!" The note of happiness in her voice turned to fear and Caspar realized that he, too, feared her emotion. He had May to think of. He could offer Ursula no more than her freedom.

He braced himself against the flood, swearing when the handle of an upturned hand-barrow washed against his leg but, as he had predicted, the water had spent much of his its force when it disgorged into the square.

"This way!" Reyna pointed towards the fountain in the middle of the square that was now gushing up a black jet of water. It stank and must have been fed from the sewerlike canals. The spout swelled into a vast curtain of water falling like a dome around the statue, completely obscuring it from view. Caspar began to run towards it, pulling Firecracker with him who in turn towed Reyna through the water.

He thought that she must know of some sort of secret passageway beneath the fountain but he was wrong. They plunged through the black waters, Firecracker shrieking in protest and nearly ripping out his arm. Once within, they were concealed by the black dome of water and hidden from view.

"What do we do now?" he shouted above the roar of the falling water.

"We wait for Elergian of course," Reyna shouted back weakly.

Caspar was concerned. She looked white and was beginning to pant weakly. Ursula took one look at the woman's belly and heaved herself off Caspar and sagged into the water beside Reyna. "For pity's sake, Spar, help her. Can't you see she's pregnant?"

Free of Ursula, Caspar put his arms under Reyna's shoulders to support her. He was surprised at her weight.

"I have to survive this." Reyna's knees sagged and Caspar braced himself to support her, praying that the mage would soon reach them.

An arm and then Elergian's face pushed through the curtain of roaring water hotly followed by Perren, Lana and then Fern who, though spluttering and shrieking, calmed himself quickly with a great show of self-control when he saw that he was upsetting the horse.

"Follow me," the mage urged excitably. "All but a couple of slaves have fled the square. The way is clear. But we've got to get out of here before that crazy slave master realizes there's no real flood danger and comes hunting for Ursula."

They plunged back through the sheet of water and ran as best they could, Perren carrying Ursula while Elergian and Caspar carried Reyna between them. They hobbled through the sloping streets against the flow of the flood and turned through a wide sluice gate into a sunken slime-coated channel that had once been a canal.

The mage smiled at Reyna, his face full of concern. "My queen, everything was just where it should have been. The ancient charts drawn up by the first queen in exile were right."

"Where are we going?" Caspar asked.

"To the mage's chambers of course. There will be no safer place in all Ceolothia," Elergian told him.

"How's that?" Caspar asked breathlessly. "And why was everyone so afraid of the flood? It was not so vast."

"Nine hundred years ago the entire city was flooded. Someone released all the waters from the canals; the walls within the city held the water in for five days. Few survived. Those in Castaguard have been fearful ever since. The city gates will be jammed now with people trying to get out."

"And with luck many slaves will escape," Ursula added with feeling. They ran along the emptied canal, the echo of the splashing feet slapping back and forth between the tall sheer walls of the narrow channel, until they came to a ledge broad enough for even Firecracker. It sloped up towards two steel doors cut into the side wall of the canal. The doors were bolted in six places.

Elergian hesitated momentarily before saying, "The right one."

"No, the left," Reyna argued.

"I remember it clearly. Your mother said it was the right door."

"The left," Reyna insisted. "Do not argue with me. She was my mother so I should know."

Caspar wondered at this logic though the mage did not seem to question it further and, with no more ado, began working at the bolts on the left-hand door. They were rusted and would not shift. He looked anxious. "Soon they'll refill the canal and we'll drown if we can't get through."

Perren pushed him aside and used nothing more than his clenched fist to hammer aside the bolts that shot back as if they had been fired from a crossbow. He heaved at the door handle but not even Perren's great strength and weight could pull the door open.

"Push it," Reyna suggested.

It slid open as if its hinges were made from butter. Ahead lay a tunnel lit from light falling through overhead grilles. The walls were lined with strange characters, moons stars, comets and sunbursts with diagrams of men and representations of witches and wizards and goblins. Caspar feared they might form a curse.

Struggling with the mage to carry Reyna along the long narrow tunnel, his arms rasped against the rock walls. Then there was sudden silence, the roar of the water and screams from the town inaudible, as Perren thumped the door closed behind them. In the new-found quiet, the squeak of rats, the drip of water and the clang of Firecracker's hooves on stone sounded loud. Caspar was unsure how far they travelled through the tunnel or in what direction. They could be in the heart of the city or way beyond the city walls; he could not tell. The dimly lit tunnel led them to a large door of black wood, undoubtedly oak. Carved into its split grain was a runic inscription.

"It might be a curse," Elergian warned. "Stand back while I cast a spell." He began to mumble in his throat.

Perren gently lowered Ursula to the ground. She doubled over, coughing. A drop of black blood trickled from her mouth into her open palm.

"Hurry!" Reyna shouted angrily at the mage. "She won't last much longer. The toad juice will have done untold damage to her lungs and stomach. We must get her inside."

Caspar sighed. "It's not a curse." The runic letters were in the tongue of the ancient Caballan, a language not dissimilar to his own, and he had understood them without too much difficulty. "It says this is the doorway to the mysteries."

Stepping past Elergian, he lifted the latch and pushed his way inside. Before them, yawned a tall hall that looked as if it once must have been sumptuously painted in vivid colours but was now coated in a thick layer of dust. Daylight fell through huge arched windows set in the domed roof onto a long table lounging before an unlit fire. Everything, even the spiders' webs that spanned from the walls to the ornate chandeliers was coated in dust.

"Untouched for seven hundred years!" the mage declared, his eyes glistening with tears.

CHAPTER TWENTY-FOUR

May squirmed and struggled just long enough to get her mouth free of the suffocating hand and scream for Amaryllis. His answering cry, as desperate as her own, swam back to her before she was enveloped in hollow darkness. Dragged into narrow fault lines and squeezed through crevices, the harsh points of the rocks snagged at her skin.

Someone tied her hands with something that felt too smooth and springy to be rope and half-dragged half-carried her deeper into the cracks in the rocks. The bumping bruising journey seemed endless but, slowly, May realised that the blackness had receded and that she could just make out the solidity of the rock walls and ceilings around her.

Amaryllis had been right! Rubies everywhere! It was rubies that gave her light. The quantities of stones were few at first, like red stars in a moonless sky, but soon their numbers increased as they passed into yet another chamber where their combined luminescence enabled May to clearly see her captor for the first time. He was not some beast of the underworld, as she had thought, but the very soldier that had attacked her in the refectory hall. But he had withered unnaturally, the flesh shrivelled on his arms and face. Somehow, the thin glow could not illuminate his features, his eyes two black sockets sucking in the light.

He dragged her on through the glistening chamber and through a tight crevice back into the dark. Now he swung her up over his shoulder and stumbled on, his bare feet scraping rhythmically on the rocks, and she wondered how he could see. Bumping along on his back, she tried to worm her tied hands towards the Egg but she could not reach the casket. Necrönd had been her last hope. Whatever this creature was, she could have driven it away, but now . . .

Then an idea kindled in the depths of her mind. She would wait. This withered creature was taking her to the depths of the mountains where no one would ever find her again. Wasn't that where she wanted to go?

The ceiling lowered suddenly and her head cracked against it. Blood trickled down her face and her senses swam. She gritted her teeth, trying to focus her mind. They had entered a wide cavern. Though it was still dark, she could tell it was a large space because of the sudden booming echo from the soldier's laboured footfalls. Again, he dragged her through a crack in the rock and on into the next cavern.

A tiny speck of light grew larger with each of the man's faltering steps until they entered a short passage that led out into a bright chamber full of glowing crystals, each appearing to hold a drop of the sun within its heart. She saw him more clearly again. His backbone at his neck was like a row of pegs jutting through the decaying skin. As if aware of her scrutiny, he plucked her from his back and thrust his shadowed face into hers.

"Help," he pleaded feebly in Ceolothian.

For a moment May saw the man, glimpsed in his eyes a spark of humanity that was all that remained of his tortured soul. Then he jerked rigid as if gripped from within, blood oozing from his mouth. A yellow and rotted tooth slipped out. Through the gory wetness, the Ceolothian voice pleaded for a swift death, then his face twisted and a sneer curled the rotting lips.

"His love!" he snarled in Belbidian, throwing her over his back. "His love. What could be better? We are nearly there now, nearly there. I nearly have it all. And then there will be no need of gods." The sound of his shod feet rattled through the dark with renewed vigour.

Fear overtook her. Was she deep enough in the mines now? How could she be rid of him? The questions rattled in her head unresolved. Though her hands were tied and she could not reach the Egg, she put all her energies into focusing on it, hoping that she could force her will over it. But she could think only of her fear and the barrier of the casket between her and the Egg. The silver casket became for her an impassable wall and it wasn't until she remembered Caspar's explanation of how he coped with daunting situations that she knew what to do.

He had told her how he had found it impossible to exercise any authority over the older boys being trained up for garrison life. The first time he had been ordered to go out alone and organize the day's target practice, something that he had done often but always under Hal's or the Captain's supervision, he had become quite witless, forgetting even the basic procedures. May understood. Three hundred youths were not easy to control and rarely listened to anyone unless the Baron was close at hand. Caspar's mother had come to his aid. "Don't focus on the problems. Don't even think about them. Look, there's Pip. Imagine it's just you and Pip and that it's a bright sunny day" – it happened to be sleeting at the time – "and you're showing just him what to do. Look at their faces and turn them all into Pip, then you'll be fine." After that, though he never had the same command as Hal, at least Caspar coped.

May imagined she was in Morrigwen's rooms that were always warm and cosy and that the Crone held her hand and reached out to touch the Egg for her.

In an instant May's mind enveloped the Egg and a rush of power swam through her. Now she was mistress of her enemies!

A shriek of pleasure from her captor shattered her moment of triumph. He seized on her thoughts and wrestled her mind for control of the Egg, his strength of will immediately stronger than hers. Beasts of the underworld, great monstrous ogres stirred within the rocks around her; tiny creatures danced in the points of light. She willed them to protect her but they only snarled and lurched at her in response to the soldier's mind. She knew she was beaten.

The moment her will weakened, he snatched more power from her. She grasped for concentration, that level of clear pure thought that would give her ultimate and sole power of the Egg but her mind was seized. It was as if something were strangling her thoughts with a garrotte that dug tighter and tighter into the soft tissues of her brain.

She was weak with pain. Her vision swam red as the soldier's terrible anger, his vilifying hatred and depravity, the lust to destroy, to avenge assaulted her mind. She wallowed in his emotions, felt his pathetic pit of sorrow and ultimate loneliness as if this creature had once known love but was now embittered and twisted and had lost all fellowship and communion with others. The horribly frightening awareness that loneliness could be the fountain of such bitter hatred clawed at her mind like a wild cat. Around her squirmed a soup of animals, their bodies combining into a sticky yolk-like whole. Into this pottage of life, she was sucked and whipped back and forth under the slime of birth fluid, like a kitten being drowned in a bucket.

She had to free her mind from the Egg. He was reaching it through her and she knew she must withdraw to keep its powers from him. But how? Her mind swirled into the maelstrom of anguished souls within the diabolised confines of the Egg. Wolves snarled out of the dark periphery of her consciousness, summoned by the blackness, and amongst them stood three tall men robed in purple with peaked hats upon their heads. They turned and laughed into her face.

I'm too weak, she thought, belatedly bemoaning her decision to take Necrönd.

She thought of home, trying to reach out for those who had loved her. She thought first of her mother and then Morrigwen but both were dead and could bring her no comfort. It was not until she thought of Caspar and imagined him galloping to her rescue and wrapping his arms around her that she gained any semblance of self-control. She didn't want to be baroness of Torra Alta; it meant nothing to her. She just wanted the gentle touch of the honest youth, to watch his nervous smile, to let him take her hand and point at the sky and say, "There flies the hawk, come let's fly with him."

The grip on her mind broke. She thought for a second that her willpower had prevailed but quickly understood that it was the other who had weakened, his concentration breaking when the image of Caspar swelled in her mind.

The stirring menace of creatures around her was swept away, directed back to the Otherworld by the sorcery of Necrönd. Now she was simply his captive again. She wondered why he did not seek to physically wrestle Necrönd from the casket chained around her neck and could not guess at his plans.

He carried her out of the glowing chamber and into the dark where her senses were numbed and her mind confused. She was only clearly aware of the rattling tap of his boots, his laboured rasping breaths and his continual, gleeful hissing of, "His beloved! His whore. I have her! Wretched little woman, forcing me all the way across the world. Wretched little creature, you will suffer now. You will suffer as I have suffered. You cannot begin to know how much. Talorcan should have spared me this but he was weak. Always, we men are seduced by the women, by sweet-smiling, silver-tongued women. The essence of womanhood is wickedness. You are evil. All of you evil!"

The soldier's maddened words filled May with terror. Mortally afraid, she prayed for the Great Mother's mercy. But her prayers died on her lips at the sight before her. Losing her self-control, she screamed in panic. Green flame lit the way ahead, its fire rising from a liquid that sizzled and hissed, spitting coils of light up through the swirling heat of the flames like dancing worms. Her own screams went unheard, drowned out by those of the agonized men she saw before her.

Around the green fire were hunched long-limbed creatures, their elongated fingers tipped by gristly suckers. Their faces were long with small noses and mouths but their eyes were disproportionately large and blinked continuously. Narrow lizardlike tongues spat, uncoiling from the front of their tiny mouths. The nearest of them snapped out its tongue to slime across May's face and coil sensuously around her eyelid.

A man, undoubtedly a slave lost or stolen from the

mines, screamed in torment as he was skewered by a spit and turned in the flames. Another beside him was long since dead, his clothes burnt away and the flesh on his skin bubbling and popping like that of a roasting pig, soon to become crisp without and succulent within. Others hung from the walls, hooked through the flesh of their shoulders. All save a very few had their eyes put out as if in ritual sacrifice.

"It hurts! It hurts!" The soldier laughed maniacally, plunging a finger into one of the slaves' empty eye-sockets and gouging deeper. "Feel how it hurts! Others must feel my pain. Tell me how much it hurts," he raged while the thin-limbed creatures with their humped backs prodded the carcasses. Some coiled lovingly around the soldier's emaciated legs, their arms worming upwards to snatch at May. Her strength spent and the emotional numbness of shock overcoming her, she could scream no longer.

She stared stupidly about her. Beyond the green glow from the fires sat a straight-backed chair, an extraordinary object to find so deep below the surface. Straps for tightly securing a man were looped over its arms and beside it upon the stone floor was a head-brace with large screws attached, designed to put out a man's eyes.

She sucked in deep breaths, determined to find her control. Poor slaves, she thought, somehow in her terror finding the means to feel pity for others. They trembled and shrieked and she prayed that the Great Mother would deliver them speedily from their torment.

The soldier laughed. "That is not for you. I have better for you, whore-woman. I have you now, and here in the depths of the world no one will come for you, no one can rescue you. You are down with the knockermen now, who simply want their larders filled and their world undisturbed. Dig too close to their homes and they fear discovery. None that go this low ever come out again."

The spitted slave was still wriggling though May could see he was weakening and at least the pungent fumes from the fire were choking his senses. She prayed he was fast losing consciousness.

The knockermen took her from the man's back and dragged her around the fire, past the chair and through the midst of a dozen of these knockermen who were hunched up over half-eaten carcasses, splintering cracks coming from the drooling mouths as they crunched on human bones. One was scooping its long tongue into an upturned skull, sucking the brains out and winding its tongue in through the empty eye holes and nose cavity. Now before her lay a broad circle of skulls surrounding a glistening bed of crystals. A chalice, a knife and a sickle were placed alongside, the dancing green light reflecting off the crystals and swirling on the metal of the three sacramental artefacts.

They tugged her through the circle of skulls and threw her onto the bed of clear crystals, where they fell on her, biting through her bonds that she now saw were of glistening gut. They pulled at her arms and legs, lashed her down by her ankles and wrists to the four corners of the bed, and pressed her onto the gleaming points of the crystals until they ground into her soft flesh. Quivering tongues wrapped around her limbs and slithered over her skin. Sticky hands wound through her hair.

Her eyes flicked between the knife, the sickle and the chalice and she wondered that they weren't going to slit open her belly and draw out her entrails before hacking out her heart while she still lived. Involuntarily her mouth opened. "Spar!" she whimpered. "Where are you? I need you!"

She thrashed and struggled, twisting her joints in her efforts to free herself but the knockermen's bonds held fast. The fleshless soldier approached. She squirmed frantically to be free. He stopped at the foot of the bed. She thought he would rip away her clothes and rape her before disembowelling her but he just stood and stared. Beads of sweat rolled from her forehead as he continued to watch. Then he buckled at the knees, heaving and retching. A black slime dripped from his mouth to form a pool at his feet. With one final convulsion, a beating mass the size of a fist forced his mouth wide and with the crack of his jaw dropped into the slime. The black pool, thick like treacle, began to seep across the ground towards the bed.

The soldier slumped to the floor, all the unnatural power gone from his body. He was sobbing, his face a picture of fear. Gone was the rigid stare of hatred.

"Close your mind," he gasped in Ceolothian and other words of warning that May barely understood for his panic. He was staring down at the shape that was trickling across the ground towards her.

Now she saw why it had not attempted to wrestle the Egg from her; it wished to possess her, to control Necrönd from within her body.

She tried to pull away as the black cold slime spiralled up the bed leg and elongated itself, stretching out for her foot. Cold crept into her, numbing her bones. Her body became leaden, unresponsive and alien. Her will was confined to one small, terrified part of her mind while her hands and arms moved to the will of another. A terrible and triumphant scream that was not her own escaped her throat.

A man's thoughts occupied her head, touching gleefully on power and revenge, and the sacrifices and the suffering he would cause to make others pay. He was owed the world. Had he not earned the right through his suffering? May could not understand his logic nor did she try. She knew only that she had experienced his cold insidious presence before and that terrified her further.

The knockermen cut the tresses that bound her to the bed of crystals and she sprang up and out of the circle. The long-limbed knockermen bowed, wriggling in supplication, their faces close to the ground and tilted eyes looking sideways like pathetic pups. She found herself striding towards the fire and heard her voice boom out that she was afraid of nothing, no one. "See, now I have the power! I bow to no gods. Scrape before me and no other for I am the one god. God of life and death, commander of souls, ruler of this life and the next."

Her hands trembled over the casket containing the Egg but the blackness within her did not yet force her body to seize it. The Dark Shadow seemed not quite prepared. Whatever evil possessed her body, she was also still there. And she had a right to be there! She would not cower in fear; she would fight. If it could place its will on her, so then surely, she could place her will on it.

Great Mother, have mercy on my soul; I am here in your womb, deep within the earth from where all life springs. Mother, hear me, she begged in prayer.

She repeated the prayer and a fit of her possessor's rage burst out from her body. Her hand flew up to cuff her ear. Her head reeled and she was sickened by the pain. The possessor laughed and shrieked and hit her again, harder and harder.

In response, she prayed more fervently, willing herself onto her knees to pray, her mind reaching out for the Mother. For a brief moment of triumph, her knees sagged. But rejoicing in the victory caused her concentration on her prayers to falter. Her body snapped upright and was forced to run for the green flames where the spitted man was now sizzling and glossy with melted fat. Her hand plunged into the flame. Searing pain jolted through her entire body as the skin swelled and blistered from her fingers.

"See, I have the power. You're weak, woman," her own mouth mocked.

She screamed within her mind but could do nothing to withdraw her arm as the greater will imposed on hers kept it there. She stared at her hand, her will withering as she was lost to pain.

"The ceremony!" her voice began. "We shall proceed with the ceremony." Her arms, one blistered and blackened, rose above her head and with authority she snapped her fingers. "Bring the crystals." Snatching up a thin blade from beside the fire, she began scratching runic characters upon the rock floor. They were meaningless to that part of her that was May.

The knockermen scurried out of the green glow of the chamber and back into the dark to appear minutes later laden with uncut sunburst rubies that they arranged in circles around her. Beyond this circle, they chiselled out thin lines in the rock to form three concentric gutters. The inner one they filled with water, and the next with the green flaming liquid. Then the chalice was taken to the neck of one of the slaves who hung by his feet upon the wall. The knife flashed and a jet of blood spurted from his jugular, gushing over the cup. His body jerked and the blood flowed. The process was repeated with six more slaves until the outer gutter was full.

"Circles of bone, circles of crystal, circles of water, circles of fire, circles of blood surrounded by runes, speak of the necromancy, talk of the passage of souls through the ether," her voice chanted. "Exorcise her soul so that I might fully possess her body. I will have her and the power."

She fought all she could to stop her body from walking into the circle. It was like jerking the strings of a puppet only to find they had been cut. She knew she had failed because she lacked willpower. Furiously, she cursed herself, realizing now why the Goddess must have chosen Caspar as guardian of the Egg. As the son of a high priestess, he would have inherited great strength of mind and she knew that was what she most loved him for.

She cursed herself for her own weakness. She was too small of mind, just an insignificant girl with delusions of grandeur. She had thought with this one great gesture of self-sacrifice that she would save Spar from the evils of the Egg. Now, far too late, she saw what foolish devilry she had stirred.

"I have Necrönd and my first task is vengeance. He must die. Only then shall I lead them all to victory and become the one God. Once I have crushed his body and imprisoned his soul within Necrönd, I shall steal away the breath of his life." May knew that her voice spoke of Caspar; his image was formed by the thoughts of the Dark Shadow within her.

"No!" she cried, her own voice at last erupting as a splutter within her throat.

The possessor's mind tensed, stunned by her resistance. She grasped that second of hesitation to fix her thoughts on the Great Mother, visualising Morrigwen, Keridwen and Brid in her mind. Morrigwen was merely a rotted corpse and Keridwen merged into the image of May's own dead mother whom she so resembled. She imagined how it must have been when her head was severed from her body by a great Vaalakan axe. Then she tried to imagine

Brid and saw her whispering and laughing in Caspar's ear. She knew now that it was her bitterness towards Brid that blocked her true love of the Great Mother.

Suddenly she doubted that she had taken Necrönd for Caspar's benefit. Had leaving him been a test, an ultimatum to see if he would finally come after her? She blamed Brid for stealing away her happiness. May was one of the Great Mother's most ardent disciples and yet she bore a bitter resentment towards the Maiden. The truth was she hated her and was horrified at the thought.

Again, the triumphant shriek from the blackness within her burst from between her lips. The Shadow latched onto her hatred with delight at such a bitterness, relishing it, feeding off it.

Mortally penitent that her thoughts so railed against the Great Mother and her chosen Trinity, May begged for Brid's forgiveness, hoped that she would understand and, in her heart, knew that she would. *I have goodness in me*, May protested inwardly. *I want no harm to anyone. I just wanted the man that I love. I want Spar*, she cried within her head, remembering those first few weeks when he had turned to her and taken her out on his fine strutting horse and she had first felt his nervous but tender touch on her hand.

"Spar!" she cried out loud, her voice suddenly strong. "Spar!" She put all the power of her thought into that cry and felt shock and repulsion from the man within her who was now struggling to gain possession of the Egg as if the sound of Caspar's name had dispossessed him of his senses. He forgot all about the ceremony, his hands moving straight for Necrönd.

Knowing that his uttermost desire was to turn the savage creatures ruled by the Egg against Caspar, she thought to break it. That would let all the wrath and terror of the ancient beasts flood back into the world, bringing with them death, disease and vengeance just as the hooded wolves had done, but it would prevent the Dark Shadow from directing them against her love.

But would it be right to sacrifice the world to save Caspar? Her conscience barely considered it. She had not been brought up to view the world on so large a scale. She understood suffering as she saw it before her and did not think beyond it. Caspar's responsibility might be for Torra Alta as the Trinity's was for humanity; but hers was for Spar. There was really no one else that mattered to her. She was decided; she must smash Necrönd.

"Spar!" she spluttered, the sound almost indistinct. Throttled noises gurgled up her throat, the sound of Caspar's name producing an acute agony in his mind. "Spar!" she screamed again, more frantically this time. She tried to hurl herself towards the flames, hoping that the fire might purify her, chasing out the devilish soul within, and possibly also destroy the Egg. The heat might crack it. But her body was ridged and swept regally back towards the circle, the blackness laughing at her.

"You have no strength, girl. You are weak. You are no one, a pawn of the vile masters of Torra Alta. When I have chased you from your body, you will be no more than a shadow roaming the earth till the end of time."

May had never walked with such pose, such confidence and she resented that it was not she who moved in that way but the power of her possessor. On stepping into the consecrated circle, she felt a cold weakness, a slow suffocation, the world around her dimming as if she were losing her sight while her other senses of touch, smell and hearing became more vivid, more painful. She was slipping away, sliding down towards the earth like snow sloughing from a sloping roof.

The blackness within her body began to chant, singing of the yew and birch symbols of death and rebirth, and of the ash tree that linked the worlds and all parts of the cosmos, giving an understanding of the greater whole. He spoke of the trees of high magic, not the simple ones that she understood, not the homely ones that spoke of intuition or strength or knowledge but rather those that controlled the soul. She was awed and afeared of this man's knowledge.

In desperation, she threw back her head and croaked like a dying beast, "Spar, I beg of you, save me. Find me! Protect my soul!"

The blackness was all enveloping and her vision nearly gone. Her hand was reaching for the Egg. Hurriedly, the blackness summoned hooded wolves out of a great void. Strangely, though the real world was a blur of blood-tinged darkness, the ghosts of the Otherworld were vivid before her. In a moment of sinking horror, May watched the three tall men, dressed strangely in long purple robes and conical hats, emerge once more from the shadows. They smiled their delight, examining their near-solid bodies. One reached for the chalice, playfully blew at it and watched in satisfaction as its shape shifted until all he held was a frog.

The blackness sapped more of her strength to give solid substance to the mages and bring them fully across the divide. Then the Shadow forced her to spin round and, though she could no longer see, she felt and sensed only through the intuition that remained in her soul, and she knew of another presence.

"You!" her possessed voice screeched in hatred. "You! You betrayed me. You will die and forever. Without a soul!"

There was no reply only a note of energy, a pure brilliant power, like the blazing sun on the zenith of midsummer's day. The energy swelled out towards her, powerful, commanding, and she knew at once that the voice belonged to Amaryllis. It was not beautiful this time but fearsome, drawn from the elements, from the great strength of the earth. And more, May thought. The energy came from the sun, she decided, remembering how Amaryllis's face had turned longingly heavenward before they had passed into the gloom of the mines.

She could see now but in an alien way, objects looming in and out of a strange, blurred world. Somehow, she saw things in greater depth but with less definition. Then she saw herself! It struck her that her soul had been expelled from her body that was now vicious and contorted, its movements alien. Lying on the earth, seeing around her things that she had never seen before, she knew she was lost. She stared at the very grain of the rocks and the Ondines, the spirits of the elements close by, those of the air dancing merrily around them without a care for her plight.

Someone was beside her, a small woman with long delicate fingers and weeping hair. A glowing aura swam about her. At once May knew her for the mysterious woman who had given her the willow bark in Kittiwake Cove. She had a sad sympathetic expression and she patted what May felt to be her hand but of course was no more than a blackness. May felt horribly cold and lonely.

"Is this all I am?" she asked.

"This is all anybody is without the vehicle of their bodies, poor child."

Looming in and out of focus, she could see the aura, the spiritual energy of all the other creatures around her. The mutilated slaves who trembled in fear were bathed in a pale blue light, her own possessed body shaded by a dark black jagged shadow. And then she saw him!

Amaryllis strode forward, spouting notes of blinding energy, a ribbon of glorious light playing about him, a vast golden glow. He was like what she had once imagined an angel might be when she had been taught the words and beliefs of the New Faith in her childhood. He was strong and potent and his light blazed at the darkness of her body's aura.

She was vaguely aware that the woman with the lovely hair, who now she realized was so reminiscent of Amaryllis, was scurrying around the circle, sweeping away the crystals and cutting new runes into the floor. May's body was flung to the back of the cave in violence as if punched by a crossbow bolt. Amaryllis towered over it, the cave shuddering with the power of his song, many of the crystals around shattering with the intensity of its pitch.

Then she knew nothing more until she was hit by the terrible pain in her scorched hand. She was grateful; the horrible cold and unbearable loneliness of her soul were gone.

Amaryllis's voice melted from one of terrorising vengeance to that of love as he gathered her up in his arms and tenderly kissed her, the energy that she had seen around him flowing into her. She drank up his strength and warmth, buried her head in his chest and sobbed like a child. "I was alone; I was out there alone, a lost soul. Where is he? Where is that thing that possessed me?"

"He's slunk away, just an empty shadow as you were, gone into the very structure of the world around."

She buried her face and clung to him, only looking up when she became aware of the mysterious golden-haired woman kneeling over her. Sympathetically, she tended May's injuries, wiping her charred hand with what looked to be simple willow bark though its touch was clearly all-healing.

May was about to thank her when the woman stiffened and looked up behind her. May followed her gaze. She could see nothing different at first then frowned in bewilderment. The air trembled with points of flickering light that thickened as she watched until the forms of many other small golden-haired men and women stepped out of the atmosphere.

"What are you doing, Saille?" a dark-skinned man with a bad-tempered face but still that extraordinary golden hair and blazing yellow eyes demanded. "You have interfered. You knew it should have been left to the fates. It is not what we agreed."

"You are pitiless, Straif! This innocent cannot be allowed to lose her soul. All I have done is give her back her body. After all, she has a right to it and has done nothing wrong, nothing against the law of nature."

"You know the High Circle must meet and discuss any matter so grave as the rights of a human soul," another with a deep voice rumbled, brandishing a heavy book in his hand as if it were a weapon.

Twelve golden-haired men and women stood before her. All were radiantly beautiful with neat elfin faces. May started. They had wings! A spread of gossamer wings that shimmered and buzzed. She gasped in disbelief; hovering before her were what she could only describe as huge living fairies. They appeared to be arguing amongst themselves, waving around wands only they were too thick, more like staves. Each bore tokens on their breasts, which she instantly recognized as embroidered tree runes. The one with the book was Phagos, the beech; the one that grumbled angrily was Straif, the blackthorn and others prominent in the debate were Nuin, the ash, and Duir, the oak. As one, they turned on Amaryllis.

"You used your voice in magic," Straif accused.

"You knew that was not part of the bargain," Phagos scratched at his long beard that evidently irritated him and plucked out a beechnut. The tree of knowledge and learning, May thought, remembering the properties of the trees.

"Her soul mattered more!" Amaryllis was vehement. "I would have lost everything if I had not fought for her soul. Everything! I would have lost her and I cannot let that happen; I love her."

May's heart pounded.

"Maybe, but your last song was a web of conjuring to make her love you. That was forbidden. You have broken our rules," Straif insisted.

"No, it was a nurturing and protecting song, a song of salvation," he contradicted.

Saille continued to soothe May's scorched hand and the bruises over the rest of her body, most of which she had forgotten about. "Soon you can go home to your mother," she said reassuringly.

"My mother's dead."

"Of course. I'm sorry, my sweet," she replied as if the matter had simply slipped her memory and she knew all about her. "Then you would return to your man, little Merrymoon."

"He loves another," she replied with equal sorrow.

"Indeed?" There was doubt in the woman's voice.

"If he had loved me, he would have come for me," May said heavily.

Saille nodded but as if she didn't mean it and pushed May's hair back from her face. "You must rest, child. Relax and let my energy flow through you."

Amaryllis continued to argue that his hand had been forced and that, if it hadn't been for him, May would never have been in any danger in the first place.

There was a mocking laugh from the most solid looking of the fairylike men before her. The symbol of Duir, the oak, was embroidered on his sash. He carried in his hand a beautifully carved wooden pipe inlaid with mother-of-pearl. "Indeed. It seems to me she put herself in danger and it has been you that has been her protector all along. And she holds the third power that is in the guardianship of man. A precarious situation indeed. Was that not what you sought all along? The third power? Your show of protectiveness is but a front."

A graceful lady who filled the air with the sweet scent of honeysuckle stepped forward and looked deep into Amaryllis's eyes. May read her emblem. Uilleand, the honeysuckle, spoke with a silken tone, "There is honesty in his words and compassion. He has gone far to discovering his own soul. He hides nothing in his heart."

"He is a verderer. They have very small hearts," the one marked with the badge of Tinne, the holly, said belligerently. "We need action here rather than this endless gossip."

"He has disobeyed the rules and the law says he must be destroyed," Phagos said solemnly, tapping the great tome.

Straif and Tinne nodded vigorously.

"But he is gaining a soul," Saille pleaded.

May was completely bewildered by the conversation. The males of the group seemed decided, even Duir who had a kindly face. "Nuin, what say you?" He turned to the most radiant of all the female fairies, her glorious hair floating lightly about her dress. She fingered a bunch of keys in her hand. May sensed deep wisdom within her.

"I think he should be given another chance," Saille loudly interrupted and Uilleand nodded vigorously, coiling her sinuous arms around her body. They continued on and on in this fashion and May had the sense of great time passing. Somehow these beings tampered with the natural laws. She inched closer towards Amaryllis and took his hand tenderly in hers. All sign of injury was gone from her scorched flesh and she knew that long weeks must have passed.

Saille had also administered a sleeping draught to her and the remaining slaves that had suffered at the hands of the knockermen, and soon she was taken into a soothing sleep, her mind wrapped in soft down that floated around her. Occasionally she woke to a restful doze and was always aware of the continuing argument over Amaryllis.

Gradually she learned, as she had always suspected, that he was not a wizard of Gorta but a creature from the Otherworld, the world that all must pass through after death in order to reach the bliss of Annwyn and join the one consciousness with the Great Mother before being reborn. It seemed that he was a soulless being, an immortal destined to live forever but he had transgressed and would die and become nothing if he did not find himself a soul.

Now she understood that indeed he had no designs on Necrönd. His need for a soul, that he might live and join the cycle of life, was paramount, obliterating all other desires.

"She does not love you. She loves another. You will not gain a soul until you have proved that a human loves you."

"But I love her," Amaryllis said humbly.

There was silence for a several long moments, the air stiff with tension.

Then Straif gave a snort of disbelief but Uilleand shook her head. "Oh no, Straif, he speaks truth."

"Still, it does not matter." Straif was unfazed. "He used the magic of his voice and transgressed the bargain. And if she had died, he would no doubt quickly go on to find another maiden to court; he had plenty enough in Rye Errish, in the Otherworld as these humans call our lands."

"No! I want no other!" he cried determinedly. "The moment she summoned me from Rye Errish with her miscast spell . . . The moment I set eyes on such innocent vulnerability and saw how she needed me, truly needed me . . . None of you can know what it is to be needed. She is helpless, utterly alone and abandoned and has taken on herself a mission far too bold and great for any human to bear alone. Yet she has done it with heart! And I would sing my song a thousand times again, however forbidden, to save her because her soul matters more than achieving mine. You see, I love her and I have discovered that that's what love means."

"Nevertheless, you have transgressed and we must send you back to Rye Errish where your body will wither and evaporate and you will become nothing but insentient dust shifting in the cosmos. You will simply cease to exist," Phagos pronounced solemnly.

"That is my fate and I would go gladly but give me time to see her through to the end of her trials. I cannot abandon her here to the knockermen. And if she survives them, she will be taken as a slave to the mines of Kalanazir. Life is harsh and vicious. I must stand with her. You must allow this. You cannot see her punished for my sins. For her sake, for what is right, I beg you, give me time to help her."

"His words are noble," Saille cried with tears streaking her smooth skin. "I say we grant him that wish."

Phagos studied the expressions on the rest of the twelve

fairylike beings and shook his head. "Saille, I believe you are outvoted. He must return to dust."

"No! Not yet." Amaryllis protested in desperation. "Do not do this to her. You must not do this. I must protect her."

May's heart went out to him. He begged only for her and the tears swelled in her eyes and she forced herself from her drug-induced sleep. Amaryllis stood before the High Circle at the far end of the cave. With steely deliberation, she swept towards him and slipped her hand into his and hung on tight. She would not forsake him. She could not reward his endeavours by spurning him. It lay in her hands to save his soul.

"Spar, forgive me," she murmured, tears of pity running down her cheeks. She dug her fingers into Amaryllis's hand and felt him squeeze back. "But I love him. You cannot take him from me," she begged. "You must not. Please, have mercy. Do not do this to him. Do not do this to me," she wept.

The Circle parted from its tight knot and Uilleand looked into her eyes. She felt an energy search out into her soul and remembered that Uilleand represented hidden secrets.

"But I do!" May found herself protesting. "I love him. I need him."

"Was it not the power of his song?"

"If anything that frightened me," May argued. "I thought he was trying to control me. No, I love him. I need him. He has protected me, been my champion despite my efforts to be rid of him. He has stood by me," she insisted and she knew in a way that her claims of love were true. Her heart had been broken. She was lonely, and no one had ever needed her before. Amaryllis was right. There was nothing in the world like being needed.

"We will give him time," Duir confirmed. "We need not yet make the decision."

There was a general nod amongst the others and May felt Amaryllis's hold tighten on hers as the air shimmered and the beings began to fade and shrink until they were no more than points of light.

She watched them fade while the still world around her began to stir. The slaves awoke, those still with eyes looking about them with bewildered fear, like young children waking with no notion of where they were. May paid them little heed. She was absorbed in Amaryllis's embrace. With his arms wrapped tight around her, he tenderly moved his lips towards hers, gently touching them. The kiss was neither demanding nor passionate but wholly giving. Her heart thrilled and her hands gripped him tightly.

Amaryllis eased back from her. "It will not take him long to find another soul receptive to his needs. We must move."

CHAPTER TWENTY-FIVE

Amaryllis's strong hand pulled May deeper into the caverns.

"But I cannot leave them," she objected.

He ignored her protests. "We have higher goals that must be achieved and have no choice. I've found the knockermen's route to the surface and showed it to the three slaves who could still see. It'll be up to them to get the rest to safety. You can't do everything, Merrymoon. If you try, you'll achieve nothing. We must get down into the bowels of the earth before the Dark Shadow finds another host."

May had no strength to argue. Amaryllis's tone was tender and caring and, when she stumbled, he finally swept her up off her feet and carried her before him like a bridegroom carrying his bride to a new life. She was too exhausted to protest.

It was eerily peaceful in the light of the green firebrand they had taken from the knockermen, the only sound the occasional crunch of bones beneath Amaryllis's feet and the stealthy padding of the knockermen behind. The fleshless, long-fingered creatures kept a wary distance from Amaryllis. Only one made an attack, leaping down from a stalagmite where it had been perched in frozen stillness, unseen until they were right beneath it.

Amaryllis was quick and sensed the knockerman long

before May was aware that anything was wrong. He caught it by the throat as it fell and crushed the life from it in his bare fist.

May gasped and clung tighter to him. She wondered how many times over the last month she had passed right by one of these slimy skeletal creatures without ever suspecting. There were plenty of slaves to fall by the wayside or to be caught in collapsed tunnels for these creatures to steal away and eat.

"We must go down below the levels of the knockermen, deeper into the earth. They will not go too deep because they will need to prey on surface creatures that venture unwittingly into their lairs. The deeper we go, the safer we shall be—"

"And then we can bury Necrönd," May finished for him.

She could see little beyond broken rocks, water-carved caverns and the weird crystalline shapes that had grown over thousands of years in the gloom. They squeezed between fissures or walked through huge underground caverns, the sound of dripping water ever present. The green smoky firebrand that they had drenched in the volatile liquid from the knockermen's fire smouldered darkly and gave off the barest light. At least May found the constant temperature pleasant as they ventured deeper and deeper into the earth.

Amaryllis halted. The fissure had closed tighter around them and, as they squeezed forward, they saw that it funnelled into no more than a hairline crack. May thought they must turn back to find another route to lead them down even deeper. Until they were at the deepest roots of Kalanazir, she would not be content. Amaryllis, however, seemed intent on going through the crack. He took a deep breath as if to sing but instead sighed and sought around for a suitable rock.

He chipped and hammered away while May, exhausted, fell asleep, too tired to even dream. When she awoke, Amaryllis was still chipping away, sweat glistening on his forehead and back. He turned and grinned at her but said nothing. May did not know what to say either and was glad of his silence. There was an uncertain tension between them, not the naturalness of lovers long together but the tension between friends when there was a tingling awareness of mutual attraction that could change everything. Before, she hadn't cared what Amaryllis thought of her but now she was embarrassed, fearing she might do or say something that would displease him.

While the desire to impress and please stole her tongue, she also sensed that Amaryllis was not himself either. At last, he had chipped out a hole big enough for them to squeeze through. They forced their way through only to find that after a very short distance along a broken fissure the ground stopped abruptly, dropping away into a chimneylike shaft in the rock. A stone dislodged beneath Amaryllis's feet and there was a long silence before they heard an echoing tinkle far below as it bounced against the sides of the shaft. Finally, after many seconds, there came a distinctive plop as it landed in water.

He turned and smiled at her. "It couldn't be more ideal. We'll climb down. Nothing has ever reached this far in centuries – if ever."

The air rising up the shaft was warm, the sultry atmosphere holding a scorched scent. May thought of the unlikely comparison to the smell of starch and sizzling hot irons. Her homely reminiscences fled as a jet of hissing steam spurted towards them.

"An abyss worm," Amaryllis muttered. "In all my thousands of years I have only ever seen one pass into the Otherworld. They are of the Great Mother, one of the creatures of the cycle but they are long-lived like the men of the rocks."

"I can't climb down there," May wailed in despair. "It's not that I'm afraid. I just don't think I can do it."

He smiled. "I wouldn't have expected you to," he said reassuringly and told her to cling to his back.

May was not particularly keen on that idea either but she obeyed and clung on fiercely, keeping her eyes tight shut. Caspar had often teased her at Torra Alta by walking along the battlements that topped the sheer wall and the precipitous cliffs, skipping along with nothing to his far side other than the horrifying drop.

With her arms wrapped around Amaryllis's neck, she listened to him grunt and fight for footholds. Every once in a while, a sudden lurch and a clatter of stones told her that the rocks had given way beneath his probing foot as he stretched down for the next toe-hold.

"Keep the light up, Merrymoon," he said with the barest hint of frustration.

She tightened her grip on the brand and prayed. Her breath was stifled by a pulse of scorched air driven up the shaft by a jet of water. The spray stopped only yards from their feet. Amaryllis pressed close against the rock as steam washed over their backs. Head tucked down, May was glad of her protective bearskin.

"But-but the abyss worm—" she stammered. The few pebbles Amaryllis dislodged now landed not too far below and her fear of the drop was replaced by her fear of the beast. "What if he takes Necrönd from us?"

"He will not," Amaryllis replied confidently. "We have delved so deep underground that here the earth itself warms the water that bubbles up from deep springs. The abyss worm's forefathers were trapped down here in the thermal spring at the beginning of time while the rest of the earthlings found their way to the top. They enjoyed the caressing warmth of the Great Mother and fed off minerals dissolved in the rocks. Such a simple beast has no need of the Egg. It would not survive anywhere but here and will have no desire to leave and therefore no need nor want nor gain from wielding the Egg. That and the boiling water make it our best guardian."

May was uncheered. She could see it; a vast, squirming beast shaped much like a slug, its head huge and eyeless, though its skin was transparent like an embryo. Its face was featureless except for a vast puckered mouth that squirted jets of sizzling water at them. A thick tail slapped the water. It plunged its head back into the pool, sucking in cavernous mouthfuls and producing swirling whirlpools on the surface. Then still half-submerged, it scooped up the rocks that Amaryllis had dislodged. From within its maw came an extraordinary grinding noise as they were pulverised within its a gullet and May wondered that it wasn't like a bird. The poulterer at the castle had told her once that hens must have grit in their meal because they didn't have teeth and the grit would work like millstones in their gullet to grind the food. She thought that this abyss worm could grind human bones to dust without the least trouble.

Holding out the green torch that sputtered in the steamy atmosphere, she could see that the shaft dropped straight into the simmering water. On the far side of the pool, a platform of rock shelved beneath the surface. There was nowhere else for them to go but it was as much help to them as if it had been on the other side of the world. The heat from the boiling pool brought a steady stream of sweat to her flushed face. She could see no way of crossing.

"Even if we are not sucked in alive and ground to

pieces by the abyss worm, we'll by boiled alive in the water." She tried to speak calmly but couldn't stop the quiver in her voice.

"I know. I have thought of that," Amaryllis replied without the least hint of trepidation.

"You have? But how can we possibly cross?"

He avoided answering her directly. "It strikes me as the perfect place for our purposes. Very few could ever find their way down here, fewer still could climb down this shaft, but there are none that could cross the boiling waters, home to the abyss worms, and reach the ledge. Think how far below the surface we are. The mines are deep yet we have travelled deeper still. As we saw, Kalanazir will soon be mined out. Then all will retreat from these mountains and there will be no lonelier place on earth."

"That still does not help us cross," May retorted a little stiffly. She was angry. Amaryllis was right. It was the most perfect resting place on earth for the Egg and yet for all that there was still no way to get across.

Amaryllis laughed. "You can't think I would let you down, Merrymoon, when you are so precious to me. I would not have brought you this far only to fail you. Trust me. My voice will—"

"No, Amaryllis! They said that you would be destroyed if you used the magic in your voice."

"They cannot – not if you . . ." His voice trailed away.

"But Amaryllis—"

"If you are true to me, they will take away only my life. No matter what they think or feel in judgement they can do nothing if you . . . If you . . . Love is above the law. You will give me a part of your own soul if you love me, do you understand? And you must prove your love by bearing my child."

"Child!" May repeated somewhat taken aback. She had been quite prepared to give him every ounce of loving sympathy but . . . To bear his child! She flushed red, her thoughts consumed with images of Caspar.

"Merrymoon, do you love me?" he asked in a voice so soft it was almost lost in the hissing steam. "Do you love me enough to bear my child?"

"I–I—" she hesitated. Her thoughts were scrambled by a jet of steam scorching her back. She squealed with the pain and Amaryllis swung her round onto a ledge out of harm's way where she clung on tightly, pressing herself forward onto the rock, her breathing rapid.

A deep and trembling note swelled out as if from his entire body. It rose and fell in both rejoicing and sorrowful tones, the sound so deeply lovely it reminded May of sparkling waterfalls dropping from the heights of the Yellow Mountains and rainbows in the summer rain. But most of all it reminded her of the first snowdrops peeking out of the crisp forest bed in mid-winter, promising that spring would come again. It was a song of promise, of love and wonderful things to come, a song rejoicing in life.

It was almost as if the very rocks sighed with pleasure at the sound and for a moment, she felt that the entire universe pivoted around Amaryllis in all his magnificent glory.

The gargantuan worm rose out of the water and May recoiled at the sight. Through its translucent skin, she could see the dark pits of its seven stomachs, churning and grinding. Glistening, fleshy horns on its head like those of a snail waved towards them, swaying to the rhythm of Amaryllis's song. Slowly the great beast rolled over and lay flat in the water, its tail swishing to and fro. Still in full voice, Amaryllis climbed down lower and put his foot on the beast. The abyss worm remained submissively passive beneath him, merely rising and shifting in the water to accommodate his weight.

Taking May's hand, he pulled her towards him and, though she didn't trust the beast not to roll over and drag her under the boiling water, she shakily surrendered to Amaryllis's coaxing tug and fell into his arms. Unbidden, the abyss worm slowly swam across the bubbling pool and rested its nose on the slab of sloping rock at the far side. May wiped the sweat from her brow.

Incredibly, someone was waiting for them. At once she recognized the dark cloak and the spike-laden staff of Straif, the being of the High Circle.

"Talorcan," he greeted him coldly. "You have disobeyed."

Amaryllis shrugged. "Do you think I care for your rules?"

"Nevertheless, the rules will be applied. Death will seek you out and, with it, eternal annihilation." A smirk soured Straif's face. "For once this will please me as much as Phagos. He has been most displeased at the way you have twisted the law."

May blinked. Duir was standing at Straif's shoulder, playing a glistening pipe. Then in a flash of light, they were gone, leaving behind only the echo of the pipe's haunting notes.

Amaryllis sighed and shrugged.

"But what will happen to you?!" May exclaimed, clasping her hands together to prevent them trembling.

"I will die," he said easily. "Like everyone else you have ever known, somewhere in my future lies death. It is not so terrible once you get used to the idea. It is there for everyone, is it not? And you do not fear it."

May shook her head. "No, of course not. The Mother is there to receive me and I will return again to walk this earth. No, I am not afraid of death, only afraid of losing the love and companionship of those closest to me. I am afraid only of loneliness."

"And I too," Amaryllis continued. "I was afraid of the loneliness of oblivion but not now, not anymore." He pulled her gently towards him as if to kiss her but she resisted and pushed him away.

A flicker of fear darkened his eyes.

"But, no, I can't," she murmured, tears welling up into her eyes. She was confused. She did love him in a way. She needed him; she was grateful to him; she respected him. But still . . . She paused for a moment and he turned away from her, busying his hands with simple tasks, trying to make May comfortable by laying out her bearskin to sit on. The torch still gave out a soft glow and the warmth from the springs was balmy. May sat on the spread bearskin and placed her hand on the casket.

"It's just," May continued uncertainly, "I came here for the love of another, to protect his soul and . . ."

She opened the casket and together they made a crisp nest for Necrönd out of the shrivelled leafy herbs that May had bought in Castaguard. Placed with the scorch mark downmost to conceal it, the ancient artefact looked quite innocent as if some rare bird had simply flown down here and laid it. Like the petrified egg of a gerfalcon or an eagle, she thought. No one would think it was anything else. The First Druid had been wise to make it as it was. When she had first seen it, she had been almost disappointed, expecting it to be red or gold with silver runes on its surface, or perhaps even made of sunburst rubies; but it was really no more than a blue and white marbled egg.

They both stood and looked down on Necrönd.

May sighed; the burden of Necrönd was lifted from her. "But I can never go back to him. If I did, one day, somehow, I might let slip the whereabouts of the Egg and he would not be able to resist coming for it."

Suddenly she knew what she must do. Throughout her journey she had wavered in her resolve and yearned to turn back to Caspar but she was now fully determined; she must turn her back forever on him. She stared long and hard at Amaryllis, and she no longer saw his handsome face and strong, lithe body, but only the love and caring in his eyes that shone strangely in the green light. The logic of the situation was plain; if she belonged to another, she could never go back to Spar. If she gave herself to Amaryllis, she would save Spar forever from the treacheries of Necrönd.

A soft smile gladdened her worried face. "Sing to me," she whispered. "But not with the power of a verderer's song but in your own voice – from your heart." She searched his eyes, revelling in his embrace, and succumbed to his tender kisses. She was still disconcerted by his eyes that seemed only to reflect her own. She paused for a moment and laughed a little nervously. "Tell me one thing first. The rubies, how did you know where they were?"

He laughed also. "I am of the Sun, an immortal being of the Sun and I sense His presence everywhere. When the rubies were formed, they trapped sunlight in their heart. That is what gives them their brilliance but it is also their warmth that I sense. But hush now; we will have much time for talk later," he said and sealed her mouth with his.

Later they lay close, his body melded with hers. Melting in his tenderness, she looked deep into his eyes, in search of the man within. As she looked, the vibrant yellow of his eyes dimmed to a natural hazel to match her own and she knew she looked in at his soul.

CHAPTER TWENTY-SIX

Caspar spread his cloak over the thick dust of the couch and lowered Ursula gently down.

Panting heavily, Reyna was stooped over a table, dust rising from her breath. "Just see to the girl," she snapped irritably at Elergian who was fussing over her. "I just need space to catch my breath."

Ursula's eyes swirled. Moaning softly, she clutched grimly at Caspar's hand, curling her legs up against some deep pain within.

"The toad juice is rotting her insides," the mage explained heavily. He lifted Ursula's head and dribbled a run of silver trinoxia into the corner of her mouth before gently easing her down. "There, brave child, you'll feel better after the three sleeps." He glanced at Caspar. "See if you can find any fresh water," he instructed before easing off the remains of Ursula's tattered clothes to examine the tears and grazes in her skin.

The youth winced. Her young body, so firm and strong yet feminine in all its curves, was horribly abused, not an inch unmarked. He swallowed at the sight. She must have seen what had happened to the wolfman and wondered when she would be strong enough to answer questions.

He pulled his eyes away and stared up at the domed ceiling to draw strength. Through a curtain of dusty webs, he peered at a pattern of stars painted on the arch of a midnight-black ceiling. Water, he reminded himself and looked around him at the hall. Much like Morrigwen's chambers, every shelf and mantle were covered with a clutter of bones, knives and chalices. The fireplace was stuffed with a thatch of twigs where generations of jackdaw nests had fallen down the chimney. Over the door, a vast curved tusk, grooved with a spiralling pattern, hung precariously, its bracket all but rusted through. The walls were lined with shelves containing vessels, vials and jars all thick with dust, and only the potions of the most vivid colour shone through the murk.

Leaving footprints in the settled dust on the floor, Caspar worked his way to the back of the domed chamber where doors led off into connecting rooms. He examined several of the dark and dusty chambers, each filled with storage barrels, pots and vials, until he came to one with a low round wall set in its centre.

Peering over the edge, he was met with his own reflection that rippled as he breathed on it. The water lay only a foot below the well mouth and looked black in the dim light but gave off no foul smell. He dipped a finger in and tentatively tasted it. The water was sweet. A pitcher lay discarded on the floor and he grabbed it only to find the wood crumbled in his hand. Remembering that one of the other rooms had many metal pitchers, some plated in gold and others that must once have been silver but were now black with tarnish, he hurried back to it. After several frustrating minutes, he found a suitable vessel that wasn't perforated and filled it from the well.

Elergian took the vessel without thanks and, mixing in a generous trickle of trinoxia, bathed Ursula's wounds. Realizing that his assistance was no longer needed, Caspar hurried to tend his horse and squirted a mouthful of the mercurial liquid under Firecracker's tongue. The stallion sucked at his tongue, snorted and rolled his eye at the unaccustomed flavour.

Reyna gave Caspar another vial of trinoxia. "I've never given any to a horse before but I think you'd better give him an extra dose. Too little and he won't pull through, too much at once and he'll burn up with excess energy. Get it right and he'll be the fittest horse in the Caballan."

Caspar smiled weakly and vigorously set to work washing and scrubbing the horse's coat to rid him of the blotches of dye. When all the scouring and washing was over, they sat back exhausted. Ursula had fallen into a still deep sleep and Firecracker was flat on his side, breathing calmly. It was hours before either stirred. Firecracker woke first, rose shakily to his feet, and for several minutes drank from a bucket that Elergian had found before slumping back down again. Ursula took longer to wake. After she too had slaked her raging thirst, Caspar seized his opportunity to ask after the wolfman.

Ursula looked at him blurrily. "I don't know. After the toads he gave Mamluc some potion as an antidote; just brewed it up out of the grasses. He gave none to me or the horse. Then he said he must leave us and hurry on ahead. It didn't make sense. He simply went berserk and ran off." Her eyes swam and she frowned in sleepy bewilderment. She closed her eyes again and, on the very brink of sleep, muttered, "Where's the dog? You haven't lost the dog? He was my friend." It was all she said before the second deep sleep overtook her.

Caspar wasn't too worried about Trog; the dog knew how to look after himself; but what of the wolf? She was his responsibility. Morrigwen had been adamant that he must look after her. And what of the wolfman and

Necrönd? Still Fern had insisted that he had smelt him in Castaguard. He fell asleep worrying.

"Where exactly are we?" Caspar asked late the next morning. Urged by Reyna, they had all partaken of the trinoxia and slept a long and invigorating sleep. Caspar felt as though he must be more than two inches taller though, when he measured himself against his bow, he was disappointed.

"Why do you want to be taller?" Perren scoffed. "It won't make you a bigger man inside." He was returning from the spring at the back of the domed chamber and was licking his fingers sensuously. Caspar guessed he had spent a long night feeling for the stories carried in the water.

"If the tales have been faithfully handed down, we are beneath the palace of Castaguard," Reyna answered Caspar's question. "It's now occupied by the descendants of the thieves who stole the crown. I believe it's used as a summer palace by Dagonet's family." She spat the king's name with contempt.

Ursula was sitting up, watching Caspar's every move. He felt intensely uncomfortable under her scrutiny but politely inquired how she felt.

She smiled back. "Quite extraordinarily well. Strong enough to go after Mamluc to get my revenge!" She laughed at the idea.

"Good," Caspar replied with feeling. "Then, I must leave at once and go after the wolfman. Fern, we must go and pick up the trail you scented as we entered the city."

Perren shook his head. "You must remember your friends first. I was wrong all those weeks ago when I tried to stop you endangering yourself in a futile attempt to rescue Ursula. You proved me wrong, for here she is. You yourself have taught me that you must never forsake your friends."

Caspar frowned at him. "My friends? Are you not all safe here—"

"I have heard more stories of heroic deeds than you could ever dream of, a number larger than your small brain can contemplate, and nowhere in any of them does a man succeed in achieving heroic deeds if he forsakes his friends."

"I don't seek to be a hero, only to find Necrönd."

"You will not find it without your friends. The Mother has picked them for you and you must trust in her judgement," Perren lectured. "You must find the wolfling and the dog. Don't you care for them?"

"They'll be all right, they're probably hiding out in the foothills, having a high old time hunting together. But Necrönd—"

"Those who would forsake their friends would forsake the world," Perren scolded him. "You must find the wolfling. She is crying for you."

"Crying for me?" Caspar queried, fingering the carved rune on the piece of bone that Morrigwen had given him; the rune of the wolf. He was suddenly fearful for her.

"She is upstream of the well and she howls for you. Calls you at her time of need."

Caspar nodded, grabbed his bow and made for the door, closely followed by the stonewight and Fern.

Ursula yelped in alarm. "Master, do not leave without me! Please, no. It is death to a slave to lose her master," she cried, her words halting Caspar before he had reached the end of the hall.

"You shall be free, my girl," Reyna assured her, waving Caspar on. "See how the trinoxia has washed away the black cross from your arm." She frowned quizzically. "Though I do not understand how those other emblems remain." She stroked the intricate pattern of coloured tattoos higher on Ursula's bare upper arm. "You must have been born with them," she joked.

"I shall never be free; I have no home, no country to call my own," Ursula said sadly. "I am a prisoner of anonymity. I am no one and yet . . ."

"And yet in your heart you know you are more," Caspar said gently, returning to her side and taking her hand in his. "But you must remain here. Your heart is strong but your body is still too weak."

She clutched his hand. "You will come back for me? Promise you will."

"Of course. You must look after Lana and my horse in my absence."

She smiled warmly at his trust. He held her stare for a long moment then turned to leave. Fern and Perren were waiting for him by the entrance.

Reyna ran after him and pressed a small vial into his hand. "This is the last of the trinoxia. Use it well. And save the wolf; only with the love of the wolf in our hearts will we break the curse over me."

Caspar nodded.

Elergian tugged at Caspar's arm. "You mustn't go back via the canals. There'll be engineers and soldiers all round them, looking for the cause of the flood."

Reyna agreed but argued hotly with Elergian about which secret passages through the palace would serve Caspar best.

"I could take you through the back chambers," Perren offered.

"But it's a dead end," Caspar and Elergian insisted in unison.

Perren shrugged his square shoulders. "Such great sorcerers should know that not all that seems rock is rock." He strode away and Caspar followed dubiously, only to scurry back and hastily retrieve one of the torches that Reyna had made from the fallen jackdaw nests that littered the huge hearth. With Fern at his heels, he trotted after Perren.

When they reached the wellroom, Perren, as usual, dipped his hand into the water and pensively chewed at his fingers before leading on to the last room. It was a small chamber formed from what appeared to be a natural fault in the structure of the rock. No other door led out from it.

Caspar took a deep breath, about to point this out, but was stopped by Fern muttering something about Perren's unbalanced mind. "You're not telling me the wolf has gone this way." He then stabbed a coarse-nailed finger at Caspar. "Why do you listen to a talking rock when you've never listened to me?"

"Hmm, indeed." Perren fetched inside his pocket for a piece of root and wafted it in front of Fern's nose. The little woodwose pursed his lips and then snatched the root from him, stuffed it in his mouth and chewed so rapidly that it made Caspar's jaw ache. The woodwose begrudgingly grunted his thanks and then pointedly butted his head against the rock.

"Giving me root doesn't stop that being rock." Rubbing his head, he kicked against the solid stone with his foot.

Caspar thrust the torch closer. It certainly looked like rock.

Perren gave a rumbling laugh. "It might just take me a little while." He rubbed his hands together and began to sing in a language that Caspar had only heard before in the stonewights' cavern. It was not beautiful but rather disturbing and made him want to wriggle. After several minutes of this grumbling aria, Perren's tone changed dramatically. Both Fern and Caspar clasped their hands to their heads at the jarring sound until he stopped.

Fern snorted disparagingly.

The stonewight glowered at him furiously then turned back to the rock. "Wake up!" he shouted angrily. "Wake up and get out of my way." He kicked the rock hard and Caspar thought he would wince but instead it was the rock that seemed to buckle and groan. It then sighed like an old man turning over in his sleep before settling back down again. Perren kicked again, harder this time. "Let me through," he demanded petulantly.

Caspar stumbled back. The stone was squirming before his eyes and a shape was forming; a huge stonewight, bewhiskered with lichen and ferns.

"I was deeply asleep, young fellow," the stonewight objected. "Asleep five thousand years and you come along belligerently demanding for me to make way. No manners at all. Youngsters! And what are you doing out and about? You are far too young. Your fathers should be ashamed, letting out a young pebble like yourself."

"Pebble!" Perren was outraged and kicked again at the rock. "Now just let me by."

"I'll never get back to sleep now," the great stonewight grumbled. "It's always the same. Youngsters have no thought for others . . . And what is that nasty little light doing down here, a snatch of the sun in my bedchamber? This is rudeness indeed. I never move aside for surface creatures. Never. And when I say never, I should point out that I remember when the world was fiery and the rocks still warm."

"I'm sure you do, wise one of the earth. Please accept our apologies for waking you," Caspar said humbly. "But we beg of you to move even if it is but a fraction. We really do need to get by and would never have disturbed you if it were not important."

Perren nodded his agreement and uttered a few grumbling words in the stonewights' peculiar tongue. The old stonewight stiffened, nearly crushing Caspar against the far rock wall.

"The Druid's Egg! Necrönd itself! We always thought the Druid foolish. Very foolish! All their eggs in one basket; is that not one of your sayings?" He peered at Caspar and Fern. "Isn't that what you fellows say?"

Fern shook his head. "No, we deer say nothing like that. Sometimes we say the stag is bigger than the hind. And the wind is in the east and the wolves in the west, may our legs have strength. And sometimes we say the spring comes and with it the shoots, but that is all."

"This fellow thinks he's a deer!" the huge stonewight laughed, his grey belly vibrating and dislodging tiny rocks from the stone around him. "Well, this was worth waking up for!" With a resounding crack, he broke free from the surrounding rock and in one smooth movement scooped up Caspar and Fern in his huge rough hands and, puckering his lips, blew out the firebrand, plunging them into darkness. "Come, youngsters, by rift and stone-fall, I shall see you through my home to the surface."

"I don't need help," Perren protested though compliantly followed, mumbling about how all fathers are the same and too eager to interfere. Caspar grinned. Once in the company of the adult stonewight, Perren behaved like an angry youth. Caspar liked him better like that; he was more human and his grumblings made a change from his stories that had no beginnings or no ends.

Caspar did not know how far they had travelled when they reached a cavern, which was lit by a thin beam of daylight falling down from above. Wind whistled and howled eerily as it skimmed over the mouth of the shaft. The air smelt fresh.

The stonewight climbed the shaft to the surface and eased them up through a thatch of birch. "My side entrance," he explained.

It was cold and bright. Caspar blinked at the daylight and hurriedly pulled his bearskin up around his neck and mouth. A stiff breeze bore flecks of snow that stung against his cheeks.

The old stonewight inspected his overgrown entrance and tutted. "I haven't been this way for years; been asleep, you know. I wouldn't have let it grow over so otherwise. The Ondines won't be impressed at all. Ondines," he sighed to himself and began pulling at the branches and grass, whistling away to himself as if Caspar and the others simply had ceased to exist.

Perren marched off without a word of thanks and only after several paces turned back to grumble at the others to follow.

Caspar ignored him and tried to take in his cold surroundings. Stark black peaks sharpened by icy winds rose all around. They must have travelled miles into the Kalanazir Mountains. He could just see the walled and moated city through a bank of low-lying cloud, the concentric circles of Castaguard's curtain walls distinctive in the landscape. He turned back to the stonewight and politely gave his thanks though the huge grey being didn't seem to hear. Apparently, he was too busy trimming back the bushes.

"Oh, yes, my pleasure," he grumbled in the old tongue of the Caballan just as Caspar was walking away, "And, by the way, young fellow," he called after Perren, "if you want to wake an old fellow like me, it's best to shout Earthquake! One moves more quickly then."

Perren scowled. "I knew that. Did you think I didn't know that?" He marched off indignantly. "And to think, in a million years I will be like him. What a terrible thought!"

"He was very pleasant. You should respect your elders," Fern scolded, keeping his chin tucked down against the wind. "So long as they have big sharp antlers, that is."

"Hush!" Caspar demanded. From somewhere in the folds of the mountains, he heard a bark that turned into a wailing howl of a dog, unmistakably Trog's cry. Following the direction of the cry, he hurried up the valley side where birch and rowan grew in profusion.

At least it was warmer in the shelter of the woods. Accustomed as he was by his home mountains, he found the climb easy on his muscles. Exposed tree roots formed natural steps in the valley sides, facilitating their climb and, even better, the leafy branches sheltered them from the sleety drizzle. Trog's howl had stopped but Caspar knew which direction to take. Fern's neck was upstretched and he had that look of distaste about his mouth. He was pointing to a spot not far ahead where a fall of white water splashed down from the head of a series of exposed rocks.

Caspar squinted. Trog, half-camouflaged in the white spray, was on his feet, his neck stretched forward in greeting. Something lay at his feet. Caspar hurried forward but stopped when Fern leapt into the air as if he had stepped on a hot poker.

"The trail!" he exclaimed. "The wolfman's trail. They found it."

Caspar began to run. As he drew close, he saw that Trog stood over the wolfling. A large blotch of red streaked her ribcage where the broken shaft of an arrow jutted from her matted fur. Runa was wet, the tips of her damp and bedraggled fur frozen into spiky fronds by the chill wind. Caspar thought it was as if she had known that Perren would hear her if she were immersed in the pool. She managed to raise a paw in greeting and Trog bounced up to give Caspar a quick lick across his face.

Runa, tried to raise her head but then slumped back in exhaustion, eyes closed. They flickered open again when he tried to dribble some precious drops of trinoxia between her lips. He cursed their extravagant use of the potion earlier. He needed it far more now. Runa's teeth were still knitted tightly together though, once she had a taste of the liquid, she lapped it up enthusiastically. It was a good sign but something had to be done about the arrow. He gritted his teeth, knowing that it must be removed though it was wedged between two lower ribs and he wasn't sure how.

"The trinoxia," Fern suggested.

Caspar agreed and poured more of the precious drops directly into the wound. Cradling Runa in his lap to keep her warm, he waited until she fell into the drug-induced sleep, her breathing slowing to a steady, quiet rhythm. Trog nuzzled her anxiously.

Wishing that Brid were there, or even May who had become quite skilful at the art of healing, Caspar steeled his nerve and yanked. A spurt of blood followed the barb as it snagged through the muscle, bringing with it slivers of flesh. It was bad but not so bad as he had feared. He packed the wound tightly with mud from the stream and bound it as he had seen Brid do, hoping that the trinoxia would do the rest.

Fern collected wood though would not come near the fire once it was lit, preferring to sit in the cold, complaining about man's thin hide and lack of fur.

"The fire won't leap up and bite you," Caspar insisted,

dragging a log to the edge of the fire so that he could avoid sitting on the frozen ground.

"You don't know that. Until yesterday I would never have believed that rocks could get up and walk, but they do, and it shakes one's faith in nature. I don't trust the water nor the air that I breathe now."

Caspar shrugged and left it at that, and before long was settling down to sleep, vowing to get a good night's rest before recommencing the search for the wolfman in the morning.

He was woken by the sound of trudging feet. Rubbing his eyes, he tried to focus. The thin grey light that precedes dawn was feeling its way through pink clouds but it was still dark below him in the valley. The creek of leather and the constant beat of feet were still audible; he hadn't been dreaming. He stiffly rose and, in the growing light, at last made out the black figures of a column of men flanked by riders on great horses making steady progress up the valley.

"Slaves on their way to the sunburst ruby mines," Perren rumbled, protectively scooping up Runa who was still sleeping peacefully.

Caspar nudged Fern awake and quickly explained what was happening. "We've got to examine the wolfman's tracks immediately." The ground was set hard but he couldn't take any risks. They couldn't afford to lose his tracks amongst those of the column.

Fern was soon on the trail, quickly singling out a particular print amongst the thousands trudging into the mountains. "It's him," the woodwose declared with certainty, rising from all fours, his nose dotted with small clods of earth.

"But it's a much shorter, wider boot," Caspar objected. "You must be wrong."

His mind churned, grappling with the unreality of the situation. Somehow the wolf's spirit must have entered the bird that the hermit had spoken of and later transferred to another man. He found the idea so incredible that he preferred not to voice the theory out loud.

Fern sucked in a deep breath of frustration. "Why do you ask me to find him, if you don't believe me when I do? Have I been wrong yet? Smell it for yourself. It reeks of wolf – reeks, I say." His words came out in a steamy haze into the cold air.

"But it's not the same tracks as the wolfling was following," Perren objected, pointing to Runa's prints that overlaid a small boot, more the size of a child's. The print was all but gone, worn away by the wind, and was only visible since the muddied ground had since been frozen by the biting wind. He guessed it was not that recent. Frozen tracks might remain a long time.

Fern barely sniffed at the smaller track. "Well, that certainly doesn't carry the scent of the wolfman!" He snorted as if Caspar's notion were quite ridiculous.

"Why was Runa following it, then?" the youth asked, clapping his hands together to get some feeling back into them.

"Do you truly understand nothing?" Fern lowered his nose to the ground and snuffled. "It is May's scent of course."

"May's!" Caspar was astounded, his brain struggling to make sense of it all. Was that why Runa ran off? Had she picked up May's scent in Castaguard? If she had, of course she would follow. And Trog too. Quite extraordinary! But May! She was headed for the slave mines, clearly as part of a column.

Suddenly he remembered the rune he had cast by Morrigwen's dead body: the triple rune of Nuin, Duir and

Huathe. He saw it now. Morrigwen wasn't trying to tell him to go to Fey Grove where the three trees grew intertwined nor look for the new Maiden; how could he have been so stupid? No, she was trying to warn him about May, whom the old woman had loved so much. Huathe was the name for the hawthorn, the may tree, and she had used the rune to represent May. He understood now. The rune, Nuin, warned of how May was linked into the grander scale of events and Duir was to tell him that she needed protection. He had been blind.

"We must move on immediately!" Caspar ordered, all thought of Necrönd pushed from his mind. The wolfman was after May. And May must already be in trouble; she had been heading for the slave mines of Kalanazir. What she was doing there he didn't care; all that mattered was that she was in need of him.

Trog was some way ahead, looking back anxiously and urging with little yips for them to follow. Perren, with Runa draped over his shoulders, was already striding after the dog and Caspar found with indignation that again he was the slowest of them all. He ran then trotted and was soon gasping for breath and finally was forced to call them to a halt so that he could recover. The freezing air stung his lungs. He rubbed at his crooked nose, hoping to get back some feeling.

Perren looked at him. "You won't slow me if you ride on my shoulders."

Caspar could not argue and clambered up the stonewight's back. It was soon after that he first looked onto the black pit of the mine's mouth.

"Perren! Quick! Get over there!" he urged Perren towards a scatter of boulders behind which they could hide.

At a rough estimate there were nearly sixty guards around the jagged teeth of stone set in a huge stone head whose gaping mouth formed the entrance to the mine. Some stood alert, scanning the incoming slaves, others checked out-going cargo, while the rest used long stock whips liberally applied to the backs of slaves to keep them in line. The procession crawled along the road, creeping over the vast split tongue of stone that lolled out from the cavernous arch of the statue's mouth, swallowing them into the mine's throat.

Disturbed by the cries for pity and moans of pain, the wolfling on Perren's shoulders trembled.

"She's in there!" the youth exclaimed. "Perren, what do I do?"

The stonewight shrugged. "Get her out of course."

"But it's a mine. Where is she, Perren? Find her for me." Caspar was clawing at Perren's thick hand and shaking it vigorously.

"Only the water will tell me." The stonewight rumbled in his throat and looked around at the hills. "I won't be able to tell from here. The water that trickles through the mine is flowing downwards, naturally, and will not be on the surface here but will emerge lower down, perhaps not before Castaguard even. If you'd asked me then—"

"Well, I didn't ask then, did I?" Caspar complained. "I'm asking now. Find her!"

"Hush!" Fern put a hand on his shoulder.

He shook him off. He had no time for comfort. Only one thing could comfort him. He paced up and down with anxiety, oblivious to the cold. "There's nothing for it but to follow her through the mine mouth. I shall go alone. I'll be less conspicuous and I cannot ask any of you to risk your lives for just one girl even if—"

Shaking his head, Fern interrupted, "Normally I would agree – wholeheartedly – but it isn't just any one girl, is it? No, this is your girl and Brid spoke highly of her. Moreover, you say she was from the Boarchase, from my own woods. You need me to help find her. I can follow her track."

Perren pulled him back. "Of course, we'll find May but not if we get ourselves caught by those guards. No, we will find another way down until I get to water that bears news of her."

Perren searched throughout the remainder of the day, having left the others to rest in the lee of a mossy boulder. Caspar spent the time shivering and picking at the hard ground in frustration.

When Perren at last returned it was nearly dark. "I've found a gorge and a spring. The rocks around have collapsed but I've moved a few and found a route down into the earth – a way in."

They slipped into the crack of rock above the spring, Perren leading, Trog and Runa snuffling along at the rear, Caspar bearing a heavy torch. The wolfling had passed through her third sleep and appeared as vigorous as ever. Caspar was immediately relieved to be out of the freezing wind. They wriggled and worked their way through narrow fissures, constantly halting while Perren, who had cast off his bandages and cloak, hammered away at any sections too narrow for them.

After some while, Caspar halted nervously when Perren broke into the old tongue of the Caballan, his rumbling voice calling out a greeting into the dimness. The rocks ahead appeared to stir and then Caspar made out the shape of an adult stonewight before them, though this one was smaller than the one they had met before but still large enough to make him feel uncomfortable. The huge being was rubbing his eyes.

"Don't apologize; I was already awake, disturbed by the terrible hammering and horrible cheeping of knockermen," the stonewight complained.

"Knockermen!" Perren exclaimed. "Ugh, how vile. Carriers of disease and evil gases."

The stonewight nodded. "I'm old, you know," he told them amiably. "Very old and riddled with faults and now I find my nest infested with knockermen. I do not want to lay me down to sleep and let my poor crumbling body take on the final rest if I am to be poked and sifted by man and desecrated by knockermen. I have no more strength to chase them out. My brothers are already at rest down there and these vile creatures sit on them. What am I to do?"

Caspar had no idea. All he could think about was May. "Please, take me down into the mines."

The old stonewight looked at him. "Haven't you forgotten something important? It's strange; I see things now that were veiled before; it is all a sign that my time approaches. You should have in your hand an object of great power; you seem to have mislaid it."

Caspar looked down at his feet, thinking that he must be treading in water for the stonewight to read him so well.

The vast rocklike being laughed, flakes of grey slate cracking away from his belly and falling about the passage. "I am so old now that I do not need the medium of water anymore. The Great Mother speaks to me straight through her bones and at last, after all these aeons, I hear and understand Her voice." He bent forward over Caspar. "You have forgotten your responsibilities because you have lost your lass and you need her. She's down here beneath my feet. I ought to go that way myself to see to the knockermen." He yawned and mumbled for a while. "But you know, I'm just too tired."

He lay down again, leaving just enough gap for them to crawl past. Perren grumbled his annoyance and, when

Caspar looked back, the ogre had turned himself back to stone.

"These are old mountains," Perren said by way of explanation.

The rock ways had smooth floors and walls and Caspar thought that they must have been formed by dragons. Perren scoffed at that the idea. "Dragons are lazy creatures; they would never delve so deep. Moreover, that old stonewight would never have let them into his lair. They steal the sapphires and rubies, you know. Quite as bad as man, they are. No, these chambers were forced open by rising gases."

After hours of trudging down deeper into the roots of the Kalanazir Mountains, the rocks underfoot grew warm and, in places, the small fissures hissed and sizzled with evaporating water. A sense of dread and weightiness dragged at Caspar's heart; Necrönd was near. Once or twice Caspar heard the pitter-patter of unshod feet but saw nothing. Each time Perren grumbled in disgust, "Foul beings."

They passed several pools of water where Perren stooped to dip his hand in but always shook his head. "Nothing but suffering, men dying of exhaustion and the foul urine of knockermen everywhere." His face wrinkled in disgust. "Man riddles the mountains with shafts and tunnels and then lets these pests run amuck. She is still below us."

When at last they delved down to one more pool that Perren probed, Caspar knew he had found her. The stonewight nodded. "Yes, she's here but I can also feel Necrönd. Its throbbing presence draws evil to her."

"The wolfman has got to her already!" Caspar despaired.

"Perhaps, perhaps not. She is close. Not far beyond my fellow stonewight here." He nodded at what looked like solid rock.

"Well, wake him up," Caspar demanded in exasperation, his voice rising to a vexed squeak of excitement. He couldn't believe that their path was blocked yet again.

The young stonewight grunted in annoyance then began to sing his deep disturbing song. The rocks shuddered. When nothing more happened, he looked irritated and frustrated then grinned and shouted, "Earthquake!"

Still the rock remained unmoved. Perren looked perplexed and sat down and groaned. "Perhaps he's been asleep too long. Perhaps his heart has finally hardened to rock." He went up to the flat wall of rock and prodded it. "Wake up!" he demanded angrily. "This is important and bedsides this is not a safe place to sleep. There are knockermen everywhere and men not too far away and they might start chiselling tunnels through you."

The wall showed no sign of moving and Caspar wondered if Perren weren't really talking to plain rock.

Perren kicked at the wall in front of him. "Get out of my way, you stubborn, obstinate fellow. I know you can hear me." He paused for a second and turned back to Caspar. "Perhaps he is dead. Perhaps he has turned to rock." Rasping his fingers over his chin thoughtfully, he returned to the pool and dipped his hand into the water, stirring it for a moment. He stiffened up with sudden resolve. "You're alive and you're just too stubborn to listen to me."

He kicked the wall and then pummelled it with his fists until, to Caspar's surprise, runnels of blood ran from his palms and spiralled around his thick forearms. The dog and the wolfling looked on in bewilderment. Soon Trog was yelping, leaping and spinning around and gnashing at the air, mad with the excitement of battle. Whimpering, Runa dropped her head, backed against the far wall and howled.

The howl sent a quiver through Caspar, who followed her staring eyes to where the light of the firebrands petered out near the tunnel roof that narrowed into a fissure. Red eyes stared down at them from the crack.

"Perren!" Caspar cried urgently.

The stonewight broke off from his hammering and in the comparative silence they heard deep grumbling clicks and knocks shuddering through the rock. The young stonewight stiffened. "Knockermen! Yuck!" He picked up a loose stone. Trog's back bristled, excited by the stonewight's belligerent behaviour and barked enthusiastically when the young stonewight hurled the rock up into the fissure.

A hail of stones came pelting back at him. Trog dodged the attack and, with relish, began leaping back and forth and spinning around in his characteristic war dance. Caspar pressed himself against the side of the passage and, shielding his face, looked up. Arms and legs were slithering down towards him, long fingers, greenish in colour, creeping into the flickering light of the firebrand. Trog finally took refuge between Caspar's legs though he still yelped with excitement.

The knockermen were dislodging great boulders and, though Perren shouldered off the blows with relative ease, Caspar noted an uncharacteristic wariness in the stonewight's bearing as even he started to retreat, though the blows from the rocks appeared to have little effect on him.

Slithering like lizards, the knockermen crawled down the tunnel sides until they touched the rock that Perren had been trying to stir. It quivered as if a distant earthquake had trembled the ground. The shape of a vast chin and a bewhiskered and deeply fissured face with heavy-lidded and drooping eyes, stirred in the rock. The massive chin lifted from where it was slumped on a huge chest. The rock shook itself and flicked out a coarse arm at the knockermen.

The great fist crushed two knockermen in one pounding movement. "Ugh, little devils! May the earth crush you." He then swore in the old Caballan tongue and thumped his foot down, flattening another's chest. Its arms and legs squirmed to crawl free, black blood oozing from its mouth. The other knockermen fled, clearly far more afraid of a fully grown stonewight than they were of Perren. The ogre crawled out of his hollow and stretched up into the dark of the tunnel above. Shrieks and cries peeled out from the dark and then three headless bodies splattered to the floor. The stonewight spat the mangled remains of the knockermen from his mouth.

"Well, that's seen to them!" Creaking and groaning, he lowered himself down so that his face was at their level and looked anxiously at Perren. "Are you all right, my lad. None of them bit you or anything?"

Perren anxiously checked himself all over and then shook his head. "No, I'm fine."

Reassured, the ancient stonewight nodded pleasantly. "Now what's one as young as you doing out alone away from the protection of the cave? What was your father thinking? Those knockermen could have bitten you and given you the crumbling disease."

Perren shuddered. "I know but there is something very important I must do. Beyond you lies Necrönd and we must rescue it before it falls into evil hands."

The vast stonewight settled himself back down into his nest and grunted in disapproval before giving out a tremendous yawn. Splinters of rock fell from the stretched corners of his mouth. "I'm too tired to bother myself with that now. This is my last sleep. The world's not the same as it was in my youth. It's gone cold. It used to be warm, beautifully warm. I have gone as deep as I can into the bosom of the earth but I still feel the cold." He yawned again.

"No, no, don't go to sleep! Don't block our way! You must help us," Caspar cried, running to tug at the stonewight's arm, surprised at the feel of cold rock. "We are nearly there. Please don't sleep. Just let us past!" He could have sat back and wept as the stonewight gave a grumbling sigh and settled his head back down on his chest. "I'll get a stone axe and hack you out of your bed," Caspar threatened.

There was no reply and the silence of despair was filled by the long, lonely howl of the wolf, who wailed on and on as if begging for help in their plight. Then Caspar thought he must be dreaming when a point of light appeared to hover before his eyes.

"You call on the Trinity," a beautiful lulling and hypnotic voice murmured. "But the Trinity is broken; the old Crone lies in the dungeons beneath Abalone, deep in the heart of Rye Errish. Your call is so desperate that it reaches her even there but we, the guardians of Rye Errish, cannot allow her to help you."

More points of light appeared before Caspar's eyes. The lights swelled and took form and he knew at once that it was the thirteen members of the High Circle that appeared before him.

Straif stepped forward, a staff of blackthorn bristling in his hands, and scowled at Caspar. "You! You take up an uncommonly large amount of our time. What mischief is it that you have done now that we should be disturbed so?"

"It wasn't him that disturbed; it was the wolf," Uilleand told Straif stiffly. "You're never any good at understanding earthlings, are you?"

"Oh, shut up!" The two began to quarrel.

"What law has been transgressed here?" Phagos demanded. "I don't see that we have any business here. We should leave."

"No, please, you must help," Caspar begged. "There is a law broken here. On the other side of this stonewight lies Necrönd and also the one that seeks to use it to gain power over life and death; a man with the scent of wolf."

"It is not our place to interfere," Phagos said.

In a twinkle of bright light, he was gone. The other ealdormen, save two, shrank back until they were no more than pinpricks of light; Beith, the birch on her sash, paused a moment to fondly stroke the wolfling's head and the other, Straif, remained, studying Caspar.

"A wolfman!" Straif snorted, testing the thorns on his staff for sharpness and sucking thoughtfully at his pricked thumb. "I can only leave it in your hands to right this wrong. For me to help, I must have the agreement of the High Circle and, as you know, that can take a very long time. But I can tell you this and leave the fates in your hand: beyond the stonewight is one that cheats death in order to steal your May. I will wake up this stonewight but you must repay me by seeing him punished."

Caspar could not think. He would do anything to save May and gave no further thought to his quest. When Straif rapped at the stonewight with his stave, Caspar drew his bow in readiness.

Perren was too mesmerised by the goings on and was still pointing into thin air where the ealdormen had been to notice Caspar. "I never saw them in the water. I never felt their presence. They are not of this world," he said in wonder.

Straif raised his thorny staff and brought it down hard on the nose of the sleeping stonewight, at the same time sounding a powerful note that thrilled the air. The stonewight groaned, shifted and reluctantly pulled his feet aside, leaving a crack in the rock just large enough for Caspar to worm through. Pushing the torch before him and dragging his bow, he forced his shoulders through the narrow crack, driven on by fear for May and a sudden sense of shame. He, a nobleman of Torra Alta, had neglected his girl. He should have gone after her and not Necrönd. He had sacrificed her for what he thought was the better good and let this terrible wrong happen.

His scalp was bleeding profusely where he had only grazed it on the rock and he knew at once that Necrönd was close. At last, he broke out beyond the narrow fissure. A pool of steaming water stretched before him, the light of his firebrand dancing on its surface, leaping from one ripple to the next and illuminating the huge tail of a great creature that sliced through the boiling water.

Beyond the steaming water, he saw May and saw too that she was held by an elflike man. He immediately recognized Talorcan, the chief verderer, the same creature who had tried to trap Brid's soul to gain her power; Caspar loathed him with every ounce of his body. The verderer clutched May in his embrace.

"May!" Caspar cried, his voice cracking with rage and jealousy. His arrow was in flight, thrumming through the steamy air, spanning the distance of the lake.

"No!" May yelled forlornly as the arrow punched into the verderer's chest.

Talorcan's gasp of pain swam back across the water. He slumped to the ground, May cradling him as he fell.

CHAPTER TWENTY-SEVEN

Hal was overly aware of the smells around him. Maybe it was because he could barely see ten paces for the impenetrable mist or perhaps it was the dampness in the air that so intensified the smells of myrtle and marsh marigolds. Sound travelled easily across the water and he was uncomfortably aware that he must also be clearly audible to anyone with an ear to the night. The damp had penetrated his clothes and he was cold.

"Wizards indeed!" he muttered. If they were so terrible how then was it so easy for him to find the causeway? It had been right there all along. They had passed it in fact and he had found it instantly when he had remembered where he had heard the ponies crunching across the shingle. True, the mist was particularly thick over the causeway, a repellent shade of green streaked with unnerving threads of smoky purple, but he had found it – and without Brid's help.

He drew his sword and smoothed his fingers down the central fuller, feeling the well of energy surge up from the metal to his mind. Secret shrieked her defiance at the mist and he patted her neck in agreement. This was just some specially brewed smoke from a trickster's fire, he told himself, not a magical mist at all. Brid was a fool to be so afraid. As was that great and noble Abelard!

He couldn't wait to see their faces when he brought

Cymbeline back after his single-handed rescue. She would be weeping with thanks and effusive with praise. That would smarten Brid up a bit when she saw how vigorously the fine princess desired him. Of course, Brid had not been overly jealous of the young marsh maidens nor should she have been even if he had given her true cause, for they had no part to play in the grand scale of the world. He thought no less of them as individuals for that; it was just that they had no widespread impact on others – unlike Cymbeline, whose disappearance had stirred kingdoms after all. And he needed to make an impact more than he needed anything else – and quite probably, he told himself, more than he needed Brid. He still couldn't forgive her for publicly slapping him – especially when he had been innocent.

Secret stumbled. The causeway was slippery and her motion beneath him somehow no longer felt as solid as it had. He had the sense that he was looking on nothing but a cushion of thought; the ground seemingly distant, unreal, swirling beneath the unresting patterns of green. He had the strangest sensation that they were somehow rising into the air, Secret's legs stretching longer and longer, and her footfall almost silent on the basaltlike surface that formed the land bridge to the black island. He shook himself. No, it was quite ridiculous. Now he was even imagining that he could see the indistinct outline of dark shapes running alongside him.

Someone was calling to him. He knew the voice; insistent, commanding, softly feminine though not melodious like Brid's. "Hal, my gallant knight."

"It is I," he called back.

"My lord, you come to rescue me."

Secret came to a sudden halt. Before him, apparently standing in the thick misty air was the image of Brid and not Cymbeline as he had anticipated. "Hal, I'm not strong enough alone. Come back! Wait till I've summoned help. All that you see is an illusion, a magic that I have no ability to contend with. It's all in your mind, Hal."

He stiffened in his saddle, trying to rid himself of the apparition and kicked on. He wasn't going to turn back. How could he? It would look like he'd been too cowardly to go on or, worse, was cowed by her will.

Strange! There was a new smell amid the marigolds and myrtle. He could smell Ceowulf, though he had never before realized that he knew what he smelt like until he detected a faint whiff of linseed oil and polished metal in the mist. Just as Hal was fastidious about oiling and sharpening his sword, Ceowulf lavished attention on his armour and even though he was not actually wearing it, he generally had it packed with him and would carefully see to it every night. Everyone took Ceowulf and his armour seriously – except perhaps Ceowulf himself.

Hal turned in the saddle, certain that his friend was there, but he could see nothing save the dark, ethereal patterns formed by the green mist. Even his breath coiling from both nostrils was green. He stopped and waited and at last heard the dull thud of a horse's hooves on the causeway, not a chime, as it should have been, but a cushioned pad.

Ceowulf's dark form seated upon his great destrier loomed large and much closer than Hal had expected.

"I thought you might have need of me, friend," he explained his presence.

Hal shrugged. "I doubt it but I am always glad of your company."

"Most gracious of you," Ceowulf replied with a laugh. "They had no want of me to help with their ceremony. They were collecting all manner of plants and singing charms, trying to lift the mist but I was of little use and when I saw that you were gone, I followed."

They rode on side by side. Hal felt a shiver run up his spine. "Is it just me or is this mist playing tricks with our minds?"

"I've the strangest feeling we're floating," Ceowulf agreed and peered down over his horse's shoulder. Both horses laboured as if walking in soft sand.

"Look out!" Ceowulf whispered urgently, his sword rasping against its scabbard as he drew it into the air. "Wolves! To our right."

Hal braced himself for the attack. Five wolves approached from what should have been the lake. It didn't seem possible. In contrast to the murky green of the mist, the red of their yawning maws was startling. They were running now, yellow teeth gnashing. Swinging Secret to face their charge and standing high in his saddle to give himself better room to manoeuvre, Hal cut in smooth arcs to left and right. His blade took the first beast in the head, slicing through its muzzle, separating teeth from the head, the open throat redly howling as the split jaws spun off into the mist.

More wolves followed. One, its eyes screwed closed, had his boot. He thrust down with his left hand, stabbing with his short dagger, piercing through behind one eye and twisting until the wolf fell away.

Secret, snorting and chafing at the bit, was ever obedient to his commands. Hal kept her broadside to the attack to protect her head from the wolves of which only a handful remained. Wary of his sword, they kept back and circled, waiting for an opening. Snatching up his throwing knives, he hurled three in rapid succession. Each found its mark. The wolves curled up like hedgehogs. Hal now had time to congratulate himself. He had never been very accurate with throwing knives but clearly, he was improving. He rested back into his saddle, breathing heavily and, feeling distinctly pleased with himself, watched Ceowulf dispatch the last of the wolves.

"We must have killed a dozen," he exclaimed, meeting Ceowulf's grin.

The knight's expression changed. "No one's ever killed that many hooded wolves."

"No!" Hal agreed enthusiastically as if that made it even better. "Ceowulf, the Wolf Slayer! Hal Wolfsbane!"

Soothing his snorting destrier, the Caldean gave Hal a derisory smile. "We might be good – and I've no doubt that we are – but no one's that good."

"But we killed them," Hal argued.

"It was too easy, much too easy," Ceowulf said ominously. "Hundreds of men have tried all year to cull these beasts and they have managed to kill a bare half dozen. We've just dispatched twice that number without suffering the slightest scratch. Don't you think that says something?"

"It does. That we are finest of fighting men," Hal continued though there was a slight nagging doubt at the back of his mind. "Anyway, there's no other explanation. No animal *allows* itself to be killed. The idea's ridiculous."

"Oh yes, but is some power controlling them, driving them onto us to give us a false sense of our own greatness, lulling us into complacency? Or perhaps they aren't real at all, just an illusion?"

Hal sniffed. He had felt the firmness of flesh at the end of his blade. He had heard . . . but, no, he hadn't. Doubt came over him. He had not heard the victory song of the runesword that came with the death of his enemy. He looked down at the blade. It was clean without a drop of blood to contaminate it.

He was angry. How dare anyone make a fool of him? He imagined Renaud laughing at him and felt his blood pump furiously against his temples. He remembered, too, what the prince's schemes had done to Branwolf, Keridwen and his nephew in Torra Alta.

Renaud would pay. No one humiliated the name of Torra Alta. "Spar, I'll show them," he brazened out loud.

"Spar?" Ceowulf queried him. "I too was thinking of him almost as if he were right here with us. How ridiculous."

Hal stiffened up, trying to gird his mind against the peculiar mist. "What did Brid say when she noticed I'd gone?"

"Hmm? Oh, not a lot," Ceowulf replied too brightly.

"You're a hopeless liar, Ceowulf. What did she say?" Hal demanded.

"Hmm. She said you were a fool to march off and you deserved to get lost in the mist. She said the only way we could safely reach the island was by dissolving away the mist with her own spell."

"Well, it hasn't worked yet," Hal pointed out. "It's as thick as ever."

Just as he spoke, a large black turret thrusting up above them appeared from out of the mist and soon they saw snatches of the black cliffs below it.

"We're climbing," Ceowulf muttered in disbelief after a while. "But how? I felt no slope nor steps."

Nevertheless, the great towers were growing closer and were now a brownish black with angry points and steel buttressing, thin rods laced between them to keep them pointing skywards. The towers bore more resemblance to the barbed points of arrows than the architectural shape of turrets. The rest of the great castle became like a huge ominous shadow behind the mist, sucking in all light, the green smoke seeping out of the arrow-slits and wafting through the portcullis.

"Oh, what wit!" Ceowulf sneered as the churning mist pulled away from the barbican, revealing the entrance to be shaped like a skull, the mouth gaping open in an expression of dread.

Three figures stepped from beneath the portcullis, waving them forward. They wore long purple gowns and tall wide-brimmed peaked hats. Hal realized in amazement that they had climbed level with the portcullis, the sea crashing against cliffs far below.

"Brid was right to be wary. They have borne us through the air to them," Ceowulf warned, "tempting us into their lair."

"How could Prince Renaud have become involved with these wizards?" Hal asked, not expecting any reply.

He raised his head at the sound of his name. A woman was crying out for him. "Hal! Hal, you've come for me. My champion! I knew you wouldn't desert me."

He dropped from his horse, looking for a way to reach Cymbeline. He didn't know how it had happened but suddenly a path came to his feet and he was running towards a high turret, climbing on a spiralling staircase of green smoke.

"No, Hal! Don't be a fool," Ceowulf yelled at his back.

Fool or not, he too leapt from his horse and came charging after him, up the insubstantial stairway. Suddenly his boots slapped on firm stone and he was clinging to a narrow ledge high on the turret wall. Hal had already worked his way along the ledge and was skirting the top of a buttress, manoeuvring towards a window from whence emerged the sound of sobbing.

His skin drained of colour, Ceowulf followed, his eyes flickering downwards whilst his fingers clung rigidly to the sheer walls. Hal looked at the knight, then around him and out over the mist.

Here, they were above the mist and he could see for miles over its churning surface. To the east and west the coastline stretched away into a thin blue-grey line and he realized the lake must be many miles across. Beyond the near southern edge of the lake, where the grey outlines of the wild ponies dipped in and out of the green fringes of the mist, Brid's fire conjured strange red smokes. Beyond that, the endless forest rose and fell in rank upon rank of oak, beach and pine, which formed verdant bands of dark and light that blended into one in the far distance. Rain clouds broken by shafts of sunlight produced patterns of shadow and fields of gold, the sun glinting here and there off a small lake or a river.

Hal was not in the least afraid of the drop. He had a good foothold on a six-inch-wide ledge so there was no possibility of falling. He stretched out his fingers, working them over the pitted stone of the walls to hook onto the window ledge.

The sound of sobbing lured him on, though a voice in the back of his mind warned him that, like the wolves and the strangely rising causeway, this might well be another illusory trick.

Forsaking his foothold and relying only on the strength in his fingers, he swung beneath the window and hauled himself up onto his elbows and in through the narrow crack.

Soft embracing arms laced around his neck and his mouth and face were smothered in kisses. "Lord Hal, I knew you would come. I knew you would never abandon me."

Hal blinked into Cymbeline's grey blue eyes, the colour of the sky seen through a veil of rain. Though she looked directly at him her gaze seemed unfocused. Instinctively, he stiffened.

"But, Hal, you swore to be my champion, my knight." Self-consciously, the Ceolothian princess adjusted one of the pink veils that was pinned to her hair and smiled coquettishly. Clad in pale fabrics woven from gossamer-thin silk, she seemed to him like a ghost. Her clothing was so light that all that gave it weight were the pearls and rubies stitched into the fabric. She threw herself into his arms again and hugged him close. "Hal, my saviour, you've come for me!"

"And your captors," Hal insisted. "They must pay for this crime."

Ceowulf clambered awkwardly in through the window, his big frame making the task difficult. One of his boots caught on the sill and, heaving it free with an ungainly lurch, he fell into the room. Without greeting or ceremony, he demanded of Cymbeline, "How do we get past the wizards to Renaud?"

"The wizards?" she queried, her head on one side.

"Yes, the wizards."

"You don't," replied a deep mocking voice from the door that was suddenly flung open. The man was tall and thin and bore a long staff etched with many runes, none of which Hal recognized though, admittedly, he was not a master of the craft. A long gown of purple decorated with yellow zigzags was thrown back over his shoulders. Hal shook his head and stared harder. When the light shone on the figure, he could see through him to the wall behind. A smile broke out on the man's weathered face and he laughed a terrible booming laugh.

Hal laughed back at him. "Wizard, you are just a ghost and I have no fear of you."

The man advanced and Hal's one thought was to protect

the princess. All their hopes were lost if she were harmed. King Dagonet would only call off his skilled and ruthless army if his precious daughter were returned in full health.

She gasped in fright and Hal stepped before her, drawing his sword. The wizard laughed derisively and muttered a dark charm.

To his dismay, his prized runesword glowed and bent, the flaccid tip drooping towards the floor, blobs of white metal dribbling from the point and sizzling where they fell on the elm boards. He tightened his grip on the scorching hilt, focusing on the runes of the blade but to no effect. The hilt burnt his hand and he dropped his sword – his precious, wonderful runesword – into the pool of sizzling molten metal. Anger flamed within him and he flung himself in mad rage at the wizard.

This was evidently the one thing the wizard had not anticipated and, clearly, nor was he or Hal expecting Ceowulf to grab Cymbeline and hold a knife to her throat.

Hal slammed his fist at the wizard's temple but swung straight through and connected with the door jamb. The wizard, however, staggered back, not from the blow passing clean through his insubstantial body but because Hal's rage had distracted him from Ceowulf. The knight was holding Cymbeline in what Hal deemed to be rather too fierce a grip. She looked startled, pained and dangerously short of breath.

"Steady there, friend," Hal advised.

Ceowulf, however, remained aggressive. "Pick up your sword!" He glared at Hal, his eyes wide, willing him to heed his words.

Hal looked from his friend to the sizzling pool at his feet and back again without moving.

"Pick it up." Ceowulf kicked at the molten mass and,

to his amazement, Hal distinctly heard the clang of cold steel. "It's all illusion; their magic isn't elemental like Brid's."

Only half believing, Hal nevertheless stooped to pick up what seemed to him to be sizzling liquid. He closed his eyes. *Great Mother, give me faith. Show me the reality of my world*, he prayed. With his eyes shut and expecting to have his fingers burnt to black sticks, he found the courage to push into the white heat of the metal only to feel the cool solid grip of his hilt in his hand. He whirled round to attack the ghostly apparition but the wizard was gone.

"Hal, Hal!" Cymbeline cried. "Get this brute off me! My father will give you anything, even the price of a lesser kingdom, if you safely return me to him. But he will not be pleased if you allow this knight to harm me. Hal, do something at once, do you hear?"

Hal did hear and he didn't understand what had got into Ceowulf. "What are you doing?" he demanded. "Let her go!"

"Open your eyes. Can't you see what's happening?" Ceowulf shouted.

"You're hurting her," Hal shouted back. Before his eyes, Cymbeline was turning a ghastly blue-grey colour. He shouldered into the bulk of the Caldean, knocking him off balance with his unexpected attack. Ceowulf staggered backwards, tripped on a low stool and fell, releasing Cymbeline, who was gasping fearfully, her eyes startled. Hal pressed his cruel-edged sword against his friend's chest and motioned Cymbeline to keep clear.

"I know the way," she cried, pulling at his sleeve and pointing towards a large drape at the rear of the room. Hal glanced back towards Ceowulf who had changed somehow, becoming threatening and sinister; his eyebrows darkening and thickening, his eyes sinking back into his skull and his lips thinning. There was a meanness in those eyes that Hal had never seen before.

"Quickly!" Cymbeline begged. "This leads to the lower floors and then the stables. No one will see us and we can plan our escape from there."

Leaving Ceowulf, who made no attempt to follow, Hal went after Cymbeline, mesmerized by her honeyed speech. "It was Hardwin and Prince Renaud," she began, hitching up her skirts and stepping lightly down the dark coiling staircase that lay behind the curtain. "The things they planned you wouldn't believe. They wanted to keep me in chains only they were afraid of my brother even though they had imprisoned him in the dungeons. We must rescue him."

"I'll get you to safety first," Hal said gallantly, "and then go back for Tudwal."

Her hair floated out behind her as she ran. "He won't want to be rescued by you." She laughed lightly.

Ceowulf still did not follow. Hal gave it little thought; his mind was elsewhere. This was his chance for glory and he would do it all single-handed – without Brid, and most definitely without Abelard, and in spite of Ceowulf. He sprinted down the stairs, barely able to keep pace with Cymbeline. Down and down, they went, her urgent voice cajoling him to hurry. At last, they came to a door that was curiously narrow with a pointed cap. It had a ring latch that Cymbeline tried to turn but, when it would not give, she looked back helplessly at Hal. "I can't."

"Allow me," he said, squeezing past her, acutely aware of her rising bosom as she drew breath. He smiled at her as the latch lifted and, still looking into her face, shouldered open the door and fell through into a starkly purple room. The walls were hung with purple drapes. The one window on the far wall was filled with purple stained-glass. The odd light from this window fell on three red-eyed creatures sitting around a large black pot, stirring a brew that belched a purple smoke. Hobgoblins, Hal decided by their evil looks.

They shrieked and cackled and Hal was so aghast that he had barely drawn his sword before the smoke, with its heady scent of violets, enveloped him and swaddled his limbs. Struggling to keep his balance, he lashed back and forth, his sword scything yellow streaks in the purple smog but could do nothing to reach the creatures.

The hobgoblins were naked save for pointed hats in mockery of the wizards. The bones of their thin bodies stood painfully proud as if at any moment they might pierce their stretched skin. As one they peeled back their thin brown lips to laugh, displaying their sharply pointed teeth. They were no bigger than children and very much thinner, every rib and hip bone jutting through their earthy brown skin. Long fingers wriggled in the pot though they occasionally withdrew them to suck them sensuously, their coiled and forked tongues flicking out and around each digit.

Hal was tiring rapidly, the smoke thickening about him like congealing porridge. It hardened around his arms and neck, slowly strangling his breathing. He couldn't convince himself that it was only an illusion as Ceowulf had warned. A swirl of smoke formed itself into a bunched fist and began to force itself into his mouth, stopping his breath. His world swam dizzily around him.

"Ceowulf!" he choked, his cry a muffled croak. Finally, he slumped into the smoke. Either he was unconscious when he hit the ground or the smoke had acted as a cushion, supporting him, but he was never aware of crashing onto the stone floor. The next thing he knew was the fiendish chattering of the hobgoblins who, unlike the ghostly wizards, were all too solidly real and no doubt had been sought out by the wizards to do their hard labour. They were astonishingly strong for their size.

Sinewy hands clasped his limbs. They lifted him as if he were a child and carried him down a series of spiralling stairs and along a long corridor, barred at intervals by doors each ominously locked and chained. Finally, they bore him through an inner portcullis set deep in the bowels of the castle.

A growing dread chilled Hal's heart. It was like descending into the depths beneath Rewik's castle at Farona. He could smell embers from hot ashes and the acrid smell of burnt fat. When they came to a steel door guarded by two more red-eyed hobgoblins armed with long knives, he knew what he would find.

They heaved open the doors and he was flung inside. The three wizards that now seemed bigger than before, towered over him. The hobgoblins ran to them and curled within their robes, clinging to their legs like children clinging to their mother. They reached up imploringly for praise and purred when their heads were stroked.

Hal found it difficult to look the wizards in the face. Thin and drawn, there was a ghastliness to them that he could not understand. Their skin was almost transparent and though their robes gave them form, their hands seemed weak and unable to grasp things. Still, they could conjure and, when one snapped his fingers and swirled his loose wrist in the air, Hal was propelled forward by a green smoke speckled with little daggers of purple that stabbed into his thighs. The hobgoblins squealed with delight as he winced.

The chains on the wall looked real enough, however, and he struggled furiously but in vain as the hobgoblins dragged him forward and clamped his wrists. The short length of chain was fixed low in the wall and prevented him from standing fully upright. He swung at the hobgoblins with his feet but they shrank back out of reach.

"We will leave you now to contemplate your fate, but rest assured we will return," the wizards spoke as one in thin croaky voices.

He took Hal's sword and chained it to the opposite wall, impossibly out of reach. Hal refrained from humiliating himself by struggling to get it though every nerve in his muscles screamed at him to try even though he knew it was impossible.

The wizards left, conversing in a language that Hal was certain was not of the Caballan Sea. Stupefied, he stared into the smoke. But what had happened to Cymbeline? He decided they must have taken her to another place of safekeeping, hopefully a little more comfortable than this. As the smoke began to clear, he heard a voice. This one was most clearly Belbidian.

"They sounded worried. And perhaps more faded than before."

Hal wondered if the voice were part of the illusion of the green smoke that was floating down from the ceiling and sleepily crawling along the fissures in stonework as if too exhausted to hang in mid-air any longer.

He glared through the thinning smoke, his pulse thumping in his throat as he beheld the man before him. His hair had grown ragged and a spiky beard now covered his jutting chin but there was no mistaking him.

"You traitor!" Hal roared, flinging himself forward in attack. He forgot his chain and, like an enraged guard dog tethered by its neck, was painfully yanked backwards when it snapped taught. "Your brother, Rewik, is torturing my brother and his wife in the dungeons of Farona because of your evildoing! He does not believe that you could turn against him. He believes you are honest to the core and . . ." Hal's words slowly died on his lips.

Prince Renaud had an expression of utter surprise. Something was wrong. Was this an illusion too? Feeling confused and cheated, he sat back against the wall and clasped his hands to his head.

"Did you not come to rescue me?" Prince Renaud's voice was high and strained. "We realized there were many goings on. The hobgoblins love to boast, you see, and they told of people forming primitive magic and I guessed it was you and your woman. Don't you think that was clever of me? I guessed, didn't I, Lord Hardwin?"

Hal hadn't noticed the squat Pisceran fellow behind Prince Renaud. He nodded at him in greeting. Both seemed vaguely hysterical, their clothes torn and their wrists and ankles ringed with such pustular sores that Hal wondered that they weren't suffering from blood poisoning.

"I'm sorry your plan failed to get us out of here," Hardwin said matter-of-factly. "Prince Renaud had such confidence in you. He said that the men of Torra Alta had never once let Belbidia down – not in matters of war, you know – but I had my doubts because of the evil done by the hooded wolves. I felt that you might not care about us."

"Where's Tudwal?" Hal cut through their inane babble. "Was he brought here too?"

The prince nodded. "They were but we've been separated since."

The hobgoblins were watching and laughing and Hal feared this was all for their benefit. He doubted whether he should be believing Prince Renaud or, for that matter, whether he were talking to him at all. He dropped his head into his hands and pondered. Surely, there had to be a way of finding out the truth. This was something that would happen to Caspar, not him. He was not easily duped. Everyone knew he was too sceptical to be fooled. He should have seen through all this.

The image of Morrigwen scolding him for being such an imbecile popped up from his subconscious. He had never been sure what to think about Morrigwen. Plainly, she had never liked him but, also, she had also never condemned his love of Brid, though the old Crone had been intensely protective over her. Smoke began rising out of the masonry and seeping up from under the door.

"They're returning!" Renaud's bewhiskered face whitened. Clearly, he was mortally afraid of the wizards and that, above any other reason, persuaded Hal to trust him. The door creaked open and the three ghostly figures stood on the threshold. They had paled, their forms more transparent and the smoke drifted through their insubstantial bodies as easily as dust through a shaft of sunlight. As Renaud had observed, they seemed worried.

"Should we dispose of him?" they asked as one.

Hal couldn't see whom they spoke to but it did not seem to be to one another. Then he saw it; a large black wolf hunched in the corner, a long trail of saliva drooling from its jaws, the mouth unable to close for the size of its fangs. Black smoke coiled around it, shrouding it from sight again but he heard the voice that came from its direction.

"Keep him. Let him draw the others to us. We shall have all of them and leave none to return. But must I do everything myself? You are beholden to me and yet you fail me; the mist is thinning. Some magic sweeps it away and soon the causeway will be clear." The voice was black with anger. "Fail me and I shall send you back to crawl forever through the marshes of the Otherworld."

From out of the black smoke a wolf leapt and bound

away through the doors. Hal yanked himself to the end of his chain, terrified for Brid's safety. It was her magic that was causing the disturbance in the mist, and he was sure that the wolf would seek her out. And, neither he nor Ceowulf were there to protect her. He prayed that Abelard was still hard by her side and drew comfort that, whatever happened, the archer would never fail her. For the first time, he felt warmth and gratitude towards the man.

"She has control of the mists and is moving them," the wizards spoke in amazement and exasperation.

"But she is alone. She cannot do it alone. The Great Mother will not answer the prayers of one alone," they answered in bewilderment.

"Raise the waters," the wizards cried before drifting away. For several seconds Hal could hear their alien chanting disappearing into the darkness.

The hobgoblins slammed the door and, by the sound of their feet slapping on the stone floor, were racing after their masters. Nothing happened for many minutes while Hal stared at the door and yelled out with all his worth for Ceowulf. He could think of nothing else.

He was beginning to believe that they had been completely abandoned when water spread from beneath the steel doors. Hal's feet were soon wet and rising water lapped against the square sides of the cell.

The water quickly rose to his calves, spilling over the top of his boots. It was cold and wet and, there was no doubt in his mind that it was real. He heaved and tugged at his chain fixed to the wall but it did not yield. Hardwin wailed in dismay.

"Lord Hal, do something. You have to save us," Renaud moaned.

Hal was exasperated by their blind faith in him. He

stood up as tall as he could, looking around for anything that might come to hand. The murky green water lapped about his thighs and a loose wooden stock floated on the bubbling surface. Surely, there was something that would help him. *Something.* The stocks came just within his outstretched grasp and he fingered them towards him, working free the metal pin that closed the stocks and used it to try to free the lock on his wrist. He struggled frantically but it would not yield.

"There will be war," Renaud moaned, "if we don't get Princess Cymbeline out of here alive. What if she drowns?"

Hal prayed Ceowulf had heard his cry. The wizards must be directing this storm at Brid and he had to do something to stop them. There had to be some way out of this. He took the length of stock, jammed it through the ring on the wall and used it as a lever to try and break the metal free from the stonework but clearly it was fixed too deep within the mortar. The water was up around his stooped shoulders as he heaved at his shackles and tried to squeeze his hand through the metal cuff but to no avail.

"Great Mother," he cried, "I have to get to Brid. Great Mother, anything, any sacrifice you name of me, whatever your will, I will do it if you save Brid," he bargained. "I have to save Brid."

Hardwin was screaming and gasping, his head back, mouth just clear of the water. A short man, he could barely stretch his neck up high enough. Beside him, Renaud was behaving like a noble Belbidian. Composed and calm, he was praying to his god for mercy and a swift death.

CHAPTER TWENTY-EIGHT

May looked towards him across the stretch of water, the verderer unmoving in her arms. At her feet was a nest of moss; Caspar knew what it contained; his heart was heavy with the burden of responsibility.

"It's all right; stay there; don't move. I'm coming for you," he cried, trying to sound calm and in control. Scrambling up onto Perren's shoulders and pulling his feet up under him to keep them clear of the steaming water, he prayed that the pool was not too deep and that Perren wouldn't slip. The stonewight had assured him that an abyss worm, something he seemed quite familiar with, could do him no more harm than the boiling water. Caspar prayed his was right on both counts. Runnels of sweat poured from his face.

When they were nearly half way across, Perren stopped. May's head was down, her hair curtained about the verderer's face. She was crying but, worse, the verderer still lived. His moans were faint but unmistakable.

"Perren, hurry! Look! The wolfman lives."

The stonewight paid him no heed and to Caspar's ears sounded quite mad as he swished his hands through the boiling water and cried, "I am blessed! The Great Mother speaks to me in the water! The clarity, the vision over such distance! I sense ice water, salt water, the Mother's tears. The rhythms are strong through the brine. Someone prays to Her, needs Her help, and I am honoured as Her voice. I must speak for them. A cry for help. They are of your blood, Spar, and they are in need."

"Perren, look out!" Caspar shouted. He hadn't been listening to a word the stonewight was saying but was fixed on the bulge of water that speared towards them. A head surfaced, its mouth open, a great lashing tail propelling the abyss worm forward.

The stonewight moved slowly, though Caspar drummed his heels into Perren's solid neck and shrieked at him to do something. At the last second, the rocklike creature bunched his fist and thrust it into the abyss worm's red maw. Evidently, he had underestimated the worm's momentum that hit like a rolling barrel. He lurched off balance and stumbled onto one knee.

Caspar clung on tightly, kicking his legs up clear of the water, splashes of it scolding his face and hands.

Perren's thick arm was swallowed up to the elbow in the creature's throat and Caspar could see the shadow of the stonewight's fingers twisting and tearing beneath the thin skin of the worm's neck.

"Perren, you'll lose your hand!" he shouted helplessly, knowing there was nothing he could do. He needed both hands to cling on or be thrown into the water.

A crunching noise ground within the worm's maw. Perren thrashed to keep upright, grunting with the effort. Then with a great cry, he sprang up from his knee, nearly sending Caspar over backwards. In his fist, Perren held a bloodied mass of gristle and tissue, fleshy tubes and purple veins dangling from his fingers. Blood vomited from the abyss worm's mouth, blinding Caspar as it sprayed over his face. Wiping the mess from his eyes, he opened them to see the creature belly up in the red foaming water.

"You ripped out his throat!" Caspar croaked in shocked disbelief.

"A fellow never knows his own strength," Perren said lightly, washing his hands in the steaming water. "Great Mother, I am sorry for the death of one of your creatures," he said reverently and waded forward.

Now that the abyss worm was dead, Caspar's eyes flickered between Talorcan, May and the Egg at their feet.

Unbelievably Talorcan was still alive though he knew he had hit him clean through the heart. He did not understand; and what he did not understand, he feared.

He had to get Necrönd. The moment Perren set him down, he ran to May, expecting her to welcome him; but she did not. He snatched up the Egg and turned it over in his fist, his hand throbbing and his heart a huge bladder of blood pulsing in his throat.

The Egg was whole! He turned it over, his heart missing a beat as he saw the jagged black scorch mark marring its creamy shell. Clearly, he had got here only just in time.

Jealously, he stepped away and clutched the Egg tight to his chest. He had it! It was safe! None could harm him or his loved ones now.

"Hal!" Perren said the name insistently.

Caspar didn't understand. What did Hal have to do with this?

The stonewight pointed to the pool excitedly. "The Great Mother demands that you use Necrönd. You must summon Morrigwen from the Otherworld. The Great Mother seeks the Trinity. You must call her."

Caspar fearfully grasped Necrönd in both hands.

CHAPTER TWENTY-NINE

Hal arched his back, craned his neck and struggled to keep his mouth above the surging water. Battling for every last second of life, he spat and swallowed the icy brine that lapped about his lips.

The level rose above his nose and the need to fight was over. Desperation left him and in the muffled world of the water, he was overwhelmed by a sudden calm. He could still see and, through the distortions of the water, he saw an extraordinary apparition floating through the dungeon door. Borne on the back of a white wolf came the ghost of an old woman, her body covered by white shrouds, a well of blood pumping from her stomach.

"He forced me to come. And to you of all people. You!" the ancient spectre groaned. "I am weak and they will punish me more. And for what? You should have obeyed Brid. How could Spar force me to take this agonising journey as a spirit when I must return whole to fulfil my duties. The pain is worse, far worse here. You will repay me, Hal," she said as her white wolf halted beside his sword on the far wall.

A red smoke seeped through the walls and two other figures, as ghostly as Morrigwen but without her deathly pallor, stood beside her. Their hands met, joining the spirits of the three high priestesses as one to do their task. Keridwen looked aged and thin; Brid, her face taut with concentration, never once glancing in Hal's direction but focusing only on the sword. With great awe, Hal knew that his prayers to the Mother had been answered.

The melded hands of the three spectres swept up the great runesword and bore it through the water towards him. Wordlessly, they placed it into his upstretched hand and their images faded though Morrigwen's lingered longer.

He saw her being sucked into a void in the atmosphere, back across the divide into the Otherworld and into a huge high vaulted dungeon where men were roasted over leaping fires. She lay spread-eagled, her shrouds pulled aside from her belly so that her entrails could be stirred by sizzling pokers.

She writhed and screamed. But every time the verderers paused in their torture, she howled like a wolf, "I will not let go! Never, not until the new Maiden is found."

The blade was in his hand and, with one swing, he sliced through the restraining chain. Head clear of the water, he forced his way through the churning flood to where Hardwin had been. Plunging down beneath the surface, he cut the bonds and pulled him up by the collar. The man gasped and shrieked, his eyes bulging with terror. One slash freed Renaud and, still choking and coughing, together they swam for the stairs.

The door was shut fast. Hal smote the bolt with his sword and the door burst open under the force of water behind. They were plunged back into the dungeon by the torrent cascading down the stairs, and hurled against the far wall. Hal hauled himself from one chain ring to the next around the edge of the rapidly filling dungeon, his success encouraging the others to follow.

Pulling themselves upward on the stair rope, they forced their way through the cascade that pounded against their thighs. Hardwin and Renaud were free like himself and he could no longer concern himself with them. His only thought was for Brid. Surely, this rising water would flood the shorelines. And what of the black wolf? "Abelard, do not forsake her," he begged out loud.

At last, he came to a door and rushed out into the barbican yard. He blinked in the sudden light. The mists had lifted though there was no sign of the causeway. A red-sailed boat bucked and strained at its moorings alongside a jetty that was being thrashed by the sudden flood. Clearly, the flood was real. He remembered Robin Longpole speaking of a sluice.

Ducking beneath the portcullis, he ran out of the castle. Scanning the far shore, he saw no sign of Brid, only a red smoke that hazed the shoreline. From here there was nothing he could do to help her; closing his eyes, he prayed for her safety.

Turning his back on the lake, he looked up at the castle. Drifts of green smoke were being swept aside from the black stone by a light breeze and the scent of triumph sweetened the air. The wizards were gone, he was sure. But where was Cymbeline? Was she drowned in the lower dungeons or had she fled back to her tower? He needed her. Her safe return was Branwolf's salvation.

Hardwin and Renaud stood by the portcullis, begging him not to abandon them.

"I'll see you well rewarded," Renaud cried but Hal doubted that Rewik would honour his brother's word if they returned without Cymbeline.

"Let go of me, you oaf," a girlish squealing voice shouted from the stable mews. Hal sprinted towards the sound. "Unhand me. I'm not leaving without my brother!" Cymbeline's voice was shrill and overexcited. She was held in Ceowulf's fierce grip but the extent of her emotion had heightened her strength and even the big Caldean was struggling to hold her as she bit his hands and kicked his shins.

Slowing to a walk, Hal took hold of Cymbeline's free wrist and almost felt like laughing. "My lady, don't worry. We'll take you safely home to King Rewik."

She stabbed him a look full of incomprehension, then her mouth flattened and formed into a regal pout. "I am not leaving without my brother."

"Well, where is he?" Hal demanded. "We shall free him."

Cymbeline pointed forlornly to the water below where the red-sailed boat was being tossed in the turbulent waters, banging its hull against the jetty. Hal could see three figures making their way towards the boat ahead of a line of men and more of those shrieking hobgoblins. He ran for the stone steps hacked into the rock wall below the castle that twisted and turned down towards the brackish waters of the lake.

Leaping the last few steps, he ran for the jetty, salty spray washing into his face as the waves crashed against the structure. A half dozen of the naked hobgoblins had hurled themselves aboard the rocking deck and were shrieking at the three men to hurry.

With sword drawn, Hal sprinted along the jetty before the three men had boarded. Two he recognized: Lord Tupwell of Ovissia; the other, Cymbeline's brother, Prince Tudwal. The third wore a black surcoat and chain mail leggings in the manner a of common mercenary.

Hal faltered. The mercenary and Tupwell were, between them, dragging the kicking and screaming Ceolothian prince towards the boat! Tudwal called frantically for Cymbeline.

Hal sprinted forward to the prince's aid, the boards of the jetty springy beneath his feet. Alarmed by his approach,

Tupwell called to the boat for help; immediately three hobgoblins slithered ashore to drag the muscular Ceolothian aboard while others cut the moorings. The boat caught the wind, swung away and surged forward on the choppy waves. Hal stood on the jetty, futilely reaching his hand out towards Tudwal as the prince cried out in despair for his sister.

There was nothing Hal could do. Puzzling over Tupwell's involvement, he climbed the steps back to Ceowulf, Renaud and Hardwin. He had the answer by the time he reached his friend who still held Cymbeline securely.

"Aren't you going to follow them?" she demanded.

"How?" Ceowulf asked rather irritably, sucking at his thumb and examining the several red teeth marks. "Would your Royal Princess expect us to swim after the boat?"

"Tupwell!" Hal blurted out when he had regained his breath. "Tupwell was behind the attack all along."

"What?!" Ceowulf exclaimed.

"I was wrong! You remember how, before the ambush, I stumbled across a torn-up parchment in the middle of the wood when Cymbeline's horse bolted. Of course, I thought that you, Renaud," he glanced at the prince, "had ordered someone to place it there. You see, when I pieced together the scraps of torn paper, they formed an instruction that Cymbeline must never reach Belbidia and I thought you were the only one with a possible motive to plan such treachery. Who else could possibly want to prevent her marrying Rewik? If Cymbeline produced an heir for the King, you lost your immediate claim to the throne; naturally I suspected you, cousin." He looked the tall prince clean in the face. "Sir, my sincerest apologies!"

"But Tupwell?" Ceowulf asked.

"Well, now that I think back with a different mind, didn't Tupwell emerge rather tardily to join the rest of the nobles? He had apparently slipped into a bog at the edge of the road but he could have easily engineered that as a distraction for the real reason for his late arrival. He must have had plenty of time to slip into the woods."

Hal paused for thought. "And the other message . . . ?" He fell silent, keeping his thoughts to himself, uncertain of the truth. Was the message he had uncovered linked to the one Brid had dug up about a find of sunburst rubies in the Yellow Mountains? Had Tupwell stolen away the princess in a way that poured suspicion on the Torra Altans? Had he really just wanted to discredit Torra Alta so that the castle might be put in Ovissian hands, better enabling him to gain access to this find of rubies in the Yellow Mountains? Yes, it had to be something like that.

"My prince, I have wronged you," he confessed to Renaud. "I have told your brother that you plotted against him and against the princess but I was mistaken."

"Indeed, you were. Hardwin and I fought so hard to protect her that in the end they were forced to take us with them as their captives. But I didn't realize that Tupwell was a part of the plot, only that he was separated from us. I presumed he was being held in other parts of the dungeons to prevent us scheming our escape together."

"I hope you will forgive me," Hal said, happy to apologize again, though his mind was no longer on the matter.

He was staring out towards the red smoke on the far shore. Long sticklike figures were emerging from it, making peculiar looping movements over the water. What manner of beast . . . ? He blinked and checked his thoughts, sheathing his sword that he had hastily pulled form its scabbard. The tall figures marching over the water were only the men of the marsh on their long stilts. And there was the tiny figure of Brid, clinging to the back of one. And Pip and Abelard also. He wasted no time and scrambled down the tortuous track cut into the cliff face to meet them.

While Robin Longpole and his men made their slow looping progress towards him, he had time to gather his thoughts and compose himself. Before they had quite reached the shore, Brid dropped from Robin Longpole's back and splashed through the shallows towards them.

She ran to him and hugged him tight before pushing him away. "You're all wet," she said critically.

"Strangely, I know," Hal replied with light sarcasm as he held her at arm's length to see her better, checking her over for signs of injury. "You're unharmed?"

She ignored his note of concern. "You were lucky. I told you to wait until I had dealt with the mist. Keridwen and I alone would never have saved you. You were lucky that somehow Morrigwen's soul was reached." Her face dropped.

"Morrigwen, she . . ." Hal didn't know what to say.

Brid nodded. "She suffers horribly." She stiffened, blinking her eyes, fighting back the tears, and raised her head to see the others above them, hurrying down the steps. "You did well. Now that we have Cymbeline and Renaud, Torra Alta's name will be cleared and we shall stay King Dagonet's arm. If we hurry, we'll get them home before midsummer. When that is done, I can turn all my attention to the search for my successor and Morrigwen's soul can be freed." She flicked back her damp plaited hair. "I'm glad you didn't listen to me."

"I doubted your power to lift the mist," Hal apologized.

"And, you were right, Hal. I didn't lift it. The wizards simply left and the mist with them." She fell pensively silent for a moment. "They could only be here at the summons of Necrönd and Spar would never have allowed such a thing. Somehow, something, perhaps one of the beasts whose breath of life is in the Egg itself was controlling it. I should not have left Spar. Necrönd was always too strong for him."

"Master Spar wouldn't have a hope of keeping control of anything," Pip shouted excitedly, running to Hal's side. "I killed one. Look!" Triumphant, he held up a knife stained with purplish blood.

"Killed what?" Hal demanded, again worriedly searching Brid for signs of harm.

"A hobgoblin," Robin Longpole informed him. "Horrible creatures came swarming over the waters, clinging to a huge black wolf. Then more came out of the forests, more than a score, I'd say. The lad did kill one but he was actually finishing him off for Abelard here, whose arrow brought him down. You don't need to worry anymore; Harle was seeing to the last of them as we left."

"You were attacked!" Hal's heart raced as he feared for what might have been.

"Yes, just when Harle and his mother were off searching for more roots and potions that Brid thought might help disperse the unnatural magic. Abelard and I drove them off," Pip boasted. "I killed one."

Abelard grinned at Pip. "I couldn't have managed without y', lad. Y're a fine fighting man!"

Hal offered his hand to the ancient archer who looked at him curiously for a moment before holding out his own. Hal gripped it firmly and shook it vigorously. Abelard's quiver was empty and he didn't need telling that it was only due to this man that Brid was safe. "I'm sorry," he started to apologize for his previous behaviour towards the archer. He seemed to be doing a great deal of apologizing of late.

Abelard smiled quietly and with great decorum retreated

a step. "It doesn't need saying, sir." Busily, he fussed over his bow.

"But it does," Hal insisted. "I owe you everything."

"Ceowulf!" Pip greeted him delightedly as the knight and the other noblemen joined them. His audience was growing and he started over again. "I killed one."

"Yes, lad," the Caldean knight acknowledged patiently. "And I'm sure you'd like to tell us all about it."

While Pip nodded happily and repeated his tale, Brid drew Hal aside. "Take us home, Hal. Take us home so that Keridwen and Branwolf can be freed."

Hal squeezed her hand, glad to be appreciated, and together they laughed at Pip, who was now telling Renaud of his triumph.

"Does he know he's talking to a prince?" Hal asked since the youth spoke to Prince Renaud with such familiarity.

Brid shrugged. "I doubt it, but knowing Pip, he wouldn't care." She looked up at the black turrets behind, watching the last of the green mist being tugged away by the breeze. "The air is nearly clean; Necrönd is safe again."

"It's with Spar," Hal said firmly.

Brid gripped his hand tight as if she would never let go.

CHAPTER THIRTY

"Amaryllis," May sobbed. "I'm sorry. I'm so sorry." Tears streamed down her face.

"His name's Talorcan," Caspar said coldly. "And he means only harm."

"No." The verderer's voice was a weak groan. "At first, I meant only to gain a soul and then to protect Merrymoon, but I have failed her. Failed . . . My Merrymoon, sweet Merrymoon, I'm dying."

May soothed the verderer's brow.

"Do not fear, Amaryllis; I love you," she whispered, tears falling onto his face. "All will be well. You already have a soul; I see it in your eyes. Reach for the Great Mother. Look for Her, find Her love and all will be well."

He sighed weakly and grasped onto May for strength, "Forgive me the wrong I did. For my part, I do not regret Caspar's good aim. Life is short for all men and I am not sorry to die. I shall wait for you, my love, on the other side." With visible effort, he turned his head towards Caspar who found himself looking into the verderer's eyes that uncannily were now an identical shade of hazel to May's. "I ask only that you look after her for me now. You must look after her."

As Caspar watched, the glint faded from Talorcan's eyes and the man lay perfectly still. May's sobs turned to a forlorn wail, her shoulders heaving.

"He protected me. And you killed him. What shall we do now? Amaryllis drove the creature away. Only Amaryllis could do it and he's dead now. You killed him. You killed him!" May flung herself at Caspar in her distress and fury. "He was there when you didn't come for me. I thought you would come. I thought you would seek me. But you never loved me; you cared only for one thing; you followed only Necrönd." She beat her fists against his chest, sobbing wildly.

Rather than fight her off, Caspar closed his arms tightly around her, pulling her head down onto his shoulders. She wept against his neck and he could feel the damp of her tears soaking through his shirt. Confused, he hugged her tightly and kissed the top of her head. "How did you take Necrönd from him?"

"He never had it," May said, her voice still shaking.

"But—" Caspar was even more confused. "But how did it get here?"

"I took it, I took it for fear that it would tear out your soul. I thought—" she pushed away from him and knelt once more beside the verderer.

"You thought I was not strong enough to be the guardian of Necrönd," Caspar finished for her. "I thought that you of all people might respect me enough." His words could have been bitter but instead they were resigned.

She looked at the Egg. "I have done much harm and have run wildly from the creatures that sought me and I know I am not strong enough. He's in the mines. There's a devilish spirit in the mines. If Amaryllis is not nearby to protect me, he tries to creep into my dreams to control the Egg. He even took my soul until Amaryllis drove him away. We're not strong enough. We need Amaryllis." Gently, she stroked back the golden hair from his still face.

"You said you loved him!" Caspar accused, sensing that

there was something that May was not telling him. She showed a physical tenderness towards the verderer.

"Yes!" she replied defensively. "He cared! To him I was everything, more important than his life, and he would do anything for me. How could I not love him?"

"But you cannot love another," Caspar said in despair. "May, you must love only me."

"Why! Why should I!" She was bitterly angry. "How dare you ask something of me that you do not ask of yourself? You say with words that you love me but your eyes have always looked to Brid; she was always your sun and moon and stars. You do not love me; you love her."

Caspar grasped her shoulders, forcing her to look at him. "May, I do love you. I was trying to tell you when we got back from Ceolothia. I love Brid, but no more than anyone else loves her as the Maiden, even as you do. I do not love her as Hal does. He crossed to the Otherworld for her when I could not because my heart belonged to you. I was overjoyed that, at last, I had found my true feelings. All I needed was time, the right moment to tell you, May, that I love you and no other. I was going to tell you at Beltane but you left me before . . ."

"I don't believe you," May sobbed. "Amaryllis loved me."

"I love you," Caspar insisted, pulling her tight to him and feeling the tension slowly easing out of her body. It was a surrender. It was as if she had girded herself up a great wall of defence against her own feelings, against the hurt and pain and now she released them, becoming limp in his arms.

"Spar, forgive me. I'm sorry I took Necrönd."

"It'll be all right, May. You were right because it brought only unhappiness upon the castle. We shall look after it together. We shall go away, leave everything behind so that no more harm shall come to those we love. Together we shall be strong enough. We shall go east over the uncharted oceans to the land beyond."

"You will look after me?" May asked, watching Caspar tuck Necrönd into her silver casket and place it under his shirt.

Absent-mindedly, he scratched at the unhealed scab on his scalp. "Of course, we shall go away alone and forever, just you and me," Caspar repeated his promise.

"Leave Torra Alta?" she queried. "You really mean it?"

He nodded.

"As equals?"

He nodded again.

"You do love me!" She laughed. "I never wanted to be a baroness!"

"Come, we have friends, many friends. They will help us." He turned to Perren who stood staring at them, tears streaming down his face.

"I was always touched by stories but I never knew how much more moving it was to see it all with my own eyes."

The wolfling was waiting for them on the other side of the pool when they eventually crossed. Runa gave May a curious sideways look and nuzzled her side.

Holding Caspar's hand and ruffling the wolfling's mane with the other, she looked back at Amaryllis. Caspar saw the sadness in her eyes and he understood; for he too knew what it was to love more than once.

The air around the verderer's body began to shimmer. Caspar was too exhausted to feel any trepidation when the thirteen members of the High Circle stepped out of a band of sparkling atmosphere to stand around Talorcan.

"He is not dust," Straif complained. "He has not been punished!"

"Is it not punishment enough that he is now no longer immortal but a part of life?" Saille asked.

No, Caspar thought. No, it is the ultimate gift. He gripped May's hand tightly and wordlessly he led her to the surface where the wet rains of Ceolothia washed away her tears.

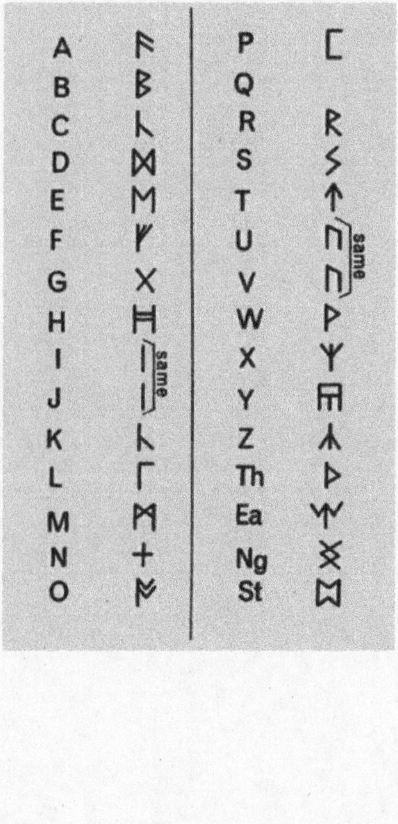

A
B
C
D
E
F
G
H
I
J
K
L
M
N
O
same
P
Q
R
S
T
U
V
W
X
Y
Z
Th
Ea
Ng
St
same